Genji & Heike

Genji & Heike

Selections from *The Tale of Genji*
and *The Tale of the Heike*

Translated, with Introductions, by
Helen Craig McCullough

Stanford University Press • Stanford, California

Stanford University Press

Stanford, California

© 1994 by the Board of Trustees

of the Leland Stanford Junior University

Printed in the United States of America

CIP data appear at the end of the book

For Amanda

Contents

Translator's Note

This book, published as a companion volume to *Classical Japanese Prose: An Anthology*, is intended for students in survey courses and others who may lack the time to read *The Tale of Genji* and *The Tale of the Heike* in their entirety. The translations are based on the texts published in *Nihon koten bungaku taikei*, Vols. 14–18 and Vols. 32–33, respectively. I am grateful to the Stanford University Press for permission to use copyrighted material.

Ages mentioned in the texts are calculated in the Japanese manner, according to the number of calendar years during which a person lives. Except in the case of fictional characters, those mentioned elsewhere are calculated in the Western manner.

For translations of characters' names in the *Genji*, I have followed the principles outlined in the Introduction. Names in the *Heike*, which appear in many different forms, have usually been reduced to given names after the initial occurrence.

Because the Japanese calendar was divided into twelve months approximately equivalent to the lunations, they did not correspond to their numerical equivalents in the Western calendar. The seventh month, for example, always included part of August, and in a given year might fall as late as the latter half of August and the first half of September. The four seasons were regarded as consisting of three months each, with spring beginning on the first day of the first month, summer on the first day of the fourth month, and so on.

Terms not defined in the footnotes and particulars on many of the historical figures of the pre-*Heike* period will be found in the Glossary. For basic information about the imperial palace and the court, see the Appendix; and for fuller information on Heian society, see McCullough and

McCullough, *Tale of Flowering Fortunes*. The following abbreviations have been used in the footnotes:

GSIS	*Goshūishū*. In Vol. 1 of SKT.
GSS	*Gosenshū*. In Vol. 1 of SKT.
IM	*Ise monogatari*. In Vol. 9 of NKBT.
IS	*Iseshū*. In Vol. 3 of SKT.
KDKYS	*Kodai kayōshū*. In Vol. 3 of NKBT.
KKKS	*Kanke kōshū*. In Vol. 72 of NKBT.
KKRJ	*Kokin rokujō*. In Vol. 2 of SKT.
KKS	*Kokinshū*. In Vol. 1 of SKT.
MYS	*Man'yōshū*. In Vol. 2 of SKT.
NKBT	*Nihon koten bungaku taikei*, ed. Takagi Ichinosuke et al. 102 vols. 1957–68.
SAS	*Saneakirashū*. In Vol. 3 of SKT.
SCSS	*Shin chokusenshū*. In Vol. 1 of SKT.
Shoku KKS	*Shoku kokinshū*. In Vol. 1 of SKT.
SIS	*Shūishū*. In Vol. 1 of SKT.
SKKS	*Shinkokinshū*. In Vol. 1 of SKT.
SKT	*[Shinpen] kokka taikan*, ed. Taniyama Shigeru et al. 5 vols. 1983–87.
SSRES	*Shinsen rōeishū*. In Vol. 2 of SKT.
TN	*Tosa nikki*. In Vol. 20 of NKBT.
WKRES	*Wakan rōeishū*. In Vol. 2 of SKT.

The Tale of Genji

Murasaki Shikibu

Introduction

The Tale of Genji (Genji monogatari) was written around the beginning of the eleventh century by a member of the middle-ranking nobility at the Japanese court, a woman known to us as Murasaki Shikibu (ca. 973?–1014?). Murasaki is not a surname, nor is Shikibu a personal name: the two together make up a sobriquet translatable as "purple ceremonial."

The polite avoidance of personal names was one of the notable characteristics of aristocratic society in the Heian period (794–1185). A brief inspection of *The Tale of Genji* itself, which adheres to contemporary practice, shows that Murasaki Shikibu's narrator and characters prefer to identify men in terms of the offices they hold, as in the case of the prominent figure Tō-no-chūjō, who serves in the dual capacity of head chamberlain (*tō*) and middle captain (*chūjō*). A clan or place-name may distinguish a character from another who holds the same title; thus, "the Reizei emperor" is the particular retired sovereign who lives at the Reizeiin, an imperial property in the capital. Feminine sobriquets may be derived from order of birth within a family (Naka-no-kimi, "second daughter"), location ("the Fujitsubo lady," a woman who lives in a building of that name at the imperial palace), or the title of an office held by the woman herself or by a male relative (Mikushigedono, "the mistress of the wardrobe"; Chūnagon "[lady related to a present or former] middle counselor"). A member of either sex may acquire a name through association with a poem (Genji's son Yūgiri, "evening mist"), a memorable incident (Yūgao, "the lady of the [flowers called] evening faces"), or a distinctive personal attribute (Kaoru, "the fragrant [gentleman]").[1]

1. Murasaki Shikibu changes the characters' sobriquets as they move from one status to another, but it is common practice to use standardized terms in referring to them. Thus, Genji

In *The Tale of Genji*, the true name of a character is seldom divulged.[2] In real life, men's personal names were probably almost always a matter of general knowledge, however infrequently they may have been used, but that seems not to have been the case for women. At any rate, relatively few full names of Heian women have been preserved, and Murasaki Shikibu's is not among them. Scholars assume that the second element in her sobriquet derives from positions her father is known to have held in the Ministry of Ceremonial (Shikibushō), and most of them believe that the first element is a reference to Murasaki, the principal feminine character in the first forty chapters of *The Tale of Genji*, whose name comes from a poem.

Little is known of the author's personal life. She belonged to a minor branch of the Fujiwara, the great clan that dominated the court during most of the Heian period. Her great-grandfather, Middle Counselor Kanesuke (877–933), had been a fairly prominent figure, the maternal grandfather of an imperial prince, but her grandfather and father had become members of the so-called *zuryō*, or career provincial governor class, men of middle-ranking status who could not aspire to important offices. Her father, Tametoki (?–?), was not even a bureaucratic success at his own modest level. He held insignificant positions in the central bureaucracy between 984 and 986, but lost them after the abdication of Emperor Kazan (968–1008; r. 984–86), the ruler who had appointed him. In 996, after a hiatus of ten years, he managed to secure appointment to the governorship of Echizen Province, but no new assignment awaited him on his return to the capital four years later, and he remained out of office until 1008, when he obtained a pair of minor posts in the central administration. He was named governor of Echigo Province in 1011 but returned to the capital in 1014, before the expiration of his four-year term. In 1016, he took Buddhist vows. The last mention of him as living occurs in a document written two years later.

Tametoki seems, in short, to have been a man who was either unable or unwilling to form and preserve the patronage relationships necessary for bureaucratic advancement—someone similar in certain respects, perhaps, to the eccentric Akashi novice in *The Tale of Genji*. But this is only one side of his story. Ever since its inception, his branch of the Fujiwara clan had produced poets distinguished enough to have their works included in imperial anthologies.[3] He himself graduated in Chinese literature from the state

---

"[member of] the Minamoto clan," is standard for the work's main character, whom the narrator sometimes calls "the young Genji lord," "the shining Genji," or the like, but more often identifies by means of an official or residential title.

2. The only exceptions in this translation are Fujiwara no Koremitsu and Minamoto no Yoshikiyo, two middle-ranking courtiers who render private services to Genji in a patronage relationship.

3. His grandfather, Kanesuke, was important both as the patron of Ki no Tsurayuki (the principal compiler of *Kokinshū*, the first imperial anthology of Japanese poetry, ca. 905) and as a poet in his own right, with 55 poems in imperial anthologies. Kanesuke's most famous

academy, where he studied under the famous scholar Sugawara no Fumitoki (899–981); and he was always regarded as one of the premier Chinese poets of the day. Whether in office or out, he composed poems at home, associated on friendly terms with leading literati, frequented the salon of the cultivated Prince Tomohira (964–1009), and participated in Chinese and Japanese poetry meetings, both at the imperial palace and in the mansions of great figures likes Fujiwara no Michinaga (966–1027), Michinaga's sister Senshi (962–1001), and his son Yorimichi (992–1074).

Tametoki seems to have been married at least twice, once to a woman of whom nothing is known except that she bore him three children, older half-siblings of Murasaki Shikibu; and later, after around 970, to Shikibu's mother, who was herself a member of a Fujiwara family of poets, and who gave birth to two daughters and a son. It is believed that she died when the second daughter, Shikibu, was still very young, and that Tametoki reared their offspring. The son, Nobunori (d. 1011), grew up to become a minor poet and minor court official. He left his post to join Tametoki in Echigo but died soon afterward. Nothing is known of the older daughter.

Shikibu is thought to have spent her girlhood with her father. She was with him during the first part of his tour in Echizen, by which time she was well along in her twenties—beyond the usual age for marriage if she was born around 973, as is tentatively assumed by many scholars. It seems reasonable to surmise that Tametoki had become concerned about providing for her future, because she almost certainly returned to the capital ahead of him to marry one of his friends, probably in 998 or 999. The bridegroom, Fujiwara no Nobutaka (d. 1001), was in his mid-forties, the father of at least three children by the numerous women in his life. Also a member of the *zuryō* class, he had been more successful than Tametoki and was in comfortable circumstances. In spite of his polygynous history, the marriage appears to have been a happy one until it was cut short by his death in an epidemic in 1001. It produced one child, a daughter, Kenshi (b. 999).[4]

In a short memoir written a few years after she was widowed, Shikibu describes her bereft existence at home as lonely and sad.[5] As was true of

composition is GSS 1102, which is said to have been written when he was worried about his daughter's future in the imperial harem: hito no oya no / kokoro wa yami ni / aranedomo / ko o omou michi ni / madoinuru ka na ("The hearts of parents are not realms where darkness reigns—yet how easily we wander in confusion on the path of love for a child!"). *The Tale of Genji* contains a number of allusions to this poem.

4. Kenshi is a personal name. It probably entered the historical record because she enjoyed an unusually successful career, including recognition as a poet, liaisons with important men, and appointment as nurse to a future emperor. Kenshi ultimately achieved junior third rank and held a prestigious position in the Handmaids Office.

5. Aside from a small collection of her poems, this memoir is our main source of information about Shikibu's life, but its biographical content is meager. Both the poetry collection and the memoir ("diary") are translated in Bowring, *Murasaki Shikibu: Her Diary and Poetic Memoirs*.

most aristocratic Heian women, even those in fortunate circumstances, she must have had many empty hours to kill, and she doubtless engaged in the usual pastimes of her sex—among them, studying old poems and writing new ones, reading romances, and looking at picture books while someone read aloud the tales that the paintings illustrated. To a modern reader, it seems unremarkable that someone with her literary antecedents should have decided to try her own hand at fiction. There were many romances available as guides, and she also possessed some knowledge of the Chinese classics and their treasure trove of stories, acquired as a result of listening while her father attempted to drum the texts into young Nobunori's ears. But the few extant pre-*Genji* romances all show evidence of male authorship, and it may well be that *Genji monogatari* is not only, by general agreement, the great masterpiece of Japanese classical fiction, but also the first significant feminine venture into a previously masculine field. As with so much else in Murasaki Shikibu's career, however, this must remain speculative. We can say only that she probably began to write *The Tale of Genji* not long after her husband's death, while she was living quietly at home.[6]

Meanwhile, the court was recovering from a power struggle. Fujiwara no Kaneie had been named regent in 986, upon the accession of his grandson, Emperor Ichijō (980–1011, r. 986–1011); and Michitaka (953–95), Kaneie's oldest son by his principal wife, had succeeded to the office after his father's death in 990. Michitaka had then secured the title of empress for his daughter, Teishi (976?–1000), also in 990, and had groomed his favorite son, Korechika (973–1010), to be his eventual replacement. Upon Michitaka's death, however, his sister Senshi (962–1001), Emperor Ichijō's influential mother, had obtained the regency for their brother Michikane (961–95), who was next in order of birth. Michikane died in an epidemic seven days later, and Senshi again intervened against Korechika (whom the emperor seems to have favored because of his love for Teishi), prevailing on her son to grant the equivalent of regental authority to the next brother, Michinaga (966–1027). Michinaga moved quickly to consolidate his position. In 996, he drove Korechika into exile; in 999, he made his eleven-year-old daughter, Shōshi (988–1074), a junior imperial consort; and in 1000

6. Scholars have suggested that Murasaki Shikibu may have been moved to try her hand at a *monogatari* ("tale") because she had read *The Gossamer Journal* (Kagerō nikki), a tenth-century feminine memoir that anticipates, on a small scale, her own probing analyses of the psychological aspects of relations between the sexes. The memoirist, known as "Michitsuna's Mother" (936?–95?) was a wife of Fujiwara no Kaneie (929–90), the clan chieftain whose granddaughter, Shōshi, was soon to employ Shikibu as a lady-in-waiting. Michitsuna's Mother was also related, very indirectly, to Shikibu herself: her sister's husband was the brother of Shikibu's maternal grandfather. It seems more likely that Shikibu would have had access to *The Gossamer Journal* after entering Shōshi's service than when she was writing the first sections of *The Tale of Genji* at home, but little is known about the way in which manuscripts circulated. Nor, indeed, is it possible even to say with certainty that *The Gossamer Journal*, which is now regarded as a landmark in the development of Japanese belletristic prose, was actually the only work of its kind available to a contemporary reader.

he saw to it that Shōshi acquired the title of empress, with the result that Emperor Ichijō became the first sovereign in Japanese history to possess two wives of imperial rank.

Michinaga exerted unparalleled influence at court for the rest of his life, ultimately becoming the father-in-law of three emperors, one retired emperor, and a crown prince; the grandfather of two emperors; and the father of two regents.

Teishi died in the twelfth month of 1000, a day after giving birth to a daughter, her second. She and the emperor had been a devoted couple for ten years, and he and his courtiers had delighted in visiting her palace apartments, where her attendants could be counted on for witty, literate conversation and amusing diversions. Now she was gone, but she had left behind a son, Prince Atsuyasu (999–1018), who represented a potential threat to Michinaga's line unless Shōshi and her future offspring could weaken old ties in the emperor's mind.

Before presenting his child-daughter in 999, Michinaga had gone to great lengths to assemble tasteful, luxurious furnishings for her apartments in the Fujitsubo, to equip her with an elaborate trousseau, and, equally or perhaps more important, to find a group of forty ladies-in-waiting capable of competing with Teishi's entourage. "Her attendants had been selected with the utmost discrimination," reports *A Tale of Flowering Fortunes* (Eiga monogatari), a contemporary history. "It was not considered sufficient for a candidate to be personable and even-tempered: even if her father held fourth or fifth rank, there was no hope for her if she was socially inept or lacking in the niceties of deportment, for only the most polished and elegant were accepted."[7] There is no specific mention in this passage of an effort to recruit literary women, but it is known that Shōshi's ladies-in-waiting included two of the most talented poets of the age, Ise no Tayū (?–?, entered ca. 1007?) and Izumi Shikibu (b. ca. 977?, entered ca. 1009?). Akazome Emon (?–?), a well-known poet who is generally accepted as the author of *Flowering Fortunes*, herself served Shōshi's mother and frequented the empress's rooms.

In view of Michinaga's interest in the creation and maintenance of a brilliant salon for Shōshi, it is no surprise to learn that Murasaki Shikibu entered the empress's service after the original chapters of *The Tale of Genji* began to circulate—probably in 1005 or 1006, when Shōshi was in her late teens and Shikibu was around thirty. Like the Akashi lady in her book, Shikibu seems to have felt ill at ease in a milieu so much more exalted than her own, particularly since she was by her own account reticent and introspective, but her memoir contains warm praise of her mistress. She considers herself Shōshi's favorite attendant and reports with satisfaction that she has tutored the empress in the poetry of Bo Juyi, keeping the sessions private to

7. McCullough and McCullough, *Tale of Flowering Fortunes*, 1: 218.

avoid being criticized for her unfeminine Chinese learning. On the whole, she was probably happier at court than she would have been at home; and the connection with Michinaga, a man of great wealth, assured her of an ample supply of paper, a precious commodity, as she continued work on the book. She is known to have moved with Shōshi to the Biwa Mansion, one of Michinaga's properties, after the death of Emperor Ichijō in 1011, and to have remained in her service as late as 1013. Many scholars believe that she died in 1014, thus predeceasing her father and, perhaps, causing his early return from Echigo. It is possible, but not demonstrable, that she continued to write *The Tale of Genji* until the end of her life.

Genji monogatari is a long work in fifty-four chapters (five volumes in modern Japanese printed editions). The standard English translation of the title implies that it is a story about someone named Genji, which is reasonably close to the truth. The dominant character in the first forty-one chapters is Genji, the shining one, a dazzlingly handsome, charismatic, gifted prince, born of a minor consort without family support, whom his imperial father has thought it best to shield from succession struggles by making him a subject with the Minamoto (Genji) surname. But an alternative translation, *Tales of the Genji*, would be equally possible, because Genji's son Yūgiri occupies the center of the stage in a number of those chapters, and Genji himself dies well before the end of the book, between Chapters 41 and 42, after which the author turns her attention to the activities of two of his descendants, one actual and one putative.[8]

There is, in a word, no single protagonist in *Genji monogatari*. Nor is there a carefully crafted plot or a clearly discernible theme. Rather, most of the work conforms to a pattern, conspicuous throughout the history of premodern Japanese prose, of bringing together a group of more or less independent parts into a loosely structured whole. If we can consider it to be in some sense an eleventh-century precursor of the Western novel, as many have done, it is largely because Murasaki Shikibu concerns herself above all with human relationships and the emotions they engender.

For purposes of discussion, Japanese scholars have found it convenient to divide *The Tale of Genji* (as we shall continue to call it) into the forty-one chapters before Genji's death and the thirteen chapters following it, and to subdivide the first and larger segment into Part One (Chapters 1–33), dealing primarily with events in Genji's life until he reaches the age of thirty-nine, and Part Two (Chapters 34–41), during which he ages from thirty-nine to fifty-two. The rationale for the subdivision is that Chapters 34 and 35, which are by far the longest in the book, mark a shift to a dark period

8. Three transitional sections, Chaps. 42–44, serve as a bridge to the final 10, known as the Uji chapters, in which the dominant male figures are Kaoru, supposedly Genji's son but actually the offspring of a liaison between Genji's young wife and another man, born toward the end of Genji's life; and Niou, Genji's grandson.

in what has been, on the surface at least, a singularly fortunate and enviable public and private career—the start of a series of events, attributable in part to long-standing flaws in Genji's character, that culminate in the loss of Murasaki, the woman who gives meaning to his life. Murasaki dies in Chapter 40, and in Chapter 41 the stricken Genji is last seen preparing to take Buddhist vows.[9]

Part One begins with two chapters that might be said to function as background for the tale that begins in earnest with Chapter 3. In Chapter 1, "Kiritsubo," the narrator runs briskly through an account of her hero's first twelve years, a period in which he loses his mother, a minor consort beloved of the emperor; lives at court as his father's favorite son; becomes a subject; develops a boyish crush on the Fujitsubo lady, a beautiful new imperial consort who is reputed to look like his dead mother; and enters into an arranged marriage with the minister of the left's daughter, Aoi, who does not interest him.

In a long episode accounting for almost all of Chapter 2, "The Broom Tree," Murasaki Shikibu prepares the way for much that is to follow in Genji's private life. The occasion is a discussion about women, which takes place on a quiet rainy night in the Kiritsubo pavilion at the palace, once the residence of Genji's mother and now assigned to Genji himself. Those present are Genji, five years older than when we saw him last, and thus in his teens; two other youths of his own age—his great friend Tō-no-chūjō and a minor courtier called Shikibu-no-jō—and a somewhat older courtier, Uma-no-kami, who seems to be in his early twenties.

Early in the conversation, Uma-no-kami introduces what has come to be known as the "hidden flower theme" in *The Tale of Genji*, describing a hypothetical situation that seems to have had a strong appeal for young nobles whose principal wives were not necessarily of their own choosing. If a girl with every advantage turns out supremely well, he says, that is no more than we might expect. "What *would* be amazing would be to discover

9. The Uji chapters are not represented in this translation, which confines itself to noteworthy events in Genji's life; and they will not be discussed here. It should be noted, however, that many people regard them as Murasaki Shikibu's finest achievement. The structure is tighter than in the rest of the book; the principal characters are few in number and brilliantly drawn; and the relationship between human emotions and the natural environment, always a concern in Heian court literature, is impressed on the reader with consummate skill as Kaoru and the women in his life try to cope with their problems against a backdrop of wild waters and brooding wintry mountains. See Seidensticker, *Tale of Genji*, the standard complete translation; and, for commentary, Ramirez-Christensen, "Operation of the Lyrical Mode." For an astute, comprehensive study of the entire work, see Shirane, *Bridge of Dreams*, which makes extensive use of the voluminous publications of Japanese specialists. The *Genji* is also discussed at length in three recent books: Field, *Splendor of Longing*; Konishi, *History of Japanese Literature*, Vol. 2; and Okada, *Figures of Resistance*. For a useful handbook, see Bowring, *Murasaki Shikibu: 'The Tale of Genji.'* An alternative to the Seidensticker translation is Waley's *The Tale of Genji: A Novel in Six Parts*, which reads well but contains many mistranslations, cuts, and additions. ("Six Parts" is a division created by Waley.)

an unbelievably sweet, appealing maiden shut up in a lonely, dilapidated, vine-choked dwelling, her very existence unknown to others. We would marvel at finding her there, and would feel strangely drawn to her just because of the way she has confounded our expectations. Her father would perhaps be old and disagreeably overweight, her brother ill-favored, but she would lead a dignified life inside her predictably undistinguished rooms, and the polite accomplishments with which she whiled away the time would seem delightful. Her skills might in fact be limited, but we'd still consider her unexpectedly interesting. I don't say she could be singled out as superb or flawless—just that it would be hard to dismiss her." Of the women with whom Genji becomes seriously involved, approximately half, including Murasaki, fall into this category.

A little later, Uma-no-kami throws out the observation that a man might do worse than "look for a completely childlike, docile woman, train her a little, and marry her," another notion that Genji seems to take to heart. He discovers Murasaki, the rarest of his hidden flowers, when he is eighteen and she is around ten, educates her with spectacularly successful results, and weds her when she is around fifteen. Seventeen years later, he makes a somewhat similar, if less wholehearted, effort to mold someone else to his liking, this time the teen-aged Third Princess, whom, at her father's request, he has brought into his household as a primary consort.

Uma-no-kami, the sophisticate, also has an opinion about how a woman should behave when a man looks elsewhere. "A husband's love will increase if a woman remains calm in every situation, merely hints at her knowledge of causes for jealousy, and speaks only in an unobjectionable, roundabout fashion of matters at which she might easily take offense. In more cases than not, he'll be moved to mend his ways," he says. We may wonder if this view was inspired by Murasaki Shikibu's experience with her own much-married husband. It is in any case the stance adopted by Murasaki and others who are successful in their relations with men in *Genji monogatari*; and the Rokujō lady, whose jealous spirit wreaks havoc in Genji's life, becomes an object lesson in the terrible consequences of feminine vindictiveness. The Rokujō lady first appears in Chapter 4, "Yūgao" (Chapter 3 in this book), as a deceased crown prince's proud, elegant widow, seven years Genji's senior and morbidly afraid of derisive gossip, whom Genji has previously managed with difficulty to seduce, and whom he neglects because of her difficult personality. "Yūgao" begins with the summer of Genji's seventeenth year, at approximately the same time as the rainy night discussion in Chapter 2. We see, then, that Genji is already involved with three women—his wife, Aoi; his stepmother, the Fujitsubo lady, for whom he nurses a secret passion; and the Rokujō lady. Later in the chapter, we are told that he has also been writing to a cousin, Princess Asagao, and in the last section of the chapter (not translated), he makes love to Utsusemi, a "hidden flower" he has chanced upon.

Chapters 3–6 describe a series of hidden-flower adventures, each centering on a different woman (or child, in one case)—Utsusemi, Yūgao, Murasaki, and the safflower lady—each taking place in the same general period, when Genji is seventeen to nineteen, and each capable of standing alone as an independent story. At the age of twenty, Genji begins an off-and-on affair with Oborozukiyo, a lady who has been chosen by her influential family for presentation to the reigning emperor;[10] and at the age of twenty-five, he is seen paying an occasional visit to an undemanding woman known as the lady from the house of the scattering blossoms.

Self-exiled in Suma to escape the ire of Oborozukiyo's relatives, who have discovered his transgression, he enters into a halfhearted liaison with the Akashi lady, another hidden flower—halfhearted because by this time he is devoted to Murasaki, who has become his principal wife after the Rokujō lady's jealous spirit has brought about Aoi's death. His return to the capital, at the age of twenty-eight, marks the beginning of a long period of happy life with Murasaki. From time to time, he is attracted to other women—Akikonomu, Asagao, Tamakazura—but never so strongly as to threaten Murasaki's place in his heart, and indeed never even to the point of physical intimacy. It is only when he reaches forty that he establishes the Third Princess as a primary wife, thereby setting in motion the chain of events that ends with Murasaki's death.

Those who regard Genji as a champion womanizer may feel that the foregoing summary makes their case. It might be argued, however, that his is not a remarkable showing, particularly in view of the prevailing standards of behavior for noblemen. Almost all of his liaisons began before he was nineteen years old. The two in his early twenties (with Oborozukiyo and the lady from the house of the scattering blossoms) were not serious; the one with the Akashi lady took place under special circumstances; and we know of no other real involvement until his lukewarm agreement to marry the Third Princess, eleven years later.

Murasaki Shikibu's own view of Genji's conduct seems ambivalent. At the beginning of Chapter 2, the narrator says, "Genji made his mistakes—so many, indeed, as to lay him open to the charge that his fine sobriquet, 'the shining one,' was a misnomer; and there even seems to have been talk (which can only be called malicious) about affairs that he tried to keep secret, afraid of acquiring a reputation for indiscretion if still more tales of his amours should be passed on to future generations. In reality, his sensitivity to the world's opinion was acute. He was the soul of circumspection, and the Katano lesser captain must have been vastly amused by his lack of romantic, interesting adventures." At times, characters in the tale remark on his roving eye; at other times, they praise his sobriety and reliability where women are concerned.

10. Genji's half-brother, the Suzaku emperor, who had replaced their father, the Kiritsubo emperor, on his retirement.

The Katano lesser captain, the protagonist of a lost tale, was presumably a romantic hero like the one in *Tales of Ise*.[11] Mentions of the captain in at least three extant Heian works attest to the popularity of such tales, as does the survival of *Tales of Ise* itself; and Murasaki Shikibu was clearly catering to contemporary taste when she created a series of entertaining stories about the amorous adventures and misadventures of an idealized young hero. It must have been the success of those initial products of her brush—some of the episodes now clustered in the early chapters of *The Tale of Genji*—that led to her appointment as a lady-in-waiting to Empress Shōshi.

Chapters 12 and 13, "Suma" and "Akashi," describe Genji's two-year sojourn in the west as an exile, a period in which he hears about the beautiful daughter of a retired provincial governor and, at her father's urgent request, favors her with his attentions. We might regard them as essentially a variation on a familiar theme—inspired, perhaps, by Korechika's sensational exile a few years earlier. But the Suma-Akashi sequence also functions as a major turning point in *The Tale of Genji*. Previously, the narrator has concentrated on Genji's love affairs and other aspects of his private life; after his return to the capital, he emerges as a powerful public figure, the man around whom court society increasingly revolves.[12]

Genji's half-brother, the Suzaku emperor, whose poor health has been a major factor in his recall, abdicates in favor of the crown prince, the Fujitsubo lady's young son. As a result, power passes into the hands of Genji, the boy's half-brother and main male relative, and of Aoi's father, the former minister of the left (who emerges from retirement to become regent and chancellor), with the Fujitsubo lady an important influence in the background. Genji rises rapidly. He becomes palace minister at twenty-eight, takes over as chancellor at thirty-two, after the death of Aoi's father, and at thirty-nine is granted "status equivalent to that of a retired emperor"—*jun daijō tennō*, an unprecedented honor—because the emperor has learned that Genji is his true father.[13]

Meanwhile, the Rokujō lady has died, committing her daughter, Akikonomu, to Genji's care; and Genji has presented the girl to the emperor, whose rear palace already houses a daughter of Tō-no-chūjō, Genji's old friend.[14] Inspired, perhaps, by accounts of the days when Emperor Ichijō's

11. *Ise monogatari* (ca. 950), a collection of poem-centered anecdotes in which an anonymous "man of the past" woos a variety of women.

12. Some scholars attribute the change to the broadening of Murasaki Shikibu's horizons after her arrival at court; some also surmise that Michinaga's example influenced the author's portrayal of the post-Suma Genji; and many point to the existence, in Japan as elsewhere, of a conventional story pattern in which a young protagonist is forced out of society, undergoes trials, and ultimately rises to an exalted status.

13. The secret of Genji's seduction of the Fujitsubo lady had been known only to Genji, the lady, one of her attendants, and a bishop in whom the attendant had confided, but the bishop had told the emperor the truth several years earlier, at the time of the lady's death.

14. "Rear palace" (*kōkyū*) is a general term for the area in the imperial palace compound where the consorts lived. Akikonomu's father was the late crown prince.

first imperial consort, Empress Teishi, was still alive, Murasaki Shikibu devotes a chapter, "The Picture Contest," to the rivalry between the two young women and their backers—a competition won by Akikonomu, who is named empress two years after her presentation, when she is twenty-four and the emperor is around fifteen. A few years later, Genji arranges a marriage between his daughter, the eleven-year-old child of the Akashi lady, and the crown prince (a son of the Suzaku emperor); and after the prince's accession, which takes place when Genji is forty-six, it is a son of this Akashi consort (later to be named empress) who promptly becomes the next heir-designate.

If Genji falls short of Michinaga's record as a maternal relative of the throne and a sire of powerful men, it is only because he has been less amply blessed with children: he possesses but one daughter, the Akashi girl, and one acknowledged son, Yūgiri.[15] In other respects, he is a public figure of equal or superior stature. Long ago, in his childhood, a skilled physiognomist had said of him, "He bears the stamp of one destined to ascend to the supreme status of emperor and become the father of the nation, but turmoil and distress may ensue if that happens," a pronouncement that had influenced the Kiritsubo emperor's decision to remove him from the possible line of succession. Now, in his maturity, the prophecy seems to have been essentially fulfilled. As we have seen, his formal status is equivalent to that of a retired emperor. Also, a few years after his return from exile, he has built the Rokujō Mansion (Rokujōin), a huge, magnificent residential complex occupying four city blocks—its size equaled in real life only by the great Reizeiin, an imperial property used by retired sovereigns—and there, in an arrangement reminiscent of the rear palace at court, he has provided accommodations for Murasaki, for the Akashi lady, for the lady from the house of scattering blossoms, and for the imperial consort Akikonomu during her stays away from the palace. When he takes the Third Princess as a wife, he does so not by visiting her at home, as was the custom among subjects, but by receiving her at the Rokujō Mansion as though she were a new consort entering the imperial palace. And when the Third Princess and Murasaki live in the mansion as dual principal wives, the relationship is not dissimilar to that of Emperor Ichijō's two principal consorts, Empress Teishi and Empress Shōshi. In his public persona, at least, Genji has indeed become the shining one who eclipses all rivals, fictional or real-life.[16]

15. His supposed second son, Kaoru, is not born until he is 48, four years before he disappears from Shikibu's narrative.

16. Scholars have pointed out that it was no longer possible in Murasaki Shikibu's day for anyone other than a Fujiwara to exercise supreme power at court. As a Fujiwara woman dependent on Fujiwara patronage, Shikibu probably meant no criticism of the status quo when she elevated Genji at the clan's expense. If we assume that both Genji and the Fujitsubo lady figured in her original early chapters, this portion of Part One is perhaps to be regarded as merely a narrative in which two important characters happen to have been born into the imperial clan. Or, as is often proposed, she may have intended to evoke romantic nostalgia for an earlier era.

A grand establishment like the Rokujō Mansion was designed primarily to serve as a luxurious setting for banquets and ceremonies.[17] In her memoir, Murasaki Shikibu describes such occasions at Michinaga's Tsuchimikado Mansion, a palatial residence that doubtless furnished a partial model for the Rokujō Mansion; and in the *Genji* she makes the Rokujō Mansion a backdrop for imperial visits and other great events illustrative of its owner's social prominence. The mansion also functions as a symbol of the domestic harmony Genji enjoys during the years between his return from Suma and the end of Part One. After some initial jealousy, Murasaki has learned to like and respect the Akashi lady, and she has known all along that the lady from the house of the scattering orange blossoms is more an object of Genji's charity than a threat to her marriage. The three women—and, when she is in residence, the quiet, gentle Akikonomu—live tranquil lives, linked but independent, the special character and taste of each reflected in the aspect of her garden.

For Murasaki, who lives with Genji in the southeast and most resplendent quarter of the establishment, and whose season is spring, Genji has provided a spring garden: "The hills were high and covered with spring-blooming trees, the pond was exceptionally spacious and tasteful, and in the garden closer at hand there were white pines, and trees and shrubs especially chosen for springtime enjoyment—red plum, cherry, wisteria, azalea, and the like—interspersed with occasional unobtrusive plantings to make a pleasant autumnal show."[18]

For Akikonomu ("Fancier of Autumn"), who owes her sobriquet to a passage in which she and Genji discuss the relative merits of spring and autumn (a perennial literary topic), there is a view designed to be at its best in autumn: "The existing hills had been planted with maples and other trees and shrubs to create a brilliant display of fall color, the clear waters of a spring had been channeled into a long stream, with additional rocks to enhance their sound and create cascades, and the total effect was of an autumn field stretching into the distance."

For the lady from the house of the scattering orange blossoms, there is a summer garden, because orange blossoms are a conventional summer image in Japanese poetry: "There was a cool-looking spring, and special attention had been devoted to summer shade. Near at hand, black bamboo gave promise of refreshing breezes, and there was a veritable forest of tall trees, their depths intriguingly reminiscent of a mountain retreat. Care had been taken to create a hedge where deutzia flowers would bloom, and there were plantings of other summer trees and grasses—the nostalgic orange, wild pinks, gentians, and so forth—as well as some spring and autumn varieties."

17. See Ōta, *Shindenzukuri no kenkyū*, p. 151.
18. From Chapter 21, "The Maiden," not included in this volume. The three passages that follow appear in the same chapter.

And for the Akashi lady, there is a winter garden, not merely because winter is the only season left, but because it was on a winter day, four years earlier, that she gave up her three-year-old daughter, whom Genji wished Murasaki to train as a future imperial consort: "A hedge of Chinese bamboo separated it from the storehouses. There were a great many pine trees, planted to offer a pleasing prospect when snow fell; also, a chrysanthemum hedge, to capture the morning frost in early winter, a grove of oaks to flaunt their color, and numbers of little-known trees transplanted from deep in the mountains."

Of the episode responsible for the Akashi lady's identification with winter, Haruo Shirane writes, "The snow, sleet, and frozen lake . . . reflect the emotional state of the heroine. . . . The snow, associated in Heian poetry and aesthetics with serene beauty, highlights her elegant figure even as it embodies her sorrow." [19] This kind of association between man and his environment is a fundamental characteristic of classical Japanese poetry; and it is obvious that Murasaki Shikibu has poetic conventions firmly in mind, not only as she deals with each of the Rokujōin gardens in its turn, but also throughout her work. Time and again, she describes a scene in nature, relates it to human emotions, which may either harmonize with the surroundings or stand in ironic contrast, and concludes with a poem, usually a soliloquy or part of an exchange, "a metaphorical fusion . . . in which the elements of the setting become the vehicle for the character's emotion." [20] In the passage below, we see Genji during the early days at Suma.

The winds of autumn, "the saddest season of all," blew at Suma. The breakers of which Yukihira speaks, in his "blowing across the barrier," sounded very close at night, even though the sea was a fair distance away; and to Genji it seemed that nothing could be as evocative of melancholy musings as autumn in such a place. Awakening alone one night, after his few attendants were all asleep, he raised his head from the pillow and listened to the howling gale. The waves seemed about to invade the room, and he wept unawares until his pillow was in danger of floating away. When he essayed a few notes on the seven-stringed koto, the sound was lonesome and uncanny, even to his own ears. He broke off and intoned the words of a poem:

koiwabite	That the breaking waves
naku ne ni magau	harmonize with these sobs
uranami wa	wrung from a grieving heart—
omou kata yori	is it because the wind blows
kaze ya fukuramu	from where someone yearns for me?

A situation of this kind in the *Genji* will almost always turn out to be classifiable under one of a small number of topics recognized in the Heian period as acceptable for serious poetic composition: the four seasons, love,

19. *Bridge of Dreams*, pp. 83–84.
20. Ramirez-Christensen, "Operation of the Lyrical Mode," p. 25.

parting, travel, laments, felicitations, and a few others (mostly lumped together as "miscellaneous"). Here the topic is travel, a rubric embracing residence away from the capital. Travel was, by definition, a lonely, depressing
experience. Murasaki Shikibu sets the stage with auditory imagery evocative
of autumnal bleakness, heightens the effect with allusions to old poems,
moves on to an exposition of Genji's feelings, which are exacerbated by the
eerie sound of the koto (an instrument considered capable of establishing
contact with unseen powers), and ends with a recapitulatory poem.

To point out that *The Tale of Genji* contains almost 800 poems is to
imply correctly that every conventional poetic category is represented in the
work. If we thumb through *Kokinshū*, the imperial anthology in which
the categories were canonized, we find a fair number of poems, usually in
the seasonal books and Felicitations, in which the speakers express happiness, admiration, uncomplicated aesthetic enjoyment, and other positive
sentiments. More typically, however, the mood is sorrowful, elegiac, or, at
best, pervaded with a gentle melancholy. Pleasure in the beauty of spring
blossoms is tempered by thoughts of their ephemerality; longing for those
left behind makes travel an ordeal; the deaths of friends and loved ones must
be mourned; the brief transports of fulfilled love lead to the lasting sorrow
of neglect and desertion; and there is an ever-present sense of the transitoriness of earthly things. Murasaki Shikibu is too good a writer to confine
herself to so narrow a tonal range, but the influence of the so-called "aesthetic of sensibility" (*mono no aware*) is visible even in the sunniest stretches
of Part One.

Quite apart from poetic tradition, Shikibu had reason to introduce prob-
lematic situations into her glowing account of the years between Genji's
return from exile and his marriage to the Third Princess. We are told more
than once that Genji and Murasaki are, in effect, living happily ever after,
an ideal married couple. But it is not without reason that authors have
tended to lay down their pens once they have straightened out the tangled affairs of their main characters. To hold our interest in this section of Part One
and, no doubt, to answer requests from Empress Shōshi and others in her
circle, Shikibu introduces extraneous subjects: brief follow-ups on some of
Genji's youthful love affairs; court politics; the maturing Yūgiri and his activities; elegant events at the Rokujō Mansion; and the long story of Tamakazura, the lost infant daughter of the lady of the evening faces (Yūgao), for
whom Genji seeks eligible suitors, posing as her father while barely restraining his amorous impulses.[21] Despite an occasional small manifestation of
jealousy, Murasaki herself seems too secure, too perfect, to be interesting,
and we hear relatively little of her.

All this changes with Chapter 34, "New Herbs: Part One," the first of
the eight chapters in Part Two. As Part Two begins, the Suzaku emperor,

21. The girl is actually Tō-no-chūjō's daughter. She marries a high court noble, Higekuro,
who later becomes the imperial regent.

ailing and desirous of taking Buddhist vows, is trying to secure the future of his favorite child, the Third Princess, who is thirteen or fourteen years old, ready for marriage by Heian standards. After considerable deliberation, he offers the girl to Genji, who accepts with mingled reluctance, gratification at the connection, and curiosity. The princess enters the Rokujō Mansion as a second main wife early in the following year, her superior social status acknowledged by the spacious quarters assigned to her and her attendants. Murasaki accepts the situation gracefully. Some seven years later, when Genji is forty-seven, Murasaki falls gravely ill, and Genji goes to stay with her at his Nijō Mansion, an earlier residence that she has always considered her home. While they are away, Kashiwagi, one of Tō-no-chūjō's sons, seduces and impregnates the princess. Genji finds out what has happened, and the birth of the child, Kaoru, is soon followed by the princess's entry into religious orders and by the guilt-ridden Kashiwagi's decline and death. Three years pass, during which the author's attention shifts to Yūgiri's affairs, and then, when Genji is fifty-one, he loses Murasaki, who has never made a complete recovery from her illness.

As this summary suggests, Part Two is shorter, less crowded with characters and events, and more tightly organized than Part One. There are some digressions—notably, the chapters dealing with Yūgiri—but they are relatively minor. The narrator concerns herself almost entirely with Genji's marriage to the Third Princess and its consequences, and with the behavior and feelings of Genji and Murasaki during the last decade of their lives.

An attentive reader will already have discovered, in the course of Part One, that Genji's character is not without its flaws. It seemed at the outset that Murasaki Shikibu might have meant to create a hero who would be the exact opposite of a man like Michinaga's father, the regent Kaneie, who emerges in *The Gossamer Journal* and other contemporary writings as entirely devoid of sensitivity, especially in his relations with women. Kaneie's indifference to the "aesthetic of sensibility" is revealed both by his callous treatment of his wife, Michitsuna's Mother, and by his poor calligraphy; Genji's perfect realization of the ideal, by his often-expressed solicitude for the feelings of others and his mastery of every polite accomplishment. Once Genji has made even a fleeting commitment, a woman need not fear abandonment: the Nijō and Rokujō mansions shelter a number of needy ladies, no longer of any particular interest to him, whom he provides with material comforts and a face-saving degree of personal attention. And all he asks in return is conformity to the model of tolerant womanly behavior set forth in Chapter 2, "The Broom Tree."

What the "Broom Tree" ideal demands, however, is that the man be given free rein to indulge in affairs with other women. For Genji, his marriage to Aoi and his relationship with the Rokujō lady are both unsatisfactory because neither woman understands that she must accept occasional neglect; his marriage to Murasaki and his relationship with the Akashi lady are smooth because neither makes inconvenient demands. As he admits to Murasaki, he has been spoiled, and despite his thoughtfulness and generosity, he is sometimes guilty of selfishness, self-pity, self-deception, and disingenuousness. When he finds himself with a dead secret mistress (Yūgao) on his hands in a mysterious deserted mansion, his first reaction is to worry about gossip; when his misconduct with Oborozukiyo forces him into exile, he blames karma from a previous existence; when the imminence of his separation from the Akashi lady intensifies a previously tepid passion, he reflects, not on the plight of the pregnant girl, but on the unkindness of the fate that seems to have doomed him to a life of unhappiness. In his opinion, he enjoys a perfect marriage with Murasaki. He finds no flaw in her, and she is always his true love. But it is precisely in this relationship that his sensitivity proves to be obtuseness, and that self-deception leads to disaster. He does not realize, or does not choose to understand, that Murasaki's view of the marriage is very different from his.

Genji is the first and only man in Murasaki's life. When she is around ten, he becomes a surrogate for the father she scarcely knows.[22] Too young for jealousy, she is merely appealingly forlorn when his affairs call him elsewhere. Later, when she is a child bride, there is little to suggest that his liaisons cause her deep distress, or that she even knows about all of them. The first real sorrow of her married existence seems to come with his departure for Suma.

The Suma-Akashi episode, which marks a turning point in Genji's life, proves equally portentous for Murasaki. Not only is Genji's confessed involvement with the Akashi lady hard to bear, but the lady produces a child— a daughter who can make him an emperor's grandfather. Murasaki herself is childless after several years of marriage, and is fated to remain so, a disturbing disadvantage for a woman married to an ambitious Heian aristocrat.[23] For the first time, she feels insecure.

After Genji's return from Suma, he takes his young daughter away from her mother and gives her to Murasaki to rear as a potential imperial consort. Murasaki's jealousy turns to pity, and she and the Akashi lady eventually become friends. During these years, Genji's fortunes flower, and we hear repeatedly of his great love for Murasaki and of the happiness of their marriage. Meanwhile, however, he courts Asagao (unsuccessfully) and takes a more than fatherly interest in his ward, Tamakazura; and the narrator reveals, in what seems almost a casual aside, that Murasaki wants to become a nun because she fears Genji will tire of her as she ages.

---

22. The high incidence of substitute figures in Murasaki Shikibu's work has been much discussed in *Genji* studies. Most of them are women: the Fujitsubo lady for the Kiritsubo lady, Murasaki for the Fujitsubo lady, the Akashi lady for Murasaki, and so forth.

23. "A woman's lot cannot be happy unless she produces a large family of children," writes the author of *The Gossamer Journal*. "I had failed to do so despite the length of my marriage, and I was tormented by thoughts of my own inconsequentiality." Quoted from McCullough, *Classical Japanese Prose*, p. 133.

As Part Two begins, Murasaki views the marriage with mixed emotions. On the one hand, she worries about her advancing age (she is thirty-one), about Genji's seeming inability to find contentment with one woman, and, no doubt, about her childless state. On the other, she has been Genji's main wife for seventeen years, unrivaled in status and, to all appearances, in his affections. Genji's marriage to the Third Princess is thus both a devastating shock and a confirmation of long-standing, half-unconscious fears and misgivings. The princess turns out to be an uninteresting little thing, nothing like the young Murasaki. It never occurs to Genji to fall in love with her, and Murasaki soon recognizes that she is no threat in that respect. It is, rather, the symbolic import of the marriage that causes her acute unhappiness. Genji now has a main wife whose exalted status demands that she be recognized as superior. Moreover, he has shown, Murasaki thinks, that he will always give his own desires priority over her happiness, confident in his ability to talk her around. How can she expect to hold the love of such a man after her beauty fades? The narrator describes her state of mind just before she falls ill:

As usual on nights when Genji was away, Murasaki stayed up late, listening to her attendants read stories aloud. In those old tales, which professed to record true-to-life happenings, a woman often got involved with a man who was fickle, licentious, and unfaithful, but he always seemed to settle down in the end. How strange that her own life should have remained so fraught with uncertainty! It was true that hers had been an unusually fortunate karma in some respects, but was she never to be free of these miserable forebodings—these worries that no woman could find endurable or acceptable? It was too much![24]

It is this unremitting mental turmoil that brings on Murasaki's illness in "New Herbs: Part Two," and that leads to her death some four years later.

The "Broom Tree" prescription for a happy marriage proves to have been a false guide. From Uma-no-kami's point of view, Murasaki's conduct has been impeccable, but she has loved Genji too well, and the psychological toll has been too great. After her death, Genji expresses the wish that he had been more careful about causing her pain, but the main lesson he draws is that he has somehow been fated to suffer more than others in this life. Ironically, Genji the shining one, the exemplar of sensitivity, has failed to comprehend the fearful strength of the emotions aroused by his conduct—a strength symbolized by the apparition of the Rokujō lady's spirit at Murasaki's bedside—and the failure has destroyed both his dearest treasure and himself. If Murasaki Shikibu is to continue her narrative, she must find a new hero.

24. Here, as repeatedly in *Genji monogatari*, the ambiguity of classical Japanese makes it impossible to tell how much of the passage is quotation and how much narratorial comment. The author's portrayal of Murasaki's unhappiness follows conventions established in the Love section of *Kokinshū*, where the grieving woman in fear of abandonment is a familiar figure.

Principal Characters

Akashi empress. Daughter of Genji and Akashi lady; consort of present emperor (q.v.); mother of crown prince, of Niou, and of three other children

Akashi lady. A consort of Genji; mother of Akashi empress

Akashi novice. Father of Akashi lady

Akikonomu. Daughter of Rokujō lady and former crown prince; empress of Reizei emperor; no children

Aoi. Daughter of minister of the left and Princess Ōmiya; sister of Tō-no-chūjō; first wife of Genji; mother of Yūgiri

Asagao, Princess. Wooed unsuccessfully by Genji

Evening faces, lady of the. *See* Yūgao

Fujitsubo lady. Daughter of a deceased emperor; consort and later empress of Kiritsubo emperor; aunt of Murasaki; mother of Reizei emperor

Genji. Son of Kiritsubo emperor and Kiritsubo lady

Hyōbukyō, Prince. Brother of Fujitsubo lady; father of Murasaki

Kaoru. Child of Third Princess; thought to be Genji's son, but true father is Kashiwagi, a son of Tō-no-chūjō

Kiritsubo emperor. Genji's father; reigning emperor at start of *The Tale of Genji*

Kiritsubo lady. Minor-ranking favorite consort of Kiritsubo emperor; mother of Genji

Kokiden lady. High-ranking consort of Kiritsubo emperor; mother of Suzaku emperor; daughter of minister of the right

Koremitsu. Minor courtier; Genji's foster-brother (*menotogo*, nurse's son), attendant, and confidant

Minister of the left. Close associate of Kiritsubo emperor; father of Aoi and Tō-no-chūjō

Murasaki. Daughter of Prince Hyōbukyō; protégée and later main wife of Genji

Niou. Son of present emperor (q.v.) and Akashi empress; Murasaki's favorite among Genji's grandchildren

Oborozukiyo. Sister of Kokiden lady; a mistress of Genji

Ōmiya, Princess. Sister of Kiritsubo emperor; wife of minister of the left; mother of Aoi and Tō-no-chūjō

Present emperor (from Genji's 46th year on). Son of Suzaku emperor; successor of Reizei emperor. *See also* Kiritsubo, Reizei, and Suzaku emperors.

Reizei emperor. Son of Genji and Fujitsubo lady; believed to be son of Kiritsubo emperor; successor of Suzaku emperor

Rokujō lady. Widow of a former crown prince; mother of Akikonomu; a mistress of Genji

Scattering blossoms, lady from the house of. A minor member of Genji's harem

Suzaku emperor. Genji's half-brother; son of Kokiden lady; succeeds father, Kiritsubo emperor; abdicates after Genji's return from Suma

Third Princess. Daughter of Suzaku emperor; wife of Genji; mother of Kaoru

Tō-no-chūjō. Son of minister of the left; friend and brother-in-law of Genji

Yoshikiyo. Minor courtier; one of Genji's attendants

Yūgao. "Hidden flower" loved successively by Tō-no-chūjō and Genji in their youth

Yūgiri. Son of Genji and Aoi

Contents of the 'Genji'

Kiritsubo

[From Genji's birth until his twelfth year]

During the reign of a certain sovereign, it happened that one rather insignificant lady enjoyed far greater imperial favor than any of the other consorts and concubines. She was regarded with contempt and jealousy by proud ladies of superior status—personages who had always taken their own success very much for granted—and her equals and inferiors among the concubines felt even more disgruntled. Perpetually agitated by her constant presence at the emperor's side, her rivals made her bear an increasingly heavy burden of resentment. And whether for that reason or another, she grew frail and melancholy, and took to staying away from court. The emperor, who pitied her with all his heart, ignored the criticism and treated her in a manner that seemed destined to go down in history as an exemplar of favoritism.

The senior nobles and courtiers averted their eyes in disapproval. "Nobody wants to watch such excessive displays of affection. This is the kind of thing that led to turmoil and trouble in China," they said. People in general also began to find the situation unpleasant and distressing—bad enough to inspire comparisons with Yang Gueifei.[1]

Reassured by His Majesty's remarkable devotion, the lady continued to appear at court despite many humiliating affronts. Her father, a major counselor, was dead, and the absence of a reliable male sponsor left her pitifully helpless in an emergency, notwithstanding the exertions of her mother, the counselor's principal wife, who was an old-fashioned woman

---

1. Yang Gueifei (719–56) was the beautiful favorite of Emperor Xuanzong of the Tang dynasty in China. When a rebel seized the capital in 755, the imperial army blamed her and her influential relatives, and the emperor was forced to agree to her execution.

of great refinement, and who saw to it that the girl appeared just as well on ceremonial occasions as influential consorts and concubines who were blessed with two parents.

Perhaps the bond uniting the lady and the emperor was a legacy from a previous existence, for she was fortunate enough to bear a male child— moreover, one who glowed like a pearl, the prettiest baby in the world. The impatient emperor lost no time in having him brought to the palace, and when he looked at him, he thought he had never seen such a beautiful face. Everyone had been fussing over the oldest son, the First Prince, whose powerful backing made his succession seem assured. (The mother, a junior consort, was the minister of the right's daughter.) But the First Prince could not begin to rival the newcomer's beauty, and the emperor made the baby his personal favorite, seeing to his needs in every possible way, and merely bestowing public marks of special esteem on the older child.

The baby's mother had not entered the palace as a mere imperial attendant. People had accepted her as someone of consequence, and she had comported herself as a noblewoman should. Her status had inevitably suffered because of the emperor's unreasonable insistence on keeping her at his side—his summoning her whenever there was an interesting musical entertainment or anything else to serve as a pretext, his penchant for detaining her while he lingered in bed in the morning.[2] But after the prince's birth she enjoyed very special imperial recognition, very special courtesies, and the First Prince's mother, the Kokiden lady, feared that the younger child might wind up in the crown prince's residence if things took a turn for the worse. The Kokiden lady had been presented at court before any of the other consorts. Her status demanded the sovereign's utmost consideration, and she was also the mother of children, so that he found her remonstrances both troublesome and pathetic.

Even though the baby's mother was sheltered by the emperor's august protection, there were many who subjected her to contempt and criticism; and the imperial affection became a source of misery, rather than of happiness, for someone so weak and fragile. Her apartments were in the building called Kiritsubo. Naturally enough, others were unhappy when the emperor went past their quarters on his constant visits to her. And when she went too often to his residence, the Seiryōden, they played unbelievably shabby tricks that ruined her attendants' skirts at bridges and galleries along the way. Or, very frequently, they conspired to torment her by locking both doors of an interior passageway she needed to use, so that she was trapped inside. Whatever the occasion, it was sure to bring some new addition to the endless list of her trials. Moved by her distress, the emperor transferred another concubine away from the Kōrōden, where she had always lived,

2. It was only women of low status who attended the emperor day and night. A recognized consort or concubine was expected to stay in her own apartments unless she received a specific summons, and to leave the imperial bedchamber before dawn.

and put those apartments at her disposal—an act for which, needless to say, she was never forgiven by the person in question.

When the young prince entered his third year, the emperor celebrated the assumption-of-the-trousers ceremony with lavish splendor, calling on all the resources of the palace storehouse bureau and the storeroom, just as he had done for his oldest son. There was much criticism of the way the event was handled, but it was impossible to dislike the boy, who was growing up with a beauty of face and disposition so uncommon as to seem quite unique. Knowledgeable people found it incredible that such a one should have been born into this world.

In the summer of that year, the Kiritsubo lady sought permission to retire from the palace because of a slight indisposition. The emperor refused to agree. Accustomed to seeing her in precarious health year after year, he said, "Stay awhile and see how you get along." But her condition worsened daily, and after a mere five or six days, she had sunk so low that her weeping mother persuaded him to release her. She resolved to depart unnoticed, leaving the young prince behind, lest she be subjected to fresh humiliation even at such a time. The emperor could postpone the parting no longer, nor, to his inexpressible sorrow, was it even possible for him to see her off. Her sweet face was emaciated, and she slipped toward unconsciousness, after struggling in vain to express her anguish. His mind in a daze, the emperor swore all kinds of tearful vows, but she lay there, unable to answer, her eyes dim and her body limp, as though she were no longer certain that she still lived.

The emperor was frantic with anxiety. He issued orders for her departure in a hand-drawn carriage, but then he went to her room, and again could not bring himself to let her go. "Didn't we promise to stay together always, even on the road to death? I know you're sick, but I don't see how you can abandon me and go your own way," he said.

She gazed at him with infinite sadness. [Her poem:]

kagiri tote	Grieved beyond measure
wakaruru michi no	to say farewell and set forth
kanashiki ni	on this last journey,
ikamahoshiki wa	gladly would I choose instead
inochi narikeri	the road of the living.

"If I had dreamed this would happen . . ." She gasped for breath. She seemed to want to say something more, but she was shockingly ill and weak.

He longed to keep her there, just as she was, so that he might witness her fate with his own eyes, but a messenger arrived with an urgent plea from her mother: "We have engaged eminent monks to conduct certain prayer rituals, which are scheduled to begin today. They will be starting tonight." He forced himself to endure the agony of letting her go.

His heart too full for sleep, he waited impatiently for the first light of dawn. He was already giving way to dismal forebodings before his messenger had had time to make the round trip. And when the messenger returned, it was with a stricken face. The people at the house, distracted and weeping, had announced that the lady had died shortly after midnight.

The emperor retreated into seclusion, shaken and dazed. His dearest wish was to keep the prince where he could see him, regardless of the mother's death, but there was no precedent for the child's remaining in the palace under such circumstances, and it was decided that he should leave. That his attendants should be weeping and wailing, and that the emperor himself should always be shedding tears, seemed strange indeed to the boy, who had no inkling of what had happened. Partings between parent and child are sad enough on ordinary occasions, but this one was indescribably moving.

There are forms that require observance, and people prepared for the cremation in the usual manner. The mother shed tears of bitter grief. "If only the smoke from my pyre might ascend with hers in a single plume!" she said. She called back one of the funeral carriages assigned to the ladies-in-waiting and got inside; and we may imagine her feelings when she reached Otagi, where solemn rituals were already under way. "Even with the body right there in front of my eyes, I was foolish enough to think of her as alive. Once I've seen the cremation site, I'll be able to accept her death," she had said earlier, in a show of bravery, but now, to the consternation of the others, she seemed in danger of tumbling out of the carriage. "This is exactly what we were afraid of," her people said.

A messenger arrived from the palace—an imperial envoy, sent to announce the Kiritsubo lady's posthumous elevation to third rank—and the proclamation of the edict called forth a fresh access of grief. The promotion had come about because of the emperor's keen remorse for his failure to so much as ensure that people should call her "Junior Consort" during her lifetime. "At least, I can raise her rank a grade now," he thought. There were many who resented even so innocuous an act.

To people of sensibility, the lady's death evoked poignant memories of her beauty and grace, of her mild, agreeable temper, and of how impossible it had been to dislike her. It was only the emperor's immoderate partiality that had made her an object of jealous spite. All the imperial ladies-in-waiting thought with affectionate regret of her sweet nature and loving disposition. It seemed that the poem "Now that she is no more" must have been composed at just such a time.[3]

The emperor never failed to send messages of condolence as the days slipped by and the various memorial rites took place. The passing of time served only to deepen his inconsolable grief, and he spent the days and nights with tear-drenched sleeves, uninterested in summoning anyone else

3. Traced in a 12th-century commentary, *Genji monogatari shaku*, to a poem not otherwise identified: aru toki wa / ari no susabi ni / nikukariki / nakute zo hito wa / koishikarikeru ("I found fault with her whenever the spirit moved while she was alive, but how dear she seems to me now that she is no more!"). See Tamagami, *Genji monogatari hyōshaku*, 1: 54.

to share his bed. Even for those who merely witnessed his misery, the autumn of that year was a dew-drenched season.

"She may be dead, but he's still so crazy about her that nobody else can feel happy," said the Kokiden lady, nursing her grievance.

Whenever the emperor saw the First Prince, he missed the young prince more, and he kept sending people to find out how the boy was getting along—trusted ladies-in-waiting, an old nurse, and so forth. One evening, when an autumn gale had brought a sudden chill to the air, his thoughts strayed to the Kiritsubo lady even more often than usual, and he decided to send a certain Yugei-no-myōbu with a message to her mother. After dispatching her by the light of a beautiful early moon, he sat lost in melancholy reverie. He had been accustomed to enjoying music at such times. The Kiritsubo lady would play the koto with incomparable skill, and if she murmured some trifling bit of poetry, it was sure to excel the compositions of the other consorts. For a moment, he seemed to see her reclining by his side, but the form and face in the vision were less substantial than earthly darkness.[4]

When Myōbu's attendants pulled her carriage inside the gate at her destination, she was saddened by the aspect of the grounds. In earlier days, the widowed mother had managed to keep up the place as a suitable residence for her daughter, but the autumn storm seemed to have wreaked havoc on the plants in the garden, which had shot up while their owner lay prostrate, lost in the darkness of parental grief; and no visitor except the moonlight had braved the tangled growths of wild vines.[5]

After the guest had been received at the south entrance to the main hall, some time elapsed before she or the mother could find words. Then the mother said, "It makes me miserable to linger on like this. And now I feel terribly embarrassed to have an exalted messenger like yourself grope her way through the dews of these mugwort-choked grounds." She wept as though indeed unable to bear her lot.

"Naishi-no-suke told His Majesty she felt much worse—really devastated—after she came here and saw things for herself. Even for an insensitive person like me, the experience is almost too much," Myōbu said. After a brief pause, she delivered the emperor's message. "His Majesty said to tell you, 'For a time, I felt like someone in a dream, and I still can't seem to awaken, even though I am a little calmer now. There is nobody here to

4. Anonymous (KKS 647): mubatama no / yami no utsutsu wa / sadaka naru / yume ni ikura mo / masarazarikeri ("It was little better than the vivid dream I dreamt—that meeting with you in earthly darkness, black as leopard-flower seeds").

5. Fujiwara no Kanesuke (GSS 1102): hito no oya no / kokoro wa yami ni / aranedomo / ko o omou michi ni / madoinuru ka na ("The hearts of parents are not realms where darkness reigns—yet how easily we wander in confusion on the path of love for a child!"); Ki no Tsurayuki (SCSS 8): tou hito mo / naki yado naredo / kuru haru wa / yaemugura ni mo / sawarazarikeri ("Though this is a house where nobody pays visits, springtime, when it comes, does not hesitate to brave the tangled growths of wild vines").

counsel me about ways of coping with this intolerable grief; I would be delighted to have you pay me a quiet visit. I worry a great deal about the little prince—it's sad to think of his living in a house of mourning. Come soon.' He could hardly talk for crying, but he was trying to control himself so as not to seem too emotional. It was a pitiful sight; I left without waiting to hear any more." She handed over the emperor's letter.

"I receive these august words as a light for one whose eyes have been blinded," said the mother. She read the letter. With great sincerity, it said, among other things, "I had been waiting to see if time would do anything to raise my spirits, but the days and months have made my pain more unbearable, and now I am quite desperate. I also worry about the little boy who lacks a mother to help rear him. Please come to the palace and bring him with you as a memento from the past." She could not bear to read all of the poem he had included:

miyagino no	At the sound of the wind
tsuyu fukimusubu	blowing to summon the dews
kaze no oto ni	of Miyagino,
kohagi ga moto o	it is the small bush-clover
omoi koso yare	to which my thoughts turn.

"Knowing as I do that longevity is a curse, I feel ashamed even to imagine the thoughts of the Takasago pines, and I surely could not presume to come and go at the imperial palace.[6] I appreciate His Majesty's many gracious messages, but I could never accept for myself. Somehow, the little prince seems to have anticipated this invitation, and he is wild with impatience to go. His eagerness is only natural, saddening though it is for me. Please tell His Majesty all these things in private, just to let him know how I feel. It would be inauspicious for the prince to keep on living with an unlucky person like me," the mother said.

Myōbu felt that she had better not take the time to see the child, who was in bed asleep. "I'd like to be able to describe everything about him, but His Majesty is probably waiting, and it's getting late," she said.

"I would welcome a chance to talk to you and gain some relief from the anguish of my loss—just to dispel a fraction of the darkness that clouds a parent's heart—so please pay me an informal visit whenever you have time," the mother said. "You used to come on happy, gratifying occasions. To see you the bearer of such a letter now . . . I know I'm repeating myself, but life is a burden to me. We pinned all our hopes on our daughter from the time of her birth, and my husband kept admonishing me about her up

6. Anonymous (KKRJ 3057): ika de nao / ari to shiraseji / takasago no / matsu no omowamu / koto mo hazukashi ("I must do my best not to reveal that I live. How embarrassing to imagine the thoughts of the Takasago pines!"). Pine trees were symbols of longevity. The poet, having outlived his contemporaries, fears that the pines may think it is past time for him to die. There were numerous pine trees at the Takasago Shrine (in southern Hyōgo Prefecture), including one particularly old specimen, best known today from the Noh play "Takasago."

to the very moment of his death. 'Be sure she's presented at court as we always intended. Don't make the mistake of giving up because I'm gone,' he said. I thought it would be better for her not to enter the palace than to live there without influential backing, but I didn't feel able to ignore his last words, so I sent her off. As it happened, His Majesty always favored her extravagantly—far more than her status warranted. I think she tried to associate with the other ladies in the usual manner, hiding the inhuman affronts she suffered, but her rivals were frightfully jealous, and her life became such a series of torments that she finally died an unnatural death. To me it seems that His Majesty's love was more an affliction than a blessing. That shows how unreasonable a bereaved parent can be." The hour grew late as she faltered on in the same vein, choked with tears.

"His Majesty feels the same," Myōbu said. "He says, 'I realize now that hers was a cruel karma: our time together was destined to be short, and that was why I adored her in a way that shocked some people. The last thing I wanted was to cause anybody the slightest disappointment, but there was much unwarranted bad feeling because of her, and at last she left me alone like this. It's more than I can do to control my grief; I've turned into a disgraceful eccentric—which, I suppose, may also be the result of acts committed in a previous existence.' He sits there weeping, saying over and over, 'If only I knew what had happened in my last life.'" She broke down. Then, mindful of the need to hurry back, she said in tears, "It's very late; I must deliver your reply before dawn."

It was not easy to leave the simple dwelling where the sky stretched clear and cloudless in the light of the setting moon, the breeze blew cool, and the insects in the grasses seemed intent on evoking tears with their wails. [Myōbu recited:]

suzumushi no	Though I were to wail
koe no kagiri o	like a shrilling bell cricket
tsukushite mo	with unstinting voice,
nagaki yo akazu	yet would the long night be too short
furu namida ka na	to end the flow of my tears.

The mother instructed a lady-in-waiting to respond:

itodoshiku	The person who comes
mushi no ne shigeki	from the place above the clouds
asajiu ni	brings ever more dew
tsuyu okisouru	to the neglected garden
kumo no uebito	where insect voices lament.[7]

"The crickets must be complaining."

Since it was not an occasion for elaborate presents, the mother gave Myōbu some of the Kiritsubo lady's things as keepsakes—a set of robes,

7. "Place above the clouds" was a term used of the imperial palace.

preserved in anticipation of just such a need, and also some toilet articles of the kind required for dressing hair in a formal coiffure.

Of course, the prince's young ladies-in-waiting were grieved by the Kiritsubo lady's death, but they considered their present surroundings boring and lonely, accustomed as they were to a busy life at court; and they also kept the emperor's melancholy state very much in mind. They declared themselves strongly in favor of an early return to the palace. But it was not a light decision for the grandmother. "People would be bound to gossip if the boy were accompanied by an unlucky woman like me. On the other hand, I'd worry if he were out of my sight for a minute," she thought.

Myōbu was touched to find the emperor still up. While making a show of interest in the luxuriant bloom of the garden, he was talking quietly with four or five especially cultivated ladies-in-waiting, whom he had summoned to act as his sole attendants. Of late, he had taken to looking day and night at a group of pictures representing scenes from "The Song of Everlasting Sorrow"—paintings commissioned by Retired Emperor Uda, who had also commanded Ise and Tsurayuki to compose verses to go with them.[8] Japanese and Chinese poems on related themes had become his favorite topics of conversation. Turning his full attention to Myōbu, he now questioned her about the visit, and she spoke in a soft voice of the deep compassion she had felt. He read the mother's letter: "I am overwhelmed by the honor Your Majesty has conferred on me. Your kind message brings new confusion to a mother's darkened heart." [Her poem:]

araki kaze	After the death of the tree,
fusegishi kage no	its protection against
kareshi yori	the blustering wind,
kohagi ga ue zo	I ponder with anxious heart
shizugokoro naki	the fate of the young bush clover.

He probably overlooked the breach of decorum because of her distraught state.[9] Determined not to make a spectacle of himself, he did his utmost to calm his feelings, but his anguish was beyond endurance. In his mind, he sought out and savored every memory of the Kiritsubo lady, including those from the days when he had barely met her; and he marveled that he had survived so long after the death of one whose briefest absence had caused him distress. His heart ached with pity for the mother. "It was always my intention to do something to repay her for going ahead with the presentation as the major counselor desired," he said, "but there's no use thinking about that now." He continued, "Even so, opportunity undoubtedly lies

8. "The Song of Everlasting Sorrow" is a poem by Bo Juyi about the tragic love of Emperor Xuanzong and Yang Gueifei (translated in Birch, *Anthology of Chinese Literature*, pp. 266–69). Lady Ise and Ki no Tsurayuki were prominent poets of the late 9th and early 10th centuries.

9. The poem could be taken to imply that the emperor would not look after the child.

ahead for the young prince, once he grows older. His grandmother must pray to live a long time."

He asked Myōbu to let him see her presents. "If only the hairpin were the one in the poem—the token brought back from a visit to the dwelling place of the dead!" he said to himself.[10] But such thoughts were vain. [His poem:]

tazuneyuku	Would that I could find
maboroshi mo ga na	a wizard to seek her out,
tsute nite mo	for then I might know,
tama no arika o	at least by hearsay, the place
soko to shirubeku	in which her spirit dwells.

There is a limit to what a brush can do, no matter how skillful the artist may be, and thus Yang Gueifei's painted face and figure lacked the warmth of life. To be sure, one could recognize in the pictures the woman to whom the poet likened the Taiyi hibiscus and the Weiyang willow; and she was probably a brilliant beauty in her Tang-style robes. But to the emperor, with his memories of the Kiritsubo lady's engaging manner and touching charm, his lost love seemed beyond comparison with the color of any flower or the song of any bird. He had sworn day and night that they should be "as two birds sharing a wing, as two trees with joined branches," and now there was only the everlasting sorrow of the death that had made a mockery of his vows.[11]

Delighted by the beauty of the moon, and having long ceased to frequent the Imperial Apartments, the Kokiden lady was making music late into the night while the sovereign sat desolate, his gloom exacerbated by the soughing wind and the chirring insects.[12] He listened with distaste, and the sound of the instruments aroused pity in the hearts of the courtiers and ladies-in-waiting who had been witness to his recent behavior. The Kokiden lady, willful and difficult by nature, probably wanted to let people know that the imperial grief was no concern of hers.

The moon set. [The emperor:]

kumo no ue mo	What light does it shed
namida ni kururu	at the neglected dwelling—
aki no tsuki	the autumn moon
ika de sumuran	whose radiance is dimmed by tears
asajiu no yado	even above the clouds?

The emperor stayed up, fretting about the grandmother and child, while his attendants trimmed and re-trimmed the lamp until the oil was gone. The

10. In "The Song of Everlasting Sorrow," a Taoist priest finds Yang Gueifei on an enchanted island, and receives from her a golden hairpin as a memento for the emperor.

11. The quotation is from "The Song of Everlasting Sorrow."

12. The Imperial Apartments (*ue no mitsubone*) were two rooms used by consorts and concubines when they came to the emperor's residence, the Seiryōden, from their quarters elsewhere in the palace compound.

voices of men from the bodyguards of the right, identifying themselves for night duty, showed that the hour of the ox [1:00 A.M.–3:00 A.M.] must have begun.[13] To avoid comment, he retired to the imperial bedchamber, but sleep refused to come. And when it was time to rise in the morning, he recalled the poem about sleeping "unaware of the dawning day,"[14] and was seemingly as indifferent as in the past to his matutinal duties of state. He made only the merest pretense of eating breakfast, and at the formal meals later in the day, he betrayed a lack of interest that made all the people serving him sigh over his pitiful mien. His closest attendants of both sexes confessed to one another that they were at their wits' end.

"Things were probably fated to turn out this way for him," some people said, "but he was wrong to ignore all the complaints and resentment and act the way he did about her; it's really too much for him to keep going on as though nothing mattered to him, not even affairs of state." There were those who sighed and made whispered comparisons with a foreign ruler.

Time passed, and the young prince came to the palace. Now that he was a bit older, the emperor discerned in him a beauty that seemed more than ever not of this world, and he fretted lest he be destined to die young.

In the following spring, when it was time to name a crown prince, the emperor wanted to disregard the First Prince's claim, but the younger child lacked influential support. Nor was the boy's nomination likely to win general acceptance—on the contrary, he feared that it might prove dangerous to him. Thus he took care to conceal his true feelings. "Besotted though he is, he does know where to draw the line," people said. The Kokiden lady breathed a sigh of relief.

Death came at last to the grandmother, the major counselor's widow—perhaps in response to her prayers, for, inconsolable in her sorrow, she had asked that she might at least be allowed to go in search of her daughter. Again, the emperor was grieved beyond measure. It was the year in which the boy turned six: he was old enough to understand this time, and he wept for his grandmother. She, for her part, had told him over and over of her sadness at leaving him behind after so many years of loving intimacy.

The boy lived entirely at court from then on. When he was seven, the emperor held the first reading, and he was so unbelievably quick and bright that his father actually worried about the significance of such brilliance.[15]

"I don't see how anyone could dislike him now," the emperor said. "Treat

13. The bodyguards of the left stood night duty during the first watch, from 9:00 P.M. to 1:00 A.M.; the bodyguards of the right, during the second watch, from 1:00 A.M. to 5:00 A.M.

14. Ise, speaking as Emperor Xuanzong (IS 55): tamasudare / akuru mo shirade / neshi mono o / yume ni mo miji to / omoikakeki ya ("Did I imagine that I would never so much as dream of her—not though I slept, blinds still drawn, unaware of the dawning day?").

15. The first reading (*fumihajime*) was usually performed when the son of a high-ranking family reached the age of seven or eight. Ostensibly designed to show the child how to read, it was a largely symbolic event, during which the young principal, dressed in elaborate robes, repeated a few words after hearing them read aloud from the *Classic of Filial Piety* or some other suitable text.

him with affection, if only because he's a motherless child." When he visited his ladies, he took the boy along and let him go inside the blinds, even at the Kokiden. The Kokiden lady, for her part, could not bring herself to keep aloof from him, for his countenance was so fair that it would have elicited smiles from the most fearsome warriors. She had borne the emperor two daughters, but their beauty was not equal to his.

The other ladies also let the child see their faces. Simultaneously intrigued and daunted by a refinement and elegance astonishing in one so young, they all treated him as a companion with whom it would not do to be too artless and open.

It was only to have been expected that the boy would excel in his formal Chinese studies, but his proficiency at the koto and flute was also the talk of the palace. Indeed, so numerous and so rare were his accomplishments that it would undoubtedly seem a disagreeable exaggeration if I were to list them all.

Around that time, the emperor learned of a skilled physiognomist who had come to the capital with a party of Koreans. Mindful of Retired Emperor Uda's injunction against summoning foreigners to the palace, he sent the young prince to the Kōrokan in great secrecy. The major controller of the right, who had been assigned general responsibility for the boy's upbringing, took him there as his own son.

The physiognomist kept cocking his head in bewilderment. "He bears the stamp of one destined to ascend to the supreme status of emperor and become the father of the nation, but turmoil and distress may ensue if that happens. We might consider the possibility that he is meant to assist with the government as an imperial surrogate, but that would contradict the signs I observe," he said.

The controller was also a learned doctor, and the two engaged in an interesting conversation. They exchanged poems in Chinese, among them a clever composition in which the physiognomist said something to this effect: "I depart for home in a day or two, but I shall feel sad now that meeting this remarkable young man has brought me such happiness." The prince produced a touching couplet, to which the Korean responded with extravagant praise and splendid gifts. There were also many gifts from the court to the Korean.

Word of the consultation inevitably spread. The emperor guarded the secret, but the crown prince's grandfather, the minister, heard about it and formed his own suspicions concerning its significance.

The emperor was both a prudent man and also something of a Japanese-style physiognomist himself; and certain personal observations had hitherto kept him from even naming the boy an imperial prince.[16] Now he made up his mind, impressed by the Korean's sagacity. "I don't want him to be set

16. Being officially designated as an imperial prince (*shinnō*) or imperial princess (*naishinnō*) conferred a social cachet and made the recipient eligible for special perquisites.

adrift as a rankless imperial prince, with no backing from any maternal relatives. And who knows how much longer I'll be emperor? The way to safeguard his future is to let him become a subject serving as a mainstay of the throne," he thought. He made sure that his son devoted increasing effort to many branches of learning. In view of the boy's remarkable intelligence, it seemed a shame to make him a subject, but he would be bound to incur suspicion if he became an imperial prince. Confirmed in this opinion by a wise astrologer with whom he took counsel, the emperor decided to name him a member of the Genji clan.

As the years went by, there was never a time when the emperor forgot the Kiritsubo lady. He arranged for the presentation of suitable consorts, hoping to find consolation, but society seemed incapable of producing anyone who might even rank in the same category, and he existed in a state of perpetual dissatisfaction.

As it happened, one of his attendants, Naishi-no-suke, had also served an earlier emperor whose fourth daughter was reputed to be a great beauty. The girl was being reared with the utmost care by her mother, the former empress. As a frequent friendly visitor at the empress's residence, Naishi-no-suke had seen the daughter from her childhood on, and she still managed to catch an occasional glimpse of her face. "I've served three emperors without encountering anyone who resembled her dead ladyship, but the empress's daughter looks very much like her now that she's grown. One seldom sees so lovely a countenance," she reported.

His hopes aroused, the emperor sent the mother a courteous request for the daughter's presentation. She temporized, alarmed by the Kokiden lady's malicious nature, and by the open contempt to which the Kiritsubo lady had been subjected; and she joined the late emperor in death while she was still trying to come to a firm decision. Recognizing that the princess had been left in a pathetic situation, the emperor sent earnest assurances that he would see to her needs just as he did for his own daughters. To her ladies-in-waiting, her guardians, and her older brother, Prince Hyōbukyō, it seemed that palace life, with its opportunities for diversion, would be preferable to a lonely private existence, and so she was presented. She became known as the Fujitsubo lady. She did indeed bear an astonishing resemblance to the Kiritsubo lady, both in face and in general appearance. Thanks to her lofty status, which predisposed people to admire her and forestalled criticism from her rivals, she did as she pleased and never had any cause for dissatisfaction. The difficulty in the Kiritsubo lady's case had simply been that people were outraged by His Majesty's open preference for someone they refused to regard as entitled to special treatment.

The emperor still thought about the Kiritsubo lady, but his affections shifted to the new consort before he knew it, and the pain of his loss was all but obliterated—a poignant reminder of the evanescence of worldly things.

As his father's constant companion, Genji was bound to see the lady the emperor visited most frequently, whether she liked it or not. I need hardly say that none of the other imperial consorts considered herself inferior in appearance, and that all were in fact beautiful. But they were a bit past their prime. The Fujitsubo lady was young and sweet, and Genji caught glimpses of her in the natural course of events, try as she might to hide her face. He had heard from Naishi-no-suke of her close resemblance to the mother he could not remember, and in his boyish heart, he came to love her with wistful nostalgia—to yearn to visit her constantly, and to see her on terms of affectionate intimacy.

The two of them were the people the emperor loved best in the world. "Don't keep him at arm's length," he told the lady. "It's odd, but I feel as though I ought to consider you his surrogate mother. You mustn't think he's rude; be loving with him. His mother's face and expression were so much like yours that you could pass for her."

Young though he was, Genji found ways of demonstrating his fondness for the Fujitsubo lady—with small gifts of cherry blossoms, for instance, or of autumn leaves. His obvious devotion rekindled the Kokiden lady's old animosity, which was aggravated by a smoldering dislike of the Fujitsubo lady herself, and she could no longer bear the sight of him.

Genji's glowing beauty was incomparably appealing, far superior to the appearance of the crown prince who was so precious to the Kokiden lady, and whom society praised to the skies. People called him "the shining one." And the Fujitsubo lady, with whom he shared the emperor's deepest love, was called "the radiant sun princess."

Although the emperor considered it a pity for Genji to discard the hairdress and robes of a child, he arranged a capping ceremony when the boy was twelve. He assumed personal charge of the event, gave it his full attention, and made additions of his own to the prescribed ritual. Everything was to be perfect; he was determined that it should create no less a stir than the crown prince's capping, which had taken place in an earlier year at the Shishinden, and which everyone had pronounced magnificent. The banquets scheduled for various places became the subject of special commands, for, he said, the officials at the palace storehouse bureau and the granary might grow careless if they merely followed regulations.

The emperor's chair was placed facing eastward in the eastern eave-chamber of the imperial residential hall, and in front of it were the seats of the initiate and the minister of state who was to confer the cap. Genji arrived during the hour of the monkey [3:00 P.M.–5:00 P.M.]. To those who saw the bright face framed in boyish loops of hair, it seemed a shame to alter his appearance. The treasury minister, who prepared the new coiffure, seemed to regret the responsibility as he cut the beautiful locks; and the emperor, looking on, found himself remembering the dead lady. If only she might have witnessed this scene! Only by stern self-discipline did he master his tumultuous emotions.

After the capping, Genji went to a retiring room and changed into a man's cloak. Then he descended to the courtyard to perform the dance of obeisance, a sight that moved all the beholders to tears. Again, the emperor was less able than others to control his feelings. He returned to the past with an anguished heart, experiencing anew the grief for which he had sometimes found solace.

Genji's beauty had increased to a startling degree, belying the misgivings of his father, who had wondered if it might not harm his looks to dress his hair in masculine style while he was still so young and delicate in appearance.

The minister of the left possessed one daughter, the offspring of an imperial princess, who had been reared with the utmost care. The crown prince had manifested an interest in her, but the minister had put him off, with the thought in mind that he might offer her to Genji instead. He spoke to the emperor, who encouraged the idea. "If that's what you want," the emperor said, "she could act as his bedmate.[17] I don't know of anyone else who is prepared to help out with the capping ceremony." And so he had reached his decision.

Genji withdrew to the courtiers' waiting room, where he took a seat below the last of the imperial princes when it came time for the company to drink. The minister of the left dropped him a hint, but he was at an easily embarrassed age, and no reply occurred to him.

A handmaid arrived with an imperial summons for the minister. When he reported, the emperor gave him some gifts as a reward for his services during the ceremony. They were the usual things: an extra-large white robe and an additional set of clothing, transmitted through His Majesty's attendant Myōbu. With the wine, the emperor offered a poem in which he called the minister's attention to a matter that was on his mind:

itokinaki	When you tied the cord
hatsumotoyui ni	to hold the young boy's hair,
nagaki yo o	did you pledge in your heart
chigiru kokoro wa	that those two should be bound
musubikometsu ya	in permanent union?

The minister replied:

musubitsuru	Great will be my joy
kokoro mo fukaki	if his interest fades no more
motoyui ni	than the deep purple
koki murasaki no	of the cord I fastened
iro shi asezuba	with a pledge of eternal ties.

17. When a prince was initiated into manhood, the event was normally climaxed by the acquisition of a feminine bed partner (*soibushi*), a girl of good family, often somewhat his senior, who usually became his principal wife later.

Then he went to the courtyard to perform the dance of obeisance, descending by way of the long bridge.[18] While there, he received a horse from the stables of the left and a perched hawk from the chamberlains' office. Gifts appropriate to their status were bestowed on the senior nobles and imperial princes ranged in lines at the foot of the stairs. By imperial command, the major controller of the right had provided the prescribed boxed delicacies and baskets of fruit for Genji to present to the emperor.

There was scarcely room for all the rice balls and chests of presents, which were even more numerous than the ones distributed after the crown prince's capping. This was in fact an occasion far more splendid than the other.

That night, the emperor sent Genji to the home of the minister of the left. During the reception ceremonies there, the minister treated the boy with a courtesy so exquisite that it seemed quite beyond precedent. Genji was still very childish in appearance, and to the host he looked almost frighteningly sweet and appealing. But to the daughter, who was a little the older of the two, the match seemed unsuitable and embarrassing.[19]

Not only did the minister enjoy the emperor's highest trust, but his consort, the daughter's mother, was His Majesty's full sister, the offspring of a former sovereign's empress. And as though those two circumstances were not enough to guarantee him a splendid position, he had now acquired Genji as a son-in-law. The marriage struck a devastating blow to the influence of the minister of the right, the crown prince's grandfather, who was expected to assume eventual control of the government.

The minister of the left had fathered a good many children by various ladies. One of them, the princess's son, held the dual positions of chamberlain and lesser captain. He was young and very handsome; and the minister of the right, unable to ignore so eligible a candidate, had arranged a marriage with his cossetted fourth daughter, even though his relationship with the boy's father was strained. The minister made it a point to treat him every bit as generously as the minister of the left treated Genji, and both sons-in-law enjoyed ideal relationships with their wives' fathers.

With the emperor constantly demanding his presence, there was little chance of Genji's settling down to life away from court. The boy cherished the secret belief that no woman could equal the Fujitsubo lady in beauty, and his love for her kept his young heart in turmoil. "If only I might marry someone like that—but there isn't anybody. His Lordship's daughter seems pretty and well-bred, but I don't really care for her," he thought.

Now that Genji had come of age, the emperor no longer allowed him inside the Fujitsubo lady's blinds as he had done in the past. The boy expressed his feelings by playing his flute in harmony with the consort's koto

18. The long bridge was a corridor connecting the Shishinden, a ceremonial building, with the Seiryōden.

19. She was 16, four years Genji's senior.

when there was music, or sought consolation in the faint sound of her voice. Naturally enough, it was only at the palace that he felt happy. His visits to his father-in-law's house were sporadic—stays of two or three days after five or six days of service at court—but the minister did everything in his power to make him comfortable and refused to find fault with his behavior, which was, he said, entirely permissible for one of his years. Both for his daughter and for Genji, the minister selected ladies-in-waiting of exceptionally high quality. He also devised amusing entertainments, and in general took great pains to please the young man.

At the palace, the emperor gave Genji apartments in the Kiritsubo, where his mother had lived, and assigned to his service all the women who had attended the dead lady at court and at home, a disposition that made it possible for the group to stay together. In accordance with imperial commands to the palace repairs office and the bureau of skilled artisans, the Kiritsubo lady's old home was refurbished with incomparable magnificence. The original groves and the artificial hill had always been attractive, and now, with much commotion, work crews set about widening the lake to make the grounds perfect. "If only I could bring someone I loved to a place like this and live there with her!" Genji thought gloomily.

People say there is a tradition that it was the admiring Korean who first called Genji "the shining one."

The Broom Tree

[Summer of Genji's seventeenth year]

Genji made his mistakes—so many, indeed, as to lay him open to the charge that his fine sobriquet, "the shining one," was a misnomer; and there even seems to have been talk (which can only be called malicious) about affairs that he tried to keep secret, afraid of acquiring a reputation for indiscretion if still more tales of his amours should be passed on to future generations. In reality, his sensitivity to the world's opinion was acute. He was the soul of circumspection, and the Katano lesser captain must have been vastly amused by his lack of romantic, interesting adventures.[1]

Around the time when he was still a middle captain, he took great delight in his court duties and seldom left the palace for his father-in-law's house. The minister's people suspected a case of "the confusion of secret love," but, to tell the truth, his was not a nature to be much attracted to frivolous, commonplace, spur-of-the-moment affairs.[2] Instead, he had a deplorable habit of very occasionally, and most uncharacteristically, setting his heart on a relationship that was bound to result in misery; and at such times his behavior was not always what it should have been.

During the unrelenting summer rains, the court observed an extended period of ritual seclusion, and Genji stayed on duty for an unusually long time. Impatient and disgruntled, the people at the minister's mansion continued to provide him with magnificent costumes, perfect down to the last

1. The Katano lesser captain, the hero of a lost romance, is said to have been an ever-successful philanderer who paid no attention to public opinion. Tamagami, *Genji monogatari hyōshaku*, 1: 160.

2. Anonymous (IM, sec. 1): kasugano no / wakamurasaki no / surigoromo / shinobu no midare / kagiri shirarezu ("Like the random patterns on this robe, dyed with young purple from Kasuga Plain, utterly confused is the heart of one secretly in love").

detail, and the sons of the house were always to be found waiting on him at the Kiritsubo. Middle Captain Tō-no-chūjō (the princess's son) was on especially close terms with him, more relaxed and informal than his brothers when there was music or some other entertainment. Somewhat heartlessly flirtatious and fickle, Tō-no-chūjō also found it distasteful to live with the daughter of the minister who treated him so well. He maintained his apartments at home in luxurious style and usually went along on Genji's visits to the family mansion, where he shared his Chinese studies and amusements day and night. Wherever Genji went, he was sure to be there. As a natural consequence of such close association, the two became great friends, their lack of reserve so complete that neither could conceal his innermost thoughts from the other.

It was a hushed evening toward the end of a long rainy day. The courtiers' hall was almost deserted, and things were also unusually quiet at the Kiritsubo. Genji sat next to a lamp, looking at books. From the cabinet beside him, he withdrew some letters on paper of various colors. Tō-no-chūjō was immediately curious, but Genji refused to hand the papers over. "I could show you a few that are harmless enough, but I'm afraid some aren't in the best of taste," he said.

"The frank ones you seem to consider 'not in the best of taste' are the very ones I want to see," his friend complained. "I can't profess to be anyone of much importance, but I do manage to carry on a correspondence suited to my status, and it produces a surfeit of humdrum, hackneyed love letters. The only ones worth reading are the ones written when the senders are full of resentment and accusations—or perhaps when they're waiting impatiently at nightfall."

If it had been a question of letters from ladies of high degree, the kind demanding strict secrecy, Genji would certainly have hidden them away instead of letting them lie loose in an ordinary cabinet. These must have been less important—nothing to worry about. Tō-no-chūjō took them up and glanced through them, one by one. "Quite a collection!" He tried to identify the authors, and some of his guesses hit the mark. To Genji's amusement, he challenged the denials even when he was wrong. Genji guarded his tongue, misled him as well as he could, and finally repossessed the letters and put them away.

"You must be the one with the big collection," he said. "How about letting me see them? I'll be glad to open this cabinet afterward."

"I fear there's nothing worth showing," Tō-no-chūjō said. "I've gradually come to realize that it's almost impossible to find a woman one can regard as beyond criticism," he continued. "There seem to be many who possess surface attractions—they write a beautiful hand, know how to make just the right reply to a letter, and in general perform rather well in terms of what might be expected of them. But even so, if I were really choosing on the basis of such accomplishments, it would be hard to find someone of whom I would think, 'I absolutely can't let her slip from my grasp.' Most of them take inordinate pride in their own skills and denigrate others in a thoroughly disagreeable manner.

"Sometimes, a man will get excited over reports of a skill possessed by a girl with a pair of doting parents who are rearing her in strict seclusion, their hearts set on a brilliant marriage. She's beautiful, gentle, innocent—and, with time on her hands because she doesn't mingle in society yet, she's become absorbed in some little art, taken up in imitation of those around her, at which she has become expert by dint of incessant practice. When the people who look after her mention her to others, they keep her weak points to themselves and talk up the reasonably good ones. And since the man has never seen her, how can he be sure that he should dismiss their reports as false, merely on the basis of guesswork? But once he gets on intimate terms with her, lured by the hope that it may all be true, she invariably disappoints his expectations." He breathed a deep sigh.

Genji smiled, as though his companion's rather intimidating display of experience had recalled a similar incident in his own past. "I wonder if there's any woman who can't boast of at least one accomplishment," he said.

"If there were, no man would let himself be persuaded to approach her. I imagine there are just about as many hopeless cases as there are paragons.

"When a girl is born into an exalted household, there will always be protective people around to conceal her faults, and she will naturally seem to be the peak of perfection. Women from the middle rank have distinct personalities and individual tastes; there are many ways of distinguishing among them. As for the lower class, they can be of no particular interest."

He seemed to have mastered every detail of his subject. His curiosity whetted, Genji said, "Now about those classes—what should the basis be for distinguishing among them? How shall we treat the high-born individual who sinks into ruin, loses rank, and scarcely lives like a human being, or the common fellow who rises to become a senior noble, decorates his house with all the self-confidence in the world, and considers himself as good as anybody else?"

Just then, Uma-no-kami and Tō Shikibu-no-jō arrived to participate in the ritual seclusion. They were great sophisticates, clever at argumentation, and Tō-no-chūjō drew them into a debate on the nature of class, delighted to see them. A good many disagreeable things were said.

"Even when a man rises in the world, people will reject him if his lineage doesn't fit his new status," Uma-no-kami declared. "And even if someone comes from an exalted family and continues to have a high opinion of himself, he'll suffer from want and be forced into unbecoming expedients if he can't make his way in the world, falls behind, and loses his popularity. Our decision should be that both belong in the second rank. Society has already defined the status of the so-called *zuryō*—the men who get involved in the job of governing the provinces—but there are gradations among them, and in times like the present, it's all right to single out some who aren't too bad and include them at the middle level of the middle class. The kind of man I personally find a refreshing improvement on a boorish senior noble is someone of fourth rank, elegible to be a consultant, who enjoys a decent reputation, comes from a respectable family, and lives in comfortable style. There seems to be nothing he doesn't have in his house, no skimping anywhere, and he probably has any number of daughters, all being reared with fantastic solicitude, and all growing up without a flaw. Many such girls enter court service and score surprising successes."

Genji laughed. "It seems we'd better concentrate on the rich ones, doesn't it?" he said.

"You don't sound like yourself," Tō-no-chūjō said with a frown.

"There's no point in discussing the girl who is born into a great house—a family irreproachable in lineage and reputation—but who is inferior both in her deportment at home and in the impression she makes on others. We can only shrug our shoulders in disgust and wonder how she managed to grow up like that," Uma-no-kami said. "If someone with the same advantages turns out supremely well, that's only natural. People think it is only to have been expected, and nobody is likely to exclaim in amazement, 'What a rare phenomenon!' Such a girl is beyond the reach of someone like me, so I won't go on about the top of the top class.

"What *would* be amazing would be to discover an unbelievably sweet, appealing maiden shut up in a lonely, dilapidated, vine-choked dwelling, her very existence unknown to others. We would marvel at finding her there and would feel strangely drawn to her just because of the way she has confounded our expectations. Her father would perhaps be old and disagreeably overweight, her brother ill-favored, but she would lead a dignified life inside her predictably undistinguished rooms, and the polite accomplishments with which she whiled away the time would seem delightful. Her skills might in fact be limited, but we'd still consider her unexpectedly interesting. I don't say she could be singled out as superb or flawless—just that it would be hard to dismiss her." He glanced at Shikibu, who remained silent. (Shikibu may have wondered if his friend was thinking of his own sisters, who had been the subject of a fair amount of praise.)

Genji must have considered the chances of such a discovery negligible, since it was impossible, after all, to find the right person at even the highest social level. He was leaning against an armrest, attired in an informal cloak that was draped with deliberate negligence over some soft white inner robes, its cords untied; and his beauty in the lamplight made it tempting to think of him as a woman. To see him was to sense the difficulty of choosing a woman who could be completely worthy of him, even if she were the highest of the high.

They talked on, comparing various types. "The world is full of women," said Uma-no-kami, "but when a man tries to pick a dependable spouse, he learns how hard it is to settle on anyone, even a person who would seem perfectly all right as somebody else's wife. It is not all that easy, I imagine, to find men with the potential to serve as pillars of state, but it takes more than one or two people to run the government, no matter how able they may be. The superior accepts help from the inferior, the inferior defers to the superior, and broad-ranging functions are performed in a spirit of accommodation. When we come to think about the lone woman who must act as mistress within the narrow confines of a household, we can see that she'll have to have a great number of indispensable qualities. It becomes a case of 'When I venture *this*, thinking, since the case is thus—when *this* is well, *that* is ill,'[3] and a man reconsiders, acknowledging the scarcity of candidates who are even marginally acceptable. It isn't that he deliberately adopts the role of a dilettante, indulging a flirtatious heart by meeting and comparing all kinds of women—no, he merely wants to satisfy himself that a girl is the wife for him, so he throws himself into the attempt to at least find someone he can love, and whose flaws are not egregious enough to require correction and instruction. His first such choice is bound to be hard.

"Once a man is married to a woman, it can be difficult for him to abandon her, even though she may not be what he could wish. People will remark on his constancy in staying with her, and, naturally, the fact that they are still together will cause others to surmise that she possesses exceptional qualities. But in all my observation of marriages, I've never encountered one that seemed unbelievably successful. And considering the problems of people like me, whose range of options is fairly wide, what kinds of alternatives are there for you young lords, who search at the very highest level?

"While women remain pretty and young-looking, they all make irreproachable behavior a point of pride. One of them may write to a man, but her ambiguous language and faint handwriting will keep him guessing. Or let's say a man calls on a woman and makes up his mind not to leave without actually meeting her. He'll be subjected to an unconscionable wait, and then, when he ventures a gallant sally, in the hope of at least eliciting a word or two, she merely murmurs a little something under her breath. All this is an excellent way to hide defects.

"Sometimes a man falls head over heels in love, fascinated by a woman's apparent gentleness and femininity, but the moment he begins catering to her whims, she turns into a tease. Of all their faults, I think this is the worst.

"Seeing to her husband's needs is the one responsibility a wife can't neglect, so it would seem just as well for her not to brood over the pathos of ephemerality, or feel an obligation to respond with sensitivity to every fleeting phenomenon, or immerse herself in elegant pursuits. On the other hand, there's the plain-looking housewife who demonstrates her sense of respon-

3. Anonymous (KKS 1060): soe ni tote / to sureba kakari / kaku sureba / ana iishirazu / ausa kirusa ni ("When I venture *this*, thinking, 'Since the case is thus,' *that* is what results. When I try *that* . . . what to say? When *this* is well, *that* is ill").

sibility by tucking her hair behind her ears and devoting herself heart and soul to domestic concerns. Her husband thinks, 'I can't talk to some outsider about everything that happens at court and elsewhere while I'm away—what people do, the good and bad things I remember seeing and hearing. If only I could discuss matters with a wife who would listen to me and understand what I say!' A smile comes to his lips, tears fill his eyes—or, often enough, he fires up with moral indignation about something or other. But what good would it do to tell her? He turns aside involuntarily, and a private recollection evokes a spontaneous laugh. 'I declare!' he says, talking to himself. He can scarcely help feeling depressed when she looks up, with her mind on something else, and asks, 'What's so funny?'

"Actually, it's not a bad idea to look for a completely childlike, docile woman, train her a little, and marry her. The man may have misgivings about her reliability, but at least he can feel that she's educable. And to be sure, he'll overlook the faults she commits in his presence the more readily because she's such an appealing little thing. But once they're apart and he sends a message about something that needs to be done, she lacks the judgment to decide how to take care of it, whether it's a matter of taste or something more practical. This is most disturbing: one feels, after all, that the flaw of undependability can be a source of infinite grief.

"And then there's the woman who's usually blunt and disagreeable but makes a wonderful appearance when the occasion calls for it." The omniscient debater heaved a deep sigh, unable to reach a conclusion.

"My present feeling," he continued, "is that I'm not going to make social position my main criterion—much less physical appearance. The one disqualification will be a terrible disposition. Otherwise, a man should simply choose for his lifetime companion anyone who is serious and placid by nature. If, in addition, she happens to be talented and discriminating, he'll rejoice. If she's a bit inferior in some respects, he won't dwell on her deficiencies: as long as she's faithful and not unreasonably jealous, he'll see that she acquires surface accomplishments in the natural course of events.

"A gentle, shy woman of the second kind may pretend not to notice things about which she might justifiably complain. To all outward appearances, she has nothing on her mind. But when she reaches the breaking point, she flees in secret to some remote mountain dwelling or isolated shore, leaving behind an indescribably poignant letter, a pathetic poem, and mementos that are sure to make the man think of her, whether he wants to or not. When I was a child listening to the ladies-in-waiting read stories, I used to feel deeply moved, even to the point of tears, by the plight of the women who made such decisions. But thinking about it now, I find their behavior rash and theatrical. Even if a wife has to put up with something at the moment, what could be more foolish than to doom herself to a lifetime of misery by ignoring her husband's sincere devotion, running away into hiding as though unaware of his feelings, and causing him no end of trouble—

all in order to test his heart? Her emotion swells, fed by people who praise her decision, and she's a nun before you know it. She seems to be in a state of enlightenment when she reaches her decision, and it doesn't occur to her that she may someday look back on her secular life with regret. But her acquaintances come to commiserate with her—'What a tragedy! To think you were ready to go this far!'—and the news of her action is greeted with tears by her husband, whom she still can't bring herself to hate. 'Why in the world did you do it when he loved you so much?' say her servants and elderly ladies-in-waiting. As she gropes for the tresses that once brushed her cheeks, her own face contorts with misery. She tries to be brave, but the tears overflow, and each time it's more than she can bear: she's so full of regrets that the Buddha must think her heart is more impure than it was before. It certainly seems to me that a woman is more likely to stray onto one of the evil paths when she's halfway enlightened than when she remains a sinful lay person. And even if the karmic bond is so strong that the man finds her before she takes the vows, the memory is bound to rankle in his mind. The truly strong, impressive marriage is the one in which the woman stays at the man's side through thick and thin, overlooking disagreeable incidents. Escapades like this are bound to leave a residue of uneasiness and constraint.

"It's also foolish for a woman to show open resentment and pick a quarrel with a man just because he gets involved in a meaningless affair with someone else. As long as he associates the wife fondly with the early days of their love, he will value the relationship, however attractive the other woman may seem; but the marriage may well end if she deluges him with complaints.

"A husband's love will increase if a woman remains calm in every situation, merely hints at her knowledge of causes for jealousy, and speaks only in an unobjectionable, roundabout fashion of matters at which she might easily take offense. In more cases than not, he'll be moved to mend his ways. On the other hand, a woman will find herself dismissed as negligible, no matter how sweet and appealing she may be, if she simply stands back, inordinately reluctant to interfere, and lets her husband do whatever he pleases. A man doesn't really get any fun out of drifting like an unmoored boat, wouldn't you agree?"

Tō-no-chūjō nodded. "It can be a serious matter when we have to doubt the fidelity of someone whose charm and appeal have captured our heart," he said. "We think we can reform the person by remaining faithful ourselves and overlooking the transgressions, but we aren't likely to succeed. On the whole, I suppose it's best to adopt an attitude of calm forbearance toward behavior at which we might take legitimate offense." This was a verdict that fit his own sister's case, he thought. He was disappointed and vexed to find that Genji had dozed off and had nothing to say on the subject.

Uma-no-kami, the expert, talked on, and Tō-no-chūjō paid close attention, eager to hear the rest of his dissertation.

"Think about some comparisons—for example, the woodworker who makes all kinds of things to suit his fancy. If one of his products happens to be a spur-of-the-moment trifle for which there is no fixed model, it may look stylish at first glance. 'Well! Here's another way to make that,' we think. As one such occasion follows another, the form keeps changing, and some of the results impress us as modern, fresh, and appealing. But when it comes to carefully fashioning a perfect piece of formal furniture—a decorative object made in the prescribed way—then the true expert demonstrates his unique skill.

"Again, there are many fine artists in the office of painting. When a group has been chosen to draw preliminary sketches in black and white, it's impossible to glance at the individual pictures and find clues to distinguish the superior from the inferior. In an extravagantly colored picture of Mount Penglai, the fairy isle no mortal has ever seen, or of fierce fish in wild seas, or horrendous Chinese beasts, or invisible spirits, the painter lets his imagination run riot to astound us the more, and the result will pass for the real thing, even though it's untrue to life. But the brush of a master is unique— far better than the efforts of a mediocre artist—when it comes to drawing ordinary mountains and streams and familiar dwellings in such a way that we think, 'That's it, exactly,' or inserting unobtrusive bits of scenery that seem appealing and gentle, or depicting range after range of densely forested rolling hills so that they seem infinitely remote from the busy world, or creating a meticulous design for a garden behind a rustic fence.

"Also in calligraphy, an ill-trained writer's characters may look skillful and stylish at first glance, with their dots running into lines and their vague aura of assertiveness, whereas the writing of someone who has mastered the essence of the art through painstaking study may appear unremarkable. But when we pick up the two specimens and compare them again, we see that the product of the competent hand is the better.

"That's the way it is in these relatively minor matters. So when it comes to the human heart, I certainly don't feel like trusting somebody who is all coquetry and surface charm. I'll tell you about one of my own early experiences, even though it may sound a bit indecent." He inched closer on his knees, and Genji awoke. Tō-no-chūjō sat opposite with the expression of a true believer, cheek on hand. It was amusingly like the scene when a learned monk delivers a Buddhist sermon, except that this was the kind of occasion on which those present find it impossible to keep from discussing their love affairs.

"Early in my career, while I still held a junior post, there was a woman I fancied. I mentioned her earlier—the one who was no beauty. Being young and setting great store by a pretty face, I considered it a minor liaison and never thought of making her my principal wife. When I got bored and sought distraction in other quarters, she flew into jealous fits. I was annoyed and wished she could be more even-tempered, but her attacks never let up. On the one hand, it was exasperating, but there were times when I felt sorry for her, too, wondering how she could keep on caring so much for someone so unreliable; and almost without realizing it, I lost the desire to roam.

"This woman paid scrupulous attention to all my needs and tried her best to see that everything was exactly as I desired. For instance, she would puzzle out ways to perform tasks she really was unequal to, determined to get them done for my sake; or she would devote tremendous effort to mastering a skill at which she didn't excel, so that I wouldn't find her wanting. I had thought that such behavior signified a strong will, but she was always submissive and gentle. She paid great attention to makeup and dress because she was afraid her ugliness might disgust me, she avoided strangers because she thought it might be a blow to my dignity for her to be seen, and in general she tried to be prudent and circumspect. As we went on together, I found no fault in her character except for the one thing—her intolerable jealousy.

"At that point, I thought, 'She seems to be an inordinately devoted, timid woman. If I can scare her just enough to teach her a lesson, she'll probably calm down and quit being so obnoxious.' It seemed to me that if I let her know I intended to break with her because I was fed up, anyone so submissive would be bound to mend her ways; and I intentionally put on a great show of coldness. Then, when she flew into one of her usual jealous rages, I said, 'Strong as our karmic bond may be, this kind of willfulness will sever it; I won't be seeing you anymore if this keeps up. If you want to break things off, just go on nursing your groundless suspicions. If you want us to stay together far into the future, you'll have to bear the hard things, learn to shrug them off, and quit being jealous. Then I'll love you with all my heart, and you'll be my principal wife when I rise to a modest prominence.'

"After I had gone on for a while in that lofty vein, satisfied that I was doing a fine job of teaching, she answered with a faint smile. 'I wouldn't be impatient or upset if it were simply a matter of accepting your present poverty and insignificance and waiting for you to move up in the world, but I can't bear the anguish of going on like this month after month and year after year, putting up with your cruelty and hoping against hope that you might change someday. The time has come for us to part.' The hostility in her voice aroused my anger, and I showered her with abuse. Too impassioned to control herself, she seized one of my fingers and bit it.

"I turned on her with exaggerated reproaches. 'I'll never be able to perform my duties at court with a wound like this. Now how am I supposed to rise above the insignificance you cast up to me? I'll just have to become a monk.' I left, holding my finger curled against my palm and saying, 'Very well, today marks the end for us.' To my parting poem I added the comment, 'You can have no complaint':

te o orite	When with my fingers
aimishi koto o	I tell over the events
kazoureba	of our married life,
kore hitotsu ya wa	I see that jealousy
kimi ga uki fushi	is far from your only flaw.

Angry though she was, she burst into tears:

uki fushi o	Your flaws I have told
kokoro hitotsu ni	in the silence of my heart
kazoekite	as time has gone by:
ko ya kimi ga te o	this is indeed the hour
wakarubeki ori	when I must bid you farewell.

"Despite the quarrel, I didn't really intend to break with her, but I was leading an unsettled life, and I let the days slip by without even sending her a note. One night when a dreary sleet was falling, a group of us left the imperial palace together, after staying late to rehearse some dances for the Kamo Special Festival, and when we separated to go our own ways, I realized that her house was the only place I thought of as home. The prospect of spending the night alone at the palace was depressing—nor could I expect much warmth at the house of a rather affected lady I had been visiting. I resolved to go where I could be sure of comfort, and also to use the occasion to test her attitude. I felt a little sheepish and shy as I entered, brushing the snow from my garments with unnecessary vigor, but I said to myself that a visit on such a night surely ought to be enough to melt even so long hardened a heart.

"A dim lamp stood facing the wall, several soft, thickly padded robes were spread on a large incense basket, and all the curtains were up, just as though she had been hoping I might appear. 'No more than I expected,' I thought smugly. But she herself was not to be seen; nobody was there but a few ladies-in-waiting who were looking after the place. 'Her Ladyship went to her father's house at nightfall,' they said in answer to my questions.

"I had already been disappointed by her behavior—shutting herself up in the house, never sending a coquettish poem or elegant note or doing anything else of interest—and now in my irritation (and little as I actually believed it), I wondered if her shrewishness might have been part of a deliberate plan to turn me against her. But the perfect dyes and impeccable tailoring of the robes laid out for me showed that they had been prepared with more than usual attention, and that, in characteristic fashion, she had been thinking about me and my needs, even after apparently deciding to break with me.

"Whatever the evidence to the contrary, I was positive she didn't want to give me up. I tried some approaches, and she accepted them. She made no effort to confuse me by hiding, nor did she embarrass me by refusing to answer any of my letters. She merely said, 'If you continue in your old ways,

I won't be able to overlook it. If you learn to settle down, I'm willing for us to live together.' 'All very well,' I thought, 'but she can't bear to part from me.' Convinced that a little discipline would do her good, I made no promise of reform, but instead subjected her to some very perverse antics. She took it dreadfully to heart and died, and only then did I realize the folly of my sport.

"When she comes to mind now, I always have the feeling that she was a woman who met every requirement for a lifetime companion. There was no matter, however large or small, on which I couldn't consult her with profit. When it came to dyeing, she was a veritable Tatsutahime, and as a seamstress she was a marvel, as deft as the Weaver Maid." As he sat remembering her, she seemed to him infinitely pathetic.

"We'd probably settle for less than the Weaver Maid's skill if we could share the Ox-Driver's good fortune in keeping his spouse forever," Tō-no-chūjō chimed in. "It sounds as though your Tatsutahime must have been truly unique among women. No wonder it's hard to find the ideal wife when we can't even count on things as trivial as blossoms and autumn leaves, which all too often display drab colors, unworthy of the season, and come and go without meriting our attention."

"Around the same time," Uma-no-kami resumed, "I was seeing something of a woman who had a nicer personality than the other one, and whose tastes seemed to be refined. She composed poetry, wrote a flowing hand, and played the koto agreeably—in fact, I didn't notice any shortcomings at all. She wasn't bad looking, either, so I paid her an occasional surreptitious visit, meanwhile relying on the nagger to look after me; and in time I fell deeply in love. When the other one died, I was dazed with grief, but it does no good to cling to the departed, and I got into the habit of paying her frequent visits. Gradually, I became aware of a somewhat flashy, flirtatious side to her character, which displeased me and led to the conclusion that she wouldn't make a trustworthy wife. My visits fell off, and presently it began to look as though she had taken a secret lover.

"As I was leaving the palace on a beautiful moonlit night in the tenth month, I met a certain courtier who joined me in my carriage. I decided to spend the night at the major counselor's place.[4]

"'I have an odd feeling of concern about a house where someone has probably been waiting for me tonight,' my companion said.

"As it happened, the woman I've been telling you about lived on the way. We could see the reflection of the moon in the lake beyond her outer wall (which was crumbling here and there), and the other man got out—unable, he announced, to go past a place where even the moon had sought a lodging. He had apparently been on close terms with my mistress for quite a

4. The major counselor was probably his father.

while, because he seated himself jauntily and gazed up at the moon from a
sort of veranda, which was attached to a corridor near the middle gate. The
white chrysanthemums had taken on a delightful reddish tinge, and the autumn leaves were scattering in the wind, as though in competition to forsake
the boughs—all in all, a moving scene. The man drew a flute from his breast
and began to play, interspersing his piping with snatches of song, such as,
'The shade is good.'[5]

"Presently, I heard the mellow strains of a six-stringed koto, already tuned
to the right key, harmonizing skillfully with the flute. The effect wasn't at
all bad, nor did the modern sound of a *ritsu* mode seem inappropriate to
the bright moonlight as it drifted from behind the bamboo blinds, summoned by the woman's gentle touch. Filled with admiration, the man
walked over to the blinds. 'I see no sign that anyone has made his way
through the autumn leaves in this garden,' he teased.[6] He picked a chrysanthemum and offered it with a poem:

koto no ne mo	Splendid beyond words
tsuki mo e naranu	both koto and moonlight
yado nagara	at this dwelling,
tsurenaki hito o	but I wonder if they have held
hiki ya tomekeru	an indifferent man.

'I really shouldn't talk that way.'

"'How about another song?' he continued. 'Don't be ungenerous when
there's someone here who can appreciate it.' To this and other jesting, familiar remarks, she returned a coquettish, affected answer:

kogarashi ni	I have no words,
fukiawasumeru	nor has my koto notes
fue no ne o	sufficient to hold
hikitodomubeki	one whose flute harmonizes
koto no ha zo naki	with the cold autumnal wind.

"Unaware that I was listening to their badinage with mounting indignation, she tuned a thirteen-stringed koto to the *banshiki* mode and began to
play in the currently fashionable manner. The music was not without its
brilliance, but I found it loathsome.

"When a man is merely involved in a casual, off-and-on affair (with a
lady-in-waiting at court, for example), it may be amusing enough, for as

5. A line from a folksong (*saibara*), "Asuka Well" (KDKYS, p. 385): "At Asuka Well—that's
where I want to spend the night. YA! OKE! The shade is good; the water is cold; the fodder is
good." The woman is expected to recall the second line, and to understand that the singer is
asking to stay with her. The small-capped words are nonce syllables.

6. Anonymous (KKS 287): aki wa kinu / momiji wa yado ni / furishikinu / michi fumiwa-
kete / tou hito wa nashi ("Now autumn has come. Fallen leaves have covered the garden, and
along the buried path no visitor makes his way").

long as the liaison lasts, to watch his fair one flirt and preen herself on her attainments. But I couldn't help turning against this woman and judging her too little trustworthy, too forward, to qualify as a partner in what I would consider a permanent relationship, even though my visits might be irregular. I used the events of that evening as an excuse for breaking with her.

"When I think over those two experiences and compare them, I see that even as a youth I recognized the unseemly, untrustworthy character of a woman who would flaunt her talents like that. I expect to hold the same view with deeper conviction in the future. You gentlemen are probably interested only in flirtatious, yielding women—dewdrops on bush clover, as it were, seemingly ready to fall if we break the branch, or hailstones on bamboo grass, ready to vanish if we pick them up. But you'll know better in another seven years or so. Take a humble man's advice: beware of the female who looks like an easy conquest. Such women commit indiscretions, and their men acquire reputations as fools."

To this advice, Tō-no-chūjō responded with his usual affirmative nod. Genji gave a slight smile in apparent agreement. "They're both rather awkward, embarrassing stories, aren't they?" he said, laughing.

"Let me tell you a story about a foolish woman," Tō-no-chūjō said. "She was someone whom I had begun to visit in strictest secrecy, and whom it had seemed worth my while to keep seeing in the same way. There was no thought in my mind of a permanent relationship, but she became dear to me as I got used to her, and I felt that it would be impossible to forget her, even though my visits were irregular. I noticed that she showed signs of regarding me as her protector; and that being the case, there were times when I couldn't help expecting her to get upset, but she didn't seem to notice that anything was wrong: however long my absence, she always seemed determined to act patient and resigned, and not to consider me a philanderer who merely dropped in now and then. Moved to compassion, I kept assuring her that she could count on me. She was a defenseless orphan, and I found it appealing that she thought, 'I'm all right; I have him,' whenever any problem came up.

"Then someone at my wife's house availed herself of an opportunity to drop a cruel, vicious innuendo in my mistress's ear. It happened during a period when I had let a long time elapse without visiting her, my mind at ease because of her mild manner; and it wasn't until later that I learned of it. Never dreaming that she had suffered such a harsh blow, I continued to stay away, without even sending a letter—though, of course, I didn't forget her. Meanwhile, she felt extremely depressed and vulnerable, especially since there was a child to consider. In desperation, she picked a wild pink and sent it to me." There were tears in his eyes.

"What did her letter say?" Genji asked.

"I don't seem to remember anything in particular. [There was a poem:]

yamagatsu no	Though the rustic's fence
kakiho aru tomo	sink neglected into ruin,
oriori ni	may the kindly dew
aware wa kake yo	descend now and again
nadeshiko no tsuyu	on the wild pink at its base.[7]

"This reminder brought me to her house. As usual, there was no coldness in her manner, but she looked terribly unhappy, and she seemed to me to resemble a character in an old romance as she gazed disconsolately at the dew-drenched grounds of the neglected dwelling, weeping as though in rivalry with the wailing insects. [I recited a poem:]

sakimajiru	Hard task though it be
hana wa izure to	to distinguish between flowers
wakanedomo	in intermingled bloom,
nao tokonatsu ni	there is still none to equal
shiku mono zo naki	the wild pink, "blossom of the bed."[8]

"My idea was to forget for the moment about the child, the 'wild pink of Yamato,' and concentrate on soothing the mother—on making it clear that I would guard her 'even against a speck of dust.' She responded with a poem, murmured as though the matter were unimportant, with no hint of serious resentment.

uchiharau	A cold gale adds its threat
sode mo tsuyukeki	to the wild pink burdened with dew
tokonatsu ni	where tears have dampened sleeves
arashi fukisou	employed to brush a dusty bed.
aki mo kinikeri	Love's autumn has truly come![9]

"She tried to keep me from noticing her tears, which seemed to cause her great embarrassment, and acted as though nothing could be more distressing than to let me see that she minded my behavior. So I didn't worry; again, I stayed away. And she simply disappeared—vanished without a trace. She must be having a hard time if she's still alive. I'd never have let her wander off like that if she had made any demands on me in the days when I was fond of her. Nor would I have neglected her for such long stretches of time; I could have arranged to give her a certain position and look after her per-

7. Fence, dew, and wild pink are metaphors for the author, Tō-no-chūjō, and the child.
8. Whereas the woman has used *nadeshiko*, "wild pink," to mean the child, Tō-no-chūjō uses *tokonatsu*, another name for the flower, to refer to the woman herself. The first two syllables of *tokonatsu* are homophonous with a word meaning "bed." The reader is intended to recall a poem by Ōshikōchi no Mitsune (KKS 167): chiri o dani / sueji to zo omou / sakishi yori / imo to wa ga nuru / tokonatsu no hana ("I have guarded them even against specks of dust since first they blossomed—those wild pinks, 'flowers of the bed' where I lie with my wife").
9. The cold gale represents Tō-no-chūjō's wife; *aki* puns on "autumn" and a form of the verb *aku*, "tire of," of which Tō-no-chūjō is the subject.

manently. The 'wild pink' was an adorable child. I want very much to find her, but I haven't been able to learn anything about her yet.

"This woman would certainly seem to be an example of your unreliable type. Deceived by her placid air, I went on loving her without realizing that her heart was seething with anger—a fruitless, one-sided love, indeed. I'm gradually forgetting her now, but I have a feeling that she can't help remembering me, that there are evenings when her heart aches with love, and she knows there's nobody but herself to blame. She was an untrustworthy person, the kind a man can't keep.

"Your nagging spouse was a memorable woman, but such jealousy would be hard to live with—and, one suspects, might produce active dislike under the wrong circumstances. In the case of the accomplished performer on the koto, we must consider her flirtatious nature a damning flaw. There is also room for doubt about the true sentiments of my unreliable mistress. If we had to choose which of the three would make the best wife, I don't believe we could do it. This kind of comparison of good and bad points is far from easy. But where is there a woman who possesses all the virtues and lacks all the faults? Some may think of Kichijōten, but she's too otherworldly and mysterious for comfort." Everyone laughed.

"Shikibu must have some interesting stories. Tell us a little something," Tō-no-chūjō urged.

"What story from the lowest of the low could merit the attention of gentlemen like you?" Shikibu-no-jō demurred.

Tō-no-chūjō was serious. "Come on," he insisted. "You're wasting time."

After mulling over possible subjects, Shikibu-no-jō began his account. "Once while I was still a student of literature, I ran across an example of the brainy woman. Just as in the case Uma-no-kami has described, she offered sage advice when I consulted her about my work, and revealed a marvelous ability to cope with the problems of everyday life. Her learning would have put some of our would-be scholars to shame, too. All in all, she was enough to make a man afraid to open his mouth.

"This happened at a time when I was visiting a certain professor to study with him. I'd been informed that he had several daughters, and when an opportunity arose, I made advances to one of them. The father heard about it and brought out the wine bowl. 'Listen while I sing of two ways,' he said.[10] I wasn't especially eager to visit the girl, but I let myself become involved with her rather than offend him. She looked after me with loving care, seasoned our pillow talk with instruction in such Chinese lore as might help me in the proper execution of my official duties, and wrote me letters in a

10. A line from a composition by Bo Juyi. The poem continues, "It's easy for a rich man's daughter to get married, but she looks down on her husband; it's hard for a poor man's daughter to get married, but she's good to her mother-in-law." The professor is offering Shikibu-no-jō his daughter.

fine, clear hand, using formal, convoluted Chinese diction, unmarred by kana. Naturally, I couldn't stop visiting her. She was the teacher from whom I learned what little I can manage in the way of composing a lame sort of Chinese, and I still thank her for that. But it seemed to me that it would be embarrassing for a man to keep letting himself be shown up as a less-than-brilliant scholar in front of a woman he cherished as a true wife. And someone like the professor's daughter would certainly have no appeal at all for young lords who can dispense with strong, active feminine support. One side of me wanted to be rid of her, but I liked her well enough to keep seeing her, possibly because of some karmic affinity. Men don't have much backbone."

The others were curious to hear the rest of the story. Tongue in cheek, they egged him on. "Well, well! A most interesting woman, indeed." Although he knew their pleas were insincere, he returned to his subject with a comical expression of satisfaction.

"Once when something took me to her house after a long absence, I was annoyed to find that she received me from behind curtains instead of in the usual comfortable room. 'How absurd,' I thought. 'Is this her way of expressing displeasure?' It occurred to me that I was being given an opportunity to break with her. But my sagacious lady was not one to indulge in rash displays of jealousy. Well aware of the conduct proper to a wife, she uttered no word of reproach. In a high-pitched voice, she said, 'For several months now, I have been afflicted with the vapors, which I am treating with the "extreme heat" garlic decoction. The odor is pungent, and I must decline an interview, but I shall be happy to execute any minor commissions with which you may wish to charge me.' Unable to frame a suitable response to this admirable formal speech, I said merely, 'I understand.' She may have felt that something more was needed, for she called out as I prepared to leave, 'Come and see me when the smell's gone.' It seemed heartless to go without a word, but I couldn't bring myself to tarry, especially after an unbearable reek of garlic began to assail my nostrils. Poised for flight, I recited a poem:

sasagani no	I don't understand
furumai shiruki	why you say, 'Come by day'
yūgure ni	on an evening
hiruma suguse to	when the spider with its web
iu ga aya naki	had told you of my visit.[11]

'What kind of excuse is that?'

"I dashed off without further ado. She sent a poem in pursuit:

11. The expression attributed to the woman, *hiruma suguse* ("Come by day"), can also mean, "Wait until the garlic smell goes." It was a popular belief that a spider spinning its web at dusk was a sign that one's lover would come that night.

au koto no	If the two of us
yo o shi hedatenu	were of those couples who meet
naka naraba	each night without fail,
hiruma mo nani ka	what embarrassment would I feel
mabayukaramashi	if you were to come by day? [12]

"It was a characteristically swift response," he concluded in a grave voice.

The others burst into appalled laughter.

"You made the whole thing up!"

"Where would anyone find such a woman?"

"I'd rather settle down with a witch. That's gruesome!" The speaker snapped his fingers.

"That can hardly be called a story," said someone in a disparaging voice. "Tell us something a little more suitable."

Shikibu-no-jō sat motionless. "What could be better than that?" he asked.

"To me it seems pathetic that an inferior man or woman always wants to show people every last bit of what little it is that he or she knows," said Uma-no-kami. "A woman will lack charm if she achieves full mastery of the three histories and five classics, the core of the Chinese curriculum. On the other hand, we can hardly say that the mere fact of her sex renders her utterly ignorant, utterly incapable of coping with what goes on in public and private. Even though she may not make a point of getting an education, her eyes and ears will naturally pick up quite a bit if she's at all bright. But if, having acquired the ability to dash off Chinese characters, she stuffs a letter to another woman more than half full of them instead of avoiding them altogether, as would be proper, then the recipient thinks, 'How disagreeable she is! Why couldn't she have chosen a more graceful style?' It doesn't occur to the writer that her calligraphy lacks grace, but to the reader, whose voice will inevitably produce stiff, harsh sounds, it seems as though she has been trying to show off. This kind of thing is by no means uncommon, even in the highest circles.

"Nothing is more annoying than the would-be poet, the slave to the art who constructs a composition around some clever historical allusion and sends it to a man who is in no mood for versification. If he doesn't answer, he's a boor; if he can't rise to the challenge, he feels humiliated. Let's say it's around the time of one of the court banquets—for instance, the morning of the fifth-month festival, when he's about to rush off to the imperial palace and can't possibly sit down for quiet reflection about sweet flags, yet she sends him a poem with a handsome root. Or he may be frantically trying to cobble together a Chinese poem on some difficult topic for the ninth-day banquet, yet she sends a reproachful missive, hinting that her tears resemble dewdrops on chrysanthemums. She's imposing a burden on him just when it's least appropriate, and she makes herself appear tactless, rather than in-

---

12. Or: "if you were here when I smelled of garlic?"

genious as she had hoped, by dispatching her effort without stopping to think that he won't be able to pay any attention to it at such a time, even though he would undoubtedly have found it novel or touching if she had just held off and let him think about it later.

"On the whole, it's surely safer for a woman not to assume stylish airs or play the aesthete if she fails to understand which occasions are the ones on which others will think, 'Why did she have to do that? Couldn't she have left well enough alone?' Any woman will be well advised not to show everything she knows, and not to speak her full mind when she has something to say."

Genji's mind had been on the Fujitsubo lady all along. To him she seemed a woman with none of those deficiencies or excesses, and his heart was full as he asked himself where her like was to be found.

The discussion trailed off inconclusively into disreputable anecdotes, and presently a new day dawned.

The weather had finally taken a turn for the better. Genji left to go to his father-in-law's house, moved to sympathy by thoughts of the minister's concern over his long stay at the palace. All was brightness, elegance, and order at the mansion and in his wife's apartments. He told himself that this lady was eminently trustworthy, just the sort of serious person his recent companions had said it would be impossible to desert, but her correct, prim manner made him feel stiff and self-conscious, and he turned in frustration to teasing Lady Chūnagon, Nakatsukasa, and others among her pretty young attendants, meanwhile loosening his robes in the heat. The attentive ladies-in-waiting found his appearance delightful. The minister arrived, sat down beyond a curtain-stand in deference to his son-in-law's dishabille, and began to chat. Genji pulled a wry face. "It's too hot to talk," he said. The ladies giggled. "Sh! Be quiet!" Genji admonished, leaning on his armrest. He seemed very much at home.

Yūgao

[Summer to tenth month of Genji's seventeenth year. Rokujō lady: 24;
Yūgao: 19; Aoi: 21]

It happened around the time when he was making secret visits to a lady in
the vicinity of Rokujō Avenue. Feeling in need of a brief rest as he was on
his way to her house from the palace, he stopped on Gojō Avenue to pay
a sick call at the home of his former nurse, Daini, who had become a nun
in search of relief from a grave illness. The carriage gate was bolted, and
he sent someone to call Koremitsu.[1]

Gazing idly at the squalid avenue while he waited, he noticed that the
house next door had a new wickerwork fence made of cypress wood. The
half-shutters above it had all been raised for a distance of four or five
bays, and from behind pale, cool-looking rattan blinds a large number of
attractive feminine foreheads were visible as their owners peeped at his
carriage. The women were apparently moving about, and it seemed to him
that they must be very tall as he tried to visualize their lower bodies. Intrigued, he wondered who they were. He had chosen a plain carriage and
had prohibited the warning shouts that usually cleared his way; and now
he ventured to expose his face for a better look, certain that he would
not be recognized. The whole of the modest establishment was in view
just inside the gate, which was only a shutter-like contrivance, raised on
a pole; and its ramshackle appearance evoked poignant thoughts of the
old poem, "What place might I single out."[2] Stately mansions are no less
ephemeral.

As though proud that they were the only flowers in bloom, some blos-

1. We learn later that Koremitsu is the nun's son, and that Genji is his foster-brother (*meno-togo*) and patron.

2. Anonymous (KKS 987): yo no naka wa / izure ka sashite / wa ga naramu / yukitomaru o
zo / yado to sadamuru ("In this world of men, what place might I single out to be my abode? I
will choose to lay my head wherever my journey ends").

soms had created exuberant splashes of white on a luxuriant green vine, which was rambling over a species of board fence.

"I would like to ask a question of the person in the distance," Genji murmured.[3]

One of his escorts knelt.[4] "Those vines, 'blooming with snow-white flowers,' are called evening faces [*yūgao*]. The name makes one think of people worth noticing—but that's a wretched fence they're blooming on."

The tangled vines had crawled along the crumbling, weakened eaves of all the dwellings in what was indeed a shabby neighborhood of mostly small, humble houses.

"Poor blossoms! Theirs is an unhappy karma," Genji said. "Pick one for me." The man went inside the raised gate and picked a flower. Modest though the household was, a pretty little girl, dressed in a long pair of thin yellow silk trousers, came to a tasteful sliding door and beckoned to him. She held out a heavily scented white fan.

"Put it on this for the gentleman," she said. "Those flowers don't have nice stems."

Just then, someone opened the gate and Koremitsu emerged. The man handed him the fan to give to Genji.

"Please forgive me; the key got lost. Nobody in this neighborhood would recognize you, but I'm sorry you had to wait in such a grubby street," Koremitsu apologized.

They took the carriage inside, and Genji got out. Koremitsu's older brother, the holy teacher;[5] the nun's son-in-law, the governor of Mikawa Province; and Koremitsu's sister had all assembled, and all expressed their gratitude for the visit, which they considered the greatest of honors. The nun herself arose from her bed. "I don't mind giving up my old way of life: if I hesitated and agonized over renouncing the world, it was only because I feared I could no longer appear in your presence like this and enjoy the honor of your gaze. But I saved my life by taking the tonsure, and now I can await Amida's glory with a pure heart, thanks to this gracious visit." She shed weak tears.

"I've kept worrying because you haven't got any better in all this time, and I feel very upset and depressed because you've become a nun. But you must live to see me rise at court. Then there won't be anything to keep you from being reborn in the highest of the nine grades. They say the mere hint of a lingering worldly concern counts against a person." Genji's voice was choked with tears.

3. Anonymous (KKS 1007): uchiwatasu / ochikatabito ni / mono mōsu ware / sono soko ni / shiroku sakeru wa / nani no hana zo mo ("I would ask a question of the person to be seen standing off in the distance: What flowers are those? I mean the ones over there, blooming with snow-white flowers").

4. Here and elsewhere in this book, "escort" translates *zuijin*, a name for a type of guard. See Glossary.

5. *Ajari*, a Buddhist title. See Glossary.

Even when a child falls below the average, a biased observer like a nurse will be foolish enough to regard him as perfect. The connection with someone as remarkable as Genji had naturally been a source of enormous pride for the nun, and she continued to weep without apparent reason, as though perhaps regretting her loss of the importance and dignity she considered herself to have acquired during her years of close personal attendance on him. Her children exchanged pained glances and nudges. Such a display of unprovoked tears in front of His Lordship could only make it seem that she was clinging to the world she had forsaken.

Genji for his part felt deep emotion. "After death claimed my natural protectors while I was a small child, there seemed to be a great many people ready to care for me, but you were the only one I felt really close to. Now that I'm grown up, there are constraints that make it impossible to see you morning and evening, or even to call and ask about your health whenever I please, but I always begin to feel unhappy when we're separated for a long time. 'How I wish that in this world there were no final partings!'"[6] He wiped away tears as he spoke, his voice quiet and confidential, and the motion of his sleeve filled the room with fragrance. Forgetting their disapproval, the nun's children wept in sympathy. "When you think about it, Mother has been blessed with an extraordinary karma," they said to themselves.

Genji issued instructions for more performances of rituals. When he was ready to leave, he told Koremitsu to bring over a torch so that he could look at the neighbor's fan. It carried an intriguing scent of perfume from the robes of someone who seemed to have made regular use of it, and on it there was a poem, written in elegant cursive script:

kokoroate ni	Just at a hazard,
sore ka to zo miru	might it perchance be his—
shiratsuyu no	the face in the twilight,
hikari soetaru	a *yūgao* enhanced
yūgao no hana	by the radiance of the dew?

Dashed off with a deliberate lack of individuality, the calligraphy suggested cultivation and taste. Genji was conscious of an unexpected stir of interest. "Do you happen to have found out who lives in the house to the west?" he asked Koremitsu.

Koremitsu wished Genji would curb his troublesome instincts, but he could not very well say so. "For the five or six days I've been here, I've been too busy with Mother, worrying and taking care of her, to find out anything about the neighbors," he answered in a snappish voice.

"I know you think I shouldn't have asked," Genji said, "but there's some-

6. Ariwara no Narihira (KKS 901): yo no naka ni / saranu wakare no / naku mo ga na / chiyo mo to nageku / hito no ko no tame ("For sorrowing sons who would have their parents live a thousand long years—how I wish that in this world there were no final partings").

thing about this fan that seems to need looking into. Call someone who's likely to know; ask him."

Koremitsu went inside, summoned the caretaker, and questioned him. "The house belongs to an honorary vice-governor," he reported. "The caretaker said, 'The husband is away in the provinces. The wife is young and fond of elegant pursuits, and she has a sister, a lady-in-waiting, who pays her frequent visits.' Considering that he's only a flunky, I don't imagine he knows anything more."

The poem would have come from the lady-in-waiting, Genji thought, noting its rather confident, familiar tone. He wondered if she might prove a severe disappointment. It was probably because of his usual susceptibility that he felt unable to ignore the overture, coming as it did from someone who had penetrated his incognito and reacted in what was, after all, a not displeasing manner. In a carefully disguised hand, he wrote a poem on a folded sheet of paper.

> yorite koso   Were it to be seen
> sore ka to mo mime   closer at hand, you might know
> tasogare ni   the evening face
> honobono mitsuru   of which you caught a glimpse
> hana no yūgao   as twilight shadows gathered.

He dispatched it by the same escort.

Although the lady had never met Genji, she had yielded to the temptation to let him know that she had glimpsed his unmistakable profile. Awkwardly enough, considerable time had elapsed without any acknowledgment on his part, but now the household was elated at having elicited a response, and the escort perceived that its members appeared to be debating a reply. That was too much, he thought. He went back to his master.

Genji set out very quietly by the dim light of his way-clearers' torches. The half-shutters had been lowered next door, and lonely rays of lamplight straggled through the cracks, fainter than a firefly's glow.

At his destination, everything bespoke a degree of comfort and elegance not to be found in the common run of dwellings—the groves of great trees, the shrubs and grasses in the gardens. The mistress was an exceptionally dignified, correct woman, and Genji probably had little leisure to remember the fence where the evening faces bloomed. He overslept the next morning. The sun was rising when he took his leave, and to those who beheld him in the early morning light, it seemed only natural that people should always be singing his praises.

On that day, also, he passed in front of the shutters. He had undoubtedly done so on earlier occasions, but the trifling incident of the fan had left an impression, and thereafter he looked at the house whenever he went by, wondering about its occupants.

Koremitsu put in an appearance several days later. "I've been taking care

of my mother, who still seems frail," he said. Drawing nearer, he a
"After receiving your instructions, I had someone question a person
knew about the house next door, but he didn't tell us much. According to
him, a certain lady has apparently been living there in strict secrecy ever
since the fifth month or thereabouts, but nobody has been told who she is,
not even the members of the household. I've looked through cracks in the
boundary fence a few times, and it's true you can make out the figures of
young women behind the blinds. They wear what look like abbreviated
trains draped around their hips—a gesture in the direction of formality, I'd
say, as though they were waiting on somebody. Yesterday, when the rays of
the setting sun were streaming into the house, I saw a beautiful woman
sitting down to write a letter. She looked unhappy, and her attendants were
trying to hide tears. I saw it all quite clearly."

Genji smiled. It would be interesting to learn more.

"A good reputation is important for someone in his position," Koremitsu
thought. "But actually, when you think about it—his youth, the deference
and praise he receives—he'd seem tasteless and dreary if he weren't a bit of
a gallant. After all, the right woman will captivate any man, even one of
those lesser mortals to whom society denies the privilege of infidelity." To
Genji he said, "I manufactured a little pretext for sending a letter to the
house, thinking that it might be a way to get a look at her, and a prompt
reply came back, written in a practiced hand. She seems to have some fairly
presentable young attendants."

"Approach her again," said Genji. "I won't be satisfied until I find out
who she is." The house fell into the category dismissed by Uma-no-kami as
the lowest of the low, but the lady seemed out of the ordinary. What if he
were to discover an undreamt-of gem in those surroundings?

Autumn arrived. Through nobody's fault but his own, there were certain
things that caused Genji overwhelming grief, and his wife existed in a state
of constant bitterness because he visited her father's mansion so seldom.

The Rokujō lady was also much to be pitied, for there had been a percep-
tible diminution in his ardor since he had overcome her stubborn resistance.
Others wondered why his present feelings lacked the passion that had driven
him before she was his. Morbidly sensitive by nature, she had feared all
along that the disparity between their ages would cause gossip if word of
the affair leaked out; and now, more than ever, despairing thoughts
crowded into her mind when she awoke during the painful nights alone.

One foggy morning, Genji left the Rokujō Mansion in response to repeated urging, sleepy-faced and sighing. Chūjō-no-menoto raised the shutters in one of the bays and moved the curtain-stand aside, as though inviting
her mistress to watch his departure, and the lady raised her head to look
out. It was as people always said: he was incomparable, lingering in seeming
reluctance to pass the riot of bloom in the garden. When he approached the
corridor, Lady Chūjō went to accompany him, a graceful, elegant figure in

a gossamer train that stood out with pleasing clarity against robes dyed in the seasonal aster combination. He looked back and drew her down to sit by the corner balustrade. Her correct posture and flowing hair seemed to him strikingly beautiful.[7] [His poem:]

saku hana ni	I would not have it said
utsuru chō na wa	that my heart has turned toward
tsutsumedomo	a flower in bloom—
orade sugiuki	yet how hard it is to pass
kesa no asagao	without plucking a "morning face"![8]

"What shall I do?" he asked, taking her hand. No stranger to elegant badinage, she responded at once with a poem in which she pretended to mistake "a flower in bloom" for a reference to her mistress:

asagiri no	The one who starts for home
harema mo matanu	without even awaiting
keshiki nite	a break in the fog
hana ni kokoro o	would seem to care but little
tomenu to zo miru	about a flower in bloom.

Genji's modish page boy had been dispatched to the garden. A pretty child whose appearance might have been designed for the occasion, he now brought back a morning-face blossom, his bloused trousers wet with dew. It would have been pleasant to paint the scene.

Everyone felt drawn to Genji, even strangers who barely caught a glimpse of him. (After all, even a coarse mountain peasant seeks out a flowering tree when he needs a rest.)[9] Of those who beheld his radiant countenance, not one well-born father but longed to send him his precious daughter, not one humble man with a presentable sister but hoped to have her serve him, in whatever menial capacity. And it was indeed unlikely that he should have been an object of indifference to any discerning person who had been exposed to his charm at first hand, even through the receipt of a poem on a suitable occasion. It is easy to imagine that Chūjō and the other ladies-in-waiting were more than a little disturbed by his failure to treat the Rokujō Mansion as home.

7. Genji has been walking along the veranda outside the Rokujō lady's bedchamber. He is now approaching a corridor leading to another building, and ultimately to the street. Lady Chūjō (Chūjō-no-menoto), shown by her sobriquet to be an upper-rank lady-in-waiting, is seeing him off. The aster combination, which was worn at the beginning of autumn, is variously said to have been light purple with a green lining, purple with a brown lining, or brown with a yellowish-green lining. "Correct posture" probably means with head modestly bowed.

8. The "morning face" (*asagao*) has been tentatively identified as the bellflower (now called *kikyō*), one of the traditional "seven plants of autumn."

9. The two *Kokinshū* prefaces (kana and Chinese) describe Ōtomo no Kuronushi's poems as "crude . . . like a mountain peasant resting under a flowering tree with a load of firewood on his back."

But to go back to the house of the evening faces. Koremitsu had been punctilious in his surveillance through the fence. "I simply can't learn who she is," he reported. "She seems bent on concealment. But I think her young ladies-in-waiting are rather bored. Sometimes they cross to the long south building, the one with the half-shutters, and peep through its blinds when they hear a carriage; and it's my impression that the one who seems to be their mistress will occasionally slip out to join them. From the little I can see of her, she is delightful. One day a carriage came along with attendants clearing the way. Some of the household were watching, and a child maid-servant called out, all excited, 'Lady Ukon! Come and see right away! Lord Tō-no-chūjō is going by!' An older lady-in-waiting appeared and signed to her to be silent. 'The idea! Hold your tongue!' she said. 'How do you know it's His Lordship? Let me see.' She started across to the long building. There's a sort of plank bridge they use when they go back and forth; and in her haste, she caught the skirt of her robe on something, stumbled, and almost fell off. 'I declare, this bridge is an absolute menace!' she said in a huff. She seemed to lose interest in the carriage.

"'His Lordship was wearing an informal cloak, and he had his escorts with him. I saw So-and-so and Thus-and-so,' the child said. She knew whose carriage it was—you could tell from the way she reeled off the names of the escorts and pages."

"I do wish I could have seen that," Genji said. It occurred to him that the nun's neighbor might be the very woman Tō-no-chūjō had told them about—the one his friend still remembered with affection. If only he could find out!

Koremitsu took note of his expression. "I've made it my business to court one of the girls; now I know every corner of their house. When I visit, I let them pull the wool over my eyes—I mean, I pretend not to notice that a certain young woman is careful to address the others as though they were all ladies-in-waiting together. They think they're being very clever about hiding the truth. There are children around, and whenever one of them uses an honorific by mistake, the grown-ups go to ridiculous lengths to distract my attention, trying to preserve the fiction that the ladies-in-waiting are the only people in the house." He laughed.

"You'll have to help me see them the next time I visit your mother," Genji said. Judging from the nature of the lady's dwelling, temporary shelter though it might be, he could only conclude that she must belong to the lowest class—the one that had been dismissed on the rainy night as beneath notice. But what if one were to be surprised by something of interest in such a quarter?

Reluctant to disappoint his master in the slightest way, and himself a seasoned philanderer, Koremitsu tried one scheme after another, and finally, through a high-handed tactic, he succeeded in introducing Genji into the mistress's bedchamber. I shall omit the tedious tale of his campaign.

Genji had not pressed the question of the lady's identity, nor had he told her his name. He set out for her house in excessively coarse attire, traveling on foot, rather than by carriage as usual. Concluding that he must really be smitten, Korechika gave him his own horse and trotted alongside. "I'll be in trouble if my lady-in-waiting sees her lover walking like a scruffy commoner," he grumbled. But Genji was determined not to be found out. His only other attendants were the escort who had picked the evening face and a page whom nobody could recognize.[10] Lest someone put two and two together, he even refrained from stopping to rest at his nurse's house.

The lady found Genji's reticence odd and disturbing. In an effort to learn where he lived, she sent people to escort his messengers home, and dispatched others to see where he went when he left at dawn, but all of them were deliberately led astray. At the same time, Genji had fallen deeply in love; the thought of not meeting her was unbearable. He castigated himself for his behavior, which he recognized as wrong and foolish, but his visits were frequent indeed. Although love has been known to cloud the judgment of the most serious, he had always avoided blameworthy conduct with admirable discretion. Now he suffered from a strange malaise, fretting in the morning because a whole day must elapse before his next visit. He would try his utmost to take a dispassionate view of the matter, to convince himself that he was irrational, that there was no reason to be carried away. In spite of her astonishingly gentle, candid nature—her lack of prudence and gravity, her childlike behavior—he was not the first man she had known. Nor was it likely that she could claim a distinguished lineage. He kept asking himself why he should feel so drawn to her.

The lady could not help finding it eerie and unsettling—quite like the behavior of a supernatural being in an old tale—that he should make a point of disguising himself in a shabby hunting robe, shield his face so that she never caught a glimpse of it, and postpone his visits until late at night, when everyone was asleep. On the other hand, she could tell merely from touching him that he was someone of high birth. Who could he be? Her suspicions fastened on Koremitsu. "I'm sure the roué next door arranged the whole thing," she thought. But Koremitsu maintained a facade of bland innocence. Assiduous as usual in his visits, he flirted and joked as though unaware of what was going on. It was quite beyond comprehension, and she worried in an oddly unconventional way.[11]

Genji's own mind was troubled. If he were to grow careless, lulled by her apparent openness, and if she were to disappear quietly, he would have no more notion than Tō-no-chūjō of where to search. With her present domicile apparently a mere temporary hiding place, who knew when she might move on to some mysterious destination? If this were a casual liaison, he

10. Murasaki Shikibu does not explain why the household would have failed to recognize the escort.

11. The usual source of a woman's concern was a man's loss of interest.

could shrug off his failure to find her, but he was far from willing to let it go at that. In desperation, he thought of smuggling her into his Nijō Mansion, that he might spare himself the intolerable anguish of spending a night elsewhere for reasons of secrecy. It would be awkward if people found out—but if they did, it would probably be because karma had ordained it. What kind of bond could have aroused a passion such as he had felt for no other woman?

"How would you like to go to a place where you could feel perfectly at ease—where the two of us would have plenty of time to talk?" he asked her.

"Everything just seems so odd! No matter what you say, I'm scared because you don't act like other people." The childish speech brought an indulgent smile to his lips. "You're right, one of us is probably a fox. Let me bewitch you," he said in a tender voice. She then became extremely submissive, willing to accept whatever he might do.

He was touched by her docility, her readiness to assent even to so shockingly unorthodox a proposal. Tō-no-chūjō's description of his lost lady came to mind at once, and he wondered again if he had stumbled on the wild pink, but he refrained from pressing her, telling himself that she must have reasons for concealing her identity. She was not one to run away suddenly into hiding just to make a dramatic gesture; she would act only if a man's visits dropped off. It even occurred to him to picture how pathetic she would be if his heart happened to stray a bit, although of course he had no intention of looking elsewhere.

It was the fifteenth of the eighth month, a brilliant moonlit night. Moonbeams streamed in through countless cracks in the board roof, affording an intriguing view of the kind of dwelling Genji seldom saw. It seemed to be getting on toward dawn; he could hear the rough voices of working people awakening next door.

"It's turned mighty cold!"

"Business is rotten this year."

"No use looking to peddle in the provinces, either. I don't know what I'm going to do."

"Hey, on the north! Can you hear me?"

As they hurriedly emerged from their sleeping quarters to begin their pathetic occupations, their gabble was a source of embarrassment for the lady who lived so close. A snobbish, affected woman would probably have fainted if she had found herself in such an environment. But this lady was a calm person, not so deeply affected by painful, worrisome, or embarrassing things as to lose her refined, equable demeanor; and she seemed to regard the neighbors' ill-mannered hubbub merely as something incomprehensible—an attitude that served better than red-faced apologies to excuse her from personal responsibility in Genji's eyes.

More appalling than thunderclaps, the crashing thumps of a mechanical pestle began to reverberate next to their pillow, worked against a mortar by someone's foot. Unlike the earlier voices, the sounds seemed intolerably noisy. With no inkling of their cause, Genji could only marvel at their strangeness and their incredible volume. It did seem to be an annoyingly inconvenient neighborhood.

They could hear the constant indistinct blows of fulling hammers on mulberry-cloth robes drifting in from near places and far, and also the cries of wild geese flying overhead—poignant reminders of autumn's sadness.[12] Genji opened the sliding door of the room, which was at the front of the house, and the two looked out together. There was an elegant clump of black bamboo in the tiny garden, and the dew on the plants in this humble place sparkled quite as brightly as at his own mansion. Insect voices shrilled in unison. Even the crickets in the walls seemed within touching distance to someone whose ears were used to hearing them from afar, but Genji found their proximity an amusing novelty—a reaction we must doubtless attribute to the passion that made him overlook every shortcoming.

The lady was a sweet, touching figure in her subdued attire—a lavender robe, no longer new, over a lined white underrobe. No particular aspect of her appearance could have been called superior, but she was delicate and frail, and something in the manner of her speech evoked affectionate compassion. Watching her, Genji thought that a little less passivity would not come amiss, but he also felt a strong desire to be with her under more relaxed circumstances.

"Let's spend the rest of the night in peace somewhere nearby. It's really too much to stay on here like this," he said.

"Why should we go someplace else? This is a very sudden idea," she objected in a placid voice.

He then swore that their union would endure beyond this life, and she readily agreed to do as he wished. What an unusual woman she was, and how little she seemed to know of men! No longer concerned about what others might think, he summoned Ukon, told her to call his escort, and ordered his carriage brought to the veranda. There were things the people in the house would have liked to know, but they trusted him, understanding from his behavior how much he loved their lady.

It was almost dawn. No cocks were crowing, but they could hear an aged voice praying as its owner prostrated himself, getting up and down with great apparent difficulty. Touched, Genji thought of the brevity of all human life, of its likeness to ephemeral morning dew, and he wondered what an old man might still find to ask for. The petitioner seemed to be purifying himself for a pilgrimage to the sacred peaks. He was intoning, "Hail to Maitreya, the Buddha of the future!"

"Listen to him," Genji said in a compassionate voice. "His thoughts aren't bent on this life alone." [He recited a poem:]

12. It was a literary convention that cloth was fulled on autumn evenings by grieving women whose husbands were far away.

ubasoku ga	Revere as a guide
okonau michi o	the faith inspiring the prayers
shirube nite	of that pious man:
kon yo mo fukaki	be true to vows that will bind us
chigiri tagau na	in the coming world as in this.

Mindful of the inauspicious occurrences associated with the Hall of Long Life, he had avoided mention of shared wings, pledging instead to be true until Maitreya's coming—a notably exaggerated commitment.[13]

[Her response:]

saki no yo no	I cannot foresee
chigiri shiraruru	a future full of promise—
mi no usa ni	not when my sorrows
yukusue kanete	show me what has been fated
tanomigatasa yo	from an earlier life.

It was a sad little answer.

The moon lingered above the horizon, and the lady, as though seduced by its example, hesitated about embarking on so unexpected an excursion. Genji set himself to overcoming her misgivings. Meanwhile, the moon ducked behind a cloud, and a beautiful dawn began to break. Unwilling to risk the embarrassment of being seen in broad daylight, he whisked her into the carriage and made his usual swift departure. Ukon rode with them.

They arrived at a certain mansion in the vicinity. Genji sent for the caretaker.[14] It was very dark under the trees as they waited outside the gate, a dilapidated structure overgrown with tiny ferns; and Genji's sleeves were drenched, merely from raising the carriage blind in the heavy, damp mist. "I've never done anything like this before," he said. "I didn't expect to feel so nervous." [He recited:]

inishie mo	Even in the past,
kaku ya wa hito no	was ever heart as perplexed
madoiken	as is mine today,
wa ga mada shiranu	following at dawn a path
shinonome no michi	I have never known before?

Her answering poem was shy:

yama no ha no	Its bright rays, I fear,
kokoro mo shirade	may vanish in mid-heaven—
yuku tsuki wa	the moon journeying on,

13. According to "The Song of Everlasting Sorrow," it was in the Hall of Long Life that Emperor Xuanzong and Yang Gueifei pledged to be "as two birds sharing a wing, as two trees with joined branches." On Maitreya, see Glossary.

14. Old commentaries identify the mansion as the Kawara-no-in, a residence of legendary grandeur built by a son of Emperor Saga, Minamoto no Tōru (822–95). Presented to Retired Emperor Uda in 895, it later fell into ruin. Murasaki Shikibu's contemporaries would have known it was nearby, and probably would have thought of it.

uwa no sora nite   powerless to probe the heart
kage ya taenan   of the rim of the hills.

"I feel so uneasy." She seemed to find the place frightening and eerie—
probably, Genji thought in amusement, because she had grown accustomed
to living in that crowded neighborhood. He had his men take the carriage
inside the grounds, and there they waited, with the shafts resting on a
balustrade, while the caretaker prepared a sitting room in the west wing.
Ukon's spirits rose as she silently recalled certain incidents in the past.
Genji's identity had become clear to her from the zeal with which the caretaker had gone about his work.

They left the carriage just as the surroundings were becoming faintly visible. Makeshift though the arrangements were, the caretaker had managed
to furnish a room in attractive style. The man was shocked by Genji's lack
of attendants. He had served him for some time as a junior steward, and
was also one of the staff at the minister of the left's mansion; and he now
came up and offered through Ukon to send for some suitable people. But
Genji bound him to secrecy. "I have purposely sought out a secluded, deserted house. Don't mention this to anybody," he said.

The caretaker hastened to produce some rice and other food, but there
were too few people to serve it in proper style. In this travel lodging, alien
to all of Genji's previous experience, there was nothing to do but pledge that
their union would rival the one in the poem about Long Breath River.[15]

When the sun was high, Genji got up and raised the shutters with his own
hands. Gazing out across the ravaged, deserted garden, he could see groves
of immense antiquity, looming like baleful presences. There was nothing of
particular interest in the trees and bushes close at hand, which looked as
though they were growing in a wild autumn field, and the lake was smoth-
ered by aquatic plants. It was an estate that had come to be more than a
little intimidating. People were apparently occupying some rooms in one of
the lesser buildings, but they were a considerable distance away.

"This has turned into an eerie place," Genji said, "but I'm sure its demon
will excuse me." He had continued to hide his face, but now he reconsidered, noting that the lady showed signs of resenting his caution. To be sure,
he thought, secrecy was inappropriate in the present state of their relations.
He recited a poem:

yūtsuyu ni   Lay it to a tie
himo toku hana wa   formed when someone chanced to see
  tamaboko no   a mere passerby—
tayori ni mieshi   the flowering of the bud,
e ni koso arikere   its bonds loosed by evening dew.

15. Uma no Kunihito (MYS 4482): niotori no / okinagagawa wa / taenu tomo / kimi ni kataramu / koto tsukime ya mo ("Even if the Okinagagawa [River of Long Breath], named for
the deep-diving grebes, were to cease to flow, never would there be an end to the words I would
speak to you").

"How do you like 'the radiance of the dew'?"[16]

With a sidelong glance, she murmured a faint response, which he chose to consider amusingly ingenious:

hikari ari to	It was a mistake,
mishi yūgao no	caused by dusk's uncertain light,
uwatsuyu wa	that led me to see
tasogaredoki no	radiance in dewdrops
sorame narikeri	on *yūgao* flowers.

Genji's beauty was indeed incomparable as he sat at his ease, and the contrast with the surroundings made him look still handsomer, almost inauspiciously so. "I wouldn't let you see my face because I resented the way you kept me at a distance," he said. "Now, though, you have to tell me who you are. For all I know, you could be a fox." But the lady clung to her privacy, very much the bashful child. "I am but the daughter of a fisherman . . . ," she said.[17]

"Oh, very well. I suppose it's my own fault." His reproaches gave way to intimate conversation, which was succeeded in turn by more reproaches and more conversation, and at length the day drew to a close.

Fruit and other dainties arrived from Koremitsu, who had managed to track Genji down. Koremitsu himself felt obliged to keep his distance, lest Ukon confront him with awkward accusations. Amused that Genji's infatuation had impelled him to become a vagabond, he could not but surmise that the lady must merit the devotion she inspired—nor could he suppress some feeling of disgust with the magnanimity that had prompted him to stand aside, instead of attempting what would probably have been a successful courtship of his own.

Genji was gazing at the evening sky, a scene quieter than anything in his experience. Upon observing that the lady seemed intimidated by the darkness inside the room, he raised the blinds next to the veranda and stretched out by her side. They looked at each other, their faces bright in the rays of the setting sun. She had considered the whole affair unbelievably strange, but now she forgot her qualms and relaxed in a delightfully appealing manner. She had clung to him all day long with a timidity that he found touchingly childish.

He closed the shutters early and called for the lamp to be lit. "You seem

16. His question is a reference to her first poem, "Just at a hazard" (p. 61). There is a pun on the bud bursting its coat and the untying of a mask, which Genji is here found to be wearing.

17. Anonymous (SKKS 1703): shiranami no / yosuru nagisa ni / yo o tsukusu / ama no ko nareba / yado mo sadamezu ("I have no abode, for I am but the daughter of a fisherman, spending my life on the shore where white waves roll in"). In the speech that follows, Genji introduces marine imagery from another poem by using the expression *warekara*, which can mean "from me" (i.e., "my fault") and is also the name of a small crustacean. Fujiwara no Naoiko (KKS 807): ama no karu / mo ni sumu mushi no / warekara to / ne o koso nakame / yo o ba uramiji ("Without blaming him, I mourn the faults that bring thoughts of the 'from me' shrimp dwelling on strands of seaweed harvested by fisherfolk").

perfectly comfortable now. I don't understand why you persist in keeping secrets," he complained.

It occurred to him that his father was probably trying to find out what had become of him. Where would the emperor's people be searching? But his chief concern was for someone he pitied. "I don't know what's got into me," he thought. "The lady at Rokujō must be terribly upset." It would be awkward if she resented his behavior—but what else could he expect? Moved by the artlessness of his present companion, he could not help comparing the two. If only he could rid the other of her excessive sensitivity, of the touchiness that made a visitor so uncomfortable!

About halfway through the first part of the night, as he lay asleep, he dreamed that a beautiful woman seated herself near his pillow. "I consider you the most splendid of men," she said, "but you can't be bothered to visit me. Instead, you bring this common creature here to bask in your attentions. It's too mortifying!" She seized his companion to pull her up. Starting awake as though from a nightmare, he saw that the lamp had gone out. The atmosphere of the room seemed ominous; he drew his sword and put it next to the pillow.[18] Then he awakened Ukon, and she came to his side with a frightened look.

"Rouse one of the men on duty in the gallery. Tell him to bring a lighted torch," he said.

"How am I supposed to get there? It's dark."

He laughed. "You sound like a child." He clapped his hands, and a ghostly echo answered. The summons had not been loud enough to arouse anyone. To the lady, trembling with fear, their situation seemed desperate. She broke out in perspiration and fell into a faint.

"She gets these absurd fears," Ukon said. "Think how she must feel now!"

"She's so very frail," Genji thought. "Even during the daytime she just kept looking off into space.[19] Poor child!" He drew Ukon closer. "I'll wake somebody up. It makes a disagreeable echo when I clap. You stay with her awhile." He pushed open the double-leafed door on the west. The light in the gallery had also gone out.

A faint breeze had sprung up, and his few attendants had fallen asleep. There were only three of them—a young personal servant, the son of the mansion's caretaker; a single page; and the escort who had plucked the *yūgao* blossom. The servant arose in answer to his call.

"Light a torch and bring it here," Genji said. "Tell the escort to twang his bowstring and keep shouting.[20] Do you think it's a good idea to drop off to

18. To ward off malignant spirits.

19. The editors of one modern Genji edition take this to be a sign of weak nerves. An early commentator saw it as a portent of death. See Abe et al., *Genji monogatari*, 1: 239, n. 16.

20. Murasaki Shikibu's mention of the sudden breeze may be intended to suggest the advent of a malignant spirit. The purpose of the bow-twanging and shouting was to warn off spirits by threatening them with military action, and with the names of Genji and his armed guard.

sleep in an isolated place like this? I thought Koremitsu was here. What's become of him?"

"Master Koremitsu was here, but he went home. He said, 'He hasn't given me any instructions. Tell him I'll come just before dawn to await his pleasure.'"

The servant, a member of the palace guards, could be heard twanging his bow with expert skill and shouting warnings against carelessness with fire as he went off toward the caretaker's room.[21] The sound reminded Genji of the imperial palace. The roll call would be over by now; the guardsmen were probably twanging their bows and proclaiming their names. It was still not very late.

He went back inside and groped his way to the lady. As before, she lay prostrate, with Ukon face down beside her. "What's the matter?" he said to Ukon. "You act scared to death. You're probably afraid of a fox or something in this deserted place, but there's nothing to worry about as long as I'm here." He pulled her to her feet.

"I'm terrified! I was lying on my stomach because I felt sick. My lady must be petrified," Ukon said.

"So it would seem." To the lady, he said, "Why are you so afraid?" When he touched her, there was no sign of life. He shook her. She was limp and seemed unconscious. She was such a child, he thought in despair. Had a malignant influence stolen her spirit?

The servant arrived with a torch. Since Ukon seemed incapable of motion, Genji pulled over the curtain-stand to shield the lady. "Bring the light up," he said.

Disconcerted by the command, which would never have been issued in the normal course of events, the servant hesitated to venture beyond the threshold of the eave-chamber.

"Come along with it! This is no place for ceremony," Genji said.

When the light illumined the lady, he saw beside the pillow a figure whose face was that of the woman in his dream—a vision no sooner glimpsed than gone. He remembered an old tale in which just such a thing had happened. It was strange and uncanny, but his first thought was for the lady. His mind in turmoil, he lay close and tried to rouse her, indifferent to his own danger. "Wake up!" he urged. But her body was icy, for she had long since ceased to breathe. Words were of no avail, nor was there any reliable person to help him. A monk might have filled the need, had one been present.

Although he had made a show of courage earlier, the sight of his dead mistress was too much for his young heart. He clasped her tight in his arms. "Come back, my darling! Don't make me suffer this agony!" But the body was cold, starting to look unpleasant.

Ukon wept in a paroxysm of grief, her previous terror forgotten.

Genji took hold of himself, encouraged by the memory of what had hap-

21. He is going to get fire for the torch.

pened in the past, when a demon menaced a minister of state in the Shishinden.[22] "No matter how things look, she's not going to die. It sounds frightful to hear someone wailing like that in the middle of the night. Don't make so much noise," he told her. But the suddenness of it all had been stunning.

He called the caretaker's son. "It's very strange . . . someone here is suffering from a spirit possession. Send word at once for Master Koremitsu to come as fast as he can. If his brother, the holy teacher, is there, ask him quietly to come too. Be discreet when you deliver the message; don't let the nun hear you. She tends to be trying about things like this." His demeanor was calm, but there was a painful tightness in his chest. It was agonizing to think that he was responsible for the lady's death—and as though that were not enough, the eeriness of the surroundings was beyond description.

Was it because the night was more than half spent that the wind had risen to a veritable gale? The soughing in the pines made it seem as though they were deep in the forest, and a strange bird uttered hollow cries. He wondered if it might be an owl.[23] Reflecting on the mansion's isolation and its unearthly atmosphere—exacerbated now by the complete absence of human voices—he regretted in vain the inexplicable impulse that had made him seek lodging in so dismal a place. Ukon clung to him in a daze, trembling like a dying woman. Was she to go too? Half-unconsciously, he held her fast. With no second rational person to consult, he felt at his wits' end. The lamplight was a mere dim flicker, and the darkness seemed impenetrable in some parts of the room, such as the area above the folding screens at the entrance to the inner chamber. He thought he heard footsteps approaching from the rear, the plank floor creaking as they advanced. If only Koremitsu would hurry! But Koremitsu was not one to spend every night in the same house, and the messenger searched place after place. The hours until dawn seemed as long as a thousand nights.

As a distant cock finally began to crow, Genji pondered his situation. What karmic bond had enmeshed him in an affair that might have cost him his life? True, he had started it himself, but what a sensation it would cause! It must be his punishment for harboring a reprehensible passion. "Once a thing has happened, it's bound to get out, no matter how hard you try to keep it a secret. His Majesty will know, people at court will talk, the street riffraff will get hold of it. I'll be a laughingstock," he thought.

Master Koremitsu arrived. Genji was annoyed. Here was the faithful attendant who stood ever ready to do his bidding—midnight or dawn, it made no difference—and he had absented himself on this of all nights.

22. According to an old story, Fujiwara no Tadahira (880–949) was accosted by a demon when passing through the deserted Shishinden on his way to execute an imperial decree. He chased it off by invoking the authority of the throne and drawing his sword. See McCullough, *Ōkagami*, p. 106.
23. Considered a bird of ill omen. The chicks were said to eat their parents.

Moreover, he had even reported late when summoned. He called him in, but what he wanted to say was too distressing; the words refused to come.

When Ukon realized who had arrived, the whole history of the affair returned to her mind, and she burst into tears. Genji was also overcome. He had continued to embrace Ukon in his role of stalwart protector, but now, with Koremitsu's arrival, he breathed a sigh of relief, and his grief welled up. For a time, he gave way to irrepressible tears.

When he had pulled himself together, he said, "Something weird has happened here: to call it astounding would be an understatement. I remember hearing that sutras need to be recited after a sudden event like this, and I sent for the holy teacher so I could commission readings and prayers, but he hasn't come. Do you know why?"

"He went up to Mount Hiei yesterday," Koremitsu said. "This is amazing! Could she have been ill before she came?"

"I'm sure she wasn't," Genji said in tears. The pathetic expression on his handsome face wrung Koremitsu's heart, and he too began to sob.

Koremitsu had come, to be sure, but it is the man of mature years, experienced in the vicissitudes of life, who serves as a source of strength in a crisis. The two of them were only boys, with no idea what to do.

"We can't let the caretaker know," Koremitsu said. "He himself could be trusted because of his ties to you, but he'll have relatives around, people who'll let it out without meaning to. The first thing is for you to get away from this mansion."

"But no place is more deserted than this," Genji said.

"That's true." Koremitsu thought about it. "We can't go to Her Ladyship's house. Her attendants would start wailing and carrying on, and there'd be all kinds of questions among the commoners in that crowded neighborhood. The truth would be bound to get out. A mountain temple—that's it! People are always being buried in such places; we wouldn't attract any attention." He thought some more. "An old acquaintance of mine, a former lady-in-waiting, has gone to live in the eastern hills as a nun. She's my father's nurse, exceedingly ancient now. The district seems fairly populous, but her cell is quiet and secluded." He had the carriage brought so that they might merge unnoticed into the homeward stream of early-morning traffic.

Since Genji appeared to be incapable of carrying the lady, Koremitsu wrapped her in a quilt and put her in the carriage. The tiny body seemed pathetic rather than repellent. He had been unable to bring himself to truss her up like a parcel, and her flowing hair was enough to blind any eye with helpless tears. Overcome by grief, Genji wanted to stay with her to the end, but Koremitsu demurred. "Take the horse and go home to Nijō before the streets get crowded," he said. He put Ukon into the carriage with her mistress, gave his horse to Genji, and tied up his trousers for walking. Then he set out on the strange, unforeseen journey to the nunnery, his pride sacrificed to the compassion he felt as he looked at Genji's stricken face.

Genji reached home in a daze.

"Where have you been? You don't seem well," the ladies-in-waiting said.

Inside the curtain-dais, he abandoned himself to thought, his hands pressed to his breast. The situation was unbearable. "Why didn't I go with her?" he asked himself. "How would she feel if she came back to life? Wouldn't she think it was horrible of me to run off and leave her?" Insinuating itself into a mind already distraught with grief, the suggestion evoked a sensation akin to nausea. His head ached, his body felt feverish, he was ill and confused. With symptoms like these, he thought, he was probably going to die too. Even after the sun rose high, he stayed in bed, too sick and depressed to respond when his puzzled attendants urged him to eat. Meanwhile, messengers arrived from the imperial palace bearing word that the emperor was troubled because his people had been unable to find Genji on the preceding day. It was the sons of the minister of the left who came.

Genji announced that he could receive only Tō-no-chūjō. "Come in, but don't sit down," he told his friend from behind the blinds. "My nurse fell gravely ill around the fifth month. She managed to rally—possibly because she cut her hair, received the commandments, and so forth—but there was a flare-up a while ago, and now she's very weak. She asked me to come to see her one last time, so I did. I thought it would seem heartless not to pay a deathbed visit to someone I'd been so close to ever since I was little. There was a sick servant in the house, and he died suddenly before he could move anywhere else. Not wanting to inconvenience me, they left him there until nightfall, but I found out about it later; and now I can't go to the palace because of the problems it would cause, what with all the rituals coming up.[24] Furthermore, I think I've caught cold; my head has been aching since before dawn, and I feel terrible. So please excuse the way I've received you."

"I'll report this to His Majesty. His men looked for you everywhere last night before the concert. He seemed displeased." Tō-no-chūjō started away. Then he turned back. "How did you really get defiled? I can't believe all that."

Genji's heart skipped a beat. "Please just tell His Majesty that I've suffered an unexpected defilement; don't go into the details. I much regret my inability to wait on him." He spoke with an air of indifference, but his thoughts were on the tragic event no words could undo, and he felt too ill to meet anyone face to face. Nevertheless, he summoned Kurōdo-no-ben and entrusted him with the same message for the emperor, speaking very seriously.[25] He also sent a letter to the minister's house, telling of his defilement and his inability to call there.

24. Defilement from contact with a corpse lasted 30 days and could be transmitted if a guest came inside and sat down. It was particularly important for a defiled person to absent himself from Shinto rituals.

25. Genji apparently has doubts about Tō-no-chūjō's reliability. Kurōdo-no-ben is Tō-no-chūjō's brother.

Koremitsu appeared at dusk. The usual visitors, told of Genji's defilement, had all departed without seating themselves, and the mansion was almost deserted. Genji called him in.

"Tell me what happened. Did you make sure there was no hope?" He wept with his sleeve pressed to his face.

Koremitsu also shed tears. "I'm afraid she's gone. I didn't think the vigil should be prolonged, and tomorrow is an auspicious day, so I've made arrangements for the funeral with a saintly old monk I know," he said.

"What about the attendant who was with her?"

"I doubt that she'll survive, either. Her mind is confused. She says she won't let her mistress go without her, and this morning she seemed ready to leap into a chasm. She wants to tell the people back at Gojō, but I've managed to put her off. 'Take a little time to pull yourself together,' I told her. 'Think things over first.' "

Genji's heart was full. "I feel terribly ill. I wonder if I'm going to die too," he said.

"Why brood about it? After all, it's karma that determines everything. This needs to be kept quiet; I'll handle all the details myself," Koremitsu said.

"You're right. I do try to see it that way. But I can't bear to think of the inevitable criticism—the accusations that I've sacrificed a human life for my own wanton pleasure. Don't let Shōshō-no-myōbu find out," he cautioned.[26] "And especially not your mother. She's always getting after me about these affairs; I simply couldn't face her."

"I won't. I've even lied to the monks," Koremitsu said. Genji was reassured.

The ladies-in-waiting overheard snatches of the conversation. "It's very odd; what can be happening?" they wondered. "He won't even go to the palace because he says he's been defiled, and now there's all this whispering and sighing."

Genji's thoughts turned to the funeral rites. "Be sure to manage things nicely," he said.

"Oh, that's nothing. There won't be much of anything to do." Koremitsu stood up to go.

Genji was overwhelmed by a sudden new access of grief. "You won't approve, but I'm going to the temple on horseback. I'll always be miserable if I don't see her one last time," he said.

Koremitsu swallowed his misgivings. "If you've decided, so be it. Please go right away; you need to get back early in the night."

Genji prepared for the journey by changing into a hunting robe, one of an assortment with which he had provided himself for his recent incognito excursions. Mindful of the previous night's horrors, he pondered the wisdom of going through with the bizarre expedition to which his bleak, tormented heart was driving him, but it was impossible to assuage his misery

26. Probably Koremitsu's sister.

in any other way. "If I don't see her now," he thought, "when in another world shall I find her looking as she did in this?" He mastered his fears and started out, accompanied by his usual attendants, Koremitsu and the escort. The ride seemed interminable.

The moon of the seventeenth night had risen, and Toribeno loomed in the distance when the party reached the riverbed, their way-clearer's torch a mere dim glow.[27] It was an eerie scene, but Genji let it pass unobserved, lost in agitated thought.

They arrived at their destination. In that area of unearthly loneliness, the nun's dwelling was a moving sight, a rude board-roofed cell with an adjoining chapel. Light from a sacred lamp shone faintly through the chapel blinds. Inside the cell, the only sound was a woman's sobbing; outside the blinds, two or three monks talked and recited the sacred name in low tones. Vespers had ended at the temples, and all was still. Off toward Kiyomizu, the glitter of many lights pointed to the presence of throngs of people.[28] The nun's son, a monk of great virtue, was intoning a sutra in a holy voice. Genji felt he must weep until his store of tears was exhausted.

Upon entering the room, Genji saw that the lamp had been turned toward the wall. Ukon was lying down, separated from her mistress by a folding screen. He could imagine her misery. To his mind, there was nothing frightening about the lady's appearance: she was as charming as ever, quite unchanged. He took her hand. "Let me at least hear your voice one last time! What kind of karmic bond could it have been? During that brief interlude, I loved you with all my heart, and yet you went away and left me to suffer this anguish, this devastating grief." He broke down in convulsive sobs. The monks knew nothing about the two, but they also shed tears, astonished by the extravagance of his grief.

"Ukon, come home with me to Nijō," Genji said.

"In all the years since I was a child, I served her without once leaving her side. How could I suddenly abandon her and go off somewhere else? Besides, I have to tell the others what's happened. Her death is sorrow enough; I really don't think I can bear it if they blame me." She began to cry. "All I want is to follow her, to be part of the smoke from her pyre," she said.

Genji tried to comfort her. "It's natural for you to feel that way, but such is life in this world. There's no parting that isn't sad. And no matter how a person may die, die he will, for every life must end. Resign yourself to it and leave everything to me." He continued, "Even though I talk this way, I feel that I can't live much longer." It was not a reassuring remark.

"Dawn seems to be approaching. I think you should start back right away," said Koremitsu.

27. The dry bed of the Kamo River was used as a thoroughfare.
28. The crowds had perhaps assembled in anticipation of the following day. The 18th of each month was considered an especially good time for the worship of Kannon, the principal divinity at the Kiyomizudera.

Genji left the cell with deep emotion and many backward glances. The wayside foliage was heavy with dew, the morning fog so impenetrable that he seemed to himself a forlorn wanderer, setting off on a journey into nowhere. As he rode, he thought of how the lady had looked lying there, the same as ever to all appearances, clad by force of circumstance in his own red singlet, which was one of the robes they had used as cover. What might have been the origin of such a karmic bond? Noticing that he seemed unsteady in the saddle, Koremitsu helped him along, but near the bank of the Kamo River, in great apparent distress, he slid to the ground from the horse's back. "I wonder if it's my destiny to die by the roadside. I just don't see how I can get all the way home," he said.

Koremitsu was nonplused. "If I'd had any sense, I'd never have taken him on an excursion like this, whether he wanted to go or not," he thought. In dismay, he cleansed his hands in the river and prayed to Kiyomizu Kannon, for he could think of nothing else to do. Genji forced himself to take heart. He offered silent prayers to the buddhas, and finally, thanks to Koremitsu's help, he managed to reach the Nijō Mansion.

The ladies-in-waiting sighed to one another over the strange errand that had kept their master out so late. "It really won't do! He's been so unusually restless lately—all those clandestine outings—and now this! Why in the world would he ramble off that way when he looked deathly ill yesterday?"

Genji took to his bed, genuinely and miserably ill, and within two or three days, he was alarmingly enfeebled. The emperor was devastated. A hubbub of continuous prayer arose at temples and shrines in every quarter: rituals addressed to the gods, yin-yang purifications, Buddhist esoteric rites—I could not possibly list them all. The general public held to the vociferous opinion that his incomparable beauty was to blame; it was an ominous sign that he was not long for this world.

Desperate though he felt his illness to be, Genji summoned Ukon to the Nijō Mansion, assigned her a room near his own quarters, and enrolled her among his ladies-in-waiting. Koremitsu was frantic with worry, but he forced himself to seem calm and did what he could to help Ukon perform her duties, aware that there was nobody else for her to turn to. Whenever Genji felt a little better, he summoned her, sent her on errands, and so forth; and she was soon at ease with the other attendants. Although she was no beauty in her deep black mourning, she was a prepossessing enough young person.

"It looks as though I must die too—as though my fate has been determined by the bond forged during that strange, fleeting interlude. I can imagine how forlorn you must feel after losing the mistress you depended on for so long, and I had meant to try to comfort you by looking after you if I lived. Unfortunately, I'll probably follow her soon." He spoke in a confidential voice, shedding weak tears.

For the moment, Ukon put aside thoughts of the one whom grief could not bring back. What a terrible waste it would be if such a life as this were extinguished!

The people in the mansion were beside themselves with worry, and messengers from the emperor came thicker than raindrops. Genji made a valiant effort to rally his spirits, awed by reports of his father's dismay.

The minister of the left bustled about on his son-in-law's behalf, paid daily calls, and made sure that the Nijō household arranged for various kinds of prayers and rites. Whether or not it was due to his efforts, Genji started on the road to recovery, with no apparent lingering effects, after more than twenty days of critical illness. The return of his health coincided with the end of the ritual seclusion imposed by his defilement, and he felt obliged to put in an appearance at the Kiritsubo pavilion on the same night, mindful of the need to show proper appreciation for the emperor's solicitude. The minister called for him there and took him in his carriage to his own house, where he went to officious lengths to ensure his observation of the ritual seclusion and other precautions required after an illness. For a time, Genji's sense of disorientation was so strong that he felt as though he had been born into another world.

It was around the twentieth of the ninth month when he recovered. His extreme emaciation served only to refine his beauty. He often sat gazing into space and sobbing, and there were those among his mystified attendants who concluded that he must be possessed by an evil spirit.

One quiet evening, he summoned Ukon for a talk. "It still seems so strange," he said. "Why wouldn't she let me know who she was? She always kept that barrier between us, as though she didn't realize I'd have loved her even if she really had been a fisherman's daughter. It was hard to bear."

"It wasn't at all that she was determined to hide who she was. There just was no opportunity to mention so insignificant a name. From the outset, she considered it strange and incomprehensible that you should be in love with her—like a dream. She felt hurt by your reticence about your own identity. 'I've guessed who he is, but he won't tell me because he doesn't take me seriously,' she said."

"Both of us were stubborn fools. I didn't want to be evasive, but I'm not used to doing things people disapprove of. I have to be very circumspect in my position—first of all, so His Majesty won't have occasion to reprimand me, but also because even a little joke addressed to a woman will cause gossip. It's an annoying situation. When I think of how strangely your mistress fascinated me after the trifling incident that night—of how I insisted on being with her—I can't help believing that her karma ordained that she should meet such an end. I pity her with all my heart, and yet I feel ill-used, too. Why did I have to love her so much if our union wasn't going to last?

"Tell me more about her. You shouldn't hold anything back now. When I commission sacred paintings to be offered during the seventh-day services, whom shall I tell myself they're for?"

"I don't want to keep anything from you; it was only that, after her death, I didn't think I ought to blurt out something she had treated as a secret. Both of her parents died prematurely. Her father was a middle captain of third rank. He loved her dearly, but he seemed to worry that his career was stagnating, and in the end he couldn't even maintain his hold on life. Later, through some little happenstance, she began to receive visits from Lord Tō-no-chūjō, who was still a lesser captain then. He kept up the relationship for three years and seemed to be very much in love, but some horrible threats came from the minister of the right's house last fall. Being an excessively timid person, my lady was terrified, and she stole away to the house of an old nurse, in the western sector of the city. It was a squalid place. She was unhappy there, and wanted to move to the hills, but that direction was unfavorable this year, so she took up residence in the shabby dwelling you know about, merely to avoid the taboo.[29] It was a sorrow to her that you found her there. She was far more diffident than most people; it embarrassed her to reveal her worries, and she always put on a placid front when you were together."

It was just as he had thought, Genji said to himself. His love and pity increased as the fragments of the lady's story came together in his mind. "I once heard Tō-no-chūjō lament the loss of a child. Did she have one?" he said.

"Yes, it was born year before last, in the spring—a sweet little girl," she said.

"Where is she? Give her to me without letting people know. It would be wonderful to have her as a keepsake of the lady whose loss is so hard to bear." He went on in a confidential voice, "I ought to tell Tō-no-chūjō about her, but he would be sure to overwhelm me with reproaches that wouldn't change a thing. In any case, I don't see what objection there could be to my rearing her. Make some excuse to the nurse, or whoever else is with her, and bring her here."

"I'd be very happy if you took her. It's sad to think of her growing up in the western sector, which is where she is now. There was nobody reliable to entrust her to at Gojō."

The quiet evening scene was like a painting—the poignant charm of the sky, the withering plants in the front garden, the feeble insect voices, the reddening maple trees. Looking out at it all, Ukon marveled that she had stumbled into such a splendid situation, and it was with a flush of embarrassment that she recalled the house at Gojō.

The throaty coo of a pigeon in the bamboo reminded Genji of how the same call had frightened the lady while they were at the ruined mansion, and a vision of her pathetic face rose before him. "How old was she?" he

29. In yin-yang cosmology, certain directions were unfavorable for an individual at certain times. If it was essential to reach a place, a person could spend one or more nights in a house from which he or she could travel in another direction.

asked. "It must have been because she was doomed to an early death that she seemed so strangely, so extraordinarily fragile."

"She would have been nineteen. After the death of my mother, who was one of her nurses, her father took pity on me and raised me with her. How can I keep on living when I remember that act of mercy? And yet I feel like the poet who regretted an intimacy he had once savored—during all those years, I relied on someone who was a rather helpless person." [30]

"It's precisely lack of strength that makes a woman appealing. Clever, unsubmissive women don't attract men. I myself am not a brisk, forceful type, and I like someone who is gentle, susceptible perhaps to masculine deception when off guard, but nevertheless basically prudent and discreet, and submissive to her husband's wishes. If a man finds such a woman, corrects her flaws to suit his taste, and makes her his wife, she'll become very dear to him," Genji said.

"When I think of how my lady was exactly what you wanted, it seems such a pity!" Ukon began to weep.

The sky had clouded over, and a cold wind was blowing. Genji stared gloomily into space. Half under his breath, he recited a poem:

mishi hito no	The evening sky itself
keburi o kumo to	becomes something to cherish
nagamureba	when I gaze at it,
yūbe no sora mo	seeing in one of the clouds
mutsumashiki ka na	the smoke from her funeral pyre.

Ukon was unable to respond. "If only she could be here with him!" The thought made her heart ache. As for Genji, even the memory of the noisy cloth fullers evoked nostalgic feelings, and he murmured, "The nights are long," as he composed himself for sleep. [31]

To mark the forty-ninth day after the death, Genji made discreet arrangements for sutra recitations at the Lotus Concentration Chapel on Mount Hiei, including unstinting, meticulous provision for costumes and other appropriate offerings. Even the sutra scrolls and the decorations for the images received careful attention. Koremitsu's brother, the holy teacher, conducted the rites with impeccable dignity. To review the petition he composed, Genji called in his Chinese teacher, a professor of literature with whom he was on close terms. With a pitiful mien, he wrote that someone dear to him, not named, had breathed her last, and that he now commended her to Amida Buddha. "That will do as it is; nothing needs to be added," the professor said. He saw that Genji seemed sunk in misery, his eyes overflowing with irrepressible tears. "Who might the lady have been?" he wondered. "She

30. The poem has not survived.
31. The quotation is part of a line from "On Hearing Cloth-fulling Mallets in the Night," a poem by Bo Juyi about wives fulling cloth while grieving for husbands absent on military duty.

must have had a splendid karma to have remained completely unknown to outsiders, and yet to have excited such remarkable grief."

Genji picked up a pair of trousers from one of the costumes he had quietly had tailored. [His poem:]

nakunaku mo	In what other world
kyō wa wa ga yuu	shall we meet with hearts at ease—
shitahimo o	in what world untie
izure no yo ni ka	the strings I fasten today,
tokete mirubeki	weeping, ever weeping?

He recited heartfelt buddha-invocations with his mind on the lady. She had been wandering up to this point; now she must be setting out on a designated path.

For no good reason, his heart beat faster whenever he encountered Tō-no-chūjō. He would have liked to let him know that the wild pink was being cared for, but he held his peace, unable to face the thought of his friend's reproaches.

Back at the Gojō house, everyone was greatly upset by the lady's disappearance, but there was nothing to go on, no way to find her. It was so odd, her attendants lamented, so strange that not even Ukon should have come back! Admittedly, there was no proof, but they whispered that appearances had pointed to Genji as their mistress's lover. They brought their complaints to Koremitsu, who professed bewilderment, talked as though he knew nothing at all, and continued to visit and flirt as before. The episode seemed increasingly dreamlike. Perhaps, they speculated, the man had been the dissolute son of a provincial governor—someone who had carried her off into the countryside because he was afraid of Tō-no-chūjō. The mistress of the house was one of three children whose mother was the nurse in the western sector. Ukon's parentage was different, and the mistress, shedding nostalgic tears, thought that she must be withholding news of the lady's whereabouts for standoffish reasons of her own. Ukon for her part thought that she would become the center of a tremendous furor if she revealed the truth; and she also knew that Genji remained set on secrecy. She felt unable even to inquire about the little girl, and the lady's people continued in the same state of stunned surprise and ignorance.

Genji mourned on. If only he might at least dream about her! Instead, on the night after the forty-ninth-day services, his dreams were visited by an indistinct figure, the exact image of the woman who had appeared at the bedside in the mansion. Looking back on the event, he could not help believing that some creature at the ruined mansion had lodged itself in his person, and that the lady had died because she happened to be present also. It was a chilling thought.

Young Murasaki

[Third to tenth months of Genji's eighteenth year. Murasaki: about 10; Fujitsubo lady: 23; Genji's wife, Aoi: 22]

Genji had begun to suffer from chills and fever. He ordered prayers for divine assistance, mystic invocations, and other rites, but nothing seemed to be able to keep the symptoms from recurring.

"There is a wonder-working monk at such-and-such a temple in the northern hills," somebody told him. "When this same sickness was going around last summer, he made many immediate cures in cases where others had produced no results with their intercessions. It would be troublesome if the others didn't succeed; I would suggest that you try him soon." He sent off a messenger, but the monk answered that age and infirmity had made it impossible for him to leave his cell.

"It can't be helped, then; I'll have to pay him a quiet visit," he said. He set out before dawn, taking only four or five trusted attendants. The cell was rather far back in the hills. In the waning days of the third month, all the cherry blossoms in the capital had passed their prime, but the trees in the mountains were still in full bloom, and there was a delightful haze in the sky. Unaccustomed to such freedom, he savored the scenery and the novelty of the journey.

The appearance of the temple inspired the utmost awe and reverence. He climbed to the sage's cell, a deep cavern on the side of a high peak. He refrained from mentioning his name, and his clothes were very shabby, but it was apparent from his bearing that he was of noble lineage. Surprised, the sage addressed him with a smile. "This is a great honor! Might you be the gentleman who summoned me the other day? But how do you happen to have come? I no longer think about this world; I've stopped performing rituals to secure worldly benefits," he said. He was indeed a most holy man.

The monk prepared appropriate charms, gave them to Genji to swallow, and chanted mystic invocations. Meanwhile, the sun rose high.

Stepping outside for a moment, Genji looked around. The high vantage point afforded a clear view of all the scattered cells lower down. Just below the winding path to the cave, there was a residence with a brushwood fence, similar to the residences of the other monks but more neatly laid out, and with trim buildings and galleries and a pleasant grove. "Who lives there?" he asked.

"That's where Bishop So-and-so has been in retreat for the last two years," said one of his attendants.

"The bishop is a man with whom one has to be on one's best behavior. It was a mistake to go to such absurd lengths with this disguise. I hope he doesn't find out I'm here."

A group of neat, pretty little girls appeared, also clearly visible as they drew offertory water and cut flowers.

"There must be a woman about the place," an attendant said.

"But surely the bishop would never install a woman there," said another.

"Who can she be?"

One of them went down and peered through the fence. "You can see a beautiful little girl, some young ladies-in-waiting, and some page girls, too," he reported.

Noting the advance of the sun as he performed his rituals, Genji wondered if the disease might be getting ready to flare up. Someone suggested doing something to take his mind off it, and he went out to look toward the capital from the mountain behind the cave. The haze extended far into the distance, softening the outlines of the trees in all directions. "It looks just like a picture," he said. "Someone who lived in a place like this could wish for nothing better."

"This scenery is nothing special. You would paint some remarkable pictures if you saw the ocean and mountains in other provinces. I'm thinking of places like Mount Fuji and Such-and-such Peak," one of his men said.

Someone else tried to amuse him with a lengthy discourse on the virtues of the bays and coasts to the west. "When it comes to places nearer at hand, nothing can compare with Akashi Bay in Harima Province," this man said. "There isn't any single feature of particular interest; it's the strangely peaceful effect of the sea view that sets it apart. A former governor of the province is rearing a daughter there—a man who's just recently taken Buddhist vows. Considering that he was either the son or the grandson of a minister of state, he ought to have had a successful career, but he was an eccentric sort, and he resigned a middle captaincy rather than take part in court life. He became governor at his own request, but his tenure was something of a fiasco because he failed to win the respect of the local people. The idea of returning to the capital as a failure didn't appeal to him, so he shaved his head after his term expired. Then he went to the coast and settled there instead of going to live in the mountains. It seems a perverse choice, and it's true that the province abounds in more suitable sites for religious retirement. But a remote mountain dwelling would have been too isolated and eerie for his young wife and child; and he himself also finds it diverting to live by the sea.

"When I visited Harima recently, I took the opportunity to call and see how he was getting along. He may not have been able to carve a niche for himself in the capital, but there in Harima he owns a magnificent residence on a huge estate. Whether he was respected or not, he did wield the power of office, and he was bent on acquiring enough resources to make him rich for the rest of his life. He's also diligent in his prayers for the life to come, so he's actually a better monk than he was a layman."

"What about the daughter?" Genji asked.

"Not bad, I hear, either in looks or in personality. It seems that one governor after another has come forward with a formal request for her hand, and other people too, but he's turned them all away. Apparently, he's always lecturing her like a man on his deathbed. 'It's bad enough that I've sunk into obscurity like this. You're my only child, and I have special plans for you. If I die before anything comes of them—if the future I have in mind doesn't materialize—then it's up to you to throw yourself into the sea,' he says."

"A most interesting tale," said Genji.

"So precious a daughter would make a fit consort for a dragon king in the sea," someone suggested.

"The father's aspirations do seem to be inconveniently lofty," laughed the narrator, Yoshikiyo. He was the present governor's son, a chamberlain who had been promoted to fifth rank that year.

"We know what a rake you are, Yoshikiyo. You've probably already made up your mind to ruin the father's plans," someone said.

"I imagine he's haunting the premises," said someone else.

"Oh, come on! Whatever the father thinks, she's probably just a country girl."

"Besides, what can you expect of someone who's spent her whole life in the wilds, catering to the whims of an old-fashioned parent?"

"I hear they've used their connections to assemble attractive young attendants and pages from the best families in the city. Apparently, the way they look after her is quite amazing," Yoshikiyo said.

"That's all very well, but what if an unpleasant character takes over as provincial governor? The father may have a hard time holding onto her."

"Why do the father's thoughts plumb the ocean depths? The seaweed there would be rather messy, I should think," Genji said.[1] He was more than a little interested. Aware of his penchant for the bizarre, his attendants surmised that he would remember the story, trivial though it was.

1. He puns on *mirume* (a kind of seaweed; "seeing eyes"), suggesting that people would criticize the father if they learned of his telling the girl to drown herself.

"It's getting late, and Your Lordship seems to have escaped an attack. You should start home as soon as possible," someone said.

The sage demurred. "It isn't merely a matter of the disease; some malignant spirits seem to be present, too. Spend tonight in quiet prayer and go home tomorrow," he said.

The attendants fell in with the suggestion, and Genji was attracted by the novel prospect of a night spent as a traveler. "All right, I'll leave at dawn," he said.

For want of other diversions to help him through the rest of the long spring day, Genji went down to the bishop's brushwood fence, trusting the hazy twilight to shield him from observation. He sent back all his attendants except Koremitsu and peered inside. There was a private icon in the west room directly in front of him, and devotions were being performed by someone who proved to be a nun. The blinds were slightly raised; flowers were apparently being offered. The nun, who seemed to be of high birth, was leaning against a pillar in the middle of the room, reciting in an infirm voice from a sutra placed on an armrest. Genji found her a moving sight—a woman in her forties, with an aristocrat's white skin, emaciated but full-faced, with attractive shoulder-length hair that seemed more pleasingly modern than if it had been left long. There were two neatly attired women with her, and small girls came and went at play. A girl of about ten came running in, dressed in a white chemise and a limp globeflower-yellow robe. Incomparably superior to all the others in appearance, she showed promise of developing into a remarkable woman. Her hair fanned out, swaying, as she moved, and her tearful face had been rubbed red.

The nun looked up. "What's the matter? Have you been quarreling with one of the girls?" she asked. Noticing a slight resemblance, Genji wondered if the child was hers.

"Inu let my baby sparrow get away. I had him under the incense basket," the child said with a woebegone look.[2]

"This really won't do!" said one of the two ladies-in-waiting. "That stupid girl needs another scolding. Where could the bird have gone? It was just getting cute, too. I hope a crow doesn't find it." She stood up and went out. She was a presentable woman with a long, flowing head of hair. It seemed that she was called Shōnagon-no-menoto, and that she was the one who took care of the child.

"Come, don't be a baby. You're a hopeless infant. It never crosses your mind that I might die any day now; all you think of is that sparrow. I keep telling you it's sinful to shut it up in a cage. What am I going to do with you? Come here," the nun said. The child knelt near her. The sweet face, the lustrous eyebrows, the forehead from which a childish hand had

---

2. Inu is a child servant. Heian women warmed and perfumed robes by draping them over wickerwork baskets called *fusego*, which were inverted above braziers containing burning incense.

brushed locks of hair, the hair itself—all were immensely appealing. Her growth to adulthood would be worth watching, Genji thought, observing her with an intent gaze. But the true source of his interest, he realized with a start, was her striking resemblance to the lady he loved so dearly, so extravagantly, that the mere thought of her brought tears to his eyes.

The nun stroked the child's head. "You hate having it combed, but it's nice hair. I worry about you, you're such an innocent. Some girls of your age are so much more grown up. My young lady already had an excellent understanding of what it meant when she lost His Lordship, her father, at the age of twelve. How in the world will you get along if I leave you now?" Tears streamed from her eyes, and Genji could not help feeling sad as he watched. Child though she was, the girl looked the nun full in the face; then she lowered her gaze and hung her head, her hair tumbling forward in beautiful shining strands. The nun:

oitatamu	It is hard for the dew
arika mo shiranu	to pass from existence,
wakakusa o	leaving the young herb
okurasu tsuyu zo	to meet an unknown future
kiemu sora naki	when it grows to maturity.

Weeping, the other woman agreed:

hatsukusa no	The dew must not think
oiyuku sue mo	of passing from existence
shiranu ma ni	while still unaware
ika de ka tsuyu no	of what full growth will mean
kiemu to suran	for the newly sprouted herb.

As she spoke, the bishop arrived from another part of the residence. "Isn't this room a bit exposed? It's a pity you chose today, of all days, to sit so close to the outdoors. I've just heard that the Genji middle captain has come to the sage's cell up above to get spells for his chills and fever. He's made a point of keeping it quiet, so I didn't know about it; I haven't gone to pay my respects, even though I've been here right along."

"Oh, dear," said the nun. "We're certainly far from presentable. What if somebody has seen us?" They lowered the blinds.

"Genji the shining one—the name on everybody's lips. What do you say to taking this opportunity to see him? Beauty like his can make a person forget his cares and live a longer life—even someone in holy orders who doesn't care about worldly things. I think I'll just drop him a note." There was an audible rustle as the bishop took his leave.

Genji started back up the hill. "What a sweet child! Considering that those philandering companions of mine are always going off on private excursions like this, they must make all kinds of unexpected discoveries. Look at what I've stumbled across, as seldom as I get out," he thought, much intrigued. "She's a perfect dear," he thought again. "Who can she be? I'd love to have her with me day and night as a consolation—a substitute for that other one." It was an idea that struck deep roots.

He was lying down when one of the bishop's disciples came and asked to see Koremitsu. The message carried to his ears in the narrow confines of the cell. "Someone has just informed me of your presence in our neighborhood. I ought to wait upon you immediately, but it troubles me that you have kept your visit a secret, knowing as you do that I am in retreat at this temple. It would also have been natural to furnish you with a lodging in the hermitage here. I am most disappointed."

Genji replied, "I began to suffer from chills and fever around the middle of the month. The constant attacks became unbearable, and when someone told me about this place, I decided on the spur of the moment to come here. I came in strict secrecy because I felt it would be awkward for so famous a healer if he failed to cure me—more embarrassing than for an ordinary monk. I shall be happy to visit you at once."

The bishop was prompt to present himself. Monk though he was, his great personal dignity and high renown made Genji self-conscious about his own casual appearance. After talking of things having to do with his period of retreat, the bishop urged Genji to visit him. "The hermitage is merely a simple brush-thatched hut like all the others, but I should like to show you the stream flowing from the spring, which is rather pleasantly cool," he said.

Genji decided to go, his desire to learn more of the appealing child outweighing the embarrassment with which he recalled the bishop's extravagant comments to the ladies who had yet to see him.

The garden was all that the bishop had promised, its trees and shrubs familiar enough in kind but meticulously arranged to create tasteful effects. Since it was the dark of the moon, basket-fires burned beside the stream, and lanterns had also been lit. The south apartment was tidily furnished.[3] An elegant fragrance drifted in from somewhere, and the scent of sacred incense hung in the air. The remarkable perfume from Genji's robes, released whenever he moved, seemed to make the hearts of the ladies inside beat faster.

The bishop told edifying stories illustrating the ephemerality of worldly things, discoursed instructively on the life to come, and so forth. Genji reflected on the frightening nature of his own sin. By setting his heart on that impossible dream, he was condemning himself to a lifetime of misery in this world—and how much greater would be his torment in the next! He longed to retire to a dwelling like his host's—but then there was his concern for the sweet child he had seen before nightfall.

3. The south room in the main hall of an aristocratic residence was used for the reception of guests.

"May I ask who might be staying with you? I had a dream about wanting to visit someone, and now I see what it meant," he said.

The bishop replied with a faint smile. "A dream out of the blue, one might say. I'm afraid the visit would be a disappointment. You may not have heard of the late inspector–major counselor, who died a long time ago, but my younger sister was his principal wife. She took religious vows after his death, and recently she has been in poor health. As you see, I don't go to the capital. She felt that this would be the best place for her, and she has joined me in retreat."

Genji thought he knew who the child was. "I have heard that the major counselor had a daughter. What became of her? I'm not asking with any romantic notion in mind; it's just a plain question."

"Yes, there was one daughter. It must have been more than ten years ago that she died. Her father took great pains with her upbringing because he wanted to present her as an imperial consort, but he died before he could manage it. The nun was left with the responsibility, and somehow Prince Hyōbukyō began to visit her in secret—I don't know who the intermediary could have been. The prince's main wife, a woman of the highest social standing, made life miserable for her in all sorts of ways, and the constant worry killed her. I saw close at hand how true it is that worry does cause illness."

Genji realized that the little girl must be the daughter's child. Was it because Prince Hyōbukyō's blood ran in her veins that she resembled the lady?[4] The thought strengthened his desire to take her under his wing. She was refined, beautiful, and unspoiled; why not bring her to live with him, educate and rear her according to his own standards, and make her his wife?

"A sad story. Did she leave no offspring as mementos?" he asked in the hope of verifying the child's identity.

"She had one child, born close to the time of her death. It was a girl, too. Now that my sister has entered her declining years, she tends to complain that the child's a problem."

It was as he had thought. "It will sound strange, but may I ask that you advise your sister to let me assume responsibility for the child? I do have something in mind. There is a lady with whom I am connected and whom I visit, but I live quite alone—possibly, I suppose, because the two of us don't get along very well. I'd be humiliated if you dismissed me as just another libertine—if you simply said, 'She's too young.' "

"Your proposal would be most welcome if she were not still a complete infant; even in jest, you couldn't treat her as a wife. Nor am I as a monk in a position to reach a decision, since it is said that the husband's behavior is what brings the wife to true maturity. I'll consult the child's grandmother and let her give you an answer."

4. Prince Hyōbukyō and the Fujitsubo lady were full siblings.

Overcome with youthful embarrassment by the bishop's brusque speech and formal manner, Genji could think of no further way to plead his cause.

"It's time for a ritual in the Amida chapel," the bishop said. "I haven't performed the vesper service yet; I'll return after I finish." He set out for the chapel.

Genji was feeling wretchedly ill. A shower brought rain pelting down, a cold mountain wind sprang up, and he could hear the roar of a waterfall whose volume had suddenly increased. The chilling sound of a sutra reading reached his ears from time to time, chanted in a slightly drowsy voice. The surroundings were enough to move the most unreflective of men, and for Genji, his mind teeming with problems, there was no question of sleep. Although the bishop had said that he was merely leaving to perform the vesper service, it was now very late.

It was clear that the people inside the hermitage were also still awake. Despite their efforts at quiet, Genji heard the faint noise of rosary beads brushing against an armrest, and there was a hearteningly familiar rustle of skirts, suggestive of elegance and refinement. The hermitage was small, and the women were nearby. A row of folding screens had been erected as an outer wall for their room. He went over to it, pushed the middle screen slightly ajar, and rapped his fan against his hand. The ladies-in-waiting seemed startled, but they could scarcely pretend not to notice, and he heard one of them inch forward on her knees. Then she moved back a bit. "How strange! Perhaps I've made a mistake," she said in an uncertain voice.

"But they say the Buddha never errs as a guide, not even in the dark."[5] His aristocratic young voice made her shrink from the thought of how her own speech must sound in comparison, but she said, "Where is it that you wish to go? I don't quite understand."

"This must seem very sudden; it's natural that you should wonder. But may I just trouble you to pass along a poem?"

hatsukusa no	Ever since that glimpse
wakaba no ue o	of the young leaf on the herb
mitsuru yori	so newly sprouted,
tabine no sode mo	never has it been free of dew—
tsuyu zo kawakanu	the sleeve of the travel robe.

"I believe you must be aware that there is nobody here who might understand such a message. To whom could I take it?" she said.

"Please tell yourself that I must have a reason for giving it to you," he said.

5. Genji's rapping was a request for help. He implies here that someone in a religious household ought to share the Buddha's attributes. The second half of his sentence is a lighthearted comparison of his own situation to that of the ignorant beings the *Lotus Sutra* describes as "entering from darkness into darkness without ever hearing the Buddha's name." See Hurvitz, *Scripture*, p. 133.

She went inside to inform her mistress. "A typical modern gallant!" the nun said. "He must think the child is of marriageable age. But how did he find out about the 'young herb'?" There was much that struck her as strange and puzzling, but it would seem discourteous to let too much time elapse. She sent back an answering poem and a comment, "Our sleeves are the ones that are hard to dry."

makura yuu
koyoi bakari no
tsuyukesa o
miyama no koke ni
kurabezaranan

Please do not compare
the dews of a single night
spent away from home
with the mossy robes of those
who dwell far back in the hills.[6]

"I don't understand at all why you communicate with me through a third person; it's not what I am used to. Forgive me, but I need to take this opportunity to have a serious talk with you," Genji answered.

"I thought he must have been misinformed," the nun said to her women. "I really feel at a loss to reply to so fine a gentleman."

"But won't you embarrass him if you don't see him?"

"You're right. I wouldn't like to speak to him if I were a young woman, but as it is . . . Besides, I can hardly ignore the honor of his saying he has something important to discuss with me." She moved forward on her knees.

"I'm sure you must consider me brash and thoughtless, but the buddhas know there is no frivolity in my heart," Genji said.

The nun sat in silence, a hint of constraint in her manner, and he felt too awkward to proceed immediately.

"Most assuredly, it is no insignificant karmic bond that brings us to converse like this on an occasion I could never have foreseen," she said.

"I wanted to speak to you about the little girl of whose plight I have heard so affecting an account. Won't you please bring yourself to accept me as a substitute for her dead mother? When I was a mere infant, I lost the one who should have been closest to me, and I have led a strangely unsettled, aimless life. It's because your granddaughter's situation is exactly the same as mine that I want with all my heart to ask you to let her be my companion. That's why I have taken this unique opportunity to address you, rude though it may seem."

"Your proposal would be welcome under different circumstances, but I fear you have been misinformed. Although there is someone here of whom I am the sole frail support, she is still a naive little girl, not a person you might take as a wife despite her shortcomings. I cannot accept your gracious offer."

"I've heard everything there is to know about her, so please don't stand

6. "Moss robes" (*kokegoromo*) was a term used of the clothing of monks, nuns, and recluses.

on ceremony; please just recognize that my intentions are not those of an ordinary man," he said.

But the nun refused to give him the answer he wanted. "He apparently doesn't understand that she's far too young for marriage," she thought.

The bishop was coming. "All right," Genji said, replacing the screen. "At least, I feel better for having brought the subject up."

It was getting on toward dawn, and the voices chanting repentance rites sounded very holy as they mingled with the sound of the waterfall, carried from the Lotus Concentration Hall by the mountain wind. [Genji recited a poem:]

fukimayou	My dreams were dispelled
miyamaoroshi ni	by voices borne on the gale
yume samete	gusting from the hills;
namida moyōsu	my eyes overflow with tears
taki no oto ka na	at the sound of the cascade.[7]

[The bishop:]

sashikumi ni	The purified heart
sode nurashikeru	of one who makes this his dwelling
yamamizu ni	remains unperturbed
sumeru kokoro wa	by the mountain stream that has evoked
sawagi ya wa suru	a visitor's sudden tears.

"This shows, no doubt, that I have grown accustomed to the sound."

The sky gradually lightened, and the mountain birds, invisible in the pervasive haze, raised a chorus of song that seemed to come out of nowhere. Moving with frequent pauses, a deer made its way through a brocade of many-colored blossoms, scattered in drifts from unidentifiable trees and bushes—a sight so novel that Genji forgot about his ailment.

Difficult though it was for the sage to move, he managed to reach the bishop's hermitage, and to perform a protective ritual on Genji's behalf, reciting the dharani with immense authority in a hoarse voice blurred by missing teeth.[8]

A number of people arrived to act as Genji's escorts for the return journey. They offered congratulations on his recovery. There was also a message from the emperor. The bishop did everything possible to welcome the visitors, sending all the way to the valley for unusual fruits and nuts. He offered Genji some wine. "I have sworn a solemn vow to stay here until the end of the year, but I can't help regretting it now, because it prevents me from going down to see you on your way," he said.

"My heart will stay with your hills and streams, but His Majesty is anx-

---

7. The poem, a polite expression of thanks for a night's hospitality, contains overtones appropriate to the circumstances: "My dreams were dispelled" can mean, "I awoke from illusion." "Sound of the Waterfall" was a chant used for repentance rites.

8. Genji has been cured; the purpose of this ritual is to keep him healthy.

ious to see me, and I must show proper respect. I'll be back very soon—
before these blossoms have passed their peak," Genji said. [His poem:]

miyabito ni	I shall go and say
yukite kataramu	to those who serve His Majesty:
yamazakura	"You must come to see
kaze yori saki ni	the mountain cherry blossoms
kite mo mirubeku	before the wind precedes you."

The splendor of his appearance and the beauty of his voice were sufficient
in themselves to dazzle the bishop:

udonge no	Savoring the feeling
hana machietaru	that at long last I have seen
kokochi shite	the *udonge* blossom,
miyamazakura ni	I have no will to turn my gaze
me koso utsurane	toward the mountain cherry tree.[9]

Genji smiled. "But a flower that 'opens once when the time is ripe' would
seem to be rare indeed."

Upon receiving the wine bowl from Genji, the sage looked at him with
brimming eyes:

okuyama no	When I set ajar
matsu no toboso o	the seldom opened pine door
mare ni akete	deep in the mountains,
mada minu hana no	I behold a face resembling
kao o miru ka na	a flower hitherto unseen.

He gave him a vajra as a talisman.[10] The bishop then presented a gauzy
silken bag, attached to a pine branch, which held a jeweled diamond-
seed rosary obtained from Kudara by Prince Shōtoku, still in the original Chinese-style box; also some medicines in dark blue jars, attached to
branches of wisteria and cherry blossoms; and various other gifts appropriate to the circumstances.[11] Genji had sent home for things to be offered to
the sage and the lesser sutra recitants, as well as for other articles required
in connection with his departure. He now made suitable gifts to everyone,
including the neighboring peasants, presented his pious donations, and prepared to leave.

9. *Udonge* is Japanese for the *udumbara*, a small deciduous tree native to South Asia that
produces clusters of small, figlike fruit. Because the flowers are well hidden, legend had it that
they bloomed only once in 3,000 years. Genji's remark below is a quotation from the *Lotus
Sutra*, which compares the rare flowering of the tree to the rarity of preaching about the true
doctrine. See Hurvitz, *Scripture*, p. 29.

10. The vajra (*toko*), a clublike metal implement, symbolized the ability of the enlightened
mind to smash all kinds of defilements.

11. "Diamond seed" (*kongōji*) probably means the hard, black fruit of the goldenrain
(*Koelreuteria paniculata*; J. *mokugenju*), a small, deciduous East Asian tree. The stones were
often used in rosaries.

The bishop went inside and told his sister exactly what Genji had proposed. "I can't say anything one way or the other now. I'll give him an answer in another four or five years if he's still interested," the nun said. Convinced that she would not change her mind, the bishop contented himself with a mere repetition of her words, an attitude Genji found deeply discouraging.

Genji sent the nun a note by a small page, one of the bishop's attendants:

yūmagure	In the uncertain dusk,
honoka ni hana no	I saw but dimly the hue
iro o mite	of the blossom;
kesa wa kasumi no	this morning I go forth
tachi zo wazurau	with vision obscured by haze.

The nun wrote back in elegant, aristocratic script, set down in an easy running hand:

makoto ni ya	I shall wait to see
hana no atari wa	if it be true—this hint
tachiuki to	from hazy skies
kasumuru sora no	of regret to leave the place
keshiki o mo mimu	where the blossom has come forth.

As Genji was entering the carriage, a large party of gentlemen, including his brothers-in-law, arrived from the minister's mansion to escort him, disturbed because he had left without telling people where he was going. Tō-no-chūjō, Sachūben, and others of the minister's sons were among those who had come in search of him. "We are always eager to accompany you on an excursion like this. The last thing we expected was to be left behind," they complained. Someone added, "It would be a shame to start back without lingering awhile in the shade of these gorgeous cherry blossoms."

They seated themselves in rows on the moss, near some rocks, and began to drink. The spot was below the waterfall, with a delightful view of the descending stream.

Tō-no-chūjō drew a flute from his breast and played with the skill of a master; Ben beat time lightly with his fan, singing, "Ah! It's west of Toyora Temple!"[12] The two were much superior to the ordinary run of courtiers, but it was impossible to look away from the peerless—indeed, uncanny—beauty of Genji's appearance as he leaned languidly against a rock. As usual, the party from the mansion included an escort who played the oboe, and there was also a gentleman, an enthusiastic amateur musician, who had brought a servant to carry his panpipes.

The bishop came out, personally carrying a seven-stringed koto. "Do play just one piece," he urged Genji. "It would be a treat even for our mountain birds."

12. From a folksong (*saibara*), "Kazuragi."

"I really don't feel at all well," Genji said. He played a little, and then they all set out. The most insignificant of the monks and pages shed tears of regret; and, of course, it was worse for the aged nuns and others inside the hermitage, who had never before seen Genji's like. One could scarcely believe that he belonged in this world, they said.

The bishop himself was affected. "What karma could have decreed the birth of such a man in this inconsequential land of the rising sun during the latter days of the Law? I find it very moving," he said, wiping his eyes.

The little girl was lost in naive admiration. "He's handsomer than His Highness, isn't he?" she said.

"If you think so, you'd better be his child," said one of the ladies-in-waiting.

She bobbed her head in vigorous assent, charmed by the idea. Whenever she played with her dolls or drew pictures, she made Lord Genji, decked him out in fine robes, and took great care of him.

Genji went first to the imperial palace, where he described his recent activities. The emperor considered him ominously thin. He asked about the sage's spiritual powers, and Genji reported in detail. "It sounds as though he merits appointment to the office of holy teacher. I wonder why I've never heard of a man who has performed so many exploits in the practice of his religion," His Majesty said in a respectful voice.

The minister of the left joined them. "I wanted to go to meet you for the return journey, but thought it best not to, in view of the private nature of your visit. Please stay with us for a day or two of quiet rest," he said to Genji. "Shall I escort you now?"

Little as Genji cared for the proposal, he felt obliged to go. The minister put him into his own carriage and got in the rear. He could not help feeling a twinge of conscience in the face of so much genuine solicitude.

The minister had made preparations at home in anticipation of the visit. During Genji's long absence, no pains had been spared to make the mansion even more perfect than before, a veritable gem of a stately dwelling.

As usual, Genji's wife seemed disinclined to emerge from the inner room in which she had secreted herself, and it was only after repeated paternal messages that she made a reluctant appearance. Like a princess in a picture, she sat where her attendants had placed her, motionless and correct. Genji thought he could love her if only she would make it worthwhile to talk to her—if only he could elicit an interesting reply by hinting at some of the things on his mind or describing his trip to the mountains. But she was so very reserved, so constrained and distant; and the formality of her manner had merely increased with the years. It was too much, too annoying. "I wish you could be more like other wives once in a while. You haven't even bothered to inquire about my health when I've been desperately ill. That's nothing new, but I do take it somewhat amiss," he said.

"Is neglect so painful?" She answered haltingly, with a sidelong glance, her face intimidatingly elegant and beautiful.[13]

"You almost never talk to me—and now I must confess to surprise. 'Visit' is hardly the word for people in our situation; it's a harsh way of putting things. But then you always make me feel small. Even though I do everything I can to try to change your mind, you just seem to dislike me more. Well, while there's life there's hope, I suppose." He entered the curtain-dais. She was slow to follow, and he stretched out with a sigh, uncertain how he might call her in. It may have been a further sign of embarrassment that he pretended to be falling asleep, meanwhile indulging in a series of gloomy reflections on his relations with women.

Much as he wanted to see the young herb mature, it was only natural that the nun should consider the child unready for marriage. The point would be hard to argue. But why not try to find some means of simply bringing her home, so that she might always be present to help him forget his troubles? He wondered how she could look so much like her aunt. Prince Hyōbukyō himself was aristocratic and elegant enough, but not particularly handsome. Could it be because the Fujitsubo lady was the prince's full sister? The child's kinship to the lady made her seem very precious, and he swore to himself that he would find a way to get her.

The next day, he sent courtesy letters to the hermitage. He probably took the occasion to drop a hint to the bishop. To the nun, he said in part, "When you seemed unwilling to consider my proposal, I felt too embarrassed to attempt a full explanation of what was in my mind. I would be so happy if this letter—this persistence—could convince you of the extraordinary depth of my feeling." There was an enclosure, a small knotted letter:[14]

omokage wa	All my heart I left
mi o mo hanarezu	with the mountain cherry tree.
yamazakura	Why, then, should its image
kokoro no kagiri	never absent itself
tomete koshikado	from what remains of me?

"I worry about the wind in the night, too."[15]

Needless to say, his calligraphy was exquisite; and the very style of the letter, with its casual wrapping, seemed superb to the dazzled eyes of the

13. "Neglect" paraphrases the lady's reply, which puts Genji on the defensive by punning on the verb *tou* ("inquire"; "visit"). Her question can mean either, "Is it painful when someone fails to inquire?" or, "Is it painful when someone fails to visit?"

14. Intended for the child Murasaki. As the name implies, knotted letters (*musubibumi*) were notes twisted into knots. They were used for love letters. More formal communications (*tatebumi*), such as Genji's letter to the nun, were written on flat pieces of paper and enclosed in envelopes bent and twisted at the ends. Genji's poem initiates Murasaki's association with cherry blossoms, her symbol throughout the book.

15. Prince Motoyoshi (SIS 29): asa madaki / okite zo mitsuru / ume no hana / yo no ma no kaze no / ushirometasa ni ("Blossoms of the plum! I arose to inspect them in dawn's early light, fearful lest the wind in the night might have carried them away").

old women. It was with difficulty that the nun framed her answer; the situation was so delicate that she scarcely knew what to say.

"I had attached no weight to what you mentioned when you stopped by, and I find it hard to reply now that you make a point of it. The child cannot as yet even write the 'Naniwazu' poem in proper cursive form; your kind letter has been wasted." [16]

arashi fuku	One cannot rely
onoe no sakura	on a heart that tarries
chiranu ma o	just for the brief span
kokoro tomekeru	before the cherries scatter
hodo no hakanasa	on the peak where the harsh wind blows.

"I worry even more."

To Genji's chagrin, the bishop replied in the same vein.

Two or three days later, Genji sent Koremitsu to the hermitage. "A woman called Shōnagon-no-menoto ought to be there. See her and go over the matter thoroughly," he told him.

"There's no possibility he won't explore," Koremitsu said to himself. "She's only a baby." He smiled as he recalled his glimpse of the child through the fence.

The bishop expressed his appreciation of the honor of another letter. Koremitsu asked to see Shōnagon, met with her, and spoke at length of Genji's sentiments and general situation. Glib as ever, he made it all sound very reasonable as he rambled on, but everyone at the hermitage considered the suggestion preposterous. What could Genji have in mind for a girl who was so obviously not of marriageable age?

Genji's letter to the nun was also written in language of the utmost sincerity. As before, he had included a note for the child. "It would give me great pleasure to see those block characters." [His poem:]

asakayama	The love I bear you
asaku mo hito o	is not shallow like the name
omowanu ni	of Shallow Mountain;
nado yama no i no	why should you stay as remote
kakehanaruran	as a rockbound mountain spring?

The nun replied:

16. KKS, kana preface: "The Naniwazu poem was composed at the beginning of an imperial reign; the Asakayama poem is a playful poem composed by a palace attendant. Those two are, as it were, the father and mother of poetry, the first lines we learn in calligraphy practice." The Naniwazu poem appears later in the preface: naniwazu ni / saku ya ko no hana / fuyugomori / ima wa harube to / saku ya ko no hana ("Flowers on the trees in bloom at Naniwazu say, 'Now the winter yields its place to springtime!' Flowers blooming on the trees!"). The Asakayama [Shallow Mountain] poem (MYS 3829), to which Genji alludes in his next note: asakayama / kage sae miyuru / yama no i no / asaki kokoro o / wa ga omowanaku ni ("The love I bear you is not like the shallow pool, mountain spring water, holding the mirrored image of Shallow Mountain itself").

          kumisomete   How can I show her
      kuyashi to kikishi   to one whose shallowness must bring
          yama no i no   regrets resembling those
       asaki nagara ya   of the traveler who sought to scoop
       kage o misubeki   water from a shallow spring?[17]

Koremitsu's report was much the same. To Genji's disappointment, Shōnagon said, "If my mistress's health improves, she'll stay here awhile longer
and then move to her house in the city. I imagine she'll be in touch with
your master after that."

The Fujitsubo lady had withdrawn from the palace because of an indisposition. Genji felt very sorry for the worried, woebegone emperor, but
he also reflected that now, if ever, was his opportunity. So great was his
mental turmoil that his visits to other quarters stopped altogether. Whether
he was at court or at home, he gazed absently into space during the daytime; and after nightfall he harassed Ō-no-myōbu with entreaties. I can't
say how Myōbu managed it, but he did meet the lady in a quite inexcusable manner. Even while he was with her, he was tormented by the feeling
that it was only a dream. For her, the mere recollection of a certain astonishing earlier event had been a source of infinite grief, and she had made a
firm resolve to prevent a repetition. Now she seemed extremely depressed
and upset; and the reserve and discretion of her demeanor made him feel
rather small, lovable and sweet though she was. He almost resented the
very qualities that set her apart from other women, the lack of any taint
of mediocrity. It was hopeless to try to express all that was in his mind,
or even to exhaust one of the innumerable subjects he wanted to broach.
He would have liked to be staying on Kurabu-no-yama [Darkness Moun-
tain], but the night was cruelly short, and he could only think, in despair,
that it would have been better if the meeting had not taken place.[18] [His
poem:]

          mite mo mata   I would become one
       au yo mare naru   with this most precious of dreams,
          yume no uchi ni   for though I see you now,
       yagate magiruru   there may never be a night
    wa ga mi to mo ga na   when we two meet again.

As he spoke, he choked with sobs. She could not help feeling sorry for him.
[Her poem:]

17. An allusion to a composition, also based on the Asakayama poem, in which the speaker
wets his sleeves scooping water, which turns out to be too muddy to drink. Anonymous (KKRJ
987): kuyashiku zo / kumisometekeru / asakereba / sode nomi nururu / yama no i no mizu ("I
regret my attempt to scoop a drink of water from the mountain spring: the pool has proved
shallow, and I have merely drenched my sleeves").

18. Kurabu[no]yama appears frequently in classical Japanese literature as a place where
perpetual night might be expected. It has been variously identified as an old name for Kura-
mayama (in Sakyō-ku, Kyoto) and as a mountain in Ōmi Province (Shiga Prefecture).

yogatari ni	Though I were to plunge
hito ya tsutaen	into an eternal dream
tagui naku	this self whose misery
ukimi o samenu	knows no peer, would not my name
yume ni nashite mo	endure in shameful legend?

Her distress seemed to him both natural and awesome.

Lady Myōbu brought his cloak and the other articles of dress she had assembled. He returned home, stretched out with tears in his eyes, and spent the day in bed. As usual, the only response to his letter was a message from Ō-no-myōbu, announcing that her mistress had not read it. He had expected nothing more, but it was hard to bear, and he spent a listless two or three days in seclusion, without even visiting the imperial palace. It was a torment to feel that the emperor must be worrying lest he had contracted some new illness.

The despairing Fujitsubo lady had concluded that some deed in a former life must have doomed her to misery in this one, and her mental turmoil worsened her illness. The emperor sent a stream of messengers urging her to return to the palace soon, but she could not decide to go. It occurred to her that her symptoms were those of a pregnancy, and she lapsed into misery and frantic anxiety about the future. During the hot weather, she arose from her bed even less often than before. After three months, her condition grew evident, and the surprise of her attendants sharpened the pain of her astonishing karma. Unaware of the facts, the ladies-in-waiting marveled that she had waited so long to inform the emperor. But there was something that only she herself knew beyond a doubt. Every detail of her appearance was familiar to her nurse's daughter Ben and to Ō-no-myōbu, the personal attendants who waited on her in the bath and elsewhere; and the two had wondered, but the matter was not one they felt free to discuss. Myōbu could only suppose, in shocked surprise, that her mistress bore the burden of an ineluctable karma.

The lady must have told the emperor that the malignant spirit responsible for her original ailment had masked the symptoms. Everyone else assumed that such was the case. The emperor showered her with solicitous inquiries, his boundless love even deeper than before. The messengers aroused a host of vague forebodings, and she existed in a state of unrelieved gloom.

Meanwhile, Genji had a dream so bizarre that he called in an expert for an explanation. The divination indicated a future that seemed utterly unattainable and unthinkable. "But there is also an unfavorable element," the man added, "something requiring circumspection on your part." It had turned out to be a delicate situation, Genji thought. "It wasn't my own dream," he said. "It was somebody else's. Don't mention this to anyone until the prophecy is fulfilled." He was still puzzling over it when he heard the news about the Fujitsubo lady. Was this how the dream would come true? More eager than ever to see her, he besieged Ō-no-myōbu with pleas, but Myōbu felt extremely nervous; in her opinion, things were now even more complicated than before, and there was no way at all to contrive a secret meeting. He no longer received even the trifling one-line replies with which the lady had occasionally acknowledged his messages.

It was not until the seventh month that the Fujitsubo lady went back to the imperial palace. The emperor was charmed by the novelty of her presence and moved by her frail appearance, and he loved her even better than before. Somewhat full of figure, with a face thin from worry, she remained a woman of incomparable beauty. As usual, he spent all his time in her apartments. With the season at hand during which music was most interesting, he also kept Genji at his side, calling on him to play the seven-stringed koto, the flute, or some other instrument. Genji did his best to behave in a discreet manner, but there were times when he failed to hide his passion; and on such occasions the lady could not help letting her thoughts dwell on things she would sooner have forgotten.

The bishop's sister had left the hermitage, her health improved. Genji learned where she was living in the city and sent an occasional letter. Naturally enough, the answer was always the same, but his longing for the Fujitsubo lady was more desperate than ever during those months, and he thought of nothing else.

Toward the end of autumn, he felt unbearably sad and depressed. One night when the moon was especially beautiful, his thoughts turned belatedly to a place where he had been accustomed to pay secret visits. Raindrops had begun to fall, perhaps the beginning of a shower. His destination was near the intersection of Rokujō and Kyōgoku avenues, which seemed rather a long distance from his point of departure, the imperial palace. On the way, he noticed a neglected dwelling shaded by ancient trees.

"That house belonged to the late inspector—major counselor," said Koremitsu, who was attending him as usual. "I stopped by there for something one day, and a lady-in-waiting told me they were beside themselves with anxiety about the nun. She's apparently sunk very low."

"Poor lady! I ought to have called. Why didn't you let me know? Go in and tell them I'm here to inquire about her," Genji said.

Koremitsu sent someone inside with the message. "Tell them His Lordship has made a special trip," he said.

The ladies-in-waiting were taken aback when the messenger announced Genji's arrival. "This is awkward. Her Ladyship has gone into a shocking decline during the last few days; she can't possibly receive anyone," they said. But it would have been disrespectful to turn him away, so they tidied the south eave-chamber and ushered him in.

"Things are in a sad state of disarray here, but we did want to thank you for your visit, at least," said one of the nun's attendants. "Please forgive our lack of preparation and the remote location of this room."

It was indeed a novelty to be received in such a place, Genji thought. He said aloud, "I've been wanting to call, but your opposition to my proposal has made me feel diffident about coming. Nobody told me you were so ill; it's most alarming."

The nun replied through an intermediary. "The malady is nothing new, but now it has entered the final stage. I only wish I could thank you directly for the honor of your visit. If you should happen to remain of the same mind about the matter you mentioned, please do take notice of the girl after she matures. The thought of leaving her in such a precarious position hinders me from setting out on the path I long to follow."

She was just in the next room, and he caught an occasional word as she addressed someone in a feeble voice. "What a great honor! I wish the child were old enough to thank him for me." Touched, he said, "I wouldn't have risked letting myself look like a lecher if I hadn't been serious. The moment I saw her, the attraction was so strong—so strangely compelling—that I am sure we must have been together in a previous existence." To the lady-in-waiting he added, "I feel as though this visit has accomplished nothing. Might I not hear a word or two from the little girl?"

"That is impossible, I fear. She went to sleep without knowing you were here."

Just then, footsteps approached from an inner room. "Grandmother, they're saying Lord Genji is here, the gentleman who came to the temple. Why aren't you looking at him?"[19]

The disconcerted ladies-in-waiting tried to hush her. "But didn't you say the very sight of him made you feel better?" she objected, pleased by the excellence of her advice.

Amused, but feigning deafness to save the attendants from embarrassment, Genji took his leave with polite expressions of sympathy. "It's true that she's a complete innocent," he thought, "but I could train her beautifully."

On the following day, he sent a courteous message of inquiry. As usual, there was a tiny note for the child:

iwake naki	Ever since the time
tazu no hitokoe	when the young crane's cry was heard,
kikishi yori	unutterable
ashima ni nazumu	the plight of the hapless boat
fune zo enaranu	seeking passage through the reeds.

"The same person . . ."[20]

Written in a deliberately childish hand, the characters were so tasteful that the ladies told the child she must use them as models.

19. If the nun had received Genji, she could have peeped at him through the panels of her portable curtain-stand.

20. Anonymous (KKS 732): horie kogu / tananashiobune / kogikaeri / onaji hito ni ya / koi-watarinamu ("Am I to love on, going back to that same person, as a tiny boat makes its way through the canal and comes rowing home again?").

It was Shōnagon who replied. "The person you asked about is going to retire to the temple in the hills; it seems that any day now may be her last. If she fails to thank you in this world, she will do so in the next." He was deeply moved.

Autumn evenings were the times when his thoughts dwelt most obsessively on the lady for whom he pined, and the season must also have increased his irrational desire to secure possession of the little girl who was related to her. Recalling the night when the nun had composed the poem about the dew's reluctance to vanish, he yearned for the child. And yet there was a twinge of apprehension. What if she proved less than he anticipated? [He composed a poem:]

> te ni tsumite   May I soon pluck it
> itsu shi ka mo mimu   and make it mine—the young herb
>   murasaki no   growing on the plain,
> ne ni kayoikeru   its roots akin to those
> nobe no wakakusa   of the purple *murasaki*.[21]

It was decided that the emperor would visit the Suzakuin in the tenth month. Everyone qualified to perform as a dancer was pressed into service—sons of exalted houses, senior nobles, and courtiers, as well as the usual professionals—and all were fully occupied with refining their skills, from princes and ministers on down.

Realizing that he had let considerable time elapse without inquiring about the nun at the temple in the hills, Genji made a point of sending off a messenger. The only response came from the bishop. "She finally succumbed on the twentieth of last month. Such is the way of the world, but I grieve for her."

He read the letter with a poignant awareness of the ephemerality of worldly things. And what of the child the nun had fretted over? At her age, she must miss her grandmother dreadfully. He dispatched a warm letter of condolence, moved by memories of his own mother's death, dim though they were. Shōnagon returned an appropriate answer.

He learned that the household had returned to the mansion in the city at the end of the mourning period, and a few days later he took advantage of a free night to call in person. The atmosphere at the neglected estate seemed

21. The *murasaki* (*Lithospermum officinale* var. *erythrorhizon*) is a gromwell common in dry meadows throughout Japan. About two feet high, it bears small, white, five-petaled flowers on its hairy-leaved stalk in summer, and its thick, purple roots yield a pigment that was prized as a dye. Here it functions as a metaphor for the Fujitsubo lady, who derives her sobriquet from the purple wisteria (*fuji*) in the courtyard (*tsubo*) of her residence at the palace; later, it becomes the child's name. Genji's poem alludes to a poem Ariwara no Narihira composed to accompany a gift of a cloak to the husband of his wife's sister (KKS 868): murasaki no / iro koki toki wa / me mo haru ni / no naru kusaki zo / wakarezarikeru ("When deep color stains the *murasaki*'s purple roots, we cannot but prize each grass and shrub on the plain stretching into the distance"). Narihira's poem says, in effect, "When a man's love for his wife is strong and deep, his affection extends to all who are associated with her; he makes no distinction between her and them."

eerie, and it was easy to imagine how frightened a child might feel with so few attendants. He was shown into the same room as before, and Shōnagon spoke of the nun's last moments and other things, weeping as she rambled on. Genji's own sleeve was soaked with sympathetic tears.

"It seems that her father proposes to take her in, but my mistress always worried about that. 'She's at an awkward age—neither an infant nor yet old enough to see through the behavior of others—and I fear her life would be miserable if she joined all the prince's other daughters in a house presided over by a woman whom my own daughter found to be heartless and cruel,' she used to say. There have been plenty of incidents to justify her misgivings, and so we do rejoice that you are kind enough to extend her this courtesy now, regardless of how you may feel in the future. We're just troubled because she's not ready for marriage—and young for her age, at that," Shōnagon said.

"Why is it that you hold back after I've explained my feelings so many times? I've realized that a special tie from another life is what makes me find her innocence so sweet and endearing. Wouldn't it be possible for me to speak to her without an intermediary?" [His poem:]

ashiwaka no	Though seaweed be scant
ura ni mirume wa	where young reeds grow in the bay
kataku tomo	at Waka-no-ura,
ko wa tachinagara	the wave will not go back to sea
kaeru nami ka wa	before it reaches the shore.[22]

"That would really be too much."

"Indeed, you pay us a great honor. But . . . :

yoru nami no	The gemweed growing
kokoro mo shirade	in Waka-no-ura Bay
waka-no-ura ni	would be indiscreet
tamamo nabikan	were it to yield to the wave,
hodo zo ukitaru	ignorant of its intent.

"I am quite at a loss," she said.

The practiced skill with which she phrased her refusal tempered Genji's annoyance. "I shall surely cross . . . ," he recited in a voice whose beauty thrilled the young ladies-in-waiting.[23]

The child was in bed, weeping for her grandmother, when some of her playmates entered. "A gentleman in an informal cloak is here. It's probably the prince," they said.

22. Wordplays yield a second meaning: "Although it may be hard to meet her, I won't leave until I do."

23. Genji announces his determination to persevere by paraphrasing a poem by Fujiwara no Koremasa (GSS 731): hito shirenu / mi wa isogedomo / toshi o hete / nado koegataki / ōsaka no seki ("My suit unaccepted, the impatience is mine alone, but though it may take years, I shall cross the barrier at the Hill of Meeting").

She got up and approached the room, asking in a sweet voice, "Shōnagon, where is the gentleman? Has Father arrived?"

"It's not the prince, but you mustn't treat me like a stranger. Come here," Genji said.

Child though she was, she recognized the voice of the splendid gentleman who had visited the temple. She went up to her nurse, afraid of having said the wrong thing. "Let's go, Shōnagon. I'm sleepy."

"Why must you hide from me now? Sleep on my knees. Come a little closer," Genji said.

"This is what I meant. She's still at the innocent age." The nurse pushed her charge toward him, and the child sat down with an unconcerned air. Genji put his hand inside the curtain. Her hair hung in silky strands above the soft robe, and the abundance of the ends suggested that it must be remarkably lovely. He took her hand.

Disconcerted and frightened by the approach of someone unfamiliar, she pulled away and retreated inside. "I said I wanted to go to bed."

Genji slipped in after her. "I'm the one who's going to care for you from now on. Don't be unfriendly."

"This is unnerving, sir. You're going much too far. Whatever you may say to her will be a waste of time," the nurse said in distress.

"She's only a child; there's no question of my doing anything. I merely want you to understand that mine is no ordinary love," Genji said.

A violent hailstorm made the night seem eerie. Tears came to Genji's eyes. "She must be dreadfully lonely with so few people around." It would be unbearable, he thought, to go off and leave her like this. "Close the shutters," he told them. "It's a terrible night out. I'll be on duty; the rest of you stay close by." He entered the curtain-dais with a matter-of-fact air.

The ladies-in-waiting were aghast. Shōnagon felt especially dismayed and indignant, but she merely sighed. There was nothing to gain by making a scene.

The terrified child trembled with apprehension, her fair skin roughening as though chilled. Moved to pity, Genji wrapped her in her singlet. Not unshocked by his own behavior, he began to talk in affectionate tones about things that he thought might please her. "How about coming to a place where there are lots of interesting pictures and dolls to play with?" he asked. His friendly, gentle speech calmed her fears, but she tossed and turned, too uneasy to sleep.

The storm raged throughout the night.

"It would have been truly lonely if His Lordship hadn't stayed. What a pity she isn't of marriageable age!" the ladies-in-waiting whispered to one another. The anxious nurse stayed as close as possible to the curtain-dais.

After the wind had died down a bit, Genji emerged in the dark, as though from a tryst. "Now that I've seen what a pitiful situation this is for her, I'll be even less able to keep from worrying. I want to move her to the place where I lead my lonely life. She simply can't stay on like this forever; it's a wonder she hasn't been frightened to death," he said.

"The prince seems to have told her he'll be coming for her, but I imagine he'll wait until after the forty-nine days expire," Shōnagon said.

"He would be a natural source of support. Still, he's always lived apart from her; she must consider him as much a stranger as I am. This is only the first time I've been with her, but I'm sure I love her better than he does," said Genji, stroking the child's hair. He set out with many backward glances.

Mist veiled the vast expanse of the sky in a delightfully unusual manner, and pure white frost covered the ground. If he had been returning from a real tryst, he would have savored the scene; as it was, he felt a vague dissatisfaction.

He realized that his route was taking him past the house of a lady he had been visiting in strict secrecy, but there was no response when he ordered someone to rap on the gate. There seemed no choice but to have an attendant with a good voice recite a poem:

asaborake	Even when I wander
kiri tatsu sora no	lost under mist-shrouded skies
mayoi ni mo	at break of day,
yukisugigataki	I cannot pass beyond
imo ga mon ka na	the gate of my beloved.

After the man had chanted the lines twice, the lady sent out a maidservant, cultivated in appearance, who chanted a reply and returned inside:

tachitomari	If you have halted,
kiri no magaki no	loath to pass the rustic fence
sugiuku wa	enshrouded in mist,
kusa no tozashi ni	the closed door of a grass-thatched hut
sawari shimo seji	should prove no obstacle.

Nobody else appeared. Dull as it seemed to go on home, Genji went back to Nijō rather than risk detection in the increasing daylight. He lay down, smiling to himself in affectionate recollection of the child's sweet face. The sun was high when he rose. He wanted to send a letter, but the message could not very well assume the usual form, and he sat racking his brains, his brush idle. In the end, he dispatched some amusing pictures.

The prince called at the house on that same day. The premises were far more rundown than in the nun's lifetime, and the sprawling old mansion seemed even more deserted and lonely than before. "You can't stay in a place like this, not even for a little while," he said, looking around. "I'm going to take you to my house. Everything will be fine. Your nurse will have a room all to herself, and there are children to play with. You'll be very happy." He called the child closer. Her clothing was saturated with the rich scent from Genji's garments—a tasteful perfume, he thought, but it was sad that she must wear robes limp with age. "Over the years while she was living with the ailing old lady, I used to urge her to come and make friends with the people at my house, but she was strangely reluctant, and my wife also seemed hesitant about stepping forward. I'm sorry she has to move under these circumstances," he said.

"But there's no need for her to go right away," Shōnagon said. "She can stay here awhile longer, lonely though it is. I'm sure it will be best if she doesn't move until she's old enough to understand what goes on around her." She added, "She never stops grieving; she won't eat a thing." The child's face was indeed very thin, but it made her look all the more refined and appealing.

"You shouldn't carry on so," the prince told his daughter. "There's no use thinking about the dead now. I'm here; everything's all right." The day drew to a close as he talked on in the same vein, and he prepared to take his leave. The child wept to see him go, her unhappiness drawing tears from his own eyes. "You mustn't take things so hard. I'll move you to my house in a day or two," he said. He set out after many repetitions of this and other soothing remarks. The house seemed empty after his departure, and the little girl shed tears of loneliness.

No worries about the future crossed the child's mind; all her thoughts were of her grandmother, the person to whom she had been close for years, with never a moment's separation, and who was now dead. The intensity of her grief brought a lump to her throat and kept her from her usual play, child though she was. There were a certain number of distractions during the daytime, but she lapsed into gloom after dark. Unable to comfort her, the nurse wept with her. "How can you go on like this?" she said.

Genji sent Koremitsu to help the household for the night. "I ought to come myself, but His Majesty has summoned me," his message said. "I feel deep concern for the child after having seen her in those sad circumstances."

"This is no way to act at the beginning of a relationship, even if it isn't a real marriage," Shōnagon said.[24]

"The prince will be sure to scold us for neglecting our duty if he hears about it," said someone else.

"Be very careful," Shōnagon told her charge. "Don't make some childish reference to Lord Genji when you happen to be talking to your father." But the child was dismayingly inattentive.

Shōnagon told Koremitsu of her concerns. "Perhaps an ineluctable fate will make her his wife at some future time. But in my opinion, she's far from ready for marriage now. I worry because I don't understand the motive behind your master's odd advances. Furthermore, her father called today and said, 'Take care of her so I don't have to worry; don't neglect your responsibility.' It's all terribly upsetting. Your master's gallantry is more worrisome

24. A man entering into a serious relationship was expected to visit the woman on each of the two nights following their initial night together.

now than if things were going along as usual." She tried to keep from sounding too distressed, afraid that Koremitsu might think Genji had seduced the girl. Koremitsu had no idea what she was talking about.

Genji could not suppress deep sympathy when Koremitsu returned with his report, but the thought of visiting the child made him feel uneasy and hesitant. If people heard about it, might they not consider him indiscreet and perverted? It would be far better to bring her to his Nijō Mansion.

He sent off a great number of letters. At nightfall, he dispatched Koremitsu with a message: "There are things that prevent me from coming. Will you think I don't really care about you?"

Shōnagon greeted Koremitsu with a few hurried words. "I have all sorts of things to do. The prince has suddenly announced that he'll be coming for us tomorrow. It's a wrench to leave the old familiar place, rundown as it is; all of milady's attendants are upset," she said. Since it was clear that they were busy with sewing and other preparations for the move, Koremitsu went back to Genji.

Genji was at his father-in-law's house, where, as usual, his wife had shown herself in no hurry to receive him. Vaguely irritated, he was strumming on a six-stringed koto, singing "I Till a Field in Hitachi" to himself in an elegant voice.[25] When Koremitsu arrived, he called him close to question him.

The news was a blow. "Once she goes to the prince's house, I'll look like a pervert if I ask for her. And if I just go off with her, people will say I've kidnapped a child. I'll have to swear her women to temporary secrecy and take her to Nijō before the prince comes for her," he thought. To Koremitsu he said, "I'll go there just before dawn. The carriage is all right as it is; just issue orders for one or two escorts to stand by." Koremitsu bowed and withdrew.

Genji could not quite make up his mind. "What shall I really do about this? They'll call me a lecher if word gets out. If only she were mature enough for people to assume we were in love, the affair would seem commonplace. Her father will probably learn where she is, and I won't be able to look him in the face." But he left the minister's house in the dead of night, unable to bear the thought of letting the child escape his grasp. His wife had been her usual indifferent, aloof self. He concealed his plans from the ladies-in-waiting by announcing that he had just remembered some pressing business at home; he would take care of it and come directly back. After putting on an informal cloak in his own apartments, he set out for the late nun's house, with Koremitsu as his only mounted attendant.

An unsuspecting servant opened the gate in response to the raps of Genji's man, and Genji had the carriage drawn inside quietly. When Koremitsu

25. Genji is waiting in his wife's apartments. She is probably intended to hear the song, a *fuzokuuta* (folksong) in which the singer declares himself guiltless of infidelity.

tapped on a corner door, clearing his throat, Shōnagon recognized his voice. She came out.

"His Lordship has arrived," Koremitsu said.

"The child is asleep. How is it that you've come so late at night?" she asked, thinking to herself that Genji was probably on his way home from an assignation.

"I heard a while ago that she was about to move to the prince's house. I have something to say to her before she goes," Genji said.

Shōnagon laughed. "What can it be? She won't produce much of an answer." To her consternation, Genji entered the room. "Some older ladies are relaxing here," she said. "They're quite unpresentable."

"Your mistress probably isn't awake yet," Genji said. "I'll get her up. How could anyone sleep through this enchanting morning mist?" He moved to the interior, where the women were too stunned to utter a word of protest.

The child was fast asleep. He picked her up and awakened her, and she opened her eyes. "Father has come for me," she thought, still half asleep. Genji smoothed her tangled hair. "Let's go. The prince has sent me for you." Puzzled and frightened, she realized that he was not her father. "Now, now, this won't do. I'm just the same as your father, you know," he said. He carried her out.

"What are you doing?" said Tayū and Shōnagon.

"I told her I wanted to take her to a nice place because I was anxious about not being able to come here whenever I pleased. Now I am dismayed to learn that she's supposed to move elsewhere, which would make things still worse; I couldn't even send her a letter. So I'm going to take her to the place I mentioned. One of you ladies come with us," Genji said.

"Today is the worst possible time. What would we tell the prince when he came? The two of you will marry some day if that's your destiny. But this is so sudden! Milady's attendants are all at a loss," said Shōnagon in great agitation.

"Very well, the attendants can come later." Genji ordered his men to bring the carriage up. The astonished women gathered in a worried cluster, unable to decide what to do. The child wept, aware that something strange was happening. Realizing that there was no way to keep her, Shōnagon picked up the robes they had sewed for her the night before, changed her own garments for more suitable attire, and got into the carriage.

The new day had yet to dawn when they arrived at the Nijō Mansion, which was close by. The men took the carriage to the west wing, and Genji got out with the child in his arms, holding her very gently. Shōnagon hesitated. "I still feel as though I'm dreaming; I don't know what to do," she said.

"Do as you please. The child is here now. If you want to go back, I'll have them take you," Genji said.

There seemed no alternative to getting out. It was all so dismayingly sudden, so agitating. What would the prince say? And what would become of the child in the end? However things turned out, it was a sad misfortune to lose those on whom she ought to have been able to rely. The nurse's eyes filled with tears, but she did her best to restrain them, recognizing that they were inauspicious.

There was no curtain-dais in the room, which was not the one Genji was accustomed to using. Genji summoned Koremitsu and had him see to the installation of folding screens and a curtain-dais. There was not much more in the way of furniture—merely a curtain-stand and some cushions. He sent someone to the east wing for his night things and lay down. The terrified child was trembling with apprehension, but she spoke without giving way to tears. "I want to sleep with Shōnagon." Her voice sounded very young.

"Now that you're a big girl, you aren't supposed to sleep with your nurse," Genji told her. She lay disconsolate, with tears in her eyes. The nurse sat dazed, incapable of sleep.

As day gradually dawned, Shōnagon looked around. The mansion and its furnishings were of course magnificent beyond anything in her experience; even the sand in the courtyard seemed to sparkle like jewels. She felt abashed in the face of so much splendor, but at least there were no fine ladies-in-waiting on duty in this wing, which was used only for the reception of guests with whom Genji was not on close terms. Nobody was around except for some menservants, waiting outside the blinds.

There were whispers among those who had caught a hint of a woman's arrival. "Who do you suppose she is? It can't be an ordinary affair."

Genji performed his ablutions and breakfasted in the west wing. The sun was high when he arose. "I'm afraid it will be inconvenient for you with no ladies-in-waiting. Why don't you call in some suitable ones from the other house this evening?" he said to Shōnagon. He sent for some page girls from the east wing—small ones only—and four pretty children arrived. The child was in bed, enveloped in one of his robes. He urged her to get up, administering her first lesson. "You'll hurt my feelings if you keep lying there. Would I treat you like this if I didn't care about you? Girls should have good dispositions." She was even prettier than she had seemed from a distance. Chatting cozily, he sent for interesting pictures, toys, and other things with which to amuse her. When she finally arose, she was charming in her limp, deep-gray mourning robes, an innocent smile on her face. The sight brought an involuntary smile to Genji's own lips.

After Genji had crossed over to the east wing, the child went to the threshold and peeped through the blinds at the trees and lake in the garden. The frost-nipped plants were delightful, quite like a picture, and the figures of gentlemen of fourth and fifth rank, new to her experience, moved back and forth in ceaseless procession, their cloaks a medley of black and red. Genji had been right; this was an entertaining place. In her naive fashion, she was soon distracted by the interesting pictures on the folding screens.

Genji went nowhere for the next two or three days, not even to the imperial palace, so that he might converse with the child and win her affection. Perhaps with the thought of letting them serve as models, he produced various things with his brush for her inspection—practice characters, pictures, and so forth. He assembled them beautifully. One especially fine calligraphic specimen bore two lines of poetry: "I sigh at the mention of Musashino."[26] She picked it up and saw a verse, written in tiny characters:

ne wa minedo	I have not seen its roots,
aware to zo omou	but it is very dear to me—
musashino no	the kin of the plant
tsuyu wakewaburu	hard to approach through the dews
kusa no yukari o	of Musashino Plain.

"Come, you must write something too," Genji said.

"I don't write very well yet."

He smiled at the artless charm with which she raised her eyes. "You mustn't refuse to write just because you can't do it well. I'll teach you," he said. Even to himself, it seemed strange that he should be utterly beguiled by the childish way in which she grasped the brush when she turned aside to write.

"I made a mistake," she said in a shy voice, trying to hide the paper. He captured it and looked at it:

kakotsubeki	I feel uneasy
yue o shiraneba	because I don't understand
obotsuka na	why you have to sigh.
ika naru kusa no	What kind of plant can it be
yukari naruran	to which I am akin?

Childish though the calligraphy looked, its amplitude promised good things in the future. The resemblance to the late nun's hand was unmistakable. She should do very well if she studied examples of a fashionable style, Genji thought. He played dolls with her, assembling a whole row of houses, and found the pastime an excellent way to take his mind off his troubles.

The ladies-in-waiting who had stayed behind scarcely knew what to say when the prince arrived and questioned them. Genji had instructed them to tell nobody for the time being; and Shōnagon, who was of the same mind, had sent word that they must maintain absolute silence. Thus they merely

26. Anonymous (KKRJ 3507): shiranedomo / musashino to ieba / kakotarenu / yoshi ya sa koso wa / murasaki no yue ("Though I have not seen it, I sigh at the mention of Musashino. And why should that be, you ask? The *murasaki* is to blame"). Genji puts his own interpretation on this poem, treating Musashino and *murasaki* as metaphors for the child and the Fujitsubo lady.

said, "Shōnagon took her off somewhere and hid her; we don't know where."

The prince could think of nothing useful to say. "Her grandmother was bitterly opposed to her coming to my house; I suppose the nurse, in a fit of officiousness, decided on her own to cast the child adrift, instead of confronting me with her objections." He set out in tears, flustering the ladies by telling them to let him know if they heard anything.

The prince also questioned the bishop to no avail. The memory of his daughter's sweet face evoked sad, nostalgic thoughts. No longer hostile toward the mother, his wife had looked forward to educating the child to her own liking, and she was distressed that it was not to be.

Ladies-in-waiting gradually assembled. Murasaki was exceptionally quick-witted and amusing, and her playmates, a group of page girls and page boys, felt delighted to participate in her games. She wept for the nun on lonely evenings when Genji was away, but thoughts of the prince seldom crossed her mind. She had always lived apart from him, and her new parent was now the one to whom she clung, and whom she loved with all her heart. Whenever Genji returned from an excursion, she was the first to welcome him home, chattering happily and entering his embrace without the least reluctance or shyness. He found her behavior immensely appealing. When a mature woman's suspiciousness and jealousy cause difficulties, the man may begin to wonder about the constancy of his own affection. He no longer feels comfortable; she for her part nurses a permanent grievance, and the unthinkable occurs without their willing it. But there were no such worries with Genji's delightful playmate. If she were his daughter, she would be too old for perfect freedom; he could never be so familiar as to lie down and get up with her. This was someone very special, very precious.

A Celebration Amid Autumn Leaves

[From the tenth month of Genji's eighteenth year to the seventh month of his nineteenth year. Fujitsubo lady: 23–24; Aoi: 22–23; Murasaki: 10–11]

The emperor's visit to the Suzakuin was to take place soon after the tenth of the tenth month.[1] Since it promised to be much more interesting than the usual imperial excursion, the consorts were upset about missing the spectacle. The emperor himself felt that something would be lacking if the Fujitsubo lady were not able to see the dances, and he arranged for a rehearsal in the courtyard outside his private residence.

Genji danced "The Waves of the Blue Sea." His partner, Tō-no-chūjō, was extraordinarily handsome and confident, but he was like a nondescript mountain tree alongside a blossoming cherry. It was a moment of absorbing interest, the music especially beautiful in the glittering rays of the setting sun; and Genji's dancing and demeanor seemed to belong to another realm of existence, familiar though the piece was. When he chanted the Chinese lines, it was like hearing the voice of a *kalaviṇka* bird in paradise. The emperor wiped away tears of admiration, and all the senior nobles and princes wept.

When Genji straightened his sleeves at the end of the chant, the waiting musicians resumed in a tempo so spirited that he flushed and looked even more radiant than usual. "His is the kind of face a heavenly spirit might take a notion to carry off. I call it creepy," said the crown prince's mother, ill-pleased by the brilliance of the performance. Her young attendants considered the remark distasteful.

---

1. The Suzakuin was a residence used by retired emperors. Judging from the title of the chapter, "A [Longevity] Celebration Amid Autumn Leaves," the purpose of the visit was to honor a former sovereign, but we are not given a full account of the occasion. Longevity celebrations (*ga*) usually took the form of decennial observances, held from a man's or woman's fortieth year on. They were sponsored by relatives, or occasionally by friends or patrons, and always included a banquet, dances, and the recitation of suitable poems.

The Fujitsubo lady thought that she might have enjoyed his dancing more if her mind had not been tormented by the heinous impropriety of their relationship, which seemed more dream than reality. She spent the night with the emperor.

"It seemed to me that 'The Waves of the Blue Sea' swept the board in the rehearsal today," the emperor said to her. "What did you think of it?"

Conscious of a strange awkwardness, she replied merely, "It was remarkable."

"Tō-no-chūjō wasn't at all bad, either," he said. "There's something distinctive about the way the son of a good house moves and gestures. Our famous professionals are highly accomplished, of course, but they can't create the same effect of fresh, youthful charm. After such a dazzling rehearsal, I'm afraid the real event under the autumn foliage may be an anticlimax, but I arranged this because I wanted you to see it."

Early the next morning, the lady received a letter from Genji. "How did the performance strike you? I've never felt as agitated as I did during my dance." [His poem:]

monoomou ni	Did you understand
tachimaubeki mo	the sentiments of the one
aranu mi no	who fluttered his sleeves,
sode uchifurishi	all but unable to dance
kokoro shiriki ya	for the burden of grief he bore?

"But I ought not to write this way."

She sent an answer, apparently unable to let the message pass in silence while the beauty of his face and figure was still vivid in her mind:

karabito no	Though I know not why
sode furu koto wa	a man of Cathay might have wished
tōkeredo	to flutter his sleeves,
tachii ni tsukete	I watched every movement
aware to wa miki	with the deepest feeling.

"I was exceptionally impressed."

For Genji, it was the most precious of gifts. "She's even a connoisseur of dance, and she's already talking like an empress with that reference to ancient China," he thought, an unconscious smile on his lips. He sat gazing at the letter, which he had spread with as much care as if it had been his special sutra.

The emperor was attended on his excursion by the entire court, princes and all. The crown prince also made the journey. The musicians' boats moved across the lake as usual, and there were innumerable dances, both Chinese and Korean. The sounds of instruments and the throbbing of drums filled the air. After having watched Genji in the late sunlight on the day of the rehearsal, the emperor had felt uneasy enough to commission sutra recitations at various temples, a precaution that received sympathetic approval from all who heard of it—all, that is, except the crown prince's disapproving mother, who considered it excessive. Nobody who was not a recognized expert had been selected for the flutists' circle, which included both courtiers and men of lower rank.[2] The two groups of dances, those of the left and those of the right, were under the supervision of two consultants, Saemon-no-kami and Uemon-no-kami.[3] The performers had been rehearsing in the seclusion of their homes, with the finest dancing masters as coaches.

The wind in the pines, a veritable mountain gale, gusted in concert with the strains of the flutes, which were played with indescribable beauty by forty men standing in a circle under the tall maple trees; and the spectacle was almost frightening to behold when Genji emerged from among the swirling colored leaves, dancing "The Waves of the Blue Sea" with dazzling brilliance. Upon observing that most of the leaves had fallen from the maple twig in his headdress, making it a poor match for his glowing face, the major captain of the left picked some chrysanthemums from the garden as a substitute. A few scattered raindrops fell in the waning light, as though the very heavens had been moved to admiration. Genji danced that day as never before, his beauty enhanced by the delightful hues of the fading chrysanthemums,[4] and his performance of the withdrawal was chilling in its perfection, a thing not of this world. Even among the menials who watched from behind trees, rocks, and piles of leaves—people who could scarcely have been expected to appreciate what they saw—those who possessed a modicum of taste were moved to tears.

Second only to "The Waves of the Blue Sea" was "The Song of the Autumn Wind," danced by the emperor's fourth son (the offspring of the Shōkyōden lady), who was still a child. The two performances exhausted the spectators' capacity for enjoyment. The other numbers attracted little attention, and actually seemed to detract from the occasion.

That night, Genji was granted senior third rank, and Tō-no-chūjō received senior fourth lower rank. All the eligible senior nobles also enjoyed suitable promotions, thanks to their association with Genji's triumph. One wondered what deed in a previous life might have enabled him to both astonish people's eyes and delight their hearts.

The Fujitsubo lady retired from the palace around that time, and Genji began to frequent her premises as usual, hoping against hope for a meeting. His neglect gave rise to complaints at his father-in-law's mansion, and

2. A feature of "The Waves of the Blue Sea" was that the dancers put on their costumes inside a ring of musicians behind the stage. Old commentaries surmise that there may have been 40 men in the ring (as indicated below) because the retired emperor's 40th year was being celebrated.

3. An indication of the importance of the occasion. Lesser officials usually oversaw such events.

4. Most of the chrysanthemums in Heian gardens were white. Contemporary taste admired the reddish, brownish, and purplish tinges they acquired as they faded.

his wife grew even unhappier when one of her ladies-in-waiting caught word of young Murasaki's discovery and abduction, and proceeded to inform her that he had brought a mistress to live in the Nijō Mansion. Her feelings were natural for someone ignorant of the facts. If she had spoken out about her discontent like an ordinary woman, he would have explained it all and set her mind at rest, but her habitual mistrustfulness made her put the worst construction on his behavior, and that was why he sometimes indulged in unfortunate frivolities. Still, she was a woman of flawless appearance and demeanor, impossible to fault. She was also the first one with whom he had been intimate, and his feeling for her was special. "She acts that way now because she doesn't realize how much love and respect I feel for her. She'll change some day. She's reasonable; she's not flighty; she's bound to come around," he thought hopefully.

Sweet, pretty, and innocent, young Murasaki grew ever more attached to Genji as she came to know him better. For the time being, he resolved to let nobody know who she was, not even the members of his household. He kept her in the isolated wing, which he had furnished with incomparable splendor, and devoted much of his time to her education. As he prepared calligraphy models and set her to writing, it seemed to him quite as though he had welcomed home a daughter who had lived elsewhere. To the bafflement of everyone but Koremitsu, he safeguarded her position by providing her with an independent administrative office, stewards, and other functionaries. Meanwhile, her father had been unable to find out anything about her.

There were still many times when the child remembered the past and missed her grandmother. She had other things to distract her while Genji was there, and he spent an occasional night at home. But more often, he would prepare to leave at dusk, bound for one of his usual destinations, and then she would sometimes protest his departure in a manner that he found tremendously appealing. Whenever he spent two or three days on duty and went straight from the palace to his father-in-law's house, she would lapse into deep gloom, and he would feel like a man with a pathetic motherless child. He no longer found it possible to pursue casual amours in a carefree spirit.

The bishop heard and rejoiced, even though it was hard for him to understand. When he performed memorial services for the nun, Genji sent impressively generous condolatory offerings.

Eager for news of the Fujitsubo lady, Genji went to her house on Sanjō Avenue one day. He was received by Myōbu, Chūnagon, Nakatsukasa, and others of the ladies-in-waiting. It galled him to be categorized so obviously as an ordinary visitor, but he concealed his displeasure and chatted about general subjects.[5] Meanwhile, Prince Hyōbukyō arrived, learned of his presence, and came to greet him. The prince was elegant, romantically inclined,

5. The attendants act as intermediaries in the conversation.

and mild-mannered—someone who would be of more than passing interest if he were a woman, Genji thought to himself. Attracted to him also because of his relationship to Murasaki and the Fujitsubo lady, he addressed him with quiet seriousness. The prince, for his part, admired the beauty of the companion who seemed so much more friendly and relaxed than usual. Always on the alert for a conquest, he thought, "What a pity he's not a woman!" Genji's desirability as a son-in-law failed to occur to him.

Genji watched with envy as the prince went inside his sister's blinds at nightfall. In the old days, thanks to his father, he had seen her close at hand and talked to her without an intermediary, and he took it rather unreasonably amiss that she should be intent on keeping him at a distance now. He ended his visit with a brusque speech. "I ought to have called more frequently, but the time slipped by because there seemed to be nothing I could do for you. Should there be anything, I will be delighted to put myself at your disposal."

Myōbu could find no way to help him. She felt both intimidated and moved to pity by the unyielding attitude of her mistress, who was more than ever convinced that the meetings with Genji were fated to cause her misery. So the empty days went by, with the two of them agonizing endlessly over the relationship that had proved so brief.

When the nurse Shōnagon thought about her charge's unexpected good fortune, she could not help seeing it as a buddha's response to the prayers the anxious nun had offered for Murasaki during her religious exercises. With a most imposing lady at the minister of the left's house, to say nothing of numerous attachments in other places, difficulties seemed all too likely to arise after the child grew up, but Genji's remarkable devotion was surely a portent of good things to come.

Genji arranged for Murasaki to discard her dark robes at the end of the twelfth month, three months being the prescribed period of mourning for a maternal grandparent. But the nun had been like a mother to her, and she wore no ostentatious colors—only semiformal outer robes in unfigured reds, purples, and yellows, in which she looked very smart and attractive.

Genji peeped into her room as he was leaving for the congratulations.[6] "Did you turn into a grown-up today?" He smiled, handsome and charming. She had already marshaled her dolls and was absorbed in play. He had provided her with accessories, kept on the shelves of a pair of three-foot cabinets, and with a group of tiny buildings, all of which now littered the floor.

"Inu said she was chasing demons and she broke this.[7] I'm fixing it," she said with a serious face.

"That was careless of her. We'll get it mended right away. This is a day

6. The congratulations (*kojōhai*) was a ceremony honoring the emperor, held at the imperial palace on New Year's Day.

7. Demon-chasing (*tsuina*) was a vigorous ritual performed on the last night of the year. Its purpose was to rid the premises of pestilence demons.

for avoiding inauspicious things; you mustn't cry." His departure with a throng of attendants was a marvelous spectacle. The ladies-in-waiting went to the veranda to watch. Murasaki also went out and looked, after which she dressed a doll as Genji and dispatched him to the palace. Shōnagon tried to make her feel embarrassed about her addiction to play. "You must act a little more grown up this year," she said. "Someone who's past ten isn't supposed to play with dolls. Now that you have a husband, you need to be quiet and gentle when you're with him, like a proper wife. As it is, you even fret when someone does your hair."

Her speech was a revelation. "So I have a husband!" Murasaki mused. "My ladies' 'husbands' are ugly, but mine is young and handsome." Despite her love of dolls, such reflections suggested that she had indeed grown a year older. The members of the household puzzled over her childishness, which was apparent on innumerable occasions, but it did not occur to any of them that she and Genji might not be sleeping together as man and wife.

Genji went from the palace to his father-in-law's mansion. His wife was her usual self, elegant and correct, with a guarded air that made him feel awkward. "I can't tell you how happy I'd be if you could at least decide to let this year mark a turning point for us, the beginning of something a little closer to a normal marriage," he said. But it was only to have been expected that she would seem even more distant and constrained than in the past, for she had heard that he was lavishing attentions on someone whom he had installed in his house, and she must have been worrying ever since about the seriousness of the relationship. Forcing herself to act as though there was nothing on her mind, she unbent and responded to his sallies in a manner distinctively her own. She was four years his senior, enough older to be in her prime, and to make him feel callow. He realized that she was a woman who left nothing to be desired, and that his own philandering was to blame for her coldness. The true cause of their estrangement was probably that they viewed their relationship in different ways. As the cosseted only daughter of the nation's preeminent minister, her mother an imperial princess, she possessed an unparalleled appreciation of her own importance and reacted with shocked indignation to any lapse on Genji's part, whereas he considered her unreasonably proud and tried to mold her into conformity with his notion of what a wife should be.

The minister was also disturbed by Genji's unreliability, but the mere sight of him was enough to make him forget his resentment and shower him with attentions. Dropping by early the next morning, as Genji was preparing to leave, he personally brought in a famous belt to go with his ceremonial robes, straightened the rear of his costume, and all but put on his shoes for him in a moving display of solicitude.

"The palace banquet will be coming up; I'll use the belt then," Genji said.[8]

---

8. The palace banquet (*naien*) was a Chinese poetry gathering, held annually in the first month of the year.

But the minister insisted that he wear it. "You'll have a better one for the banquet; I just brought this because it looks a little unusual," he told him. It was in fact only when he was fussing over Genji and admiring his beauty that his life seemed worth living. Infrequent though the visits were, there could be no greater pleasure than seeing such a man come and go as his daughter's husband.

Although Genji had announced that he intended to pay New Year calls, he visited only a few places: the imperial palace, the residences of the crown prince and the retired emperor, and the Fujitsubo lady's house on Sanjō Avenue.

"His Lordship looks remarkably handsome today. The more he matures, the more beautiful he seems; it makes one quite nervous," said the Fujitsubo lady's admiring attendants. Many thoughts crowded into their mistress's mind as she peeped at him through a gap in her curtains.

It was cause for some concern that the twelfth month had passed with no sign of the Fujitsubo lady's delivery. Her people continued to wait—the child was bound to arrive in the first month, they said—but the first month also went by, disappointing their expectations. To the lady's dismay, the gossips began to speculate. Might a malicious spirit be impeding the birth? It would surely be the death of her, she lamented. Sunk in misery, she fell ill. Genji made quiet arrangements for esoteric rites at numerous temples, more convinced than ever that the child must be his. He mulled over the situation with a sinking heart. Was her death to mark the end of a fleeting moment in a world of impermanence? But she gave birth to a son toward the middle of the second month, and the emperor and her household rejoiced, their worries forgotten. She felt now that she must cling to life. It was a painful decision, but she began a gradual recovery, spurred by the thought that news of her demise would produce a gleeful response from the Kokiden lady, who was said to have referred to her in language that amounted to a curse.

The emperor could hardly wait for his son to arrive in the palace. Burdened with his secret and consumed with worry, Genji went to the Sanjō house at a time when no other visitors were present. "His Majesty says he is eager to see his son. I wonder if I might see him; then I can tell him what he looks like," he said.

"I'm afraid he's still at the ugly newborn stage," the lady demurred.

Her refusal sounded not unreasonable, but the truth of the matter was that nobody could mistake the child's astonishing, almost uncanny resemblance to Genji. Her conscience nagged. "Once people see him, everyone will know I've committed a transgression so terrible I can hardly believe it myself. People are always ready to find fault, even when it's nothing of importance—nothing like this. What will happen to my reputation?" Beset by such thoughts, she seemed to herself the victim of a uniquely bitter fate.

From time to time, Genji saw Lady Myōbu. Making use of every conceivable argument, he implored her to arrange a meeting with her mistress, but it need hardly be said that his efforts were futile. He badgered her with pleas to let him see the baby. "Why be so unreasonable? You'll see him soon enough in the natural course of events," she said. Inwardly, she was as distressed as he. Too embarrassed to come to the point, he said, "I wonder if there will ever be a time when I can talk to her without an intermediary." He was a pathetic figure, his eyes brimming with tears. [His poem:]

ikasama ni	What was the nature
mukashi musuberu	of the karma we fashioned
chigiri nite	in a time gone by,
kono yo ni kakaru	that in this world we suffer
naka no hedate zo	separation such as this?

"I just don't understand this kind of thing," he said.

Myōbu, a witness to the lady's anguish, could not bring herself to rebuff him. She murmured a soft reply:

mite mo omou	The one who sees grieves.
minu hata ika ni	And what must be the sorrow
nagekuran	of the one who sees not?
ko ya yo no hito no	Might this be the darkness
madou chō yami	where humans are said to stray?[9]

"It distresses me that neither of you should know a moment's peace."

Since he could find no way to send in a message, Genji left. The Fujitsubo lady, worried about gossip, told Myōbu not to dream of helping him. She no longer admitted her attendant to the trustful intimacy of old, and there must have been times when she showed displeasure with her, even though she treated her well enough to avoid comment. Myōbu must have felt very forlorn and disappointed.

The baby was taken to the imperial palace in the fourth month. He was large for his age and precocious, already showing signs of wanting to sit up. The emperor was not at all suspicious of his amazing resemblance to Genji. "It's just as they say; two supremely handsome individuals do tend to look very much alike," he thought. He was enchanted. His affection for the infant Genji had been equally warm, and he still much regretted that fear of public disapproval had kept him from naming the boy crown prince. It had been a sorrow to watch him develop into someone whose bearing and appearance were far too distinguished for a subject. But now he possessed a son with the same radiant beauty, born of a mother whose status was irreproachable; and he treated him as a flawless gem. Meanwhile, the Fujitsubo lady existed in perpetual apprehension and gloom, worried as much by the emperor's joy as by the child's appearance.

One day, when Genji was participating as usual in a musical gathering at the Fujitsubo pavilion, the emperor came out with the baby in his arms. "Of

9. An allusion to Kanesuke's poem on parental love ("Kiritsubo," n. 5).

all my sons, you were the only one I saw constantly, beginning with the days when you were just this young. Perhaps it's the association of ideas, but I seem to notice a close resemblance. I wonder if all babies look alike when they're tiny." He gazed at the child with deep affection.

Genji was sure he was changing color. Trepidation, shame, joy, tenderness—one emotion seemed to follow another, and his eyes brimmed with tears. The baby looked almost ominously appealing as it cooed and smiled. Though he said it himself, it was no small thing to resemble such a paragon, he thought rather egotistically. The Fujitsubo lady perspired in an agony of embarrassment.

Despite the eagerness with which he had looked forward to seeing the child, Genji found the experience so unsettling that he left the palace. Back in his own apartments, he lay down to rest. He would go on to his father-in-law's house after he regained his composure.

Wild pinks were blooming in the garden outside, a splash of color against a green background. He picked one and sent it to Lady Myōbu, with a letter that probably ran on at considerable length. [His poem:]

yosoetsutsu	Small consolation
miru ni kokoro wa	to gaze at the pink in bloom,
nagusamade	mindful of another:
tsuyukesa masaru	the tears I shed outnumber
nadeshiko no hana	the dewdrops on its petals.

"I had looked forward to the flower's bloom, but ours is a hopeless situation."

A suitable opportunity must have arisen, for Myōbu showed the letter to her mistress. "Please do send him an answer on a petal, even if it's no more than a speck of dust," she said.[10]

The Fujitsubo lady herself was wrestling with painful emotions. She produced what seemed half an answer, a single poem written in faint characters:

sode nururu	Though I tell myself
tsuyu no yukari to	it is the source of dewdrops
omou ni mo	dampening sleeves,
nao utomarenu	I cannot look with dislike
yamatonadeshiko	on the wild pink of Yamato.

Myōbu sent it on, happy even with so little. Genji had been lying down in wretched spirits, staring into space, with no expectation of anything but the usual silence. The poem made his heart beat wildly, and he shed tears of joy.

No matter how long he might lie there moping, he thought, his spirits would be unlikely to revive. He went to seek diversion in the west wing, as

10. An allusion to Mitsune's poem ("The Broom Tree," n. 8).

was his custom at such times. Blowing a pleasant air on his flute, he peeped into Murasaki's room, his hair untidy and his robes rumpled. She reminded him of the dewy pinks as she leaned against an armrest, looking bewitchingly sweet and pretty. Apparently piqued by his failure to come as soon as he reached home, she kept her face averted in uncharacteristic fashion. He knelt at the threshold. "Come here," he said. As though she had not heard, she murmured a line from a poem: "A rock when the swelling tide rolls in."[11] She raised a sleeve to her mouth in a delightfully coquettish gesture.

"You're not being nice at all. When did you learn to talk that way? I don't want you to get a surfeit of seaweed."[12] He told someone to bring a koto for her. "The second string on the thirteen-stringed instrument doesn't stand up very well to high notes. It would be a nuisance to have it break," he said. He took it down to the *hyōjō* mode, played a few notes to tune it, and pushed it away. She stopped pouting and began to play with childish grace, looking very sweet as she bent her tiny body to twang the strings with her left hand. Charmed, he coached her while he played the flute. She was so bright that a single hearing was all she needed to master a difficult melody. Her lively intelligence and delightful disposition were exactly what he had hoped for. He gave "Hosoroguseri" a spirited rendition that made its ugly name seem acceptable, and she accompanied him in perfect time, her touch immature but rich with promise.

The servants lighted the lamps, and the two of them looked at pictures.

Since Genji had announced that he would be going out, his attendants began to clear their throats. "It looks like rain," a voice said. As usual, Murasaki's spirits sank. She turned away from the pictures and lay facedown, a pathetic sight. He stroked the abundant hair tumbling over her shoulders. "Do you miss me when I'm away?" he asked. She bobbed her head.

"It's very hard for me, too, if I have to go without seeing you for a day. But I feel I can be at ease with you while you're still a little girl, and there are some jealous ladies whom I don't want to offend. They're being rather difficult, so I'm going to have to go out like this for a while. I'll never go anywhere after you grow up. The reason I don't want anyone to hate me is that I hope to live a long life and spend it happily with you." His long explanation left her abashed and speechless. She put her head on his lap and promptly fell asleep. Overcome with compassion, he told the ladies-in-waiting that he had decided not to go out that evening, and they all went off to bring his dinner to the west wing.

11. Anonymous (MYS 1398): shio miteba / irinuru iso no / kusa nare ya / miraku sukunaku / kouraku no ōki ("Seldom do I see you, often do I yearn for you. Yet you are not seaweed on a rock that vanishes when the swelling tide rolls in").

12. Genji uses *aku* to mean "surfeit" instead of "one's fill," twisting the meaning of the anonymous poem he quotes (KKS 683): ise no ama no / asa na yū na ni / kazuku chō / mirume ni hito o / aku yoshi mo ga na ("I long for a means of seeing my fill of you—seeing like the weed, the 'see weed' Ise fishers harvest morning and evening"). There is a pun on *mirume* ("seeing," "seeing eye"; a type of seaweed).

He woke Murasaki up. "I've decided not to go out," he said. She sat up, her good humor restored, and they dined together. She toyed with her food. "Well, then, please go to bed," she said, as though afraid he might change his mind. How could he ever leave such a one, even to set off on the Shide Mountain road itself?

There were many times when Genji was detained in the same way. People naturally heard about what was happening, and the stories were passed along to the household of the minister of the left. "Who can she be?" the ladies-in-waiting at the mansion asked one another. "It passes belief! Still not a word about her identity, and look at the way she hangs onto him like a spoiled child! She can't have much to recommend her in the way of birth or refinement; she's probably someone he met at the palace or some place, fell in love with, and hid for fear of criticism. Maybe that's why they say she's childish and unreasonable."

The emperor heard that Genji was keeping a woman at home. "It's pitiful that the minister of the left should feel so unhappy," he told his son. "He's been doing everything imaginable for you ever since you were a child, and it's not as though you weren't old enough now to understand what you owe him. What makes you so heartless?" Genji preserved a respectful silence. "Poor lad," the emperor thought. "He doesn't seem to care much for his wife." He continued, "And yet I don't see or hear anything to suggest that you're promiscuous or infatuated with one of the ladies-in-waiting here or the women you see elsewhere. What kind of hole-in-the-corner affair is it that's causing so much resentment?"

Despite his advancing years, the emperor retained an eye for an interesting woman, bestowing special praise and favor on anyone who was attractive and bright, even a waitress or seamstress; and his was a reign during which many clever and accomplished women served at court. These attendants seldom failed to take Genji up on a casual remark, but he seemed curiously detached, whether because he knew all of them too well, or for some other reason; and if one ventured a flirtatious overture, he merely kept answering long enough to save her from embarrassment, with no real interest in the game. Some of them considered him much too sober.

The emperor's staff included an assistant handmaid, no longer young, who was well-born, clever, elegant, and popular, but extremely coquettish and promiscuous. Why should a woman of her age retain such a lively interest in men, Genji wondered. He flirted with her a bit out of curiosity. It was something of a shock to discover that she perceived nothing incongruous in an affair with him, but he persisted until they shared a moment of intimacy, assuring himself that it would be a novel experience. Later, to her indignation, he treated her with studied indifference, unwilling to let it be known that he had dallied with an old woman.

One day, after this same handmaid, Naishi-no-suke, had finished doing the emperor's hair, His Majesty summoned a dresser and went to have his

robes changed, leaving her alone with Genji. She had got herself up to look
positively seductive, her general appearance prettier than usual, her pose
and coiffure alluring, her robes gay and worn with a dashing air. Genji
observed the effect with distaste, finding it unbecoming that she should cling
to youth with such desperation, but he could imagine what she was thinking, and it seemed impossible to ignore her. He gave the end of her train a
suggestive tug.[13] She responded with a languorous sidelong gaze from behind a gorgeous fan, her half-lowered discolored eyelids sagging, and her
exposed tresses lamentably rough. The fan seemed to him scarcely suitable.
He took it from her to look at it, presenting his own in exchange. It was
decorated with a grove of tall golden trees, painted on red paper, its color
bright enough to reflect onto the user's face. The unpainted half contained
a snatch of poetry, scribbled in an outmoded but not inelegant hand: "Now
that they have aged—these grasses under the trees."[14] He could not help
smiling. What could have possessed her? It was not as though other possibilities had been lacking.

"Summer seems to have visited the grove," he said.[15]

He quailed at the prospect of being caught addressing frivolous remarks
to an inappropriate partner, but the lady thought otherwise. She murmured
a poem in an inviting voice:

kimi shi koba	Past their prime they may be—
tanare no koma ni	those grasses under the trees—
karikawan	but if you will come,
sakari sugitaru	I will cut them as fodder
shitakusa naritomo	to feed your favorite horse.

[He replied:]

sasa wakeba	I fear a challenger
hito ya togamemu	were I to tread the bamboo grass
itsu to naku	in the shady grove
koma natsukumeru	where other people's horses
mori no kogakure	seem so very much at home.

"There are too many complications," he said, getting to his feet. She
caught hold of his sleeve and burst into hysterical tears. "Nothing like this
has happened to me before. I've never been so humiliated," she sobbed.

13. They are both seated.

14. Anonymous (KKS 892): ōaraki no / mori no shitakusa / oinureba / koma mo susamezu /
karu hito mo nashi ("Now that they have aged—these grasses under the trees at Ōaraki
Woods—no horses come to eat them, no reapers come to cut them").

15. "On the contrary, you seem to have lots of admirers." Minamoto no Saneakira (SAS 28):
hototogisu / kinaku o kikeba / ōaraki no / mori koso natsu no / yadori narurame ("That we
hear cuckoos come with voices raised in song is surely because Ōaraki Woods has become their
summer home").

"I'll be in touch soon. It's not that I don't care." He freed himself and started to leave. She seized his robe again, crying in a reproachful voice, "Am I a bridge pillar?"[16]

The emperor, his toilet complete, had observed the scene from behind a sliding partition. An ill-assorted pair, he thought in amusement. "My attendants are always fretting about your primness, but here's one opportunity you didn't reject," he said to Genji with a laugh. Naishi-no-suke felt somewhat embarrassed, but she made no very vigorous attempt to assert her innocence, possibly because she was one of those people who enjoy having their names linked with attractive members of the opposite sex, whether mistakenly or not.

Tō-no-chūjō got wind of the affair, which seems to have become a subject of gossip among the emperor's surprised attendants. "I like to explore whatever possibilities there are, but I see that I've overlooked something," he thought. He proceeded to woo and win Naishi-no-suke, his interest aroused by the notion of an intrigue with a woman whose amorous instincts had survived so many years. He was no ordinary man, and Naishi-no-suke thought he would do to take her mind off Genji's unkindness, but it was Genji on whom her heart was set—perhaps a little too fastidiously.

The lady kept her new romance so quiet that Genji caught no inkling of it. She reproached him whenever she saw him. He pitied her because of her age and thought about consoling her, but the prospect held little appeal, and much time elapsed while he procrastinated.

One evening, as he was strolling in the dark near the Unmeiden, enjoying the cool aftermath of a shower, he heard her playing the lute with an expert touch. Her skill at the instrument was unsurpassed—so remarkable that she often joined the gentlemen when they made music for the emperor—and it was moving to realize that he was hearing a performance by a woman disappointed in love. She sang, "Shall I wed a melon farmer?" in an accomplished voice. It made a somewhat unpleasant impression, but he listened with attention, wondering if the voice admired by Bo Juyi at Ezhou had sounded equally beautiful.[17] The lute broke off, as though the musician were too distraught to continue.

16. Probably a reference to a poem cited in an old commentary, or to one like it: tsu no kuni no / nagara no hashi no / hashibashira / furinuru mi koso / kanashikere ("How grievous it is to be as far gone in years as the bridge pillars on the Bridge of Nagara in the province of Settsu!"). Nagara Bridge appears often in classical literature as a symbol of advanced age.

17. He has reference to a woman Bo Juyi overheard singing on a boat anchored near his. Naishi-no-suke's song, the *saibara* "Yamashiro," impresses Genji because it is a complaint against him, only slightly veiled. "Yamashiro" (KDKYS, p. 398): "The melon farmer near Koma in Yamashiro! NA! NAYOYA! RAISHINA YA! SAISHINA YA! The melon farmer, the melon farmer! HARE! The melon farmer says he wants me. What shall I do? NA! NAYOYA! RAISHINA YA! SAISHINA YA! What shall I do? What shall I do? HARE! What shall I do? Shall I marry him before the melons ripen? YA RAISHINA YA! SAISHINA YA! Before the melons ripen? Before the melons ripen?" (The words in small capitals are meaningless chants.)

Genji went closer, singing "Curve-roofed House" in a soft voice, and she chimed in when he reached the line, "Push it open and come in!"[18] It did not seem the sort of thing most women would have done. She recited a poem in plaintive accents:

tachinururu	How hard it seems
hito shimo araji	that rain must drip from the eaves
azumaya ni	of the curve-roofed house,
utate mo kakaru	where there is but little chance
amasosogi ka na	of someone's standing in the wet!

He was unlikely to be the only man to whom her reproaches might apply, he thought. It was unpleasant of her to indulge in such blatant complaints. [His response:]

hitozuma wa	Trouble must ensue
ina wazurawashi	from visiting a woman
azumaya no	claimed by another.
maya no amari mo	I think I would be ill-advised
nareji to zo omou	to get too friendly with you.[19]

Although he wanted to leave, he decided to make himself agreeable rather than hurt her feelings, and they exchanged some lively jokes—a conversation he found interesting enough in its way.

Genji treated Tō-no-chūjō to frequent solemn lectures about his philandering, a habit not appreciated by his friend, who had formed the distinct impression that Genji was involved in a number of clandestine liaisons himself, in spite of his affectation of rectitude. It was Tō-no-chūjō's great ambition to catch him out; and now, to his glee, he discovered him in Naishi-no-suke's room. He decided to give him a small fright—just enough to fluster him—so that he could say, "Let this be a lesson to you!" He waited around to let him have time to relax.

A cool breeze came up, and it began to get late. Concluding that the two were probably asleep, he stole toward the room. The sound of a footstep startled Genji, who had not felt comfortable enough to doze off. Never dreaming that the intruder was Tō-no-chūjō, he thought, "It must be Suri-no-kami; they say he can't forget her." He picked up his cloak and retreated behind a folding screen, intent on avoiding the embarrassment of being caught by an older man in a demeaning situation. "This is too much!" he

18. Like "Yamashiro," "Curve-roofed House" (*azumaya*) was a *saibara* (KDKYS, p. 384): "He: I stand here drenched by raindrops falling from the eaves of your curve-roofed house, of your gabled house. Open the door! She: That door I would fasten had I a latch, had I a bolt. But push it open and come in! Am I someone else's wife?"

19. Genji's poem contains a reference to "Curve-roofed House" in the form of an ornamental preface (*jo*, omitted in the translation): "the eaves of your curve-roofed house, of your gabled house." The juncture to the rest of the poem is through a pun on *amari* ("eaves"; "too").

said. "I'm going! How could you inveigle me into staying, when you must have known he'd be coming?"

Smothering his laughter, Tō-no-chūjō went over to the screen and banged the folds together, making as much noise as he could. Naishi-no-suke was a sophisticated, voluptuous woman, no stranger to disconcerting incidents even at her age. She was not so agitated that she failed to worry about what harm might befall Genji, and she caught hold of the intruder with a trembling hand, bent on restraining him. Still unaware that it was Tō-no-chūjō, Genji wanted to leave but hesitated, thinking what a fool he would look from the rear, with his cap crooked and his robes in disarray.

Maintaining silence to keep Genji from recognizing his voice, Tō-no-chūjō drew his sword and produced an imitation of a man maddened by rage.

"Spare my lover!" Naishi-no-suke begged. She faced him with her hands joined in supplication. It was all he could do to keep from laughing. With her seductive air and youthful toilette, she presented a not unattractive outward appearance, but she was a woman of fifty-seven or fifty-eight; and now, unabashedly disheveled and distraught, she cut a most unbecoming figure as she knelt in terror between the two handsome twenty-year-olds.

Tō-no-chūjō's efforts to disguise himself with a ferocious appearance served only to expose his identity to Genji, who recognized sheepishly that it was all a prank. His friend had known he was inside. He promptly grasped Tō-no-chūjō's sword arm and gave it a severe pinch. Tō-no-chūjō regretted that the game was up, but he could no longer restrain his mirth.

"I really do question your sanity. You don't seem to understand how to play a joke. Well, I'll put on my cloak," Genji said. Tō-no-chūjō seized it and refused to let go. "All right, we'll both do without." Genji pulled his belt loose and tried to strip off his cloak. Tō-no-chūjō resisted, and they struggled until a seam on Genji's robe burst and unraveled. [Tō-no-chūjō recited a poem:]

tsutsumumeru	Through the opened seam
na ya moriiden	of an inner robe damaged
hikikawashi	in a tug of war,
kaku hokoroburu	word will doubtless leak out
naka no koromo ni	of the love you sought to hide.

"The truth will be sadly visible if you don't wear anything over it."
[Genji:]

kakure naki	It was ill-advised
mono to shirushiru	to come on such an errand
natsugoromo	while well aware
kitaru o usuki	that your own romances
kokoro to zo miru	can easily be brought to light.

With amity restored after this passage, they both left the palace, looking distinctly untidy.

Genji went to bed, smarting over Tō-no-chūjō's discovery. On the following morning, his trousers, belt, and other discarded articles arrived from Naishi-no-suke, who had been dumbfounded by the whole affair. [Her poem:]

uramite mo	It would do no good
iu kai zo naki	were I to utter complaints.
tachikasane	The waves in turn
hikite kaerishi	approached, the waves in concert
nami no nagori ni	receded—and in their wake . . .

"The bed must have been visible." [20]

She was shameless! Genji was disgusted, but the memory of her consternation evoked a characteristic impulse of sympathy. This was his only reply:

aradachishi	I am not angry
nami ni kokoro wa	with the wave that approached
sawaganedo	so violently,
yoseken iso o	but how could I fail to resent
ikaga uraminu	the beach that invited it?

The belt belonged to Tō-no-chūjō. Genji saw that the color was too dark to be his, and also that he was missing a cuff.[21] He took the experience to heart. It had been a discreditable series of events. And no doubt a confirmed roué was always landing himself in such ridiculous situations.

To his annoyance, Tō-no-chūjō sent him his cuff, neatly wrapped, from his quarters in the palace, together with a suggestion that he lose no time in reattaching it. How could he have got hold of it? Fortunately, Genji had the belt. He dispatched it, wrapped in paper of the same color, together with a poem:

naka taeba	Worried lest you two
kagoto ya ou to	reach a parting of the ways
ayausa ni	and I bear the blame,
hanada no obi wa	I have not even ventured
torite dani mizu	to look at this blue belt.

The reply:

20. Naishi-no-suke's poem includes words that can mean "shore," "sea," and "seashell." She continues the water imagery with a reference to an anonymous love poem (scss 937): wakarete no / nochi zo kanashiki / namidagawa / soko mo arawa ni / narinu to omoeba ("After our parting, I was overwhelmed by grief. I can only think the bed of my river of tears must have become visible").

21. From his cloak. By convention, belt and cloak were the same color, lighter shades indicating higher status. The "cuff" was actually an ornamental strip of cloth just above the sleeve opening.

kimi ni kaku	I must complain
hikitorarenuru	of a shattered romance,
obi nareba	a casualty
kakute taenuru	of the situation
naka to kakotan	in which I lost the belt to you.

"You won't be able to escape my wrath."

That afternoon, both of them were in the courtiers' hall. Genji treated his friend with formal courtesy, the picture of composure. Tō-no-chūjō was amused, but it was a day on which there was much official reporting to the throne and handing down of edicts, and he was required to comport himself in a solemn, dignified manner. The two could not help smiling when they looked at each other.

Tō-no-chūjō went over to Genji when they happened to be alone. "I hope you've learned a lesson about secret affairs," he said, fixing him with a stern sidelong glance.

"Not at all," Genji said. "I just feel sorry for the fellow who had to wait around and go home with nothing to show for it. To tell the truth, though, I'm worried about gossip." They ended by agreeing that neither would speak of it.

In subsequent verbal jousts, Tō-no-chūjō never missed an opportunity to exploit the incident, and Genji must have come to realize, with increasing clarity, what a mistake it had been to get involved with such a nuisance of a woman. To his annoyance, Naishi-no-suke still insisted on favoring him with arch reproaches. Tō-no-chūjō had decided to say nothing to his sister; it was a threat he would hold in reserve.

The emperor made his special affection so clear that everyone felt obliged to defer to Genji, even princes born of high-ranking consorts, but Tō-no-chūjō challenged him on the most trivial points, determined not to be over-awed. He was the only full brother of Genji's wife, and in his view, the sole difference between him and Genji was that Genji's father happened to be an emperor. He was a princess's son, reared with incomparable care by a father who was the sovereign's favorite minister, and he could not see that there was anything inferior about his status. Nor was he deficient in personal attributes: everything was ideal, nothing was lacking. The rivalry between the two in matters of the heart took some odd turns, but it would be distasteful to dwell on the subject.

The Fujitsubo lady was named empress in the seventh month, and Genji became a consultant. The emperor was getting ready to retire. He intended to make his baby son the next crown prince, but fretted because there would be nobody to act as regent after the boy ascended the throne. The maternal relatives all belonged to the imperial clan, and members of the Genji were ineligible for the regency.[22] He had therefore decided that he would at least

22. It was always a Fujiwara who served as regent.

give the mother a solid base from which to support the child.[23] The Kokiden lady was upset, of course, but he told her not to worry. "Your son will be emperor very soon, and then you're sure to be named grand empress," he said.

As usual, the gossips made censorious remarks. "No wonder she's bitter. One would have thought it would be hard to set aside a woman who is not only the crown prince's mother but also a consort of more than twenty years' standing," they said.

Genji served as a member of the entourage on the night the Fujitsubo lady made her formal entry into the palace. There was, perhaps, nothing novel about being in the presence of an empress, but this one was an empress's daughter, as radiant as a jewel, and the sovereign's dearly beloved consort; and the gentlemen in the retinue treated her with very special respect. The unhappy Genji found his thoughts straying inside the palanquin. Tormented by the feeling that she was now hopelessly inaccessible, he was hard put to maintain his composure, and he murmured a poem with a full heart:

> tsuki mo senu   I stray in the dark
> kokoro no yami ni   of a spirit tormented
>   kururu ka na   by undying love
> kumoi ni hito o   when I see my dearest one
> miru ni tsukete mo   as remote as the clouds.

The empress was greatly distressed by the baby's resemblance to Genji, which became more striking as he grew older, but nobody seemed to wonder at it. "To be as handsome as Genji, a person would have to look exactly like him; any difference would be a mark of inferiority. They're like the sun and the moon—two similar orbs shining in the sky," people said.

23. By making her empress.

Aoi

[From the fourth month of Genji's twenty-second year to the first month of his twenty-third year. Fujitsubo lady: 27–28; Genji's wife, Aoi: 26; Murasaki: 14–15; Rokujō lady: 29–30.

The emperor, Genji's father, has retired, and the new emperor's mother and his maternal grandfather, the minister of the right, have gained power at the expense of Genji's father-in-law, the minister of the left.]

Genji felt discouraged and unhappy after the changes at court. His more exalted status also made it hard to indulge in frivolous secret excursions, and his altered behavior caused much uncertainty and grief in various quarters.[1] As though in karmic retribution, he never ceased to pine for the one who treated him so coldly. That lady now spent more time than ever with his father, and was in fact always at his side, exactly like an ordinary housewife. It was a state of affairs that doubtless annoyed the new emperor's mother, the grand empress, for she chose to remain entirely in the imperial palace, leaving the Fujitsubo lady untroubled by the presence of a rival.

Whenever the occasion arose, the retired emperor held musical entertainments and other events whose magnificence was the talk of society, and his general situation was actually better than before. The only flaw in his happiness was that he missed the crown prince dreadfully. Worried because there was nobody to look after the boy, he assigned full responsibility to Genji, who felt both embarrassed and pleased.

Meanwhile, the Rokujō lady's daughter by the late crown prince had been named Ise Virgin, and the mother, dubious about Genji's reliability, had been thinking of using the girl's youth as an excuse for going to the province with her.[2] The retired emperor spoke to Genji when he heard about her misgivings. "The crown prince held her in the very highest esteem and loved her dearly. It's sad to hear people say that you're toying

---

1. Already a consultant, Genji had received the additional title of major captain as a parting gift from his father. As such, he is now expected to travel with an escort of eight armed guards.

2. The daughter is known as Akikonomu, from an episode later in the book.

with her, as though she were just another woman. Furthermore, I think of
the Virgin exactly as I do of my own daughters. You would do well to
avoid treating the lady with discourtesy, both for the prince's sake and for
mine. This kind of self-indulgent philandering exposes you to criticism,
you know." Genji maintained a respectful silence, aware that his displeasure was justified.

"Never embarrass a woman," the emperor continued. "Whoever she
may be, keep things friendly so she won't begin to hate you."

Genji wondered what he would do if his father learned of that other
matter, that truly unpardonable affair. He took his leave, horrified by the
very idea.

The retired emperor's reprimand had made it clear that the affair with
the Rokujō lady could lead to unfortunate results for both parties. Genji
would look like a philanderer; she would be an object of pity. More than
before, Genji realized that she was someone he must view with concern,
someone he could not simply drop. But he still avoided a public, formal
commitment. Embarrassed by the disparity in age, she had seemed to keep
him at arm's length, and he had responded by drawing back as though intimidated. Now everyone knew about the relationship, even his father—
and yet, to her great distress, his regard seemed lukewarm at best.

Princess Asagao had heard the rumors.[3] Determined not to share the Rokujō lady's misfortune, she almost never returned even a trifling answer to
any of Genji's messages. At the same time, she managed to avoid irritating
or embarrassing him, an evidence of breeding in which he found confirmation of his opinion that she differed from ordinary women.

Although his wife was unhappy about the roving eye that led him into
such adventures, she made no display of anger, possibly because she considered it useless to protest against behavior in which he indulged openly,
as a matter of course. She was with child, pitifully uncomfortable and in
miserable spirits. Genji was delighted and sympathetic. Her parents and
the others around her rejoiced, but they also saw to it that she observed
various precautions, mindful of the possibility that things might go wrong.
Genji became preoccupied with such matters, and there must have been
many times when he failed to appear elsewhere, even though he intended
no neglect.

The Kamo Virgin retired around that same time, and the position went
to the Third Princess, the retired emperor's daughter by the Kokiden lady.
The girl's withdrawal from lay life saddened her imperial parents, who
were especially devoted to her, but there was no other eligible princess.

3. The princess was Genji's cousin, a daughter of one of his father's brothers. Toward the
end of "The Broom Tree," in a section not translated, there is brief mention of her as the
recipient of a poem sent by Genji in what was apparently a continuing, if sporadic, courtship;
and she figures later as one of the few women who resist him to the end. Her sobriquet, Asagao,
derives from the flower of that name (see "Yūgao," n. 8).

Much was done to increase the impressiveness of the usual religious cere-monies. There were also to be numerous events in addition to the ones regularly sponsored by the court for the Kamo Festival, and some stunning spectacles were promised, thanks to the new Virgin's special importance.

Regulations limited the number of senior nobles who could accompany the Virgin on the day of her purification, but each of the men chosen was outstanding in reputation and bearing, and great attention was paid to every aspect of their appearance—the colors of their robes, the designs on their trousers, and even their horses and saddles. Genji joined them by special imperial decree.

Sightseeing carriages, decked for the occasion, filled every available space along Ichijō Avenue, creating a positively frightening degree of congestion. The scattered viewing stands had been embellished with all the splendor human ingenuity could conceive, and they were a marvelous sight, even to the displays of feminine sleeves from behind the blinds.

Genji's wife seldom went to witness such events, and the thought was especially far from her mind now that she was pregnant. But her young ladies-in-waiting protested. "It won't be any fun if we just sneak a look at the procession by ourselves," they told her. "They say everyone is dying to see His Lordship, even people who have no connection with him, like peas-ants from the hills. Men are bringing their families from distant provinces! It's too much for Your Ladyship not to go." Her mother, Princess Ōmiya, heard them. "It looks as though you feel all right today, and your attendants seem upset about missing the parade," she said. She ordered carriages on the spur of the moment, and thus it was decided that the lady would join the spectators.

Making an unpretentious departure toward noon, the party advanced in a sedate procession. They searched without success for a vacant spot on the avenue, which was filled to capacity with parked carriages. Since many of the carriages seemed to belong to women of high birth, the head groom chose a place where there were no groups of servants and told his men to clear away everything in that area. Among the threatened earlier arrivals, there were two wickerwork vehicles, not quite new, with elegant inner cur-tains. The occupants were seated far back, with the obvious aim of appear-ing inconspicuous, and nothing was to be seen of them except indistinct glimpses of beautifully colored sleeve openings, formal trains, and young girls' trailing robes. Their men refused to let anyone touch the carriages. "These aren't the kind of carriages you can chase off like this!" they insisted. Some of the men on both sides were young and drunk, and a fierce brawl broke out. The lady's way-clearers, who were older, tried in vain to restrain her grooms.

In the hope of finding a little surcease from her unhappiness, the Rokujō lady had decided to pay a quiet visit to the scene of the procession. Her people tried to guard her privacy, but the other side soon realized that the two carriages were hers. "It's not for the likes of you to warn us off! You seem to think you can hide behind your connection with Lord Genji," they said.

Some of Genji's own men had accompanied his wife's carriages. Their sympathies were with the Rokujō lady, but they stood aside, afraid of making matters worse by trying to intervene.

In the end, the party from the mansion aligned their carriages in a row and pushed the Rokujō lady's carriages behind the attendants, back to a place where it was almost impossible to see anything. The lady was angered by their insolence, of course, but it was the public exposure of her attempted disguise that truly infuriated her. Both of her carriage stands had been broken, and the grooms had had to prop the yokeboards onto the hubs of strangers' wheels. Unspeakably embarrassed, she regretted in vain the impulse that had led her to come. She would have liked to go straight home without waiting for the procession, but there was no room for her carriages to make their way out. Meanwhile, voices in the crowd proclaimed the arrival of the vanguard, and she felt a sudden urge to await the appearance of the man whose indifference had caused her so many heartaches. It was very weak of her. He passed with no acknowledgment of her presence—possibly because the Hinokuma River was nowhere near—and she felt worse than if she had not come.[4]

As I have mentioned, the spectators' carriages were turned out with far more care than usual. They were filled to overflowing with ladies who had been determined not to miss the show, and there were some toward which Genji directed smiling sidelong glances, without quite appearing to do so, when he glimpsed the occupants through gaps in their curtains. His expression was grave as he passed his wife's unmistakable carriage, and his attendants went by with every manifestation of respect. It was a crushing, bitter defeat for the Rokujō lady. Her tears overflowed as she murmured a poem:

kage o nomi   It brings home to me
mitarashigawa no   the misery of my plight
tsurenaki ni   as never before—
mi no uki hodo zo   the coldness of one but glimpsed
itodo shiraruru   by the purifying stream.

It was humiliating to be seen in tears, but she would not willingly have missed the startling beauty of Genji's mien and face, which showed to particular advantage on public occasions like this. The members of the Virgin's entourage appeared to have taken immense pains with their costumes and those of their attendants, and the senior nobles looked especially grand, but Genji's radiance outshone them all. Except for the most magnificent impe-

---

4. Anonymous (KKS 1080): sahinokuma / hinokumagawa ni / koma tomete / shibashi mizu kae / kage o dani mimu ("Rein in your young horse at Hinokuma River, at Hinokuma, and let him drink there awhile, that I may at least see your back").

rial progresses and similar events, chamberlain-lieutenants did not usually serve as special escorts for major captains, but Genji was attended on this occasion by a member of the bodyguards who held that title. His other escorts, handsome men in dazzling costumes, provided further evidence of people's readiness to put themselves at his disposal—an attitude so universal that it seemed the very grasses and trees must share it. The spectators included women of quite good birth, wearing sedge hats and veils, as well as others who had renounced the world—nuns and the like—all losing their footing and tottering in the crush. People would ordinarily have frowned on such excessive displays of determination, but they seemed only natural today. Toothless lower-class dames with their hair tucked into their robes brought joined palms to their foreheads in comic worship as Genji passed. Even the male commoners smiled all over their faces, without caring how they looked. It was also interesting to see how the daughters of insignificant provincial governors—women Genji could scarcely have been expected to notice—sat self-consciously in their extravagantly decorated carriages, their hearts in their mouths. And there were many among the spectators, ladies he had favored with discreet visits, who mourned in private the lack of consequence that had never seemed so apparent before.

Watching from his viewing stand, Prince Shikibukyō told himself with some concern that his nephew was turning into a man of dazzling beauty; there seemed danger of a spirit's taking notice.[5] Asagao felt a surge of affection. Genji's courtship over the years had been remarkable for its tenacity, she thought—enough to evoke a response even if he had been someone quite ordinary. How could she possibly regard this paragon with indifference? But she had no intention of getting on closer terms with him. Her younger ladies-in-waiting sang his praises at tiresome length.

Genji's wife decided not to go out on the day of the festival.

Meanwhile, someone told Genji all about the struggle for carriage space, a recital that made him feel pity for the Rokujō lady and annoyance with his wife. It was unfortunate, he reflected, that his wife happened to be a dignified woman who was a little deficient in human kindness, a little inclined to snobbish brusqueness. She herself had probably not sought a confrontation, but she refused to recognize that she and the Rokujō lady might owe each other a degree of consideration, connected as they were; and it was doubtless something in her attitude that had encouraged her servants' wrongheaded behavior. He could imagine the emotions of the Rokujō lady, a personage whose sensitivity and tact often put him to shame. He went to see her, his heart swelling with sympathy, but the Virgin was still at home, and her mother used the demands of ritual purity as an excuse for not receiving him. Although he admitted that her behavior was natural, he could not help saying to himself, "Why does it have to be this way? I wish they wouldn't treat each other as enemies."

5. The prince is Asagao's father.

On the day of the Kamo Festival, Genji was staying apart from his wife at the Nijō Mansion, and it was from there that he proposed to set out to watch the parade. He went to the west wing and told Koremitsu to have some carriages brought up. "Are you ladies-in-waiting ready?" he teased Murasaki's girl attendants. Their young mistress looked very sweet in her dainty holiday finery. Gazing at her with a smile, he said, "Now then, you and I are going to watch together." He stroked her hair, which was even more beautiful than usual. "It looks as though it hasn't been trimmed for a while. I know this is an auspicious day," he said. He summoned a calendar doctor to see if the hour was suitable. Meanwhile, he inspected the smart little girls, announcing that the "ladies-in-waiting" were to leave first. Their pretty hair had been trimmed carefully at the ends, and the abundant tresses stood out in sharp relief against their float-patterned trousers.

"I'll trim your hair myself," he said to Murasaki. The task proved troublesome. "It's much too thick. What will it be like when it gets longer?" he said. "Even ladies with very long hair seem to have rather short strands near their cheeks. It wouldn't be interesting not to have any stray locks at all." He stopped cutting and pronounced an auspicious phrase, "A thousand *hiro*."[6] The nurse Shōnagon watched with awe and gratitude.

Genji recited a poem:

hakari naki	I alone shall guard
chihiro no soko no	the future growth of this hair
mirubusa no	abundant as seaweed
oiyuku sue wa	in the thousand-*hiro* depths
ware nomi zo min	of the unfathomable sea.

With engaging childishness, Murasaki chose to write out her reply, which was a skillful one:

chihiro tomo	Who knows if the sea
ika de ka shiran	be a thousand *hiro* deep?
sadame naku	For in ceaseless change,
michihiru shio no	the restless tide rolls in,
nodokekaranu ni	only to withdraw again.

Genji was delighted.

On this day, too, the entire roadside was choked with carriages. Genji looked without success for a vacant spot near the pavilion at the riding grounds used by the imperial bodyguards. "It's crowded around here; the place seems to be full of senior nobles' carriages," he said. As he hesitated, someone beckoned with a fan to one of his attendants from an elegant woman's carriage, which was filled to overflowing with ladies-in-waiting. "Won't your master stop here? We'll make room for him," she said. She

6. "May your hair grow ever longer." Long hair was a main criterion of feminine beauty. A *hiro* was the distance between the index fingers of two outstretched arms.

would seem to be something of a flirt, Genji thought, but it was a choice location, and he ordered his men to draw up alongside her carriage.

"I wondered how you managed to get such an excellent place; I couldn't help coveting it," he said.

She replied with a message on a strip of paper, torn from the edge of a stylish fan:

hakanashi ya	How foolish of me!
hito no kazaseru	Unaware of that other
au hi yue	decked out in heartvine,
kami no yurushi no	I looked forward to this day
kyō o machikeru	on which the gods sanction meetings.[7]

"I see no way of penetrating the rope barrier."[8]

To his surprise, Genji recognized the hand of the elderly Naishi-no-suke. She was absurd, he thought in disgust—putting on youthful airs instead of acting her age. His reply was curt:

kazashikeru	I must think you fickle
kokoro zo ada ni	when I see you thus bedecked.
omōyuru	This is a day, it seems,
yasoujibito ni	for meeting anyone
nabete au hi o	who happens to come along.

Embarrassed, she countered:

kuyashiku mo	Far better had I
kazashikeru ka na	dispensed with these decorations.
na nomi shite	Faithless to their name,
hitodanome naru	they are but leaves
kusaba bakari o	inspiring unmerited trust.

Jealous pangs troubled many hearts as Genji sat without raising the blinds, an unidentified feminine companion at his side. There was much gossip and speculation. "He was formality itself at the purification, but he's relaxing today. I wonder who's in the carriage with him. You can bet she isn't bad looking," people said.

Genji was dissatisfied with the exchange about the carriage decorations, which did not suit his notion of a battle of poetic wits, but anyone less brazen than Naishi-no-suke would have felt constrained by his companion's presence and shy about sending him any response at all.

7. The poet has seen that Genji is sharing his carriage with a feminine companion. Her composition puns on words that were homophonous at the time: *au hi*, "day of meeting," and *aoi*, the name of a vine with heart-shaped leaves (*Asarum caulescens* Maxim), for which Edward Seidensticker has coined the English name "heartvine." This poem and Genji's composition below are the source of the chapter's title, and also of the name by which Genji's wife is identified.

8. "Barred by another, I see no way of meeting you." The metaphor is chosen to suit the occasion, which is a Shinto festival. Rope barriers cordoned off sacred areas at shrines.

More than ever before, the Rokujō lady suffered from conflicting emotions. She had accepted Genji's indifference as fact—yet she knew she would feel miserable, and perhaps incur ridicule as well, if she simply put an end to the relationship by going off to Ise. But when she thought that it might be best to stay in the city after all, she feared that her demeaning situation might make everyone look down on her. Perhaps it was the constant agonizing—the indecision that made her wonder if her mind might be "a float like the ones the fishers cast"—that caused her to feel physically ill and mentally as unstable as the floats in the poem.[9]

Instead of forbidding her to go, or interfering with her plans, Genji picked quarrels with her, not really caring whether she stayed or went. "It's natural that you should want to break with an ordinary fellow like me," he said, "but it would show that our vows meant something if you stayed anyway, worthless as I am." Such speeches made it harder for her to reach a decision. And when she had gone to watch the purification procession, hoping to forget her problems for a while, it was only to encounter the violent affront that made the whole world seem hateful.

Meanwhile, everyone at the minister's mansion was lamenting the great suffering of the lady Aoi, which showed signs of being caused by a malignant spirit. It was not a time for private adventures, and Genji seldom went out, even to visit his own Nijō Mansion. He had not always got along with Aoi, but he regarded her with very special respect, and her illness caused him deep concern, especially since she was with child. He arranged for numerous esoteric rites and prayers to be performed in his rooms. Among the many spirits who came forward to identify themselves (some of them belonging to living people), there was one that clung with great obstinacy, frustrating every effort to transfer it to a medium. It did not inflict horrendous pain, but it never left for an instant. There seemed small likelihood that the spirit of an ordinary person would be so persistent—so impervious to the exhortations of the greatest wonder-working monks—and people at the mansion began to speculate about Genji's affairs of the heart. "The ladies at Rokujō and Nijō seem to be the only ones he really cares about. Both of them probably hate Her Ladyship," they whispered. They consulted diviners, but the findings were inconclusive. None of the spirits claimed to hold Aoi in any special enmity. They were a heterogeneous, insignificant lot—some of them apparently deceased nurses, others the wraiths of men with hereditary grudges against the family, taking advantage of her weakness. Aoi sobbed and wept incessantly, and sometimes vomited and retched as though in unbearable pain. Watching with fear and pity, her parents and Genji asked themselves what was to become of her. Genji's father, the retired emperor, sent a steady stream of inquiries, and went so far as to concern himself with

9. Anonymous (KKS 509): ise no umi ni / tsuri suru ama no / uke nare ya / kokoro hitotsu o / sadamekanetsuru ("However I try, I cannot steady my heart. Might it be a float, like the ones the fishers cast into the sea at Ise?").

prayers on her behalf, a gracious act that made the possibility of her loss even more devastating.

The Rokujō lady found it hard to maintain her composure as she listened to reports of all these expressions of concern. In the past, there had been no very strong spirit of rivalry between Aoi and herself, but the trivial dispute over carriage space had stirred emotions of which the people at the mansion had no conception. Beset by tumultuous thoughts, she fell into a lingering illness, which made it necessary to move to a place where she could have esoteric rites performed. Genji heard of her condition and paid her a somewhat reluctant visit. His neglect had not been at all intentional, he explained in his most disarming manner; he begged her to understand about his wife's illness.

"I myself don't feel any great alarm, but her parents are pitiful, and I feel I should stay with her until she gets better. It would make me very happy if you could manage not to let it bother you," he coaxed. That she should look uncharacteristically pathetic was only natural; his heart went out to her.

He departed toward dawn, at the end of a visit that had turned out to be stiff and uneasy. His appearance as he left shook her resolve to break with him. But she told herself that he would probably settle down with Aoi, a lady he held in the highest esteem, and to whom he must henceforth be attached even more closely than before. She would live in constant misery if she continued to hang on his visits. Last night's meeting, she felt, had merely revived her old forlorn longing.

There was a letter toward evening, nothing more. "The lady here had seemed better, but she has taken a sudden disconcerting turn for the worse. I fear I ought not to leave her," he wrote. Another of his excuses, she thought, but she replied with a poem and a comment:

sode nururu	Wretched is the one
koiji to katsu wa	who sets foot on the path of love,
shirinagara	hapless as the peasant
oritatsu tago no	who goes into the paddy,
mizukara zo uki	knowing the mud must drench his sleeve.

"It would be only natural to mention the water of the mountain spring."[10]

As Genji read, he told himself that her handwriting was in a class by itself. His life seemed peculiarly difficult. There was nobody among his ladies whose disposition and appearance were such that he could discard her, nor was there anyone he could fix upon to the exclusion of all the others. It was well after nightfall by then, but he sent an answer. "What can I think when

10. Anonymous (KKRJ 987): kuyashiku zo / kumisometekeru / asakereba / sode nomi nururu / yama no i no mizu ("I regret my attempt to scoop a drink of water from the mountain spring: the pool has proved shallow, and I have merely drenched my sleeves"). Puns yield a second meaning: "Would that I had not got involved with this man, whose shallow feelings make me weep until my sleeves are wet."

you talk about getting your sleeves wet? It sounds as though there is little depth to your affection." [His poem:]

asami ni ya	You must walk, it seems,
hito wa oritatsu	where the water is shallow.
wa ga kata wa	I find the path of love
mi mo sobotsu made	a mire in whose muddy depths
fukaki koiji o	my whole body is drenched.

At the minister's mansion, Aoi was in dreadful pain from the harassment of a malignant spirit. The Rokujō lady heard that people were saying it might be either hers or her late father's, and she pondered the matter. Concerned only with her own unhappiness, she felt no desire to bring misfortune on anyone else, but spirits were reported to wander when their owners brooded, and she recognized the possibility that hers had gone astray. For years she had suffered from all kinds of painful thoughts without breaking down like this, but then there had been that trifling incident on the day of the purification—that day when Aoi had seemed to treat her with contemptuous indifference—and now she was unable to control her agitation. Possibly for that reason, she had been having a recurrent dream, even during short naps, in which she went to a handsome apartment that seemed to belong to Aoi, heaped abuse on the occupant, and fell to beating her, overcome by a fierce, wild recklessness alien to her waking self. There were times when she felt that she was not herself, and she wondered in revulsion if her spirit had indeed strayed from her body.[11] People never gave each other the benefit of the doubt, not even in minor matters; this illness of Aoi's would be a golden opportunity for the gossips, and no doubt their tongues would soon begin to wag about her. "It's common enough for a person to hold fast to a worldly grudge after she dies, but that in itself seems to me a grave sin—a gruesome way to act. What a miserable karma, to be accused of that loathsome kind of behavior while I'm still alive! No matter what it costs, I've got to stop thinking about a man who cares so little for me," she told herself, changing her mind again. But the thought itself was a thought of Genji.

Her daughter, the Ise Virgin, was supposed to have moved to the imperial palace in the year just past, but obstacles had forced a postponement until this autumn. Since the girl was to go straight on to the Shrine in the Fields in the ninth month, preparations for the second purification had to follow hard on the heels of those for the first. But the mother was beset by an odd lassitude, and she spent most of her time sick in bed. The Virgin's perturbed attendants offered prayers of many descriptions for the lady. There was nothing dramatically wrong; she merely went on feeling vaguely ill, day

11. Ōshikōchi no Mitsune (KKS 977): mi o sutete / yuki ya shinikemu / omou yori / hoka naru mono wa / kokoro narikeri ("Perhaps it went off, abandoning my body. The heart, I perceive, is far from being a thing that does just what one wishes").

after day. Genji made regular inquiries about her health, but the dreadful sufferings of a more important lady always seemed uppermost in his mind.

Aoi suddenly went into labor before the baby was due, catching everyone off guard. The family ordered even more numerous and more potent prayers than before, but the same obstinate spirit resisted every effort to transfer it to a medium. The famous wonder-working monks were astonished and baffled. Their efforts did press the spirit hard, and it wept as though in excruciating pain. "Please relax your zeal. There's something I need to tell Lord Genji," it pleaded.

"Just as we thought! It must have something on its mind," the attendants said. They ushered Genji in to the curtain-stand near the bed. The end seemed near, and the minister and his wife moved back, thinking that their daughter wanted to address a last word to her husband. Genji raised the curtains to look inside. It was enough to wring anyone's heart, let alone a husband's, to see her lying there with her beautiful face and high belly; and he naturally felt the greatest sorrow and pity. Her long, luxuriant tresses lay bound at her side, their color a vivid contrast to the white robe. It seemed to him that a new sweetness and charm had made her more beautiful than usual. He took her hand. "This is so terrible! You're breaking my heart." He choked and fell silent. Her eyes, which had always made him feel uncomfortable and defensive, now looked up at him with a languid, steadfast gaze. Presently, they brimmed with tears. How could he have watched without deep emotion?

The fast-falling tears seemed to him a sign that she pitied her parents and mourned the final parting with himself. In the hope of comforting her, he said, "You mustn't feel so gloomy. You're sick, but you're going to get well. Even if you did die, you and I would meet again; husbands and wives always do. And the ties between parents and children are too strong to break between incarnations, so you must believe that a time will come when you will be reunited with the minister and the princess."

"No, no, this isn't what you think. I just wanted to tell the monks to stop awhile, to give me a little respite from my terrible suffering. I never meant to come here like this, but I know now that what people say is true; the spirit of someone who grieves does wander," she said in a gentle voice. She murmured a poem, looking and sounding quite unlike his wife—quite like a different person:

nagekiwabi	Behind the hem of the robe,
sora ni midaruru	where it overlaps in front,
wa ga tama o	hold fast the spirit
musubitodome yo	that roams in a daze, driven forth
shitagai no tsuma	by grief beyond endurance.

After a scant moment of stunned reflection, it came to him that the speaker must be the Rokujō lady. He had dismissed the rumors about her as mere ill-natured gossip—but now, he said to himself with a shudder, their truthfulness had been demonstrated before his very eyes. It was revolting. "You talk like this, and yet I don't know who you are," he said. "Please let me be clear about it." She did as he asked. Shall I say that he was astonished, incredulous, dismayed? No such words could do justice to his emotions. He was embarrassed even by the presence of the ladies-in-waiting outside the curtains.

The voice from the bed fell silent, as though the pain were in remission. The mother brought hot water. Aoi sat up, supported by an attendant, and the baby arrived almost at once. Everyone was overjoyed by the safe delivery, but the disappointed spirits stormed and blustered in the mediums, giving cause for worry about the afterbirth. The parents and Genji swore innumerable vows, and then—perhaps for that reason—everything went along without a hitch. The Tendai abbot and the other august monks hurried off with smug faces, wiping away sweat.

The consuming anxiety felt of late in so many quarters was now relieved; the worst seemed over. Although the family began additional esoteric rites, the whole household relaxed, absorbed for the moment in the pleasant task of caring for a new baby.

On each night of the birth celebrations, everyone exclaimed over the rarity and impressiveness of the gifts presented by the retired emperor and by all the princes and senior nobles.[12] The baby was a boy, which made the ceremonies especially joyous and splendid.[13]

The news upset the Rokujō lady. "They said she was in critical condition, but she's given him a child after all," she thought. She continued to feel that she was not herself, and a strange smell of poppy seed clung to her garments, persisting even after she washed her hair and changed her clothes.[14] As loathsome as it was to fear that her own spirit was at fault, it would have been worse to discuss the possibility with others—to set them to gossiping and shuddering. She could only brood alone, in ever-increasing anguish.

Now that Genji was less anxious about Aoi, his thoughts kept returning with distaste to the spirit's disclosures on that amazing occasion. He regretted the pain his long neglect must be causing the Rokujō lady, but it would also be sad for her if—as would probably happen—he found it impossible to resume their intimacy without feelings of revulsion. After much pondering, he merely sent her a letter.

12. Heian families held formal celebratory banquets, with poetry and music, on the 3rd, 5th, 7th, and 9th nights after a birth. Prior to each event, relatives and friends sent presents of white clothing for the mother and child, special foods, articles of furniture, etc. Each banquet had a different sponsor (usually a maternal relative), but all took place at the mother's residence.

13. Genji's son by Aoi is known as Yūgiri ("Evening Mist") through association with a poem composed later in the story (not translated).

14. Poppy seeds were burned during exorcism rituals.

Everyone felt the need for caution during the fragile convalescence of the lady who had been so desperately ill, and Genji naturally refrained from going out on private errands. She was not well enough for normal conjugal relations.

From the moment of the birth on, Genji made a great fuss over the baby, whose beauty verged on the inauspicious. The delighted minister of the left felt that all his prayers had been answered. He worried because Aoi had yet to make a complete recovery, but took comfort in the thought that she was merely suffering from the aftereffects of an uncommonly severe illness.

The new baby bore a striking resemblance to the crown prince, especially in the sweet expression of his eyes; and seeing him made Genji miss his other son so much that he decided to visit the palace. "I feel nervous about having stayed away all this time; I think I'd better venture out today," he told Aoi. In a reproachful voice, he added, "Since I'll be gone for some time, I'd like to sit a little closer while we talk. I don't understand why you seem determined to keep me at arm's length."

His complaint seemed natural to the women in attendance. It was not as though this were a relationship in which their mistress needed to play the coquette. She was very thin, to be sure, but that was no reason for keeping him outside the curtains. They arranged a seat near the bed, and he came inside to chat. Her replies were intermittent and weak. Even so, the conversation took on a dreamlike quality as he recalled how she had looked when he had given her up for dead. He talked of the moment when she had seemed to be breathing her last—and, in doing so, remembered how she had suddenly rallied and burst into fluent speech. A feeling of revulsion overcame him. "Well, I have lots more to say, but you still seem quite tired," he said. He told her to drink her medicine and otherwise made himself useful, causing the ladies-in-waiting to marvel at his expertise. Weak and haggard, his beautiful wife looked very appealing and pathetic as she lay there, scarcely conscious. The hair spreading over her pillow was a rare vision, every strand in place. Somewhat to his surprise, he could not take his eyes off her. What was it that he had found lacking during all those years?

"I'm going to visit Father and so forth; then I'll be right back," he said. "It would make me awfully happy if I could keep on seeing you in this same easy manner. I've forced myself to stay away because your mother is always around; I've been afraid she might consider it rude for me to come in while she was here. Please recover your strength—just a little at a time—and go back to your own apartments. The princess does tend to treat you like a child; I think that may be one reason why your convalescence has been slow." He set out, an elegant sight in his court robes, and she watched from the bed, her eyes lingering on his departing figure as they had never done in the past.

The minister also left, it being the date for decisions about the fall appointments list; and the sons of the house followed in turn, each with a case for promotion to present, and each determined not to leave his father's side.

After silence had descended on the all but deserted mansion, Aoi felt a sudden familiar nausea and experienced agonizing pain. She ceased to breathe before there was time to get word to the imperial palace.

Everyone rushed out of the palace in a panic. (It would seem that the appointments ceremonies had to be canceled.)

The uproar had started around midnight, too late to call in the Tendai abbot and other prominent clerics. Even though the illness had lingered, the people at the mansion had stopped worrying, convinced that the worst was over, and now they were numb with shock. Messengers thronged in, bearing expressions of sympathy from many quarters, but the distraught household was in no condition to cope with them. It was frightening to witness the anguish of those who had been closest to the lady.

Mindful of how malignant spirits had more than once taken control of her body, the parents and Genji watched over her for two or three days, during which time her pillow and bedclothes remained untouched, but signs of change gradually appeared, and they resigned themselves to their loss. It was a heartrending moment for all of them.

With another matter to worry about besides his grief, Genji felt a profound disenchantment with affairs of the heart. He would have preferred not to receive the condolences that arrived from special quarters.

The saddened retired emperor sent a personal expression of sympathy. An honor received as an unexpected consequence of misfortune, the message brought a degree of happiness to the stricken minister, who seemed to be forever weeping from either sorrow or joy.

At someone's suggestion, they ordered all kinds of imposing prayer rituals, just in case she might possibly return to life. It was a frantic last expedient, undertaken in spite of visible marks of decay, and it did no good. After several days had passed, she had to be taken to Toribeno. There were many pathetic scenes on the way.

The vast plain was filled with mourners from different places, and with monks who had come from their temples to chant the sacred name of Amida Buddha. Messengers arrived in rapid succession from the retired emperor, the empress, the crown prince, and others, bearing word of inexpressible regret and sympathy. Everyone pitied the minister, who could not manage to stand erect. "Think of it! An old man like me outliving a daughter in the flower of her youth! I just don't know what to do," he said, shedding shamed tears.

Impressive ceremonies continued all through the night, and then, in the darkness before dawn, with nothing left of the lady but her fragile bones, the mourners all set out for home. Funerals are commonplace enough, but Genji had had little experience of such events—perhaps only of one—and that circumstance may explain why his heart overflowed with passionate love for Aoi. It was late in the eighth month, the time when the moon lingers into the daytime. There was much in the aspect of the sky to stir human emotions, but the minister wandered lost in the darkness of parental love.[15] To Genji his father-in-law's behavior seemed natural and infinitely pathetic. His own eyes drawn upward, he gazed intently at the heavens as he recited a poem:

noborinuru	I cannot tell which cloud
keburi wa sore to	took shape from the risen smoke,
wakanedomo	but there is something
nabete kumoi no	evoking deep emotion
aware naru ka na	in the whole expanse of the sky.

Wide awake back at the mansion, Genji thought about his years with Aoi. "Why was I so sure she would begin to trust me someday—so carefree about the whole thing, so willing to hurt her in order to indulge my own idle whims? She lived and died thinking I was a man she couldn't feel close to, couldn't relax with." Regret followed regret, all of them useless now.

It seemed a dream that he was wearing light black robes. If he had been the one to die first, her robes would have been dyed a darker color. Moved by the thought, he murmured:

kagiri areba	Because rules exist,
usuzumigoromo	the black of these mourning robes
asakeredo	is not deep-dyed,
namida zo sode o	but there are depths where the tears
fuchi to nashikeru	have made pools of my sleeves.

He chanted some prayers, his appearance even more elegant than usual, and proceeded to recite a sutra in a soft voice, more impressive than a veteran monk as he intoned, "Fugen, the bodhisattva whose meditative powers embrace all creation."

The sight of the baby moved Genji to tears. "What would there be to serve as a reminder of her?"[16] He took comfort in the reflection that his sorrow would be greater if he lacked this memento.

Aoi's mother, the princess, kept to her bed, brokenhearted. Fearing for her life, the alarmed minister ordered prayers on her behalf.

Time slipped by, and the minister made arrangements for the services, his grief welling up constantly as he went about tasks he had never dreamed of performing. His feelings seem all the more natural when we consider the

15. Another allusion to Kanesuke's poem ("Kiritsubo," n. 5).

16. A quotation from a poem written by a woman's nurse when, after the woman's death, it was decided to send her two children to live with relatives. Nurse of Kanetada's Mother (GSS 1187): musubiokishi / katami no ko dani / nakariseba / nani ni shinobu no / kusa o tsumamashi ("What would there be to serve as a reminder of her if I were deprived even of the children she left as mementos?").

affection parents lavish on children who are mediocre or downright inferior. The couple had always longed for more than one daughter, which made the loss an especially stunning blow—worse than the proverbial shattering of a jewel on a sleeve.

Genji never went out at all, not even to his own Nijō Mansion. He spent the days in fervent prayer, his heart aching with love and grief. To his various ladies he merely sent notes. The Ise Virgin had moved into quarters assigned to the gate guards, and her need to observe stricter ritual purity furnished a convenient excuse for not exchanging messages with the Rokujō lady.[17]

Already disenchanted with life in society, he had now begun to look on the world as a thoroughly distasteful place. Were it not for certain encumbrances, he would follow his true desire and take the tonsure. But that train of thought led at once to Murasaki, and to the loneliness she must be enduring.

Even though he was surrounded by hovering ladies-in-waiting, it was lonely at night inside the curtain-dais. He often lay awake, with the old poem running through his mind, "Why, of all seasons . . ."[18] Toward dawn, he would hear the sacred name chanted by his attendant monks, holy men who had been chosen for the beauty of their voices, and his anguish would seem unbearable.

The nights were interminable for someone unused to sleeping alone. It was only too true, he thought, that the sound of the wind added new poignance to the sadness of autumn as the season advanced.

One foggy morning, just as the first light dawned, someone appeared with a letter, put it down, and left. It was written on dark gray paper tinged with green, and had been attached to a chrysanthemum stem bearing a freshly opened flower. He inspected it, impressed by the sender's taste, and recognized the Rokujō lady's hand. "I wonder if you can guess how I have felt during this time when I haven't written," it said. [Her poem:]

> hito no yo o   I am moved to tears
> aware to kiku mo   by news of that lady's death,
>   tsuyukeki ni   but it is sadder still
> okururu sode o   to imagine the drenched sleeves
> omoi koso yare   of the one she has left behind.

"The weather this morning is deeply saddening; I could not keep from writing."

In spite of everything, he was conscious of a certain reluctance to set aside

17. The Rokujō lady has accompanied her daughter to the Virgin's temporary quarters in the palace compound. Genji's mourning robes render him ritually impure.

18. Mibu no Tadamine (KKS 839): toki shi mo are / aki ya wa hito no / wakarubeki / aru o miru dani / koishiki mono o ("Why, of all seasons, did he take his leave of us in these autumn days, when loneliness chills our hearts even at sight of the living?").

a specimen of calligraphy that struck him as even finer than usual, but the feeling gave way to disgust at what he regarded as the hypocrisy of her expressions of sympathy. And yet she would be a pathetic figure, her reputation compromised, if he simply broke off the relationship without a word. His mind was in turmoil. He could accept the apparent fact that Aoi had been fated to die. If only he had not seen and heard the cause of her death, clearly and beyond dispute! That was what made it impossible to think of the Rokujō lady with anything but loathing. There was also the Virgin's purification to consider. Would it not be troublesome for her household to receive a letter from someone in mourning? After long hesitation, he decided that it might seem cruel to ignore a letter she had taken special pains to send. He wrote on blackish-purple paper. "Please forgive my long silence. I have thought of you but have hesitated to write during my period of mourning. I feel sure you will understand." [His poem:]

tomaru mi mo	For the one who stays,
kieshi mo onaji	as for the one who has gone,
tsuyu no yo ni	life is but a dewdrop.
kokoro okuran	Nothing can be achieved
hodo zo hakanaki	by attachment to worldly things.

"Please free your own mind from worldly entanglements.[19] I fear you may be reluctant to read a letter from someone in mourning, so I shall say no more."

The Rokujō lady happened to be staying at home when the letter arrived. As she perused it in private, the meaning of Genji's hint imposed itself on her uneasy conscience with painful clarity. So he knew! The realization was almost too much. She must be the most unlucky woman in the world! What would the retired emperor think if he heard such talk? Of all the imperial brothers, her late husband, the crown prince, had been the one closest to him. The prince had earnestly commended the couple's daughter to His Majesty's care, and the emperor had said, time and again, that he would simply take up where the prince had left off with the girl. More than once, he had urged the widow to stay on in the greater imperial palace, but she had scrupled to do even that much, concerned lest it lead to undesirable consequences. And now, at an age when she ought to have put such things behind her, she had stumbled into a situation that might end in scandal. Her anguish took its toll, and her health continued to be poor.

Nevertheless, she was a woman who had long been famous for her refinement and cultivation, and she devised all sorts of intriguing novelties when the Virgin moved to the Shrine in the Fields. Word reached Genji that the more elegant among the courtiers were making it their business to brave the dews of the fields morning and night. It was only to have been expected; she

---

19. A subtle reminder that emotions like jealousy and vindictiveness are powerful hindrances to enlightenment.

was a woman of impeccable taste. He could not help recognizing that he would feel the loss if she forsook her old life for Ise.

The prescribed religious services came and went, but Genji stayed at the minister's mansion to await the final rites on the forty-ninth day. He seemed to find the unfamiliar lack of occupation a trial, and Tō-no-chūjō attempted to divert him with frequent visits, during which he talked about happenings in the outside world, some of them serious and others of the frivolous kind they both enjoyed. One of the people he joked about was Naishi-no-suke. Tongue in cheek, Genji reproved him for making fun of a pathetic old woman, but he was always amused. They discussed a certain occasion in autumn—a night when clouds had obscured the full moon—and gave each other complete accounts of various other romantic adventures. Sometimes their stories led to talk of the pathos of human existence, and they ended in tears.

One such visit took place on a melancholy evening, during a wintry shower. Recently changed out of deep mourning, Tō-no-chūjō cut a dashing figure in his gray cloak and baggy gray trousers. Genji was leaning on the balustrade near the west door, looking out at the frostbitten garden. The raindrops streaming earthward in the gusting wind made him feel that his eyes must hold an equal number of tears. He rested his cheek on his hand, murmuring under his breath a line from a Chinese poem: "Has she become rain, has she become a cloud? Now there is no way to tell."[20] Seated nearby, his friend observed him closely. "If I were a woman who died before him, I know my spirit would stay behind," he thought, his mind running in its usual erotic channel. Aside from fastening his cloak at the throat, Genji had made no effort to correct the casual disarray of his costume. In his sober mourning garb—a summer cloak darker than Tō-no-chūjō's, worn over a lustrous red jacket—he was a sight of which it would have been difficult to tire.

Tō-no-chūjō gazed at the sky with sad eyes:

ame to nari	When we fix our gaze
shigururu sora no	on the floating clouds in the sky
ukigumo o	whence come these showers,
izure no kata to	have we a way to find out
wakite nagamemu	which of them might be she?

"Who knows where she is?" he murmured, as if to himself.

When Genji replied, his appearance bore witness to the depth of his feeling:

20. From a poem by Liu Yuxi (772–842). The ultimate allusion is to the famous story of how the king of Chu spent a night with the goddess of Wu Mountain, who disappeared after telling him, "In the morning, I become a morning cloud; in the evening, I become the falling rain." See Schafer, *Divine Woman*, p. 36.

mishi hito no	Now with these showers,
ame to narinishi	darkness veils even the sky—
kumoi sae	the heavens wherein
itodo shigure ni	she whom I used to meet
kakikurasu koro	has been transformed into rain.

It was strange, Tō-no-chūjō thought. Time after time over the years, he had felt sorry for Genji because he seemed to be plodding along in an unhappy marriage, trapped by the retired emperor's worried comments on his lack of ardor, the minister's pathetic attentions, and the difficulty of breaking with the daughter of his own aunt, Princess Ōmiya. But now it was apparent that he had regarded Aoi as a special person, someone whose status demanded high esteem; and the realization made her death all the more tragic. The world seemed dark and gloomy, a place where a light had gone out.

Gentians and wild pinks had begun to bloom in the frostbitten undergrowth. Genji picked some, and after Tō-no-chūjō's departure, he asked the baby's nurse, Lady Saishō, to take them to Princess Ōmiya. [His poem:]

kusagare no	The wild pink
magaki ni nokoru	lingering by the rustic fence
nadeshiko o	in the season of frost
wakareshi aki no	I prize as a memento
katami to zo miru	of departed autumn.

"I wonder if you may consider your grandson less beautiful than his mother."

The baby's face, wreathed in innocent smiles, was in truth immensely appealing.

The princess's tears were always near the surface. The mere sound of the wind made them fall faster than the fragile leaves scattering from the trees, and now they flowed in fresh abundance. She could not pick up Genji's letter. [Her poem:]

ima mo mite	The sight of it now
nakanaka sode o	serves but to increase the tears
kutasu ka na	that rot these sleeves—
kakio arenishi	the wild pink of Yamato,
yamatonadeshiko	growing by a ravaged fence.

Still dull and depressed, Genji found himself thinking that Princess Asagao would understand how sad the weather made him feel, even though she was not the most sympathetic of correspondents. He sent off a note, despite the fact that it was already dark. It had been a long time since his last letter, but he had always written at irregular intervals, and she read his poem and comment without resentment. His gray Chinese paper matched the color of the sky.

wakite kono	For many a year,
kure koso sode wa	I have felt the sadness
tsuyukekere	that autumn brings,
mono omou aki wa	but my sleeves this evening
amata henuredo	are drenched as never before.

"Wintry showers always fall . . ."[21]

He had taken special pains with his calligraphy, and the result was even more splendid than usual. She could not ignore it, her ladies told her. She felt the same. With flawless taste, she restricted herself to a few words in faint black ink. "My heart has gone out to you during this period of mourning, but there did not seem to be anything for me to say."

akigiri ni	Ever since hearing
tachiokurenu to	of how you were left alone
kikishi yori	in the autumn mists,
shigururu sora mo	I have imagined your grief
ikaga to zo omou	when wintry showers have fallen.

Ours is a world in which reality seldom seems to exceed expectation, but it was Genji's nature to feel especially drawn to those who kept him at arm's length. "Even though a woman may act standoffish, there can be lasting affection if she demonstrates sensibility when the occasion calls for it. On the other hand, she will seem less than ideal if she draws excessive attention to her refinement and taste. I don't want to rear Murasaki in that mold," he thought. He never forgot his ward. With little to keep her busy, she would be longing to see him. But his mind was at ease where she was concerned; she was the motherless child he had taken under his wing, not someone who would entertain troublesome suspicions about his absence.

Darkness had fallen. Calling for a lamp to be brought close, he asked Aoi's principal attendants to come and chat. He had bestowed discreet favors on one of them, Lady Chūnagon, for a number of years, but had shown no interest in her during the mourning period. The very fact that the coast was now clear had made him reluctant to act, an attitude understood and admired by Chūnagon. He addressed the group as a whole, speaking in a gentle, intimate manner. "We've all become very close during these past days—much more so than before. We'll miss each other, won't we, if it can't always be like this? Quite apart from the sorrow of your mistress's death, there are many reasons why I can scarcely bear to think about the future."

"We can reconcile ourselves to that black grief," someone said, "but when we think of how we'll feel when you leave this house for good . . ." She broke off, weeping.

21. An early commentator identifies this as an allusion to an otherwise unknown poem: kannazuki / itsu mo shigure wa / furishikado / kaku sode hizuru / ori wa nakariki ("I have been aware that showers always fall in the godless month [tenth month], but never has there been a time when my sleeves have been drenched like this").

Moved, Genji looked at each of them in turn. "I certainly don't mean to disappear altogether. You seem to think I'm a flighty type. With a little time and patience, you will soon learn better—but then, it's hard to tell how long anyone may live." He looked very handsome as he turned his pensive gaze on the flickering lamp, his eyes brimming with tears.

It was only natural, Genji thought, that Aoi's favorite page girl, an orphan, should feel especially miserable. "Now that your lady is gone, Ataki, you must depend on me," he said. The child burst into tears. She was attractively dressed, her little inner robes darker than those of the others, her topmost robe, with its floating panels, also black, and her trousers orange.

He urged the women to be patient. "Please, those of you who remember the past, don't desert the baby—put up with the boredom and stay on. Nothing will be left from the old days if you all go away, and I'll feel more forlorn than ever," he said. But they were disconsolate, for they suspected that he would come even less often than before.

Without making a point of it, but with due regard for differences in status, the minister distributed Aoi's things among the ladies—trifling baubles and also more substantial keepsakes.

In need of a respite from the gloomy pattern of his days, Genji decided to visit his father. Just as the men brought up the carriage and the way-clearers gathered, raindrops came pelting down, as though to accentuate the poignance of the moment. A gusting wind sent leaves flying from the trees. Sorrow overwhelmed the women who were serving him, and their tears drenched sleeves that had only recently begun to dry. One by one, his personal attendants went off to wait for him at the Nijō Mansion, where they expected him to spend the night after his visit to the retired emperor. It was not as though he would never come to the minister's mansion again, but their departure seemed unbearably sad. For the minister and Princess Ōmiya, the events and atmosphere of the day brought a new access of grief.

Genji sent Princess Ōmiya a note. "Father has let it be known that he is impatient to see me, so I plan to visit him today. Even thinking about a little excursion like this makes me wonder how I have survived to attempt it. I feel terribly upset; I fear it would merely add to your sorrow were I to try to say goodbye in person." His message brought more grief, and the princess felt unequal to a reply, her eyes blinded by tears. Instead, the minister put in a hasty appearance. He was a heartrending sight, all but overcome, with his sleeve in front of his face. Tears of deep emotion filled Genji's own eyes as he pondered the many implications of human ephemerality, but they did not mar the beauty and elegance of his appearance.

After a considerable lapse of time, the minister managed to pull himself together. "Tears come easily to the aged, even over trifles; my eyes are never dry any more. I just can't get hold of myself. If other people saw me, they'd think that I looked a mess—that I'd lost my pride—so I can't very well visit your father. Please explain it to him when you have the chance. Ah, it's bitter for an old man to lose a child at the very end of his life!" It was painful to see the effort it cost him to speak in a calm voice.

Genji blew his nose more than once as he replied. "We know there's no telling whether a person will die early or late in this world, but nothing can compare with the anguish of firsthand experience. I'm sure Father will understand when I tell him," he said.

"Well, it doesn't look as though the rain's going to let up. Leave before it gets dark," the minister urged.

Looking around him, Genji was moved to discover that at least thirty ladies-in-waiting had assembled behind curtain-stands, beyond open partitions, and in other places where there was a clear view, all of them dressed in varying shades of gray and black, and all shedding forlorn tears.

"I know you won't forget the child who will stay here," the minister said. "I console myself by thinking, 'Anyway, he'll stop in occasionally for one reason or another.' But these ladies aren't very reflective. They seem to despair of your ever returning to this home after today—to feel that this is the end of all those months and years when they were sometimes privileged to render you personal services. It's only natural for them to consider such a loss harder to bear than a death. I always believed things would work out for you and Aoi eventually, even though the two of you were never on easy terms, but it proved to be wishful thinking. The women are right; it's a gloomy evening." He began to weep again.

"It's foolish of them to be upset. During the days when I was trying to give their mistress time to learn to like me better, my visits may have been infrequent, it's true; but there's no cause for negligence now. You'll see how it will be." Genji took his leave.

After seeing him off, the minister went back inside. All the furnishings and other things looked just as usual, but to him the room suggested a cicada's discarded husk. Genji had left a few objects scattered in front of the curtain-dais—an inkstone and some pieces of paper used for calligraphy practice. The minister picked up the papers and looked at them, repeatedly screwing his eyes tight to squeeze away tears. Desolate though the ladies-in-waiting felt, it was a sight to make some of the younger ones smile. Genji had jotted down a variety of touching phrases from old Chinese and Japanese poems, some in cursive script and others in block characters. "What a wonderful hand he writes!" the minister thought. He looked up at the sky with an absent gaze—saddened, it may be, by the realization that such a one would no longer continue as a member of his household. Genji had written a poem of his own composition next to a line of Chinese verse, "With whom might he share the old pillow, the old quilt": [22]

22. From a variant text of "The Song of Everlasting Sorrow." The best-known version reads, "The quilt [embroidered with] kingfisher wings was cold; with whom might he share it?"

naki tama zo	It was always hard
itodo kanashiki	to leave the bed where we slept.
neshi toko no	My misery grows
akugaregataki	as I wonder if her spirit
kokoronarai ni	might feel the same way now.

Next to another quotation, "The frost flowers were white," he had written:

kimi nakute	How many nights
chiri tsumorinuru	have I wiped away teardrops,
tokonatsu no	lying on the bed
tsuyu uchiharai	where dust has accumulated
ikuyo nenuramu	now that you are gone?[23]

Among the scraps of paper, there lay a withered pink, probably from the nosegay he had picked the other day.

The minister showed his finds to Princess Ōmiya. "I've tried to come to terms with the situation," he said. "I've accepted her death, I've forced myself to believe that our grief isn't unique, I've realized that it was our karma to suffer the agony of losing her so soon, and I've focused my bitterness on a previous existence instead of on this one. But I miss her worse every day, and now there's the added sorrow of knowing that Lord Genji won't be part of our household anymore. I can't help feeling miserable. When I think of how it troubled me when he stayed away for a day or two, I don't see how I can go on living if I'm to be altogether deprived of the radiant presence that brightened my mornings and evenings." He began to sob. The older ladies-in-waiting all broke down in sympathetic wails, and the gathering dark suddenly seemed chilly.

The younger women assembled here and there in melancholy talk with their friends. "We ought to console ourselves by taking care of the baby, as His Lordship urged, but an infant is a fragile memento," some of them said. Others announced that they intended to go home for a short time and then return, and many affecting incidents took place as they said their farewells.

When Genji reached the retired emperor's palace, his father was alarmed to see how thin his face looked—probably, he surmised, because his diet had been restricted to vegetarian fare for so long. He ordered up food and fussed over him in an awesome display of concern.

Genji went on to the apartments of the empress, the Fujitsubo lady, whose attendants were delighted to see him after his long absence. The lady sent out Myōbu with a message. "There is so much to keep my own grief alive. I wonder how you manage to get through the days."

23. The quotation is also from "The Song of Everlasting Sorrow," which, however, reads, "the frost flowers were thick." Wordplay in Genji's poem yields "wiped away dew from the wild pink" as an alternative meaning for lines 3 and 4 (line 2 in the translation)—a reminder of the poem by Mitsune quoted earlier ("The Broom Tree," n. 8).

"I knew in a general way that nothing lasts in this world, but having the truth brought home has made many things seem distasteful; it has cost me great mental anguish. That I have survived this long is thanks entirely to the comfort I've received from your occasional notes of sympathy," Genji replied. He was a pathetic sight, revealing in his face both the sorrow of bereavement and the misery he always felt because of this lady's inaccessibility. In his mourning attire—the unpatterned court cloak, the gray underjacket, the rolled strip of cloth behind his cap—he looked even more elegant than when he wore brilliant robes.

Genji also told the crown prince that he was concerned because he had been unable to visit him for so long. By then it was late, and he left the palace.

The whole staff was awaiting his arrival at the Nijō Mansion, where every room had been cleaned and polished. All the higher-ranking ladies-in-waiting had returned to duty, their beautiful costumes and meticulous makeup eloquent of spirited competition. The sight evoked poignant memories of the rows of despondent women at the minister's house.

He changed and went to the west wing. The furnishings installed for the change of dress were clean and bright, and the pretty young ladies-in-waiting and page girls looked most attractive. The nurse Shōnagon had done an efficient, tasteful job, he thought.

Murasaki was very sweet in her autumn attire. "You've grown up amazingly while I've been away all this time," Genji said. When he raised the curtains from the low stand, she avoided his eyes in embarrassment, her appearance flawless. Looking at her profile and hair in the lamplight, he was elated to see that she was developing into the very image of the woman he loved. He moved closer to speak of how much he had worried about her. "I'd like to tell you all about what's been going on, but it's an inauspicious story. I'll come back after I've rested awhile in the other wing. From now on, I'm going to be with you all the time; I'm afraid you may begin to think I'm a nuisance," he said.

Shōnagon was glad to hear him talk that way, but she had her doubts. He was seeing a number of important ladies in private, and she feared that one of them might replace Aoi as his principal consort. It was disagreeable of her.

Genji went to his own quarters, asked an attendant, Lady Chūjō, to massage his legs, and fell asleep. On the following morning, he sent a letter to those who were caring for his baby son, and he read the touching answer with great sadness.

He was bored at home, prone to fits of melancholy, but it seemed too much trouble to go out, even to pay a discreet visit or two. Besides, Murasaki was now a beautiful grown woman, and he considered her to have reached an age at which marriage would not be inappropriate. He experimented with occasional suggestive remarks, all of which seemed to go over her head.

With time on his hands, he gravitated to the west wing, where he spent the days playing *go*, character parts, and other games. Even in such trivial pursuits, Murasaki's natural wit and charm made her an enchanting partner. In the days when he had regarded her as too young for marriage, her appeal had been merely that of a child, but now he found it impossible to contain his passion, reluctant though he was to distress her. With their sleeping arrangements as they were, no third person could tell when their relationship changed, but there came a morning when he rose early and she rose not at all.

The ladies-in-waiting were upset. Why was she staying in bed? Was she ill? Genji set out for the east wing, first thrusting an inkstone box inside the curtains. Alone for a moment, Murasaki raised her head with a languid motion. There was a piece of paper near the pillow, twisted into a knot. Listlessly, she opened it and looked at the scribbled poem:

ayanaku mo	Night upon night
hedatekeru ka na	have we spent together
yo o kasane	in intimacy.
sasuga ni nareshi	That inner robes should part us
naka no koromo o	made no sense whatsoever.

She had never dreamed that he had any such thing in mind, and her shock and dismay were correspondingly great. How could she have put all her trust in someone whose true nature was so odious?

He came back to the west wing around noon. "You seem to be ill; what's wrong? I'll feel disappointed if I can't play *go* today." He peeped inside. She was still lying down, a robe over her head. The ladies-in-waiting moved back, and he came closer. "Why are you acting like you hate me? I didn't think you could be so mean. Your ladies must consider this behavior awfully odd, too," he said. Pulling the quilt away, he saw that she was drenched in perspiration. Even the hair on her forehead was soaked. "Come, this won't do at all. This is terrible." He tried his best to soothe her, but she maintained a stubborn silence, offended from the bottom of her heart. "All right, then. I won't inflict myself on you any longer. You make me very uncomfortable," he said in a pettish voice. He opened the inkstone box and found it empty. What a child she was, he thought with a rush of affection. He spent the rest of the day inside the curtain-dais, trying without success to divert her. There was something peculiarly endearing about her refusal to be cajoled.

Piglet cakes were brought in toward nightfall.[24] With Genji in mourning,

24. Colored, piglet-shaped cakes (*inoko mochi*) were eaten on the first day of the boar in the tenth month to ward off disease. Their consumption also represented a prayer for flourishing progeny (because pigs produce large litters).

no great fuss was made over the ceremony; cakes of various colors were merely arranged in elegant cypress-wood boxes and presented to Murasaki alone. After seeing them, Genji went to the south side of the building to summon Koremitsu. "Bring some of those cakes tomorrow evening, but not such a big assortment. Today isn't a lucky day." He spoke with a smile, and the quick-witted Koremitsu understood at once.[25]

Koremitsu made his acknowledgment in oblique language. "Yes, Your Lordship would need to choose the right day before partaking of cakes to mark the beginning of 'sweetness.' " With a grave face, he inquired, "How many 'ratlet cakes' will I need to get?"[26]

"One for every three of these will do quite well," Genji said.[27] Koremitsu left with his assumption confirmed. He never seemed to be at a loss, Genji thought in admiration.

Without a word to anyone, Koremitsu had the cakes prepared at his own house, supervising the process with such care that he might as well have made them himself.

Murasaki's rejection of Genji's blandishments made him feel as though she were a woman he had just abducted. It was an intriguing situation; he realized that his old compassionate affection had been nothing in comparison with his present feeling. There was no accounting for the human heart! Now it would be unbearable if they were apart for a single night.

Koremitsu brought the cakes late at night to avoid notice. In the prudent thought that it might embarrass Murasaki to have them delivered by a grown woman like Shōnagon, he took the precaution of asking for the nurse's daughter Ben. "Deliver this in private," he told the girl, thrusting a box of the kind used to hold incense jars inside the curtains. "It's to celebrate something, and it absolutely must go beside milady's pillow. Don't be careless, whatever you do."

Ben was puzzled by the admonition, but she took the box. "Inconstancy is something I don't know anything about," she said.[28]

"Come to think of it, that's a word you need to avoid right now. Be sure not to let it slip out," he said.

Too young to guess the truth, she took the box away and pushed it inside the curtains on the stand near Murasaki's pillow. Genji probably assumed his usual role of teacher.

25. A man's ritual consumption of "third-night cakes" constituted formal recognition of the woman as a wife.

26. Koremitsu uses "sweetness" as a substitute for "marriage." He coins "ratlet" (*nenoko*) because the day of the rat follows the day of the boar, and probably also because *ne* ("rat") is homophonous with a word meaning "bed."

27. The author probably uses the number three here so there can be no mistaking Genji's meaning. According to an old romance, *Utsubo monogatari*, the bridegroom was supposed to eat three cakes on the third night, and the bride as many as she chose.

28. She misunderstands Koremitsu's use of the word *ada*, which can mean both "careless" and "inconstant."

The other attendants were still in no position to understand what had happened, but those who were closest to Murasaki began to put two and two together in the morning, after Genji told them to remove the box. When could anyone have got hold of such plates? The stands with their carved legs were exquisite, and the cakes had been prepared with exceptional care and taste.

Shōnagon had never dreamed that Genji would make so much of the occasion. She burst into tears of gratitude, awed that he should have gone to such lengths.

"This is all very well, but why didn't His Lordship drop a word in *our* ears about needing cakes? Imagine what Koremitsu must have thought!" the women whispered among themselves.

From then on—and to his considerable bewilderment—Genji felt uneasy and lonely whenever he was away from Murasaki, even during short visits to the imperial palace or to his father's residence. He experienced an occasional twinge of pity when he received a reproachful letter from one of the ladies he had been in the habit of visiting, but he was reluctant to distress his bride by leaving for a single night, and his replies always strove to create the impression that he was ill. He would hope to see the writer as soon as he felt better.

Oborozukiyo, the mistress of the wardrobe, still thought only of Genji.[29] "Well, after all, it wouldn't be a bad match for her, now that his wife has died," the minister of the right said. But the Kokiden lady hated Genji, and she had made up her mind that the girl must be offered to the emperor. "She'll be a big success if she'll just exert herself," she said.

Genji held Oborozukiyo in high esteem and regretted the family's decision, but there was no room in his heart for anybody but Murasaki now. "Life is too short to keep running after women; I'll settle down with this one. Feminine anger is best avoided," he thought, chastened by experience.

As far as the Rokujō lady was concerned, he pitied her but was convinced that he could never feel at ease with her as his principal wife. If she was willing to continue on the old basis, he would enjoy being in touch when the occasion arose. In spite of everything that had happened, he was reluctant to contemplate a final break.

Society at large had yet to learn who Murasaki was. Recognizing that it must seem as though she was a nobody, Genji resolved to inform her father, the prince. With an extraordinary display of devotion, he immersed himself

29. Without being certain of her identity, Genji had met and spent the night with this lady after a festive occasion described in an earlier chapter (not translated). Both that meeting and a second one, about two months later, had taken place in the year before Aoi's death. The lady is the daughter of the minister of the right, and thus the sister of the reigning emperor's mother, the Kokiden lady, who is now grand empress and the most influential woman at court. In accordance with customary practice, she is identified here by a sobriquet: Oborozukiyo ("[the lady of] the misty moonlit night").

in plans for a splendid ceremony to mark her assumption of the train, even though no general announcement was made. But to Murasaki herself, he was an object of intense aversion. What a fool she had been to put all her trust in him, to cling to him for so many years! It was deeply mortifying; she could not look him in the face. His jests pained and annoyed her, and she brooded in most uncharacteristic fashion. Genji reacted with a mixture of amusement and compassion. "It upsets me for you to act so standoffish. I've shown you for years how much I love you," he told her.

Amid such reproaches, the year came to an end.

Genji paid the customary call at his father's palace on New Year's Day, visiting also the imperial palace and the residence of the crown prince. He then went to the minister of the left's mansion. The seasonal festivities were a matter of indifference to the minister. Lonely and miserable, he had just begun to reminisce about the past, and Genji's arrival brought on a fresh access of emotion, which he strove without success to control. Perhaps because Genji was a year older now, a new impressiveness in his bearing made him even handsomer than before. He went from the minister's quarters to Aoi's old rooms, where the ladies-in-waiting were reduced to tears by his appearance after so long an absence. With a heavy heart, he gazed at the little boy, who had grown a great deal and smiled all the time. The expression in the child's eyes and the shape of his mouth were exactly like the crown prince's. He wondered uneasily if people might ask questions about the resemblance. The furnishings in the room were unchanged. The usual costume hung ready for him on the clothing rack, lonely and forlorn with no feminine robes beside it. There was a message from Princess Ōmiya: "I am trying my best to suppress my grief today, but your visit makes it harder to bear." She added, "We have prepared the robes as we used to do, but my eyes have been blinded by tears during these last months, and I fear you may find the colors unattractive. Poor as they are, I hope you'll change into them, just for today." She had provided other garments as well, all tailored with the utmost care. The color and weave of the underjacket were extraordinary. She had hoped he would wear it today, and he put it on so that her kindness should not go unappreciated. He was glad he had come; the poor lady would have been terribly disappointed otherwise. In his reply, he wrote, "I came to show you that spring has arrived at last, but now I find myself speechless, overwhelmed by memories."

amatatoshi	The past returns,
kyō aratameshi	and tears threaten to fall,
irogoromo	when, as for all those years,
kite wa namida zo	I change today into robes
furu kokochi suru	of resplendent beauty.

"My emotions are quite beyond control."

The princess replied:

atarashiki	Although a new year
toshi to mo iwazu	has come to replace the old,
furumono wa	something old remains:
furinuru hito no	tears overflowing the eyes
namida narikeri	of one far advanced in age.

Theirs was no ordinary grief.

CHAPTER SEVEN

Suma

[From the third month of Genji's twenty-sixth year until the third month of his twenty-seventh year. Fujitsubo lady: 31–32; Murasaki: 18–19; Rokujō lady: 33–34; Akashi lady: 17–18; Yūgiri, 5–6; crown prince: 8–9; Suzaku emperor: 29–30.

Four years have elapsed since the events described in "Aoi." The fates have not been kind to Genji: his father died three years ago, the minister of the left has withdrawn from court, the Fujitsubo lady has become a nun, the Rokujō lady has gone to Ise with her daughter, Asagao has left the capital to serve as Kamo Virgin, and Oborozukiyo has become a principal handmaid and imperial concubine. Worst of all, Oborozukiyo's father, the minister of the right, has discovered her and Genji in bed together, and her sister, the Kokiden lady, has made up her mind to drive Genji from the court. As we learn below, Genji has been stripped of his offices and faces the possibility of banishment on a trumped-up charge of treason.]

In miserable spirits as one disheartening event succeeded another, Genji came to feel that he would merely invite further misfortune by staying in the capital as though nothing were amiss. He thought about going to Suma but hesitated after someone told him, "People from the court did live there long ago, but it's terribly isolated and lonely now. Even a fisherman's house is a rarity." On the other hand, it would scarcely be desirable to live in retirement at a place where one would keep open house for throngs of visitors. Still, Suma was very distant; he would worry about things at home. It was embarrassingly difficult to sort out his thoughts and reach a decision.

All sorts of distressing things came to mind as he pondered every aspect of his situation, from the past to the future. Determined though he might be to leave the place he now found so distasteful, it was impossible to contemplate the move itself without realizing how many things he could not bear to part with. Above all, there was the wrenching pity whenever he looked at Murasaki, whose misery increased with every passing morning and evening. Even on occasions when it was possible to keep in mind the poet's words about following different ways to certain reunion, a mere separation of a day or two was enough to worry him and depress her, but this was not to be an absence of a predetermined number of years; rather, his departure might well mark their last farewell in an uncertain world, even though he would set out with meeting her again as his final objective.[1] The thought was so painful that he sometimes toyed with the idea of quietly taking her along, but he always reconsidered. It would never do to carry off such a fragile, helpless creature to a cheerless shore where the winds and waves would be their only visitors; besides, having her there would make him worry more. Hurt, she tried to persuade him that she would be happy in the worst of places, if only he would agree not to leave her behind.

Naturally enough, the prospect of his departure caused great distress at the house of the scattering orange blossoms, for he was the sole stay of the lady's sad, pathetic life, even though he seldom visited her.[2] There were many others who grieved in private, women with whom he had once had casual liaisons. And from the Fujitsubo lady there came a stream of solicitous secret messages, sent in spite of her fears about gossip. If only she had been so warm, so sympathetic, in the old days, Genji thought, recalling the past. It was bitter to feel that their relationship had apparently been fated to produce nothing but misery.

He left the capital soon after the twentieth of the third month. There was no preliminary announcement; he simply set out in an unobtrusive manner, accompanied only by seven or eight faithful attendants. By way of farewell to certain ladies, he merely sent discreet private messages. (Some of the letters were long and deeply affecting, undoubtedly worth reading, but I was too upset to make the proper inquiries.)

Two or three days before his departure, he visited the mansion of the minister of the left under cover of darkness. It was sad, almost dreamlike, to witness his furtive arrival in a shabby wickerwork carriage, its curtains lowered to suggest that the occupant was a woman. Aoi's old apartments seemed lonely and desolate. Upon learning of his rare visit, the boy's nurse, the pages, and Aoi's remaining attendants all assembled; and even the feckless younger ladies wept to see him, abruptly and poignantly aware of the ephemerality of worldly things.

1. To heighten the emotional intensity of Genji's soliloquy, Murasaki Shikibu uses phrases from two old poems. Ki no Tomonori (KKS 405): shita no obi no / michi wa katagata / wakaru tomo / yukimegurite mo / awamu to zo omou ("Although we part now, following our different ways, we will meet again, like an underbelt's two ends circling to come together"). Ōshikōchi no Mitsune (KKS 611): wa ga koi wa / yukue mo shirazu / hate mo nashi / au o kagiri to / omou bakari zo ("I cannot be sure where this love of mine may lead, or how it may end. I know only that meeting is my final objective").

2. This minor character, introduced in the chapter immediately preceding "Suma" (not translated) and usually called Hanachirusato ("[the lady from] the house of the scattering [orange] blossoms"), lives with her sister, one of the late emperor's lesser consorts. Both women depend on Genji for economic assistance.

The little boy came romping up, a captivating child. "I'm touched to see that he hasn't forgotten me after all this time," Genji said. He took him on his knee, looking as though the parting might be too much.

The minister came to greet him from another part of the mansion. "I've gathered that you've been home with time on your hands, and wanted to call for a chat about old times, but since I've pleaded illness as grounds for ceasing to perform my duties and resigning my rank, I felt that the gossips would sneer, 'He doesn't seem to have any trouble getting around on private business.' I ought not to have to worry about public opinion anymore, but people are merciless nowadays; it's frightful. And when I see what's happening to you, it seems that this must be an era of degeneracy, a time when longevity becomes a curse. Life isn't worth living when I see you in circumstances I could never have imagined, not if the world had turned upside down." He broke down in tears.

Genji's reply was lengthy. "They say everything is the result of a cause from a previous existence, so this is simply my bad karma. I've heard that in all civilized countries, people consider it a grave transgression for anyone under official censure to go on with his life as usual, even a minor offender who hasn't been stripped of rank and offices as I have; and in my particular case, it seems, the crime would be so heinous that the penalty could be distant-banishment. I can't run the risk of acting unconcerned just because my conscience is clear; I've decided to get away from the city before I suffer a worse humiliation," he said.

The minister began to speak of the old days, and of the late emperor and his aspirations for Genji. He found it impossible to keep his sleeve from his eyes, and Genji's efforts to maintain his own composure also failed. The innocent little boy ran around, claiming the attention of first one and then the other in a manner that seemed infinitely pathetic to both.

"I never forget the one who has left us, never cease to grieve, even for an instant," the minister said. "But now that this is happening to you, I take comfort in the thought that she escaped a nightmare by dying young. If she were alive, her anguish would be unbearable. What's sadder than anything is that the child will have to stay on here indefinitely in the company of two old people, without the experience of being close to his father. It never used to be that a man would have to face this kind of punishment, even when he was guilty of a genuine offense. True, lots of ill-fated innocent people like you have suffered, even in China, but it's always been because there were specific charges against them. I just don't understand it." He ran on in the same vein.

Tō-no-chūjō arrived, and the hour grew late as they drank. Genji decided to spend the night. He summoned Aoi's attendants for conversation and observed with silent compassion the misery to which his secret favorite, Lady Chūnagon, could not give voice. He made it a point to engage her in intimate talk after the others had fallen asleep. (It was probably because of her that he stayed.)

When dawn approached, he prepared to set out in the dark, under a delightful late moon. A thin mist hovered over the garden, which looked very white with so little shade from the cherry trees now that the blossoms had gradually passed their prime; and the hazy, indistinct scene was far more moving than if the season had been autumn. He looked out for a while, leaning against the balustrade at the corner of the building. Lady Chūnagon opened the door and waited as if to see him off.

"I'm afraid we won't be able to see each other again. It never occurred to me that anything like this might happen; I didn't feel a need to rush things in the days when meeting would have been easy," he said. She wept in silence.

Lady Saishō, the boy's nurse, brought a message from Princess Ōmiya. "I wanted to speak to you myself, but I was so upset that I hesitated, and now they say you're leaving while it's still pitch black—such a change from the old days, I can't help thinking. It would be nice if you could wait until our little sleepyhead wakes up."

With tears in his eyes, Genji murmured a poem as though it were not intended to be an answer.

toribeyama	Will the smoke resemble
moeshi keburi mo	the plume from the pyre that burned
magau ya to	at Mount Toribe?
ama no shio yaku	I go to view the shore
ura mi ni zo yuku	where seafolk tend their salt fires.

"I wonder if partings at dawn are always this painful. You probably know about such things," he said.

The nurse seemed deeply affected. "They say the word 'parting' is unpleasant at any time, but I don't think it could ever be as sad as it is this morning," she said in a tearful voice.

To the princess, Genji replied, "There are innumerable things I want to say to you, but . . . Please try to imagine the state of my emotions. I would never be able to leave this hateful city if I were to look at the boy; I must pluck up my courage and hurry off."

The ladies-in-waiting peeped out to watch him go. Elegant, handsome, and melancholy, his appearance in the brilliant light of the sinking moon was enough to bring tears to the eyes of tigers and wolves. And for these women who had served him since his boyhood, his incomparable beauty seemed too sad to bear.

I almost forgot the princess's answer:

naki hito no	If you do not stay
wakare ya itodo	beneath the heavens where she
hedataranu	ascended as smoke,
keburi to narishi	you will be farther still
kumoi narade wa	from the one who is no more.

Confronted by this new grief while they were still mourning the loss of their mistress, the women felt as though there were no end to their sorrows, and they all wept over his departure in a manner that verged on the inauspicious.

Back at the Nijō Mansion, Genji found his ladies-in-waiting assembled in separate clusters. They had apparently stayed up all night, appalled by the things that were happening. There was nobody in the waiting room used by his male attendants. The men closest to him had probably gone off to say their private goodbyes, resolved to share his journey; and the others feared that a farewell call might be enough to expose them to censure and persecution. The quiet, deserted street, which had once barely accommodated the crush of visitors' horses and carriages, brought home the realization of what a cruel place the world could be. There was dust on some of the individual dining tables, and a number of seating mats had been put into storage. If things looked this way while he was still here to see, he could imagine the process of decline that would follow.

He crossed to the west wing, setting off a flurry of activity among the small page girls who had been lying about on the veranda, more than half asleep, while Murasaki sat in pensive thought, her shutters still unlowered. The children were a delightful sight in their nightdresses, and he reflected gloomily that they would probably disperse in time, unable to face the long wait until his return. It was a concern that would not ordinarily have given him pause.

"It got late last night, what with one thing and another, so I slept at the minister's house. You probably thought I was doing something distasteful again. I want to be with you every instant while I'm still in the city, but there are many things on my mind, of course, and I haven't been able to stay home all the time. Life is so uncertain; it would be sad to hurt people by letting them think I didn't care about them," he said.

She said only in reply, "No 'distasteful thing' could possibly be worse than what's happening now." It was natural that she should feel Genji's departure more than others, for it was he with whom she had felt at home since childhood. Her father, the prince, had always been a remote figure, and now, unwilling to risk gossip, he was holding himself more aloof than ever, neither writing to her nor even calling to ask how Genji was faring. Embarrassed to have her ladies know of his neglect, she wished he had never found out where she was. She had learned through certain channels that her stepmother had said, "Her sudden prosperity didn't last long, did it? What a karma! One way or another, she loses everybody who cares about her." And since then she had broken off all communication, deeply wounded. With nobody but Genji to turn to, she was in a pathetic situation.

"If I should have to stay there indefinitely without a pardon, I'll send for you, even if the place is only a cave in the rocks, but it wouldn't do for people to hear that I was taking you with me now.[3] They say it's a major offense for anyone under official displeasure to lead a normal life, or even to go outside and look at the sun and moon. I believe it must be my karma to suffer unmerited hardships; the blind irrationality at court makes me feel that my troubles would only increase if I ignored the precedents and took along someone I loved," Genji explained. He stayed in bed until the sun was high.

Prince Sochi and Tō-no-chūjō arrived, and he put on an informal cloak to receive them.[4] The garment was made of unfigured silk, appropriate for someone without rank or office, but its very plainness created an effect of elegant simplicity. He moved closer to the mirror-stand to comb his hair. Even to his own gaze, his thin face looked refined and handsome. "I didn't realize I'd lost so much weight. It shows in this mirror. What a sad business it's been!" he said. Murasaki watched him with steadfast, tearful eyes, an unbearably pathetic figure. [Genji:]

mi wa kakute	Although my body
sasuraenu tomo	may wander off like this,
kimi ga atari	my reflection
saranu kagami no	will never leave the mirror
kage wa hanareji	that remains by your side.

Murasaki replied as though talking to herself:

wakarete mo	Were your reflection
kage dani tomaru	something that might stay behind
mono naraba	after you had gone,
kagami o mite mo	then it would be comforting
nagusametemashi	to look into this mirror.

She seated herself beside a pillar to hide her tears, and Genji's gaze lingered involuntarily on her figure. To see her was to realize that none of his other ladies could compare with her.

Prince Sochi stayed, conversing quietly, until the day ended.

Naturally, Genji had been receiving frequent communications from the dismayed residents of the house of the scattering blossoms.[5] Afraid that the consort's sister would take it amiss if he failed to pay her a visit, he decided to go out again that night. He went with reluctance, and it was very late when he arrived.

"That you should deign to honor us with this visit, just as though we

3. Anonymous (KKS 952): ika naramu / iwao no naka ni / sumaba ka wa / yo no ukikoto no / kikoekozaramu ("Within what manner of cavern, bounded by rocks, might one seek shelter to divorce oneself from news of the sorrows of the world?").

4. Prince Sochi, Genji's half-brother, is better known as Prince Hotaru ("the Firefly Prince"), from an incident later in the story.

5. Probably in connection with their material needs.

were people of consequence!" The consort expressed her appreciation in language it would be tedious to report in full. He could not help imagining the bleak future confronting this household, which for so long had barely survived through his assistance. The building was hushed, and the sight of the wide pond and the densely wooded hill, lonely and cheerless in the misty moonlight, brought to mind the "cave in the rocks" where he might dwell.

The consort's sister in the western apartment had been sunk in gloom, not daring to hope that Genji would take the trouble to visit her, but he came along in the soft, quiet light of the sad moon and slipped inside, his motions releasing an incomparable fragrance. She moved forward on her knees to greet him and sat gazing at the moon. They began to talk, and presently it was almost dawn again.

"The nights are so short now," Genji said. "To think that even another meeting like this will probably be impossible . . . If only I had used my time better! I see now that I've always been too worried about the gossip someone in my position attracts." There were repeated cockcrows as he reminisced, and he prepared to hurry off so as not to be noticed. As usual, she could not put away the sad feeling that he was vanishing along with the setting moon. The moonlight on the wet sleeve of her purple robe recalled the old poem about tears on the face of the moon, and she recited:[6]

tsukikage no	Narrow though they be—
yadoreru sode wa	these sleeves that give lodging
sebaku tomo	to the rays of the moon—
tomete mo mibaya	how I long to detain
akanu hikari o	the light of which I never tire!

Moved by her distress, he tried to comfort her despite his own unhappiness:

yukimeguri	Do not gaze at the sky
tsui ni sumubeki	where clouds may briefly obscure
tsukikage no	the light of the moon—
shibashi kumoramu	the orb that will make its rounds
sora na nagame so	and shine bright again at last.

"But when you get down to it," he said, "my return does look uncertain. One's eyes are simply blinded with the tears that come from not knowing what lies ahead."[7] He left in the gray light of dawn.

He saw to everything that needed attention, parceling out degrees of responsibility at the Nijō Mansion among those of his intimate attendants

6. Ise (KKS 756): ai ni aite / mono omou koro no / wa ga sode ni / yadoru tsuki sae / nururu kao naru ("How fitting it seems that tears should dampen the face even of the moon, whose image visits my sleeve as I sit lost in sad thought").

7. Minamoto no Wataru (GSS 1333): yukusaki o / shiranu namida no / kanashiki wa / tada me no mae ni / otsuru narikeri ("These tears that fall, plain for all to behold, will serve as witness to the sorrow of one who knows not what lies ahead").

who had refused to truckle to the ruling clique, and selecting all the men who were to accompany him on the journey. As furnishings for his rustic dwelling, he chose to take only certain essentials, all of the plainest, most unadorned sort, a box containing the collected poems of Bo Juyi and other necessary books, and a single seven-stringed koto. There were to be no ostentatious articles of furniture, no magnificent robes; his guise would be that of a humble mountain peasant. Murasaki was to take charge of his ladies-in-waiting and everything else that might come up. He gave her the deeds to his estates, pasturages, and other properties. To help her administer these and lesser resources—storehouses, treasures, and so forth—with the assistance of his trusted stewards, he explained the necessary procedures to her nurse, Shōnagon, whose abilities he held in high regard.

For Nakatsukasa, Chūjō, and others of his favored ladies-in-waiting, having him in the house had served as consolation for his neglect. Now they felt deprived of all comfort, but he gave them mementos appropriate to their status and sent them off to the west wing, high and low alike. "It may be that I will survive long enough to return. Anyone who wants to wait for me should please serve Her Ladyship," he said. Needless to say, he also sent tasteful farewell presents to the boy's nurses and the people at the house of the scattering blossoms—nor did he forget to add practical gifts.

He took the risk of sending Oborozukiyo a letter. "I know it's only natural that you haven't written . . . Facing up to leaving everything is the saddest and most painful experience of my life."

ōse naki	Unable to see you,
namida no kawa ni	I sank beneath the flowing
shizumishi ya	river of my tears.
nagaruru mio no	Might that have been the origin
hajime nariken	of the tide that bears me off?

"That unforgettable love is the only crime to which I must plead guilty." He wrote little, apprehensive lest the letter fall into unfriendly hands before it could be delivered.

The lady tried to hide her anguish, but there was nothing she could do about the tears that overflowed her sleeve. [Her poem:]

namidagawa	The bubble afloat
ukabu minawa mo	on a river of tears
kienubeshi	is doomed to vanish.
nagarete nochi no	It cannot await reunion
se o mo matazute	with the one who drifts away.

Set down in a hand that hinted at the writer's tearful, distraught state, the calligraphy was delightful. Genji felt that it would be a pity to leave without seeing her one last time, but on second thought he decided not to press the point, mindful of his numerous enemies among her relatives, and of her own terror of discovery.

He was to set out in the morning. Toward nightfall, he left the mansion with the intention of paying his respects at his father's grave in the northern hills. At that time of month, the moon would not rise until almost dawn, so he went to call on the Fujitsubo lady first. Someone placed a cushion for him just outside the blinds, and she talked to him without an intermediary, the crown prince's future much on her mind. Both were people of rare sensibility, and their conversation must have called forth deep emotion.

The change to the religious life had not diminished the lady's old sweetness and charm. Genji felt tempted to hint at the pain her coldness had caused, but he knew she would consider it improper for him to talk that way to a nun; also, to do so would add to his own distress. He allowed himself only a brief remark, one that sounded reasonable in the circumstances.

"I can think of but one explanation for these astonishing charges—one that makes me fear the judgment of heaven. Life is unimportant to me; I wouldn't mind dying if I could be sure the boy would have a safe reign," he said. Perfectly aware of his meaning, she was too agitated to respond. He sat weeping over the memories that crowded into his mind, an indescribably refined and elegant figure.

"I'm going to visit Father's grave," he said. "Do you have a message for him?" She struggled with her emotions, slow to reply. At length:

mishi wa naku	Weeping, I go on,
aru wa kanashiki	nothing gained from renouncing
yo no hate o	the sad, fading world,
somukishi kai mo	where he whom I knew has died
nakunaku zo furu	and he who lives meets with grief.

They were both too distraught to express all of their thoughts in verse. Genji replied:

wakareshi ni	I drained the dregs of grief
kanashiki koto wa	in parting with my father,
tsukinishi o	but now I discover
mata zo kono yo no	in this present existence
usa wa masareru	a source of greater sorrow.[8]

He left when the moon rose. He rode on horseback, accompanied by only five or six close attendants and some trusted servants. Needless to say, there was little resemblance to the way in which he had once traveled. The whole party was in wretched spirits. One of them was the chamberlain-lieutenant who had served as his special escort on the day of the purification.[9] After

8. *Kono yo*, "this present existence," is homophonous with a phrase that can mean, "my child's situation."

9. That is, for the Kamo Virgin's purification ceremony four years before, as described at the beginning of "Aoi."

waiting in vain for a promotion he had had every right to expect, he had finally lost both his entrée into the courtiers' hall and his offices, and he was now leaving with Genji because he felt too embarrassed to show his face at court. Reminded of the past by the sight of the lower Kamo Shrine, which was visible in the distance, he dismounted, grasped the bit of Genji's horse and recited a poem:

hikitsurete	Recalling the day
aoi kazashishi	when I decked my hat with heartvine
sono kami o	as your attendant,
omoeba tsurashi	I resent the unkindness
kamo no mizugaki	of the Kamo divinities.

Genji pitied him. How must he feel to have come to this, after outshining all his peers? He dismounted also, bowed toward the shrine, and asked leave of the gods to depart:

ukiyo o ba	Now I bid farewell
ima zo wakaruru	to this wearisome life.
todomaramu	If there is talk of me,
na o ba tadasu no	I trust you to show the truth,
kami ni makasete	deities of Tadasu.[10]

To the lieutenant, who was an impressionable youth, he seemed a moving and splendid figure.

When Genji arrived at the grave, the memory of his father was so vivid that he seemed to see him before his eyes, looking just as he had looked during his lifetime. It was painful to realize that communication with the dead is impossible, even in the case of an emperor. No matter what tearful tale he might unfold, there was no hope of a discernible response, no point in asking what had become of all those anxious dying instructions to the present ruler.[11]

Dew from the rank vegetation on the path had drenched his robes, which were already damp with tears. The moon had disappeared behind some clouds, and the dense woods were shrouded in eerie darkness. Not at all sure that he would be able to find his way out again, he performed his obeisance, and as he did so, his father's face rose before him with uncanny clarity. [Genji:]

nakikage ya	When he sees me thus,
ikaga miruramu	what is his spirit thinking?
yosoetsutsu	Clouds darken the moon,
nagamuru tsuki mo	the orb at which I gaze,
kumogakurenuru	likening it to his face.

10. Tadasu, the name of a wooded area where the Kamo Shrine was situated, can be taken to mean "investigate and determine the truth."

11. Genji's father had told the new emperor to make Genji his principal adviser.

Upon returning home after sunrise, he decided to send the crown prince a message. He addressed the letter to Ō-no-myōbu, who was acting as a surrogate mother for the boy, and attached it to a cherry branch from which all the blossoms had scattered. "At long last, I intend to leave the capital today. The greatest of my many sorrows is that I have been unable to visit you. Please imagine my feelings and convey them to the prince." [His poem:]

itsu ka mata   When will he see again
haru no miyako no   the cherry blossoms of spring
hana o mimu   in the capital—
toki ushinaeru   the mountain-dwelling peasant
yamagatsu ni shite   shunted aside by the times?

Ō-no-myōbu showed the letter to the prince, and he looked at it with sober attention, young though he was. "How shall I reply?" she asked. "Say, 'I miss you even when I don't see you for a little while. What will it be like when you're far away?'" he told her. It seemed a pathetically childish answer. She could not help remembering everything—the days when Genji was consumed by a hopeless passion, the times when he and her mistress had actually met. Both of them should have enjoyed happier lives, but he had deliberately chosen a darker path—and for that, she felt, she herself was solely to blame. Her answer was somewhat disjointed, probably because she was in a state of extreme agitation. "I can find no words. I gave His Highness your message. It was very sad to witness his grief."

sakite toku   It is painful
chiru wa ukeredo   that blossoms must scatter so soon,
yuku haru wa   but please view them next year,
hana no miyako o   when the spring that now departs
tachikaerimi yo   shall have returned to the city.

"Once the time comes . . ."

Afterward, the ladies-in-waiting fell into melancholy conversation, and furtive tears were shed throughout the prince's palace.

Every one of the crown prince's attendants had grieved to see Genji brought low, even those who had merely caught glimpses of him. The people in service at the Nijō Mansion were, of course, far more deeply affected. Favored with the rarest of generosity, which extended all the way down to maids and chamber-pot cleaners, menials of whose existence Genji could scarcely have been aware, they were dismayed by the prospect of any absence on the part of their master, no matter how brief. And in society as a whole, not a soul shrugged off his departure as a matter of indifference. There was nobody who had not depended on his good offices or profited from his kindness, for he had been with his father day and night since the age of seven, and none of his requests had ever been denied. Many senior nobles, controllers, and other powerful figures owed him debts of gratitude, and the numbers of his lesser beneficiaries were beyond calculation. Such men were not unaware of their obligations, but all of them avoided the Nijō Mansion, intimidated by the punitive atmosphere at court. They may have felt that they could do nothing for Genji by visiting him at the sacrifice of their own careers, even though they felt deep distress at his departure and inwardly criticized and resented the court's behavior. In many cases, their aloofness verged on the indecent, and Genji was constantly made to feel that the world was a dreary place.

He set out late at night in the usual manner, after a day spent in quiet conversation with Murasaki. His hunting robe and other travel accouterments were all very plain. "The moon has risen all the way," he said. "Won't you come out a little way to see me off? I know I'm going to think of all sorts of things I needed to tell you. It's strange how depressed I feel whenever we're apart, even if it's only for a day or two." He rolled up a blind and coaxed her toward the veranda. Trying to control her tears, she crept forward hesitantly, very lovely in the moonlight. He worried about how she would get along once he had severed his ties with the fickle world, but to speak of such things would only add to her distress. Instead, he tried to make light of the situation:

ikeru yo no	I swore to be true
wakare o shirade	until the day of my death,
chigiritsutsu	not realizing
inochi o hito ni	that separations may occur
kagirikeru ka na	while people are still alive.

"It was foolish to think there wouldn't be times when we'd be apart."
She replied:

oshikaranu	If only I might
inochi ni kaete	win a brief postponement
me no mae no	of today's parting
wakare o shibashi	in exchange for the life
todome te shi ga na	I would gladly sacrifice!

He felt certain that those were her true feelings. It was hard to leave, but he hurried away, conscious of how awkward it might be if dawn overtook him.

Murasaki's image never left him as he journeyed, and it was with a heavy heart that he boarded the boat.

Thanks to the long days at that time of year, and to the help of a following wind, he arrived at Suma in daylight, before the hour of the monkey [3:00 P.M.–5:00 P.M.]. None of his short excursions had served as preparation for such a trip, and he felt that he had now experienced both the trials and the pleasures of travel for the first time. The Ōe Lodge was in ruins, distinguishable only by its pine trees.[12] [His poem:]

karakuni ni	Shall I perhaps lodge
na o nokoshikeru	in dwellings more uncertain
hito yori mo	than those of the one
yukue shirarenu	who has left behind a name
iei o ya semu	in the land beyond the sea?[13]

Watching the waves advance toward the shore and then retreat, he murmured, "With envious eyes . . ."[14] The quotation was a familiar one, but his unhappy attendants felt as though they were hearing it for the first time.

When he looked behind him and saw haze dimming the mountains he had passed, he could not restrain the tears that fell like spray from the boatman's oar; he seemed indeed "three thousand leagues from home."[15] [His poem:]

furusato o	The haze on the peaks
mine no kasumi wa	screens off the royal city.
hedatsuredo	Might it be, at least,
nagamuru sora wa	that this sky I gaze upon
onaji kumoi ka	is the very one they see?

No aspect of the journey but gave rise to pain.

The place where he was to live was close to the site of the dwelling where Middle Counselor Yukihira had "wept as salt seaweed dripped."[16] It was in the hills just behind the coast, a site forbidding in its loneliness. Everything about it struck him as remarkable, even the fences. There were thatched buildings and other thatched structures that looked like corridors, the whole done in excellent taste. It was all very novel, perfectly suited to the situation. Remembering some of his old romantic adventures, he knew it would have delighted him if the circumstances had been different. He summoned officials from his manors nearby, and Yoshikiyo, serving as his steward, issued

12. The lodge is said to have stood on the bank of the Yodo River at Ōe (now a part of Ōsaka) and to have been used by Ise Virgins returning to the capital.

13. Thought to be a reference to the Chinese poet Qu Yuan (340 B.C.–278 B.C.) and his wanderings in exile.

14. Genji quotes a poem attributed to a courtier traveling eastward from the capital in self-imposed exile. Anonymous (IM, sec. 7): itodoshiku / sugiyuku kata no / koishiki ni / urayama-shiku mo / kaeru nami ka na ("With envious eyes, I watch the returning waves—now, more than ever, borne down with nostalgia for all that lies behind me").

15. A hyperbolic expression, derived from a poem by Bo Juyi in which the speaker is a lonely traveler.

16. Ariwara no Yukihira (KKS 962): wakuraba ni / tou hito araba / suma no ura ni / moshio taretsutsu / wabu to kotae yo ("If, by any chance, someone should ask after me, answer that I pine, weeping as salt seaweed drips on the beaches of Suma"). Yukihira, a prominent 9th-century courtier and poet, was forced into temporary self-exile at Suma for a reason that is no longer known.

orders and supervised the execution of necessary tasks, a role pathetically different from the one he had enacted in the capital.

Before long, Genji had succeeded in creating very attractive surroundings for himself. He had made a deep garden stream and done some planting, and now, as though in a dream, he found himself quite reconciled to the idea of living there.

The governor of the province, who was one of his protégés, showed his sympathy by performing discreet services on his behalf.

With so many people going in and out, it was hard to believe that this was only a travel dwelling, but there was nobody with whom to converse on equal terms, and Genji felt very much a stranger in a strange land. He wondered gloomily how he would manage to get through the months and years.

As things gradually settled down and the rainy season began, his thoughts turned to the capital, and to the many people he missed, especially Murasaki, whose grieving figure haunted his memory; also the crown prince, and the little son who had run from one person to another in innocent play. He decided to send a messenger to the city. When he tried to write to Murasaki and the Fujitsubo lady, blinding tears forced him to break off. To the Fujitsubo lady he sent a poem and a note:

matsushima no	In this season
ama no tomaya mo	when the shore-dweller at Suma
ika naramu	weeps as saltweed drips,
suma no urabito	how is it in the fisher's
shio taruru koro	thatched hut at Matsushima?[17]

"I have felt unhappy all along, but now the past and the future seem equally dark; the river threatens to overflow its banks."[18]

As usual, his message to Oborozukiyo took the form of a private communication to her attendant Chūnagon. In an enclosure, he wrote, "I have little to occupy me, and memories of the past keep coming into my mind." [His poem:]

korizuma no	Unrepentant, I yearn
ura no mirume mo	for the *mirume* seaweed
yukashiki o	on Suma strand—
shio yaku ama ya	but how feels the fishermaid
ikaga omowan	tending the salt-burning fire?

You can probably imagine the detailed letters he addressed to other quarters. One message went to Aoi's father, and there was another instructing the nurse Saishō to take good care of the boy.

17. Puns yield another meaning: "In this season when my tears fall like rain, what are the thoughts of the nun who awaits my return?"

18. Ki no Tsurayuki (KKRJ 2345): kimi oshimu / namida ochisoi / kono kawa no / migiwa masarite / nagarubera nari ("When the tears I shed, loath to bid you farewell, fall into its waters, this river will be certain to overflow its banks").

Many people in the capital suffered great anguish as they read these messages. To the dismay of Murasaki's women, who tried in vain to comfort her, she lay prostrate with the letter in her hand, wracked by passionate longing. She grieved for him as though for the dead, treasuring his personal belongings, the koto on which he had strummed a few notes, the scent from a discarded robe, and other such things. Her behavior seemed positively inauspicious; Shōnagon asked the bishop to offer prayers. The bishop performed esoteric rites for both Genji and Murasaki. Moved to compassion, he prayed that she might find surcease from her grief, and that he might return and be as he had been.

Murasaki prepared bedclothes and other necessities to send to the country. Saddened by the sight of informal cloaks and bloused trousers made of plain white taffeta, all so different from his usual attire, she remembered his poem about the mirror. The promised reflection appeared in her mind's eye, but it afforded small comfort. She choked up whenever she looked at an entrance he had used or a pillar he had leaned against. When we consider that such a parting would have saddened anyone, even a woman of mature years, profound discernment, and much experience in the ways of the world, her desperate longing seems only natural, for she had been torn apart from the one person with whom she was most comfortable, the one person who had cherished and reared her in the place of a father and mother. Nothing could have been done about it if he had died; she would probably have begun to forget as time went on. But she never ceased to agonize over the impossibility of telling how long this parting might last, even though he was apparently not very far away.

I need not say that Genji's departure had also come as a great blow to the Fujitsubo lady, who had relied on his support for the crown prince. In any case, she could not have shrugged off the misfortune of someone to whom her own karma was linked by such close bonds. Worried about gossip in past years, she had held her feelings in check and cultivated a pose of indifference to his love, telling herself that there might be criticism if she seemed at all sympathetic, but she could not help remembering with nostalgia that his firm control of his tumultuous emotions, and his skill at concealment, had kept their relationship safe to the end from the tongues of the capital. Her reply was warmer than usual:

> shio taruru
> koto o yaku nite
> matsushima ni
> toshi furu ama mo
> nageki o zo tsumu

> She amasses stores
> of firewood—the fisher who dwells
> at Matsushima
> year after year, her sole concern
> the burning of seaweed for salt.

"Still more now . . ."[19]

19. "Your plight deepens the sorrow of the nun whose sole occupation is weeping for the dead."

Oborozukiyo sent a brief message, which was enclosed in Lady Chūna-gon's reply:

ura ni taku	Because this passion
amata ni tsutsumu	must be concealed from many eyes,
koi nareba	there is no escape
kuyuru keburi yo	for the smoldering smoke
yuku kata zo naki	from the fire in my breast.

"So much goes without saying. I simply can't . . ."

Chūnagon wrote a full account of her mistress's unhappiness. She included many pathetic details, and Genji's heart ached for the girl.

Murasaki's letter, a response to his own loving message, contained much to stir his emotions. She had included this poem:

urabito no	Compare it to the sleeve
shio kumu sode ni	of the dweller by the shore
kurabemi yo	dipping salt water—
namiji hedatsuru	the robe worn at night by one
yoru no koromo o	beyond the waves of the sea.

The bedclothes she sent were beautifully dyed and tailored. She did everything so very well. How ideal it would be to live here quietly with her, free of other demands on his time and energy—and how frustrating to be denied that pleasure! Her face stayed with him day and night, a source of unbearable memories. Should he not, after all, bring her to Suma in secret? But no. In this world of sorrows, he must at least try to atone for his sins. He restricted himself to vegetarian fare and read the scriptures all day long.

It was also saddening to receive news of Yūgiri from Aoi's parents. Genji told himself that he and the boy would meet again, and that there could be no cause for anxiety while he was in such reliable hands, but no parent can keep from worrying about a child.

With all that was going on, I forgot to mention that Genji had written to the Rokujō lady at Ise. There now arrived a letter from her, sent by a messenger who had had to search to find him. It was full of tender sentiments, and the peerless elegance of its verse and calligraphy served as a reminder of her erudition and taste. "I have felt lost in an endless night since hearing of your move to that unbelievable place. I imagine you will return to the capital soon, but it will probably be a long time before I see you, sinner that I am." [20]

ukime karu	O dweller at Suma,
ise o no ama o	the shore where saltweed drips,
omoiyare	please sympathize

20. She will presumably stay at Ise until a new emperor selects a replacement for her daughter. Proscriptions against Buddhism were observed at the shrine; hence she is a sinner in the eyes of Buddhists.

moshio taru chō	with the fisher of Ise
suma no ura nite	who reaps the floating wrack.[21]

"Everything seems so dreadful! How will it all end?" It was a long letter. [Her second poem:]

iseshima ya	That I should live on
shiohi no kata ni	seems as pointless as to comb
asarite mo	the Ise beaches
iu kai naki wa	at low tide, seeking shellfish
wa ga mi narikeri	where none such can be found.

Overcome by painful emotions, she had more than once laid her brush aside and taken it up again, until she had filled four or five pages of white Chinese paper with characters in beautiful shades of black and gray. Genji pitied her. His own conduct seemed inexcusable. It was his mistake—his letting one incident transform his old affection into repugnance—that had driven her to her desperate act of renunciation. The timing of the letter strengthened its effect. Even the messenger seemed like a special friend, and Genji detained him for two or three days in order to hear his tales of Ise. The fellow was young and handsome, one of the Virgin's attendants. In Genji's straitened circumstances, even someone of negligible status naturally came close enough to catch a glimpse of him, and tears rose in the youth's eyes as he beheld his splendid figure.

You may imagine the language in which Genji answered the lady's letter. He wrote in part, "If I had known I would have to leave the city, I'd have followed you to Ise. It's boring and depressing here."

isebito no	Instead of reaping
nami no ue kogu	floating wrack, I might have ridden
obune ni mo	in a small boat
ukime wa karade	rowed out over the waves
noramashi mono o	by a dweller at Ise.[22]

ama ga tsumu	How long must I live
nageki no naka ni	gazing into the distance
shio tarete	at Suma shore,
itsu made suma no	shedding briny tears where seafolk
ura ni nagamemu	pile wood to burn their saltweed?

"It's dreadfully distressing not to know when I can see you again."

He kept in touch with all his ladies in this manner.

There were sad replies from the sisters at the house of the scattering blos-

---

21. "You who weep like Yukihira at Suma: sympathize with someone who lives in misery at Ise."

22. Genji alludes to a *fuzokuuta* (folksong) popular at court (KDKYS, p. 441): "A dweller at Ise is a very queer person. Why is that, you ask? Because he gets into a small boat and rows out over the waves! And rows out over the waves!"

soms. It was a novel experience to read their elegant epistles in his present surroundings, and he read and reread them with mingled pleasure and gloom. The younger sister had sent this poem:

aremasaru	As the long rains fall,
noki no shinobu o	dewdrops cluster on the sleeve
nagametsutsu	of one sick at heart
shigeku mo tsuyu no	who gazes at the creeping moss-fern
kakaru sode ka na	on the moldering eaves.

Yes, he thought, there was nobody but the weeds and wild vines to look after them now. Upon learning that the rains had collapsed the tile-capped earthen walls of their house in several places, he sent orders to his steward in the capital to muster repair crews from his estates in neighboring provinces.

Conscious that people were laughing at her, Oborozukiyo had sunk into a deep depression, and her doting father, the minister, kept after the emperor and the Kokiden lady to do something about it. The emperor decided that he should reconsider. She was an official at court, not a recognized imperial consort whose conduct was governed by strict rules; and furthermore, it was solely because of the unfortunate incident with Genji that she had been punished. He decreed that she should be pardoned and allowed to return to court. But there was no room in her heart for anybody but Genji.

She returned to court during the seventh month. The emperor, who still loved her dearly, kept her at his side as before, ignoring the gossips, and alternating tender reproaches with vows of eternal fidelity. He was a splendid-looking man, handsome in face and figure, but memories of Genji haunted her mind in a most disrespectful fashion. One time, while they were enjoying a little music, he said, "I miss Genji, and I can imagine that there must be many others who find his absence still more painful. I'm always feeling as though a light has gone out." He went on, "I ignored Father's last wishes, which is bound to count as a sin." He choked with tears, and Oborozukiyo also wept.

"I have learned from experience that life is no fun, and I feel sure I won't be around much longer. I hate to think my death will mean less to you than your separation from someone who isn't so very far away. He wasn't much of a lover, the poet who said, '. . . while I am still alive.'" [23] He spoke with gentle sincerity. Observing that her cheeks were wet with tears, he said, "Ah, you're crying! For whom, I wonder?"

"I'm sorry you haven't given me children. I'd like to adopt the crown prince as Father asked me to, but I fear it would cause problems," he said.

23. Said to be an allusion to a poem by Ōtomo no Momoyo (sis 685): koishinamu / nochi wa nani sen / ikeru hi no / tame koso hito no / mimaku hoshikere ("What would be left after I had perished, unhappy in love? My goal is to be with her while I am still alive"). A proper lover hoped to continue the relationship in another life.

Certain people were conducting public affairs in a manner not to his liking, and there was much to distress a sovereign who was too young and weak to impose his will.

The winds of autumn, "the saddest season of all," blew at Suma.[24] The breakers of which Yukihira speaks, in his "blowing across the barrier,"[25] sounded very close at night, even though the sea was a fair distance away; and to Genji it seemed that nothing could be as evocative of melancholy musings as autumn in such a place. Awakening alone one night, after his few attendants were all asleep, he raised his head from the pillow and listened to the howling gale. The waves seemed about to invade the room, and he wept unawares until his pillow was in danger of floating away. When he essayed a few notes on the seven-stringed koto, the sound was lonesome and uncanny, even to his own ears. He broke off and intoned the words of a poem:

> koiwabite   That the breaking waves
> naku ne ni magau   harmonize with these sobs
> uranami wa   wrung from a grieving heart—
> omou kata yori   is it because the wind blows
> kaze ya fukuramu   from where someone yearns for me?

His attendants awakened. Saddened by the beauty of his voice, they pulled themselves listlessly erect, trying not to show that they were blowing their noses. He could imagine their feelings, and his heart went out to them. It was for his sake alone that they had embraced this life of uncertainty, parting with their parents, their brothers and sisters, and the beloved homes from which any absence at all would have been hard to bear. How depressing it must be for them to see him moping like this!

During the days that followed, he enlivened his conversation with small jests, and put his leisure time to use by pasting together pieces of colored paper and writing out poems on them. He also amused himself by painting pictures on fine Chinese damask, producing folding screens splendid to behold. Now that he saw with his own eyes the ocean and mountains of which his attendants had once told him, and which he had hitherto merely pictured from afar, he recognized that this was indeed a coastline of matchless beauty, and he painted its many aspects with incomparable skill. It was a

24. Anonymous (KKS 184): ko no ma yori / morikuru tsuki no / kage mireba / kokorozu-kushi no / aki wa kinikeri ("To see moonlight come filtering through the branches is to awaken to the coming of autumn, the saddest season of all").

25. Ariwara no Yukihira (ShokuKKS 868): tabibito wa / sode suzushiku / narinikeri / seki fukikoyuru / suma no urakaze ("A wind on the beach at Suma, blowing across the barrier: a traveler remarks on the coolness of his sleeves"). Commentators have suggested that Murasaki Shikibu may actually have had in mind a poem by Mibu no Tadami (SKKS 1599): akikaze no / seki fukikoyuru / tabi goto ni / koe uchisouru / suma no uranami ("Each time the autumn wind blows across the barrier, the waves breaking on the seashore at Suma chorus in harmony"). Nothing is known about the barrier.

great pity, his men said to one another, that he could not summon the leading painters of the day, Chieda and Tsunenori, to add colors to his sketches. His friendliness and good cheer made them forget their troubles, and four or five of them were always in attendance, happy to associate with him on such intimate terms.

On a pleasant evening when the flowers in the garden were in profuse bloom, Genji strolled out to a corridor from which the sea was visible, and his almost uncanny beauty, strangely exotic in such surroundings, made him seem a visitor from another world as he lingered there. He was wearing a deep blue cloak, its ties casually loose, over robes of soft white damask and a pair of aster-colored baggy trousers. Intoning, "I, a disciple of Śākyamuni Buddha," he began a slow recitation of a sacred text, and to his attendants it seemed that no other voice could be so beautiful.

They could hear boisterous voices raised in song from fishing boats at sea. The boats were barely visible, a lonely sight in the distance, like little birds afloat on the waves. A line of wild geese flew by, their cries like creaking oars, and Genji's tears overflowed as he watched. The hand he raised to wipe his eyes, very white in contrast to the black prayer beads, comforted the men whose thoughts were with women in the capital. He recited a poem:

> hatsukari wa
> koishiki hito no
> tsura nare ya
> tabi no sora tobu
> koe no kanashiki

> That the first wild geese
> raise sad voices as they wing
> through travel skies—
> might it be through friendship
> with the one for whom I yearn?

Yoshikiyo replied:

> kakitsurane
> mukashi no koto zo
> omōyuru
> kari wa sono yo no
> tomo naranedomo

> It is not as though
> the wild geese were my friends
> in days gone by,
> yet they evoke a train
> of memories of the past.

Koremitsu:

> kokoro kara
> tokoyo o sutete
> naku kari o
> kumo no yoso ni mo
> omoikeru ka na

> I once imagined
> I shared nothing in common
> with crying wild geese
> who had chosen of their own will
> to leave their distant home.

The former guards lieutenant:

> tokoyo idete
> tabi no sora naru
> karigane mo
> tsura ni okurenu
> hodo zo nagusamu

> They find comfort
> in being with their comrades—
> even those wild geese
> who go from their far-off land
> to wing through travel skies.

"Imagine what it would be like to get separated from one's companions." He had accompanied Genji instead of surrendering to the temptation to join his father, the new vice-governor of Hitachi Province. The decision must have cost him secret anxiety, but he maintained an attitude of confident cheer.

The brilliant moon rose, a reminder that it was the fifteenth of the month. Genji thought with nostalgia of music in the courtiers' hall. In other places also, people would be looking skyward. He gazed intently at the face of the moon, chanting: "In the moonlight, my thoughts turn to an old friend two thousand leagues away."[26] Once again, his attendants could not help weeping. With a full heart, he recalled the time when the Fujitsubo lady had sent him the poem about intervening mist.[27] Other memories of the lady followed, and he wept aloud.

His attendants mentioned the lateness of the hour, but he lingered outside. [His poem:]

miru hodo zo	Distant though it be—
shibashi nagusamu	the celestial palace
meguriawamu	I long to see again—
tsuki no miyako wa	I find brief consolation
haruka naredomo	in gazing at the moon.[28]

He remembered the night when the emperor had engaged him in friendly conversation about the past, and recalled with nostalgia how much he had looked like their father as he talked. Murmuring, "The garment His Majesty conferred is beside me now," he went inside.[29] He did indeed keep always at his side just such a robe. [He composed another poem:]

ushi to nomi	I cannot feel
hitoe ni mono wa	simply that he was cruel.
omōede	Conflicting emotions
hidari migi ni mo	have dampened both of my sleeves,
nururu sode ka na	the left and the right alike.

26. From a poem by Bo Juyi, composed, like Genji's, on the fifteenth of the eighth month, the night of the harvest moon. The "old friend" was his boon companion, Yuan Zhen.

27. The lady had gone to the imperial palace to see her son, the crown prince, before taking religious vows, and Genji had visited her there on a moonlit night. Her poem: kokonoe ni / kiri ya hedatsuru / kumo no ue no / tsuki o haruka ni / omoiyaru ka na ("Might it be because layers of mist intervene? I must content myself with picturing from afar the moon above the clouds"). Wordplays and metaphors yield another meaning: "There are those in the imperial palace who dislike me and the crown prince. Is that why I am denied access to the present emperor?"

28. "Celestial palace" renders *tsuki no miyako* ("moon palace"), which here is an elegant way of referring to the capital. The notion that there was a palace in the moon came from China.

29. From a poem in Chinese by the exiled statesman-literatus Sugawara no Michizane (845–903): "Last year on this night, I served at the Seiryōden; in my 'Autumn Thoughts' poem, I spoke of secret anguish. The garment His Majesty conferred is beside me now; raising it high, each day I revere the lingering scent."

Around that time, the assistant viceroy of Kyushu was returning to the capital from his post. What with all his relatives, the entourage assumed imposing proportions, and it was decided that his wife should go by boat, taking with her the numerous daughters whose presence would complicate a journey by land. As they progressed, hugging the shoreline and enjoying the scenery, the women were charmed by the special beauty of Suma. And when they learned of Genji's presence, the romantic younger girls fussed nervously over their appearance—just as though there were any chance of his seeing them while they were in the boat. The Gosechi lady was even more reluctant to be towed on past.[30]

They heard the sound of a distant koto, carried on the wind. The loneliness of the spot, the plight of the musician, and the melancholy voice of the instrument drew tears from all in the party who were capable of refined feeling.

The assistant viceroy sent Genji a message. "I had meant to pay my respects and hear news of the capital from you as soon as I returned from the back country. It's a sad shock to find you living in a place like this. So many acquaintances and other people have come to meet me that I would risk causing you trouble if I were to call. It's a great disappointment; I look forward to another opportunity soon."

It was his son, the governor of Chikuzen Province, who brought the message. Indebted to Genji for an appointment as chamberlain and other favors, the son felt great sympathy and indignation but thought it best not to tarry, for people were watching and there were the gossips to consider.

"It has been difficult to see any of my old friends since I've been away from the capital," Genji said. "Thank you so much for taking the trouble to drop by." His answer to the assistant viceroy was much the same. The governor wept as he left, and the assistant viceroy and his entourage of greeters shed many tears, overcome by grief that verged on the inauspicious as they listened to the messenger's description of Genji's living arrangements.

The Gosechi lady managed to send off a note:

koto no ne ni	Is my lord aware
hikitomeraruru	of an agitated heart
tsunadenawa	unsteady as the rope
tayutau kokoro	slackened when our vessel halts,
kimi shirurame ya	charmed by the sound of a koto?

30. The Gosechi lady appears to have been one of Genji's minor interests. She has been mentioned once before, in "The House of the Scattering Blossoms" (not translated), where Genji says to himself, "The Gosechi dancer from Kyushu was an especially attractive girl." We learn now that she is the assistant viceroy's daughter. On the Gosechi dancers, who figured prominently in the court's harvest thanksgiving ceremonies, see McCullough and McCullough, *Tale of Flowering Fortunes*, 1: 376–77. Towropes, manned by sailors, were often used to move boats along shorelines.

"If I seem forward, 'please do not find fault with me.'"[31]

Genji smiled, looking so handsome that his men felt positively uncomfortable. He replied:

kokoro arite	If, through affection,
hikite no tsuna no	you wavered like a drawn rope,
tayutawaba	would you be likely
uchisugimashi ya	to travel on beyond
suma no uranami	the seashore at Suma?

"I never expected 'to find myself reeling in a fisherman's line.'"[32]

The lady was more deeply moved than the stationmaster who was favored with the Chinese poem;[33] she only wished that she might leave the boat and stay there.

As time went by in the city, the emperor and others missed Genji on many different occasions. The crown prince thought of him always, shedding furtive tears that wrung the hearts of his nurses—and also, most especially, that of Lady Myōbu.[34] For the Fujitsubo lady, ever apprehensive on the prince's behalf, the absence of the boy's father was a source of additional worry.

In the early days of Genji's exile, his brothers and his friends among the senior nobles sent him solicitous letters. A number of touching Chinese poems traveled back and forth, and Genji's compositions attracted universal acclaim. The Kokiden lady made her displeasure clear when she heard about it. "They tell us a man under imperial censure is supposed to have a hard time finding enough to eat, but this fellow sits around in his stylish house criticizing everybody. His toadies remind me of the sycophants who called a deer a horse," she said.[35] People grew nervous when unpleasant rumors of such remarks made the rounds, and Genji's correspondents stopped writing.

The passing of time brought no respite from grief for the lady at the Nijō Mansion. When Genji's attendants from the east wing first moved to the west wing, all of them doubted that Murasaki would prove to be the paragon their master seemed to think her, but they soon learned to appre-

---

31. Anonymous (KKS 508): ide ware o / hito na togame so / ōbune no / yuta no tayuta ni / mono omou koro zo ("You who are watching: please do not find fault with me, for this is a time when love makes me as unsteady as a ship riding the waves").

32. He echoes the lady's imagery and quotes a poem composed in exile by Ono no Takamura (KKS 961): omoiki ya / hina no wakare ni / otoroete / ama no nawa taki / isari semu to wa ("Did I ever think to find myself reeling in a fisherman's line, away from all my old friends, cheerless in a distant land?").

33. The reference is to a poem that Sugawara no Michizane, the most famous of all Japanese exiles, recited to a sympathetic stationmaster he encountered at Akashi, near Suma, as he was making his way to Kyushu, his place of banishment. See McCullough, *Ōkagami*, p. 97.

34. The go-between who had helped Genji meet the Fujitsubo lady in private.

35. According to *Shi ji*, a treasonous official of the Qin dynasty tested the loyalty of subordinates by seeing if they would agree with him when he called a deer a horse.

ciate both her sweetness and elegance and her generosity and concern for their well-being; and not one of them left the mansion. Those of higher rank, who were sometimes privileged to glimpse her in person, considered it only natural that Genji should have loved her better than any of his other ladies.

The longer Genji stayed in Suma, the less able he felt to live there without Murasaki. But how could he bring her to a dwelling whose hardships seemed, even to himself, so severe that they must undoubtedly represent a punishment for misdeeds in a former life? He changed his mind; it was no place for her. Everything was so different in the country. He was unaccustomed to witnessing the daily life of commoners who knew nothing about him, and their activities struck him as bizarre and—if he did say so—not the kind of thing to which he ought to be exposed. From time to time, columns of smoke rose nearby. He attributed them to fishermen's salt fires, but they turned out to come from brushwood, smoldering in the mountains behind the house. Intrigued, he composed a poem:

> yamagatsu no Would that someone at home—
> iori ni takeru one for whom I yearn—might visit me
> shibashiba mo time and time again,
> kototoikonan as burn the fires of brushwood
> kouru satobito at the huts of mountain folk.[36]

It was winter, the season of snowstorms. To Genji's pensive eye, the sky seemed bleaker than ever, and he sought consolation in his koto, directing Yoshikiyo to sing and Koremitsu to blow the flute. With meticulous care, he played a series of melodies so haunting that the others fell silent, wiping away tears. His thoughts strayed to the lady who was sent to the barbarian lands long ago, and to the Han emperor whose misery must have exceeded his own. What if he were required to send his beloved Murasaki away like that? The mere idea made him shudder; it was as though it might actually happen. "Dreaming after frostfall," he chanted.[37]

A brilliant moon shone, its beams penetrating every cranny of the rustic dwelling. From his seat on the floor, he could see the late night sky. The light of the setting moon seemed unutterably lonely, and he murmured under his breath, "I simply journey toward the west."[38] Also to himself:

36. The English version is a rough approximation of the Japanese, which puns on *shiba* ("brushwood") and *shibashiba* ("time and again").

37. A Han emperor, Yuandi (r. 48 B.C.–31 B.C.), was tricked into sending off a beautiful consort, Wang Zhaojun, to marry a barbarian chieftain. The quotation is from a Chinese poem about the consort by a Japanese literatus, Ōe no Asatsuna, which reads in part (WKRES 702): "The sound of the barbarian flute: an end to dreaming after frostfall. Thoughts of the Han capital a myriad leagues away: heartbreak under the moon."

38. From "A Reply on Behalf of the Moon" (KKKS 511) to "I Ask a Question of the Autumn Moon" (KKKS 510). The full line reads, "I simply journey toward the west; it is not that I have been sent into exile." Both poems were composed in exile by Sugawara no Michizane.

izukata no	Over what cloud paths
kumoji ni ware mo	might I also be destined
madoinan	to go wandering?
tsuki no miruramu	It is embarrasssing
koto mo hazukashi	even to be seen by the moon.

Wakeful as usual toward dawn, he heard the plaintive cries of plovers.

tomochidori	Even when I wake
morogoe ni naku	in bed alone, it is cheering
akatsuki wa	to hear my friends,
hitori nezame no	the plovers, crying with me
toko mo tanomoshi	as daybreak approaches.

Nobody was stirring yet; he lay there, repeating the poem to himself.

Sometimes he devoted himself to pious recitations during the small hours of the night, after first cleansing his hands and mouth with water; and this also seemed to his attendants so remarkable and praiseworthy that they found it impossible to leave him, even for brief stays in their own homes.

It was no distance at all to the coast at Akashi. Remembering the Buddhist novice's daughter, Yoshikiyo sent off a letter to which she made no response.[39] Her father invited him to drop by to see him—there was something he wanted to discuss, he said—but Yoshikiyo decided against it. The prospects looked discouraging. His suit would probably fail, and he would look like a fool if he let himself get involved, only to come away empty-handed.

The father cherished extravagant notions of his own importance. The great ambition of others in the province was to form a connection with the ruling governor, but this eccentric gentleman bided his time, contemptuous of any such alliance. When he heard about Genji, he spoke to the girl's mother. "People tell me that the court has censured Genji, the shining one, the Kiritsubo lady's son, and that he has come to live in Suma. It must be our girl's karma that something so astonishing should happen. This is our chance to give her to him."

"What a wild idea!" the mother said. "From what they say in the capital, he already has all kinds of high-ranking wives—and there's even talk of a secret affair with one of the imperial concubines. A man who's attracted so many fine ladies isn't going to be interested in a plain country girl."

He flared up and answered with stubborn pride. "It's apparently too much for you to comprehend. My view of the matter is different. Just make up your mind to it. I'm going to find a way to get him here." He proceeded to furnish the house with dazzling splendor and to lavish all kinds of attentions on his daughter.

"Fine gentleman or not, why should our first choice for the girl be an

39. The girl and her father, the former governor of the province, were discussed by Genji and his companions in "Young Murasaki."

exiled criminal? And it's not as though he might fall in love with her, you know. The whole thing is just out of the question—not even worth joking about," the mother said.

The novice muttered to himself in an angry voice. "No matter whether it's in China or here, anyone as outstanding as Genji—as different in every way from ordinary men—can't help being accused of some crime or other. Do you know who he is? His mother was the daughter of my uncle, the inspector—major counselor. Everyone praised her to the skies, and Uncle sent her to court. Jealous rivals hounded her to death because the emperor made too much of her, but happily she left this son behind. A woman needs to aim high. Genji won't disdain our girl just because I live in the country."

The daughter was not a remarkable beauty, but in sweetness, refinement, and intelligence, she could have held her own against any great lady, just as her father believed. She was resigned to her unfortunate situation. Convinced that no man of any real consequence would notice her, she was resolved not to marry anyone more suitable to her own status. If she outlived the parents who loved her, she would become a nun, or perhaps drown herself in the ocean. Her solicitous father saw to it that she visited the Sumiyoshi Shrine twice a year, and himself offered secret prayers for divine assistance.

With the arrival of the new year, the days grew tediously long at Suma. The newly planted cherry saplings put forth their first hesitant blossoms, the air was balmy, and Genji often found himself in tears, his mind full of sad memories. With an aching heart, he remembered the pathetic figures of those who had mourned his departure from the capital late in the second month of last year. Now would also be the time when the cherry tree outside the Shishinden would be in full bloom. He thought of that cherry-blossom banquet in a bygone year—of his father's high spirits, and of the present emperor's refined beauty as he chanted one of Genji's own verses.[40]

itsu to naku	I never cease to miss
ōmiyabito no	the men of the great palace,
koishiki ni	but now the day has come,
sakura kazashishi	the very day when I adorned
kyō mo kinikeri	my cap with cherry blossoms.

Just when he was feeling bored to distraction, Tō-no-chūjō paid him a sudden visit. His friend was now a consultant, a fine-looking man with an excellent reputation, but court life had lost its savor without Genji, whose absence he felt on every occasion; and he had finally decided that he would not care if people heard about his trip and charged him with wrongdoing. As soon as he laid eyes on Genji, he shed tears of nostalgic joy.

40. The occasion is described in "The Cherry-blossom Banquet" (not translated). In the poem below, Genji refers to a sprig of blossoms presented to him by the then—crown prince when he was about to perform a dance.

The place where Genji lived seemed the ultimate in Chinese taste. The scenery was as beautiful as a painting, and the encircling fence of woven bamboo, the stone steps, and the pine pillars conveyed an impression of novelty and elegance despite their crudity.[41] Genji was dressed with deliberate rustic simplicity, his yellowish-red underjacket and greenish-gray hunting robe and trousers suggestive of a mountain peasant, but his beauty evoked an involuntary smile. There was a makeshift look to his personal belongings, and his whole sitting room was exposed to view. The *go* and backgammon boards, stones, and so forth were all of rustic make, as were the tiddlywinks pieces; and there were prayer beads and other Buddhist objects to attest to his custom of invoking Amida's sacred name.

When food was served, it was apparent that pains had been taken to make the meal interestingly appropriate to the surroundings. Some seafolk had come bearing a catch of shellfish, and Tō-no-chūjō summoned them. In response to his questions about their life on the shore, they launched into tales of insecurity and suffering. It was hard to follow their gabble, but he felt for them, moved by the realization that all men share the same emotions. He gave them robes and other presents, which made them think their lives had been worth living after all.

Genji's horses were kept nearby. Tō-no-chūjō watched in fascination as someone fetched their rice straw from a distant structure, which hardly seemed to qualify as a granary. He chanted a snatch of "Asuka Well,"[42] and then began to talk about the past months, punctuating his remarks with frequent tears and laughter. "The little boy's innocence breaks Father's heart," he said. "He worries about him day and night." For Genji, the thought of his son was almost too much.

It would be hopeless to try to record all that was said; I could not even do justice to a small part of the conversation.

They stayed up all night, composing poetry in Chinese. Tō-no-chūjō was in a hurry to get back, worried about gossip despite his protestations. He took up the wine bowl, and the two of them chanted in unison: "Melancholy in my cups, I sprinkle the springtime wine bowl with tears."[43]

Their attendants all wept, sorry to see their masters part after so brief a visit.

A line of wild geese flew across the dawn sky. Genji:

furusato o	I look with envy
izure no haru ka	at geese winging homeward.
yukite mimu	In what springtime

41. The images in this sentence are all drawn from Bo Juyi's description of his hermitage at the foot of Incense-burner Peak. See Tamagami, *Genji monogatari hyōshaku*, 3: 129, on the substitution of "pine" for the "cinnamon tree" of the original.

42. Presumably the line "the fodder is good." For the full song, see "The Broom Tree," n. 5.

43. From a poem composed by Bo Juyi when he parted from his best friend, Yuan Zhen, after meeting him for the first time in several years.

urayamashiki wa	will I set forth from here
kaeru karigane	to see again the capital?

Reluctant to depart, Tō-no-chūjō answered:

akanaku ni	Well may it lose the way
kari no tokoyo o	to the city of blossoms—
tachiwakare	the wild goose that leaves
hana no miyako ni	before it has had its fill
michi ya madowamu	of the far-off fairyland.

He had brought appropriate souvenirs from the capital, all very tasteful. Genji gave him a black horse in appreciation of the visit. "You'll probably think it's unlucky to receive a present from someone in my situation, but he has a tendency to neigh when he feels the wind," he said.[44] The horse was a remarkable animal. In return, Tō-no-chūjō gave him a few little things, including a fine flute, an instrument of some renown, about which he said, "Please value it as a keepsake." Neither of them could make his presents magnificent enough to risk criticism.

The sun had gradually risen. Tō-no-chūjō started off in a flurry of activity, recognizing that he should have left earlier. He looked back again and again, and Genji watched him go, his appearance so pathetic that it seemed he might have been better off without the visit.

"I don't know when I'll see you again. But you surely won't be here forever."

Genji replied:

kumo chikaku	Look at me, O crane,
tobikau tazu mo	from the heavens where you fly
sora ni mi yo	close to the clouds:
ware wa haruhi no	my conscience is as clear
kumori naki mi zo	as a perfect day in spring.

"I feel sure I'll be able to go back. On the other hand, men in my position have found it very hard to resume successful careers, even when they were distinguished figures before, so I really don't have any great desire to see the capital again."

Tō-no-chūjō:

tazuka naki	Yearning for the friend
kumoi ni hitori	with whom he flew wing to wing,
ne o zo naku	the crane flies alone,
tsubasa narabeshi	raising his plaintive voice
tomo o koitsutsu	in the cheerless realm of the clouds.

44. The horse, like its owner, misses the capital when the wind blows from that direction. Genji paraphrases part of a line from one of the Nineteen Old Poems in the Chinese anthology *Wen xuan*: "A Tartar horse likes a wind from the north." For a translation of the poem, see Liu and Lo, *Sunflower Splendor*, p. 30.

"There are many times when I wish I had never accustomed myself to the privilege of your friendship . . ." He hurried off without further speech, leaving Genji to spend the rest of the day in even deeper gloom than usual.

On the first day of the snake in the third month, someone who made rather a fetish of being well-informed said, "It would be a good idea for a person with problems like yours to purify himself today." Genji had been wanting to see the ocean anyway, so he went to the shore. He used bunting to create a makeshift enclosure, summoned a yin-yang master who traveled back and forth between the capital and the province, and had the ritual performed. The sight of the big doll, launched outward in the boat, reminded him of his own plight: [45]

shirazarishi	No common sorrow
ōumi no hara ni	wears down the wanderer
nagarekite	who has drifted here,
hitokata ni ya wa	doll-like, on the alien plain
mono wa kanashiki	of the mighty ocean.

The bright, expansive setting lent an inexpressible beauty to his seated figure. The vast expanse of the sea was perfectly still. Who could tell where those waters were bound? His thoughts moved on to his own situation—his past, his future—and he recited another poem:

yaoyorozu	The manifold host
kami mo aware to	of gods heavenly and earthly
omouramu	must surely pity me,
okaseru tsumi no	for I have been guilty
sore to nakereba	of no offense whatever.

A sudden wind sprang up, and the sky blackened. The purification ritual gave way to an agitated stir. A terrific downpour began, throwing his attendants into such confusion that they failed even to hoist the folding umbrella for his return home. Everything in sight was blown away by the phenomenal wind, which had been completely unexpected, and terrifying breakers made the party run for their lives. The surface of the sea glistened like a silk quilt; the heavens reverberated; lightning flashed. They struggled back to the house, in fear and trembling of being hit by a thunderbolt.

The men were bewildered. "I've never seen anything like it," one of them said.

"A wind will usually give you some warning."

"Totally bizarre."

The sound of thunder filled the air, and the pelting raindrops seemed capable of piercing whatever they struck. Gloomy and perplexed, the men wondered if this might not be the way the world would end. Genji recited a sutra in a calm voice.

45. During a purification ritual, a person rubbed his body against a specially prepared doll to transfer his troubles to it. The doll, usually made of paper, was then set adrift.

The wind continued into the night, but the thunder trailed off around sunset, as though in answer to the attendants' many vows.

"The waves would have swept us into the sea if it had gone on much longer," one of them said.

"I've heard that a tsunami will kill a person in an instant," said someone else.

"I've never seen the like."

Toward dawn, they all began to nod, and Genji dozed off into a dream in which an unidentifiable figure was searching for him. "You've been summoned to the palace; why don't you come?" it demanded.

"The dragon kings in the sea love beauty; one of them must have his eye on me." It was a chilling thought, one that made his present abode seem unendurable.

Akashi

[From the third month of Genji's twenty-seventh year to the eighth month of his twenty-eighth year. Fujitsubo lady: 32–33; Murasaki: 19–20; Rokujō lady: 34–35; Akashi lady: 18–19; Yūgiri, 6–7]

The rain and wind never ceased in the ensuing days, nor did the thunder subside. Innumerable things conspired to exacerbate Genji's loneliness, and he lost his habitual fortitude as he pondered his bleak past and future. What could he do? People would laugh if he let the weather drive him back to the capital without a pardon. And if he simply disappeared into the deep mountains, as was tempting, the gossips would probably say it was only because he had been afraid of the wind and waves, and he would go down in history as an exemplar of skittishness. His dreams were haunted every night by the same figure as before.

The days passed with no rifts in the clouds, and the lack of news from the capital grew increasingly worrisome. Was he destined to rot here like this forever? But the weather was too harsh for anyone to put his head outdoors, and no messengers arrived.

There was one exception—a wretched emissary from the Nijō Mansion, who was soaking wet when he finally reached them. It was inappropriate to his own station in life, Genji realized, and also a sign of vanishing self-respect, that he should feel as though he had found a long-lost friend in this humble fellow—a man whom he would have scarcely been able to identify as human if he had met him on the road in the old days, and whom his attendants would have promptly chased out of the way.

Murasaki had written, "This unbelievable stretch of rainy weather makes me feel that the very skies must be choked with grief. I lack even the consolation of looking out toward Suma."

   urakaze ya   In days when waves of tears
  ika ni fukuramu   ceaselessly drench the sleeves of one
   omoiyaru   who worries from afar,

| sode uchinurashi | how great must be the fury |
| namima naki koro | of the gales that blast your shore! |

There was much else of a sad, affecting nature. New tears rose in Genji's eyes the moment he opened the letter—enough to "make the beaches more damp"—so that was almost blinded.[1]

"People in the capital say this wind and rain are a terrible divine message; I've heard talk of a Benevolent King service. And the senior nobles going to the palace . . . all the streets are blocked; the government's at a standstill." The messenger's speech was halting and uncouth, but Genji called him in for questioning, eager for any news of the city.

"The rain hasn't let up for days, and the wind never stops blowing. It's so unusual, everybody's amazed. But we haven't had this thunder all the time, or this hail that's hard enough to drill holes in the ground." The man was obviously terrified by the fury of the elements at Suma, and his woebegone face made Genji's attendants feel gloomier than ever.

More than once of late, Genji had been beset by an irrepressible feeling that this might be the way the world would end. But on the following day, beginning before dawn, a violent wind blew up, a high tide came flooding in, and mighty waves crashed ashore, their violence menacing the very rocks and mountains. The thunder and lightning were beyond description. Fearful of being struck at any moment, the attendants all panicked. "What crimes in a previous existence can have brought us to this extremity?" they lamented. "Are we to die without ever meeting our parents again—without ever seeing the faces of our dear wives and children?"

Genji pulled himself together, seeking reassurance in the thought that he had committed no sin for which he must die on this shore. To calm his agitated men, he made offerings of colored strips of cloth, accompanied by many fervent petitions. "O gods of Sumiyoshi, it is you who protect these environs. If you are truly manifestations of Buddhist divinities, come to my aid!" he prayed. His attendants feared for their own lives, of course, but they were also dismayed by the possibility that a man like their master might meet an unprecedented death in the sea, and some of them managed to summon up enough courage and composure to raise a loud chorus of prayer to the buddhas and gods. "I offer my life in exchange for his," each of them shouted. They turned toward the Sumiyoshi Shrine and offered all kinds of petitions.

"Our lord was reared in the emperor's great palace and enjoyed every pleasure, but that did not keep him from rescuing innumerable sinking souls all over Japan with his largesse. For what transgression must he now be

1. Ki no Tsurayuki (TN i.7): yuku hito mo / tomaru mo sode no / namidagawa / migiwa nomi koso / nuremasarikere ("The rivers of tears on the sleeves of one who goes and one who remains rise until they overflow and make the beaches more damp").

punished by drowning in these evil angry seas? Make your judgment, gods of heaven and earth!" they demanded. And again, "Why, when he has already been falsely accused, stripped of offices and rank, and driven from house and home to spend his days in constant uncertainty and sorrow— why should he also have to suffer this terrible experience, which may cost him his life? He wonders if this might be a punishment for a sin committed in a previous existence, or if he is being repaid for a transgression in this life. If the gods and buddhas are just, let them put an end to his travail!"

Genji prayed also to the dragon kings in the sea and to the myriads of gods, but the thunder crashed louder than ever. Lightning struck a gallery adjoining his quarters, and leaping flames burned it to the ground. His distracted attendants moved him to a rear building—a kitchen, by the look of it—and all of them crowded inside, regardless of rank, their frantic shouts rivaling the thunderclaps. When night fell, the sky already looked as though someone had rubbed it with an inkstick.

In time, the wind blew itself out. The rain subsided and the stars began to shine. Genji's men thought about escorting him back to the main building from his squalid shelter, which was an appallingly inappropriate lodging, but the surviving apartments were themselves unappealing, bereft of their blinds, which had all blown away, and full of confused people trampling noisily around. They vacillated, wondering if it might not be best to wait until morning. Meanwhile, Genji intoned pious words and pondered his situation with an uneasy mind. After the moon rose to reveal the closeness of the high tide mark, he opened the rude door and gazed absently at the surf, which was still turbulent in the wake of the storm. There was no discriminating person in the immediate vicinity—nobody capable of taking the past and present into account and understanding exactly what was going on. The only visitors were a group of humble seafolk, come to stand guard over their exalted neighbor. He found their incomprehensible chatter odd, but his men could not very well shoo them away. "The tide would have swept everything away if the wind had kept up a little longer. The gods really helped us!" a voice said. It would be a sad understatement to say that he felt forlorn as he listened. [His poem:]

umi ni masu	But for the succor
kami no tasuke ni	of the divinities
kakarazuba	who dwell in the sea,
shio no yaoai ni	I would have been swept away
sasuraenamashi	by the mighty tidal flow.

He had kept his composure while the wind raged all day, but it was an exhausting ordeal, and he dozed off unawares. As he slept, leaning against a support that was all the comfort his rude accommodations could provide, he thought the late emperor came and stood before him. "What are you doing in this sordid place?" his father asked. He took him by the hand and pulled him to his feet. "Get into a boat and leave this coast immediately; let the Sumiyoshi gods be your guides," he said.

Genji was overjoyed to see him. "My life has been one sorrow after another since I bid farewell to your respected person. Right now, I feel like dying on this shore," he said.

"That wouldn't do at all! This is nothing but a small karmic retribution. I was guilty of no misgovernment during my reign, but I committed some sins without realizing it, and I have been too busy expiating them to concern myself with this world. Still, I couldn't bear to witness your misery, so I plunged into the sea and emerged on this shore. Tired as I am, I need to use this opportunity to speak to His Majesty; I must hurry off to the capital." He started away.

Saddened that the parting should come so soon, Genji burst into tears. "I want to go with you," he said. He looked up and saw only the shining countenance of the moon. He had no feeling of having dreamed. His father's presence seemed to linger, and a cloud trailing across the sky evoked poignant emotions. He had been vouchsafed a brief but vivid glimpse of the face for which he had yearned, fretting at his inability to see it even in a dream; and the vision, at least, was something he could always summon to mind. With a full heart, he thought, "He flew to help me when I was in the depths of despair, almost ready to die." It came to him that the storm had been a good thing, and in the aftermath of the dream, he felt trustful and happy. Then, with a sudden overwhelming surge of emotion, disappointment at the brevity of the encounter made him forget the problems of his waking existence. Why had the dream ended before he could answer? On the chance that his father might visit him again, he tried his best to return to sleep, but his eyes refused to close, and presently it was almost dawn.

A small boat came in to the shore, and two or three men approached the travel lodging. When Genji's attendants asked who they were, one of them said, "The new Buddhist novice, the former governor of this province, has fitted out a boat and come here from Akashi. If Yoshikiyo, the Minamoto lesser captain, is here, he would like to meet him and explain."

Yoshikiyo was surprised and puzzled. "I knew him when I was in Harima and have been friendly with him for several years, but there's a little bad feeling between us at the moment, a private matter, and we haven't exchanged any letters for a long time, not even perfunctory greetings. I can't imagine why he'd come here in these rough seas," he said.

With his dream in mind, Genji said, "Go and meet him right away."

Yoshikiyo went to the boat and met the novice. He could not understand how he had managed to set sail in such a violent storm.

"Early this month," the novice said, "a strange figure visited my dreams and told me something I could scarcely believe. 'I'll give you a clear sign on the thirteenth. Fit out a boat, and be sure to head for Suma as soon as the wind and rain die down,' he said. Just to see what would happen, I did equip a boat, and then there was this terrifying rain and wind and thunder. Today is the thirteenth, and considering that there have been people who have saved the state by trusting their dreams—many in foreign lands, too—I thought I shouldn't let night fall without reporting the matter to His Lordship, even if he didn't consider it worth bothering about. When I launched the boat, a strange wind blew just behind us, and that's how we reached this shore. It's an unmistakable case of divine guidance. I am wondering if His Lordship recollects anything that might have happened here. May I impose on you to tell him all this?"

Yoshikiyo conveyed the message in private. Genji pondered his past and future in the light of the unsettling dreams and happenings that had seemed so much like divine communications. If he tried to avoid the criticism of posterity by rejecting what might be a true offer of divine assistance, he would run the risk of incurring more ridicule than if he accepted the novice's story at face value. It was bad enough to oppose the will of a living mortal. Even in trifling matters, it was appropriate, after all, to defer to seniors, and also to men of high rank and reputation, and to be guided by their opinions. Didn't the ancient sage say, "Follow others and avoid reproach?" Salvaging his posthumous reputation was by no means an overriding concern for someone who had just passed through an almost fatal series of horrifying experiences. And then there were his father's instructions in the dream. What need for further doubt? He framed a reply.

"I have suffered every conceivable bizarre trial in this alien place, but no messenger has come from the capital to ask after me. I've simply stared at the sun and moon, watching them journey toward their unknown destinations, and looking on them as friends from home. 'Great, then, is my delight when I behold the fishing boat.'[2] Might there be a quiet retreat for me on your shore?"

Delighted, the novice made grateful assent.

Genji's men urged him to embark before daybreak. He did so, taking along only four or five intimates, and arrived at Akashi like a bird in flight, thanks to the same strange wind. The two shores were almost within crawling distance of one another—a mere half hour apart[3]—but still, there was something uncanny about the wind's behavior.

Just as Yoshikiyo had said, the beauty of the coastal scenery at Akashi was incomparable. It would have been wholly to Genji's liking if only there had not been so many people around. The novice owned land both on the coast and in the mountains, and there were many noteworthy buildings in various places, erected with careful regard for the seasons and the environ-

2. Ki no Tsurayuki (GSS 1224): nami ni nomi / nuretsuru mono o / fuku kaze no / tayori ureshiki / ama no tsuribune ("Great is my delight when I behold the fishing boat of a beach dweller, sped by the wind to one whose sleeves are wet as from waves"). Composed to welcome an unexpected visitor.

3. An hour by modern Western count.

ment—a reed-thatched cottage at the beach, from which to enjoy the changing seasons; a majestic Concentration Hall beside a stream from the hills, a location suitable for rituals and calm reflection on the life to come; and, to meet the needs of the present world, groups of rice storehouses containing the bounty of the autumn fields, reaped and stored as sustenance for the owner's remaining years.

Alarmed by the high tides, the novice had recently moved his daughter and the others to a house at the foot of the hills, and Genji was able to go to the main residence with an easy mind. The sun had already risen when he left the boat for a carriage, and a mere glimpse of his face was enough to make the novice forget his advanced age and feel like a man with years left to live. He offered an immediate prayer of thanksgiving to the Sumiyoshi gods, his face wreathed in smiles. To his mind, he held the light of the sun and the moon in his hands; it was only natural that he showered the guest with attentions.

The setting was superb, of course. Only a painter of perfect sensitivity could have done justice to the tastefulness of the buildings, the charm of the groves, rocks, and grasses in the garden, and the indescribable beauty of the coastal waters. It was infinitely more cheerful and appealing than the place where Genji had been staying during the past months. The furnishings were as elegant as Yoshikiyo had said: the owner's lifestyle equaled that of the most august personages in the capital, and, indeed, seemed rather to surpass such establishments in luxury and brilliance.

After Genji had regained some of his composure, he wrote letters for the capital. He summoned Murasaki's messenger, who was still at Suma bemoaning the difficulties of the route and the miseries of the journey; gave him many presents, all finer than his station warranted; and dispatched him. He probably sent detailed descriptions of recent events to the prayer monks with whom he was on close terms, and also to other people with whom he would naturally have wanted to keep in touch. To the Fujitsubo lady alone, he related the strange circumstances of his escape from death. The response to Murasaki's loving expressions of concern did not come easily, and his letter to her was composed in a different way from the others, with frequent pauses to wipe his eyes.

"Now that I have suffered every imaginable disaster, just one thing after another, I simply want to turn my back on the world, but never for an instant do I forget your face as you said, '. . . to look into this mirror,' and the thought of taking religious vows without seeing you again is so painful that my other troubles pale into insignificance."

haruka ni mo	I have followed the shore
omoiyaru ka na	to a place even more remote
shirazarishi	than the one once unknown.
ura yori ochi ni	How great is the distance now
urazutai shite	from which I send my thoughts to you!

"I still feel as though I were dreaming: I'm writing this without awakening, and it may not make much sense."[4]

His letter was indeed rambling and incoherent, scribbled in a state of manifest distraction, which made his attendants curious about its contents. They realized that Murasaki occupied a unique place in his affections. Each of them probably sent home gloomy tidings of his own.

The persistent rains had ceased, the skies had cleared all the way to the horizon, and the fishermen seemed in good humor. Unlike Suma's lonely strand, where even a shore-dweller's rocky shelter was a rarity, Akashi was too populous to suit Genji, but the new surroundings offered much that was novel and interesting, and his spirits took a turn for the better.

The novice devoted himself to religious pursuits with admirable sincerity. He did worry about his daughter's future, however, and there were numerous occasions when he unburdened himself to Genji in a pathetic manner. To Genji, who had heard earlier of the girl's charms, his unexpected, roundabout arrival at Akashi seemed to suggest a bond from a previous existence. At the same time, he felt that he ought to confine himself to religious matters so long as he remained in his present predicament. There was also Murasaki in the capital to consider: she would regard it as a breach of his promises if he suddenly took up with somebody else, and he would be ashamed to face her. Thus he avoided any hint of interest in the daughter. But this is by no means to say that he viewed her with indifference, for many small things had conspired to convince him that she was exceptional in character and appearance.

Respectful of Genji's privacy, the novice stayed in a separate minor building and seldom visited the main hall. It was not a state of affairs to his liking. He would have wished to be with the guest morning and night; and he prayed harder than ever to the gods and buddhas for the fulfillment of his heart's desire. Although he was around sixty, he was a dapper man, appropriately thin from the practice of austerities. As a result, perhaps, of the good stock from which he had sprung—and despite a certain eccentricity and elderly vagueness—he was also knowledgeable about ancient customs, free of any taint of vulgarity, and well educated. Genji found a little relief from his boredom by encouraging him to tell tales of the past. In bits and pieces, he related stories of earlier public events—matters concerning which Genji had had little opportunity to become informed, engrossed as he had been in his own official duties and private affairs—and some of his yarns were so interesting that Genji actually thought he would have been the poorer if he had not come to such a place and met such a man.

4. This sentence, ambiguous in the original, can also be taken as an apology for future behavior: " . . . there may be many lapses on my part while I stay in this dream." Genji senses that he is caught up in a fated sequence of events, which will ultimately ensure his ascendancy by giving him a daughter who can become an imperial consort. (Murasaki is childless and remains so.)

The novice thus associated with Genji on fairly intimate terms, but he was too awed by his noble bearing and magnificent presence to speak out on the subject that was closest to his heart, regardless of his previous assertions. It was a frustrating, tantalizing situation, he lamented in his discussions with the girl's mother. As for the daughter herself, she had been made poignantly aware of her own inferior status by the sight of Genji's breathtaking beauty, coming as it did in a place where there were not even any ordinary fellows who could be called handsome; and she considered him hopelessly beyond reach.[5] Her parents' scheming appalled her; she felt worse than if no such paragon had appeared.

The fourth month arrived. The novice provided tasteful robes, curtain-dais hangings, and other things for the change of dress. Genji regarded his eagerness to leave nothing undone as pathetic and a bit officious, but he let him do as he pleased, aware that he was a man of proud and noble character.

A steady stream of solicitous messages arrived from the capital.

On a peaceful moonlit night, when the sea was visible to the horizon under a cloudless sky, the quiet waters merged in Genji's mind with the lake at home, and he was overcome by a feeling of unutterable yearning for he knew not what. The only land in sight was the distant silhouette of Awaji Island. He intoned, "In the distance . . . wondering, 'Can that be it?'"[6] [His poem:]

a wa to miru	This evening's moon
awaji no shima no	evokes in encompassing light
aware sae	Awaji Island,
nokoru kuma naku	where one wonders, "Can that be it?"—
sumeru yo no tsuki	and all my sorrow as well.

Taking his long-neglected seven-stringed koto from its bag, he struck a few notes, and his attendants watched with deep emotion, saddened by the incongruity of the setting. Then he played "Kōryō" with all the skill at his command.[7] The music-loving young ladies-in-waiting thrilled to the sound as it reached the house below the hill, mingling with the soughing of the pines and the murmur of the waves. Humble folk from here and there were lured forth to saunter along the beach and catch cold in the wind—people who would have seemed incapable of telling one song from another. And the novice hurried off to join his guest, unable to concentrate on his rituals.

"I can't help remembering the world I've left behind; it all comes flooding

5. It is not clear how the girl can have seen Genji, since they live in different places.

6. Ōshikōchi no Mitsune (SKKS 1515): awaji nite / awa to haruka ni / mishi tsuki no / chi-kaki koyoi wa / tokorogara ka mo ("Perhaps the place explains the closeness this evening of the moon I saw in the distance at Awaji, wondering, 'Can that be it?'"). There is a pun on the first two syllables of Awaji (the name of an island visible from Akashi) and *a wa*, "[as for] that."

7. "Kōryō" is said to have been a "secret melody" of Chinese origin.

back again. This place tonight must be very like the pure land in which I pray to be reborn," the novice said in tearful praise. Genji's own thoughts strayed to the kinds of things he and others had done at seasonal concerts in the past—to how one person or another had played on strings or flute, or had sung, and how he had always been singled out for praise, and had been made much of by everyone from the emperor down. As his fingers moved over the strings now, he felt that this could only be a dream, and the chill sounds he evoked drew tears from the listeners' eyes.

Servants were sent to the hill house for a lute and a thirteen-stringed koto, and the novice performed one or two interesting and unusual pieces of the kind associated with itinerant lutanists in clerical robes.[8] He offered the koto to Genji, who played a little while, long enough for the novice to realize that he was a master of that instrument as well. Even a performance of no great distinction may sound impressive in the right circumstances, but here an unbroken expanse of sea stretched far into the distance, the fresh charm of the flourishing natural groves surpassed the choicest spring blossoms or autumn leaves, and a clapper rail's call brought moving thoughts of the poem, "Who . . . bars the gate?"[9]

Genji was moved by the peerless tone of the novice's instruments and the gentle appeal of his touch. "What's really pleasant is to hear a woman play the thirteen-stringed koto in an intimate, relaxed manner," he said. It was a general observation, but the novice misunderstood him. He replied with a broad smile. "No woman's touch could be more appealing than Your Lordship's. I was taught by one of Emperor Daigo's pupils, and although my own lack of ability has caused me to abandon and forget worldly things, I've turned to the strings when I've felt especially low. There's someone here who has imitated my style with amazing fidelity, and who consequently plays very much as my teacher, the prince, did. But I am a mountain rustic with poor ears; perhaps it's only the wind in the pine trees that I hear.[10] I'd like very much to try to arrange for you to listen to her in private." He trembled with excitement as he spoke, all but weeping.

Genji put the instrument aside. "I should have known better than to play in a place where people wouldn't hear my koto as a koto," he said.[11] "For

8. *Biwa hōshi*, best known as reciters of *The Tale of the Heike.*

9. Identified in a Heian-period commentary as an allusion to an otherwise unidentified poem: mada yoi ni / uchikite / tataku / kuina ka na / ta ga kado sashite / irenu naruramu ("The night is still young when the clapper rail taps. Who might it be—that someone who bars the gate and won't let it come in?"). The clapper rail, or ruddy crake, is a small, secretive bird whose single note suggests the sound of a knock at the door.

10. Old commentary: matsukaze ni / mimi naretekeru / yamabushi wa / koto o koto to mo / omowazarikeri ("The mountain rustic, his ears attuned to the voice of the wind in the pines, is unable to recognize a koto as a koto"). See Tamagami, *Genji monogatari hyōshaku*, 3: 191.

11. Genji twists the meaning of the same poem: "I am clearly an amateur in the company of experts—people who will scarcely consider my koto a koto."

some reason, it's always been women who have made a study of the thirteen-stringed koto. Emperor Saga gave personal instruction to his fifth daughter, and she is supposed to have been the finest musician of her time, but nobody keeps her style alive. Our famous contemporaries merely strum the instrument as a pastime. It's fascinating that the tradition should have survived here without anyone's knowing about it. I must hear your pupil."

"No problem! If you want to call her in, that's fine, too. We know there was once somebody who won praise as a lutanist, even though she was only a merchant's wife.[12] Speaking of the lute, few musicians in any era have been able to elicit that instrument's true tones, but this same person plays it with really superior fluency and charm. I don't know how she's managed to master it. It hurts to hear such music merge with the noise of crashing waves, but on the other hand, there are times when her playing takes my mind off my troubles."

Intrigued by the refinement of his taste, Genji gave him the koto to play in place of the lute, and he addressed the instrument in a style that was indeed superior to the ordinary run of performances. He played strains no longer to be heard in our day, employing a brilliant Chinese fingering technique, and agitating the strings with his left hand to produce deep, silvery tones. They were not on the shores of the Sea of Ise, but Genji told the good singers among his men to sing, "Let's pick up the seashells on the clean strand" and other songs.[13] From time to time, he took up the clappers and joined the chorus, causing the novice to pause and offer words of praise.

The novice presented an array of ingenious tidbits to accompany the wine, plied the gentlemen with drink, and otherwise saw to it that the night became an occasion for forgetting their woes.

A cool wind blew through the pine trees as the night advanced, and the setting moon shone ever brighter as it neared the horizon. In the pervading quiet, the novice unburdened himself without reserve, speaking in fits and starts of his worries during his early days at Akashi, and of his present religious activities, and voluntarily bringing up the subject of his daughter. It was amusing that he should be so forward about the girl, but some of his remarks touched Genji's heart.

"Awkward as it is to say so, I believe that the gods and buddhas I've prayed to for years may have decided to subject you to temporary hardships because they pitied me, and that that explains why you have come like this, however briefly, to a place where you could never have dreamed of living.

12. A reference to the former singing girl, now a tea merchant's wife, who is the subject of Bo Juyi's "Lute Song." For a translation of the poem, see Bynner and Kiang, *Jade Mountain*, pp. 125–29.

13. "The Sea of Ise" (a *saibara*): "On the clean strand of the Sea of Ise, of the Sea of Ise, let us when the tide is out pluck the sea grape! pick up the seashells, YA! pick up the gemlike pebbles, YA!"

It's been eighteen years since I first placed my faith in the gods of Sumiyoshi. Ever since my daughter was a baby, I've had plans for her, and I've never failed to visit the shrine twice a year, once in the spring and once in the fall.[14] I hope to be reborn in the pure land, of course, but when I perform the six daily devotions, I merely pray to have my high aspirations for her fulfilled. Even though I've turned into a miserable mountain peasant because of bad karma from a previous existence, my father was a minister of state. I used to fear that this descent into rusticity would doom my posterity to complete obscurity, but I've had something to hope for since the girl's birth. My heart is set on offering her to a high-ranking gentleman in the capital, so I've offended many whose status is as low as my own, and have borne the brunt of numerous unpleasant experiences. But none of that bothers me in the least. I tell her, 'As long as I'm alive, I'll manage to take all the care of you my meager resources permit. If I die while you're still single, be ready to drown yourself in the sea.' " Weeping, he said many other things of which I could not hope to give a proper report.

Genji's eyes filled with tears as he listened, for it was a time when his own mind was also beset by worries. "I couldn't understand what I'd done wrong—why I had to suffer from unjust accusations and wander in alien places—but when I take into account what you've said tonight, I feel from the bottom of my heart that the two of us must be linked by a firm bond from a previous existence. You were well aware of it; why didn't you tell me sooner? Once I left the capital, I turned against the transitory world and concentrated on religious matters; and as time passed, I lapsed into a state of unrelieved depression. I had heard a little about your daughter, but my self-confidence was shattered: I believed you'd think it was unlucky to get involved with someone as insignificant as I've become. So, then, it seems that you'll be kind enough to guide me? It will be a comforting change, too, from the loneliness of an unshared bed," he said.

The novice was beside himself with joy. [His poem:]

> hitorine wa   Do you too understand
> kimi mo shirinu ya   how it is to sleep alone—
> tsurezure to   the dreariness
> omoiakashi no   of lying bored and wakeful
> urasabishisa o   nightlong at Akashi Shore?

"And please imagine how much more discouraged I myself have felt during all these years of constant worry." A-tremble with excitement, he still retained his air of gentility.

"But surely," Genji said, "it must be less lonely for someone like yourself who has grown accustomed to these shores." [His poem:]

14. The daughter, who now appears to be around 18 by Japanese count, would have been only nine when Yoshikiyo described her in "Young Murasaki."

tabigoromo	Beset by the grief
uraganashisa ni	of one who wears travel garb
akashiwabi	I long in vain for dawn,
kusa no makura wa	unable to weave a dream
yume mo musubazu	from my pillow of grass.

Sitting there at his ease, radiating charm, he was a figure of indescribable elegance.

The novice rattled on, but it would be tedious to write down everything he said. As it is, I have sometimes erred in recording his speeches, and I may have made him look more foolish and eccentric than he was.

Around noon on the following day, while the novice bided his time with heightened spirits and cautious optimism, Genji sent a message to the hill house. In view of what he had heard about the daughter's accomplishments, which promised to put his own in the shade, he gave serious attention to the possibility that this obscure corner might conceal an unexpected treasure, someone superior to many a fine city lady. He took immense pains with his note, which he inscribed on a sheet of saffron-colored paper from Korea:

ochikochi mo	I call where treetops
shiranu kumoi ni	mark the house of which faint tidings
nagamewabi	reached me while I gazed,
kasumeshi yado no	sunk in gloomy thought, at skies
kozue o zo tou	where I know not near or far.

"'. . . by the ardor of my love.'"[15] I believe I am correct in thinking that he wrote nothing more.

The novice had gone in private to wait at the hill house, and when the messenger made his expected appearance, he served wine until the man's senses reeled.

The daughter was very slow to reply. The novice went inside to hurry her up, but she declined to listen. Too embarrassed and diffident to try to answer a letter of such intimidating elegance, and overwhelmed by the vast gulf between Genji's status and her own, she pleaded illness and lay down against a support. Despairing of talking her around, the novice wrote in her stead. "Perhaps because rustic sleeves cannot accommodate such graciousness, my daughter is too awestricken to look at your letter.[16] Watching her, I have thought this:

15. Anonymous (KKS 503): omou ni wa / shinoburu koto zo / makenikeru / iro ni wa ideji to / omoishi mono o ("How very firmly I had decided to hide it—and yet my resolve has been vanquished by the ardor of my love").

16. Similar sentiments are expressed in an anonymous old poem (KKS 865): ureshiki o / nani ni tsutsumamu / karakoromo / tamoto yutaka ni / tate to iwamashi o ("In what might I wrap the great happiness I feel? Had I foreseen it, I would have said, 'Make wide sleeves on this robe of Chinese silk'").

nagamuramu	That her gaze, like yours,
onaji kumoi o	should turn in pensive thought
nagamuru wa	to those selfsame skies—
omoi mo onaji	surely it must be because
omoi naruran	the thoughts are also the same.

"Forgive me for straying into the realm of romance."

The letter was written on Michinoku paper in an old-fashioned hand, embellished with smart flourishes. He did seem interested in matters of the heart, Genji thought in some surprise.

As a reward for his services, the novice gave the messenger a superb set of women's robes.

Genji wrote again on the following day. "I've never received a surrogate letter before."

ibuseku mo	Overcome with gloom,
kokoro ni mono o	I suffer agonies
nayamu ka na	in my inmost heart,
ya yo ya ika ni to	for nobody cares to ask,
tou hito mo nami	"Come, now, how is it with you?"

"I cannot speak . . ."[17]

This time, he wrote in a beautiful hand on very soft, thin paper. No young girl could have looked at it with indifference—not unless she was irremediably shy and retiring. To the daughter it seemed quite wonderful, but she considered a relationship with him out of the question for someone of her inferior status; it was merely cause for tears that he should approach her as an equal. She adopted the same immobile pose as before, and only after a veritable barrage of entreaties did she consent to write a few words on a sheet of heavily scented purple paper, varying the blackness of the ink to conceal any possible calligraphic flaws:

omouramu	What is the extent
kokoro no hodo ya	of the love you profess?
ya yo ika ni	Has rumor sufficed
mada minu hito no	to trouble the mind of one
kiki ka nayamamu	who has never yet met me?

Her handwriting and literary address were aristocratic, not vastly inferior to those of a great lady.

Genji was diverted by the correspondence, which brought back memories of his life in the capital, but he preferred not to attract comment by appearing overeager. He wrote at intervals of two or three days, choosing plausible occasions—tedious evenings, lonely mornings before daybreak, and other

17. Old commentary: koishi to mo / mada minu hito no / iigatami / kokoro ni mono no / nagekashiki ka na ("An indefinable feeling of melancholy pervades my spirit; I cannot speak of my love to one I have never met").

times when he guessed that her feelings might resemble his—and her replies were never inadequate. Impressed by her apparent prudence and dignity, he felt a strong desire to meet her. On the other hand, he remembered with some distaste that Yoshikiyo had talked as though she were his private property. It would be a sore blow to him if Genji thwarted his longtime ambition by snatching her from under his nose.

Now that he had traveled beyond the Suma Barrier, he worried about Murasaki more than ever. What would he do if anything happened to her? It was no time for silly games.[18] He sometimes weakened to the extent of wondering if he might not smuggle her into Akashi, but he always reconsidered. Surely he would not have to go on like this year after year. Why expose himself to criticism now?

One divine message followed another at court that year, and there were many causes for uneasiness. On the thirteenth of the third month, during a stormy night of thunder, lightning, rain, and wind, the emperor dreamed that his late father came to the foot of the stairs, near the *kawatake* bamboo, and stood scowling at him with a highly displeased expression on his face. He straightened up respectfully, and his father addressed him at length. It would seem that he probably talked about Genji. Frightened, but also moved to deep pity, he reported the dream to his mother, the Kokiden lady.

"When it rains and storms at night, people tend to dream about things that are on their minds. It's nothing to get into a panic about," she said.

Whether or not it was because he had met the full force of his father's glare in the dream, the emperor developed a distressing eye complaint. He and the Kokiden lady both performed every conceivable abstinence ritual. Then the chancellor, his grandfather, died. In view of the old gentleman's age, his passing was only to have been expected, but it was one more in a series of disturbing incidents. Then the Kokiden lady herself began to suffer from a vaguely debilitating ailment. It was most upsetting for the emperor. If Genji had truly committed no offense to justify his present adversity, karmic retribution was sure to follow. He told his mother more than once that he would like to restore Genji to his old position, but she always countered with a sharp reproof. "They'll criticize you for being flighty. What will people say if you pardon a malefactor before he's even been gone from the city for three years?" Time passed as he hesitated, and the health of both declined.

At Akashi, the shore wind blew with the special loneliness of autumn, and Genji felt very forlorn in his empty bed. From time to time, he suggested to the novice that he find a way to bring his daughter to the beach house without attracting attention. (He could not see his way clear to going to the hill house.) But the lady was of no mind to cooperate. In her view, only the

18. Anonymous (KKS 1025): arinu ya to / kokoromigatera / aimineba / tawaburenikuki / made zo koishiki ("When I stay away, just as a trial, to see if I can get along, my passion grows too intense to allow such silly games").

humblest country maid, someone in truly dire straits, would fling herself into the arms of a flirtatious visitor from the capital. She would face a future of abject misery if she yielded to a man who considered her unworthy of serious consideration, as Genji undoubtedly did. As long as she continued to live a sheltered life at home, her parents could cling to their impossibly extravagant hopes for her, but such a marriage would bring them endless anguish, not the joy they expected. It was sufficient happiness to exchange notes while he stayed at Akashi. For years, tucked away in her remote corner, she had heard talk of him and wished to catch a glimpse of such a paragon some day; and now, of all things, he was living where she could actually see him, if imperfectly—where she could hear the wind-borne strains of the koto he was reputed to play with unmatched skill, and could be cognizant of all his daily activities. Furthermore, he had gone so far as to acknowledge her existence and write to her. It was more than enough for a girl stranded among fishermen. Eternally conscious of the disparity in their statuses, she could not bring herself to think of meeting him on closer terms.

To her parents, it had seemed that their prayers of many years were about to be answered, but now they began to reconsider, beset by misgivings. It would be terrible for her if they blithely brought the two together, only to have Genji refuse to take her seriously. Despite his glittering reputation, the outcome could be devastating. Had it been a mistake, after all, to form their entire plan on the basis of indications from unseen powers, without considering either the man's attitude or the girl's karma?

Genji kept after his host. "As I listen to the waves nowadays, I long to hear the koto you told me about. Otherwise, the season will go to waste," he said.

The novice gave a diviner quiet instructions to choose a suitable day. He personally fussed over his daughter's room until it shone, paying no attention to his wife's nervous flutterings and saying nothing to any of the servants. And when a brilliant moon rose on the night of the thirteenth, he sent Genji a note, which consisted of a single phrase: "On a night too fine to waste."[19] A bit suggestive, Genji thought, but he put on an informal cloak, groomed himself, and set out late at night. He rode on horseback instead of using the resplendent carriage provided by the novice, which struck him as excessive; and he went alone, except for Koremitsu and a servant or two.

The full expanse of the shoreline was visible as he rode toward the hill house, which was a fair distance away. Gazing at the moonlit bays, "scenes to be viewed with dear comrades,"[20] he thought of his precious Murasaki,

---

19. Minamoto no Saneakira (GSS 103): atarayo no / tsuki to hana to o / onajiku wa / aware shireran / hito ni misebaya ("All being equal, it is to someone of rare taste that I would display the moon and blossoms on a night too fine to waste").

20. Old commentary: omoudochi / iza mi ni yukamu / tamatsushima / irie no soko ni / shizumu tsukikage ("Come, dear comrade! Let's set out together to see the moonlight on the bottom of the inlet at Tamatsushima Island").

and was seized by an urge to go past his destination and head toward the capital. He murmured a poem under his breath:

aki no yo no	Fly through the heavens,
tsukige no koma yo	O horse with moon in your coat.
wa ga kouru	That I may see her,
kumoi ni kakere	even for a little while,
toki no ma mo mimu	fly to the beloved city![21]

Set far back in a grove of trees, the house was worthy of note, an exceptionally elegant residence. In contrast to the one on the shore, which was grand and fashionable, its appearance suggested that the occupants must lead lonely lives. Anyone who lived there would run through all the melancholy thoughts a mind could store, Genji thought in an access of pity. From the chapel nearby, the novice's handbell rang in mournful accompaniment to the wind in the pines; and the exposed roots of the pines growing from the rocks made their own contribution to the tasteful effect. Insect voices chorused in the gardens.

Genji surveyed the scene. The daughter's private residence had been polished to perfection, and moonlight entered where a handsome wooden door stood the slightest bit ajar. He spoke a hesitant word or two, but the unhappy lady made no reply, determined to avoid meeting him on intimate terms. She was irritatingly high and mighty, he thought. In his experience, not even the proudest and least accessible of women had spurned a courtship carried to this stage. Was she snubbing him because he had come down in the world? He tried to decide what to do. To force himself on her in these particular circumstances would be a mistake. On the other hand, it would be humiliating to emerge the loser in a battle of wills. One would indeed have liked to "show him to someone of rare taste" as he stood there, agitated and annoyed.[22]

A nearby curtain streamer brushed against a thirteen-stringed koto, eliciting a faint sound. In his mind's eye, he saw her as she must have sat at the instrument, relaxed and unselfconscious, making music to pass the time. It was an interesting picture. He launched forth into a series of pretty speeches. Would she not even play the koto he had heard so much about? [He recited a poem:]

mutsugoto o	I long for a partner
katariawasemu	in intimate talk—for the chance
hito mo ga na	of awakening,
ukiyo no yume mo	halfway through, from this dream
nakaba samu ya to	of a world of sorrows.

21. Commentators describe the coat of the "moon-coated" (*tsukige*) horse as resembling the plumage of the Japanese crested ibis (*toki*), a white bird with "pale pink flight feathers, tail and beneath-wings." Description from Yamashina, *Birds in Japan*, p. 145.

22. See Saneakira's poem, n. 19, above.

[She replied:]

akenu yo ni   For one who wanders
yagate madoeru   ever lost in eternal night,
kokoro ni wa   it is impossible
izure o yume to   to speak with understanding
wakite kataramu   of which is dream, which reality.

The aura of breeding conveyed by her shadowy presence was a potent reminder of the lady who now lived in Ise.

Dismayed by these happenings, which had caught her completely off guard, the daughter fled to a neighboring room and managed to fasten the door shut. Genji gave no sign of trying to break his way in. But it could hardly have been expected that the matter would end there.

The lady was very aristocratic—tall and slender—and Genji felt quite at a disadvantage. He found it moving to reflect on the strength of the karmic bond that must have forced this relationship into being. No doubt his ardor was warmer now that the two had actually met. Usually so disagreeable, the long autumn night seemed to rush toward its close, and he took his leave with many loving words, uneasy lest others learn of his visit.

He dispatched his morning-after note in strict privacy. (One wonders if his conscience had proved troublesome.) Equally concerned to keep the secret, the people at the hill house refrained from bestowing lavish presents on the messenger, for whom the novice felt very sorry.

Afterward, Genji visited the lady from time to time, always with precautions to avoid notice. There were occasions when he stayed home, unwilling to risk a chance encounter with a gossipy fisherman—which was all too likely, he felt, in view of the fairly long distance between the houses—and at such times, she thought in despair that it was no more than she had always expected. Her father, who shared her misgivings, forgot about his prayers for rebirth in paradise and spent all his time waiting for Genji to put in an appearance. It seemed a pity that such mental turmoil should afflict a man who had made it a point to divorce himself from worldly concerns.

Genji knew—and from this we may understand the depth of his love— that he would feel penitence and shame if Murasaki learned about the Akashi affair from other people, even through whispers on the wind, and if she were to turn against him, even in jest, for keeping it a secret. Recalling times when she had reacted to his adventures with anxiety and indignation, gentle though she usually was, he asked himself why he had let such meaningless distractions cause her pain, and wished that he might live the past differently. His longing unassuaged by his visits to the Akashi lady, he wrote Murasaki a more detailed letter than usual. Toward the end, he said, "It's painful even to remember the times when my impulsive and irresponsible behavior made you angry with me; but now again, I've dreamed a strange, fleeting dream. Please realize that I confess this because I don't ever want to keep any secret from you. 'The promises I swore . . .'[23]

"No matter what the occasion . . ." [he assured her]:

shioshio to	The transient seaweed
mazu zo nakaruru	has served the fisherman
karisome no	as a diversion,
mirume wa ama no	but he remembers someone else,
susabi naredomo	and salt tears fill his eyes.

Her answer was mild and endearing. At the end, she wrote, "I was reminded of many things when I read about the dream you couldn't conceal":

ura naku mo	Mine was a naive heart.
omoikeru ka na	Because of the vows we spoke,
chigirishi o	I waited for you,
matsu yori nami wa	trusting that waves would never cross
koeji mono zo to	Sue-no-matsu Mountain.[24]

Greatly affected by this uncharacteristic hint of resentment, which belied the placid tone of the rest of the letter, he stared at the paper as though unable to put it down, and the lingering effect made him cease his visits to the hill house. The Akashi lady felt that the anticipated disaster had clearly occurred, and that the time had come when she ought indeed to cast herself into the sea. It was far worse than she had pictured it in her imagination. "With nobody to rely on except two aging parents, I couldn't hope to amount to anything in the future," she thought, "but at least I didn't have any real troubles in my simple life. It's agonizing to be involved in a relationship like this." Nevertheless, her manner toward Genji was calm, with no trace of resentment. Moved, he grew fonder of her as time passed, but he slept alone more often than not, for it was deeply distressing to imagine the anxiety with which a certain great lady must be enduring the long months, his plight never absent from her mind. He painted many different kinds of pictures, assembled them, and added poems to express his thoughts, leaving room for the replies he hoped to hear someday. The blank spaces would have touched the heart of anybody who saw them. Somehow, as though their minds had met in the empyrean, Murasaki had begun to keep a record of her own, a sort of diary, jotted down on pictures that she painted and assembled in the same way when she could find no other solace for her unhappiness. What did fate hold in store for them?

A new year began. The emperor was in poor health, and rumors flew. He

23. Old commentary: wasureji to / chikaishi koto o / ayamataba / mikasa no yama no / kami mo kotoware ("May I bow beneath the judgment of the gods at Mount Mikasa if I break the promises I swore never to forget").

24. Anonymous (KKS 1093): kimi o okite / adashigokoro o / wa ga motaba / sue no matsu-yama / nami mo koenamu ("Would I be the sort to cast you aside and turn to someone new? Sooner would the waves traverse Sue-no-matsu Mountain").

possessed a son, the offspring of the Shōkyōden consort (a daughter of the current minister of the right), but the child was barely two, so young that it seemed necessary to yield the throne to the crown prince.[25] When the emperor pondered the question of who was to stand behind the new ruler and conduct affairs of state, he felt all the pathos and injustice of Genji's unhappy situation; and finally, in disregard of the Kokiden lady's remonstrances, he issued a decree of pardon. The Kokiden lady herself had been suffering from the attacks of a malignant spirit since the year before, and a series of portentous occurrences had also begun, all very unsettling to everybody at court. Now there was even a resurgence of the emperor's eye trouble, which had seemed to be clearing up (thanks, perhaps, to the assiduity with which he had practiced ritual seclusion). In wretched spirits, he gave instructions for the promulgation of a second decree, which commanded Genji to return to the capital. It was shortly after the twentieth of the seventh month.

Although Genji had believed that the court would relent in the end, he had worried about his chances of survival in a world of change, and the sudden recall was cause for rejoicing. But his happiness was tinged with sorrow, for he knew that his departure from these shores would be a final one. As for the novice, a weight seemed to settle on his chest when he heard the news, even though he had known it was only to be expected; but he cheered himself with the thought that Genji must first rise in the world if his own aspirations were to be fulfilled.

Around that time, Genji spent every night with the daughter, who had been showing pathetic signs of indisposition ever since the sixth month. Perversely, perhaps, his affection had warmed now that he was soon to leave her in such circumstances, and he thought gloomily of the strange fate that seemed to have doomed him to a life of unhappiness. The lady was desolate, as was only natural.

Miserable as the unexpected journey to Suma had been, Genji had taken comfort in the belief that he would return to the capital someday. Now that he was to set out toward that cherished destination he felt only poignant regret as he realized that he would never see these shores again.

His attendants rejoiced, each according to his own circumstances. People came from the city to accompany the party home, and high spirits reigned. Only the host, the novice, spent his days in tears as the month drew toward its close.

As though the parting were not hard enough to bear, it was now midautumn, a season when the very aspect of the sky calls forth deep emotion. His thoughts in turmoil, Genji wondered why he had always gone out of his way to involve himself in love affairs that threatened to ruin his life. Those

25. Having forced the withdrawal from public life of Genji and the Fujitsubo lady, who had been the crown prince's main supporters, the Kokiden lady's faction had apparently hoped to shunt the boy aside when the time came for the emperor to retire.

who knew him well grumbled as they watched him. "What can you do? It's the same old story. All this time, he's been lukewarm about her, just sneaking in for the odd visit when he was sure nobody would notice; now, he turns around and acts in a way that's bound to hurt her," they complained among themselves. It irked Lesser Counselor Yoshikiyo to hear them whisper that he had been the one to give Genji his first inkling of the girl's existence.

Two days before his departure, Genji went to the hill house without waiting until his usual late hour. It was his first good look at the daughter's elegant, aristocratic face and figure, and he asked himself, in sudden sadness, how he could possibly abandon such an astonishingly beautiful woman. He would find a way to send for her. To comfort her, he told her of his intention. I need not dwell on the splendor of his own appearance, which was handsomer than ever now that years of austerities had refined his features. To see him as he swore eternal love, his face shadowed with sorrow and his eyes brimming with tears, made her feel as though this alone were all the happiness she could want, quite enough to satisfy any woman—and, at the same time, served as a tormenting reminder of the social gulf between such magnificence and herself. Carried on an autumn wind, the noise of the waves sounded even more depressing than usual, and faint trails of smoke from salt fires added to the characteristic loneliness of the scene. [Genji murmured a poem:]

kono tabi wa	Though I leave you now,
tachiwakaru tomo	we shall be together soon,
moshio yaku	just as plumes of smoke
keburi wa onaji	from seaweed burned for salt
kata ni nabikamu	follow a common direction.

[She replied:]

kakitsumete	The tumult in my breast
ama no taku mo no	resembles a fire from seaweed
omoi ni mo	gathered by fishers,
ima wa kai naki	but there would be no point now
urami dani seji	in uttering vain reproaches.

Sobbing pitifully, unable to speak at length, she managed an accomplished reply when silence would have been rude.

Genji took it amiss that she had never played the koto for him, much as he had wanted to hear her. "If you really don't intend to reproach me, won't you at least play a piece as a parting gift, a memory for me to cherish?" he said. He sent for the koto he had brought from the capital and played a soft tune of exceptional interest, the clear notes resounding with incomparable beauty in the deep night. The novice, moved beyond endurance, brought a thirteen-stringed instrument and thrust it under the blinds. The lady herself was moved to tears, and she began to play in a quiet, exceedingly refined manner, probably because there seemed no other way to bring her emotions under control. Genji had always believed that nobody in the world could match the tones elicited from the thirteen-stringed koto by the Fujitsubo lady. Hers was indeed a skill so flawless that the listener was ravished by the modishness and brilliance of the performance, and even felt able to form a mental picture of the musician's physical appearance. The Akashi lady's playing was enviably pure and elegant. Even to Genji, listening with a connoisseur's ear, her music sounded fresh and moving, and it was tantalizing to have her break off at the very moment when an unfamiliar melody had engaged his full attention. Overcome with regret, he asked himself why he had not prevailed on her to play for him during all these months—insisting, if necessary. He showered her with fervent promises about the future.

"I'll leave my koto as a keepsake until we play together again," he said. She half-whispered a poem:

> naozari ni   Shedding ceaseless tears,
> tanomeoku naru   I shall cherish the memory
>   hitokoto o   of facile promises
> tsukisenu ne ni ya   left behind, like this koto,
> kakete shinobamu   to make me rely on you.

Annoyed, he replied:

> au made no   Take care not to change
> katami ni chigiru   the key of the middle strings
>   naka no o no   on the koto I leave
> shirabe wa koto ni   as a keepsake until we meet,
> kawarazaranamu   as a symbol of our vows.[26]

"We'll definitely meet before the strings need retuning," he assured her. But she shed bitter tears, unable to think of anything except the misery of parting. It was only natural.

Genji left her house well before daybreak on the morning of his departure. It was hard to concentrate amid the bustle of his entourage, but he managed to find a private moment in which to get off a poem:

> uchisutete   My heart swells with grief
> tatsu mo kanashiki   as I depart from this shore,
>   uranami no   leaving you behind.
> nagori ika ni to   But more painful is the thought
> omoiyaru ka na   of your feelings, here alone.

The reply was a frank avowal of her thoughts:

> toshi hetsuru   This thatched cottage,
> tomaya mo arete   my home for many years,
>   ukinami no   will fall into ruins.

26. Wordplays add another meaning: "Don't stop loving me."

| kaeru kata ni ya | I wish only to follow |
| mi o taguemashi | the path of the retreating waves. |

He strove for self-control as he read, but tears rolled down his cheeks. People who were ignorant of the facts drew their own conclusions. "It's not much of a place, but he's lived here a long time; of course, it must be a wrench for him to leave," they said. Yoshikiyo was irritated. "He seems to be serious about the girl," he thought.

Despite their happiness, Genji's men went around with long faces. I believe they expressed sympathy with their master's feelings and exchanged lachrymose remarks about never seeing those shores again, but I must be excused from recording their conversations.

The novice made splendid arrangements for the departure. There were attractive traveling costumes for the attendants, even the very lowest. One wondered how he had had time to finish them all. I need not mention the magnificence of the garments he provided for Genji. And there were many chests of clothing to be taken along, carried by Akashi people. Chosen with taste and with meticulous attention to detail, the farewell presents were souvenirs worthy of being taken to the capital. A poem from the lady was attached to the hunting costume presented for Genji's use that day:

yoru nami ni	These robes for travel,
tachikasanetaru	sewn and layered in a place
tabigoromo	where the waves roll in—
shiodokeshi to ya	will you find them distasteful
hito no itowan	because they are wet with salt?

Despite the commotion around him, he composed a reply and changed his clothes.

katami ni zo	There could be no doubt
kaubekarikeru	that I would change into robes
au koto no	bestowed as keepsakes—
hikazu hedaten	middle robes to bridge the days
naka no koromo o	until we two meet again.

"It was so very nice of you." He sent her the robes he had been wearing, keepsakes that seemed likely to become still another source of sad memories. Fragrant and incomparably beautiful, they could scarcely have failed to move her.

Although the novice had supposedly turned his back on worldly things, he longed to escort Genji on the homeward journey, and much regretted, he said, that it should be impossible for one in his position. Oddly contorted with grief, his face probably made some of the younger people smile, pitiful though it was. [His poem:]

| yo o umi ni | Many are the years |
| kokora shiojimu | I have lived by the salty sea, |

> mi to narite
> nao kono kishi o
> e koso hanarene

> rejecting the world;
> it remains beyond my power
> to get away from this shore.[27]

"I know my mental turmoil will increase after you leave—my worries for her sake. If only I could at least go as far as the boundary of the province!" he said. To probe Genji's intentions, he continued, "I fear it may sound forward, but if you should happen to think of her sometimes, please send her a line or two."

To Genji it seemed a heartbreaking situation, and there was a redness around his eyes that made him look marvelously handsome. "I couldn't abandon her in her present condition. You'll soon come to understand what I have in mind. It's just that right now it's very hard for me to leave this house. I scarcely know what to do," he said. [His poem:]

> miyako ideshi
> haru no nageki ni
> otorame ya
> toshi furu ura o
> wakarenuru aki

> Not inferior
> to the grief of departure
> from the city in spring—
> this autumn when I leave the shore
> where I have watched the years go by.

More and more distraught, the novice cried harder than ever as he watched Genji wipe away tears. He was dismayingly unsteady on his feet.

The daughter's feelings were beyond comparison. Anxious to conceal her grief, she strove for composure. But she could not overcome her resentment at being left behind, reasonable though it seemed when she considered her humiliating status, nor could she forget the face that haunted her thoughts, and she lacked the strength for anything but tears. Her mother was at a loss to comfort her. "Why did we think of a thing that could cause this kind of misery?" she said to her husband. "You're so headstrong; I should never have listened to you."

"Quit complaining," he told her. "He may be leaving, but he'll think of the girl; he won't forget her when she's in this condition." To his daughter, he said, "Cheer up! Take a little sip of your medicine, at least. It's unlucky to carry on like that." He sat down in a corner.

The mother and the girl's nurses had much to say to one another about the novice's wrongheadedness. "For years, I hoped that someday soon, somehow, I could see her well settled, but look at the terrible thing that's happened—right at the outset, too, just when it seemed my dream had come true," the mother lamented. The sight of her gloomy face stirred piteous feelings in the daughter and made the novice more vague and absentminded than ever. He took to sleeping through the day, getting up at night with a show of briskness, seating himself in front of his icon, and rubbing his hands

27. On one level, the novice laments his inability to progress spiritually from this world (*kono kishi, shigan,* "this shore") to "the other shore" (*higan*)—that is, enlightenment. On another, he apologizes for not being able to see Genji partway on the journey.

together in lieu of his prayer beads, which, to his surprise, seemed to have got lost. His disciples made snide remarks. Going outdoors on a moonlit night with the intention of pacing the grounds while reading a sacred text, he fell into the stream and struck his hip against the edge of one of his elegant rocks. He nursed his pain in bed, and it was only during that period that he managed to forget some of his worries.

Genji arrived in the vicinity of Naniwa, performed a purification ritual, and sent a messenger to Sumiyoshi, with instructions to announce his intention of visiting the shrine later, in fulfillment of vows of thanksgiving for a safe voyage. He was unable to go in person this time because his retinue had suddenly burgeoned to unwieldy proportions.

He hurried straight to the capital, without pausing for side excursions. When he reached the Nijō Mansion, it was like a dream for everyone, both those who had waited and those who had gone with him; and there ensued an almost inauspicious hubbub of reunion, accompanied by floods of happy tears. Murasaki must have rejoiced in the life she had once considered meaningless.[28] She had matured delightfully into a woman of classic beauty, and her hair, which had been almost too rich and thick, had thinned to perfection during the years of grief and worry. For Genji, there was deep contentment in the thought that he could always be with her like this from now on, but his very peace of mind led him to imagine, with painful clarity, the unhappiness of the lady from whom he had parted while their love was new. It looked very much as though his life was never to be free of worries associated with the opposite sex.

He told Murasaki all about the Akashi lady. His manner as he reminisced suggested an interest that was more than casual, and Murasaki, as though surmising that the affair might be serious, murmured a line from an old poem, "about my forgotten self," adopting an offhand manner that he found amusing and lovable.[29] He marveled that he had been able to endure the years of separation from one of whom he could never tire—of whom the very sight was deeply satisfying—and he burned with indignation as he recalled the machinations that had driven him into exile.

The court soon made him a provisional major counselor, which was a promotion from his former office. When appropriate, his men were restored to office, and they blossomed forth in society like withered trees revisited by spring.

Genji went to the palace in response to an imperial summons. He looked more splendid than ever, and people asked themselves how he could have endured the years in those remote places. His presence stirred sad memories

28. A reference to her farewell poem in "Suma."

29. Ukon (SIS 870): wasuraruru / mi o ba omowazu / chikaiteshi / hito no inochi no / oshiku mo aru ka na ("I do not worry about my forgotten self; my only concern is for the life of the one who vowed by gods and buddhas"). The poet suggests that the divine powers may punish the faithless man with death.

in some of the ladies-in-waiting, decrepit old women who had served the late emperor, and who now wept aloud as they praised him, recalling the past as though it were yesterday.

Somewhat abashed, the emperor paid special attention to his costume before coming out. Although he was weak from his long illness, he had been feeling a little better for the last day or two, and he carried on a quiet conversation with Genji until nightfall. As a brilliant full moon cast its light on the hushed surroundings, memories of the past filled his mind, and he wept into his sleeve. No doubt he was in a depressed mood. "It's been a long time since we've had music—so very long since I've listened to your instruments as I used to," he said. Genji responded with a poem:

>   watatsumi ni   Like the leech child
>   shizumiurabure   unable to stand erect,
>   hiru no ko no   I lived for three years,
>   ashi tatazarishi   miserable and ruined,
>   toshi wa henikeri   by the shores of the sea.[30]

Conscious of both sympathy and shame, the emperor answered in a gentle, refined manner:

>   miyabashira   Now that you have come
>   meguriaikeru   full circle, as when the gods
>   toki shi areba   went round the pillar,
>   wakareshi haru no   let no resentment persist
>   urami nokosu na   from that parting in springtime.

Genji's first concern was to begin arrangements for an eight expositions service to benefit the late emperor's spirit.

He visited the crown prince, who had matured to an astonishing extent, and who received him with a surprised delight that he found infinitely touching. The boy was an excellent scholar, so bright that he already seemed capable of reigning.

He called on the Fujitsubo lady after he felt a little more composed, and we may imagine that that was another moving occasion.

I almost forgot to mention the letter he sent to Akashi by the novice's returning party. It seems to have been an affectionate message, written in privacy. "I worry about how it is for you on those nights when the waves roll in," he said. And:

>   nagekitsutsu   Sharing your sorrow,
>   akashi no ura ni   I picture Akashi Shore

---

30. One version of the Japanese creation myth says: "After the sun and moon, the next child born was the leech child. When this child had completed his third year, he was still unable to stand upright. The reason why the leech child was born was that in the beginning, when [the god] Izanagi and [the goddess] Izanami went around the pillar, the female deity was the first to utter an exclamation of pleasure, and the law of male and female was thus broken." Translation adapted from Aston, *Nihongi*, p. 20.

<table>
<tr><td>asagiri no</td><td>veiled in morning mists—</td></tr>
<tr><td>tatsu ya to hito o</td><td>vapors evoked by someone</td></tr>
<tr><td>omoiyaru ka na</td><td>who sighs the nights away.[31]</td></tr>
</table>

The assistant viceroy's daughter, the Gosechi lady, had decided to get over her secret crush on Genji, the futility of which had become apparent. She told someone to leave a note for him, with only a wink as a clue to the sender's identity. [Her poem:]

suma no ura ni	I would that I might
kokoro o yoseshi	show you the moldering sleeves
funabito no	of the seafarer
yagate kutaseru	whose heart went out to you
sode o misebaya	on the waters of Suma.

Though the hand was much improved, he recognized it. He sent off an answer:

kaerite wa	On the contrary,
kagoto ya semashi	it is I who must complain.
yosetarishi	The wave that approached
nagori ni sode no	left in its wake a sleeve
higatakarishi o	I have sought in vain to dry.

Her letter rekindled fond memories of a lady whom he had once considered enchanting, but he seems to have determined, around that time, not to get involved in indiscreet adventures. Even the lady in the house of the scattering blossoms received only notes, and his failure to appear in person made her feel worried and resentful.

31. This rather strained conceit is a conventional one, dating back to *Man'yōshū* (8th c.).

New Herbs: Part Two

[From the first month to the sixth month of Genji's forty-seventh year.
Murasaki: 39; Akashi lady: 38; Akashi imperial consort: 19; Third Princess:
21 or 22; Yūgiri: 26; Tō-no-chūjō's son Kashiwagi: 31 or 32.

Approximately 20 years have elapsed since Genji's return to the capital.
The throne has changed hands twice in the interim, passing from Genji's
half-brother, the Suzaku emperor, who was reigning in "Akashi," to Genji's
"other son" (the Reizei emperor) and then, on his retirement, to the present
sovereign, a son of the Suzaku emperor. At 47, Genji is the most important
figure in court society. His official status is equivalent to that of a retired
emperor, his daughter by the Akashi lady is an imperial consort and the
mother of the crown prince, and he has acquired a prestigious second main
wife, the Third Princess, who is the daughter of the Suzaku emperor (now
living in retirement as a Buddhist novice). In the seven years since the
marriage, the princess has lived at his magnificent Rokujō Mansion, where
she associates on friendly terms with the other residents—Murasaki, the
Akashi lady, and the lady from the house of the scattering blossoms. Though
Murasaki remains Genji's great love, she is tormented by feelings of insecurity and thinks of becoming a nun. As this passage from "New Herbs: Part
Two" begins, Genji has been giving the Third Princess private lessons on the
seven-stringed koto, which she is to play during a long-planned visit to her
father.]

"Someone in the wing keeps wanting to hear your seven-stringed koto being
played," Genji said to the princess. "I'd like very much to try a ladies' concert—your instrument and the thirteen-stringed koto and lute of others.
The great musicians of the present day aren't at all superior to the talent
we have right here at the mansion. I can't claim to have mastered more
than a fraction of the tradition, but in my youth I wanted to learn everything there was to know, and I did my best to study with all the famous
teachers and acquire the secret lore of all the experts in noble families. As
it turned out, I met nobody who seemed so marvelously accomplished that
it was embarrassing to play in his presence. And it seems to me that our
young musicians nowadays are affected and overrefined, shallower than
their predecessors. That's true especially of the seven-stringed koto; they

tell me nobody makes a serious study of it any more. I would guess that hardly anyone has learned to play as well as you do."

The princess responded with a naive smile, happy to have improved enough to deserve such commendation. At twenty-one or twenty-two, she still seemed extremely young and immature, her slender, delicate figure like that of an appealing child. "It's been years now since your father has seen you. When you meet, you'll have to do your best to show him how much you've grown up," Genji told her whenever he could.

"It would be even harder to hide her childishness if she didn't have someone like His Lordship to look after her," her ladies-in-waiting said to themselves.

The skies were balmy as the twentieth of the first month approached. Warm breezes blew, the plum trees near the veranda gradually came into full bloom, buds swelled on all the other flowering trees, and haze extended all the way to the horizon.

Genji arranged for Murasaki to go to the main hall. "Once this month ends, there'll be a rush to get ready for the celebration, and the gossips might dismiss your concert as a mere rehearsal. Do it now, while things are quiet," he said.[1] All of her woman were eager to join the audience, but she eliminated everyone whose knowledge of music was deficient, choosing those and only those with a true understanding of the art, even though some of them were rather old. As pages, she summoned only children of superb appearance and demeanor—four beautiful little girls, whom she dressed in red mantles, trailing white paneled robes with red linings, inner robes of figured lavender silk, float-patterned silk trousers, and glossy red singlets.

As befitted the start of a new year, the furnishings in the imperial consort's quarters were even more splendid than usual, and nothing could have equaled the fresh beauty of her women's costumes, each of which had been assembled with painstaking care in a spirit of keen competition. Her page girls were all dressed alike in green mantles, trailing pink paneled robes lined in deep red, Chinese damask trousers, and yellow Chinese damask inner robes.

The Akashi lady had turned out her pages in modest fashion—two in red mantles with purple linings, and two in white with red linings. All four wore trailing paneled robes of pale green, inner robes in different shades of purple, and beautiful lustrous singlets.

The princess had also paid special attention to her pages' costumes after learning that the other ladies would assemble in the main hall. They wore

1. The celebration is to honor the Suzaku emperor's 50th year. The present concert is to take place in the main hall of the southeast complex, the Third Princess's residence at the Rokujō Mansion, and (as we learn below) the ensemble is to include both the Akashi lady and the Akashi consort, who is home on a visit. The Third Princess lives in the western part of the hall; the consort is staying in the eastern part.

yellowish-green mantles, trailing white paneled robes with green linings, and grape-colored inner robes—nothing remarkably clever or original, but an incomparably dignified and aristocratic total effect.

The inner partitions had been removed from the eave-chamber, leaving only curtain-stands here and there to establish boundaries, and a seat had been prepared for Genji in the central space. In the thought that it would be well to bring in children as accompanists, Genji had arranged for Higeku-ro's third son (Tamakazura's first) and Yūgiri's oldest boy to play the pan-pipes and flute on the veranda. Inside the room, rows of cushions were set out, and stringed instruments were placed in front of the musicians. Precious instruments were removed from beautiful grayish-blue bags—a lute for the Akashi lady, a six-stringed Japanese koto for Murasaki, and a thirteen-stringed koto for the imperial consort. For the Third Princess, Genji tuned the seven-stringed koto on which she usually practiced, not altogether sure of how she might acquit herself on a more celebrated instrument.

"The thirteen-stringed koto's strings don't loosen up, but the bridges tend to get dislocated when it's played in concert. One needs to take care; women seldom seem able to get the strings tight enough. We'd better call on Yūgiri. These little wind players aren't old enough to be reliable when it comes to setting the pitch," Genji laughed. He told an attendant to summon his son.

The prospect of having Yūgiri present made the ladies self-conscious and nervous, and Genji's own emotions were similar.[2] All of them except the Akashi lady were his prized pupils, and all would need to be impeccable with Yūgiri listening. He was not worried about the consort, who was used to participating in musicales presided over by the emperor, but he could not help feeling sorry for Murasaki. Although the six-stringed koto produced only a small number of notes, its very limitations might lead a woman into error, because there were no guidelines to follow. Might she not go astray in a situation like this, which required a harmonious ensemble?

Yūgiri himself felt tense. The pressure on this occasion would be much greater than if it were an elaborate formal rehearsal in the imperial presence. He selected a dazzling new cloak and some heavily scented inner robes, perfumed his sleeves with care, and arrived after sunset, groomed to perfection. In the delightful dusky air, the branches of the plum trees drooped beneath blossoms whose abundance might have been mistaken for last year's lingering snow; and the gentle breeze mingled indescribably pleasant perfumes from within the blinds with the sweet smell of the trees, filling the surroundings with a fragrance to "lure the warbler forth."[3]

Genji pushed the end of a thirteen-stringed koto outside the blinds. "For-

2. They all feared that the performance might not measure up to Yūgiri's exacting standards.

3. Ki no Tomonori (KKS 13): hana no ka o / kaze no tayori ni / taguete zo / uguisu sasou / shirube ni wa yaru ("To a wind letter, I will attach the fragrance of the flowering plum, and let it become a guide to lure the warbler forth").

give my asking, but would you tune the strings and test them? We can't very well let an outsider come in here to do it," he said.

Yūgiri performed an obeisance, took the instrument with impressive caution, tuned the third string in the *ichikotsu* mode, and waited without playing.

"Try a song to check the tune—just to be sociable," Genji said.

Yūgiri's demurral seemed a bit overdone. "I don't feel at all qualified to participate in today's music-making," he said.

Genji laughed. "Even so, don't you think it would be a shame if people said, 'He ran off because he couldn't keep up with the ladies'?'"

Yūgiri finished his tuning, played an interesting air just long enough to verify the results, and returned the koto.

Charming in their informal cloaks, the little boys piped away, their playing immature but rich in intriguing hints of future skill.

When all the instruments were tuned and the ladies began to play, it would have been impossible to rank one performance above another, but the Akashi lady seemed especially skillful on the lute, her archaic style producing delightful crystal-clear notes. Both Genji and Yūgiri listened to the six-stringed koto with close attention. Its music sounded gentle and charming when Murasaki used her left hand, and strikingly modish when she used her right, an effect no less brilliant than the melodies and tones elicited by the pretentious technique of famous professionals. It was amazing that the instrument could be played in that manner. The splendor of her performance showed how hard she had practiced, and Genji listened in admiration, his worries dispelled. Music of appealing, gentle beauty emanated from the thirteen-stringed koto, an instrument whose unobtrusive voice emerges when others fall silent. Although the Third Princess's playing was still immature, she was engaged in an intensive course of study, and her seven-stringed koto harmonized flawlessly with the other instruments. She had achieved an elegant touch, Yūgiri thought. He took up the beat and began to sing. Genji joined in occasionally, keeping time with his fan and singing in a voice that seemed better than in the past—a little deeper and more impressive. Yūgiri had also been blessed with an excellent voice, and the concert proceeded in an indescribably agreeable manner as the night grew ever more quiet.

It was the time of month when the moon is slow to rise; Genji had had lamps hung here and there to provide suitable light. Stealing a look in the princess's direction, he noticed that she seemed much smaller than most women—pathetically appealing, almost as though nothing were there but a set of robes. Not a ripe beauty but pleasingly aristocratic in appearance, she called to mind a green willow, just stirring to life around the twentieth of the second month, its drooping branches so fragile that the breeze from a warbler's wings might twist them into tangles. Her hair also resembled the trailing branches of a willow as it overflowed on both sides of her white semiformal jacket, which was lined with red in the cherry-blossom combination. A woman of that appearance could only be someone of the highest birth.

The imperial consort's beauty was equally refined and a bit more glowing; and her manners and bearing were elegant and tasteful. One might have compared her to a luxuriant wisteria vine, blooming on into summer to bask unrivaled in the morning sun. Uncomfortably great with child, she had pushed her koto aside to prop herself against an armrest. She looked very pathetic, leaning heavily and seeming to stretch her tiny body to accommodate to the support, which was of the usual size. (One would have liked to furnish her with a smaller model.) She was a figure of incomparable charm in the lamplight, her beautiful hair tumbling over a red semiformal outer robe, which was lined with purple in the red-plum combination.

Murasaki was wearing a red semiformal jacket over a rich brown semiformal outer robe, which I think may have been lined with blue in the grape combination. Her hair lay in masses on her skirts, its graceful curves almost too dazzling to be real; her height was ideal; and her perfect beauty seemed to infuse the surroundings with radiance. There was no flower to which one could compare her, not even the cherry blossom. She was in a class by herself.

Some might have expected that the Akashi lady would be overshadowed in such company, but that was by no means true. There was in her demeanor a hint of qualities that might put others to shame, a suggestion of intriguing depths, an indefinable air of nobility and elegance. She wore a green bombycine semiformal jacket, lined with white in the willow combination, and a semiformal outer robe, dyed a yellowish-green, I believe. In deliberate acknowledgment of her inferior birth, she had put on an inconspicuous gossamer train, but it would have been impossible to slight anyone whose bearing and character bespoke such obvious refinement. Making respectfully slight use of a cushion edged in green Korean brocade, she sat with her lute in front of her and played in an unassuming manner, the grace with which she wielded the plectrum even more rare and delightful than the sound of the instrument. If was as if one were inhaling the scent of a branch laden with flowers and fruit, broken from the orange tree whose blossoms "await the fifth month's coming."[4]

His senses alive to signs of the seriousness with which all the ladies treated the occasion, Yūgiri could not help wanting to look inside the blinds. Ever since the time when he had caught sight of Murasaki, he had been obsessed with the desire to see her again, convinced that she must be growing more and more beautiful. And in the case of the Third Princess, a slightly better karma would have made her his. Why had he been so lukewarm? It was

---

4. Anonymous (KKS 139): satsuki matsu / hanatachibana no / ka o kageba / mukashi no hito no / sode no ka zo suru ("Scenting the fragrance of orange blossoms that await the fifth month's coming, I recall a perfumed sleeve worn by someone long ago").

annoying to recall that the Suzaku emperor had given him repeated hints and had spoken of him to others as a potential husband for her. On the other hand, there had been indications that the princess was a bit shallow, and he had felt no great interest in the match (without at all looking down on her). With Murasaki, it had been a question of complete inaccessibility year after year—of frustration and unhappiness because there was no way simply to let her know of his admiration. It was not at all that he nurtured an improper or forbidden passion; any such impulses were firmly suppressed. . . .

[On the day after the concert, Genji talks to Murasaki in a reflective mood.]

"From my infancy on, I enjoyed special treatment and was reared with the greatest partiality; and my present reputation and way of life are such as few have known. But I have also been unusual in another respect—in the sheer number of extraordinary misfortunes that have come my way. In the first place, I have lost one after another of the people who loved me; and now, left behind in my declining years, I still must cope with a host of painful thoughts. I also fret to a rather strange extent about the misdeeds of the past. Mine has come to be a sad existence, and it has occurred to me to wonder if that may be why I've lived longer than I expected—if longevity may be my recompense.

"Aside from that one separation, I don't think you've had any cause for real worry. Imperial consorts enjoy exalted positions, but they all have their troubles—the empresses, and even more the women of lesser status. Moving in those high circles, they're always anxious, always competing, never at ease. Other women don't have the peace of mind you've known, living as though you were still the cherished object of parental devotion. Do you realize what an extraordinarily good karma yours has been in that respect? The princess's unexpected presence must seem a little disagreeable, but perhaps you may be too closely involved to notice how much it has strengthened my love for you. Still, you always seem to see to the bottom of things; I'm sure you understand that she's no threat."

"It must seem to outsiders that I have had far more luck than a friendless waif could expect, just as you say, but I do believe the only thing that has kept me alive has been the constant tension of one unbearable grief after another—my substitute, I suppose, for the prayers on which others rely." She broke off, seemingly unfinished, with an abashing air of nobility.

"I truly do feel that I haven't much longer to live," she resumed. "It makes me very uneasy to go on ignoring the fact that this is a dangerous year. If I might just have your permission to do what I've asked about before . . ."[5]

5. She has asked for permission to take Buddhist vows. Genji has mentioned previously that this is her 37th year, which was considered a dangerous one for women. (If she was around 10 in "Young Murasaki," she should actually be around 39 now.)

"That's absolutely out of the question. What would be the point of my existence if you weren't here? Ours is an uneventful life, but I couldn't conceive of any greater happiness than just being with you day in and day out. Let me show you to the end what a very special place you hold in my heart." He said no more; it was the same old disappointing answer. Tears came to her eyes.

Moved to compassion, he tried to distract her with talk of other things. "I haven't had a great deal of experience with women," he said, "but after coming to know some of them fairly well, I've reached the conclusion that few possess mild, steady dispositions, even though they can all lay claim to various other merits.

"My connection with Yūgiri's mother began when I was only a boy. To me she was worthy of the highest respect, a wife from whom it would have been inconceivable to part, but we never got along, and I still felt conscious of a distance between us when she died. Thinking about it now, I pity her, and I regret that things couldn't have been different. At the same time, I tell myself in private that I was not the only one at fault. She was decorous and dignified; one couldn't point to a single flaw. But perhaps she was too reserved, too punctilious, a little too much the intelligent woman—reliable enough, but uncomfortable to be with.

"The empress's mother, the widow of the crown prince, was a very special person, one who comes to mind at once as an exemplar of refinement and elegance, but I found our association awkward and difficult.[6] Granted that she had a right to resent certain things, it was hard to bear the way she brooded over her grievances and magnified them. It was a tense, embarrassing relationship. Both of us felt too constrained to live together in casual intimacy. I went to great lengths to appear in a good light because I feared her scorn. And so we finally drifted apart. She grieved pathetically because she had left herself open to unpleasant, degrading rumors, and I felt guilty when I thought about her high status. It was to atone for my desertion that I lent my support to her daughter, even though it meant incurring criticism and alienating certain people. (Of course, I don't deny that the girl's karma has also had something to do with her success.) I hope the lady thinks more kindly of me now, there in the other world. Past and present, I've indulged in many idle diversions—whims that have put people in pitiful situations and made me regret my behavior."

Little by little, he brought up other women with whom he had become involved. "At first, I dismissed the Akashi lady as insignificant, a mere toy, but she is far from shallow—in fact, she's a woman of immeasurable depth. Her submissive, gentle exterior conceals a rather formidable firmness."

"I can't say anything about those other ladies, because I never knew them, but there have naturally been chances for me to learn what the Akashi lady

6. Genji is speaking here of the Rokujō lady, whose daughter, Akikonomu, is the consort of the (now retired) Reizei Emperor.

is like, even without meeting her face to face; and obviously, she is indeed someone of formidable dignity. It's embarrassing to wonder how my own deplorable lack of reserve must look to her, but I tell myself that the consort probably overlooks my faults," Murasaki said.[7]

It was admirable, Genji thought, that her affection for the consort had led her to make friends with a woman she had once resented and shunned. "Even when you have certain private reservations, you always come up with a tactful, sympathetic word, something exactly right for the person you're talking to and for the circumstances. Of all the women I've known, there's never been one to compare with you. I can tell what you're really thinking by the look on your face," Genji said with a smile.

He left for the Third Princess's apartments around nightfall, saying that he wanted to thank her for playing so well. She was practicing with childish absorption, no thought in her mind of any possible resentment on Murasaki's part. "Please let me have some time off now, and take a little rest yourself," Genji said. "Your music teacher is more than satisfied. Thanks to your long, hard practice, you've turned into an expert; there's nothing left for me to worry about." He pushed the koto aside and went to bed.

As usual on nights when Genji was away, Murasaki stayed up late, listening to her attendants read stories aloud. In those old tales, which professed to record true-to-life happenings, a woman often got involved with a man who was fickle, licentious, and unfaithful, but he always seemed to settle down in the end. How strange that her own life should have remained so fraught with uncertainty! It was true that hers had been an unusually fortunate karma in some respects, but was she never to be free of these miserable forebodings—these worries that no woman could find endurable or acceptable? It was too much! Those thoughts were succeeded by many others, and it was late when she went to bed. Toward dawn, her chest began to hurt. Doing their best to nurse her, the ladies-in-waiting suggested that someone get in touch with Genji, but she refused to hear of it. She spent the rest of the night in almost unbearable pain. In the morning, she was feverish and miserable, but nobody told Genji, who was taking his time about coming to the wing.

A note of invitation arrived from the imperial consort. Murasaki replied that she was unwell, and the consort sent a shocked message to Genji. He rushed over in great alarm and found her looking dreadfully ill.

"How do you feel?" Her skin was hot to his touch, and his heart sank as he recalled yesterday's talk of the precautions she needed to take this year. His attendants brought his meal to the sickroom, but he ignored it. He stayed beside her all day long, attending to her every need with an anguished heart.

Day after day, Murasaki lay prostrate, rejecting all food, even small pieces of fruit. Frantic with apprehension, Genji commissioned innumerable

---

7. The imperial consort, Genji's daughter by the Akashi lady, is Murasaki's foster-daughter.

prayers and summoned monks to perform mystic invocations. It was hard
to tell just what was the matter; she merely felt very ill, with occasional
bouts of almost unbearable chest pain. The countless prayers at shrines and
temples met with no apparent response.

Even when an illness is desperate, there is room for optimism if the patient
shows some small sign of improvement, but Murasaki seemed to get no
better at all. Disheartened and miserable, Genji gave no thought to other
matters; the bustle of preparation for the celebration died down. The Suzaku emperor heard of her sickness and sent many kind messages of inquiry.

Two months went by in the same way. Inexpressibly worried, Genji
moved her to the Nijō Mansion to see if the change might prove beneficial.
There was great turmoil throughout the Rokujō Mansion, where many
people feared the worst. The Reizei emperor was also grieved by the news.
Yūgiri did everything he could think of to help, convinced that Genji would
turn to a life of religion if Murasaki died. He took care of the usual esoteric
rites and ordered additional special ones on his own initiative.

Whenever Murasaki's mind cleared a little, she uttered the same reproachful words. "It's so cruel of you not to let me do as I ask." Genji
always repeated the same refusal, feeling that to lose her to death would be
the lesser of two evils; the disappointment and sorrow would be beyond all
endurance if he were to watch with his own eyes while she voluntarily assumed a nun's garb and renounced the world. "For years, it's been my own
fervent wish to take religious vows," he said. "If I've gone on all this time,
it's because I've felt sorry for you—because I haven't wanted you to be
unhappy alone. Are you going to turn around and desert me?" But it began
to look as though there was little hope; she was failing, and there were many
times when death seemed imminent. What ought he to do? His mind in
turmoil, he stayed away from the Third Princess's apartments altogether.

The musical instruments had been put away for lack of interest, and everyone had assembled at the Nijō Mansion, leaving the Rokujō Mansion
like a place where the fires have been extinguished, vacant except for
women. It seemed that all the mansion's brilliance had emanated from a
single source.

The imperial consort came to Nijō to help Genji with the nursing. Murasaki managed to speak through her pain. "Malignant spirits can be a terrible menace to someone in your condition. Please go back to the palace
right away." The sight of the consort's sweet little daughter made her weep.
"Ah! I can't watch her grow up. She'll forget all about me," she said. The
consort could not repress tears of pity.

"You mustn't have these inauspicious thoughts," Genji said. "It's attitude
that determines what happens to people. If they're generous, fortune smiles
on them; if they're narrow-minded, they never feel quite serene, even though
their karma may elevate them to great heights; if they're impetuous, they
can't maintain their positions; if they're relaxed and calm, they're likely to

live a long time." He prayed in a similar vein to the buddhas and gods, pointing out to them the rare beauty of Murasaki's character and her innocence of all but the most trivial sins. That he should speak in such frantic terms seemed extraordinarily pathetic to the holy teachers who conducted the esoteric rites, and also to the eminent monks who maintained nighttime vigils nearby; and they threw themselves into their own prayers with all the energy at their command.

For five or six days running, there would be indications that Murasaki might be holding her own, but her condition invariably worsened again. Time went by, and the grieving Genji wondered how it would all end. Would she never recover? No possessing spirit came forward to announce itself. The ailment seemed to have no focal point; she merely weakened each day, and Genji lived in misery.

[Around the middle of the fourth month, Kashiwagi, one of Tō-no-chūjō's sons, takes advantage of the situation to force himself on the Third Princess. Afterward, the princess says that she is unwell, and Genji visits her. While he is there, someone comes from Nijō to tell him that Murasaki has stopped breathing. The time is the day after the Kamo Festival.]

Dazed, with a terrible blackness in his heart, Genji set out for Nijō. He traveled in desperate haste, and as he neared his destination he saw agitated crowds, assembled as far away as the adjacent avenues. Inside the grounds, there was the ominous sound of wailing voices. "She had seemed a little easier for the last few days, but then this suddenly happened," her attendants told him. Utterly distraught, they were all begging not to be forced to live on without their mistress. The altars had been dismantled, and all the monks except the usual officiants were making brisk preparations to depart. It could only mean that Murasaki's life had ended. Genji's despair and misery were beyond comparison.

He tried to quiet the women. "Even though she may have stopped breathing, it's just an evil spirit that's causing it. Don't make such a racket," he said. He redoubled his petitions and pledges to the supernatural powers.

"She may have reached the limit of her destined life span, but please grant her a brief extension. There is the great vow pronounced by the holy Fudō; let her at least live that much longer," the monks begged, praying so hard that smoke seemed to rise from their own heads.[8]

"Please look into my eyes one last time. It's devastating, heartbreaking, that I couldn't be with you at the end," Genji said. We may imagine the feelings of the witnesses to his agitation, which was so great that it seemed he would not live much longer either.

8. According to an old commentary, Fudō has vowed to extend the alloted life spans of human beings by six months. A fierce foe of evil, he is usually depicted in Buddhist art with a halo of flames.

Perhaps a buddha deigned to look into Genji's stricken heart. The possessing spirit, which for months had been adamant in its refusal to appear, now took control of the medium, a small girl, and began to cry out. To Genji's joy, terror, and bewilderment, Murasaki breathed again.

Pressed by the exorcist, the spirit spoke. "The rest of you will please leave. What I have to say is solely for His Lordship's ears . . .

"I had intended to punish you for the heartlessness with which you and your prayers have harassed me during these last months, but I wouldn't be here if some of my old feelings had not survived the transformation into my present shameful form; after all, I can't ignore the pity I feel, seeing you so distraught that your very life seems at stake; and that's why I've shown myself at last. I had never meant to let you know who I was." The girl tossed her hair over her face and wept, looking exactly like something he had seen in the past.[9] Chilled by the resemblance to the apparition that had so shocked and horrified him before, he took the child's hand and sat her down to restrain her indecorous behavior.

"Is that really you? People say the reputations of the dead are blackened by the evil ravings of crazed foxes. Make your identity clear. Or else tell me something nobody else would know—something I'd be sure to remember. Then I might be able to put some credence in what you say," he told her.

The medium broke down in tears:

wa ga mi koso	My own appearance
aranu sama nare	is not as it was in the past,
sore nagara	but you, my lord,
soraobore suru	remain the same as ever,
kimi wa kimi nari	always pretending ignorance.

"I hate you!" She sobbed and shrieked—yet he was conscious of a familiar reserve, which now seemed eerie and alienating. He resolved to ask no more questions.

"Flying through the sky, I've watched your care of my daughter, the empress, with pleasure and gratitude," the spirit said, "but I wonder if people may cease to feel any strong attachments, even to their children, once they have left the world of the living. My only remaining impediment to enlightenment is the old bitterness against you. What I've found most offensive hasn't been the way you slighted and discarded me while I was alive; no, the really hateful thing was the way you called me difficult and disagreeable when you and your lady were talking. I had expected you to forgive my shortcomings after my death—or, at least, to conceal whatever might have exposed me to disparagement; it's the mortification of that betrayal that has turned me into an avenging spirit and reduced your wife to this extremity. I don't bear her any particular grudge, but your own protection is very

9. Just before Yūgiri's birth, when Aoi seemed on the point of death.

strong: I can barely hear your voice, much less get close to you. Please have prayers said to lighten my burden of sin now. Alas! All this hubbub of esoteric rites and sutra readings is merely a torment, a nightmare of engulfing flame; not a word of the sacred texts reaches my ears.

"Tell the empress this. 'While you serve His Majesty, never engage in jealous struggles for his favor. And be sure to make pious offerings to atone for the sins you accumulated as [Ise] Virgin. I wish you had never held that office.' "[10] She ran on in the same way, but he shut the child in an inner chamber, afraid of causing comment by conversing with a spirit. He took quiet steps to move Murasaki into another room.

Rumors of Murasaki's death had spread everywhere, and there were condolatory calls that Genji considered most inauspicious.

Senior nobles heard the reports on their way home from watching the Kamo return.

"A terrible thing! She was a woman fortune smiled on—someone for whom life was truly worthwhile. No wonder it's started to drizzle; a sun's rays have been extinguished today," some of them said.

Others whispered among themselves.

"Paragons never manage to live very long."

"Remember the old poem, 'What could anyone prefer to blossoms of the cherry.' "[11]

"It would have caused grief in other quarters if she'd kept monopolizing the good things year after year. The princess ought to come into her own now. It's been pitiful to see how she's suffered in the competition for his attention."

After having moped at home through the preceding day, Kashiwagi had put his two younger brothers, Sadaiben and Tō-no-saishō, into the rear of his carriage and gone to watch the return. Shocked by what he overheard, he murmured, "Does anything last for long in this insubstantial world?"[12] The three of them started off toward the Nijō Mansion.

Kashiwagi thought it would be inauspicious to offer condolences on the strength of rumors that might turn out to be false; he would restrict himself to a conventional inquiry about Murasaki's health. But the weeping and wailing at the mansion seemed distressing proof that she had died. Her father, the prince, arrived and went inside with a stricken face. It was beyond his power to deliver messages. Yūgiri came out, wiping away a tear.

10. As Shinto priestesses, the Ise and Kamo virgins were required to avoid all aspects of Buddhism.

11. Anonymous (KKS 70): mate to iu ni / chirade shi tomaru / mono naraba / nani o sakura ni / omoimasamashi ("If, when we said, 'Wait,' they held fast to the branches, never scattering, what could anyone prefer to blossoms of the cherry?").

12. Anonymous (IM, sec. 82): chireba koso / itodo sakura wa / medetakere / ukiyo ni nani ka / hisashikarubeki ("It is just because the cherry blossoms scatter that they win our praise. Does anything last for long in this insubstantial world?").

"How are things here?" Kashiwagi asked. "We've heard some inauspicious rumors; I can't believe they're true. We're sorry Her Ladyship has been ill so long; we thought we'd call to ask how she is."

"She has been gravely ill for months, and she stopped breathing around dawn this morning. But a malignant spirit seems to have been at the bottom of it. We've been told that she has gradually begun to breathe again, which is a great relief for everyone, but it's still too early to feel at all secure. We're worried to death." Yūgiri's face bore the traces of many tears; his eyes were a little swollen. Kashiwagi studied his appearance. Was it merely his own errant heart that made him wonder why this gentleman should seem so perturbed about a stepmother—someone with whom he was surely not on intimate terms?

Genji heard that visitors had arrived. "Our patient here has been in critical condition, and she suddenly seemed to stop breathing. Her attendants panicked," he sent word. "I found it impossible to maintain my own composure, which I fear is still much shaken. I hope to thank you later for taking the trouble to call." Kashiwagi received the message with an agitated heart. The ignoble secret festering in his mind made him cringe at the thought of being so close to this man, whom he could never have brought himself to visit in less compelling circumstances.

Still apprehensive after Murasaki's return to life, Genji commissioned an even more exhaustive array of solemn rites than before. When he remembered what an intimidating presence the Rokujō lady had seemed in life, he could picture the appalling guise she might have assumed in the other world, and the mental image was so repellent that he even felt disinclined to see to the needs of her daughter. When you got down to it, all women were causes of grievous sin; all relations between the sexes were distasteful. And how disagreeable to have to recognize that the malignant spirit—the eavesdropper who had thrown in his face his few private, confidential remarks to Murasaki—was none other than the Rokujō lady, and that he could never permit himself to utter a careless remark!

Because Murasaki had set her heart on becoming a nun, he arranged for a token tonsure (a few locks snipped from the top of her head), and for the administration of five of the ten precepts, in the hope that the deed might ensure her recovery. With many impressive holy phrases, the preceptor spoke to the Buddha of the worthiness of her act; and Genji sat by her side, almost too close for appearances, wiping away tears as he joined her in prayer. The scene made one realize that not even the most splendid of men can control himself when he is confronted with a truly harrowing experience. Day and night, he thought only of saving her life, whatever the cost—of somehow keeping her in this world. He seemed dazed, oblivious of all else, and his face began to look gaunt.

Although Murasaki could not have been expected to feel very well during the rains of the fifth month, she did seem a little better than before. But the relentless pains continued. Genji arranged for daily dedicatory readings of the complete *Lotus Sutra*, and for other solemn rituals. He also saw to it that there were perpetual sutra recitations near her bed, performed only by monks with impressive voices. The spirit made only an occasional pathetic statement after its initial appearance, but it never went away.

To Genji's indescribable distress, Murasaki weakened steadily in the summer heat, which left her gasping for breath. Half unconscious, she nevertheless grieved to see the state he was in. As far as she herself was concerned, the prospect of death would not cause any regrets at all, but it would be unfeeling to slip out of his life when he was already so terribly upset. She forced herself to sip her medicinal decoctions, and in the sixth month she was able to raise her head once in a while—thanks, perhaps, to the restorative powers of the draughts. Her beauty seemed to Genji so extraordinary as to augur ill for the future; he did not risk even a brief visit to the Rokujō Mansion.

The Third Princess had felt vaguely out of sorts and ill ever since the shocking experience that had caused her such dismay; and from the fifth month on, she had stopped eating and grown very pale and thin. Goaded to recklessness by his passion, Kashiwagi paid her an occasional fleeting, dreamlike visit, but she considered his behavior atrocious. Very much in awe of Genji, she could scarcely have failed to recognize that her husband was quite a different order of man from Kashiwagi, both in appearance and in character. To most observers, the proud, elegant Kashiwagi would have seemed superior to the ordinary run of young men, someone to admire, but to the princess he was merely odious, accustomed as she had been since childhood to Genji's incomparable presence. It was a pitiful karma that had doomed her to suffer because of his actions. Her nurses had realized that she must be pregnant, and they exchanged indignant whispers about Genji's failure to come more often.

Impelled by reports of the princess's illness, Genji finally decided to go to the Rokujō Mansion. Murasaki had had her hair washed to gain relief from the oppressive heat, and she was feeling somewhat refreshed. Spread behind her as she lay in bed, the hair was slow to dry, but it fell in beautiful ripples, not a strand out of place. Her face was wan and thin, its skin a pure, almost transparent white of incomparable beauty. She was still shaky, as frail as an insect's discarded husk.

The interior of the Nijō Mansion was a bit rundown because of Genji's long absence, and it seemed unbelievably cramped. Alert enough to look outside during the past two or three days, Murasaki felt happy to have survived to see the stream and the garden, which had been tended with meticulous care and was now a vision of delight.

Lotuses bloomed everywhere on the cool lake, their fresh green leaves sprinkled with gemlike dewdrops.

"Look at the lotuses," Genji said. "Every one of them seems to be boasting of its coolness." Tears of joy sprang to his eyes when she sat up to look into the distance. "It's like a dream to see you so well," he told her. "There were times when I was terribly afraid it was the end for both of us—for me as well as for you."

Moved, Murasaki recited a poem:

kietomaru	My life is like the dew
hodo ya wa fubeki	clinging to a lotus leaf:
tamasaka ni	can I hope to live
hachisu no tsuyu no	as long as the dew may require
kakaru bakari o	to vanish of itself?

[Genji:]

chigiri okamu	Let's stay together,
kono yo narade mo	in the next world as in this,
hachisuha ni	like sparkling dewdrops
tama iru tsuyu no	on a single lotus leaf:
kokoro hedatsu na	don't ever set yourself apart.

CHAPTER TEN
[40]

The Rites

[From the third month to the autumn of Genji's fifty-first year. Murasaki: 43; Akikonomu: 42; Akashi lady: 42; Akashi empress: 23; Yūgiri: 30; Genji's grandson Niou: 5.

Almost four years have elapsed. Murasaki recovered soon after the events described in "New Herbs: Part Two," and she and Genji have moved back to the Rokujō Mansion, where she has kept busy with Genji's grandchildren.[1] Kashiwagi is dead, and the Third Princess is now a nun, having taken Buddhist vows shortly after giving birth to Kaoru, Kashiwagi's son. Two of Genji's old flames, Oborozukiyo and Asagao, have also become nuns.]

Very frail since her terrible illness, Murasaki had long been suffering from a vague malaise. There were no dramatic symptoms, merely a steady, progressive weakening as the months slipped by. Genji was frantic with grief, unable to bear the thought of outliving her by an instant. With no remaining worldly aspirations and no children to worry about, she felt no desire to cling to life, but she could not help grieving in secret when she thought of the pain she would inflict by breaking the bond that had united them for so many years. She commissioned many pious works to ease her lot in the next world, and thought and spoke constantly of somehow satisfying her cherished desire—of becoming a nun so that she might devote all her energies to religious matters for the remainder of her life, however brief the time might be. But Genji refused to hear of it. He had formed his own private resolve to renounce the world, and it occurred to him, when she pressed her point, that he might take the opportunity to set out on the same path. He had resolved, however, that he would never look back at the old life, not even for a moment, once he had become a monk. Although he and Murasaki were a devoted couple, pledged to share a lotus pedestal in paradise, he would arrange matters so that they lived apart

1. As was customary among the aristocracy, the children were being reared in their mother's family home.

while they performed their devotions in this world; they might retire to the same mountains, but intervening peaks would keep them from seeing each other. Still, his search for spiritual purity in a mountain retreat would produce only a sullied mind, for it would be impossible to keep from worrying if he left her while she seemed hopelessly ill. It was probably such considerations that caused him to vacillate, and to lag far behind those who rushed into a halfhearted sort of religious life as soon as the idea struck them. In Murasaki's opinion, it would not be seemly for her to take the vows without his permission, nor would she feel right if she did; and his refusal was the one thing she held against him. Might it be, she worried, that she was partly to blame—that she was suffering retribution for grave sins of her own?

She had decided to hurry ahead with a service of personal prayer for salvation—an offering of a thousand sets of the *Lotus Sutra*, which she had had scribes copying for a number of years. She would hold the event at the Nijō Mansion, the place she thought of as home. For each of the seven monks, she provided vestments appropriate to his status, beautiful costumes, masterpieces of dyeing and tailoring. The results were always impressive whenever she took charge of any Buddhist rite. Since she had not told Genji that she intended to make this an elaborate affair, he had not coached her in the details, but she was the best of feminine planners, knowledgeable even in sacred matters. It seemed to him that nothing was beyond her powers; he limited his contributions to a few general arrangements. Yūgiri assumed responsibility for the musicians and dancers.

The rewards for sutra recitations and other offerings presented by the emperor, the crown prince, the empresses, and the ladies at the Rokujō Mansion were splendid in themselves, but everyone had been caught up in the affair, and some of the results were almost too elaborate.[2] One wondered when Murasaki could have set so many complicated preparations in motion. She must have made her vow long, long ago.

The lady from the house of the scattering blossoms and the Akashi lady came to the Nijō Mansion. Murasaki sat in a walled chamber on the west side of the main hall, with the doors open to the south and east, and the other two ladies occupied small rooms in the northern eave-chamber, separated only by sliding partitions.

It was the tenth of the third month. The cherry trees in full bloom and the delightful balminess of the weather called to mind the beauties of Amida's paradise; one felt that everyone present would be freed of sin, even those whose faith was not especially strong. Chanted by the great assemblage of monks, the firewood-procession hymn reverberated with majestic volume, and Murasaki felt the full effect of the lonely silence after it

2. We learn here that Genji's daughter, the Akashi consort, has been named empress. Akikonomu, the Rokujō lady's daughter, also holds one of the imperial titles (see Appendix).

ended.[3] Everything saddened her nowadays. She sent the Third Prince, Niou, to the Akashi lady with a poem.[4]

oshikaranu	Little as I mind
kono mi nagara mo	bidding farewell to life,
kagiri tote	it is sad to feel
takigi tsukinan	that now the time has arrived
koto no kanashisa	when the firewood must burn out.

The Akashi lady must have feared that a poem in the same melancholy mood would expose her to charges of tactlessness later, for she answered in bland language:[5]

takigi koru	Long will be the future
omoi wa kyō o	of your quest for the doctrine
hajime nite	in this world—
kono yo ni negau	the quest that begins today
nori zo harukeki	with the cutting of firewood.

It was interesting to hear the steady beat of the drum, which harmonized with the sacred chants throughout the night.[6] In the first dim light of dawn, flowers of many colors appeared through rifts in the haze, their glorious profusion seemingly designed to ensure universal homage to spring, Murasaki's season; and birds burst into song, their warbles no less delightful than the sound of flutes.[7] Just when it seemed that nothing could be more moving or more intriguing, the "Ryōō" dance was presented; and when the tempo quickened, the musicians gave the finale a brilliant, lively performance, inspiring the whole company to strip off robes and offer them as tokens of appreciation—and thus to create a display of variegated color peculiarly appropriate to the surroundings. Those who were expert musicians performed with all the skill at their command, princes and senior nobles in-

3. The *Lotus Sutra* describes how the historical Buddha, Śākyamuni, came into possession of that sutra by gathering firewood and drawing water for the seer Asita. Though the rites here seem to resemble the conventional eight expositions service, which included an imposing "firewood procession" of chanting monks and laymen with ritual offerings of wood and water, those services usually continued over a period of four days.

4. Niou, son of the present emperor and the Akashi empress, was Murasaki's favorite among Genji's grandchildren. The poem alludes to the *Lotus Sutra*, in which the death of a buddha named Sun-and-Moon-Glow is described as having been "like firewood burning out, like a flame being extinguished." For a translation of the passage, see Hurvitz, *Scripture*, p. 15, where the simile is rendered as "without residue."

5. Her poem compares Murasaki to the king who achieved enlightenment by listening to a seer preach the *Lotus Sutra*. Hurvitz, *Scripture*, p. 195.

6. This was probably a small handdrum (*kakko*), tapped to regulate the tempo of the chant.

7. "Through rifts in the haze," a phrase from a poem by Tsurayuki, is an oblique reference to the flowering cherry, Murasaki's symbol. Ki no Tsurayuki (KKS 479): yamazakura / kasumi no ma yori / honoka ni mo / miteshi hito koso / koishikarikere ("I yearn for someone glimpsed for a fleeting instant, as through rifts in the haze we perceive the dim outline of the wild mountain cherry").

cluded. Everyone of every status seemed happy and interested, but for Murasaki, awaiting the end that was soon to come, the sight of their enjoyment merely evoked melancholy reflections.

On the following day, Murasaki felt much too ill to rise, possibly because she had deviated from her usual custom by sitting up all day on the tenth. Wondering if she was seeing and hearing everything for the last time today—the faces and figures of people who had always attended such events over the years, their several talents, the strains of their kotos and flutes—she fixed her sad gaze on individual faces, even those that would ordinarily have had no special claim to her attention. And what of her feelings about the ladies with whom there had perhaps been an inevitable, semi-serious spirit of rivalry in matters as small as summer and winter concerts and other seasonal entertainments, but to whom she was bound by ties of mutual sympathy and affection? Granted that ours is not a world where anyone can count on staying for long, it was deeply moving to think, and think again, that it was she, and she alone, who would soon set forth into the unknown. When the guests prepared to leave after the services, she felt that it was a final parting. She sent a poem to the lady from the house of the scattering blossoms:

taenubeki	The merit of these rites,
minori nagara zo	the last to be held by one
tanomaruru	who is soon to die,
yoyo ni to musubu	safeguards the tie that binds us
naka no chigiri o	through past, present, and future lives.

The reply:

musubioku	Were these splendid rites
chigiri wa taeji	merely the usual thing,
ōkata no	yet would the bond they forge
nokori sukunaki	forever link Your Ladyship
minori nari tomo	to this insignificant self.

Immediately after the dedicatory services, they took care to begin repentance rites, continuous sutra recitations, and other impressive rituals. The labors of the monks yielded no significant results, and Genji arranged for uninterrupted performances of esoteric rites at many different temples and holy places.

Summer came. Even under ordinary circumstances, there had been times when Murasaki had almost fainted from the heat, and now the episodes occurred more often than ever. The illness had not settled in any specific part of her body; she merely weakened, free of repugnant or embarrassing symptoms. When her attendants considered her chances of recovery, they were blinded by grief, devastated by the thought of losing their precious mistress.

With Murasaki in such a state, the Akashi empress decided to go to Nijō. She was to stay in the east wing, and Murasaki went to the main hall to wait for her. The arrival ceremonies merely followed the usual pattern, but to Murasaki their every aspect seemed moving. How she would have liked to watch the empress's children grow up! When the senior nobles announced themselves, she identified every man by his voice. An exceptionally large group had joined the entourage.

Savoring the rare opportunity to be with her foster-daughter, whom she had not seen for a long time, Murasaki engaged her in affectionate conversation.

Genji came in. "I'm not needed tonight, I see; I feel like a bird barred from its nest," he said. "I'll sleep somewhere else." He went off again. It had been a joy to see Murasaki up, a brief moment in which to entertain a delusion of hope.

Murasaki lingered awhile. "I couldn't presume to ask you to come to my apartments, nor am I strong enough to come here again," she said. The Akashi lady joined them, and they talked with quiet sincerity.

There were many things on Murasaki's mind, but she avoided portentous references to the period after her death. She merely offered a few calm remarks about the uncertainties of life in general, uttered with a gravity more moving, and a sadness more unmistakable, than if she had expressed her feelings in explicit language. She looked at the imperial children with tears in her eyes, her flushed face very lovely. "I did so want to watch them grow up. Could it have been because part of me has clung to life, frail as I am?" The empress also began to weep. Why was her mind obsessed with such thoughts?

Although Murasaki took care to say nothing inauspicious, she spoke of her concerns whenever the occasion offered. "There are certain ladies who have served as my intimate attendants for many years—people like So-and-so and Thus-and-so—and who are pathetically alone in the world. Please be sure to look after them when I'm gone."

The empress retired to her usual quarters for the sutra readings.[8]

Of all the imperial children, Prince Niou seemed especially appealing as he ran here and there; Murasaki liked to have him sit nearby during her easier moments. "Will you remember me after I'm gone?" she said when nobody was listening.

"I love you a lot, better than Father or Mother. I'll feel terrible if you're not here." He was charming, rubbing his eyes to make the tears disappear; and Murasaki's own eyes overflowed as she smiled at him.

8. This is said by commentators to refer to a recitation of the *Great Wisdom Sutra* (Daihan-nyagyō) on the empress's behalf. Such rites (*ki no midokkyō*, "seasonal sutra readings") were usually performed semiannually, in the second and eighth months. Since it is now summer (fourth to sixth months), the spring service has apparently been delayed. Or perhaps this is a special summer observance, a reversion to an earlier day when there were four a year.

"When you grow up, you must live here at Nijō; and when the plum trees and cherry trees bloom outside this wing, you mustn't forget to enjoy them. I'd like it if you would offer some of the flowers to the Buddha, too, when the time is right," she said. He bobbed his head with an intent look and went away on the verge of tears. His rearing and that of the First Princess had been her special responsibility, and she could not help feeling regret and sorrow at leaving her task half finished.

The long-awaited autumn arrived, bringing with it a measure of relief from the heat. Murasaki acted as though she felt refreshed, but there was little excuse for optimism. Although it was still too early for the piercing autumn wind that would naturally have evoked melancholy reflections, her sleeves were often dewy with tears.

The empress was getting ready to return to the palace. Murasaki had not tried to dissuade her. Much as she would have liked to plead for a slightly longer stay, she was afraid of seeming forward. And then there were all those messengers from the emperor, arriving with worrisome frequency. Since she could not go to the east wing, the empress came to her. It was an honor of which she felt unworthy, but she arranged a special seat near the bed, unable to bear the thought of not seeing Her Majesty again. Instead of marring her appearance, Murasaki's extreme emaciation had merely refined the nobility and elegance of her face and figure. In the past, when she was at the height of a beauty almost too radiant and dazzling, one could have likened her to the fairest of the world's flowers, but now she looked infinitely sweeter and more appealing. Nothing could have been as pitiful, as ineffably saddening, as to recognize in her the look of one who had come to regard this world as a fleeting abode.

A strong wind had begun to blow. Murasaki sat up, leaning on an armrest, so that she could look out at the twilit garden, and Genji saw her there when he crossed to the west wing. "It's wonderful to see you sitting up today. Having Her Majesty here seems to have done you a world of good," he said. It was pitiful, she thought, that he should rejoice in so tiny a hopeful sign. What misery would he suffer after her death? In an access of sadness, she murmured:

> oku to miru   Only for the moment
> hodo zo hakanaki   do we behold those dewdrops
>   to mo sureba   on the bush clover,
> kaze ni midaruru   for it is the way of dew
> hagi no uwatsuyu   to scatter in the wind.[9]

Genji felt the justice of the comparison to the dew, which was clinging precariously to blossoms tossing in the wind. And as though that were not

9. A wordplay yields another meaning: "You see me up, but not for long: the dew that is my life must soon scatter before the wind of impermanence."

enough, the very season evoked unbearable emotions.[10] He broke down in tears. [His poem:]

yaya mo seba	In this transient world,
kie o arasou	where man and his works resemble
tsuyu no yo ni	dewdrops competing
okuresakidatsu	to vanish, I would have no gap
hodo hezu mo ga na	between the first and the last.

The empress composed a reply:

akikaze ni	Who can believe
shibashi tomaranu	that in this transient world,
tsuyu no yo o	where dew cannot for long
tare ka kusaba no	withstand the autumn wind,
ue to nomi min	the only risk is on a leaf?

To Genji, she and Murasaki were all that any man could ask, two women of flawless beauty, and he yearned for a way to prolong their life together for a thousand years. It was bitter to realize that such matters are not arranged to suit our wishes—that it is beyond our power to detain the dying.

"Please go now," Murasaki said. "I've started to feel very ill. There's no more hope, but it would be discourteous to make you look at me when I'm like this." She pulled the curtain-stand close and lay down, looking even nearer to death than on past occasions.

"How are you feeling?" The empress took her hand and gazed at her with tears streaming down her face. It seemed that Murasaki was indeed vanishing like a dewdrop; innumerable messengers went rushing off to commission prayers. Mindful of the earlier time when she had returned to life, Genji suspected the machinations of an evil spirit. Throughout the night, he tried to save her by every possible means, but it was all in vain. She faded away as the new day dawned.

It was cause for deep emotion that the empress had not left yet, and that she was able to be present at the end. Neither she nor Genji reflected that the separation imposed by death is a natural one, or that others had suffered similar bereavements; their loss seemed to them uniquely terrible, and I need hardly say that they felt like dreamers lost in the gray light of dawn. Neither of them was in any condition to make sober judgments. All of Murasaki's attendants were in shock.

Genji was, of course, far more distraught than any lady-in-waiting. When Yūgiri arrived to be with him, he called him over to the curtain-stand. "See, this is how she looks at the end. My poor, poor lady! She died here without achieving her heart's desire. It sounds as though the dignitaries who were

10. By literary convention, autumn was the saddest of the seasons, and a windy autumn night was particularly lonely and depressing. Deaths in *The Tale of Genji* tend to take place in these months.

offering prayers and the other monks reciting sutras have all stopped and
gone away. But somebody must still be here. If there's no hope for her in
this world, I can at least make a pious plea for divine assistance as she treads
the dark path. Have somebody get ready to cut her hair. See if a qualified
monk isn't still around," he said. He seemed to be straining for composure,
but there was a stricken look on his face, and he could not suppress tears.
His feelings seemed all too natural to the sympathetic Yūgiri.

"It could be that a spirit is trying to torment you by making her seem
dead," Yūgiri said. "That would explain why she isn't breathing. And in
that case, it would be an excellent idea to have her take the vows. According
to holy writ, it would ensure her rebirth in paradise, even if she only lived
one more day. But if she's really dead, I doubt that she would derive much
benefit in the other world from having her hair cut off; it would only increase the sorrow of the people who see her. I wonder if it would be wise."
He proceeded to summon monks to perform the necessary offices, choosing
them with care from among a group who had remained behind, desirous of
assisting during the mourning period.

Without ever harboring any improper fantasies, he had hoped for years
that he might see Murasaki someday, even if it was only a glimpse as fleeting
as that other.[11] To think that he had never so much as caught the faint sound
of her voice! Now he would not hear the voice, and this would be his last
chance to see the face and figure, lifeless though they had become. He broke
down and wept, unable to keep up appearances. At the sight of his tears,
the women all began to wail, and he raised the curtains on the stand and
looked inside, acting as though his only concern was to restore quiet. "Do
try to be less noisy; control yourselves awhile," he said.

Objects were still indistinct in the faint light of dawn; Genji was looking
at Murasaki with the assistance of a lamp that he had brought close to the
bed. Shattered by the loss of a face so flawlessly sweet and beautiful, he
seemed to lack the will to block Yūgiri's vision when he realized that his son
was stealing glances at her.

"She still looks just the same, but you can tell she isn't alive." He pressed
his sleeve to his face. Yūgiri forced the blinding tears from his own eyes and
looked at the body. It would have been better, after all, to deny himself the
privilege; he was saddened beyond comparison, and his presence of mind
almost deserted him.

Murasaki's hair lay untouched, abundant and glossy, its ideal beauty unmarred by the slightest tangle. Her white skin seemed to glow in the bright
lamplight—fairer now that she lay dead and insensible than in the days
when she had concealed its natural color under cosmetics. To describe it as
flawless would be a waste of words. Yūgiri recognized that such beauty was

11. He had seen her through an open door during a typhoon some 15 years earlier.

not merely unusual. No, it was incomparable. He found himself harboring an unreasonable desire to keep the departed spirit with the body.

Since Murasaki's usual attendants were stupefied with grief, Genji forced himself to regain control of his senses and make the funeral arrangements. He had never borne a similar responsibility before, even though he was no stranger to sad losses; and it seemed to him that his present anguish must remain unique, unmatched in the future as in the past.

There was to be no delay; the cremation would take place that very day. Constrained by the harsh world's prescriptions, Genji was denied even the small consolation of gazing at the "cicada-husk shell." [12]

Despite the grandeur and impressiveness of the ceremonies on the vast moor, which was filled to overflowing, and despite the mourners' familiarity with such events, the monks were unable to lead the congregation to calm acceptance; it was a wrenching experience to see Murasaki rise in the air as a forlorn wisp of smoke. All who were present, including the most ignorant of commoners, wept to see the great Genji arrive on foot, leaning on an attendant as though incapable of feeling the ground under his feet. The ladies-in-waiting in the cortège felt even less in touch with reality, and the carriage men were hard pressed to keep them from falling out.

Thinking back to the small hours of the night after Aoi's death, Genji remembered that he had noticed the brightness of the moon—a sign, perhaps, that his brain had been functioning as usual. But tonight he groped in darkness. Murasaki had died on the fourteenth; it was now almost daybreak on the fifteenth. [13]

The sun rose in brilliant splendor, flooding the surroundings with light. The dewdrops sparkling in every corner of the fields set Genji to pondering the ephemerality of life in this world, which he now regarded, with increasing aversion, as merely a source of intolerable grief. True, he had survived her, but for how long? Sunk in misery, he yearned to go ahead with his old idea of becoming a monk. But people would be sure to call him weak and impulsive if he took the tonsure immediately; he would wait until after the danger of criticism had passed. It was a painful decision, almost unbearable.

Yūgiri sequestered himself at Nijō during the mourning period, never leaving for even a brief absence, but staying at Genji's side morning and evening, and doing everything possible to help him bear his anguish, which he found natural and pitiful. One evening, a violent wind evoked nostalgic memories of the time in the past when he had caught a fleeting glimpse of

12. Murasaki's body has been sealed in a coffin for the journey to the cremation site. Bishop Shōen (KKS 831): utsusemi wa / kara o mitsutsu mo / nagusametsu / fukakusa no yama / keburi dani tate ("It had helped a little that we could see the body's cicada-husk shell. Send up, at least, a plume of smoke, O Mountain of Rich Grasses").

13. This probably means that Murasaki died just before dawn on the night of the 14th (morning of the 15th), and that it is now almost daybreak on the night of the 15th (morning of the 16th).

Murasaki. His thoughts moved on to the dreamlike experience at the time of her death and to other private reminiscences, and he felt an overwhelming sense of desolation. Lest he reveal the nature of his grief, he began to chant, "Amida Buddha, Amida Buddha," telling a bead with each repetition, and trusting to the diversion to dry his tears.

inishie no	Fondly I recall
aki no yūbe no	an autumnal evening
koishiki ni	in a time now past—
ima wa to mieshi	but ah! that parting vision,
akegure no yume	that dream in dawn's gray light!

The very memory hurt.

Illustrious monks had been summoned to recite the *Lotus Sutra*—and, of course, to chant the prescribed invocations. All the services called forth deep emotion.

Genji's tears never dried, either when he tried to rest or when he was up and about; night and day, he saw the world through misty eyes. He thought much about the past. It had been evident, even from his reflection in the mirror, that he was different from others; ever since his youth, the buddhas had encouraged him to understand the misery and ephemerality of this world. His stubborn insistence on living an ordinary lay life had ended in a sorrow for which there could be no parallel in the past or future. And now, with Murasaki gone, no misgivings remained; there should be nothing to prevent his devoting himself heart and soul to religious matters. But, he worried, would it not be impossible to set foot on that longed-for path unless he could govern his mental turmoil? He intoned the sacred name of Amida Buddha. "Deign to mitigate this grief—let me forget a little, as any other mortal would do."

The emperor and less exalted personages sent innumerable condolatory messages, some of which went far beyond the customary expressions of grief. Now that Genji had decided to become a monk, nothing ought to have distracted his eyes, ears, or mind, but there was his reputation to consider. He did not want to give the appearance of having lost control of his life—to let people say later, "In his declining years, he took religious vows because he was too weak to overcome his obsession with her death"—and thus the messages actually increased his unhappiness by keeping him from doing as he wished.

There were frequent messages from Tō-no-chūjō, who was as punctilious in expressions of sympathy as in everything else, and who felt real regret and sorrow at the early death of a woman as peerless as Murasaki. One lonely evening, he sat in pensive thought, saddened by the recollection that his sister, Yūgiri's mother, had died at the same time of year. "How many of the people who mourned her have died since then! Some of us are left

behind and others go ahead, but the distinction means little in this world."
Moved by the somber sky, he sent off one of his sons, Kurōdo-no-shōshō,
with a letter full of sympathetic grief. There was a poem at the end:

inishie no	I feel as though
aki sae ima no	that long-gone autumn itself
kokochi shite	were present now:
nurenishi sode ni	dewdrops add their moisture
tsuyu zo okisou	to sleeves already drenched.

As it happened, Genji was in a reminiscent mood. He had just been absorbed in a nostalgic review of that autumn's events, and he composed his
answer in a state of great agitation, his face wet with tears:

tsuyukesa wa	I cannot perceive
mukashi ima to mo	differences between the dews
omōezu	of past and present:
ōkata aki no	every autumn seems to me
yo koso tsurakere	an unendurable season.

"I have been delighted to receive your many kind messages." He had taken
pains to temper the tone of his reply with a note of thanks, aware that Tō-
no-chūjō, who was that kind of man, would pounce on it as a sign of weakness if he revealed the true extent of his misery.

He was wearing robes a little darker than the ones he had written about
after Aoi's death.[14]

There are women in the world who may be fine human beings, but who
nevertheless incur universal envy and spite simply because fortune has
blessed them; and there are others, born to high position, who cause suffering because of their inordinate pride. But Murasaki was a remarkable person, as charming as she was efficient in every situation: her slightest action
received general praise, and she enjoyed amazing popularity, even among
people of no special discernment. In those days, complete outsiders—people
who could not really have been expected to mourn—were all moved to tears
by the soughing of the wind or the chirring of insects. For anyone who had
ever caught a glimpse of her, the grief was inconsolable. And to the women
who had served as her intimate attendants for years, it seemed bitter and
wrong that they had outlived their mistress even briefly; there were those
among them who made up their minds to live as nuns in remote mountain
dwellings.

A steady stream of heartfelt messages arrived from Akikonomu. In one,
she set down this poem, after speaking of her unending grief:

karehatsuru	That the dead lady
nobe o ushi to ya	cared but little for autumn—

14. In "Aoi" (p. 145).

> naki hito no   might it have been
> aki ni kokoro o   because she felt no liking
> todomezarikemu   for expanses of withered fields?

"Now, at last, I understand her reason."

Though he was scarcely able to concentrate, Genji read and reread the note, unable to put it down. She, at least, was left—the one person from whom it was still worthwhile to seek such distraction as literature could afford. It was a train of thought that made him feel a little better, but the tears overflowed when he recognized its implications, and he was too busy wiping his eyes to write a proper answer. [His poem:]

> noborinishi   From the realm of clouds
> kumoi nagara mo   to which you have ascended,
> kaerimi yo   please look back at me.
> ware akihatenu   This autumn I have wearied
> tsune naranu yo ni   of the transitory world.

Even after wrapping it, he sat lost in thought for a time.

Unable to keep up a facade of courage, he had moved to the women's quarters to hide his many displays of weakness, which he himself knew to be excessive. He performed quiet devotions in front of a sacred image, with only a few attendants nearby. How cruel it was to be parted by death from the one with whom he had hoped to spend a thousand years! Now he thought only of the world to come, praying with unflagging zeal that no worldly hindrance should prevent him from joining Murasaki on her lotus pedestal. (I am sorry to say, though, that he worried about what people would think if they learned of his behavior.)

He gave no definite instructions about the prescribed services for the dead. Yūgiri took charge of them.

Time after time, Genji resolved that he would take his vows today—and yet the empty days and months slipped by in dreamlike procession.

There was never an instant when the empress and the others forgot Murasaki or ceased to miss her.

The Tale of the Heike

Introduction

As the twelfth century waned, no thoughtful Japanese could have failed to recognize that the long Heian interlude of peace, economic security, and cultural florescence was nearing its end, and that a new political force was threatening the imperial court's hegemony. The signs were unmistakable.

In the countryside, there had been a steady evolution away from the institutions established by the seventh-century Taika Reforms, which had brought all rice lands under state control and had created organs of local government to collect taxes and maintain order. At the time of the reforms, some powerful families had stayed on the land, where they had typically occupied subordinate government offices; others had moved to the capital and, as members of a new aristocracy, had helped create the brilliant civilization depicted in the eleventh-century *Tale of Genji*.[1] Over the years, the court's preoccupation with the immediate concerns of aristocratic life had led to the discontinuance of the periodic land allotments on which the Taika economic system was based; to the widespread growth of private landholdings, known as *shōen*; and to the rise of a provincial armed élite, brought into existence by the government's military impotence.

Many among the new warrior class traced their roots to pre-Taika forebears who had remained in the provinces; others were aristocrats who had come from the capital as *shōen* managers and provincial officials, or were the descendants of such men. The court had become accustomed to calling on them in case of need, and during the tenth century, in particular, had used some of their prominent leaders to quell two protracted civil disturbances in eastern and western Japan, the rebellions of Taira no Masakado and Fujiwara no Sumitomo, respectively. The result had been a great in-

---

1. After frequent early moves, the court had settled first at Nara (8th c.) and then at Heian[kyō] (794 on; modern Kyoto).

crease in the power and prestige of two warrior clans of aristocratic lineage, the Taira, or Heike ("House of Taira"), and the Minamoto, or Genji ("Minamoto Clan"), whose chieftains had become actual or potential overlords for large numbers of local warriors and warrior bands. The main Minamoto strength was in the east; the Taira had established themselves both in the east and in the west, where they had grown rich through the China trade.

In the capital, little heed had been taken of the potential threat such power bases represented. The court aristocrats had continued throughout to view the rural warriors as bumpkins, useful for punishing rebels, furnishing guards to make city life safer, and repulsing incursions of soldier-monks from the Enryakuji, Kōfukuji, and Tōdaiji temples (which had developed a tendency to press their grievances by marching on the imperial palace), but otherwise unworthy of serious notice, except insofar as the economic resources of the wealthier ones might be tapped. Their attention remained fixed on the annual round of public and private ceremonies, amusements, and religious observances in the capital, and on the ceaseless quest for influence and preferment in the Chinese-style central bureaucracy, which was another Taika legacy.

In theory, the Taika Reforms had made the emperor the supreme figure at court, the source of all social status and bureaucratic position. As early as the ninth century, however, one clan, the Fujiwara, had succeeded in controlling the sovereigns—many of them children who either died young or abdicated after a few years—by providing them with Fujiwara mothers, uncles, grandfathers, and regents; and had consequently monopolized the desirable offices, acquired large numbers of *shōen*, and otherwise prospered. Their ascendancy had endured until late in the eleventh century, when Emperor Go-Sanjō, the able, mature offspring of an imperial princess, had abdicated and established what was thenceforth to function as a second center of prestige and power, the Retired Emperor's Office (*innochō*), with edict-issuing authority comparable to that of the emperor.

The principal figures in the *innochō* were a small group of from five to twenty *kinshin* ("close attendants"), who typically included rich provincial governors, relatives of the former sovereign's nurses, talented figures with no future in the bureaucracy, and men who enjoyed the retired emperor's personal favor. Rivalries and shifting alliances involving the *kinshin*, the members of the regular bureaucracy, the Fujiwara regent, and the reigning and retired sovereigns had exacerbated the already fierce competition for rank and office, affected the distribution of economic plums, and, in the absence of a rule of primogeniture, vastly complicated the selection of new emperors.

It was under such circumstances that the imperial succession fell vacant in 1155. Complex, deep-seated animosities flared after the retired emperor of the day, Toba, chose the future Emperor Go-Shirakawa; and Toba's death in 1156 set off the brief armed clash known as the Hōgen Disturbance. With the aid of the Minamoto and Taira clan chieftains, Yoshitomo and Kiyomori, Go-Shirakawa's supporters triumphed over their opponents, who had relied on Yoshitomo's father, Tameyoshi (the retired Minamoto chieftain), and a minor Taira named Tadamasa. But in a larger sense both sides lost, because the affair brought the warrior class forward as an independent power, capable of determining events at the highest political level.

Less than four years later, Go-Shirakawa, by then the retired emperor, encountered a second challenge from a faction resentful of the privileges granted to his *kinshin*; and Kiyomori again defeated the insurgents, whose chief military support had come from Yoshitomo, Kiyomori's erstwhile ally. After that clash, known as the Heiji Disturbance, the Minamoto were leaderless, bereft of Tameyoshi (who had been put to death earlier), Yoshitomo, and Yoshitomo's heir, Yoshihira. It was only thanks to the intercession of a compassionate Taira woman, Lady Ike, that the next in line for the chieftainship, Yoshitomo's fourteen-year-old son Yoritomo, was spared and allowed to live as an exile in eastern Japan. Kiyomori and his relatives, on the other hand, entered a period of prosperity such as no military clan had dreamed of.

The groundwork for the Taira ascendancy had been laid by two members of the clan's western branch, Kiyomori's father and grandfather, Tadamori and Masamori, who had managed to break into court society as *kinshin* of Go-Shirakawa's great-grandfather and father, Retired Emperors Shirakawa and Toba. As a result of their military services, and of their lavish expenditures on projects dear to the imperial hearts, Kiyomori himself had received significant preferment in office and rank from his twelfth year on. His exploits in the Hōgen and Heiji disturbances were rewarded with substantial appointments: by 1160 he had already joined the exalted ranks of the senior nobles (*kugyō*), and in 1167 he advanced from the lowest ministerial office, palace minister, to the pinnacle of the bureaucracy, the chancellorship, without passing through the intermediate positions of ministers of the right and left. Following the usual practice of ambitious courtiers, he also established kinship ties in high places. His principal wife was sister to Go-Shirakawa's favorite, Kenshunmon'in, and thus aunt to Kenshunmon'in's son, Emperor Takakura; one of his daughters, the future Kenreimon'in, became a consort of Emperor Takakura; and other daughters married important Fujiwara nobles.

Retired Emperor Go-Shirakawa, under whose auspices Kiyomori's spectacular rise occurred, seems to have been willing enough to bring the Taira leader and his relatives forward. The clan's military support was vital to his position, and his interests and Kiyomori's coincided during the period when both were maneuvering to place Kenshunmon'in's son on the throne. Moreover, Kiyomori carried out his activities with considerable prudence—not only during the tense early 1160's, when Go-Shirakawa and the reigning emperor, Nijō, were at odds, but throughout his public career, which ended in 1168, when he took Buddhist vows in consequence of an illness.

But Kiyomori's circumspection disguised the fact that his clan had become a potentially dangerous power center. By the mid-1170's, dozens of its members had acquired coveted offices, profitable provincial governorships, and extensive *shōen* holdings; the retired emperor found himself competing with Emperor Takakura's Taira kinsmen for his son's ear; and Kiyomori's daughter was an imperial consort, the potential mother of a future sovereign. Members of the clan had begun to display an arrogance that was profoundly offensive to the established aristocracy, many of whose members remained unreconciled to the presence of military upstarts in their midst. Kenshunmon'in's brother, Taira no Tokitada, had been heard to remark, "All who do not belong to this clan must rank as less than men," and one of Kiyomori's young grandsons, Sukemori, had created a scandal in 1170 by insulting the regent—an incident particularly galling because the boy's conduct had been defended by his father, Shigemori, Kiyomori's successor as head of the clan.

In 1177, Retired Emperor Go-Shirakawa attempted to neutralize the Taira threat. With his encouragement, a group of his *kinshin* planned a military coup against the clan, relying on the assistance of Yukitsuna, a minor Genji warrior from nearby Settsu Province. The plot collapsed when Yukitsuna betrayed his associates, and the *kinshin* were arrested and punished as Kiyomori saw fit.

No issue was made of Go-Shirakawa's involvement, but the affair left an irreparable breach between the retired emperor and Kiyomori. There was a period of uneasy truce, during which the two came together in a show of amity for the birth of their mutual grandson, the future Emperor Antoku, in 1178. Then, in 1179, the Taira suffered a devastating blow: Shigemori, their forceful, able leader, died at the age of forty-one and was succeeded as chieftain by his brother Munemori, whose cowardice and poor judgment were to be among the causes of the clan's ruin. Go-Shirakawa seized the opportunity to deprive the clan of tax rights and properties to which Kiyomori felt entitled, and to decide against Kiyomori's candidate for an important court office. Kiyomori promptly took an army to the capital from his villa at Fukuhara (in modern Kobe), terminated the official appointments of more than three dozen of the retired emperor's *kinshin* and other supporters, and confined the former sovereign to the Toba Mansion, an imperial villa outside the city.

Kiyomori made his démarche toward the end of 1179. A few months later, he completed the sweep of actual and potential rivals by installing his infant grandson on the throne, which Emperor Takakura was forced to vacate. But the Taira clan had become a vulnerable target for anyone who chose to identify himself as a defender of the imperial house and the traditional order. At the instigation of Minamoto no Yorimasa, a respected elderly Buddhist novice (*nyūdō*) who lived in the capital area, one of Retired Emperor Go-Shirakawa's sons, Prince Mochihito, summoned the provincial Genji (Minamoto) to arms within two months of the young Emperor Antoku's accession.

Before the year was out, two ambitious Genji, the now grown Yoritomo and his cousin, Kiso no Yoshinaka, were fighting Heike armies in the provinces. Yoritomo won an important psychological victory at the Fuji River in late 1180. He then retired to his headquarters in eastern Japan, where, as the "Kamakura Lord," he concentrated on establishing feudal relationships with local warriors, to whom he guaranteed land rights in exchange for allegiance (a tactic the Taira sought in vain to counter by recruiting men through bureaucratic channels).

In early 1181, the Taira, already at a disadvantage, were further staggered by the death of Kiyomori, which left the hapless Munemori in control of the clan's destinies. Widespread famine and pestilence produced a lull in the fighting, but by mid-1183 Yoshinaka was threatening the capital. Munemori fled westward at the head of his kinsmen, overriding the objections of his brother Tomomori and others who wanted to mount a last-ditch stand, and taking along Emperor Antoku in an attempt to legitimate the clan's status. The retired emperor promptly enthroned another of his young grandsons, the sovereign known to history as Emperor Go-Toba.

Meanwhile, three days after the flight of the Taira, Yoshinaka made a triumphant entry into the city, accompanied by his uncle Yukiie. Hailed as a savior at first, he soon wore out his welcome. His men foraged for provisions in the famine-stricken countryside, the volatile Yukiie slandered him to Retired Emperor Go-Shirakawa, his rustic ways alienated the snobbish aristocrats, and his efforts to launch an effective campaign against the Taira in the west failed miserably. Four months after his grand entry, the retired emperor mustered a ragtag collection of soldier-monks and local warriors and ordered the "savior" to withdraw from the capital. Yoshinaka crushed the imperial forces, carried out wholesale demotions of high court officials, made a futile attempt to persuade the Heike to ally themselves with him against his cousin Yoritomo, with whom the retired emperor was in active communication, and finally died at the hands of Yoritomo's eastern forces, which were commanded by two of the Kamakura Lord's half-brothers, Noriyori and Yoshitsune.

Less than a month later, the eastern forces attacked Ikuta-no-mori and Ichi-no-tani, the eastern and western entrances to a stronghold the Taira had established between the mountains and the sea, in what is now the area of Kobe. Thanks to a surprise assault from the mountains behind Ichi-no-tani, executed by Yoshitsune and a few of his men, the stronghold fell, and the Taira fled over the water to Yashima on Shikoku Island, crippled by the loss of many of their leading clansmen and retainers.

Noriyori returned to Kamakura after the victory at Ichi-no-tani, but Yoritomo sent him westward later in 1184, with instructions to seek out and attack the Taira. Meanwhile, Yoshitsune had been guarding the capital. Yoritomo had indicated to Retired Emperor Go-Shirakawa that he would also send Yoshitsune against the Taira, but now he changed his mind, angered because the retired emperor had granted his brother two desirable court offices without consulting him. Noriyori therefore advanced alone to Suō and Nagato provinces, where he presently found himself bottled up by two Taira forces—one, under the able Tomomori, threatening the Kyushu sea lanes from Hikoshima, and the other, imperiling his rear, dispatched to Kojima in Bizen Province from Yashima, where Munemori remained with Emperor Antoku. Further hampered by supply problems and a lack of boats, Noriyori idled away several months.

Finally, in early 1185, Yoritomo ordered Yoshitsune into action. Yoshitsune crossed to Shikoku during a storm, took the Taira by surprise, and drove them from Yashima. Munemori joined forces with his brother Tomomori, and the opposing sides met in a last major engagement, the naval battle of Dan-no-ura, which ended with the defeat of the Taira and the deaths of Emperor Antoku, Kiyomori's widow, and most of the male members of the clan. Thereafter, Yoritomo and Go-Shirakawa reached a tacit understanding, with ultimate authority exercised by the court in form and by the new military government at Kamakura in fact. The Genji dominated Japan, and Kiyomori's descendants disappeared from the pages of history.

Like other dramatic events of far-reaching importance, the rise and fall of the house of Taira, and especially the protracted five-year struggle known to scholars as the Genpei War, constituted a rich source of materials for the storyteller. Even before the final defeat of the Heike in 1185, tales must have been circulating about isolated events in the conflict. And at some point, probably early in the thirteenth century, the ancestor of the present *Heike monogatari* made its appearance.[2]

The Tale of the Heike is known today in numerous versions, probably dating from the thirteenth century to the Edo period (1600–1868): some are relatively short, some very long; some have variant titles; some are written in Chinese; some were seemingly designed to be read; and some contain internal evidence suggestive of use by Buddhist preachers (*sekkyōji*). By far the most characteristic, however, are texts of intermediate length, known to have been narrated by a class of blind men called *biwa hōshi*. *Biwa* is the Japanese name for the *pipa*, a Chinese musical instrument resembling a lute, which had entered Japan with the introduction of Buddhism many centuries earlier; *hōshi* ("master of the doctrines") designates a monk or, as in this case, a layman in monk's garb.

---

2. Japanese scholars classify the *Heike* as a "military tale" (*gunki monogatari, senki monogatari*), a historical or quasi-historical narrative in which warriors and their activities play a prominent role.

The *biwa hōshi* had appeared in the countryside several centuries earlier. Many of them frequented Buddhist temples, where they probably first learned to play the *biwa*, and where they may have acquired the habit of wearing clerical robes. Thanks to their attire, to their acute nonvisual senses, and to their mastery of the *biwa*—which, like other stringed instruments, was considered an efficacious means of establishing contact with unseen powers—they seem to have impressed country folk as capable of communicating with the otherworld, and they were called upon to drive away disease gods and pacify angry spirits. They also functioned as wayside entertainers, telling stories (often of a sermonizing nature), reciting poems, and singing songs.

By the thirteenth century, large numbers of such men had congregated in the capital, where they must have encountered a demand for stories about the Genpei War—in particular, tales of tragic or violent death, which, when related with sympathy, would serve to quiet the restless spirits of the deceased. Some of them are known to have frequented the Enryakuji Temple on Mount Hiei, the home base of a school of preachers famous for their eloquence and erudition; some almost certainly used their art to become acquainted with mid-level court nobles, the kind of men who collected oral stories as a hobby. Although the details are elusive, the ancestral *Heike monogatari* almost certainly emerged from such circumstances—from a pooling of the talents and practices of religiously oriented professional entertainers with the literary skills of educated men.

Medieval writings proffer several explanations of our work's origins. The best known appears in *Tsurezuregusa* (Essays in Idleness), a collection of jottings set down around 1330 by Yoshida Kenkō, a monk and former courtier with a reputation as a scholar and an antiquarian:

In Retired Emperor Go-Toba's time, the Former Shinano Official Yukinaga won praise for his learning. But when commanded to participate in a discussion of *yuefu* poetry, he forgot two of the virtues in the "Dance of the Seven Virtues," and acquired the nickname "Young Gentleman of the Five Virtues." Sick at heart, he abandoned scholarship and took the tonsure.

Archbishop Jien [the abbot of the Enryakuji Temple] made a point of summoning and looking after anyone, even a servant, who could boast of an accomplishment; thus, he granted this Shinano novice an allowance. Yukinaga composed *The Tale of the Heike* and taught it to a blind man, Shōbutsu, so that the man might narrate it. His descriptions of things having to do with the Enryakuji were especially good. He wrote with a detailed knowledge of Yoshitsune's activities, but did not say much about Noriyori, possibly for lack of information. When it came to warriors and the martial arts, Shōbutsu, who was an easterner, asked warriors questions and had Yukinaga write what he learned. People say that the *biwa hōshi* of our day imitate Shōbutsu's natural voice. (*Tsurezuregusa*, Sec. 226)

If we assume that Emperor Go-Toba's "time" means both his reign (1183–98) and his period of authority as retired emperor (1198–1221), and if scholars are correct in ascribing the original *Heike monogatari* to the early thirteenth century, then Kenkō's dating is approximately correct. Moreover, Yukinaga is a historically identifiable figure of the right period. In the absence of independent evidence, we cannot go further, but Kenkō's statements probably reflect the kind of thing that actually happened, even though they may be wholly or partially inaccurate in their particulars. The same may be said of the attributions to other authors put forward in other sources, along with purported information about textual evolution. Although none of those attributions can be substantiated, they seem to support the assumption that a number of different people had a hand in the work's creation, and that some versions, at least, were the product of collaboration between *biwa hōshi* and mid-level courtiers or monks (or both).

The available evidence also suggests that a number of texts were in existence by the end of the thirteenth century. It is impossible to know how much the earliest versions may have resembled one another in content and style, or whether they all sprang from a single original, but we *can* say that any versions entirely unrelated to our present texts have disappeared without a trace. Although there are many points of difference between extant texts, they have all descended from a common parent, even the huge forty-eight-chapter *Tale of the Rise and Fall of the Minamoto and the Taira* (Genpei jōsuiki), which bears a unique title and was once considered an independent work.

This Introduction is not the place for a discussion of the immensely complicated, ill-understood connections between surviving *Heike* texts. We shall be concerned only with the version perfected over a thirty-year period and recorded in 1371 by a man named Kakuichi, a *biwa hōshi* who took traditional materials, reshaped them into a work of literary distinction, and established a standard text, memorized and narrated by many successive generations of blind performers.

By the first half of the fourteenth century, the *biwa hōshi* in the capital had become sufficiently specialized in what came to be called *heikyoku*, or "*Heike monogatari* narration," to form a guild, the Tōdōza, with a noble house as patron. A court noble's diary tells us that Kakuichi was active in the guild by 1340, when he is conjectured to have been about forty years old. There is no reliable information concerning his earlier life—merely a legend preserved in a seventeenth-century collection of Tōdōza traditions and precepts, *Saikai yotekishū*, which identifies him as having been a monk at Shoshazan.[3] According to that work, he became a *biwa hōshi* after the sudden loss of his vision, went to the capital, joined the Tōdōza, and rose to the guild's top ranks. Whatever his origins, by 1340 he was presenting *heikyoku* performances that the same noble diarist described as "different" (*ikei*), a comment probably inspired not only by his textual revisions but

---

3. Shoshazan was another name for the Enkyōji, a Tendai temple on Mount Shosha in Harima Province (now in Himeji City, Hyōgo Prefecture). Monk Jigu, *Saikai yotekishū*, p. 94.

also by his performance style, which seems to have been more complex, colorful, and melodic than anything previously attempted by the members of the guild.

Some scholars have hypothesized that Kakuichi drew on the Buddhist chants (*shōmyō*) in vogue at Shoshazan. We know that Shoshazan was a recognized center of Buddhist music by the fifteenth century, but it is not certain whether this was the case in Kakuichi's day—or, indeed, whether there is any truth in the legend associating him with the temple. Nevertheless, he undoubtedly revolutionized *heikyoku* performance. During his lifetime, and probably soon after the appearance of the original Kakuichi text, the Tōdōza split into two schools, the Ichikata-ryū and the Yasaka-ryū. Personalities and other issues may have been involved, but the main reason for the disagreement seems to have been that a conservative faction, the future Yasaka-ryū, refused to accept the innovations introduced by Kakuichi and adopted by the rest of the community, who became the Ichikata-ryū.

Thanks largely to Kakuichi, *heikyoku* won upper-class acceptance and became recognized as the leading contemporary performing art. Both the Ichikata-ryū and the Yasaka-ryū continued to flourish in the so-called golden age of *heikyoku* narration, the century from Kakuichi's death in 1371 to the Ōnin War, which was fought in the capital between 1467 and 1477. Five or six hundred *biwa hōshi* are reported to have been active in the city in 1462, and the best of them enjoyed the patronage of aristocrats and prominent warriors, for whom they sang on demand. But the Ōnin War marked a turning point in *heikyoku* history. Thereafter, other types of entertainment became more popular—for example, the Noh drama, the comic kyōgen play, and the recitation by "narrator monks" (*katarisō*) of another military tale, *Taiheiki* (Chronicle of Great Peace).

This does not mean that *Heike monogatari* fell into obscurity. Stories about the Genpei epoch were never to lose their appeal, and *The Tale of the Heike*, the principal repository of such materials, continued to attract readers. *Heike monogatari* also served as a model for medieval chronicles of later military campaigns, and as a point of departure for countless dramas and prose stories. Of the sixteen warrior pieces (*shuramono*) in the modern Noh repertoire, a majority are based on *Heike monogatari*, and many follow its text closely, a practice specifically recommended by Zeami, the revered Noh dramatist. Other types of Noh plays retell *Heike* anecdotes about music and poetry, or center on some of the work's pathetic figures. *Heike* heroes appear as protagonists in thirty-three of fifty extant ballad dramas (*kōwakamai*, a form prominent in the sixteenth century). They figure in innumerable kabuki and puppet plays (*jōruri*) as well, many of which continue to enjoy great popularity, as do modern films and television dramas dealing with the Genpei period. *Heike* characters also play important roles in all of the half-dozen or so popular prose fiction genres of the Edo period. As a measure of the work's enduring appeal, we may note that a potboiler called *Shin Heike monogatari* (New Tale of the Heike) was a national best-seller as recently as the 1950's. There are medieval and later *Heike* picture books, songs, comic verses, and parodies.[4]

It would be wrong to claim direct influence from *Heike monogatari* on all of the hundreds of literary and artistic productions inspired by the Genpei campaigns. Some authors retold old anecdotes missing from *Heike monogatari*; others launched Genpei figures on adventures of their own devising. But we can probably say that no single Japanese literary work has influenced so many writers in so many genres for so long a time as the *Heike*, and that no era in the Japanese past can today match the romantic appeal of the late twelfth century. It is not surprising that one of the two *heikyoku* performing schools managed to survive the medieval period despite the competition of newer entertainments. The Yasaka-ryū dropped out of sight around 1600, but the Ichikata-ryū secured shogunal protection, lingered into the twentieth century, and still boasts a handful of performers.

In seeking an explanation for the Ichikata-ryū's greater longevity, we may point to its tighter organizational structure, an advantage traditionally credited to Kakuichi, who is said to have created its four grades and sixteen subgrades of performers. The school also possessed a superior text, as is evident from a comparison with extant Yasaka-ryū texts. And, finally, it seems to have offered a more appealing performance style.

There are comments on performance in various Tōdōza documents, including extensive discussion in a seventeenth-century collection, *Saikai yotekishū*,[5] and there are also Edo-period scores, compiled when sighted amateurs took up *heikyoku* as a hobby. In view of the prestige enjoyed by Kakuichi and his text, and of the generally conservative nature of the Japanese arts during and after the medieval period, it can probably be assumed that such sources, and the modern performers who use them, reflect Kakuichi's own practice to a considerable extent.

Drawing on these sources, then, we can say that the performer was silent while the *biwa* was played; that the *biwa* music was relatively uncomplicated, as compared with, say, the samisen accompaniment in the *jōruri* puppet theater; and that the *biwa* passages were short. The instrument sounded the opening pitch for a vocal passage, gave the pitch for the succeeding passage, or heightened the mood conveyed by the text. The vocal part of the performance was a combination of declamation and singing. For each section (*ku*)—that is, each titled subdivision of a chapter (*maki*)—there was a prescribed *katari*, or narrative, pattern, designed both to suit the context

4. There are also three complete English translations—by A. L. Sadler; Hiroshi Kitagawa and Bruce T. Tsuchida; and Helen Craig McCullough. *Heike monogatari* has received extensive scholarly attention in Japan (much of it devoted to the vexed question of textual transmission), but little has been written in the West, aside from brief treatments in surveys of Japanese literature. For a consideration of some aspects of the work, see McCullough, *Heike*, Appendix A, "The 'Heike' as Literature."

5. Summarized in Ueda, *Literary and Art Theories*, pp. 114–27.

and to provide the variety and drama necessary to capture and hold an audience's attention. There are said to have been as many as thirty-three types of melodies in use at one time or another, of which some eight or nine were especially important. A brief look at four of them will give a general idea of their nature.[6]

The most musical was the *sanjū* ("threefold"), used for passages that dealt with the imperial court, the supernatural, the arts, or the classical past, or wherever an effect of gentle, elegant beauty was desired. High-pitched and leisurely, it was compared in *Saikai yotekishū* to the flight of a large crane rising from the reed plains: the voice soared, wavered gracefully as though flapping its wings, and settled slowly to earth again.

A quavering, slow melody called *origoe* ("broken voice") was employed in pathetic or tragic passages, such as the description of little Emperor Antoku's death by drowning, or to express heroic resolve, or to convey an address to the throne, or for letters, some kinds of dialogue, and soliloquies.

A livelier melody, *hiroi* ("picking up"), was associated especially with fighting and deeds of valor, but might also be prescribed for descriptions of disasters, scenes of confusion, or any other sort of dramatic action.

For straightforward narrative, the performer might employ *kudoki* ("recitation"), a relatively fast, simple melody close to ordinary speech. Narrative was also rendered in *shiragoe*, "plain voice," a brisk, declamatory style making no use of melody.

Kakuichi's art as a performer manifested itself not only in the development of a superior repertoire of melodies, but also, and more significantly, in the painstaking combination of individual melodic elements into patterns that were dramatically effective and appropriate to the content. Armed with the model he provided, which regulated every nuance of every section, the rank and file of the Ichikata-ryū enjoyed an invaluable advantage over their competitors. We cannot appreciate that advantage fully, nor can we recapture the medieval audience's experience, even if we are fortunate enought to witness a brief performance by a modern narrator. Limited for all practical purposes to the printed page, we find ourselves in the position of those who must read a script instead of seeing the play performed. But just as the best dramatists surmount such obstacles, so Kakuichi and his colleagues have created an independent literary work of lasting interest and importance. It is the translator's fault, not theirs, if this abbreviated English version fails to convey the heroic spirit, humor, and lyricism with which the original is so richly endowed.

6. Monk Jigu, *Saikai yotekishū*, pp. 48–55.

Principal Characters

Antoku, Emperor (1178–85, r. 1180–85). Son of Emperor Takakura and Kenreimon'in; grandson of Kiyomori

Atsumori, Taira (1169–84). Son of Tsunemori; nephew of Kiyomori. Died at Ichi-no-tani.

Dainagon-no-suke. Daughter of Gojō Major Counselor Kunitsuna; wife of Shigehira; one of Emperor Antoku's nurses; lady-in-waiting to Kenreimon'in

Go-Shirakawa, Retired Emperor (1127–92, r. 1155–58). Son of Retired Emperor Toba and Taikenmon'in; exercised authority during the reigns of Emperors Nijō, Rokujō, Takakura, Antoku, and Go-Toba. An instigator of coup against Taira clan. Nijō and Takakura were his sons; Rokujō, Antoku, and Go-Toba his grandsons.

Kagetoki, Kajiwara (d. 1200). Trusted lieutenant of Yoritomo; figures in *Heike monogatari* as provoking Yoritomo's enmity toward Yoshitsune

Kamakura Lord, *see* Yoritomo

Kanehira, Imai. Foster-brother and chief lieutenant of Yoshinaka

Kenreimon'in (1155–1213). Daughter of Kiyomori and nun of second rank; full sister of Munemori, Tomomori, and Shigehira; consort of Emperor Takakura; mother of Emperor Antoku. Taken prisoner at Dan-no-ura; died as a nun.

Kiso, *see* Yoshinaka

Kiyomori, Taira (1118–81). Son of Tadamori; head of clan after father's death; dominated court despite nominal retirement in 1168

Koremori, Taira (?–?). Oldest son of Shigemori; committed suicide after taking the tonsure

Michimori, Taira (d. 1184). Son of Norimori; nephew of Kiyomori; died at Ichi-no-tani

Mochihito, Prince (1151–80). Second son of Retired Emperor Go-Shira-kawa; nominal leader of anti-Taira revolt of 1180. Called Prince Takakura.

Mongaku, monk (1139–1203). In *Heike monogatari*, incites Yoritomo to rebellion; later gains reprieve for Rokudai, Koremori's son

Munemori, Taira (1147–85). Son of Kiyomori and nun of second rank; clan head after Shigemori's death; palace minister. Executed in 1185.

Narichika, Fujiwara (1138–77). Close associate of Retired Emperor Go-Shirakawa; brother-in-law of Shigemori; father-in-law of Koremori. Executed for plotting against Taira in 1177.

Naritsune, Fujiwara (d. 1202). Son of Narichika; son-in-law of Norimori. Exiled after anti-Taira plot of 1177.

Norimori, Taira (1128–85). Son of Tadamori; brother of Kiyomori; father-in-law of Naritsune. Died at Dan-no-ura.

Noritsune, Taira (?–?). Son of Norimori; nephew of Kiyomori. Depicted in *Heike monogatari* as a leading Taira commander.

Noriyori, Minamoto (?–?). Son of Yoshitomo; half-brother of Yoritomo. One of Yoritomo's two principal commanders in the Genpei campaigns.

Nun of second rank (1126–85). Taira no Shishi (Tokiko), principal wife of Kiyomori and mother of Munemori, Tomomori, Shigehira, and Kenreimon'in. Died at Dan-no-ura.

Rokudai, Taira (d. ca. 1200?). Son of Koremori; grandson of Shigemori. Prospective head of Taira clan after Genpei War.

Shigehira, Taira (1157–85). Son of Kiyomori and nun of second rank. Important Taira commander; captured at Ichi-no-tani and later executed.

Shigemori, Taira (1138–79). Oldest son and heir of Kiyomori, whom he succeeded as clan head; palace minister

Tadanori, Taira (1144–84). Son of Tadamori; brother of Kiyomori. Known as a poet. Died at Ichi-no-tani.

Takakura, Emperor (1161–81, r. 1168–80). Son of Retired Emperor Go-Shirakawa and Kenshunmon'in; nephew of Tokitada; married to Kenreimon'in; father of Emperor Antoku

Takakura, Prince, *see* Mochihito

Tokimasa, Hōjō (1138–1215). Yoritomo's deputy in the capital after the breach with Yoshitsune

Tokitada, Taira (d. 1189). Member of a branch family. Brother of Kenshun-mon'in; uncle of Emperor Takakura; brother of nun of second rank; provisional major counselor

Tomomori, Taira (1152–85). Son of Kiyomori and nun of second rank. Figures in *Heike monogatari* as a military leader. Died at Dan-no-ura.

Tsunemasa, Taira (d. 1184). Oldest son of Tsunemori; nephew of Kiyomori. Known as a poet and musician. Died at Ichi-no-tani.

Tsunemori, Taira (1124–85). Brother of Kiyomori; consultant

Yorimasa, Minamoto (1104–80). Distant relative of Yoritomo; military leader in revolt of Prince Mochihito

Yorimori, Taira (1132–86). Half-brother of Kiyomori; son of Yoritomo's benefactor, Lady Ike; provisional major counselor

Yoritomo, Minamoto (1147–99). Son and eventual heir of clan chieftain Yoshitomo; eastern hegemon; founder of Kamakura shogunate after victory in Genpei War

Yoshinaka, Minamoto (1154–84). Son of Yoshikata; cousin of Yoritomo. Leader of northern anti-Taira forces; killed in battle against Noriyori's army.

Yoshitsune, Minamoto (1159–89). Son of Yoshitomo; younger half-brother of Yoritomo. As one of Yoritomo's two principal commanders, won pivotal victories in the Genpei campaigns. Later hounded by forces of the jealous Yoritomo.

Yukiie, Minamoto (d. 1186). Son of Tameyoshi; uncle of Yoritomo. Known at first as Yoshimori. Military leader; allied successively with Yoritomo, Yoshinaka, and Yoshitsune.

Contents of the 'Heike'

Chapter 6

Chapter 7

Chapter 8

Chapter 9

Chapter 10

Chapter 11

Chapter 12

The Initiates' Chapter

Chapter 1

Time: seventh month of 1169 to around fifth month of 1177
Principal subject: growth of bad feeling between the Taira clan and the court
Principal characters:

> Go-Shirakawa, Retired Emperor. Head of the imperial clan
> Jōken. Prominent Buddhist monk; holds title Dharma Seal
> Kiyomori (Taira). Retired head of the Taira clan; main power at court
> Motofusa (Fujiwara). Imperial regent
> Narichika (Fujiwara). A favorite courtier of Retired Emperor Go-Shirakawa; the principal Shishi-no-tani conspirator
> Naritsune (Fujiwara). Son of Narichika; son-in-law of Norimori
> Norimori (Taira). Brother of Kiyomori; father-in-law of Naritsune
> Shigemori (Taira). Eldest son of Kiyomori, on whom he is a restraining influence; clan head
> Shunkan, Bishop. High official at Hosshōji, an important Buddhist temple; a Shishi-no-tani conspirator
> Takakura. Reigning emperor; son of Retired Emperor Go-Shirakawa
> Yasuyori (Taira). A minor member of the Taira clan; a Shishi-no-tani conspirator

1.1. *Gion Shōja*

The sound of the Gion Shōja bells echoes the impermanence of all things;
The color of the *śāla* flowers reveals the truth that the prosperous must decline.
The proud do not endure; they are like a dream on a spring night;
The mighty fall at last, they are as dust before the wind. . . .

1.6. *Giō*

[This is one of a series of early episodes describing the rise and increasing arrogance of the Taira and their leader, Kiyomori.]

Now that Kiyomori held the whole country in the palm of his hand, he indulged in one freakish caprice after another, undeterred by the censure of society or the scorn of individuals. For instance, there were two famous and accomplished *shirabyōshi* dancers who lived in the capital in those days, sisters called Giō and Ginyo. They were the daughters of another dancer, Toji. Kiyomori took a great fancy to Giō, the older one, which meant that Ginyo, the younger, became a popular favorite. He also built a fine house for the mother, Toji, installed her in it, and sent her five hundred bushels of rice and a hundred thousand coins every month. So the whole family was exceedingly prosperous and fortunate.

When the other dancers in the capital heard about Giō's good luck, some of them felt envious and others felt spiteful. The envious ones said, "Giō has all the luck! I wish the same thing would happen to me. It must be the 'Gi' in her name. I'll use it, too." One called herself Giichi, another Gini, another Gifuku, another Gitoku, and so forth. The spiteful ones, of whom there were many, stuck to their own names. "What difference could a name or part of a name make?" they sniffed. "Good luck is something a person gets from a previous existence."

After things had gone on like that for three years, another famous dancer arrived in the capital from Kaga Province. Her name was Hotoke, and she was sixteen years old. Everybody in the city showered her with praise, high and low alike. "We've had lots of *shirabyōshi* ever since the old days, but we've never seen dancing like this," people said.

"No matter how famous I am, I'm disappointed that I've never been called in by Kiyomori, the most important man in the country," Hotoke thought. "What's to keep me from volunteering to perform for him? It's usual enough." She went to Kiyomori's house at Nishihachijō, and someone announced her.

"Hotoke is here, the dancer they're talking about in the capital nowadays."

"What's that you say? Entertainers like her aren't supposed to just show up without being called. What makes her think she can do this? Besides, she has no business coming to the place where Giō lives, whether she's a god or a buddha.[1] Throw her out!" Kiyomori said.

As Hotoke was about to leave after that harsh dismissal, Giō spoke to Kiyomori. "It's quite customary for an entertainer to appear without an invitation. And they say Hotoke's very young, too. Now that she's plucked up the courage to come, it would be cruel to send her home with that harsh dismissal. As a dancer myself, I can't help feeling involved; I'd be miserable. You'd be doing her a great kindness if you just received her, even if you didn't watch her dance or listen to her sing. Won't you please bend a little and call her back?"

"Well, my dear, if you're going to make a point of it, I'll see her before she goes," Kiyomori said. He sent a messenger to summon Hotoke.

1. A pun on Hotoke's name, which can mean "Buddha."

Hotoke had entered her carriage after that harsh dismissal.[2] She was just leaving, but she returned in obedience to the summons. Kiyomori came out to meet her. "I shouldn't have received you today; I'm just doing it because Giō made a point of it. But I may as well listen to a song as long as I'm here. Let's have an *imayō*," he said. Hotoke assented respectfully:

kimi o hajimete	Now that it has encountered
miru ori wa	this lord for the first time,
chiyo mo henubeshi	it will live a thousand years—
himekomatsu	the seedling pine tree.
omae no ike naru	Cranes seem to have come in flocks
kameoka ni	to disport themselves
tsuru koso mureite	where Turtle Island rises
asobumere	from the garden lake.

She chanted the song three times, and the beauty of her voice astonished everyone. Kiyomori felt a stir of interest. "You sing *imayō* nicely, my dear. I suspect you're a good dancer, too," he said. "I'll watch you do a number. Call the drummer." The drummer was set to his instrument and Hotoke danced.

A beautiful girl with a magnificent head of hair and a sweet, flawless voice could hardly have been a clumsy dancer. Her skill was beyond imagination, and Kiyomori was dazzled, swept off his feet.

"What can this mean?" Hotoke said. "It was my own idea to come, and I was thrown out for my pains, but then I was called back because Giō spoke up for me. What would she think if I were kept here? It's embarrassing even to wonder about it. Please let me go home now."[3]

"That's out of the question. If you're hanging back because of Giō, I'll get rid of her," Kiyomori said.

"I couldn't dream of such a thing! It would be bad enough if you kept the two of us here together, but I couldn't possibly face the embarrassment if you sent her away and kept me by myself. Please let me go today. I'll come any time you happen to remember me."

"What! What! That's out of the question. Tell Giō to get out of the house right now." He sent Giō three separate messages.

Giō had resigned herself to this possibility long ago, but she had never dreamed that it might happen "so very soon as today."[4] Now, with Kiyo-

2. Conventional storyteller's phrases, such as "that harsh dismissal," occur fairly often in *The Tale of the Heike*. As will be seen later, they are especially numerous in episodes having to do with warriors.

3. We are to understand that Kiyomori has decided to keep Hotoke as a mistress. In some versions of the tale, this speech occurs after a retainer has carried her off into another room. See Nagano, *Heike monogatari no kanshō*, p. 23.

4. A phrase from Ariwara no Narihira's death poem (KKS 861): tsui ni yuku / michi to wa kanete / kikishikado / kinō kyō to wa / omowazarishi o ("Upon this pathway, I have long heard others say, man sets forth at last—yet I had not thought to go so very soon as today").

mori insisting on her immediate departure, she prepared to leave as soon as the room was swept and tidied.

Every parting causes sadness, even when two people have merely sheltered under the same tree or scooped water from the same stream. With what regret and grief did Giō prepare to bid farewell to her home of three years, her eyes brimming with futile tears! But she could not linger; the end had come. Weeping, she scribbled a poem on a sliding door before she set out—perhaps to serve as a reminder of one who had gone:

moeizuru mo	Since both are grasses
karuru mo onaji	of the field, how may either
nobe no kusa	be spared by autumn—
izure ka aki ni	the young shoot blossoming forth
awadehatsubeki	and the herb fading from view?[5]

She got into her carriage, rode home, and fell prostrate inside the sliding doors, sobbing wildly.

"What's the matter? What's wrong?" her mother and sister asked. She could not answer. They had to learn the truth by questioning the maid who had come with her.

The monthly deliveries of rice and coins ceased, and it was the turn of Hotoke's connections to prosper. All kinds of men sent Giō letters and messengers. "People say Kiyomori has dismissed her. Why not see her and have some fun?" they thought. But she could not shrug everything off and lead a gay social life. She refused to receive the letters, much less the messengers, and spent more and more time in tears, her gloom deepened by their importunities.

The year ended, and in the following spring a messenger came to Giō's house from Kiyomori. "How have you been since we parted? Hotoke seems bored these days; come and amuse her with some *imayō* and dances." Giō made no reply.

"Why don't you answer? Do you refuse to come? If so, speak up. There are steps I can take," Kiyomori sent word.

Giō's mother, Toji, was upset. "Do give him some kind of answer, Giō," she urged tearfully. "That would be better than having him scold you like this."

Giō still refused to answer. "I'd promise to go at once if I meant to obey him, but I don't mean to, so I don't know what to say. He says he'll 'take steps' unless I obey his summons, but the most he can do is banish or kill me. Banishment wouldn't matter to me, or death, either. I can't face him again after the contemptuous way he treated me," she said.

Her mother offered some more advice. "No living creature in our country

5. The poem puns on *karuru* ("wither"; "separate") and *aki* ("autumn"; "satiety"). "Young shoot" (*moeizuru* [*kusa*]) and "fading herb" (*karuru* [*kusa*]) are metaphors for Hotoke and Giō.

can disobey Kiyomori. The bonds linking a man and a woman are forged before this life begins. Sometimes a couple may part early, after having sworn to stay together forever; sometimes a relationship that had seemed temporary may last a lifetime. A sexual liaison is the most uncertain thing in the world. That you enjoyed Kiyomori's favor for three years was an unusual show of affection on his part. Of course he won't kill you if you don't obey his summons; he'll simply expel you from the capital. You and your sister are young; you'll probably survive very nicely, even among rocks and trees. But your feeble old mother will be banished too, and my heart sinks when I think of living in some strange country place. Won't you please let me finish out my life in the capital? I'll regard it as a filial act in this world and the next."

Giō told herself that she had to obey her mother, hard though it was. She was pitifully distraught as she set out, her eyes brimming with tears. Unable to bring herself to go alone, she traveled to Nishihachijō in a carriage with her sister, Ginyo, and two other dancers.

It was not to her old place, but to a much inferior seat, that she was directed.

"What can this mean?" she wondered. "It was misery enough to be discarded through no fault of my own; now I have to accept an inferior seat. What shall I do?" She pressed her sleeve to her face to hide the tears, but they came trickling through.

Hotoke was overcome with pity. "Ah, what's this?" she said. "It might be different if she weren't used to being called up here. Please have her come here, or else please excuse me. I'd like to go and greet her."

"That's entirely out of the question!" Kiyomori made her stay where she was.

Then Kiyomori spoke up, with no regard for Giō's feelings. "Well, how've you been since we parted? Hotoke seems bored; sing her an *imayō*."

Now that she was there, Giō felt unable to refuse. She restrained her tears and sang:

hotoke mo mukashi wa	In days of old, the Buddha
bonbu nari	was but a mortal;
warera mo tsui ni wa	in the end, we ourselves
hotoke nari	will be buddhas too.
izure mo busshō	How grievous that distinctions
gu seru mi o	must separate those
hedatsuru nomi koso	who are alike in sharing
kanashikere	the Buddha-nature![6]

She repeated the words twice, weeping, and tears of sympathy flowed from the eyes of all the many Taira senior nobles, courtiers, gentlemen of fifth rank, and samurai who sat in rows looking on.

6. The song, an adaptation of a Buddhist chant, puns on Hotoke's name.

Kiyomori was diverted by the performance. "An excellent entertainment for the occasion," he said. "I'd like to watch you dance, but some urgent business has come up today. Keep presenting yourself from now on, even if I don't summon you; you must amuse Hotoke with your *imayō* and dances." Giō departed in silence, suppressing her tears.

"I forced myself to go to that hateful place because I didn't want to disobey Mother, and now I've been humiliated again. The same thing will keep happening if I stay in society. I'm going to drown myself," Giō said.

"If you do, I'll drown with you," said her sister, Ginyo.

The mother, Toji, was greatly distressed. In tears, she offered more advice. "It's only natural for you to feel bitter. I'm sorry I urged you to go; I didn't dream things would turn out that way. But if you drown yourself, your sister says she'll do the same, and then what will become of your feeble old mother, even if she manages to linger on after the deaths of her two daughters? I'll drown with you. I suppose a person would have to say it's one of the five deadly sins to make a parent drown before her time. The world is only a transient shelter; it doesn't matter if we suffer humiliation here. The truly hard thing is the darkness of the long afterlife. This life is nothing; I'm just worrying about your having to face the evil paths in the next one."

After hearing her mother's tearful plea, Giō suppressed her own tears. "You're right. There's no doubt that I'd be committing one of the five deadly sins if we all killed ourselves. I'll give up the idea of suicide. But I'd just have to suffer more if I stayed in the capital, so I'm going somewhere else."

Thus it was that Giō became a nun at the age of twenty-one. She built a brush-thatched hermitage deep in the Saga mountains, and there she dwelt, murmuring buddha-invocations.

"I vowed to drown myself with my sister," Ginyo said. "Why should I hang behind when it comes to renouncing the world?" Most pitifully, that nineteen-year-old girl also altered her appearance and secluded herself with Giō to pray for rebirth in paradise.

"In a world where even young girls alter their appearance, why should a feeble old mother cling to her gray hair?" the mother, Toji, said. She shaved her head at the age of forty-five and, like her daughters, performed buddha-invocations in earnest prayer for rebirth in paradise.

Spring passed, summer waned, and the first autumn winds blew. It was the season when mortals gaze at the star-meeting skies and write of love on the leaves of the paper-mulberry, the tree reminiscent of an oar crossing the heavenly stream.[7]

One afternoon, the mother and daughters watched the setting sun disappear behind the rim of the western hills. "People say the western paradise lies where the sun sets. Someday we'll be born into a peaceful life there," they said. The thought evoked memories and brought many tears.

7. The passage, written in poetic seven-five meter, contains a pun on *kaji* ("paper-mulberry tree"; "oar," a reference to the Tanabata legend). On Tanabata, see Glossary.

After the twilight faded, they fastened their plaited bamboo door, lit the dim lamp, and settled down to intoning buddha-invocations in unison.

While they were chanting, they were frightened by the sound of someone knocking on the door.

"A malevolent spirit must have come to interfere with our humble invocations," they said. "What mortal would wait until late at night to visit a brush-thatched mountain hermitage, a place where nobody ever calls, not even in the daytime? The door is just plaited bamboo; it would be the easiest thing in the world to smash it if we refused to open it. We'd better let him in. If he's a merciless creature bent on our destruction, we must rely firmly on the original vow of Amida, the Buddha in whom we have always placed our trust; we must just keep repeating the sacred name. The heavenly host comes to meet believers when it hears their voices, so it will be sure to take us to the pure land. We'll simply have to be careful not to falter in our recitations."

Reassuring one another in that manner, they opened the door. But the visitor was not a malevolent spirit. No, it was Hotoke.

"What in the world!" Giō said. "Can it really be Hotoke? Am I awake or dreaming?"

Hotoke tried to restrain her tears. "What I say will probably sound self-serving, but it would seem callous to keep quiet about it, so I want to go over the whole story from the beginning. I went to Kiyomori's mansion on my own initiative and was turned away, but then I was called back, thanks entirely to Giō's intervention. A woman is a poor, weak creature who can't control her destiny. I felt miserable about being kept there. When you were summoned again to sing the *imayō*, it brought my own situation home to me. I couldn't feel happy when I knew my turn would come some day. I also realized that you spoke the truth in the lines you left on the sliding door, 'How may either be spared by autumn?' Later on, I didn't know where you'd gone, but I heard that the three of you were living together as nuns. I envied you after that, and I kept asking for my freedom, but Kiyomori wouldn't let me go.

"When we stop and think about it, good fortune in this world is a dream within a dream; happiness and prosperity mean nothing. It's hard to achieve birth in human form, hard to gain access to the Buddha's teachings. If I sink into hell this time, it will be hard to rise again, no matter how many eons may pass. We can't count on our youth; the old may outlive the young in this world. Death refuses to wait for the space of a breath; life is more evanescent than a mayfly or a lightning flash. I couldn't bear to keep preening myself on my temporary good fortune and ignoring the life to come, so I stole away this morning, put on this appearance, and made my way here." She removed the robe that had covered her head, and they saw that she had become a nun.

"Now that I've come to you in this new guise, please forgive my past offenses," she pleaded, with tears streaming down her face. "If you say you forgive me, I want to recite the sacred name with you and be reborn on the same lotus pedestal. But if you can't bring yourself to do it, I'll wander off—I don't care where—and then I'll recite buddha-invocations as long as I live, lying on a bed of moss or the roots of a pine tree, so that I can be reborn in the pure land."

Giō tried to restrain her tears. "I never dreamed you felt that way. I ought to have been able to accept my unhappiness here at Saga, for sorrow is the common lot in this world, but I was always jealous of you. I'm afraid there would have been no rebirth in the pure land for me. I seemed stranded halfway between this world and the next. The change in your appearance has scattered my old resentment like dewdrops; there's no doubt now that I'll be reborn in the pure land. To be able to attain that goal is the greatest of all possible joys. People have talked about our becoming nuns as though it were unprecedented, and I've more or less thought the same thing, but it was only natural for me to do it when I hated society and resented my fate. What I did isn't worth mentioning if it's compared with the vows you've just taken. You weren't resentful, you knew no sorrow. Only true piety could instill such revulsion against the unclean world, such longing for the pure land, in the heart of someone who's barely turned seventeen. I look on you as a teacher. Let's seek salvation together."

Secluded in a single dwelling, the four women offered flowers and incense before the sacred images morning and evening, and their prayers never flagged. I have heard that all of them achieved their goal of rebirth in the pure land, each in her turn. And so it was that the four names, "the spirits of Giō, Ginyo, Hotoke, and Toji," were inscribed together on the memorial register at Retired Emperor Go-Shirakawa's Chōgōdō Hall. Theirs were touching histories.

1.11.   *Horsemen Encounter the Regent*

Retired Emperor Go-Shirakawa became a monk on the sixteenth of the seventh month in the first year of Kaō [1169]. He continued to deal with affairs of state after taking the tonsure, and there was no way to distinguish between him and the reigning sovereign. The senior nobles and courtiers closest to him, and even the warriors in his north guards, received offices, ranks, and emoluments beyond their deserts, but some of them were dissatisfied, human nature being what it is. They exchanged whispered complaints with their friends. "If only So-and-so would die, somebody else could be appointed to his province," they said. "If Thus-and-so died, I might get his office." In private conversations, the retired emperor expressed similar sentiments. "Since early times, many men have subdued the court's enemies in one reign or another, but nothing like this has ever happened before," he would say. "When Sadamori and Hidesato put down Masakado, when Yoriyoshi crushed Sadatō and Munetō, when Yoshiie conquered Takehira and

Iehira, their only rewards were provincial appointments.[8] It's not right for Kiyomori to do whatever he pleases; it's because the court has lost its authority in these latter days of the Law." But there never seemed to be a chance for him to administer a reprimand.

Meanwhile, the Taira bore the court no particular ill will. But then, on the sixteenth of the tenth month in the second year of Kaō [1170], something happened that was to plunge the nation into chaos.

At that time, Shigemori's second son, Middle Captain Sukemori, was only a thirteen-year-old boy, with the title Governor of Echizen. Charmed by a light snowfall, which had created interesting effects in the withered fields, he decided to lead thirty young mounted samurai on an outing to Rendaino, Murasakino, and the riding grounds of the bodyguards of the right. He took along a great many hawks, spent the day hunting larks and quail, and turned back toward Rokuhara as twilight fell. Meanwhile, Lord Motofusa, the imperial regent, happened to be on his way to the palace from his mansion near the intersection of Naka-no-mikado and Higashi-no-tōin avenues. He was traveling south along Higashi-no-tōin Avenue and west along Ōi-no-mikado Avenue, intending to enter through the Yūhōmon Gate, when Sukemori met his procession at the intersection of Ōi-no-mikado Avenue and Inokuma Street.

"Who goes there?" asked the regent's men. "You're breaking all the rules. This is the regent's procession. Get off your horses! Dismount!"

Sukemori was arrogant and high-spirited, and all of his samurai were in their teens. None of them understood the niceties of social conduct. It meant nothing to them that they had encountered the regent, nor did it occur to them to pay him the courtesy of dismounting. Instead, they tried to gallop through.

Unaware that the leader of the band was Kiyomori's grandson (or, perhaps, making a pretense of not recognizing him in the dark), the regent's men retaliated by pulling them all off their horses in a most humiliating fashion.

When Sukemori went dragging back to Rokuhara with his tale, Kiyomori flew into a rage. "I don't care whether he's the regent or not! He's supposed to defer to my relatives," he said. "It was a hateful thing to do—to just go blithely ahead and insult a young boy. That's the kind of thing that leads to more slights. I'll teach him a lesson if it's the last thing I do. I'll get even!"

"Why worry about nothing?" Shigemori said. "It would be a real disgrace if a Genji like Yorimasa or Mitsumoto insulted us. It was rude for a son of mine not to dismount when he met a regental procession." He called in the samurai who had gone with Sukemori. "Remember this from now on," he told them. "I'm going to apologize to the regent for your discourtesy." Then he went home.

8. Sadamori, Hidesato, Yoriyoshi, and Yoshiie were court-appointed warriors who defeated powerful local rebels in the 10th and 11th centuries. See Glossary.

Later, without a word to Shigemori, Kiyomori called in sixty or so rural warriors—Nanba, Senō, and other rustics, who feared nothing except his commands. "The regent will go to the palace on the twenty-first to consult about the emperor's capping ceremony. Intercept him wherever you please, and give his way-clearers and escorts haircuts to avenge Sukemori," he said.[9]

Without the faintest suspicion of any such thing, the regent traveled west along Naka-no-mikado Avenue toward the Taikenmon Gate, which he was scheduled to use that day. He was to stay awhile in his palace apartments to make arrangements about the capping officiant and the promotions for the ceremony in the following year, so his procession was somewhat grander than usual.

When he reached the vicinity of Inokuma and Horikawa streets, a party of helmeted and armored horsemen from Rokuhara surrounded him and shouted a great battle cry from every direction, more than three hundred strong. They chased down his way-clearers and escorts, who were magnificently attired for the day's event, dragged them off their horses, abused them with scurrilous remarks, and cut off their hair. One of the ten escorts was Takemoto, an aide in the bodyguards of the right. Before the warriors sheared Fujiwara Chamberlain Takanori, one of them said in a loud, clear voice, "Don't consider this your hair. Think of it as your master's."

After that, all the warriors poked their bow ends inside the regent's carriage, pulled the blinds down, cut loose the rump and chest ropes from the ox, and perpetrated other outrages. Then they went off to Rokuhara with victorious whoops. "Well done!" Kiyomori told them.

One of the regent's attendants was a former messenger to Inaba named Toba no Kunihisamaru, a man of low status but delicate feeling. In tears, he took hold of the shafts and pulled the regent home to his Naka-no-mikado Mansion. Words cannot describe the wretchedness of the state in which Lord Motofusa returned, the sleeve of his court robe raised to hold back tears. Never in all the generations since Yoshifusa and Mototsune had such an experience been visited on an imperial regent. (I need say nothing of Kamatari and Fuhito.)[10] This was the first of the Taira clan's evil deeds.

Shigemori showed his displeasure by dismissing all the participants in the attack. "No matter what unexpected order my father might issue, it was your responsibility to at least give me a hint of it," he said. He sent Sukemori away to Ise Province for a time. "It was all your fault," he told him. "'The sprout of the sandalwood already smells fragrant.' When a boy is twelve or thirteen, he's old enough to understand and obey the rules of courtesy. Your rudeness has blackened your grandfather's name; you have no conception of filial piety." His conduct won praise from the emperor and everyone else.

9. According to reliable historical sources, it was actually Shigemori who ordered the retaliatory action. The *Heike* consistently presents Shigemori in a favorable light in order to contrast his character with Kiyomori's.

10. Yoshifusa, Mototsune, Kamatari, and Fuhito were heads of the Fujiwara clan.

1.12. *Shishi-no-tani*

As a consequence, the deliberations concerning the imperial capping were postponed. They took place on the twenty-fifth in the courtiers' hall at the retired emperor's residence. It would not have been proper to leave the regent as he was, so an imperial edict was issued on the ninth of the eleventh month, notifying him that he would be elevated to the chancellorship on the fourteenth. He proffered his expressions of gratitude on the seventeenth. Nevertheless, the incident left a disagreeable aftertaste.

The year drew to a close. Emperor Takakura performed the capping ceremony on the fifth of the first month in the new year, the third of the Kaō era [1171], and paid a formal visit to his parents on the thirteenth. When they received him, the retired emperor and his consort, Imperial Lady Kenshunmon'in, must have found him very appealing in his new man's cap. He was given one of Kiyomori's daughters as a consort—a fifteen-year-old girl whom the retired emperor had adopted.

Around that time, Fujiwara no Moronaga resigned as major captain of the left. People said Tokudaiji Major Counselor Sanesada was next in line for the post, but Kazan'in Middle Counselor Kanemasa aspired to it, and it was also eagerly sought by New Major Counselor Narichika, the third son of the late Naka-no-mikado Middle Counselor Ienari.

Prayers of various descriptions were begun by Narichika, who was one of the retired emperor's favorites. He sequestered a hundred monks at Yawata with instructions to perform a full seven-day reading of the *Great Wisdom Sutra*. One day, while those holy men were keeping up a diligent chant, three turtledoves flew from the direction of Otokoyama, lit in an orange tree in front of the shrine, and pecked one another to death. Dharma Seal Kyōsei, the superintendent, reported the matter to the throne, perplexed because the doves, Hachiman's favorite messengers, had behaved that way at the Iwashimizu Hachiman Shrine. The diviners in the department of shrines performed their rituals, and the oracle predicted a political disturbance. But there was no need for the emperor to be careful, it said; a subject was the one for whom discretion was indicated.

Narichika saw no reason for alarm. For seven nights running, under cover of darkness, he walked to the upper Kamo Shrine from his house at Naka-no-mikado-Karasumaro. On the seventh night, he went home, stretched out to rest, and had a dream in which he went back to the shrine. Something pushed the sanctuary door open, and he heard an unearthly, majestic voice chant a poem:

> sakurabana
> kamo no kawakaze
> uramu na yo
> chiru o ba e koso
> todomezarikere

> Attach no blame,
> cherry blossoms, to the wind
> where Kamo's stream flows.
> The wind has not the power
> to prevent your scattering.

Still unworried, he sent a Buddhist ascetic to the shrine, telling him to perform the Dagini ritual for a hundred days at an altar inside a hollow cryptomeria tree, which stood behind the sanctuary.[11] While the monk was there, lightning struck the mighty tree and set it afire. A throng of priests and others ran over and put out the blaze, which had endangered the shrine. They tried to eject the performer of the heretical ritual, but he refused to go. "I made a solemn vow to shut myself up in this shrine for a hundred days. This is only the seventy-fifth day, so I can't leave," he said.

The shrine officials reported to the imperial palace. "Follow your own rules," the emperor commanded. "Throw him out!" Some of the lower servants at the shrine beat the ascetic on the nape of the neck with unpainted wooden staffs, and chased him off southward beyond Ichijō Avenue.

Even though we are told that the gods reject improper petitions, Narichika went ahead and prayed for a major captaincy, a post to which he was not entitled. That may be why those weird things happened.

In those days, ranks and offices were not conferred at the discretion of the retired and reigning sovereigns, nor yet by regental decision, but solely as the Heike saw fit. Neither Sanesada nor Kanemasa won the captaincy; instead, a shocking thing happened. Kiyomori's oldest son, Shigemori, who had been major counselor and major captain of the right, switched to major captain of the left; and the second son, Munemori, who was a mere middle counselor, leapfrogged over several of his seniors to become major captain of the right. It was especially galling that Munemori took precedence over Sanesada, who was the senior major counselor, a member of a family eligible for the highest offices, an outstanding scholar, and the heir of the house of Tokudaiji. People made private predictions that Sanesada would leave secular life to become a monk, but he simply resigned as major counselor and retired to his mansion, where he awaited future developments.

"I could have put up with it if I'd been passed over for Sanesada or Kanemasa," Narichika said, "but I can't abide the thought of yielding place to Kiyomori's second son. This is what comes of letting the Taira run everything. I'll find a way to bring them down and get what I want!" An appalling speech! Even though his father had been a mere middle counselor, he himself, the youngest son of the family, had risen to major counselor with senior second rank. He had received revenues from a number of large provinces; and imperial favors had also been bestowed on his children and other dependents. What possible cause for dissatisfaction did he have? He must have been possessed by an evil spirit. He had been threatened with execution because he supported Nobuyori during the Heiji Disturbance, and it had been thanks entirely to Shigemori's pleas that his life had been

11. The Dagini ritual was a prayer designed to enlist the aid of demons called *dagini* (Skt. *dākini*) in gaining an end. It was considered heretical because *dagini* did not belong to the Buddhist pantheon.

spared.[12] Yet he forgot his obligation and devoted all his time to wooing warriors and assembling secret stockpiles of weapons.

The area in the eastern hills known as Shishi-no-tani was a perfect natural fortress, adjacent to the Miidera temple grounds at the rear. Bishop Shunkan had a villa there, and in that villa Narichika and his cronies held regular meetings to plot the destruction of the Heike. Once Retired Emperor Go-Shirakawa went to pay them a visit, accompanied by Dharma Seal Jōken, a son of the late novice Shinzei. The retired emperor broached the subject to Jōken while the conspirators were banqueting that night.

"This is unbelievable!" Jōken exclaimed. "With all these people listening! Word won't take long to leak out; there'll be a crisis."

Narichika scowled. He jumped up, the sleeve of his hunting robe overturning the wine bottle in front of the retired emperor.

"What does that mean?" His Majesty asked.

Narichika resumed his seat. "The downfall of the *heiji*!"[13]

The retired emperor smiled. "Everybody come forward and do a *sarugaku* turn," he said.[14]

Police Lieutenant Yasuyori advanced. "We have entirely too many *heiji* here; I'm drunk," he announced.

"What shall we do about them?" Bishop Shunkan asked.

"Off with their heads!" said the monk Saikō. He decapitated a bottle as he left the stage.

Dharma Seal Jōken was speechless with amazement. To be sure, it was shocking behavior.

If you are curious about the identities of the conspirators, they were the novice Renjō; the Hosshōji administrator Bishop Shunkan; Yamato Governor Motokane; Senior Assistant Minister of Ceremonial Masatsuna; Taira Police Lieutenant Yasuyori; Koremune Police Lieutenant Nobufusa; New Taira Police Lieutenant Sukeyuki; and Tada no Kurando Yukitsuna of the Settsu Genji, as well as many members of the north guards.

12. Nobuyori was the principal court noble involved in the Heiji Disturbance of 1159, an abortive attempt to overthrow the Taira and their allies. One of Narichika's wives was Shigemori's sister, and Shigemori's son Koremori was married to Narichika's daughter.

13. *Heiji* can mean both "wine bottle" and "Taira clan."

14. *Sarugaku* was a type of comic dance. The next three speakers are performers.

Chapter 2

Time: sixth month and later, 1177
Principal subject: consequences of the Shishi-no-tani conspiracy, which has
    been discovered by the Taira. Narichika and the other conspirators have
    been arrested.
Principal characters:
    same as Chapter 1

2.8. The Exile of the Major Counselor

On the second of the sixth month, Kiyomori's men took Major Counselor Narichika to the senior nobles' reception room at Nishihachijō for a meal, but he was too choked with emotion to raise the chopsticks.[1] Then they brought up a carriage and urged him to get in. He entered with reluctance, and warriors took up positions on all sides. There was no sign of any of his own people. He asked to meet Shigemori again, but it was not to be.

"Even when a man is charged with a heinous crime, he always takes one of his people with him when he goes to a distant province." The plaintive murmur inside the carriage made all the warrior-guards weep into their armor sleeves.

As Narichika traveled westward and then south along Suzaku Avenue, he gazed at the imperial palace in the distance. Even his ox-driver and other old servants wept until their sleeves were drenched, and it is moving to think of the far more poignant grief of his wife and young children, whom he was leaving behind in the capital. When he passed the Toba Mansion, he thought with a heavy heart of how he had never failed to accompany the retired emperor on a single one of his visits there.[2] His own Suwama villa stood nearby, but he passed on, seeing it only from a distance. They emerged in front of the mansion's south gate.

The warriors were impatient. "What's holding up the boat?" they asked.

"Where are you taking me? If I have to die, let it be here near the capital,"

1. The Nishihachijō Mansion was one of Kiyomori's residences.
2. The Toba Mansion was Retired Emperor Go-Shirakawa's magnificent villa at Toba, just south of the capital.

Narichika pleaded. He asked the name of the chief warrior. "Nanba no Jirō Tsunetō," the man replied.

"Some of my people may be nearby. I have something to say before I go on board; find one of them and have him come here," Narichika said. The warriors ran around searching, but they found nobody who would admit to being in his service.

"When I was prospering, there must have been a thousand or two thousand men who claimed me as a patron. It's hard that not one of them should come to see me off, even in a surreptitious way," he said. Tears came to his eyes, and the fierce warriors wept into their sleeves.

Ever-flowing tears were now the only things left to the major counselor. It is easy to imagine the feelings of this man, who had once made pilgrimages to Kumano and the Tennōji Temple, traveling aboard ships with double keels and triple cabins, with twenty or thirty other vessels in his wake, and who now left the capital forever, to sail distant seas in a mean craft with a makeshift curtained cabin, escorted by unknown warriors. That day he traveled as far as Daimotsu Harbor in Settsu Province.

It was thanks to Shigemori's intercession that the sentence imposed was merely exile and not death, the one that was to have been expected.

Earlier, while Narichika was still a middle counselor, he served for a time as governor of Mino Province. Some shrine servants from Hirano-no-shō, a property owned by Mount Hiei, came to sell arrowroot cloth to the deputy governor, Uemon-no-jō Masatomo, during the winter of the first year of Kaō [1169]. Masatomo, who was in his cups, scribbled ink on the cloth, told the sellers to shut up when they complained, and subjected them to physical abuse. Before long, several hundred shrine people burst in on him, and he killed more than ten of them, defending himself as prescribed by the regulations. The Hiei monks rose in a body on the third of the eleventh month in that same year, demanding the exile of the governor, Narichika, and the imprisonment of his deputy. The court condemned Narichika to exile in Bitchū Province, and he was sent as far as Shichijō Avenue in the western sector of the capital, but the retired emperor chose to bring him back after five days for reasons of his own. People said the monks were calling down horrible curses on him, but he received the additional offices of commander of the right gate guards and police superintendent on the fifth of the first month in the second year of Kaō [1170]. Sukekata and Kanemasa were passed over for his benefit at that time. Sukekata was a senior figure, and Kanemasa was a man for whom everything went well. It was bitter that the heir of a household should be set aside like that, but Narichika was reaping the reward of having built the Sanjō Mansion.[3] He was granted senior second rank on the thirteenth of the fourth month in the third year of Kaō [1171], at which time Naka-no-mikado Middle Counselor Muneie

3. Narichika appears to have assumed responsibility for additions to the Sanjō Mansion, an imperial residence near the Sanjō-Muromachi intersection.

was passed over; and he rose from provisional middle counselor to provisional major counselor on the twenty-seventh of the tenth month in the first year of Angen [1175]. "All this, even though he was supposed to have been cursed by the Hiei monks!" the cynics said. But perhaps it was because the curses were effective, after all, that he found himself in this dreadful predicament now. Sometimes the punishments of gods and the curses of men work swiftly, and sometimes they are slow to take effect.

There was a commotion on the third when a messenger from the capital arrived at Daimotsu. Narichika asked if he had brought orders for his death, but that was not it: instead, he was to be exiled to Kojima Island in Bizen Province. There was a letter for him from Palace Minister Shigemori. "I used every argument I could think of to have you taken to some remote mountain place near the capital, but I simply didn't have enough influence to manage it. Still, I did persuade my father to spare your life." Shigemori had also sent Tsunetō instructions to show Narichika every courtesy, and to do nothing to displease him; and he had made careful arrangements for Narichika's requirements on the journey.

So Narichika was doomed to separation from the sovereign who had made him a favorite, and from the wife and children whom he had never wanted to leave, not even for an instant. "Where am I going? I'll never get back to the capital, never see my family again," he thought. "When the Hiei monks got me exiled that other time, His Majesty recalled me from western Shichijō because he wasn't willing to let me go, but he isn't the one who's punishing me now. How can this have happened?" He raised his eyes to the skies and flung himself to the ground, he wept and lamented, but it was all useless.

Too soon, at dawn on the next day, the crew launched the boat. For Narichika it was a tearful journey. Short though his future seemed, his dewlike existence continued. The white waves rose in the wake, the capital receded ever farther into the distance, and the province of his exile drew closer as the days accumulated. The sailors brought the boat in to Kojima in Bizen, and the warriors deposited him in a squalid brush-thatched shack, a commoner's dwelling. As is usually true of islands, mountains rose to the rear, the sea stretched out in front, the winds sighed through the shore pines, and the waves crashed on the beach. It was all unbearably depressing.

2.10.   *The Death of the Major Counselor*

Before long, Bishop Shunkan, Taira no Yasuyori, and Lesser Captain Naritsune were exiled to Kikai-ga-shima Island in Satsuma Bay.[4] Kikai-ga-shima can be reached from the capital only after many long, hard days at sea; no vessels call there in the ordinary course of events. The few inhabi-

4. Shunkan and Yasuyori were two of the Shishi-no-tani conspirators; Naritsune had been arrested because he was the son of the ringleader, Narichika. Kikai-ga-shima has not been identified.

tants are unlike people in this country. Black as oxen and inordinately hairy, they are unable to comprehend what others say to them. The men wear no caps; the women do not let their hair hang free. They do not dress in clothing, and thus they do not resemble human beings. They lack foodstuffs, and thus they place a premium on the slaughter of living things. Because there are no farmers tilling mountain paddies, there is no rice; because there are no people picking mulberry leaves in orchards, there is no silk. In the interior, there is a high mountain where eternal fire burns, and where sulfur occurs in such abundance that the island is sometimes called Io-ga-shima [Sulfur Island]. Ceaseless thunder rolls up and down the mountain; torrential rains fall at its base. It does not seem the kind of place where a man might survive for a day or an hour.

Major Counselor Narichika had been wondering if Kiyomori might not be disposed to relent. But then he heard of his son's exile to Kikai-ga-shima. "If it's come to this, it won't do any good to keep up a brave front and hope for the best," he thought. He found an opportunity to let Shigemori know that he had decided to take the tonsure, and the retired emperor approved the request when it was transmitted to him. Without further ado, he renounced the world, exchanging the sleeves of flowering fortunes for the shabby black garb of someone who dwells far from the transitory concerns of society.

Narichika's wife was living in concealment near the Urin'in Temple in the hills north of the capital. Even under the best of circumstances, it is depressing to stay in unfamiliar surroundings, but for that lady the days were truly hard to endure, fearful as she was of people's eyes, and lost in memories of the past. Whether through fear of criticism or through reluctance to be observed, none of the mansion's many former ladies-in-waiting and samurai came to see her. There was only one exception, a kindhearted samurai called Genzaemon-no-jō Nobutoshi, who paid regular calls. One day, she summoned him. "I'm sure I'd heard that Narichika was at Kojima in Bizen Province, but people have been saying lately that he's in a place called the Ariki Ascetics' Cloister, or something like that.[5] I do wish I could manage to send him a letter and get an answer back," she said.

Nobutoshi tried to keep from crying. "His Lordship was always good to me, ever since I was a child; there was never a time when I wasn't at his side. I begged to be allowed to share his exile, but the authorities at Rokuhara wouldn't hear of it. I can still hear his voice as it sounded when he used to summon me; I can never forget a word he said when he scolded me. It doesn't matter what happens to me; I'll start out with the letter right away," he answered. Overjoyed, the lady made haste to write something, and each of the children also composed a message.

Nobutoshi traveled with the letters over the long road to the Ariki Ascet-

5. The Ariki Ascetics' Cloister was on the border between Bizen and Bitchū provinces. Narichika had been taken there from Kojima.

ics' Cloister in Bizen. He explained his mission to the head warrior, Nanba no Jirō Tsunetō, and Tsunetō willingly granted him permission to see Narichika, moved by his loyalty.

"Nobutoshi has arrived from the capital," they told the prisoner. Narichika had just been talking about the capital, and his spirits were very low. He shifted quickly to a formal posture, wondering if it might be a dream. "Have him come in!" he said.

Nobutoshi entered. It was bad enough to see how his master was living, but the monkish black robes made his senses reel. He handed over his mistress's letter and also reported her exact words. Blurred with tears, Narichika's eyes could scarcely make out the characters. She had written, "It's sad to see how dreadfully the children miss you, and my own longing is quite unbearable—it just never stops." In a fresh access of grief, he felt that his earlier loneliness paled by comparison with his present emotions.

Four or five days passed. "I'd like to stay here to see His Lordship to the end," Nobutoshi said. But Tsunetō refused to agree, and Narichika had to order him back to the capital. "I'll probably be put to death before long," he said. "Be sure to pray for me when you hear that I'm gone." He wrote out an answer. Nobutoshi took it, asked permission to leave, and prepared to set out. "I'll be sure to come again," he said.

"I don't think I can wait that long. It's hard to say goodbye. Stay just a little bit longer," Narichika said. He called him back repeatedly, but the parting could not be postponed forever. Nobutoshi restrained his tears, set out for the capital, and finally delivered the letter. When Narichika's wife opened it, she saw a lock of hair at the end of the scroll—proof that he had already become a monk. She prostrated herself and wept, unwilling to look again. "This very keepsake is now a source of misery," she said.[6] The children also wailed and lamented.

The warriors took Narichika's life on the nineteenth of the eighth month. It happened at a place called Kibi-no-nakayama in Niwase-no-gō, on the border between Bizen and Bitchū. There were different rumors about his last moments, but it appears that Tsunetō's men planted pronged spikes at the bottom of a twenty-foot cliff and pushed him off to die on their tips, after having tried unsuccessfully to kill him with poisoned wine. People felt that it would be hard to find a parallel for such cruelty.

"I hesitated about becoming a nun until today," Narichika's wife said when she heard of his death. "I kept hoping that somehow I might see him unchanged just one more time, and be seen unchanged by him. But what's the use of waiting now?" She went to a temple called the Bodaiin, changed into a nun's habit, and performed the prescribed rituals as prayers for Narichika's enlightenment in the life to come.

6. Anonymous (KKS 746): katami koso / ima wa ata nare / kore naku wa / wasururu toki mo / aramashi mono o ("This very keepsake is now a source of misery: if it were not here, there might be fleeting moments when I would not think of you").

That lady was the daughter of Yamashiro Governor Atsukata. A great beauty, she had been the dearly beloved favorite of Retired Emperor Go-Shirakawa, who had presented her to Narichika as a mark of special esteem.

Most touchingly, the children also picked sprays of blossoms and drew holy water to pray for their father in the next world.

Thus do times change and things depart. Even as the five signs of decay herald the deaths of heavenly beings, so must change come to mortals in this world.

2.15. *Yasuyori's Prayer*

Meanwhile, the exiles at Kikai-ga-shima survived like dewdrops on the tips of grasses. Although life was not something to be cherished under such circumstances, regular shipments of food and clothing came to the island from Kase-no-shō, a property in Hizen owned by Lesser Captain Naritsune's father-in-law, Norimori; and the gifts helped Bishop Shunkan and Yasuyori to stay alive too.

At the time of his banishment, Yasuyori had taken the tonsure at Muro-zumi in Suō Province, adopting Shōshō as his religious name. He recited a poem to show how long he had wanted to become a monk:

tsui ni kaku	I regret only
somukihatekeru	not to have cast them aside
yo no naka o	earlier than this—
toku sutezarishi	the worldly concerns on which
koto zo kuyashiki	I have turned my back at last.

Yasuyori and Naritsune were both fervent adherents of the Kumano faith. "If we could just find places on the island for branches of the three Kumano shrines, we could pray there for our return to the capital," they said. Bishop Shunkan, an irreligious man, refused to be party to the plan, but the other two ranged the island in search of an area that resembled Kumano. They discovered a place beside a river where there was a splendid grove of trees, their colored foliage like embroidered red brocade, and where there were extraordinary peaks soaring above the clouds, their slopes like shimmering green gossamer. From the mountains to the trees, it was a site of transcendent beauty. To the south, the distant waves of the boundless sea merged into clouds and mist; to the north, a waterfall a hundred feet high surged over a mighty precipice. The chill, awesome sound of the water and the pervasive aura of sanctity, heightened by the soughing of the wind in the pines, called to mind Nachi, the mountain where the deity of the waterfall dwells enshrined, and they promptly gave the place that name. Then they named two lower peaks Hongū and Shingū, and identified other places with minor shrines on the pilgrim route. Every day from then on, they prayed as Kumano pilgrims for a return to the capital, with the novice Yasuyori acting as spiritual guide, and with Naritsune following along behind. "Hail, Kongō

Dōji! We beseech you to take pity on us. Return us to the capital! Grant that we may meet our wives and children again!" they implored.

When time brought the need for freshly sewn sacramental garb, they substituted hemp robes; when they scooped purifying water from a marsh nearby, they thought of it as the unsullied flow of the Iwada River; when they climbed a height, they identified it with the Awakening of Faith Gate.[7] On each pious visit, Yasuyori recited a prayer, holding aloft sprays of blossoms in lieu of the orthodox offerings he could not make for lack of paper.[8] These were the words he intoned:

This year is the first of the Jishō era [1177]. The number of its months is twelve, that of its days more than three hundred and fifty. After having chosen an auspicious day and a propitious hour, we, the true believers and generous donors Fujiwara no Naritsune of the imperial bodyguards and the novice Shōshō, humbly venture in utmost sincerity, and with body, word, and thought in full accord, to utter this respectful petition before the august buddha-manifestations and bodhisattva-manifestations of the three Kumano shrines, the greatest miracle workers in Japan, and before the Great Waterfall Bodhisattva-manifestation. The Great Bodhisattva Shōjō [at Hongū] is a manifestation of Amitābha, the teacher who saves us from the sea of suffering and takes us to the other shore, the enlightened one fully manifested in the three bodies. The divinity of Hayatama is a manifestation of Yakushi, the Healing Lord who reigns over the Jōruri Paradise in the east, the Tathāgata who cures all disease. The divinity of Nachi is a manifestation of Thousand-armed Kannon, the teacher who dwells on Mount Fudaraku to the south, the bodhisattva who has passed through all the stages leading to enlightenment. The divinity of Nyakuōji is a manifestation of Eleven-headed Kannon, the lord of the world of men, the bodhisattva who rescues us from fear, who exhibits the visage of enlightenment atop his head, who answers all prayers from sentient beings. Never is there a failure to respond when anyone who seeks tranquility in this world or salvation in the next, whether emperor on high or commoner below, scoops pure water and washes away the defilement of illusion in the morning, or faces the deep mountains and chants the sacred name in the evening.

Comparing the heights of these sheer, soaring peaks to the loftiness of the divine virtue, likening the depths of these precipitous valleys to the profundity of the bodhisattva vow, we part the clouds in ascent and brave the dews in descent. Why would we tread the tortuous paths if we did not trust in the beneficent bodhisattvas as in the earth itself? Why would we create shrines in this remote district if we did not revere the compassion of those who manifest themselves on earth to help mankind? Therefore we entreat you, Great Bodhisattva Shōjō and Great Bodhisattva of the Waterfall: gaze on us with the compassionate eyes that resemble green lotus leaves, hearken to us with the ears that resemble those of stags! Recognize our peerless sincerity; grant our heartfelt desire!

Moreover, in order to lead the sentient beings who believe in Buddhism, and to

7. The Iwada River was a stream in which pilgrims to Kumano Hongū purified themselves; the Awakening of Faith Gate was the main entrance to the main shrine at Kumano Hongū.

8. Strips of paper (*gohei*) are still presented as offerings at Shinto shrines. Paper was rare and expensive in the Heian period.

save the hosts of unbelievers, through means suited to the quality of each individual, the bodhisattvas manifested as Musubu and Hayatama have left their magnificent, jewel-decked abodes, dimmed the radiance of their eighty-four thousand distinguishing marks, and come to tread the dust of the six paths and three existences. And therefore we worship them without cease; we hold aloft offerings and written petitions, sleeve to sleeve, in the hope that fixed karma may be changed for the better, and long life may be obtained by asking for long life. We wear the robes of meekness, offer the blossoms of the wisdom road, and pray with fervor strong enough to move the shrine floor, our devout hearts as pure and full as the pond where sentient beings achieve salvation.[9] If the deities listen to us with favor, why should our wishes lack fulfillment? With raised eyes, we beseech you, O buddha-manifestations and bodhisattva-manifestations of the Twelve Places: spread your wings of salvation, fly far away to the heavens above this sea of suffering, end the sorrows of our exile, and let us realize our dream of returning to the capital.

We bow twice.

2.16.   *Stupas Cast Afloat*

Some of Naritsune's and Yasuyori's regular Kumano pilgrimages took the form of all-night vigils. One time, they spent the night singing *imayō*.[10] Dozing off toward dawn, Yasuyori dreamed that a small boat with a white sail came rowing toward him from the open sea. Twenty or thirty women in red divided skirts stepped ashore and sang three choruses of a beautiful song, meanwhile beating drums:

> More than the vows of all the buddhas,
> Trustworthy is the pledge of the Thousand-armed One;
> Flowers will bloom, fruit will grow in an instant,
> Even on withered trees and grasses.

In the next moment, they disappeared.

Yasuyori awakened, filled with wonder and awe. "Those ladies must have been manifestations of dragon kings. It is Thousand-armed Kannon whose manifestation is called the western deity of the three Kumano shrines. And since a dragon king is one of Thousand-armed Kannon's twenty-eight attendants, we can be absolutely sure of an answer to our prayers," he thought.

Again, when the two had fallen asleep after another vigil, one of them dreamed that an offshore wind blew two leaves against their sleeves. Picking them up out of idle curiosity, they saw that they belonged to an evergreen tree native to the vicinity of Kumano. The leaves contained the words of a poem, which seemed to have been formed by the gnawing of insects:

> chihayaburu   Because your prayers
> kami ni inori no   to the mighty deities
> shigekereba   have been so fervent,

9. To offer the flowers of the wisdom road is to make floral offerings as one who strives for enlightenment. "Pond" is a metaphor for the gods who help sentient beings.

10. To entertain the deities.

nado ka miyako e   you will most assuredly
kaerazarubeki   return to the capital.

Homesick for the city, Yasuyori set himself to fashioning a thousand stupas, on each of which he wrote the Sanskrit letter "A," the date, his given name and surname, and two poems:[11]

satsumagata   Go tell my mother,
oki no kojima   O wind over distant seas,
  ware ari to   that I cling to life
oya ni wa tsuge yo   on an island far from shore
yae no shiokaze   in the Bay of Satsuma.

omoiyare   Sympathize with me:
shibashi to omou   a man feels nostalgia
  tabi dani mo   for the capital
nao furusato wa   even when he is assured
koishiki mono o   of an early homecoming.

He took the stupas to the beach and tossed one of them into every white wave that retreated toward the offing. "Hail! All hail! I touch my head to the ground in obeisance. Bonten, Taishaku, Four Great Heavenly Kings, Earth Deity, Guardian Deities of the Land, and especially Deities of Kumano and Itsukushima: send at least one of these to the capital!" he said. Because he consigned each new stupa to the sea as soon as it was finished, and because the total number increased with the passing of time, one among the thousand was cast ashore in front of the Itsukushima Shrine in Aki Province. (Yasuyori's fervor may have turned into a fair wind, or the gods and buddhas may have sped the stupa on its way.)

It happened that a certain monk, one of Yasuyori's friends, had begun a pious journey through the western provinces, in the hope of finding a chance to cross to Kikai-ga-shima and seek the novice out; and that he had just then reached Itsukushima, his first stop. That monk encountered a layman dressed in a hunting robe, someone who looked as though he might be connected with the shrine, and he fell into conversation with him.

"By the by," the monk asked, "the buddhas and bodhisattvas are reputed to assume many forms when they dim their radiance and descend to earth in aid of sentient beings—but through what karmic tie are the divinities of this shrine linked to the fish of the sea?"

"Our chief goddess is the dragon king Sāgara's third daughter, the one who is a manifestation of Vairocana Buddha," the other replied. He proceeded to speak of extraordinary occurrences at the shrine, from the goddess's advent until the present age, in which she continues to help sentient beings achieve salvation. Perhaps that is why the shrine possesses eight

11. In esoteric Buddhism, "A," the first syllable in the Sanskrit syllabary, is regarded as symbolic of the unity of all things. Making 1,000 stupas is advocated in a Buddhist work as a means of ensuring that a wish will come true.

buildings, with tiled roofs soaring side by side.[12] The structures face the sea, and the clear moon lodges nearby as the tides ebb and flow. When the waters rise, the great torii and the sacred fence seem made of red gems; when they recede, the white sand resembles frost, even on a summer night.

With increased reverence, the monk began to recite a sutra as an offering. The sun sank lower and lower, the moon rose, and the tide flowed in, carrying all manner of seaweed and other flotsam. The monk noticed a stupa-shaped object, picked it up out of curiosity, and saw the words, "I cling to life on an island far from shore." Carved in the wood, the letters remained clearly visible in spite of having been immersed in the sea.

The monk was amazed. He put the stupa in the top of his pilgrim box, went to the capital, and showed it to Yasuyori's aged mother, the nun, and to his wife and children, all of whom were living in seclusion at Murasakino, north of Ichijō Avenue. The family broke into laments. "Why did this stupa make its way here? It's just a reminder of our sorrow! Why didn't it drift off to China?" they said.

News of the discovery spread everywhere, even to the retired emperor's distant ears. His Majesty inspected the stupa in person. "What a pitiful sight! So they're still alive then." He wept as he spoke. He sent the stupa to Shigemori, who showed it to his father, Kiyomori.

Kakinomoto no Hitomaro's thoughts pursued a tiny boat "going island-hid"; Yamanobe no Akahito watched cranes among reeds; the Sumiyoshi god thought of his shrine's crossbeams; the Miwa god pointed to the cedar at his gate.[13] Ever since the divine Sosanoo created the thirty-one-syllable poem long ago, gods and buddhas alike have expressed their many emotions in verse.[14] Even Kiyomori seemed moved by pity when he spoke of Yasuyori—for, after all, he was not an insensate rock or tree.

12. In earlier versions of *Heike monogatari*, where the "layman dressed in a hunting robe" does not appear, the first sentence of this paragraph takes the form of an authorial comment, and the second is missing. "Perhaps that is why," at the start of the third sentence, presumably means that the imposing size of the shrine may be attributable to the deity's importance.

13. Anonymous, sometimes attributed to Kakinomoto no Hitomaro (KKS 409): honobono to / akashi no ura no / asagiri ni / shimagakureyuku / fune o shi zo omou ("In dawn's first dim light, my thoughts follow a small boat, going island-hid through the morning fog and mist at Akashi-no-ura"). Yama[no]be no Akahito (MYS 924): waka no ura ni / shio michikureba / kata o nami / ashihe o sashite / tazu nakiwataru ("There is no dry beach when the tide comes flooding in at Waka-no-ura Bay; the cranes fly calling toward the place where tall reeds grow"). Anonymous, sometimes attributed to the Sumiyoshi god (SKKS 1855): yo ya samuki / koromo ya usuki / katasogi no / yukiai no ma yori / shimo ya okuran ("Does the cold I feel come from the chill of the night or from thin garments—or might it be that frost falls through the crumbling crossbeams?"). Anonymous, sometimes attributed to the Miwa god (KKS 982): wa ga io wa / miwa no yamamoto / koishiku wa / toburaikimase / sugi tateru kado ("I live in a hut at the foot of Mount Miwa. If you should miss me, please come and pay a visit—the gate where the cedar stands").

14. Sosanoo (or Susanoo), the obstreperous brother of the sun goddess Amaterasu, was exiled by the other gods to Izumo Province, where, according to the two *Kokinshū* prefaces, he composed the first *tanka* (31-syllable poem).

Chapter 3

Time: first month of 1178 to end of 1179
Principal subject: consequences of the Shishi-no-tani conspiracy (cont.)
Principal characters:
　　same as Chapter 1

3.1. The Pardon

The New Year felicitations took place at Retired Emperor Go-Shiraka-wa's palace on the first of the first month in the second year of Jishō [1178], and the emperor made his filial visit on the fourth.[1] But although the usual forms were observed, the retired emperor was still angry about the loss of Major Counselor Narichika and many others of his intimates during the past summer. Affairs of state had grown distasteful to him, and he was always in a bad humor. Kiyomori, for his part, had mistrusted the former sovereign ever since Yukitsuna's revelations.[2] He seemed his usual self on the surface but was very much on guard inside, and his smiles never came from the heart.

A comet appeared in the east on the seventh of the first month, one of the kind called Chi You's Banner, or Red Spirit.[3] Its brilliance increased on the eighteenth.

Meanwhile, to the distress of the court and the nation, Kiyomori's daughter Kenreimon'in fell ill. (She still held the title of empress at the time.)[4] Sutra readings began at various temples; official messengers were dispatched with offerings to shrines. The doctors prescribed all their medicines, the yin-yang masters exercised all their arts, and the monks performed every large

1. The New Year's felicitations (*hairei*) was a ceremony of obeisance to a retired emperor or regent, similar in import to the congratulation of the emperor on the same day.

2. The Shishi-no-tani conspirators had been betrayed by Yukitsuna, a Genji warrior from Settsu Province, whom Narichika had suborned with bribes and promises.

3. Any comet was considered an ominous portent.

4. Kiyomori's daughter Tokushi (1155–1213) had become a consort of Emperor Takakura (1161–81; r. 1168–80) in 1171. She held the title of empress (*chūgū*) from 1172 until her son, Emperor Antoku (1178–85; r. 1180–85), made her an imperial lady (*nyoin*) late in 1181. She then became known as Kenreimon'in.

and secret ritual. But presently it was reported that the difficulty was no ordinary sickness; no, she was pregnant. Although Emperor Takakura was eighteen years old and she was twenty-two, she had yet to give birth to a child of either sex. "Won't it be wonderful if it's a boy!" the Heike said, as delighted as though a male child had already been born. "With that clan prospering the way it is, it's bound to be a boy," people from other families told one another.

Once the pregnancy was confirmed, wonder-working monks of high rank and saintly reputation were instructed to perform large and secret rituals, and prayers for a boy were addressed to stars, buddhas, and bodhisattvas. The empress assumed the sash of motherhood on the first of the sixth month. The Ninnaji abbot, Priestly Imperial Prince Shūkaku, came to the imperial palace to perform the *Peacock Sutra* ritual as a prayer for divine protection.[5] The Tendai abbot, Priestly Imperial Prince Kakukai, came in the same manner to perform rituals designed to transform a female fetus into a male.

The empress began to feel worse as time went by. It seemed that Lady Li of Han, whose single smile was reputed to cast a hundred spells, must have looked the same when she lay ill in the Zhaoyang Hall; that even Yang Gueifei of Tang must have looked less pitiful when she grieved like a spray of pear blossoms drenched by springtime rain, or a lotus blossom drooping in the wind, or a maidenflower bowed down by dewdrops.

A number of stubborn spirits took advantage of the lady's condition to invade her body. The monks called on Fudō's help to transfer them to mediums, and they revealed themselves to be the Sanuki retired emperor, Uji Fearsome Minister of the Left Yorinaga, Major Counselor Narichika, the monk Saikō, the Kikai-ga-shima exiles, and others.[6] Kiyomori decided that measures would have to be taken to placate both the living and the dead. The Sanuki retired emperor was hastily granted a posthumous designation, "Emperor Sutoku," and the Uji Fearsome Minister of the Left was made a posthumous chancellor of first rank.

Kadowaki Consultant Norimori spoke to Shigemori when he heard the news. "People say that prayers of all kinds are being offered for the empress's confinement. Nothing would be better than a general amnesty, no matter how you look at it. And especially, no act could be as meritorious as the recall of the Kikai-ga-shima exiles."

Shigemori went to call on his father. "It's pitiful the way Norimori keeps pleading for Naritsune," he said. "Judging from what I've heard, harass-

5. The *Peacock Sutra* ritual (*Kujaku myōōkyō no hō*) was a specialty of the Shingon sect. Its central object of worship was Daikujaku Myōō (Skt. Mahāmayūrī-vidyā-rājñī), a peacock-riding deity considered efficacious in bringing rain, ending droughts, healing ailments, protecting women in childbirth, and so forth.

6. All of the men named had suffered death or exile because of involvement in either the Shishi-no-tani plot (Narichika, Saikō, Kikai-ga-shima exiles) or an earlier failed coup, the Hōgen Disturbance of 1156.

ment by Narichika's departed spirit is one of the main causes of the empress's suffering. People say, 'It's the major counselor's spirit that's behind it.' If you want to pacify Narichika, you'd better call his son, Naritsune, back to the capital. If you relieve the sorrow of others, you can gain your own objective; if you grant the wishes of others, your own petitions will receive prompt answers. The empress will give birth to a son and our fortunes will flourish."

Kiyomori responded with uncharacteristic mildness. "Well, well! Then what should we do about Shunkan and Yasuyori?"

"Recall them, too. It would be a sin to leave one of them there by himself."

"That's all right as far as Yasuyori's concerned. Shunkan owes his whole career to me, but in spite of everything I've done for him, he went ahead and made his own villa at Shishi-no-tani into a headquarters for the most despicable kind of activity, which he justified on the flimsiest of pretexts. It wasn't as though plenty of other places weren't available, either. I wouldn't even consider a pardon for him."

When Shigemori went home, he summoned his uncle, Consultant Norimori. "Naritsune will definitely be pardoned. Don't worry about it anymore," he told him.

Norimori rejoiced with clasped hands. "When he left, he seemed to be wondering why I hadn't arranged to be his custodian. It was pitiful to see how his eyes filled with tears every time he looked at me," he said.

"I know how you feel; every parent loves his child.[7] I'll discuss the whole matter with my father." Shigemori went inside.

Before long, there was a formal decision to recall the Kikai-ga-shima exiles, and Kiyomori handed down the pardon. An official messenger prepared to set out from the capital. Overjoyed, Norimori instructed a private envoy to go with him. The two were told to travel day and night with all possible speed, but sea journeys do not always go as people might wish, and they suffered from the vagaries of the winds and waves. Although they left the capital late in the seventh month, it was around the twentieth of the ninth month when they reached Kikai-ga-shima.

3.2. *The Foot-Drumming*

The official messenger, Tan Zaemon-no-jō Motoyasu, went ashore with his party. "Are the exiles from the capital here?" they shouted. "The Tanba lesser captain, the Hosshōji administrator, the Taira police lieutenant—monk?"

Naritsune and Yasuyori were away on one of their regular Kumano pilgrimages, but Bishop Shunkan had stayed behind.

"Have I thought about this so long that I've started to dream?" the bishop

---

7. Norimori's real concern is the happiness of his daughter, Naritsune's wife.

said to himself. "Or are those the deceitful voices of devils from the world of desire? I can't believe they're real." He rushed up to identify himself to the messenger, stumbling in his excitement. "What's your business? I'm the exile Shunkan," he said.

The messenger produced Kiyomori's pardon from a letter pouch, which he had had a servant carry around his neck. He handed it over, and Shunkan read it. "In consideration of the distant-banishment you have endured, your grave offense is pardoned. Prepare to return to the capital immediately. A general amnesty is to be granted as a prayer for the empress's safe delivery; therefore, we pardon the Kikai-ga-shima exiles Lesser Captain Naritsune and Monk Yasuyori," it said. That was all; the name "Shunkan" was missing. Certain that it must appear on the outer wrapper, the bishop sought it there in vain. He read the letter from end to beginning and from beginning to end, but only two people were mentioned. There was nothing about a third.

Naritsune and Yasuyori arrived soon afterward. Whether it was Naritsune who took the letter and read it, or whether it was Yasuyori, the outcome remained the same: there were only two names, not three. When they said to themselves, "It's in dreams that such things happen; can we be dreaming?," they knew they were awake; when they wondered if it were really true, it was like a dream. To make matters worse, the messengers had been entrusted with innumerable letters from the capital for Naritsune and Yasuyori, but there was nothing for Shunkan, not even a note to ask how he was getting along. "The three of us were found guilty of the same offense and banished to the same place," Shunkan said. "When a pardon is issued, why should two be recalled and one be left here? The Heike must have forgotten about me—or maybe the secretary made a mistake. How can this have happened?" He looked up to the skies, flung himself down on the earth, and wept and lamented, but it was all in vain.

"Your father's wretched conspiracy is to blame for my predicament," Shunkan said, clinging to Naritsune's sleeve in an agony of despair. "You can't just wash your hands of me. I know I can't go all the way to the capital without a pardon, but please let me travel on this boat as far as the Nine Provinces.[8] News naturally came from the city once in a while while you two were here, just as swallows come in springtime and wild geese visit the rice paddies in autumn, but how can I ever hear anything from now on?"

Naritsune tried to comfort him. "I know how you feel. Glad as I am to be recalled, I almost don't have the heart to leave when I see you like this. I'd be only too happy to take you with us on the boat, but the messenger from the capital says it can't be done. Besides, there could be trouble if people found out that all three of us had left the island, even though we hadn't all been granted permission. I'll go on ahead to the capital, talk to people, find out what Kiyomori's feelings are, and send someone to get you.

8. A name for Kyushu.

In the meantime, you'll just have to keep up your spirits and be patient. The main thing is to stay alive. You're bound to be pardoned sooner or later, even if they did leave you out this time," he said. But Shunkan wept and lamented, without caring who saw him.

The crew began to make noisy preparations for the departure. Shunkan tried his best to go too, scrambling up and falling back, falling back and scrambling up. Naritsune left him a quilt as a keepsake, and Yasuyori left a copy of the *Lotus Sutra*. When the sailors untied the hawsers and pushed off, Shunkan clung to a rope, letting himself be dragged until the water reached his hips, and then his armpits, and then his head. After he lost his footing, he caught hold of the boat. "Are you really going to abandon me? I didn't think you could be so hardhearted. So much for our old friendship! Can't you stretch a point and let me get in? At least, take me as far as the Nine Provinces," he begged over and over. But the official messenger said, "It's out of the question." They pried his hands loose and rowed away.

In despair, Shunkan went back to the beach, threw himself down, and beat his feet against the sand, just like a child who wants his nurse or mother. "Let me go with you! Take me!" he shrieked. But the vessel went off, leaving behind only a wake of white waves, as is the way with journeying boats.[9] Although it had not gone far, he was blinded by tears. He raced to a hilltop and beckoned toward the offing. It seemed that not even Lady Sayo of Matsura could have felt greater misery when she waved her scarf, desolated by the departure of the Chinese ship.[10]

The boat disappeared and the day drew to an end, but Shunkan did not return to his rude shelter. He spent the night on the beach, his feet washed by the waves and his garments wilted by the dew.

"Still, Naritsune's a kindhearted fellow. He'll speak up for me," he thought. Only that vain hope kept him from drowning himself on the spot. Now, at last, he could understand the misery of Sōri and Sokuri, the boys who were sent off to Kaigakusen Island long ago.[11]

3.7. *The Lesser Captain's Return to the City*

Lesser Captain Naritsune started toward the capital from Kase-no-shō in Hizen Province during the last third of the first month in the new year, the third of the Jishō era [1179]. Although he traveled with all possible speed, the weather was still bitterly cold, and the waves were so high that they had to tack from island to island along the coast. It was not until around the

9. Monk Mansei (SIS 1327): yo no naka o / nani ni tatoen / asaborake / kogiyuku fune no / ato no shiranami ("To what may man's life in this world be compared? A wake of white waves, left by a boat rowing off as the day begins to dawn").

10. Lady Sayo was a legendary woman who waved a scarf frantically from a hilltop when her husband sailed for Korea.

11. According to legend, these two little Indian boys were sent off by their stepmother to die of starvation on Kaigakusen, a desert island.

tenth of the second month that he reached Kojima in Bizen Province. From there, he sought out the place where his father, Narichika, had lived. When he went inside to look around, he saw idle scribblings on the dilapidated sliding partitions and bamboo pillars. "Calligraphy is the best of mementos. He wrote those things and now we can see them," he said. He and Yasuyori read and wept, wept and read. "Twentieth day, seventh month, third year of Angen [1177]: took sacred vows"; "Twenty-sixth day: Nobutoshi came." That was how he learned of Nobutoshi's visit. An inscription on the wall nearby said, "I rely on the welcome of Amitābha and his two attendants; I have no doubt of being reborn in the pure land of nine grades." "Yes, of course, he would want to try to be reborn in paradise when he found himself in that dreadful plight," Naritsune said. Despite his anguish, he spoke as though there were still something to be happy about.

They discovered the grave in a pine grove, unmarked by anything that could be called a mound. Naritsune chose a spot where the ground seemed a little higher than elsewhere, joined his sleeves, and uttered a long, tearful speech, as though to a living presence: "I heard a vague rumor about your death in Kikai-ga-shima, but I wasn't free to do as I pleased; I couldn't rush off here. Needless to say, I feel happy to have survived my banishment on the island, and glad to have been recalled after two years, but my survival wouldn't really have meant anything to me unless I had been able to see you while you were still alive. I came as fast as I could, but I don't feel like hurrying during the rest of the trip."

If Narichika had been alive, he surely would have said, "Tell me how you got along," or something of the kind; but an unutterably sad distance separates the living from the dead. Who can answer from under the moss? There was only the sound of pine trees sighing in the wind.

Naritsune paced around the grave with Yasuyori all night long, chanting buddha-invocations; and on the following day he made a new mound, encircled by a stake fence. Then he spent seven days and nights in a temporary shelter opposite the grave, chanting invocations and copying sutras. On the last day, he put up a big stupa with an inscription: "May the holy spirit of the departed leave the realm of reincarnation and attain full enlightenment." Below the date he wrote, "His loving son, Naritsune." Even humble, unlettered woodcutters wept into their sleeves at the sight, telling themselves that there was no greater treasure than a child. For Naritsune himself, the years might come and the years might go, but never would he forget the loving kindness with which he had been reared. It all seemed a dream, a phantasm. Nothing remained but the endless flow of his yearning tears. The buddhas and bodhisattvas of the three worlds and the ten directions must have pitied him. And how pleased Narichika's departed spirit must have felt!

"It would be proper for me to amass merit by reciting invocations a while longer, but the people waiting in the capital are probably anxious. I'll be sure to come again." With those words of farewell to the dead, Naritsune went away in tears. The parting must have been just as painful for Narichika under the grass.

Naritsune reached Toba before nightfall on the sixteenth of the third month. His father's mountain villa, the Suwama Mansion, stood nearby. During the years of desertion and neglect, tiles had vanished from earthen walls, and doors from gates. When he entered the garden, there was no sign of human life, nothing but thick moss. On the lake, he saw mandarin ducks and white gulls paddling where white waves rippled in the spring breeze from Autumn Hill; and he wept without cease, yearning for the one who had delighted in such scenes.[12]

The house itself had survived, but the latticework was in ruins, and the shutters and sliding doors had disappeared.

"Father did thus-and-so here," Naritsune said. "He went out of this corner door in such-and-such a way. He planted that tree over there with his own hands." Every word showed how much he missed Narichika.

Since it was only the sixteenth of the third month, there were still a few cherry blossoms left; and boughs of arbutus, peach, and damson flaunted their colors as though claiming the season for their own. Perhaps they were flowers that could not forget the springtime, even though their former master was gone.[13] Standing under a tree in bloom, Naritsune recited some old Chinese and Japanese verses:[14]

> Peach and damson speak no word: how many springs have passed?
> Smoky hazy leaves no track: who might have dwelt there once?

furusato no	If only the flowers
hana no mono iu	in this familiar place
yo nariseba	were gifted with speech,
ika ni mukashi no	how many are the questions
koto o towamashi	I would ask about the past!

To Yasuyori the quotations seemed strikingly apposite, and he wept until his black sleeves were drenched.

Although Naritsune had meant to leave around sunset, he could not help lingering until late at night. In the way of moldering houses, gaps in the old eave boards admitted moonlight, which flooded the chambers with ever more radiance as the hours went by. When dawn began to break over the hills, he still felt no desire to speed on his way, but he could not go on like that forever, and he set out from the mansion in tears, reminding himself

---

12. Autumn Hill was a man-made prominence on the grounds of the Toba Mansion.

13. An allusion to a poem written in exile by Sugawara no Michizane (SIS 1006): kochi fukaba / nioi okose yo / ume no hana / aruji nashi tote / haru o wasuru na ("If an east wind blows, send me your fragrance by it, blossoms of the plum: do not forget the springtime because your master is gone").

14. The quotation in Chinese is from a poem by the literatus Sugawara no Fumitoki (WKRES 548); the waka is by Dewa no Ben (GSIS 130).

that it would be inconsiderate to delay the reunion with those who had sent a carriage for him, and who now awaited his arrival.

It is easy to imagine the mingled sorrow and joy with which the travelers entered the capital. Someone had sent another carriage for Yasuyori, but he had chosen to ride in the back of Naritsune's. "It's very hard to say goodbye now, after all we've been through together," he said. The two could scarcely bring themselves to go their separate ways when they reached the Shichijō riverbed. We suffer a pang of regret when we so much as bid farewell to someone with whom we have enjoyed a half day under blossoming cherry boughs or a single night of moon-viewing, or to a fellow wayfarer with whom we have shared a sheltering tree during a passing shower. To Naritsune and Yasuyori, it must have seemed that only a strong tie from a previous existence could explain their joint karma and its consequences, the harsh island existence and the dangerous sea voyage.

Naritsune went to the home of his father-in-law, Consultant Norimori. His mother, who had been staying at Ryōzen, had gone to the house that morning to wait for him. When she saw him come in, she uttered only a single phrase, "Because I still live."[15] Then she sank to the floor and lay prostrate, a robe over her head. Norimori's ladies-in-waiting and samurai crowded around, weeping for joy. And how much greater must have been the happiness of Naritsune's wife, and of Rokujō, his nurse! Unremitting sorrow had turned Rokujō's black hair completely white, and Norimori's gay, pretty daughter had wasted away until she almost seemed another person. Only three at the time of his father's exile, Naritsune's son was now grown up enough to wear his hair in loops.[16] There was a smaller child of about three at his side.

"And that one?" Naritsune asked.

"Yes, that one . . ." Rokujō wept with her sleeve to her face, unable to continue.

"Yes," he thought, "I had to leave her when she was pregnant, but she's managed to bring the child up all right." He was saddened again by the memory.

Naritsune was reinstated in the retired emperor's service and rose to become a consultant and middle captain.

Yasuyori went to stay at his villa in the part of the eastern hills known as Sōrinji. His first act was to express his feelings in verse:

> furusato no   Moss has blanketed
> noki no itama ni   the gaps between the eave boards
> koke mushite   at the old dwelling.

15. Monk Nōin (SKKS 799): inochi areba / kotoshi no aki mo / tsuki wa mitsu / wakareshi hito ni / au yo naki ka na ("Because I still live, I have gazed on the moon this autumn as well, but there is no night when I meet the one from whom I have parted"). The poem puns on *yo* ("night"; "world").

16. Boys wore their hair in loops until they performed the capping ceremony.

omoishi hodo wa   Fewer than I had surmised—
moranu tsuki ka na   the moonbeams filtering through.

A recluse with the bitter past always on his mind, he wrote the tales called
A Collection of Treasures.

3.8. Ariō

Of the three exiles on Kikai-ga-shima, two had been recalled to the capital, leaving Bishop Shunkan as the sole pitiful warden of the island where
life had been so hard for them all.

There was a youth, Ariō by name, whom the bishop had petted and kept
in his service ever since he was a child. Having heard that the exiles were to
enter the capital on a certain day, this Ariō went to Toba to meet them, but
his master was nowhere to be seen. It would be inadequate merely to say
that he was upset by the answer to his inquiries: "They left that one on the
island; he was adjudged too guilty to be forgiven." For a time, he hung
about near Rokuhara in the vain hope of hearing that Shunkan was going
to be pardoned. Then he went to the place where the bishop's daughter was
living in retirement.

"They passed over my master in the recent amnesty; he hasn't come to
the capital. I feel that I have to go to the island to find him, and I'd like to
take a letter from you," he said. In tears, the girl wrote something.

Having been told that vessels bound for China weighed anchor in the
fourth and fifth months, and having perhaps concluded that he would be
too late if he waited for the change to summer clothing, Ariō set out from
the capital as the third month was ending. (He felt certain that his father
and mother would never consent to his going, so he started without getting
their permission.) He reached Satsuma Bay after a long, arduous sea voyage.
At the Satsuma port of embarkation for Kikai-ga-shima, he was stripped of
his robes by people who said he looked like a suspicious character, but the
experience was not enough to make him regret his original decision. (The
daughter's letter was hidden in his tophair.) He reached the island aboard a
merchant vessel.

The vague rumors he had heard in the capital had done little to prepare
him for the reality. There were no rice paddies, no farm plots, no villages,
no hamlets. He encountered a few human beings, but their speech was
unintelligible.

"Excuse me," he said, in the hope that some of them might know about
his master.

"What is it?" they answered.

"Do you know where I can find a man called the Hosshōji administrator,
a person who was exiled here from the capital?"

There might have been an answer if they had understood "Hosshōji" or
"administrator," but they shook their heads and said, "I don't know."

One of them did understand. "Let me see. There were three men like that here, but two of them were recalled to the capital. The other, the one who was left, he wanders around from place to place. I don't know where he is now."

In the thought that the bishop might be in the mountains, Ariō climbed peaks and descended gorges deep in the interior. But white clouds obliterated footprints and hid paths; winds in the green trees shattered the dreams in which he might have seen his master's face. In the end, the mountain search for the bishop failed. And when Ariō investigated the seashore, he met nobody of whom to ask directions—unless it might have been the gulls making tracks on the sandy beaches, or the plovers congregating on the white sandbars offshore.

One morning, a man as thin as a dragonfly came lurching into view from a rocky beach. Bits of seaweed and other ocean debris clung like a crown of brambles to his hair, which stuck straight up, as though he might once have been a monk. His joints poked out, his skin hung in folds, and it was impossible to tell whether his clothing had originally been made of silk or of some other material. In one hand, he held a strand of edible seaweed, in the other a fish given to him by a fisherman. Although he gave the appearance of walking, he staggered sideways without making any progress.

"I've seen plenty of beggars in the capital," Ariō thought, "but never one like this. The scripture says, 'The various asuras dwell beside the great ocean.' And the Buddha has explained that the evil paths of the asuras lie deep in the mountains and alongside the mighty ocean. Can it be that I've come to the world of hungry spirits?"

Meanwhile, the two approached each other. Ariō thought that even a wretch like this might possibly give him news of his master, so he spoke to him.

"Excuse me."

"What is it?"

"Do you know where I can find a man called the Hosshōji administrator? He's someone who was exiled from the capital."

Although Ariō had failed to recognize Shunkan, how could the bishop have forgotten him? "I'm the man!" As the words left his mouth, he cast away his burdens and fell flat on the sand. That was how Ariō learned of his master's sad fate.

Ariō cradled the unconscious bishop in his lap. "I'm here," he sobbed. "Please don't make me suffer like this, just when I've found you. It makes it seem as though I wasted my time by going on that long, hard sea voyage to look for you."

Presently, the bishop began to regain consciousness. With Ariō's help, he got to his feet. "I can't praise you enough for what you've done, coming all this way to find me. I never think of anything but the capital, day or night; sometimes I have visions in which my dear ones appear. And now that I'm so thin and weak, I can't tell whether I'm awake or dreaming. It seems that your arrival must be nothing but a dream. If it is, what shall I do after I wake up?"

"I'm really here," Ariō said. "When I look at you, it's like a miracle that you've survived so long."

"I suppose so. I must leave it to you to imagine how I felt after Naritsune and Yasuyori abandoned me last year. I was going to drown myself when they left, but Naritsune's an unreliable fellow if there ever was one, and he talked me out of it. 'Wait for further news from the capital,' he said, and I was foolish enough to try to stay alive, hoping against hope for a pardon. There's nothing to eat on this island. While I still had the strength, I used to go to the mountains and dig sulfur; then I gave it to traders from the Nine Provinces in exchange for food. But now I'm too weak to keep it up. I go to the beach when the sun's warm, as it is today, and there I join my palms and bend my knees and ask the net and hook fishermen for fish. When the tide recedes, I gather shellfish, pick up seaweed, and eat the mossy shore growth to preserve my dewlike life. That's how I've survived this long. How else could I have managed? There are lots of other things I'd like to talk to you about—but come, let's go to my house."

"To look at him, nobody would think he *had* a house," Ariō said to himself. When they arrived, he saw that the bishop had erected pillars of bamboo driftwood in the middle of a pine grove, improvised crossbeams from bundles of reeds, and added thick layers of pine needles above and below. It was not a structure that seemed likely to withstand wind or rain.

It was strange that such a dire fate should have overtaken a man who had once been responsible for administering more than eighty estates, all owned by the Hosshōji Temple, and who had lived inside ridgepole gates and flat-topped gates surrounded by four or five hundred attendants, lesser servants, and family members. There are numerous kinds of karma: some actions bear consequences in the present life, some in the next, and some in a later incarnation. This bishop, who had never owned anything that was not the rightful property of a temple building or a buddha, had apparently been made to suffer in the present life for his sinful and callous appropriation of the offerings of the faithful.

3.9.   The Bishop's Death

Once the bishop had convinced himself that he was awake, he said, "There were no letters from my people when the men came to get Naritsune and Yasuyori last year, and nobody has given you any either. Does this mean nobody has anything to say to me?"

Ariō fell prostrate, choked with tears. For a time, he was silent. Then he rose, controlled his sobs, and spoke. "Officers came to the house soon after you left for Nishihachijō. They arrested our men, questioned them about the plot, and put them all to death. Worried about hiding the child, milady went to a secret retreat far back in the Kurama mountains, and I was the only one who visited there once in a while to help her. Everyone felt sad, but the child missed you especially. Whenever I appeared, he used to say, 'Ariō, go to that island—Kikai-ga-shima or whatever it's called—and take me with you.' He died of smallpox earlier this year, in the second month. Milady fell into a deep depression, grieving over his death and worrying about you, and she finally passed away on the second of the third month. Your daughter is the only one left now. She's been staying with her aunt in Nara. I've brought a letter from her." He took it out and handed it to him.

When Shunkan opened the letter, he saw that it contained exactly what Ariō had just told him. At the end, the girl had written, "Why is it that two of the three who were exiled have been recalled but you're still gone? Nothing is worse than being a girl. I'd go to that island of yours if I were a boy. Please come back right away with Ariō."

"Look, Ariō," he said, weeping. "See what a childish letter she writes. Isn't it sad that she tells me to come back right away with you? I would scarcely have spent three years here if the decision had been mine. She's turned twelve this year, I believe, but how can anyone so immature look out for herself by getting married or going into court service?" His sorrow brought home the truth of the old poem:

hito no oya no	The hearts of parents
kokoro wa yami ni	are not realms where darkness reigns—
aranedomo	yet how easily
ko o omou michi ni	we wander in confusion
madoinuru ka na	on the path of love for a child![17]

"Since I've been exiled on this island, I haven't had a calendar to help me keep track of the date," Shunkan said. "I simply know it must be spring when the blossoms scatter, and autumn when the leaves fall. When the sound of cicadas sends off the spring wheat harvest, I assume that summer has come, and when snow accumulates, I assume that it's winter. Watching the waxing moon interchange with the waning, I've distinguished the passing of thirty days; counting on my fingers, I've known that this is my little boy's sixth year. And now I learn that the child has died before me. It seems only the other day that he begged to go with me when I left for Nishihachijō, and I comforted him by saying I'd be right back. If only I'd known it was our final farewell, I'd have stayed there awhile, just to look at him. If it's true that parents are linked to children, and husbands to wives, by bonds transcending this world, why didn't I know sooner that those two had died before me—even through a dream or a vision? If I hadn't had my heart set

17. Fujiwara no Kanesuke (GSS 1102).

on seeing them again, I wouldn't have disgraced myself by these desperate struggles to stay alive. My daughter is the only thing I have left to worry about, but at least she's survived; she'll eke out an existence, even though it may be a sad one. It would be selfish of me to make you suffer by trying to linger on here." He stopped eating even his former meager fare, chanted the name of Amida Buddha constantly, and prayed for correct thoughts in his final hour. And at the age of thirty-seven, on the twenty-third day after Ariō's arrival, he died in his rude shelter.

Ariō clung to the corpse, looked up at the skies, collapsed onto the earth, and wept and lamented, all to no avail. After he had cried himself out, he said, "It would be fitting for me to join you immediately in the next world. But even though her young ladyship is still alive, there's nobody left in this world who can offer proper prayers for your enlightenment. I'll stay alive awhile to intercede on your behalf." Without touching the bed, he tore down the hut on top of it, added a covering of dry pine branches and withered reeds, and transformed his master's body into salt-fire smoke. When the cremation was complete, he picked up the white bones, put them in a bag to hang around his neck, and went back to the Nine Provinces on a trading vessel. Then he went to the bishop's daughter and told her everything that had happened.

"He felt even sadder after he read your letter. He couldn't answer it, because he didn't have an inkstone or paper; everything that was in his mind perished unexpressed. No matter how many births and deaths you may experience, you'll never hear his voice or see him again," he said. The girl fell prostrate in an agony of grief, weeping aloud. Most pitifully, she promptly became a nun, aged twelve, and devoted herself to prayers for her father and mother at the Hokkeji nunnery in Nara.

Ariō ascended Mount Kōya with Bishop Shunkan's remains around his neck, laid the bones to rest in the inner cloister, and took the tonsure at Rengedani. After that, he wandered as an ascetic over the seven circuits, praying for his master's enlightenment in the afterlife.

A dreadful fate menaced the house of Taira, the cause of such an accumulation of human suffering.

3.18. *The Exile of the Retired Emperor*

[Shigemori dies in the eighth month of Jishō 3 (1179), and Kiyomori, freed of his son's restraining influence, is now bent on making Retired Emperor Go-Shirakawa suffer for his hostility toward the Taira.]

On the twentieth [of the eleventh month of Jishō 3], warriors surrounded the retired emperor's Hōjūji Mansion. Someone said they intended to set fire to the buildings and burn the occupants alive, as Nobuyori had done to the Sanjō Mansion during the Heiji era; and the ladies-in-waiting and maids came running out in frantic haste, without even stopping to cover their heads.[18] The retired emperor was also greatly alarmed.

Munemori brought up a carriage. "We ask that His Majesty get in quickly," he said.

"What's the meaning of this? I'm not aware that I've done anything wrong. I suppose you mean to banish me to some distant province or remote island, just as you did with Narichika and Shunkan. I've merely taken a hand in matters of state because of the emperor's youth; if that isn't acceptable, I'll stop from now on," the retired emperor said.

"There's no question of anything like that. My father wants you to stay in the Toba Mansion until we can restore order," Munemori said.

"In that case, Munemori, you come with me," the retired emperor said. But Munemori refused, afraid of Kiyomori's displeasure.

"Ah," said the former sovereign, "this is another illustration of Munemori's vast inferiority to his older brother. I almost suffered the same fate earlier, but Shigemori prevented it at the risk of his life; that's why I've been safe until now. Kiyomori is doing this because there's nobody left to oppose him. What's to become of me?" Most awesomely, tears streamed from his eyes.

The retired emperor got into the carriage. No senior nobles or courtiers escorted him; his only attendants were lower-grade north guards and a shaven-pated porter called Kongyō. A single nun rode in the rear of the carriage—his former nurse, the Kii lady of second rank. As the party traveled westward on Shichijō Avenue and south on Suzaku, even the humblest commoners of both sexes wept until their sleeves were drenched, desolated that he should be exiled.

"The great earthquake on the seventh was a warning that something like this was going to happen," people said. "No wonder the bowels of the earth shook hard enough to frighten the earth deity!"

After the retired emperor entered the Toba Mansion, he summoned Master of the Palace Table Office Nobunari, who had managed to slip in, and who was waiting nearby. "I feel certain that I'll be put to death tonight. Can you arrange for me to have a bath?" he said.

Already benumbed by the events of the morning, Nobunari received the command with profound awe. He tied back the sleeves of his hunting robe with a sash, demolished a brushwood fence, and split up some supports from a veranda. Then he drew water, heated it, and presented it in the proper manner.

Dharma Seal Jōken went to Kiyomori's house at Nishihachijō. "I've heard that the retired emperor has gone to the Toba Mansion, and that he lacks attendants there," he said. "That seems a shocking state of affairs to me. What harm could it do if you let me join him? I want very much to go."

18. The burning of the Sanjō Mansion, Go-Shirakawa's residence, was the most dramatic event of the Heiji Disturbance.

Kiyomori gave his permission. "You aren't the kind of man who creates problems," he said. "Go along."

Jōken went to the Toba Mansion, left his carriage in front of the gate, and entered. The retired emperor was intoning a sutra in a resonant voice. Stealing in, the monk saw tears falling onto the scripture. He raised his vestment sleeve to his face, overcome with sorrow, and presented himself in tears. The former sovereign's sole attendant was the nun.

"Ah, Jōken, His Majesty hasn't eaten anything since breakfast yesterday at the Hōjūji Mansion—no dinner last night, no breakfast this morning. And he didn't sleep a wink last night. I'm afraid his life is in danger."

Jōken restrained his tears. "Nothing lasts forever. The Taira have prospered for more than twenty years, but their wickedness has gone too far; they'll soon be destroyed. Amaterasu and Hachiman won't desert His Majesty. Furthermore, the gods he trusts, the divinities of the Seven Shrines at Hiyoshi Sannō, have sworn to protect the One Vehicle, and they'll certainly defend him by visiting his *Lotus Sutra* as long as their pledges endure. He'll control the government again; the evildoers will vanish like bubbles on a stream." His words made the retired emperor feel a little better.

Emperor Takakura had already been much distressed by the banishment of the regent and the deaths of so many of his subjects. After he learned that the retired emperor had been confined to the Toba Mansion, he refused food and retreated to the imperial bedchamber, saying that he was ill. Every night from the day of the retired emperor's imprisonment on, he worshipped the Grand Shrine of Ise at the lime altar in the Seiryōden.[19] His prayers were explained as special expressions of piety, but their real purpose was to intercede for his father.

Although Emperor Nijō was a wise ruler, he had persisted in disobeying the retired emperor, justifying himself by saying that a sovereign possesses neither father nor mother. Perhaps that is why he founded no line, and why his chosen successor, Emperor Rokujō, had died unexpectedly at the age of thirteen, on the fourteenth of the seventh month in the second year of Angen [1176].[20]

3.19. *The Seinan Detached Palace*

"In all that a man does, he should put filial conduct first. . . . A wise sovereign governs the realm with filial piety."[21] Thus we are told that Tang Yao revered an aged, infirm father, and that Yu Shun paid honor to an obstinate mother. We must admire the sentiments of Emperor Takakura,

19. The lime altar, floored with a mixture of dirt and lime, was a Shinto sanctuary where the emperor performed matutinal rites in worship of Amaterasu and other deities, assisted by women from the handmaids' office.

20. This paragraph emphasizes the author's approval of Emperor Takakura's filial conduct. Go-Shirakawa's immediate successors were his son Nijō, Nijō's son Rokujō, and Takakura.

21. From the Chinese *Classic of Filial Piety*.

who had very probably taken to heart the example of those two sage kings.

A secret message went from the imperial palace to the Toba Mansion at around that time. "What can I accomplish by staying on the throne with things the way they are? I intend to follow in the footsteps of Emperors Uda and Kazan—to take religious vows, leave society, and roam the mountains and forests as an ascetic."

"You must do no such thing," Retired Emperor Go-Shirakawa answered. "My only hope is in having you there as emperor. Where could I look for help if you became a monk and dropped out of sight? Please wait until you've learned all there is to know about this old man's fate." The emperor shed bitter tears, with the reply pressed to his face.

A ruler is a boat; his subjects are the water. The water supports the boat but may also capsize it; the subjects sustain the ruler but may also overthrow him. Kiyomori had supported the sovereign in the Hōgen and Heiji eras, but now in the Angen and Jishō eras he was treating him with contempt.[22] It is exactly as the *Book of History* tells us.

Ōmiya Chancellor Koremichi, Sanjō Palace Minister Kinnori, Hamuro Major Counselor Mitsuyori, and Nakayama Middle Counselor Akitoki had all died earlier. Of the old faces, only Nariyori and Chikanori remained, but both had now taken Buddhist vows in the prime of life and dropped out of society, convinced that it would be futile to try to prosper through court service as matters stood, even though they might rise to middle and major counselorships. Popular Affairs Minister–Novice Chikanori made companions of the Ōhara frosts, Consultant-Novice Nariyori dwelt amid the Kōya mists, and both, it was said, devoted themselves to pious exercises in the hope of achieving enlightenment in the next life. Since there were those in antiquity who hid in the Shang Mountain clouds and purified their minds under the Ying River moon, it was natural that two such learned and upright men should also forsake society.[23]

"I was wise to become a monk," Nariyori said at Kōya when he learned about the things that were happening. "The world is the same, though I am different; still, it would have been far worse to witness those events at first hand as someone personally involved. The Hōgen and Heiji disturbances seemed shocking enough, but these are the latter days of the Law; that's why matters have come to this. What are we to expect next? I wish I could climb even higher—through the clouds, if necessary. I wish I could penetrate even deeper into the wilds—beyond the mountains, if necessary." The world seemed, indeed, not one in which a man of sensitivity would wish to linger.

22. A reference to the Hōgen and Heiji disturbances. Hōgen: 1156–58; Heiji: 1159; Angen: 1175–76; Jishō: 1177–80.

23. In China, four men are said to have retreated to Shang Mountain to escape the excesses of the Qin regime (221 B.C.–206 B.C.). The Ying River is famous as the place where Xu You, an upright ancient, washed his ears after Emperor Yao announced his intention of abdicating in his favor.

On the twenty-third, the former Tendai abbot, Archbishop Meiun, returned to his old position as the successor to Abbot Kakukai, who had expressed an urgent desire to step down.

Despite Kiyomori's arbitrary actions, he appears to have decided that there was no cause for anxiety as long as he continued to be the empress's father and the regent's father-in-law. He went off to Fukuhara, leaving instructions that Emperor Takakura was to take charge of all affairs of state.[24] Munemori hurried to the palace with the news, but the emperor refused to consent. "I won't rule unless the retired emperor chooses to cede the responsibility to me," he said. "Talk to the regent and handle things as you please, Munemori."

The retired emperor had now lived at the Seinan Palace until midwinter.[25] Howling gales swept in from the mountains and fields; the moon shone cold and bright on the frozen garden. No mortal foot left its track where fallen snows accumulated in the courtyard; the flocks of birds had disappeared from the ice-bound lake. The sound of the bell at the Great Temple evoked thoughts of Yiaisi; the color of the snow on the western hills suggested the appearance of Incense Burner Peak.[26] The faint, chill echoes of fulling mallets reached the imperial pillow through the frosty night; carriages grating over the ice toward dawn left traces stretching into the distance outside the gate. As the former emperor observed the travelers and horses bustling along the thoroughfare, he was moved by the realization that man's journey through life is no different. Most awesomely, he said, "I wonder what karma from a previous existence links me to the guards at the gate, that they should watch here day and night." There was nothing that was not a source of pain. The rural surroundings themselves evoked floods of nostalgic tears, as his mind turned again and again toward his sightseeing excursions on this occasion and that, his visits to shrines and temples in various places, and his splendid celebrations.

The old year gave way to the new, the fourth of the Jishō era [1180].

24. Kiyomori possessed a villa on the coast at Fukuhara (now a part of Kobe).
25. Seinan Palace was another name for the Toba Mansion.
26. "Great Temple" was an informal name for the Shōkyōmyōin, a temple near the Toba Mansion. The comparisons are to places associated with the poetry of Bo Juyi.

Chapter 4

Time: fifth month of 1180
Principal subject: a second attempt to overthrow the Taira, led by Minamoto
    no Yorimasa
Principal characters:
    Kiō. A samurai in Yorimasa's service
    Mochihito, Prince. Son of Retired Emperor Go-Shirakawa
    Munemori (Taira). Second son of Kiyomori; now clan head with Shi-
        gemori's death
    Nakatsuna (Minamoto). Son of Yorimasa
    Yorimasa (Minamoto). An aged warrior

4.6. Kiō

[At the instigation of Yorimasa, Prince Mochihito has agreed to lead a revolt against the Taira, but the plot has been discovered, and he is forced to flee the capital.]

Prince Mochihito traveled northward on Takakura Street, eastward on Konoe Avenue, and across the Kamo River to Nyoiyama Mountain. Long ago, we are told, Emperor Tenmu fled to the Yoshino mountains, disguised as a young woman, after having been attacked by rebels during his days as crown prince; and now this prince found himself in the same situation. Because he was unaccustomed to such travel, blood from his feet reddened the sand as he plodded nightlong over the unfamiliar mountain paths, and the heavy dew on the luxuriant summer foliage must have increased his discomfort. He arrived at the Miidera Temple as dawn approached.

"My life isn't worth much, but I don't want to lose it, so I've come to you for protection," he said. Awed and happy, the monks prepared the Hōrin'in Hall as a residence for him. Then they took him inside and offered him refreshment.

On the next day, the sixteenth [of the fifth month in the fourth year of Jishō, 1180], the capital was thrown into an uproar by the news that Prince Mochihito had rebelled and disappeared.

"The cause for rejoicing predicted by Yasuchika was my departure from the Toba Mansion; the cause for sorrow is this," said Retired Emperor Go-Shirakawa.[1]

If we ask why Yorimasa started a rebellion in that particular year, after having survived so long by remaining passive, the answer is to be sought in the reprehensible behavior of Kiyomori's second son, Munemori. This lesson teaches us that a man must be very careful about permitting himself to indulge in improprieties of speech and conduct, merely because he happens to be blessed with prosperity.

Yorimasa's heir, Nakatsuna, had owned a horse that was famous throughout the capital. It was an incomparable bay with a black mane, easier to ride, faster, and better natured than any other mount could possibly have been. It was named Konoshita [Under the Trees]. Munemori heard about it and sent Nakatsuna a message. "I'd like to take a look at that famous horse I've heard about," he said.

"I did have a horse like that, but I sent him to the country for a short rest; he was tired from having been overridden lately," Nakatsuna answered.

"Well, all right." Munemori let the matter drop. But later, when a large party of Heike samurai were seated in rows at the mansion, several men said, "That horse was in the capital as late as the day before yesterday," "He was here yesterday, too," and, "They were riding him around the courtyard this very morning, training him."

"In other words, Nakatsuna just doesn't want to send him here! That's beneath contempt! Go tell him I want the horse!" By urgent samurai messenger and letter, Munemori asked for Konoshita five or six or seven or eight times in a single day.

Yorimasa called Nakatsuna in. "Even if the horse were made of gold, you couldn't hold onto him with Munemori pressing you like that. Send him off to Rokuhara now," he said. There was nothing for Nakatsuna to do but obey. He composed a poem to go with the horse:[2]

koishiku wa	If it attracts you,
kite mo mi yo ka shi	please come to see it here:
mi no soeru	how might I manage
kage o ba ikaga	to detach and send away
hanachiyarubeki	something that is my shadow?

Munemori sent no answer to the poem.[3] "Yes, he's a fine horse, magnificent. But the owner was stingy. Brand him with his owner's name," he said.

---

1. A few days earlier, on the 12th, some weasels had appeared in the Seinan Palace (Toba Mansion), where Retired Emperor Go-Shirakawa was still confined. When asked to explain the significance of the visitation, Abe no Yasuchika, the head diviner, had said, "Joy and sorrow will visit His Majesty within three days." Subsequently, on the 13th, Kiyomori had allowed the retired emperor to move back to the city.

2. In a variant *Heike* text, *Genpei jōsuiki,* the poem appears after Munemori's initial request, a more suitable location. There is a pun on *kage* ("shadow"; "bay horse").

3. An act of rudeness. Poems required responses in kind.

He had Konoshita branded "Nakatsuna" and put him in his stable. Whenever a visitor asked to see the famous animal, he would say, "Saddle Nakatsuna and lead him out," "Mount Nakatsuna," "Whip Nakatsuna; give him a wallop," and so forth.

Nakatsuna was furious. "It was bad enough for that bully to seize a horse that was as dear as life to me. Now he's using him to ridicule me. I won't stand for this!" he said.

"The Heike make those humiliating remarks because we're objects of contempt to them," Yorimasa told him. "They think we have to take whatever they dish out. A life like this isn't worth living; I'm going to look for a chance to do something." As became evident later, he did not attempt a private revenge; instead, he persuaded Prince Mochihito to act.

In that connection, as in so many others, people remembered Palace Minister Shigemori with nostalgia. One time when Shigemori called in at the empress's apartments during a visit to the imperial palace, an eight-foot snake coiled itself around the left edge of his bloused trousers. "It may upset the ladies-in-waiting and alarm the empress if I make a fuss," he thought. He held down the snake's tail with his left hand, took hold of its head with his right, and put it inside the sleeve of his cloak. Then he stood up and calmly called for a chamberlain of sixth rank. The summons was answered by Nakatsuna, who was a chamberlain at the time. Shigemori gave him the snake. Nakatsuna took it, went past the archery hall to the small courtyard outside the courtiers' hall, and called over a page from the Giyōden storeroom, but the page ran off, shaking his head. Nakatsuna had to summon a retainer of his own, Palace Guard Kiō. He gave Kiō the snake, and Kiō took it and got rid of it.

The next morning, Shigemori had someone saddle a good horse, which he sent to Nakatsuna. "You handled yourself very well yesterday. This horse is a pleasure to ride. Use him when you leave the guard quarters at night to visit a pretty woman," he said. Nakatsuna's reply was a suitable one to address to a minister of state: "I am delighted to respectfully receive Your Excellency's gracious gift of a horse. May I say that your actions yesterday resembled the 'Return to the Castle'?"[4]

How could Munemori have been so different from his admirable brother? That he should have failed to achieve quite the same high standard was not surprising, but it was disgraceful to plunge the country into turmoil, just because he coveted someone else's favorite horse and took it away.

After dark on the sixteenth, Yorimasa, his oldest son Nakatsuna, his second son Kanetsuna, Rokujō no Kurando Nakaie, Nakaie's son Kurando Tarō Nakamitsu, and others burned their houses and went off to the Miidera Temple—more than three hundred mounted men altogether.

One of Yorimasa's samurai, Palace Guard Kiō, stayed behind because he

---

4. A court dance in which a performer dressed as a Central Asian introduced a snake into his sleeve.

had failed to join the others in time. Munemori summoned him.[5] "Why did you stay behind instead of going with Yorimasa?" he asked.

"I always meant to be the first to gallop forward and give my life for him in a crisis," Kiō said respectfully, "but for some reason he didn't say a word to me about it."

"Well, do you plan to side with Yorimasa, the traitor? You've been in and out of our houses too. Do you want to prosper in the future by serving us? Say what you really think."

Kiō shed tears. "My family and His Lordship's have been close for generations, but I can't cast my lot with a traitor. I want to serve you."

"Then do so. You'll find us quite as generous as Yorimasa," Munemori said. He went inside.

From morning until evening on that day, Munemori kept asking his samurai if Kiō was around. The answer was always yes. He went outside toward nightfall, and Kiō addressed him in a respectful voice. "They say Yorimasa has gone to Miidera. You must be planning to send a punitive force against him. He's not very strong; there's probably nobody with him except the Miidera monks and some men from Watanabe, whom I know quite well. I'd like to kill one of his best men, but a so-called friend of mine stole the horse I keep for fighting. Could you lend me one of yours?"

"I'll be glad to," Munemori said. He had a good saddle put on a valuable horse, a whitish roan named Nanryō [Silver], and gave it to him.

Kiō went home. "I'm going to ride this horse to Miidera the minute it gets dark; I'll be the first man in Lord Yorimasa's force to gallop out and die in battle," he said.

When night came at last, he sent his wife and children into hiding. Then, with a full heart, he prepared to leave for Miidera. He put on a hunting robe with a three-colored design and large chrysanthemum-shaped braided seam decorations, a hereditary suit of armor with flame-red lacing, and a helmet with silver studs. At his waist, he hung a magnificent oversized sword; on his back, he placed a quiver containing twenty-four arrows, the white feathers of each marked with broad black bands, as well as a pair of target-shooting arrows fledged with hawk feathers, which he may have included through a wish to honor the etiquette observed by the palace guards.[6] He picked up a rattan-wrapped bow, mounted Nanryō, and assigned a man to ride a remount and a groom to carry a shield under his arm. Then he burned his house to the ground and galloped off toward Miidera.

Shouts arose at Rokuhara. "Kiō's house is on fire!" Munemori hurried out. "Is Kiō here?" he asked. No, he was not. "I gave that fellow the benefit of the doubt, and now he's turned around and cheated me! Catch up with him and kill him!" he said. But Kiō was a superb archer, famous for his

5. Kiō is said in other *Heike* texts to have lived near Munemori in the Rokuhara area.

6. The palace guards (*takiguchi*), the group of archers to which Kiō belonged, made it a practice to add a target-shooting arrow or two to their quivers.

speed with the bow, and a strong, brave man. "He'll kill twenty-four opponents with those twenty-four arrows in his quiver," Munemori's men said. "Don't volunteer." Not one of them was willing to face him.

At the very same time, the warriors at Miidera were discussing Kiō. "I wish we could have brought him with us," said a member of the Watanabe League.[7] "Terrible things might be happening to him back there at Rokuhara."

Yorimasa knew Kiō. "That one will never let himself be captured," he said. "He's devoted to me. Wait and see; he'll show up any minute now." Kiō appeared before he finished.

"What did I tell you?" Yorimasa said.

Kiō spoke respectfully. "I've brought Nanryō, a horse from Rokuhara, in exchange for Lord Nakatsuna's Konoshita. Here, he's yours." He gave Nakatsuna the horse.

Nakatsuna was delighted. He cut off Nanryō's mane and tail, branded him, and had him chased inside the gate at Rokuhara in the middle of the following night. The horse went into the stable and began to exchange nips with his fellows.

"Look who's here! It's Nanryō!" said the startled grooms.

Munemori hurried out to see. The horse's brand said, "Taira Buddhist Novice Munemori, formerly Nanryō."[8] In a rage, he swore revenge. "I gave that cur the benefit of the doubt and he turned around and cheated me. Take him alive the minute we start the attack on Miidera! I'll behead him with a saw," he said. But Nanryō's mane did not grow back, nor did the brand disappear.

4.11. *The Battle at the Bridge*

[Prince Mochihito has left Miidera for Nara, escorted by Yorimasa's men and a group of soldier-monks.][9]

Prince Mochihito fell off his horse six times between Miidera and Uji. "He didn't get any sleep last night; that's what's the matter," the others said. They ripped up the planking of the Uji Bridge as far as the third pillar, and took him into the Byōdōin to rest awhile.

Meanwhile, the men at Rokuhara said, "What do you know! It looks like the prince is fleeing toward Nara. Go after him and kill him."

A force of more than twenty-eight thousand riders crossed Kohatayama

7. A league was an association of middle- and low-level local warriors, usually based on blood ties.

8. The horse's cropped mane was meant to suggest a monk's shaven head.

9. Soldier-monks (*sōhei*) were fighting men maintained by temples to safeguard their property and support them in disputes. The best-known aggregations were at the Enryakuji, the Onjōji (Miidera), and the great temples of Nara, notably the Kōfukuji and the Tōdaiji.

Mountain and bore down on the Uji Bridge, led by these commanders-in-chief:

> Commander of the Military Guards of the Left Tomomori
> Head Chamberlain—Middle Captain Shigehira
> Director of the Stables of the Left Yukimori
> Satsuma Governor Tadanori

And by these samurai commanders:

> Kazusa Governor Tadakiyo
>   His son Kazusa no Tarō Hangan Tadatsuna
> Hida Governor Kageie
>   His son Hida no Tarō Hangan Kagetaka
> Takahashi no Hangan Nagatsuna
> Kawachi no Hangan Hidekuni
> Musashi no Saburōzaemon Arikuni
> Etchū no Jirōbyōe-no-jō Moritsugi
> Kazusa no Gorōbyōe Tadamitsu
> Akushichibyōe Kagekiyo

The Taira saw that the enemy warriors were inside the Byōdōin. They shouted three rounds of battle cries, and the prince's men answered with shouts of their own.

"They've pulled up the planks! Watch it! They've pulled up the planks! Watch it!" the Heike vanguard yelled. But their cries failed to carry to the men in the rear, who were pressing ahead in the hope of gaining the lead. More than two hundred of the foremost riders were pushed into the river, where they drowned and floated away.

Archers from the two sides took their places at the bridge for the exchange of arrows.[10] The prince's men—Shunchō, Habuku, Sazuku, and Tsuzuku no Genta—released a flight of arrows that pierced both armor and shields.

Yorimasa was wearing a heavy silk tunic and a suit of indigo-laced armor with a white fern-leaf design. As though to show that he expected that day to be his last, he wore no helmet. His heir, Nakatsuna, wore a red brocade tunic and a suit of black-laced armor. He had left off his helmet so that he could wield his bow more easily.

Tajima strode onto the bridge alone, with his mighty spear unsheathed.[11]

"Shoot him down, men!" the Heike commander ordered.

Expert archers stood in a row and let fly a fast and furious barrage of arrows, but Tajima calmly ducked under the high ones, jumped over the low ones, and used his spear to fend off the ones that came straight at him. The

10. The arrow exchange was a declaration of mutual intent to do battle.
11. Tajima was a soldier-monk from Miidera.

men on both sides watched in admiration, and from then on people called him Tajima the Arrow-scatterer.

Jōmyō Meishū of Tsutsui, one of the worker-monks, was wearing a dark blue tunic, a suit of black-laced armor, and a helmet with five neckplates. At his waist, there was a sword with a black lacquered hilt and scabbard; on his back, there was a quiver containing twenty-four arrows, all fledged with black eagle-wing feathers. Grasping a lacquered, rattan-wrapped bow and his favorite long, plain-handled spear, he advanced onto the bridge and announced his name in a mighty voice.

"You must have heard of me long ago; see me now before you! Everyone at Miidera knows me—the worker-monk Jōmyō Meishū from Tsutsui, a warrior worth a thousand! If anybody here considers himself my equal, let him come forward. I'll meet him!" He let fly a fast and furious barrage from his twenty-four-arrow quiver, killing twelve men instantly and wounding eleven others. Then, with one arrow left, he sent the bow clattering away, untied and discarded the quiver, took off his fur boots, and ran nimbly along a bridge beam in his bare feet. Other men had been afraid to cross, but Jōmyō might as well have been on Ichijō or Nijō Avenue. He mowed down five enemies with his spear and was engaging a sixth when the blade snapped in the middle. He abandoned the weapon and fought with his sword. Hard-pressed by a host of adversaries, he struck out in every direction, employing zigzag, interlacing, crosswise, dragonfly reverse, and water-wheel maneuvers. He cut down eight men on the spot, and struck the helmet of the ninth such a mighty blow that the sword snapped at the hilt rivet, slipped loosed, and splashed into the river. Then he fought on with desperate fury, using his only remaining weapon, a dagger.

Fighting in Jōmyō's wake, there was a strong, agile monk called Ichirai, an attendant of Holy Teacher Keishū at the Jōenbō Cloister. Ichirai wanted to pass Jōmyō, but the beam was too narrow. "Pardon, Jōmyō," he said. He put his hand on Jōmyō's helmet, bounded over his shoulder, and fought on.

Ichirai died in battle. Jōmyō crawled back, took off his armor and helmet on the grass in front of the Byōdōin, and counted sixty-three arrow dents. Five shafts had penetrated the leather, but none of the wounds was serious. He treated the places with moxa, wrapped his head in a cloth, and donned a white clerical robe. Then he broke his bow to make a staff, shod his feet in low clogs, and set off toward Nara, chanting the name of Amida Buddha.

One after another, the monks from Miidera and the men of the Watanabe League dashed across the beams as Jōmyō had done. Some returned with trophies; others, mortally wounded, cut open their bellies and jumped into the river. The battle on the bridge raged like a fire.

One of the samurai commanders on the Heike side, Kazusa Governor Tadakiyo, went to the commanders-in-chief. "Look what's happening!" he said. "There's fierce fighting on the bridge. Now would be the time for us to ford the river on horseback, but it's flooding from the summer rains. We'd probably suffer heavy losses of horses and men. Would it be best to head toward Yodo and Imoarai, or should we go around by the Kawachi Road?"

A warrior came forward: Ashikaga no Matatarō Tadatsuna, a resident of Shimotsuke Province. "It's not a question of summoning warriors from India or China to send to Yodo, Imoarai, or the Kawachi Road; we'd be the ones to go. If we let these enemies reach Nara instead of destroying them when they're right in front of us, there are men in Yoshino and Totsukawa who won't waste any time in joining them, and then there could be trouble.

"A great waterway, the Tone River, forms the boundary between Musashi and Kōzuke provinces. Once when the Chichibu and the Ashikaga had fallen out and were always fighting, the Ashikaga decided to make a frontal attack across the ford at Nagai and a rear attack across the fords at Koga and Sugi. But the Chichibu destroyed all the boats that had been assembled at Sugi by the Nitta novice of Kōzuke, who was allied with the Ashikaga. 'It will be an eternal disgrace to us as warriors if we don't get across now,' Nitta said. 'If we drown, we drown. Come on! We'll ride across!' And cross they did, probably by means of horse rafts.[12]

"When we see an enemy across a river, we eastern warriors don't make a habit of picking and choosing between shallow and deep. This stream's no faster or deeper than the Tone. Follow me, men!" He led the way into the water, and more than three hundred riders entered after him, foremost among them Ōgo, Ōmuro, Fukazu, Yamagami, Naba no Tarō, Sanuki no Shirōdaifu Hirotsuna, Onodera no Zenji Tarō, and Heyako no Shirō—and among the retainers, Ukukata no Jirō, Kiriu no Rokurō, and Tanaka no Muneda.

"Put the strong horses upstream and the weak ones downstream," Tadatsuna shouted. "As long as they can stand, let them walk with the reins slack. If they start to struggle for footing, tighten the reins to make them swim. Anyone who sees a straggler, have him catch hold of the end of your bow. Hold hands and stay shoulder to shoulder while you cross. Get a firm seat in the saddle; put plenty of weight on your stirrups. Pull your horse's head up if it goes under, but not so hard that it submerges again. If the water gets deep enough to go over your head, move back to the rump. Try to keep your weight off the horse; make the river carry you. Don't use your bow while you're in the water, not even to answer enemy fire. Keep your neck-guard down all the time, but don't bend so far that they can hit the top of your helmet. Cross in a straight line; don't let yourself be carried downstream. Don't try to head upstream. Come on! Come on!" Thanks to his instructions, the three hundred riders surged onto the opposite bank without losing a man.

12. A military technique. The mounted warriors crossed in compact parallel rows, with the foot soldiers clinging to the horses.

Chapter 5

Time: last three months of 1180
Principal subject: unrest in the provinces as a consequence of Prince Mochi-
    hito's call to arms
Principal characters:
    Go-Shirakawa, Retired Emperor. Head of the imperial clan
    Kiyomori (Taira). Retired head of the Taira clan and principal power
        at court
    Koremori (Taira). Son of Kiyomori's dead heir, Shigemori
    Mongaku. Eccentric Buddhist monk
    Motomichi (Fujiwara). Regent to the infant Emperor Antoku
    Munemori (Taira). Son of Kiyomori; leader of the Taira clan
    Shigehira (Taira). Son of Kiyomori
    Tadakiyo (Fujiwara). A senior samurai in the service of the Taira
    Tadanori (Taira). Brother of Kiyomori; known as a poet
    Takakura, Retired Emperor. Father of the infant Emperor Antoku
    Tomomori (Taira). Son of Kiyomori
    Yoritomo (Minamoto). Heir to the chieftainship of the Minamoto clan
        living in exile in the eastern province of Izu

[The leaders of the revolt against the Taira, Prince Mochihito and Yorimasa,
have lost their lives, but Kiyomori has now invited more trouble by forcing
the court to move from Heian-kyō (modern Kyoto) to his seat of power in
Fukuhara (within modern Kobe).]

5.3. *Strange Occurrences*

Inauspicious dreams preyed on the nerves of the Taira after the move to
Fukuhara, and there were many strange apparitions. As Kiyomori was lying
down one night, a huge face peered in at him, big enough to fill all the space
between two pillars of the room. He glared back at it, and it vanished at once.

On another night, people heard the sound of a great tree crashing to the
ground near the hill palace, followed by a burst of laughter, which seemed
to come from twenty or thirty throats.[1] That palace had just been built;

1. The hill palace is mentioned again in "The Flight from Fukuhara" (Sec. 7.20), where it
is said to have been designed as a place from which to view spring blossoms.

there were no big trees near it. In the thought that goblins were probably responsible, the Taira created a "whizzing-arrow watch," made up of a hundred men who were to be ready to release whizzing arrows by night, and fifty who were to be ready by day. Not a sound was heard when the archers shot toward the place where the goblins seemed to be lurking, but there was boisterous laughter when they shot in other directions.

Again, Kiyomori left his curtain-dais one morning, pushed open the outer door, and found the inner courtyard full of skulls, an immense number of them, clashing and rebounding with a frightful clatter and rumble, and rolling up and down and in and out. He called for his attendants. "Is someone on duty? Is anyone around?" But nobody happened to be within earshot. All the skulls merged into a single enormous whole, bigger than the garden—a veritable mountain, a hundred and forty or fifty feet high. In that great head, there appeared thousands and tens of thousands of big human eyes, all fixed on him with an unblinking, angry stare. He stood his ground calmly, glaring back, and the wrath of his gaze wiped out the great skull without a trace, just as the sun melts frost or dew.

Furthermore, one night a mouse made a nest and gave birth in the tail of a horse on which Kiyomori had lavished special attention, housing it in his best stable and assigning many grooms to cater to its needs. He ordered seven yin-yang masters to divine the significance of the birth, and the seven reported, "You must observe great caution." The horse had been presented to him by Ōba no Saburō Kagechika, a resident of Sagami Province, who had told him that it was the finest mount in the eight eastern provinces. It was black, with a white forehead, and its name was Mochizuki [Full Moon]. Abe no Yasuchika, the director of the Bureau of Divination, received it as a gift. (During Emperor Tenchi's reign, so the *Chronicles of Japan* tell us, an insurrection broke out abroad after a mouse built a nest and gave birth in the tail of an imperial mount.)

Also, there was a man, a young samurai in the service of Minamoto Middle Counselor Masayori, who had an ominous dream. It seemed that a throng of senior officials, all dressed in formal attire, had assembled for a conference in what looked like the office of the department of shrines at the greater imperial palace, and that they were expelling someone who sat in a low seat, and who gave the impression of belonging to the Taira faction.

"Who is it that they're expelling?" the dreamer asked an old man.

"The deity of Itsukushima," the ancient answered.

Then the dignified occupant of the highest seat spoke. "The Sword of Commission, which had been entrusted temporarily to the house of Taira, is now to be presented to Yoritomo, the Izu Exile."

"Please give it to my grandson after that," said another old man by his side.

When the dreamer asked about the speakers, he was told, "It was the Great Bodhisattva Hachiman who said the sword was to go to Yoritomo, and it was the Kasuga divinity who asked to have it go to his grandson next. I am the Takeuchi divinity."[2]

The samurai told people about his dream, and the story reached Kiyomori, who sent Gendayū no Hangan Suesada to Masayori. "Tell your young samurai, the one who had the dream, to report here at once," he said. The samurai took to his heels, but the matter was allowed to drop after Masayori hurried to Kiyomori's house with assurances that there was absolutely no truth to the rumors. It was sad, others observed, that the house of Taira, hitherto the bulwark of the throne and the protector of the land, should now seem in danger of losing the Sword of Commission for having disregarded the imperial will.

When news of these events reached Consultant-Novice Nariyori at Mount Kōya, he said, "The Heike won't last much longer! It was understandable that the Itsukushima divinity sided with them. But I'd always heard that that divinity was feminine, the third daughter of the dragon king Sāgara. Also, it was natural for the Great Bodhisattva Hachiman to propose to give the Sword of Commission to Yoritomo, but I can't see why the Kasuga divinity should have said, 'Give it to my grandson next.' Can it mean that military supremacy will pass to the descendants of Kamatari, the sons of the regental house, once the Taira have been destroyed and the Genji have replaced them?"

"Buddhas and bodhisattvas can assume many forms," said another monk who happened to be present. "Sometimes they may appear as mortals, sometimes as goddesses. We call the Itsukushima divinity a goddess, it's true, but she is a miracle-working deity, possessed of the six supernatural powers and three insights: it isn't impossible for her to assume human form."

It would have been correct for such men to make enlightenment their sole concern, seeing that they had rejected this transitory world for the path of truth, but it is only human nature to admire good government and deplore injustice.

5.4. The Fast Courier

On the second of the ninth month in that same year [1180], Ōba no Saburō Kagechika of Sagami Province sent a message to Fukuhara by fast courier. "The Izu Exile, the former assistant guards commander Yoritomo, sent his father-in-law, Hōjō no Shirō Tokimasa, to challenge the deputy governor of Izu Province, Izumi no Hangan Kanetaka, and Kanetaka was killed in a night attack on his Yamaki Residence on the seventeenth of the eighth month. Later, about three hundred men established a stronghold at Ishibashiyama—Toi, Tsuchiya, Okazaki, and others. I led a thousand Taira par-

---

2. The Itsukushima, Hachiman, and Kasuga shrines were associated with the Taira, Minamoto, and Fujiwara clans, respectively. The Takeuchi divinity was worshipped at a shrine in the Iwashimizu Hachiman complex.

tisans against them, attacked, and reduced them to seven or eight horsemen, including Yoritomo himself. Yoritomo fled to Sugiyama in the Toi region after a desperate last stand. Hatakeyama rallied to our side with five hundred men, and the sons of Miura no Ōsuke Yoshiaki joined the Genji with three hundred. Hatakeyama retreated to Musashi Province after losing to the Miura in engagements at the Yui and Kotsubo beaches, but then he attacked the Kinugasa stronghold of the Miura with a force of three thousand riders, made up of his kinsmen (the Kawagoe, the Inage, the Oyamada, the Edo, and the Kasai) and members of the Seven Leagues of Musashi. Yoshiaki was slain; his sons crossed by boat from Kurihama beach to Awa and Kazusa provinces."

There was foolish talk among the young senior nobles and courtiers of the Heike clan, for whom the transfer of the capital to Fukuhara had already lost its novelty. "If only something would happen soon! Nothing would suit us better than to be part of a punitive force," they said.

Hatakeyama no Shōji Shigeyoshi, Oyamada no Bettō Arishige, and Utsunomiya no Saemon Tomotsuna happened to be in the capital as members of the provincial guards. "There must be some mistake," Shigeyoshi said. "It's impossible to be sure about the Hōjō because they're very close to Yoritomo, but I can't believe those others would join a traitor. There's bound to be a correction to Ōba's report before long." Some people agreed with him, but many others whispered, "Oh, no! There's going to be a national crisis."

Kiyomori flew into a rage. "Yoritomo would have been executed if Lady Ike hadn't persuaded us to reduce his sentence to exile," he said.[3] "Now he's taking up arms against us, just as if he didn't owe us a thing. The gods and buddhas won't stand for behavior like that. Heaven will punish him soon enough!"

5.7. Mongaku's Austerities

On the twentieth of the third month in the first year of Eiryaku [1160], as a consequence of his father Yoshitomo's revolt in the twelfth month of the first year of Heiji [1159], the fourteen-year-old Yoritomo had been sentenced to live in exile at Hirugashima in Izu Province; and there he had remained for more than twenty years. If we ask why he started a rebellion in that particular year, after having survived for so long by lying low, some say the answer is to be found in the exhortations of the monk of Takao, the saintly Mongaku.

Mongaku was known in lay life as Endō Musha Moritō, the son of Watanabe no Endō Mochitō.[4] At the age of nineteen, while he was a minor functionary in Jōsaimon'in's service, he experienced a religious awakening,

3. Lady Ike, Kiyomori's late stepmother, is said to have pitied Yoritomo because he reminded her of a son who had died young.
4. Probably to be associated with the Watanabe League in Settsu (Sec. 4.6).

renounced the world, and resolved to embrace the life of a wandering ascetic.[5] To find out how painful the austerities might be, he made his way into a thicket on a hillside during the sixth month, on a day when not even a blade of grass was stirring under the blazing sun. He stretched out on his back and lay motionless, while swarms of horseflies, mosquitoes, wasps, ants, and other poisonous insects settled on his body and bit him. He stayed there for seven days, and on the eighth he got up.

"Does it hurt about this much to perform austerities?" he asked someone. The other person answered, "Nobody could survive if it did."

"Then there's nothing to worry about." He embarked on his travels.

He decided to make a retreat at Kumano Nachi. First, he went to the base of the famous waterfall, with the idea of braving the torrent as a brief preliminary exercise. By then, it was past the tenth of the twelfth month. The snow was deep, the ice was thick, the valley streams had fallen silent. There was a freezing wind blowing from the mountaintops, icicles had formed in the waterfall, and everything was perfectly white, even the branches on the trees. Mongaku waded into the pool below the falls, submerged himself to the neck, and began to recite a set number of invocations to Fudō. He managed to go on for two or three days, but on the fourth or fifth day he lost his footing and floated to the top. Was there any chance that he might stay there, in spite of the rush of the great waterfall? The current swept him away and carried him downstream, rising and sinking amid knife-edged rocks, for six or seven hundred yards. Then a handsome youth appeared and pulled him ashore by the hands. An amazed bystander built a fire to warm him, and he regained consciousness very soon. (It was not in his karma to die just then.)

The moment Mongaku came to his senses, his eyes began to blaze. "I made a solemn vow to stand under the waterfall for twenty-one days and recite the name of Fudō three hundred thousand times. Today is only the fifth day. Who dared to bring me here before I had even finished the first week?" he demanded. The other people felt too frightened to answer.

Mongaku went back to the pool and stood under the waterfall. On the second day, eight youths came to pull him out, but he fought them off as hard as he could. On the third day, he finally stopped breathing. There may have been some concern lest the pool suffer defilement, for two divine youths with their hair dressed in side loops descended from the summit of the waterfall. With warm, fragrant hands, they stroked him from the top of his head to the fingernails and palms of his hands and the soles of his feet, and he awakened as though from a dream.

"Who are you who treat me so kindly?" he asked.

"Kongara and Seitaka, messengers from the Mystic King Fudō. Our master commanded us to come here. 'Mongaku is undertaking heroic austerities in accordance with a supreme vow. Go and help him,' he told us," they said.

5. Jōsaimon'in (1126–89) was Retired Emperor Go-Shirakawa's sister.

"Now tell me, where is the Mystic King Fudō?" Mongaku shouted.

"He is in the Tuṣita Heaven." The two ascended into the distant skies.

Mongaku joined his palms in prayer. "The holy Fudō himself knows of my austerities," he thought with a confident heart. He returned to the pool and stood under the waterfall again. Thanks to the divine protection, the gales no longer pierced his flesh and the descending waters felt warm. Thus he accomplished his mighty vow to stay under the falls for twenty-one days.

After spending a thousand days in retreat at Nachi, Mongaku visited Ōmine three times and Kazuragi twice. He also made pious journeys to all the other holy places in Japan—Kōya, Kokawa, Kinpuzen, Shirayama, Tate-yama, Mount Fuji, Togakushi in Shinano Province, and Haguro in Dewa Province. When he finally decided to return to the capital (possibly because not even he was impervious to homesickness), he brought with him a repu-tation as a miracle worker with razor-sharp skills, someone who could pray a flying bird down from the sky.

5.8.   The Subscription List

After that, Mongaku devoted himself to pious exercises far back in the mountains at Takao, where there was a temple called the Jingoji, founded by Wake no Kiyomaro during Empress Shōtoku's reign. Long fallen into disrepair, the building was shrouded in haze during the springtime and filled with mist in autumn. Its doors lay moldering under fallen leaves, brought low by the winds; its roof tiles exposed the very altar to the sky, ravaged by the rains and dews. There was no abbot, nor were there any visitors, except for occasional shafts of moonlight and sunlight.

Mongaku swore a mighty vow to restore the temple, no matter what the cost. Then he began to make the rounds with a subscription list, looking for donations. One day, he arrived at Retired Emperor Go-Shirakawa's Hōjūji Mansion.[6] A concert was going on, and the former sovereign brushed aside his request for a contribution. To this most audacious and self-assertive of monks, it seemed that someone must have failed to deliver his message. He burst into the inner courtyard without worrying about the proprieties. "You are a supremely merciful, supremely benevolent lord. How can you turn me down?" he bawled. He unrolled the subscription list and began to chant in a sonorous voice:

The novice Mongaku speaks with respect. A request for donations, in order that with the assistance of noble and base, clerical and lay, I may build a hall on the holy

6. This episode takes place before Retired Emperor Go-Shirakawa's stay at the Toba Man-sion (late 1179–fifth month of 1180), and thus before the transfer of the court to Fukuhara in the sixth month of 1180. The name of the retired emperor's residence was derived from a nearby temple, the Hōjūji, which is said to have been located southeast of the present Sanjū-sangendō, in Higashiyama-ku, Kyoto.

site at Mount Takao and offer prayers to attain the great boon of happiness in this world and the next.

When we consider it, absolute reality is vast and great. "Sentient being" and "Buddha" are mere provisional terms. But ever since the true nature of the phenomenal world has been covered by the thick clouds of distracting notions, which trail over the peaks of the twelve-linking chain of dependent origination, the light of the moon of the lotus-pure Buddha nature has been too dim to appear in the sky of the three virtues and four mandalas. How lamentable it is that the Buddha-sun should already have set, should have left the world of transmigration enveloped in darkness! Human beings founder in lust and wine; they cannot emancipate themselves from illusions that resemble mad elephants and leaping apes. Immoderate in their slanders against others and against the dharma, how may they escape punishment at the hands of Enma's torturers?

Although I have shaken off the dust of the world to don the garb of religion, evil is still strong in my heart, battening day and night; virtuous words still offend my ears, suffering rejection morning and evening. How bitter it is to know that I must return again to the firepits of the three evil paths, that I must long remain bound to the grievous wheel of the four births!

Thus it is that the millions of scrolls in Śākyamuni's teachings show us how to attain Buddhahood. We may reach the opposite shore of enlightenment either through the provisional instructions or through the teachings of absolute truth. And thus, moved to tears by the transitoriness of all things, I have resolved to call on monks and laity of high and low degree to assist in the creation of a site sacred to Buddhism, so that they may attain rebirth in the highest level of paradise.

Takao is a lofty mountain, a veritable Vulture Peak, with tranquil valleys resembling the mossy grottoes of Shang Mountain. Its white waters echo among the boulders; the monkeys on its heights call as they play in the branches. Human habitations are distant; noise and dirt are absent. The site is excellent, most appropriate for religious pursuits. I ask only a trifling donation: can there be anyone who will withhold assistance? We hear that even when a child builds a pagoda of sand, the deed instantly becomes a cause leading to Buddhahood.[7] How much greater must be the merit of one who gives a sheet of paper or half a coin from his personal belongings!

I ask that I may succeed in my vow to build the hall; that the imperial petition for the safety of the imperial palace and the tranquility of the reign may be fulfilled; that the praises of a rule as restrained and benign as those of Yao and Shun may resound from city and country, from far and near, from officials and commoners, from clergy and laity; and that we may enjoy peace as enduring as the leaves of the *chun* tree.[8] And in particular, I ask that the spirits of all who die, whether early or late, high or low, may go immediately to lotus pedestals in the pure land of which the *Lotus Sutra* tells, and that they may assuredly bask in the moonlight of the myriad merits of the three bodies.

Thus it is that I have undertaken the pious work of soliciting contributions.

> In the third month of the third year of Jishō [1179]
> Mongaku

7. Mongaku's source is the *Lotus Sutra*. See Hurvitz, *Scripture*, p. 38.

8. The mythical *chun* tree "counted 8,000 years as one spring and 8,000 years as one autumn." See Watson, *Complete Works of Chuang Tzu*, p. 30 (where the tree is called the Rose of Sharon).

5.9. *Mongaku's Exile*

As it happened, there was great animation behind the jeweled blinds and brocade curtains just then. Chancellor Moronaga had been playing the lute and chanting *rōei* to most delightful effect in the imperial presence; Major Counselor Sukekata had been singing *fuzoku* and *saibara*, beating time to accompany himself; Suketoki and Morisada had been playing the six-stringed koto and singing *imayō*; and the retired emperor had joined the supporting chorus, caught up in the pleasure of the occasion. Mongaku's loud voice made the singers stray off-key and the rhythm-beaters falter in confusion.

"Who is that? Hit him on the head!" the retired emperor said. Some impetuous youths raced toward Mongaku, and one of them, Police Lieutenant Sukeyuki, dashed out in front. "What are you jabbering about? Get out of here!" he said.

Mongaku stood his ground. "I'm not budging until His Majesty donates an estate to the Takao Jingoji," he said. Sukeyuki tried to hit him on the head, but Mongaku knocked off his cap with the subscription list, flattened him with a blow to the chest, and sent him skulking back to the veranda, minus his cap. Then Mongaku drew from his breast a dagger with a hilt bound in horsehair, unsheathed its glittering blade, and waited, ready to stab anybody who came near him. Prancing about, with the subscription list in his left hand and the naked blade in his right, he seemed to the stunned spectators to be brandishing two forged weapons. The bewildered exclamations of the senior nobles and courtiers put an end to the concert, and the palace was thrown into an uproar.

Andō Musha Migimune, a resident of Shinano Province, was serving in the Military Office at the time. He came running up with his sword to see what was wrong. Mongaku sprang at him. Perhaps out of reluctance to shed a monk's blood, Migimune turned his blade sideways and used the flat edge to deliver a powerful blow to Mongaku's dagger arm. Then, as Mongaku faltered, Migimune dropped the sword and grappled with him. "I've got you!" he shouted.

Although Mongaku had been thrown, he managed to stab Migimune in the right arm; although Migimune had been stabbed, he held fast. Two exceptionally strong men, they rolled over and over, now on top and now underneath. Newly courageous onlookers of various statuses came forward and hit Mongaku wherever they could, but the fearless monk merely showered them with abuse.

At last, Mongaku was dragged outside the gate and turned over to some lackeys in the service of the police, who started to march him off. As they tugged at him, he glared at the retired emperor's palace. "I say nothing about your refusal to make a donation. But I'll have my revenge for this outrageous treatment. The three worlds are a burning house; not even an imperial palace can escape destruction. You may pride yourself on your imperial position now, but you won't escape the torments of the ox-headed and horse-headed torturers after you go to the Yellow Springs!" he yelled, hopping up and down.[9] Outraged by his insolence, they clapped him in jail.

Sukeyuki stayed away from court for a while, humiliated by the loss of his cap. As a reward for having wrestled with Mongaku, Migimune became a third-level official in the stables of the right, without having passed through the highest post in the Military Office.

Mongaku was soon pardoned, thanks to a great amnesty occasioned by the death of Lady Bifukumon'in.[10] But instead of going away somewhere to practice austerities for a while, as would have been suitable, he resumed his solicitations with the subscription list. Furthermore, he kept on making shocking statements during his rounds. "Things are terrible! The country is on the brink of chaos. The ruler and his courtiers are all doomed to destruction," he would say.

In retaliation, the court sentenced him to distant-exile in Izu Province.[11] "That monk can't be allowed to frequent the capital," they said.

Nakatsuna, the oldest son of Minamoto no Yorimasa, was the governor of Izu at the time. He issued orders for Mongaku to be transported by sea, via the Eastern Sea Road, and two or three minor police functionaries were detailed to accompany him on the journey to Ise.

"When we policemen perform this kind of duty, we always try to be nice to the prisoner," the guards told Mongaku. "How about it, Reverend Sir? You must have friends, even though you've met with this misfortune and have to go into exile. Ask them for farewell presents and food."

"I don't have any friends I can call on for favors like that. But come to think of it, I do know somebody in the eastern hills quite well. I'll send him a note," Mongaku said.

The guards located a piece of cheap paper, but he threw it back at them. "I can't write on paper like that," he said.

They found some thick paper for him. He laughed. "I don't know how to write," he said. "You write it." He dictated a message: "While I was soliciting contributions to build and dedicate the Jingoji Temple at Takao, I came up against the sovereign who's ruling now. Needless to say, I haven't accomplished my vow. Furthermore, I've been thrown into jail, and now I've been banished to Izu Province. It will be a long trip, and I'll be greatly in need of

---

9. *Lotus Sutra*: "There is no safety in the three worlds [i.e., the types of existence into which the unenlightened are reborn]; they resemble a burning house." Hurvitz, *Scripture*, p. 72. Yellow Springs was a term for the nether regions, including the Buddhist hells. Jailers in the hells were believed to have heads like those of horses and oxen.

10. Bifukumon'in, the favorite consort of the late Emperor Toba, was a power at court for many years. She had actually died in 1160, 19 years before the date of Mongaku's subscription list.

11. The legal codes recognized three degrees of exile, of which distant-exile (*onru*) was the most severe. The other two were near-exile (*konru*) and intermediate-exile (*chūru*).

farewell presents and food. Please give something to the bearer of this message." One of them made a careful record of his words.

"How shall I address it?" the scribe asked.

"Write, 'To the Reverend Kannon at Kiyomizu Temple.'"

"You're trying to make us look like fools."

"No, not at all. I have absolute faith in Kannon. And there's nobody else I can turn to," Mongaku said.

The party set out to sea from Ano Harbor in Ise Province. When they reached Tenryū Bay, offshore from Tōtōmi Province, a sudden gale whipped up huge waves. The sailors and helmsman did their best to keep the boat from capsizing, but the wind and waves raged with mounting fury. Some of the passengers intoned Kannon's name, others recited the ten buddha-invocations of the dying. Mongaku lay oblivious, emitting loud snores, until, at the very last minute, something made him jump up. He stationed himself in the bow and glared toward the offing. "Are you there, Dragon Kings? Are you there?" he shouted. "What's the idea, trying to capsize this boat when it's carrying a monk who's sworn a mighty vow like mine? Heaven will visit instant punishment on you, Dragon Kings!" Perhaps that is why the elements subsided almost at once, allowing the boat to reach Izu Province.

On the day of his departure from the capital, Mongaku had begun to repeat a prayer. "If it's my destiny to return to the capital, and to build and dedicate the Takao Jingoji, I won't die; if my vow is to come to nothing, I'll perish on this journey." For lack of fair winds, the boat had to follow the coastline and hug the islands all the way to Izu, and no food passed his lips for thirty-one days. But he kept up his ascetic practices with as much vigor as ever. There were many indications that this was no ordinary man!

5.10.   *The Retired Emperor's Fukuhara Edict*

In Izu Province, Mongaku lived far back in the area called Nagoya, under the surveillance of a man named Kondō no Shirō Kunitaka. While he was there, he made it a practice to visit Assistant Commander of the Military Guards Yoritomo, and to amuse him with talk of the past and present.[12] One day, he said to him, "Shigemori was the steadiest and wisest of all the Heike, but he died last year in the eighth month. I wonder if that wasn't a sign that the luck of the Heike is ending. These days, there's nobody, Genji or Heike, whose face shows the marks of a supreme military commander the way yours does. Rebel now! Rule Japan!"

"I've never dreamed of anything like that," Yoritomo said. "The late Ike nun saved my worthless life; my only thought now is to pray for her salvation by reciting the *Lotus Sutra* every day."

12. Here and elsewhere, as a sign of respect, the *Heike* gives Yoritomo a title of which he had been stripped.

Mongaku persisted. "The book says, 'He who refuses heaven's gifts incurs heaven's censure; failure to seize opportunity leads to disaster.'[13] Do you think I'm just trying to feel you out? See for yourself whether I'm on your side or not." From his breast he drew a skull swathed in white cloth.

"What's that you have there?" Yoritomo asked.

"It's the head of your father, the late chief of the stables of the left. After the Heiji fighting, it stayed in front of the prison, buried under the moss, and nobody offered prayers for His Lordship. For my own reasons, I persuaded the warders to let me have it, and I've carried it around my neck for more than ten years, visiting many mountains and temples and praying. I think he's been rescued from a kalpa of suffering. You can see that I've done my best to help him."

Yoritomo found the tale hard to believe, but tears of longing filled his eyes when he heard Mongaku say the skull was his father's. From then on, he talked to him without reserve. "How could I lead a rebellion? I'm still under imperial censure," he said.

"Oh, that's no problem. I'll go to the capital right away and get you a pardon," Mongaku said.

"Don't be ridiculous. You're under censure yourself. You can't promise to get a pardon for someone else."

"I'd be wrong to claim I could try to get one for myself, but there's nothing to prevent me from speaking up for you," Mongaku said. "I can reach the new capital at Fukuhara in three days, at the most. I'll spend one day getting the edict from the retired emperor. The whole trip won't take more than seven or eight days." He hurried off.

Mongaku went back to Nagoya, told his disciples that he was going to spend seven days in private retreat at Oyama Shrine in Izu, and set out. In three days, just as he had anticipated, he arrived at Fukuhara. There he went to call on the former commander of the military guards Mitsuyoshi, a man with whom he had a slight acquaintance. "Tell the retired emperor this: 'The Izu Exile, Yoritomo, says that he is prepared to mobilize his family's retainers in the eight eastern provinces, crush the Taira, and restore peace, if only he receives a pardon and an edict from His Majesty,' " he said to him.

"Well, I don't know," Mitsuyoshi said. "This is a bad time for me; I've lost all three of my court offices. Also, the retired emperor is being held in confinement, so I'm not sure how things will work out. But I'll try to let him know."

The moment Retired Emperor Go-Shirakawa received Mitsuyoshi's secret report, he issued the edict. And on the third day after that, Mongaku arrived in Izu Province, with the edict around his neck.

Yoritomo had been fearing all kinds of misfortunes because of Mongaku's lack of discretion. But on the eighth day, at the hour of the horse [11:00

13. A quotation from the Chinese *Records of the Grand Historian* (Shi ji).

A.M.—1:00 P.M.], Mongaku arrived and turned over the document. Awed by the word "edict," Yoritomo cleansed his hands, rinsed his mouth, donned a new cap and a white robe, and made a triple obeisance to the paper. When he opened it, he read:

In recent years, the Taira have governed as they pleased, contemptuous of the imperial family. They have violated the Buddhist Law and have sought to bring down the imperial authority.

Our country is the land of the gods. Ancestral shrines stand side by side; divine power works miracles. Consequently, during all the thousands of years since the founding of the imperial line, failure has met every attempt to interfere with the imperial rule and jeopardize the state.

Therefore, I command that you make haste to chastise the house of Taira and eliminate the enemies of the court, placing your reliance on divine aid and following the instructions of this imperial edict. Win prominence for yourself and prosperity for your family by perpetuating the martial tradition of the Genji and surpassing the loyal service of your ancestors!

The above edict of His Majesty the Retired Emperor is hereby transmitted.

   Fourteenth day, seventh month, fourth year of Jishō [1180]
   Received by Mitsuyoshi, the former commander of
    the military guards of the right
   To the former assistant commander of the military guards of the right

People say that Yoritomo put the edict in a brocade bag and wore it around his neck, even during the battle of Ishibashiyama.

5.11. *Fuji River*

Meanwhile at Fukuhara, a council of senior nobles decided to dispatch a punitive force against Yoritomo before he could recruit allies. More than thirty thousand horsemen left the capital on the eighteenth of the ninth month [of 1180], with Lesser Captain Koremori as commander-in-chief and Satsuma Governor Tadanori as deputy commander. They reached the old capital on the nineteenth, and set out promptly toward the east on the twentieth.

The commander-in-chief, Koremori, was twenty-three years old, more splendid in deportment and attire than any painter's brush could depict. He had ordered his heirloom suit of armor, Karakawa [Chinese Leather], to be carried in a Chinese chest. For the journey, he wore a red brocade tunic and a suit of green-laced armor, and he rode a white-dappled reddish horse with a saddle edged in gold. The deputy commander, Tadanori, wore a blue tunic and a suit of armor with flame-red lacing, and he rode a stout and brawny black horse with a gold-flecked lacquer saddle. The army was a magnificent sight as it departed—the horses, the saddles, the armor, the helmets, the bows and arrows and swords—even the daggers seemed to gleam.

For several years, Tadanori had been intimate with a certain princess's daughter. One evening, he arrived at her house to find her engaged in a long conversation with a feminine caller of high birth. The guest showed no signs of leaving, even when it got very late. After loitering under the eaves for a while, Tadanori rattled his fan. In an elegant voice, the princess's daughter murmured two lines from a poem:

no mo se ni sudaku	The voices of insects
mushi no ne yo	everywhere in the fields![14]

Tadanori immediately stopped his fanning and went home. Later, when he came again, the lady asked, "Why did you stop fanning the other night?"

"Because I heard someone saying I was noisy," he said.

Now, saddened by the prospect of his long journey, that same lady sent him a poem with the gift of a short-sleeved robe:

azumaji no	There will be more dew
kusaba o waken	drenching the sleeve of the one
sode yori mo	bowed down by sorrow
taenu tamoto no	than wets the sleeve of the one
tsuyu zo koboruru	who parts the eastland grasses.

He replied:

wakareji o	What need to lament
nani ka nagekan	the parting of the ways
koete yuku	when we remember,
seki mo mukashi no	"The barrier we cross now
ato to omoeba	is the one of bygone days?"

There was great refinement in the lines, "The barrier we cross now is the one of bygone days." He must have been thinking about the time when Taira Commander Sadamori went east to subjugate Masakado.

In the past, before a commander left the capital to defeat an enemy of the court, he went to receive a Sword of Commission at the imperial palace. The emperor proceeded to the Shishinden, the bodyguards formed ranks at the foot of the stairs, two ministers of state supervised the ceremonies inside and outside the Shōmeimon Gate, and there was a banquet, attended by all the nobles of sixth and higher rank. Swords were received by both the commander-in-chief and the deputy commander. But now it was decided that the precedents set in the Shōhei and Tengyō eras [931–37, 938–46] were too ancient for successful imitation.[15] Instead, the authorities merely gave Koremori a bell, citing the example of Taira no Masamori's march to

14. The lines are from a *rōei* (SSRES 313): kashigamashi / no mo se ni sudaku / mushi no ne ya / ware dani mono o / iwade koso omoe ("Despite my passion, I long for you in silence—how clamorous the voices of insects, everywhere in the fields!") Tadanori's mistress comments to the guest on the insects in the garden, while saying to her lover, "I can't offend this lady; I must yearn for you in silence."

15. Shōhei and Tengyō were the eras during which Masakado and Sumitomo rebelled, respectively.

Izumo Province to subdue Minamoto no Yoshichika.[16] Koremori gave it to a servant to carry around his neck in a leather bag.

In the past, three commitments had been required of a commander who went out from the capital to crush an enemy of the court. On the day when he received the Sword of Commission, he forgot his lineage; when he prepared to leave home, he forgot his wife and children; and when he engaged the foe on the battlefield, he forgot his life. It is moving to think that those same resolves must have been in the minds of the two Heike leaders, Koremori and Tadanori.

On the twenty-second [of the ninth month in the same year], Retired Emperor Takakura began another pilgrimage to Itsukushima in Aki Province.[17] He had gone once before, in the third month, and, perhaps as a result, there had followed a month or two of tranquility in the country and well-being for ordinary people. But now, because of Prince Mochihito's revolt, the land was troubled and everything was unsettled. The retired emperor hoped to restore peace, and he also wanted to pray for his own return to good health. He was starting from Fukuhara, so he would be spared the trials of a long journey. He composed his prayer himself, and the regent, Motomichi, wrote out a fair copy:

We are told that the true nature of the phenomenal world is like an unclouded moon, soaring high and bright on the fourteenth or fifteenth night of the month, and that the profound wisdom of the Itsukushima deity resembles the alternating winds of yin and yang. The Itsukushima Shrine is a place whose name is invoked far and wide, a source of incomparable miracles. The high peaks encircling it are nature's parallel to the lofty eminence of the goddess's supreme mercy; the boundless sea at its feet symbolizes the depth and breadth of the goddess's vow.

In the beginning, I was an ordinary man granted the great honor of occupying the imperial throne; now, obedient to the teachings of Laozi, I savor a quiet, free life in the abode of a retired sovereign. Nevertheless, I journeyed once before, pure in heart, to the holy shrine on this solitary isle; I went to the sacred fence to seek divine benevolence; I prayed until sweat bathed my body; and I was vouchsafed an oracular response, which remains graven in my mind. I was warned to exercise special caution in late summer and early autumn. And, indeed, I fell victim to a sudden illness, against which medical treatment proved ineffectual. As time passed, I recognized with renewed clarity the truth of the divine response. Although I commissioned prayers, the burden of my suffering was not lifted. Thus I came to believe that I could not do better than to undertake another pilgrimage to Itsukushima, a journey made with peerless sincerity.

My dreams during travel were shattered by incessant blasts from cold gales; my eyes traced distant routes in the lonely, pale light of the autumn sun. Now, having reached the shrine at last, and having reverently prepared a purified seat and copied sacred writ, I offer the *Lotus Sutra* in black graphs on colored paper; the *Sutra of Innumerable Meanings* and the *Sutra of Meditation on the Bodhisattva Universal*

16. Official travelers rang such bells to requisition men and horses at post stations.
17. He had ceded the throne to his 15-month-old son, Antoku, in the second month of that year (1180).

Virtue; the *Small Amitābha Sutra* and the *Heart Sutra*, each in one scroll; and the Devadatta Chapter of the *Lotus Sutra*, which I have inscribed myself in graphs of gold. As I do so, the shade from the luxuriant evergreen trees nurtures the seed of auspicious benefit, the resonant ebb and flow of the sea harmonizes with the voices chanting in praise of the Buddha.

The time has been short, a mere eight days, since this disciple of the buddhas left the imperial seat. But that I should have braved the western seas a second time brings home the strength of the ties binding me to Itsukushima. More than one are those who come here in the morning to pray; numbered in thousands are those who make pious journeys in the evening. Yet I have heard of no visits by retired sovereigns or princes, other than Priestly Retired Emperor Go-Shirakawa, even though many exalted personages have paid homage to the goddess. Emperor Wu of Han could not distinguish the Buddha's tempered radiance in the moonlight at Mount Songgao; the supernatural beings of Penglai Grotto were concealed by intervening clouds.[18] I raise my eyes and pray to the goddess, I prostrate myself and beseech the *Lotus Sutra*. Take heed of my fervent petition now; grant me the unique blessing of your divine response!

> Twenty-eighth day, ninth month, fourth year of Jishō [1180]
> The retired emperor

Meanwhile, the Heike were following the thousand leagues of the Eastern Sea Road after their departure from the ninefold capital.[19] It was all too uncertain whether they would return unharmed. They borrowed lodgings from the dew on the plains and slept on the moss of lofty peaks; they traversed mountains and rivers. Day succeeded day, until finally, on the sixteenth of the tenth month, they arrived at Kiyomi Barrier in Suruga Province. They had left the capital with only thirty thousand horsemen, but additional musters along the way had swelled their numbers to more than seventy thousand. The rear guard was still at Tegoshi and Utsunomiya when the vanguard reached Kanbara and the Fuji River.[20]

The commander-in-chief, Koremori, summoned the samurai commander, Kazusa Governor Tadakiyo. "I think we ought to cross the Ashigara Mountains and fight east of the pass," he said.

18. Emperor Wu of Han (157 B.C.–87 B.C.; r. 141 B.C.–87 B.C.) is said to have made a pilgrimage to Songgaoshan, one of the five sacred peaks of Han China, and to have sent an envoy to the eastern seas in an unsuccessful search for the elixir of immortality, which was believed to exist on the mythical Penglai Island (J. Hōrai; also called Mount Penglai and Penglai Grotto). Retired Emperor Takakura is apparently requesting a more favorable divine response than the Chinese monarch received. (According to the dynastic history *Han shu*, the Songgaoshan mountain god, who is represented here as having refused to appear for Wudi, actually manifested himself as a mysterious voice wishing the emperor a long life.)

19. "Ninefold" (*kokonoe*) is a word derived from the nine gates through which it was necessary to pass to gain access to a Chinese imperial palace. It usually modifies "palace" or substitutes for it. Here it complements the hyperbole of "thousand leagues."

20. The Fuji River (128 km) flows southward to Suruga Bay through what was once the middle of Suruga Province (now the middle of Shizuoka Prefecture). Tegoshi and Utsunomiya were slightly west of the river, in what is now Shizuoka City. Kanbara was a post station on the site of the present town of the same name.

"When you left Fukuhara, Lord Kiyomori ordered you to be guided by my military judgment," Tadakiyo said. "All the warriors in the eight eastern provinces have cast their lot with Yoritomo; he must be able to deploy hundreds of thousands of horsemen. It's true that we have seventy thousand, but they've rushed to join us from many different provinces. They're exhausted, and so are their horses. Furthermore, there's no sign yet of the forces from Izu and Suruga that we expected. You need to keep the Fuji River in front of you and wait for more allies to arrive." There was nothing for Koremori to do but halt the advance.

Yoritomo crossed the Ashigara Mountains to Kisegawa in Suruga, and the Genji from Kai and Shinano galloped to join him. During a muster at Ukishima-ga-hara, the names of more than two hundred thousand horsemen were recorded.[21]

A lackey in the service of Satake no Tarō, one of the Genji from Hitachi Province, had set out toward the capital with a message from his master. Tadakiyo, riding in the Heike vanguard, stopped him and took it away from him. When it turned out to be a letter to a woman, he gave it back, concluding that there would be no harm in letting it go through. Then he asked the man, "By the way, what's the size of Yoritomo's force?"

"All during my trip—seven or eight days by now—every field, mountain, seashore, and river has been swarming with armed men. I know how to count up to four or five hundred, or maybe a thousand, no further; I can't say whether the army's large or small. I did hear someone mention yesterday at Kisegawa that there were two hundred thousand horsemen," the man said.[22]

"If only our commander-in-chief hadn't been so lackadaisical!" Tadakiyo thought.[23] "If he had sent us out right away, and if we'd crossed the Ashigara Mountains into the eight provinces, Hatakeyama's family and the Ōba brothers would have been sure to join us, and then every grass and tree east of the pass would have bowed down." But his regrets were useless.

Koremori summoned Nagai no Saitō Bettō Sanemori, a man who was known to be familiar with conditions in the east. "Tell me, Sanemori, how many men in the eight provinces handle a strong bow as well as you do?" he asked.

Sanemori gave a derisive laugh. "You call my arrows big? They're just barely thirteen fists long. Lots of eastern warriors can say the same; nobody's a long-arrow man there unless he draws a fifteen-fist shaft. For an easterner, a strong bow is a weapon that it takes six powerful men to string.

21. Kisegawa was the name of an area in the eastern part of the province, on the east bank of the small Kisegawa River (now a part of Numazu). Ukishima-ga-hara was a stretch of sand dunes between the two rivers (now inside the cities of Numazu and Yoshiwara).

22. There would also have been many foot soldiers. Sizes of military forces tend to be exaggerated in the *Heike*, sometimes grossly.

23. This seems to be a reference to Munemori, who has stayed in the capital.

It's nothing for one of those mighty archers to penetrate two or three suits of armor.

"Every big landholder can command at least five hundred horsemen. Once a rider mounts, he never loses his seat; and no matter how rugged the terrain is, a galloping horse never falls. If a man sees his father or son cut down in battle, he just rides over the body and keeps fighting. In battles fought in the west, a man leaves the field if he loses his father, and nobody sees him again until he's made his offerings and mourned awhile. A man who loses a son is too broken up to come back at all. When westerners run out of commissariat rice, they stop fighting until the fields are planted and harvested. In summer, they think it's too hot to fight; in winter, they think it's too cold. Easterners are entirely different.

"The Genji from Kai and Shinano know this area. I wouldn't be surprised if they're planning to circle around behind you from the base of Mount Fuji.

"I'm not trying to scare you. As they say, it's strategy, not numbers, that wins battles. But I don't expect to get back to the capital alive from what we're up against."

All the Taira warriors trembled.

The twenty-third of the tenth month arrived. It had been decided to hold the arrow exchange on the following day, at the Fuji River.

Looking out toward the Genji positions that night, the Heike lost their courage when they saw the cooking fires of the local people—peasants from Izu and Suruga, and others who had gone into the fields, or hidden in the mountains, or taken to the rivers and the sea in boats, terrified by the prospect of warfare. "Look at all those Genji campfires!" the shaken warriors lamented. "It's true; every field, mountain, seashore, and river is alive with enemies. What are we going to do?"

Midway through the night, there was a sudden commotion—a huge flock of water birds, rising from the Fuji marshes, where they had congregated, with a noise of flapping wings like a typhoon or a thunderclap. Who knows what startled them?

"The Genji host has launched its attack!" the Taira warriors yelled. "It's just like Sanemori said; some of them must be coming around from the rear. We can't hold out if they surround us. Fall back! Set up defensive lines at the Owari River and Sunomata!"[24] They fled in desperate haste, abandoning their possessions. Some of them grabbed their bows and forgot their arrows in the confusion; some mounted others' horses; some saw their horses mounted by others. Some leaped onto tethered animals and rode in circles around picket stakes. Screams rose from the lips of innumerable

---

24. Both of these places were far to the rear, closer to the capital than to the Fuji River. The Owari River, now called the Kiso, flowed along the boundary between Mino and Owari provinces. Sunomata was a strategic point on the Nagara River (a tributary of the Kiso) in Mino Province.

courtesans and harlots, women who had been fetched from neighboring post stations to entertain the men, and who now sustained grievous injuries from kicks to the head, or suffered broken hips from being trampled underfoot.

At the hour of the hare [5:00 A.M.–7:00 A.M.] on the next day, the twenty-fourth, the two hundred thousand Genji horsemen swooped down on the Fuji River with three battle cries, each mighty enough to rattle the heavens and shake the earth.

5.12. *The Matter of the Gosechi Dances*

Not a sound broke the silence at the Heike campsite; the scouts reported that the entire army had fled. Some of them came back with armor discarded by the foe; others brought abandoned tents. "There's not even a fly stirring in the enemy positions," they said.

Yoritomo dismounted and took off his helmet. He washed his hands, rinsed his mouth, and knelt facing the capital. "I can claim no credit for what's been accomplished. The Great Bodhisattva Hachiman planned it," he said. To show that he was claiming the territory at once, he assigned Suruga Province to Ichijō no Jirō Tadayori and Tōtōmi Province to Yasuda no Saburō Yoshisada. He might have been expected to pursue and attack the Heike, but he turned at Ukishima-ga-hara and headed back to Sagami Province, concerned about possible threats to his rear.

There was laughter among the courtesans at the post stations on the Eastern Sea Road. "Isn't it disgusting? What a disgrace! The commander-in-chief of a punitive force runs back toward the capital without shooting a single arrow! It's bad enough for a man to run when he sees enemies on the battlefield, but that fellow took to his heels the minute he heard a noise," they said.

Many lampoons appeared. Because Munemori was the commander-in-chief in the capital, and because Koremori, the leader of the punitive force, was serving at court as a provisional assistant commander in the guards, someone wrote this poem, punning on "Heike" and *hiraya*:

> hiraya naru   The ridge guardian
> munemori ika ni   at the one-story dwelling
> sawaguramu   must be in despair
> hashira to tanomu   after seeing the downfall
> suke o otoshite   of the mainstay he trusted.[25]

[Another poem:]

25. The two graphs used for writing "Heike" can be read *hiraya*, "one-story house." *Munemori* puns on "ridge guardian"; *suke* on "assistant commander" and "mainstay"; and *otoshite* on "let fall" and "let flee." The poem can mean, "Munemori, the man responsible for the house of Taira, must be in a terrible state after the flight of the assistant commander on whom he relied to avert the clan's ruin."

fujigawa no	Ah, the Ise Heiji!
seze no iwa kosu	Their flight is even faster
mizu yori mo	than the swift descent
hayaku mo otsuru	of the Fuji River's stream
ise heiji ka na	where rapids cross the rocks.[26]

Someone composed a poem about Tadakiyo's abandonment of his armor at the Fuji River:

fujigawa ni	You left your armor
yoroi wa sutetsu	beside the Fuji River.
sumizome no	You had best put on
koromo tadakiyo	black-hued robes, Tadakiyo,
nochi no yo no tame	and devote yourself to prayer.[27]

[Another poem:]

tadakiyo wa	Tadakiyo rode
nige no uma ni zo	a horse colored fleeting gray.
norinikeru	It did him no good
kazusa shirigai	to gallop with a crupper
kakete kai nashi	made in Kazusa Province.[28]

On the eighth of the eleventh month, Commander-in-Chief Koremori arrived at the new Fukuhara capital. Kiyomori was furious. "Exile Koremori to Kikai-ga-shima! Put Tadakiyo to death!" he said.

On the ninth, all the Heike samurai, old and young alike, met to discuss whether Tadakiyo should be sentenced to death. Police Lieutenant Morikuni came forward. "I've never heard anybody call Tadakiyo a coward," he said. "As I remember, he was eighteen years old when the two worst desperadoes in the home provinces took refuge in the treasury at the Toba Mansion. Nobody wanted to go after them, but Tadakiyo jumped over the wall and got inside, all alone, in broad daylight—and he killed one and captured the other. That's something people will still be talking about long after we're gone. The way I see it, there was something mysterious about his failure the other day. I'd say their lordships should offer every possible prayer to try to end this disturbance."

On the tenth, Koremori was made a middle captain in the bodyguards of the right. "He commanded a punitive force, but he didn't accomplish much. Why are they rewarding him?" people whispered to one another.

Once in the past, Taira Commander Sadamori and Tawara Tōda Hide-

26. There is a pun on *otsuru* (a form of *otsu*, "descend," "fall"; "flee"), and probably another on *heiji* (surname; "wine bottle"). The Fuji River was known as one of the "three swift rivers of Japan."

27. The poet advises Tadakiyo to become a monk because he has been disgraced. There is a pun on *tada ki yo* (man's name; "You had best put on").

28. There are puns on *nige* ("gray horse"; a form of *nigu*, "flee") and *kake* (from *kaku*, "gallop"; "attach"). Kazusa, known for its fine cruppers, was the province Tadakiyo governed.

sato went into the eastern provinces with orders to hunt down Masakado, but found it hard to destroy him. A council of senior nobles dispatched another punitive force under Fujiwara no Tadafun, with Kiyowara no Shigefuji as junior deputy commander. One night, when the second force was staying at Kiyomi Barrier in Suruga Province, Shigefuji gazed into the distance across the boundless sea. In a sonorous voice, he chanted a Chinese couplet:[29]

> Reflections of fishing-boat fires: cold, they kindle the waves.
> Sounds of post-road bells: by night, someone crosses the mountains.

The elegance of his gesture moved Tadafun to tears.

Meanwhile, Sadamori and Hidesato had started toward the capital with the head of Masakado, whom they had finally managed to kill. They met the relief force at the barrier, and the two commanders went back together.

When rewards were designated for Sadamori and Hidesato, the question of rewards for Tadafun and Shigefuji arose in the senior nobles' council. "Tadafun and Shigefuji marched eastward as commanded, after the original punitive force had experienced difficulty in defeating Masakado, but Masakado was killed before they arrived. They certainly deserve rewards," said Kujō Minister of the Right Morosuke. But the regent of the day, Ononomiya Lord Saneyori, decided against it. "The *Record of Ritual* says, 'When in doubt, do nothing,'" he announced. Tadafun was so angry that he starved himself to death. "I'll treat Saneyori's descendants like slaves," he swore, "but I'll be an eternal guardian to Morosuke's." That explains why Morosuke's descendants have enjoyed wonderful good fortune, and why Saneyori's line has vanished without producing anybody of importance.

Kiyomori's fourth son, Shigehira, became middle captain of the left.

On the thirteenth of the eleventh month, the emperor moved into the newly completed palace at Fukuhara. It would have been proper to hold a Great Thanksgiving Service. But the emperor goes to the Kamo River late in the tenth month to perform the purification for such a service. A sanctuary is built in the fields north of the imperial palace, and sacred robes and sacred utensils are made ready. A structure called the Kairyūden is erected below the Dragon-tail Walkway in front of the Great Hall of State, and the emperor performs ablutions there. Great Thanksgiving shrines are built parallel to the walkway to receive the sacred food offerings. There are performances of sacred and profane music. An accession audience takes place in the Great Hall of State, sacred music is played at the Seishodō, and banquets are held in the Court of Abundant Pleasures. But there was no Great Hall of State at the new capital, and thus no place for an accession audience. There was no Seishodō, and thus no place in which to present sacred music. There was no Court of Abundant Pleasures, and thus no place for banquets. The senior nobles decided in council that only a First Fruits Service and

29. From a composition by the Tang poet Du Xunhe (WKRES 502).

Gosechi dancing should be attempted that year. Furthermore, the First Fruits Service was held at the department of shrines in the old capital.

Now as regards the Gosechi: on a certain windy, moonlit night at the Yoshino Palace, the Kiyomibara Emperor Tenmu was peacefully playing the zither when a heavenly maiden descended from the sky and fluttered her sleeves five times. That was the first Gosechi performance.

5.13. The Return to the Old Capital

With ruler and subjects grieving over the transfer of the capital, and with the Enryakuji, the Kōfukuji, and the other temples and shrines all condemning the move as improper, the stiff-necked Kiyomori finally yielded. "All right," he said. "The court will return to the old capital." A tremendous commotion followed.

The return took place abruptly, on the second of the twelfth month [of 1180]. The site at Fukuhara rose high to the north where it adjoined the mountains, and sank low to the south where the sea pressed close. The roar of the waves never stopped; the winds swept ashore with frightful velocity. Retired Emperor Takakura had gradually sickened there, and he left as fast as he could, eagerly attended by the regent, the chancellor, and the other senior nobles and courtiers. Kiyomori and the rest of the Taira notables also made haste to leave.

Who would have wished to linger for an instant in the dismal new capital? From the sixth month on, members of the court had been dismantling their houses for shipment, bringing in their household effects and other belongings, and establishing themselves in makeshift quarters, but now they abandoned everything without a backward glance, obsessed with the idea of returning home. Since none of them possessed houses, even people of impressive social standing went to Yawata, Kamo, Saga, Uzumasa, and the remote areas of the eastern and western hills, where they found accommodation in the corridors of temples and the oratories of shrines.

If we ask the true reason for the move to Fukuhara, the answer is to be sought in the proximity of the old capital to the Kōfukuji and Enryakuji temples, whose monks seized the slightest pretexts to create turmoil with the sacred tree from Kasuga and the sacred palanquins from Hiyoshi.[30] People said Kiyomori made his decision because he thought that such disruptive behavior would be impossible at Fukuhara, which lay beyond mountains and inlets and was also a considerable distance away.

On the twenty-third of the twelfth month, a total of more than twenty thousand mounted warriors set out for Ōmi Province under the command of Left Military Guards Commander Tomomori and Satsuma Governor

---

30. When a temple considered its interests threatened, its soldier-monks frequently marched to the imperial palace to seek redress, taking along an object imbued with divine authority, such as a god's palanquin or a sacred tree from Kasuga (a shrine associated with the Kōfukuji Temple), as a means of intimidation.

Tadanori, with the purpose of attacking the Minamoto rebels there. One by one, they defeated all the Genji who lived in various scattered locations— the Yamamoto, the Kashiwagi, the Nishigori, and others. Then they crossed into Mino and Owari provinces.

5.14. *The Burning of Nara*

Meanwhile, the Kōfukuji monks were up in arms because they had heard that people in the capital were saying, "The monks of Nara became enemies of the court in the first place by siding with Prince Mochihito when he went to the Onjōji, and then again by going out to meet him, which was even worse. The Kōfukuji and the Onjōji are both going to be attacked." The regent, Motomichi, told the monks that he was ready to transmit anything they wanted to say to the throne, no matter how many visits it might take, but they paid no attention. He sent them an emissary, Superintendent Tadanari, but they yelled, "Drag that fellow out of his filthy carriage! Cut off his topknot!" Tadanari blanched and went back to the capital. Next, the regent sent Chikamasa, an assistant commander in the gate guards, but the monks threatened his topknot, too, and he beat a hasty retreat. On this second occasion, two men in service at the Kangakuin lost their topknots.[31]

The monks made a big wooden ball, which they dubbed "Kiyomori's head," and urged one another to hit it and trample on it. As has been said, "Talk easily accessible to others is the handmaiden of disaster; imprudent speech is the pathway to destruction."[32] Only devils could have prompted the use of such language about a man who was His Sacred Majesty's maternal grandfather!

It would have been too much to expect Kiyomori to tolerate the monks' behavior. Determined to put a quick end to their excesses, he made Senō no Tarō Kaneyasu chief of police in Yamato Province; and Kaneyasu prepared to set out toward Nara with five hundred horsemen.

"Be careful," Kiyomori warned as he sent him off. "Even if the monks get violent, don't retaliate with violence. Don't wear your armor; don't carry bows and arrows." But the monks knew nothing about his instructions. They seized more than sixty of Kaneyasu's men, cut off all their heads, and hung the heads in rows beside Sarusawa Pond.

"All right! Attack Nara!" said Kiyomori in a rage.

More than forty thousand horsemen set out for the southern capital, with Shigehira as commander-in-chief and Michimori as deputy commander. Seven thousand monks of all ages put on helmets and waited for them at the Narazaka and Hannya roads, which they had trenched and barricaded with shields and branches.[33]

31. The Kangakuin was a private academy for the education of Fujiwara youths. It also handled matters having to do with the clan's tutelary shrines and temples.

32. *Chen gui*, a Tang ethical text.

33. Both roads were approaches to Nara from the capital.

The Heike split their forty thousand horsemen into two parties and swooped down on the fortifications at the two roads, uttering mighty war whoops. The monks were all unmounted men with forged weapons, but the court's warriors were horsemen with bows and arrows, and they galloped after the monks in all directions, hitting every one of them with fast and furious barrages of arrows. The battle began with an arrow exchange during the hour of the hare [5:00 A.M.–7:00 A.M.] and raged all day long. After nightfall, the positions on the two roads both went down in defeat.

One of the routed monks was Saka no Shirō Yōkaku, a brave warrior who surpassed everyone in the seven great temples and fifteen great temples in swordsmanship, archery, and physical strength. He wore armor with black lacing over a corselet with green lacing, and his five-plated helmet was fitted over a metal cap. Holding in one hand a long, unlacquered spear, curved like cogon grass, and in the other a great sword with a lacquered hilt, he slashed his way out of the Tegai Gate at the Tōdaiji, surrounded by a dozen monks from his cloister. He held his ground for a time, scything horses' legs and felling many opponents. But the waves of attacks from the court's huge army cut down all his companions, leaving him alone with his back unprotected, and he fled toward the south, brave though he was.

Now the battle was being fought in the dark. "Make a fire!" Shigehira ordered, standing in front of the gate at the Hannyaji Temple. One of the Heike warriors was a man named Tomokata, a functionary from the Fukui estate in Harima Province. This Tomokata promptly set a commoner's house on fire, using a torch made from a broken shield. There was a strong wind blowing, as was usual enough for the season—it was late in the twelfth month, the night of the twenty-eighth—and the gusts spread the fire from the initial location to many different buildings in the temple precincts.

The battles at the Narazaka and Hannya roads had claimed the life of every monk who had feared disgrace and prized honor; and the others who could walk had fled toward Yoshino and Totsukawa. Aged monks unable to walk, eminent scholar-monks, pages, women, and children had fled helter-skelter into the Kōfukuji, and also into the Great Buddha Hall, where more than a thousand had sought refuge on the second floor, with the ladders removed to save them from the pursuing enemy.[34] When the raging flames bore down on them, they uttered shrieks that seemingly could not have been surpassed by the sinners in the flames of the Tapana, Paritāpana, and Avīci hells.[35]

The Kōfukuji was the hereditary temple of the Fujiwara clan, founded by vow of Tankaikō. It was grievous beyond measure that it should all have been reduced to smoke in an instant—the image of Śākyamuni Buddha in

34. The Great Buddha Hall (Daibutsuden) at the Tōdaiji Temple still houses an enormous statue of Vairocana Buddha, erected during the Nara period (710–84).

35. In Buddhism, three of the eight great hells: the hell of burning (J. *shōnetsu*), the hell of fierce heat (J. *daishōnetsu*), and the hell of suffering without intermission (J. *mugenabi*).

the Eastern Golden Hall, which had been brought to Japan during the first days of Buddhism; the image of Kannon in the Western Golden Hall, which had sprung spontaneously from the earth; the corridors on all sides, as beautiful as rows of gems; the two-storied Nikaidō Hall, resplendent in vermilion and cinnabar; the two pagodas, their nine rings glittering in the sun.

At the Tōdaiji, there had been a gilt bronze statue of Vairocana Buddha, one hundred and sixty feet tall, erected by Emperor Shōmu (who had personally helped with the polishing), and designed to serve as a representation of the eternal, indestructible, enlightened being whose physical body appears in the Land of Buddha-reward in Reality and the Land of Tranquility and Wisdom. The *uṣṇīṣa* on its head had towered high, hidden by clouds in midair; the white curl between its eyebrows had inspired the pious to ever-renewed devotions.[36] But now the head of that holy image—that face resplendent as a full moon—melted and fell to earth, and the body fused into a mountainous heap. Like an autumn moon, the eighty-four thousand signs of buddhahood vanished behind the cloud of the five deadly sins; like stars in a night sky, the ornaments signifying completion of the forty-one stages flickered in the wind of the ten evils. Smoke filled the sky; flames filled the air below. Those present who witnessed the scene averted their eyes; those afar who heard the story trembled with fear. Of the Hossō and Sanron scriptures and sacred teachings, not a scroll survived. It was impossible to imagine such a devastating blow to the Buddhist faith in India or China, to say nothing of our own country.

After all, even the fine gold statue sculpted by King Udayana and the red sandalwood image carved by Viśvakarman were merely the size of a man.[37] How much more ought the Buddha of the Tōdaiji, unique and unparalleled in this human realm, to have endured for eternity! Yet now it mingled with the dust of the profane world, its ruin a source of everlasting sorrow. Bonten, Taishakuten, the Four Heavenly Kings, the dragons and others of the eight kinds of guardian gods, the functionaries and demons in the realm of the dead—all must have been astonished and dismayed. And what can have been the thoughts of the Kasuga god, the protector of the Hossō sect? The dew on Kasuga Plain changed color; the tempest from Mount Mikasa shrieked in protest.

When the scribes made a careful record of those who had burned to death in the flames, the total amounted to more than three thousand five hundred people: more than seventeen hundred on the second floor of the Great Buddha Hall, more than eight hundred at the Kōfukuji, more than five hundred in this temple building, more than three hundred in that. More than a thou-

36. The *uṣṇīṣa*, a protuberance of the skull, and the white curl, which emits light, are two of the 32 distinguishing marks of a buddha.

37. According to Buddhist sources, it was King Udayana, the ruler of a central Indian state, who carved the sandalwood statue of the Buddha, and Viśvakarman, the patron deity of artisans, who made the golden Buddha.

sand monks had been killed in battle. The victors hung a few heads in front of the gate at the Hannyaji and carried a few others back to the capital.

On the twenty-ninth, Shigehira returned to the capital, leaving Nara in ruins. Kiyomori greeted the outcome of the expedition with vindictive glee, but the empress, the two retired emperors, the regent, and everyone else lamented. "It might have been all right to get rid of the soldier-monks, but it was a terrible mistake to destroy the temples," people said. The original plan had been to parade the monks' heads through the avenues, and to hang them on the trees in front of the jail, but the court refused to issue the necessary orders, appalled by the destruction of the Tōdaiji and the Kōfu-kuji. The heads were discarded in gutters and ditches.

In a document written in his own hand, Emperor Shōmu had declared, "If my temple prospers, the realm will also prosper; if my temple declines, the realm will also decline." Thus it seemed that the realm was certainly doomed to decline.

The terrible twelvemonth drew to an end, and the fifth year of Jishō [1181] began.

Chapter 6

Time: first, second, and intercalary second months of 1181
Principal subjects: revolts of Yoshinaka and others in the provinces; death of
    Kiyomori
Principal characters:
        Go-Shirakawa, Retired Emperor. Head of the imperial clan
        Kiyomori (Taira). Retired head of the Taira clan
        Munemori (Taira). Son of Kiyomori; clan head
        Yoritomo (Minamoto). Heir to the chieftainship of the Minamoto clan;
            leader of anti-Taira forces in the east
        Yoshinaka (Minamoto). Cousin of Yoritomo; leader of anti-Taira forces
            in the north

[The new year, 1181, has begun with the death of Retired Emperor Takakura,
the son of Retired Emperor Go-Shirakawa. "He had been distressed to the
point of physical illness by Retired Emperor Go-Shirakawa's confinement in
the Toba Mansion two years earlier, by Prince Mochihito's slaying in the year
just past, by the shocking disruption of the move to the new capital, and by
other such happenings. To the intense grief of his father, the priestly retired
emperor, he sank very low after learning of the destruction of the Tōdaiji and
the Kōfukuji; and he finally breathed his last at the Rokuhara Ikedono Mansion on the fourteenth of the first month"; Sec. 6.1.]

6.5. The Circular Letter

Kiyomori himself may have felt that he had been inhumane, for he tried
to placate Retired Emperor Go-Shirakawa by giving him his eighteen-year-
old daughter, an elegant, beautiful girl whose mother was one of the attendants at the Itsukushima Shrine. Many carefully selected ladies-in-waiting
of high status entered the former sovereign's palace with her, and a great
assemblage of senior nobles and courtiers accompanied the procession, just
as though a new imperial consort were arriving. People whispered that it
was inappropriate for such an event to take place within fourteen days of
Retired Emperor Takakura's death.

Meanwhile, there began to be talk of a Minamoto in Shinano Province called Kiso no Kanja Yoshinaka. This Yoshinaka was the son of Captain Yoshikata of the crown prince's guards, who was the second son of the late Rokujō Police Lieutenant Tameyoshi. After the slaying of his father, Yoshikata, at the hands of Kamakura no Akugenda Yoshihira on the sixteenth of the eighth month in the second year of Kyūju [1155], the two-year-old child's weeping mother carried him in her arms to Shinano Province, and there she went to Kiso no Chūzō Kanetō. "Please raise the boy as you think best; make a man of him," she said. Kanetō worked hard at his ward's upbringing for more than twenty years, and the child grew into a man of outstanding strength and peerless bravery. "He's a stronger archer than you'll ever see. On horseback or on foot, he's the equal of Tamuramaro, Toshihito, Koremochi, Tomoyori, Yasumasa, his own ancestors Yoshimitsu and Yoshiie, and all the other great warriors of the past," people said.

One day, Yoshinaka summoned his guardian, Kanetō, to hint at something that had been on his mind. "They say Yoritomo has rebelled and seized control of the eight eastern provinces; I hear he's getting ready to march against the capital from the Eastern Sea Road and drive the Taira out of the city. I want to subjugate the Eastern Mountain and Northern Land circuits and dash on to defeat the Heike. To tell you the truth, I think I'd like to have people call me one of the Two Commanders of Japan," he said.

Kanetō was delighted. "That's just why I've taken care of you all this time," he said, with a respectful bow. "Those words prove your descent from Yoshiie." He set to work at once to plan the rebellion.

With his guardian as escort, Yoshinaka had often visited the capital to observe the activities and behavior of the Taira. He had gone to the Hachiman Shrine for his capping ceremony when he was thirteen, and there, in the presence of the bodhisattva, he had offered a prayer. "My great-grandfather Yoshiie became the son of this august divinity and assumed the name Hachiman Tarō [Hachiman's Eldest Son]. I intend to follow in his footsteps." Then he had put up his hair in front of the shrine and taken the name Kiso no Jirō [Second Son] Yoshinaka.

"The first thing we need to do is to send around a circular letter," Kanetō said.

In Shinano Province, they approached Nenoi no Koyata and Unno no Yukichika, and both men agreed to join them. Then other warriors did the same; not a grass or tree but bowed. The warriors of Tago District in Kōzuke Province were also unanimous in their declarations of allegiance, because there were old ties between them and Yoshikata. Thus it was that the Genji tried to satisfy long-standing ambitions by taking advantage of the weakness of the Taira.

6.6. *The Arrival of the Couriers*

The area known as Kiso is situated at the southern edge of Shinano Province, on the border with Mino Province, which is no distance at all from the capital. Thus there was a great commotion when the Heike learned of Yoshi-naka's activities. "It was bad enough to have the eastern provinces in revolt. What are we going to do now?" they asked one another.

"We don't need to worry about Yoshinaka," Kiyomori said. "Even if the warriors in Shinano Province do join him, Taira no Koremochi's descendants in Echigo Province, Jō no Tarō Sukenaga and his brother Jō no Shirō Sukeshige, are both men who control large forces. They'll take care of him any time the emperor gives the command, just like that." But many other people expressed whispered doubts.

On the first day of the second month, Jō no Tarō Sukenaga was appointed governor of Echigo. People said it was to get him to subdue Yoshinaka.

On the seventh day, ministerial and lesser families prepared and offered copies of the *Enlightened One Darani* and pictures of Fudō, hoping to end the revolts through prayer.

On the ninth day, it was reported that Musashi Gon-no-kami Yoshimoto and his son Ishikawa no Hangandai Yoshikane, two men who had been living in the Ishikawa District of Kawachi Province, had rebelled against the Taira and reached an agreement with Yoritomo, and that they were about to flee to the east. Kiyomori immediately ordered the dispatch of a punitive force. The force's commanders, Gendayū no Hangan Suesada and Settsu no Hangan Morizumi, set out with more than three thousand horsemen. The defenders at the Ishikawa stronghold numbered barely a hundred men—Yoshimoto, Yoshikane, and some minor figures. The besiegers yelled a war whoop, fired some preliminary arrows, and attacked in relays for several hours. Many of the warriors who were inside perished after desperate struggles. Yoshimoto died in battle, and Yoshikane was taken prisoner, severely wounded.

On the eleventh day, the victors brought Yoshimoto's head into the capital and paraded it along the avenues. (It was said that the precedent for such an act during a period of national mourning had been set after the death of Emperor Horikawa, when the head of Minamoto no Yoshichika was paraded.)

On the twelfth day, a courier arrived from Chinzei with a message from Kinmichi, the head priest at the Usa Hachiman Shrine. "Okata no Saburō Koreyoshi, Usuki no Jirō Koretaka, the Hetsugi, and all the other warriors in Kyushu, including the Matsura League, have turned against the Heike and cast their lot with the Genji," he said. The Heike struck their palms together in frustration and alarm. "It was bad enough when the eastern and northern provinces revolted. What shall we do now?" they said.

On the sixteenth day, a courier arrived with news from Iyo Province. Beginning around the winter of the year just past, it seemed, Kōno no Shirō Michikiyo and the lesser warriors in Shikoku had all turned against the Heike and cast their lot with the Genji. The Naka novice Saijaku of Bingo Province, a loyal Taira partisan, had crossed into Iyo Province and killed Michikiyo at the Takano stronghold, on the boundary between the eastern and central districts of the province.

At the time of Michikiyo's death, his son, Kōno no Shirō Michinobu, had been absent on a visit to his maternal uncle Nuta no Jirō, who lived in Aki Province. Determined to avenge his father, Michinobu awaited an opportunity to kill Saijaku.

After disposing of Michikiyo, Saijaku went on to subjugate the other rebels in Shikoku. Then, on the fifteenth of the first month, he crossed over to Tomo in Bingo Province, and began to drink and carouse with a troop of courtesans and harlots. Michinobu and a hundred daredevil confederates swooped down on him while he was in his cups. Saijaku's force numbered more than three hundred men, but the suddenness of the attack created tremendous confusion, and the defenders who managed to resist were either shot down or put to the sword. Michinobu captured Saijaku, took him to the Takanō stronghold in Iyo Province (the place where his father had met his end), and cut off his head with a saw—or, according to another version of the story, crucified him.

6.7. *The Death of Kiyomori*

After that, all the warriors in Shikoku swore allegiance to Kōno no Shirō Michinobu. There were rumors that Tanzō, the superintendent of the Kumano shrines, had also gone over to the side of the Genji, in spite of everything that he owed to the Taira.

The east and the north were in revolt; the south and the west were as we have described. Tidings of barbarian rebellions shocked every ear; portents of war were reported one after another. All men of discernment lamented, whether they belonged to the Taira clan or not. "The barbarians in the four directions have risen overnight; the regime is doomed," they said.

At a council of senior nobles, held on the twenty-third of the second month, Munemori proposed that he himself should be named commander-in-chief of a new expedition against the east, since the first one had not accomplished anything worth mentioning. The suggestion met with effusive praise, and Retired Emperor Go-Shirakawa proceeded to decree that Munemori was to command a campaign against the rebels in the east and north, and that the army was to include in its ranks those courtiers and senior nobles who occupied military posts or were experienced in the martial arts.

On the twenty-seventh, Munemori postponed the force's eastward march, which had been about to begin, because his father had fallen ill. From the twenty-eighth on, word spread that Kiyomori was in critical condition. There were whispers in the city, and also at Rokuhara. "Aha! His deeds have come home to roost!"

After the disease took hold, Kiyomori could swallow nothing, not even a sip of water. His body was as hot as fire; people could hardly bear to stay within twenty-five or thirty feet of the bed. The only words that passed his lips were, "So hot . . . so hot." Apparently, it was no ordinary ailment.

The staff at the mansion filled a stone tub with water, which they drew from the Thousand-armed Well on Mount Hiei, but it boiled off into steam as soon as Kiyomori got in to cool off.¹ Desperate to give him a little relief, they sent a stream onto his body from a bamboo pipe, but it spattered away without reaching him, as though recoiling from red-hot stone or iron. The few drops that struck burst into flame, sending black smoke throughout the hall and tongues of fire swirling toward the ceiling. For the first time, those who witnessed these things understood what Bishop Hōzō must have experienced when he asked about the site of his mother's rebirth while he was visiting King Enma's court at the king's invitation: the sympathetic king sent him to the Tapana Hot Hell with an escort of torturer-guards, and inside the iron gate he saw flames like shooting stars, ascending into the sky for hundreds of *yojanas*.²

Kiyomori's wife, the nun of second rank, had a terrible dream. In it, some people brought a flaming carriage inside the gate, attended before and behind by creatures with the faces of horses and oxen. On the front of the carriage, there was an iron tablet, inscribed with the single graph *mu* [without].

"Where has that carriage come from?" the nun asked.

"From Enma's tribunal. It's here to get Kiyomori," a voice answered.

"What does the tablet mean?" she asked.

"The tribunal has decided that Kiyomori is going to fall to the bottom of '[the hell of suffering] without intermission' [*mugen*] because he is guilty of burning the one-hundred-and-sixty-foot gilt bronze Vairocana in the world of men. Enma has written the *mu* of *mugen*, but he hasn't put in the *gen* [intermission] yet."

The nun started awake, wet with perspiration; and all the people she told felt their hair stand on end. The family showered wonder-working shrines and temples with gold, silver, and the seven treasures; they even sent off horses, saddles, armor, helmets, bows, arrows, swords, and daggers—but there was no sign of a divine response. Kiyomori's grieving sons and daughters gathered at the head and foot of his bed, racking their brains for something to do, but there seemed little chance that things would turn out as they hoped.

On the second day of the intercalary second month, the nun went up to her husband's pillow, steeling herself against the unbearable heat. "As I watch you, I can't help feeling that it's getting more and more hopeless every day. If there's anything in the world you want, tell me when your mind is clear." She wept as she spoke.

A painful whisper issued from the lips of the man who had been so formidable a presence. "Since Hōgen and Heiji, I have subdued enemies of the

1. The well was a source of holy-water offerings for a nearby image of Thousand-armed Kannon. Since the name of the well was sometimes written with graphs meaning "thousand years," it was probably selected in the hope of prolonging Kiyomori's life through word magic.

2. A Hindu measure of distance; one *yojana* usually equaled about five miles.

court on more than one occasion, and my rewards have been beyond my deserts. I've become a chancellor and the grandfather of an emperor; I've seen my prosperity shared by my children. There's nothing left for me to desire in this life. The one thing that bothers me is that I have yet to see the severed head of Yoritomo, the Exile of Izu. Don't build any halls or pagodas for my sake after I die; don't dedicate any pious works on my behalf. Just send the punitive force off immediately, take Yoritomo's head, and hang it in front of my grave. That's the only dedication I need." Those were words steeped in sin!

On the fourth, they tried to ease his suffering by laying him on a board soaked with water, but it did no good. He writhed in agony, fell to the floor unconscious, and died in convulsions.

Horses and carriages galloped in every direction, making enough noise to set the heavens echoing and the earth trembling. If death had claimed the imperial master of all the realm, the lord of a myriad chariots, the agitation could have been no greater.

Kiyomori had turned sixty-four that year. It was not an age at which death was necessarily to have been anticipated, but his karma had decreed that he should live no longer: the large rituals and the secret rituals lacked efficacy, the power of the gods and the buddhas vanished, the heavenly spirits offered no protection. What could mere mortals do? There were tens of thousands of loyal warriors seated in rows high and low at the hall, each ready to exchange his life for his lord's, but none of them could hold off the invisible, unconquerable messenger from the land of the dead, not even for an instant. Kiyomori must have been all alone when he started on his journey through the nether regions, over the Shide Mountains from which no man returns, and past the River of Three Crossings. Most sadly, his sole escorts must have been the evil deeds of which he had so often been guilty, coming to greet him in the form of torturers with the heads of horses and oxen.

Since matters could not go on like that forever, they cremated the remains at Otagi on the seventh. Dharma Eye Enjitsu hung the bones around his neck, took them to Settsu Province, and buried them at Kyō-no-shima Island.

Kiyomori's fame and power had extended over the whole length and breadth of Japan, yet his flesh rose into the skies above the capital as a transitory plume of smoke, and his bones survived only briefly before becoming one with the earth, indistinguishable from the sands of the beach.

Chapter 7

Time: fourth to seventh month of 1183
Principal subjects: fighting in the north between Yoshinaka and the Taira; the
flight of the Taira from the capital
Principal characters:

Go-Shirakawa, Retired Emperor. Head of the imperial clan
Kenreimon'in. Daughter of Kiyomori; consort of the late Emperor Ta-
kakura; mother of the young Emperor Antoku
Koremori (Taira). Son of Shigemori; grandson of Kiyomori
Michimori (Taira). Son of Norimori; nephew of Kiyomori
Motomichi (Fujiwara). Imperial regent
Noritsune (Taira). Son of Norimori; nephew of Kiyomori
Shigehira (Taira). Son of Kiyomori
Tadanori (Taira). Son of Tadamori; brother of Kiyomori
Tomomori (Taira). Son of Kiyomori
Tsunemasa (Taira). Son of Tsunemori; nephew of Kiyomori
Yoshinaka (Minamoto). Cousin of Yoritomo; leader of anti-Taira forces
in the north
Yukiie (Minamoto). Son of Tameyoshi; uncle of Yoritomo and
Yoshinaka

[The expedition planned in 1181, before Kiyomori's death, has yet to take
place. Fighting in the provinces has continued, and Yoshinaka, in particular,
has been successful against Taira partisans. "The Heike in the capital shrugged
off the news from the provinces. On the sixteenth [of the ninth month of
1182], Munemori was reappointed to the office of major counselor, and on
the third of the tenth month he became palace minister. When he went to
make his formal expression of gratitude on the seventh, he was attended by
twelve Taira senior nobles and preceded by sixteen courtiers on horseback,
including the two head chamberlains. But there seemed little substance to such
magnificent occasions, staged as they were in frivolous disregard of the coming
storm, while the Genji in the east and north swarmed like hornets, poised for
an attack on the capital"; Sec. 6.12.]

7.2. The Expedition to the Northern Provinces

Meanwhile, there were rumors that Kiso no Yoshinaka, the master of the Eastern Mountain and Northern Land roads, was about to attack the capital with more than fifty thousand horsemen. Ever since last year, the Heike had been proclaiming their intention to give battle "when the horses are fed young grass next year"; and warriors had been pouring in like clouds from the Mountain Shade, Mountain Sun, Southern Sea, and Western Sea roads. Men had arrived from the provinces of Ōmi, Mino, and Hida on the Eastern Sea Road, but none had come from Tōtōmi or anywhere farther east. (Those in the west all came.) Nobody came from Wakasa or farther north on the Northern Land Road.

It had been decided that a punitive force would be sent to the Northern Land Road to defeat Yoshinaka, and that it would go on to attack Yoritomo. During the first quarter of the hour of the dragon [7:00 A.M.–9:00 A.M.] on the seventeenth of the fourth month in the second year of Juei [1183], a combined total of more than a hundred thousand horsemen headed northward from the capital. They were led by six commanders-in-chief, and by more than three hundred and forty principal samurai commanders.

> The commanders-in-chief:
>   Komatsu Middle Captain of Third Rank Koremori
>   Echizen Governor of Third Rank Michimori
>   Tajima Governor Tsunemasa
>   Satsuma Governor Tadanori
>   Mikawa Governor Tomonori
>   Awaji Governor Kiyofusa
> The main samurai commanders:
>   Etchū no Zenji Moritoshi
>   Kazusa no Taifu no Hangan Tadatsuna
>   Hida no Taifu no Hangan Kagetaka
>   Takahashi no Hangan Nagatsuna
>   Kawachi no Hangan Hidekuni
>   Musashi no Saburōzaemon Arikuni
>   Etchū no Jirōbyōe Moritsugi
>   Kazusa no Gorōbyōe Tadamitsu
>   Akushichibyōe Kagekiyo

The army had received authorization to live off the provinces, and it seized everything in its path from Ōsaka Barrier onward, even rice and other official tax commodities levied from powerful landowners and great houses. The common people all scattered into the mountains and fields, driven beyond endurance, as the host gradually looted its way through Shiga, Karasaki, Mitsukawajiri, Mano, Takashima, Shiotsu, and Kaizu.[1]

1. All places near Lake Biwa.

7.3. *The Visit to Chikubushima*

The commanders-in-chief, Koremori and Michimori, had pressed ahead, but the deputy commanders, Tsunemasa, Tomonori, and Kiyofusa, had halted at Shiotsu and Kaizu in Ōmi Province. Tsunemasa was an expert poet and musician. Ignoring the turmoil around him, he cleansed his mind of impure thoughts and went down to the shore to look at an island in the lake. He asked an attendant, Tōbyōe Arinori, to tell him its name, and Arinori said, "That's the famous Chikubushima."[2]

"It is? I've heard of it, of course. Let's go over there." He crossed in a small boat, accompanied by Arinori, An'emon Morinori, and three or four other samurai.

It was the eighteenth day of the fourth month. A touch of spring still seemed to linger on the green branches, the songs of the warblers in the valleys had lost their freshness, and the cuckoos everywhere were raising their long-awaited voices to herald the new season. Tsunemasa sprang from the boat and gazed in delight at the scene, which was beautiful beyond imagination or description. Very similar must have been the appearance of Mount Penglai, the unattained goal of the youths, maidens, and magicians who had been sent out by Emperors Shihuangdi and Wudi to seek the elixir of immortality, and had frittered away their lives in ships on the vast deep, pledged not to return without reaching their destination. A sutra says, "In the world of men, there is a lake, and in that lake, sprung from the bowels of the earth, there is a crystal isle where heavenly maidens dwell."[3] This was that very island.

Tsunemasa knelt in front of the shrine. "Daibenkudokuten is the same as Śākyamuni Buddha; she is a bodhisattva who manifests the absolute nature of the buddha-mind. Two are the names Benzai and Myōon; one is the true form of this divinity, the bringer of salvation for sentient beings. It is said that those who worship here even once will have every wish granted: thus I face the future with hope," he said. For a time, he recited sacred texts.

The evening shadows gradually gathered, and the eighteen-day-old moon rose. The broad expanse of the lake shone; the shrine glittered ever more brightly. Charmed by the scene, the resident monks brought Tsunemasa one of the shrine's lutes. "We know of your skill," they told him.

He began to finger the strings. Then he played two secret compositions, "Heaven" and "On the Rock," and the clear tones, echoing inside the shrine, moved the goddess to manifest herself above his sleeve in the form of a white dragon. Shedding tears of awed joy, he expressed his emotions in verse.

chihayaburu	That she has appeared
kami ni inori no	in form plainly visible—

2. In the northern part of Lake Biwa.
3. The sutra has not been identified.

> kanaeba ya might it signify
> shiruku mo iro no the goddess's acceptance
> arawarenikeru of my prayers at her shrine?

There could be no doubt that the detested enemy would soon be subdued—no doubt that the rebel forces would soon be attacked and crushed. Immensely cheered, he returned to the boat and left the island.

7.4. *The Battle at Hiuchi*

While he was still based in Shinano Province, Kiso no Yoshinaka built a stronghold at Hiuchi in Echizen Province and provided it with a garrison of more than six thousand horsemen—the Heizenji abbot Saimei, Inazu no Shinsuke, Saitōda, Hayashi no Rokurō Mitsuakira, the Togashi novice Bussei, Tsuchida, Takebe, Miyazaki, Ishiguro, Nyūzen, Sami, and others. The position was a formidable one, surrounded by lofty rocks and peaks, with mountains in front and behind. There were also two rivers in front of it, the Nōmigawa and the Shindōgawa, and the defenders had built an elaborate dam at their confluence, felling great trees and dragging them into place to make barricades. Thus waters lapped at the base of the mountains on the east and west, just as if the stronghold had been facing a lake.

> Blue and vast, the surface steeped the southern mountains;
> Red and patterned, the waves engulfed the westering sun.[4]

On the bottom of the heatless lake, there is gold and silver sand;[5] by the shore at Kunming Lake, there were the boats of virtuous government; and at this artificial lake near the Hiuchi stronghold, there was a dam with roiling waters, constructed to deceive an enemy.

Since the lake could not very well be crossed without boats, the great army of the Heike idled away the days at camps in the mountains on the far side.

Now there was one member of the garrison, Abbot Saimei, whose secret sympathies lay entirely with the Taira. Saimei went out along the base of the mountains, put a letter inside a whizzing arrow, and shot it into the Heike camp when nobody was watching. "There is no natural depression under the lake; the people here have merely blocked a mountain stream. The waters will soon subside if you send out some foot soldiers at night to destroy the dam. The footing for horses is good; cross quickly. I'll shoot arrows at the defenders from the rear. Heizenji Abbot Saimei."

The commanders-in-chief were delighted. They hastened to send out foot soldiers, and the soldiers cut the dam away. In spite of the lake's impressive

4. From a poem by Bo Juyi about Kunming Lake, a body of water created southwest of the Changan capital for naval maneuvers during the reign of Emperor Wu (Wudi) of Han.

5. In Buddhist cosmology, the heatless lake is said to lie at the center of Enbudai (Skt. Jambu-dvīpa), the world in which we live.

appearance, it was nothing but a mountain stream. Its waters soon ebbed, and the great Heike force surged across. The warriors inside the stronghold held out for a while, but there seemed little chance that so few could prevail against so many.

Saimei declared allegiance to the Heike and became their loyal man. Still defiant, Shinsuke, Saitōda, Mitsuakira, and Bussei abandoned the stronghold, retreated to Kaga Province, and dug in at Shirayama and Kawachi, but the seemingly invincible Heike followed hard on their heels into Kaga and burned the two strongholds defended by Mitsuakira and Bussei. Then, from nearby post stations, the victorious host sent couriers to the capital, where their news was received with extravagant relief and rejoicing by Munemori and the other members of the Heike clan who had stayed behind.

On the eighth of the fifth month, the Heike mustered at Shinohara, in Kaga Province, and divided their hundred thousand horsemen into frontal and rear assault forces. The frontal force, seventy thousand strong, set out toward Tonamiyama, on the border between Kaga and Echizen, with Koremori and Michimori as commanders-in-chief and Etchū no Zenji Moritoshi as the main samurai commander. The rear force, thirty thousand horsemen, proceeded toward Shio-no-yama on the border between Noto and Etchū, with Tadanori and Tomonori as commanders-in-chief and Arikuni as the foremost samurai commmander.[6]

While staying in the capital of Echigo Province, Yoshinaka learned of the Taira movements. He made hasty preparations to confront the enemy with fifty thousand horsemen. In the belief that his earlier campaign had set an auspicious precedent, he divided his army into seven groups.[7] His uncle Yukiie went to meet the Taira at Shio-no-yama with ten thousand men. Nishina, Takanashi, and Yamada no Jirō were sent toward Kitagurosaka with seven thousand men as a rear assault force, and Higuchi no Jirō Kanemitsu and Ochiai no Gorō Kaneyuki were sent toward Minamigurosaka with seven thousand men.[8] Ten thousand men were stationed in ambush at the entrance to Tonamiyama, at the base of Kurosaka, at Yanagihara in the area of Matsunaga, and at Gumi-no-kinbayashi. Imai no Shirō Kanehira crossed the Washinose shallows with six thousand men to take up positions at Hi-

6. Tonamiyama is a mountainous area on the boundary between the present town of Tsubata in Kahoku District, Ishikawa Prefecture, and the city of Oyabe in Toyama Prefecture. The old Hokurikudō (Northern Land Road) crossed it at Kurikara Pass. Shio-no-yama, the destination of the Taira rear force, is thought to have been in the vicinity of the present town of Shio in Hakui District, Ishikawa Prefecture.

7. An earlier episode (Sec. 6.12; not translated) tells how Yoshinaka won a victory in 1182 at Yokotagawara, in Shinano Province, by outwitting a much larger enemy force. He divided his men into seven groups, who rode slowly toward the enemy, displaying red Taira banners. At the last minute, the groups merged, whipped up white Minamoto banners, and charged. Caught off guard, the Taira warriors suffered total defeat.

8. The objectives of these and the other Minamoto forces named below have not all been identified, but all appear to have been in the general area of Tonamiyama and the approaches to it.

nomiyabayashi, and Yoshinaka himself crossed the river at Oyabe-no-watari and camped with ten thousand men at Hanyū, just north of Tonamiyama.

7.5. *The Petition*

"The Heike must intend to cross Tonamiyama to the plains and stage a frontal attack with their huge army," Yoshinaka said. "In a battle like that, it's numbers that determine victory. We won't win if we let them exploit their size. But if we send standard bearers ahead with white flags, they'll see them and stay in the mountains. 'Here comes the Genji vanguard!' they'll say. 'Their army must be enormous! They know the terrain and we don't. They'll surround us if we burst out onto the plains. As long as we stay in these rugged mountains, our rear is safe; we'd better dismount and let the horses rest awhile.' In the meantime, I'll pretend to be trying to engage them, and then as soon as it gets dark, I'll drive their whole army down into Kurikara Valley." He ordered his men to plant thirty white banners on top of Kurosaka Hill.

When the Heike spotted the banners, they dismounted at a place in Tonamiyama called Saru-no-baba, just as Yoshinaka had foreseen. "Here comes the Genji vanguard!" they said. "Their army must be enormous! They know the terrain and we don't. They'll surround us if we burst out onto the plains. As long as we stay in these rugged mountains, our rear is safe. There seems to be good forage and water here; we'd better dismount and let the horses rest awhile."

Looking out from his camp at Hanyū, Yoshinaka descried a sacred red fence and a shrine with beveled crossbeams nestled among the green trees on the summer peaks. There was a torii in front. He called for a man who knew the province. "What shrine is that?" he asked. "What deity is worshipped there?"

"Hachiman. This is Hachiman's land," the man said.

Yoshinaka was delighted. He summoned Taifubō Kakumei, whom he had brought along to serve as his scribe. "This is a great stroke of luck! It's my chance to visit a shrine dedicated to Hachiman before the battle. Now I know I'm going to win! How would it be if I offered a written petition, both as a prayer and as something for posterity?"

"That sounds very suitable," Kakumei said. He dismounted and prepared to write.

Kakumei was wearing a dark blue tunic and a suit of armor with black leather lacing. At his waist, he wore a sword with a black lacquered hilt and scabbard, and on his back there was a quiver containing twenty-four arrows, fledged with black hawk's-wing feathers. His lacquered, rattan-wrapped bow was at his side; his helmet hung from his shoulder-cord. He took a small inkstone and some paper from the quiver, knelt in front of Lord Kiso, and began to write out the petition. What a splendid combination of the civil and military arts he seemed!

This Kakumei belonged to a family of Confucian scholars. After serving at the Kangakuin, where he was known as Chamberlain Michihiro, he became a monk and took the name Saijōbō Shingyū.[9] He paid frequent visits to Nara, and it was he whom the monks of Nara had commissioned to reply for them when letters were sent to Mount Hiei and Nara after Prince Mochihito's arrival at the Onjōji. Kiyomori took violent exception to one of his sentences—the one that said, "The novice Kiyomori is the dregs of the Taira clan, the scum of the warrior class."

"Why does that renegade Shingyū think he can get away with calling me the dregs of the Taira clan and the scum of the warrior class? Arrest him and execute him!" he said. So Shingyū had fled from Nara to the northern provinces, and there he became Lord Kiso's scribe and adopted the name Taifubō Kakumei.

This was the petition:

All hail! I touch my head to the ground in obeisance.

The Great Bodhisattva Hachiman is the lord of the Japanese court, the ancestor of our generations of illustrious sovereigns. To guard the imperial throne and benefit mankind, he manifests himself as the three august divinities and assumes the temporary guise of the three deities.[10]

For some years now, a person called the Taira Chancellor has dominated the four seas and distressed the populace. He has been a foe to the Buddhist doctrine and an enemy to the imperial law. Though humble, I spring from warrior stock; though inadequate, I pursue my father's calling. The thought of the Taira Chancellor's foul deeds prohibits selfish calculation: I entrust my fate to heaven and dedicate my life to the nation.

I have mustered warriors to suppress the evildoers. But although our two opposing forces are now face to face, my men have yet to display martial spirit, and I have been fearful of defections. At this juncture, here on this field of battle where I raise my banners, I suddenly behold a shrine where the true essence of the three deities diffuses his tempered radiance. It is clear that my prayers will be heeded; it is beyond doubt that the evildoers will be put to death. My tears of joy overflow; my gratitude is profound.

Ever since my great-grandfather, the former governor of Mutsu Yoshiie, dedicated himself to Hachiman's service and took the name Hachiman Tarō, all of his descendants have worshipped at Hachiman's shrines. Many years have passed since I first bowed my head before the god as one of their number. In undertaking this great task now, I am like a child measuring the vast ocean with a seashell, like a praying mantis opposing a mighty chariot with its forelimbs.[11] But I act for nation and sovereign, not for family or self. My sincerity is apparent to the divine eyes. Great is my faith, great my joy! Prostrate, I beseech the unseen and seen Buddhas to lend their strength

9. On the Kangakuin, see Chap. 5, n. 31.

10. "Three august divinities" is probably a reference to Amida and his chief attendants, Kannon and Seishi, who were regarded as the true forms (*honji*) of the "three deities"—that is, Emperor Ōjin, Empress Jingū, and Himeōkami, the principal objects of worship at Hachiman shrines.

11. Similes from *Han shu* and *Zhuangzi*.

and the holy gods to exert their powers. Secure my victory at once! Drive the enemy back in every direction!

If this prayer has been accepted, if the visible and invisible powers will protect me, I ask to be shown a sign.

> Eleventh day, fifth month, second year of Juei [1183]
> Minamoto no Yoshinaka

Yoshinaka and twelve of his men took the top arrows from their quivers and presented them to the shrine with the petition. Did the great bodhisattva recognize the suppliant's peerless sincerity from afar? Most reassuringly, three wild doves flew out of the clouds and fluttered above the white banners of the Genji.

While Empress Jingū was attacking Silla once in the past, there was a time when the weakness of her army and the strength of the foe made victory seem impossible. The empress prayed to heaven, three supernatural doves appeared in front of her shields, and she defeated the enemy. Also, when the ancestor of these Genji, Yoriyoshi, attacked Sadatō and Munetō, his force was weak and the rebel army was strong. He lit a fire in front of the enemy position. "This is not in any sense a private blaze; it is a divine fire," he said. At that instant, a wind engulfed the enemy in flames and burned down Sadatō's headquarters, the Kuriyagawa stronghold. The rebels were defeated later on, and Sadatō and Munetō were destroyed.

With these precedents in mind, Lord Kiso dismounted and took off his helmet. Then he washed his hands, rinsed his mouth, and bowed to the supernatural doves with confidence in his heart.

7.6. *The Descent into Kurikara*

Meanwhile, the Genji and the Heike took up positions facing each other. The two sides were barely three hundred and fifty yards apart. The Genji did not advance closer, nor did the Heike.

The Genji ordered fifteen strong archers to ride out from behind their defensive shields and shoot humming-bulb arrows into the ranks of the Heike. The unsuspecting Heike retaliated with fifteen humming-bulb arrows from fifteen of their horsemen. The Genji sent out thirty horsemen to shoot; the Heike responded with thirty horsemen and thirty humming-bulbs. The Genji sent out fifty; the Heike matched them with fifty. The Genji sent out a hundred, and the Heike matched them with a hundred, so that each side had a hundred horsemen in front of its lines. But although the warriors on both forces were eager to fight, the Genji commanders restrained their men. It was too bad for the Heike that they let the day slip by in such encounters, never dreaming that the Genji meant to delay until nightfall so that they could drive their huge army down into Kurikara Valley.

As the evening shadows gradually lengthened, the ten thousand men in the rear came forward from the north and south to assemble near the Kuri-kara Hall.[12] They began to yell battle cries, beating on their quivers.

When the Heike looked back, they saw clouds of white banners behind them. "What's happening?" they shouted. "How could they get behind us with all these cliffs here?"

Yoshinaka's frontal attack force chimed in with battle cries of their own, and there were simultaneous shouts from the ten thousand Genji lying in wait at Matsunaga-no-yanagihara and Gumi-no-kinbayashi, and from Imai no Shirō Kanehira's six thousand men at Hinomiyabayashi. To the men who heard the roar of those forty thousand voices from the front and rear, it seemed that the very mountains and rivers must disintegrate.

As Yoshinaka had planned, the Heike began to waver, unnerved by the growing darkness and the attackers' yells. There were plenty of men who cried, "Don't disgrace yourselves! Come back!" But the retreat could not be reversed, once started, and the warriors galloped pell-mell into Kurikara Valley. Unable to see the vanguard, they took it for granted that there was a road at the bottom. Sons followed fathers in the descent, younger brothers older brothers, kinsmen and retainers lords. Men piled onto horses and horses onto men, layer upon layer. Deep though the valley was, the seventy thousand Heike riders filled it to the top. Streams of blood flowed from rocks; corpses mounted into hills. People say arrow gouges and sword marks can be seen in that valley to this very day.

Three of the clan's most valued retainers died in the avalanche of bodies: Kazusa no Taifu no Hangan Tadatsuna, Hida no Taifu no Hangan Kage-taka, and Kawachi no Hangan Hidekuni. A Genji warrior, Jirō Nagazumi of Kaga Province, captured Senō no Tarō Kaneyasu of Bitchū Province, a warrior renowned for his strength. The Genji also captured Saimei, the Hei-zenji abbot who had switched loyalties at the Hiuchi stronghold in Echizen. "Kill that damned monk before you do anything else!" Yoshinaka said. They put him to the sword. Commanders-in-Chief Koremori and Michimori retreated to Kaga Province, fortunate to escape with their lives. Only two thousand of their seventy thousand horsemen remained.

On the following day, the twelfth, two superb horses reached Yoshinaka, a gift from Hidehira in Michinoku Province. He promptly fitted them out with gold-mounted saddles and presented them to the Hakusan Shrine.[13]

"Everything's all right here," Yoshinaka said, "but I don't feel easy about the battle Yukiie is fighting at Shio. I think I'd better see how he's doing."

After picking and choosing from among his forty thousand men and their

12. At the summit of Kurikara Pass. The hall was dedicated to the worship of Fudō. The rear forces sent to the north (Kitagurosaka) and the south (Minamigurosaka) were earlier said to number 14,000 riders.

13. Fujiwara no Hidehira (d. 1187; not related to the clan of that name in the capital) was the quasi-independent lord of Ōshū (Michinoku Province). Other *Heike* texts say that Yoshi-naka had prayed to Shirayamahime, the goddess worshipped at the Hakusan Shrine, for victory in the approaching battle.

mounts, he hurried toward Shio-no-yama with twenty thousand horsemen. The tide happened to be full when they reached the crossing at Hibi-no-minato, and they drove ten saddled horses into the water to test its depth. The animals reached the opposite shore in safety, the pommels and cantles of the saddles dry except at the lower edges. "It's shallow! Cross!" Twenty thousand strong, the great force plunged across.

As it turned out, Yukiie had been beaten back. Yoshinaka found him resting his horses. "I thought so," he said. His twenty thousand fresh warriors galloped into the middle of the thirty thousand Heike, yelling, whipping their horses, and attacking until the sparks flew. The Heike warriors put up a brief resistance, but they finally went down to defeat on that battlefield as well, crushed by the Genji assault. A Heike commander-in-chief, Tomonori, fell in battle. He was Kiyomori's youngest son. Many samurai also perished.

Yoshinaka crossed Shio-no-yama Mountain and camped in front of the tumulus called Shin'ō-no-tsuka, at Odanaka in Noto Province.

7.8.   *Sanemori*

[This episode takes place nine days later, on the twenty-first of the fifth month. Yoshinaka has again attacked the Heike, who had withdrawn to Shinohara, and he has again won.]

Even though all the others were running away, Nagai no Saitō Bettō Sanemori of Musashi Province kept turning back alone to meet the enemy and put up a defense. With a special plan in mind, he had donned a red brocade tunic, a suit of armor with green lacing, and a horned helmet, had armed himself with a gilt sword with bronze fittings, a quiver containing arrows fledged with black-banded eagle feathers, and a rattan-wrapped bow, and had mounted a white-dappled reddish horse with a saddle trimmed in gold.[14] One of Lord Kiso's men, Tezuka no Tarō Mitsumori, singled him out as a good opponent. "You're putting on quite a show! Who is this hero, this fellow who stays behind after all his friends have run away? Let's hear your name," he said.

"Who are you?" Sanemori asked.

"Tezuka no Tarō Kanezashi no Mitsumori of Shinano Province."

"We're well matched! I don't mean to be insulting, but there's a reason why I'd rather not give you my name. Come on, Tezuka! Let's wrestle!"[15]

Sanemori spurred forward. One of Mitsumori's retainers galloped up from the rear, pressed ahead to protect his master, and gripped Sanemori as hard as he could.

14. His "plan" was to pass for a young man. Older men favored a more sober appearance.

15. A standard tactic in mounted combat. As indicated below, the object was to wrestle the opponent to the ground, pin and kill him, and take his head.

"Congratulations! You want to wrestle with the strongest man in Japan!" said Sanemori. He grabbed the warrior, pulled him against the pommel of his saddle, cut off his head, and tossed it away.

After seeing his man killed, Mitsumori got around to Sanemori's left, lifted the skirt of his armor, stabbed him twice, and wrestled him to the ground as he staggered. Sanemori was still full of fight, but he was tired from all his earlier engagements. Also, he was no longer young. In the end, Mitsumori pinned him.

Mitsumori turned over Sanemori's head to another retainer, a man who had galloped up later, and hurried to report to Lord Kiso. "I've just killed an odd sort of fellow in a wrestling match. He might have been a samurai except that he was wearing a tunic made of brocade. Yet where were his men if he was a commander? I kept asking for his name, but he wouldn't give it. He talked like an easterner," he said.

"This looks to me like the face of Saitō no Sanemori," said Lord Kiso. "I saw him in Kōzuke Province when I visited there as a child, but his hair was already turning gray. It would have to be white by now. How can he have a black beard and black hair? Higuchi no Jirō Kanemitsu has known him a long time; he ought to recognize him. Tell Kanemitsu I want him." [16]

One look was enough for Kanemitsu. "Poor fellow! Yes, that's Sanemori," he said.

"Then he must be over seventy. He ought to have white hair. How is it that his hair and beard are black?" Lord Kiso said.

Kanemitsu broke down in tears. "I meant to explain that, but I felt so sorry for him that I couldn't help crying. Even on trivial occasions, a warrior ought to say things people will remember. Saitō always used to tell me, 'If I fight a battle after I'm past sixty, I'll dye my hair and beard so I'll look young. I know it's childish to try to compete with the young fellows for first place, but I couldn't face the humiliation of having them write me off just because of my age.' Sure enough, he did dye his hair. Have it washed; see for yourself."

"You may be right," Lord Kiso said. He had the hair washed, and it turned white.

Here is how Sanemori happened to be wearing a tunic made of brocade. When he went to take his final leave of Palace Minister Munemori, he said, "Even though I wasn't the only one, it's the shame of my old age that I didn't fire a single arrow when we marched toward the east that year—that I just ran back to the capital from Kanbara in Suruga, scared to death because

16. Kanemitsu was the brother of Imai no Shirō Kanehira, Yoshinaka's foster-brother (*me-notogo*) and best friend. A typical name of a provincial warrior, such as Imai no Shirō Kane-hira, consisted of what we may call a surname, derived from the locality in which the man lived (in this case, Imai), a sobriquet indicating his order of birth within a male sibling group (Shirō, fourth son), and a given name (Kanehira). The particle *no* ("from," "of") appears to have been used inconsistently. Brothers who lived in different localities, like Kanemitsu and Kanehira, might have different surnames.

some birds flapped their wings. I've made up my mind to die on the battle-field during this northern campaign. I was born in Echizen Province, though I've lived at Nagai in Musashi these past few years as an official on one of your properties. There's a saying, 'Wear brocade when you go home,' so could you please let me wear a tunic made of brocade?" Moved by his gallantry, Munemori granted the request. Might we say that Sanemori had now won fame on northern soil, just as Zhu Maichen waved brocade sleeves at Huijishan long ago?[17] How pitiful that his empty name alone should have survived, impervious to corporeal decay, while his mortal remains have become one with the northern soil!

The Heike army had seemed invincible when its hundred thousand horsemen set out from the capital on the seventeenth of the fourth month, but it numbered scarcely more than twenty thousand on its return late in the fifth month. "You can catch a lot of fish if you fish out a stream, but there won't be any next year. You can capture a lot of game if you burn a forest while you're hunting, but there won't be any next year. They would have done well to reserve some men for the future," people said.

7.13. *The Emperor's Flight from the Capital*

On the fourteenth of the seventh month, Sadayoshi, the governor of Higo Province, entered the capital with Kikuchi, Harada, the Matsura League, and others—a total of more than three thousand horsemen—after subjugating the rebels in Chinzei. But although the Heike had managed to restore peace in Chinzei, they were unable to end the fighting in the eastern and northern provinces.

Around midnight on the twenty-second, there was a tremendous uproar in the vicinity of Rokuhara. Horses were saddled, girths were tightened, and people took their belongings off to hiding places in every direction. It seemed that an enemy invasion must be imminent.

The next morning, people learned what had happened. During the Hōgen Disturbance, a certain Sado no Emon-no-jō Shigesada, one of the Mino Genji, had captured Chinzei no Hachirō Tametomo, who had fled in the wake of his side's defeat, and had turned him over to the authorities. As a reward, he had been promoted from lieutenant in the military guards to lieutenant in the gate guards. Ostracized by his relatives for his conduct, he had proceeded to ingratiate himself with the Heike. And the commotion had started because he had galloped to Rokuhara in the middle of the night, and had announced that Kiso no Yoshinaka had invaded from the north with an army of fifty thousand horsemen. "They're swarming all over the eastern base of Mount Hiei," he said. "One of Yoshinaka's retainers, Tate

17. The Chinese general Xiang Yu is said to have remarked, "Not to return to one's old home after having become rich and famous is like going out at night dressed in brocade. Who will know you are wearing it?" Zhu Maichen, originally a poor man, rose in the service of Han Wudi and went home in brocade.

no Rokurō Chikatada, and his scribe, Kakumei, have rushed to the top of the mountain with six thousand men, and the three thousand monks have gone over to their side. The combined force is ready to invade the city!"

In great agitation, the Heike dispatched warriors in all directions. Commanders-in-Chief Tomomori and Shigehira left the capital, leading a total of three thousand horsemen, and occupied quarters at Yamashina. Michimori and Noritsune garrisoned the Uji Bridge with two thousand horsemen, and Yukimori and Tadanori guarded the Yodo Road with a thousand horsemen. But then there were rumors that Yukiie of the Genji was going to invade by way of the Uji Bridge with several thousand horsemen, that Yada no Hangandai Yoshikiyo was advancing on the capital from Ōeyama, and that untold numbers of Genji from Settsu and Kawachi were about to descend on the city like clouds.

The Heike called all their men back. "Now that it's come to this, make your last stand together," they said.

"The capital is a place where men compete for fame and fortune; after cockcrow, there is no rest."[18] If that can be said of a peaceful society, how much more must it apply to troubled times! The Heike would have liked to retire to the innermost recesses of the Yoshino mountains, but all the provinces and the seven circuits had risen against them. Where could they have found a tranquil shore? "There is no safety in the three worlds; they resemble a burning house." That is the miraculous language of the *Lotus Sutra*, the scripture containing the Buddha's golden words, so how could it be even a tiny bit wrong?

In the dead of night on the twenty-fourth day of the seventh month, Munemori went to the Rokuhara Mansion, the place where Kenreimon'in was staying. "I thought we could manage this situation somehow, but things look hopeless now," he said. "The others want to make a last stand in the capital, but I can't bear to expose you to distress here; I've decided to take you, the retired emperor, and the emperor to the western provinces."

"Whatever happens, I'll do as you think best." She could not restrain the tears that overflowed her sleeve, and the minister also wept until his sleeve dripped.

Retired Emperor Go-Shirakawa may have heard that the Heike were secretly planning to flee from the capital that night, and that they intended to take him with them, for he stole away from his mansion and went to Kurama, attended only by Major Counselor Sukekata's son Suketoki. Nobody else knew about his departure.

Now there was a Heike samurai named Kichinaizaemon-no-jō Sueyasu, a bright fellow whom the retired emperor also made use of. This Sueyasu happened to be on duty at the Hōjūji Mansion that night. He noticed much agitated whispering near the former sovereign's private apartments, and he also observed that the ladies-in-waiting were sobbing quietly. He pricked up

18. Paraphrased from a poem by Bo Juyi.

his ears, and presently he heard someone say, "His Majesty has just suddenly vanished! Where can he be?" In great perturbation, he galloped off to report to Munemori at Rokuhara.

"There must be some mistake!" Munemori said. Without another word, he rushed to the Hōjūji Mansion to see for himself. The retired emperor was indeed nowhere to be found, and Lady Tango and his other personal attendants also seemed to be missing.

"What's happened? What's going on here?" Munemori asked. But everybody at the palace seemed flabbergasted. Not one voice said, "I know where he went."

Pandemonium broke out in the city when people learned of the retired emperor's disappearance. It seemed that the Heike could not have been any more upset if enemy soldiers had been invading their homes. (There is, after all, a limit to what can happen on such occasions.) For the members of the clan, busy with preparations to take both the retired emperor and the reigning sovereign off with them to the western provinces, this desertion was like being rained on under a tree where they had sought shelter.

"Well, let's take the emperor, at least," the Heike said. They brought up a travel palanquin early in the morning, during the hour of the hare [5:00 A.M.–7:00 A.M.], and the six-year-old emperor got blithely inside, too young to understand what was happening. His mother, Kenreimon'in, joined him.

The Mirror, the Bead Strand, and the Sword were brought out.[19] "Take the official seals, the treasury keys, and the clock from the Seiryōden, also Kenjō and Suzuka," Major Counselor Tokitada ordered.[20] But many possessions were left behind in the confusion, among them the sword from the emperor's Daytime Chamber. His Majesty's only attendants were three men in court attire—Tokitada himself, Director of the Palace Storehouse Bureau Nobumoto, and Sanuki Middle Captain Tokizane.

The imperial palanquin proceeded west on Shichijō Avenue and south on Suzaku, escorted by members of the bodyguards and by palanquin-cord holders who wore armor and carried bows and arrows.

The new day was the twenty-fifth of the seventh month. Already, the sky had brightened where the river of heaven flowed.[21] Clouds trailed from the peaks to the east, the dawn moon shone white and cold, and cocks raised their busy voices. Not even in a dream could anyone have envisioned such a scene. When people remembered the turmoil caused by the move to the new capital, they recognized that those earlier events were portents of what was happening now.

The regent, Motomichi, had set out to accompany the imperial proces-

19. The imperial regalia, or Three Treasures. See Glossary.
20. Kenjō (Arcane Supremacy), a lute, and Suzuka (Hind), a koto, were heirloom instruments.
21. "River of heaven" was a name for the Milky Way.

sion, but a young boy, his hair looped on the sides, suddenly dashed past the front of his carriage at Shichijō-Ōmiya, and Motomichi saw that his left sleeve bore the legend, "Springtime Sun." He was immensely heartened. "The graphs for 'Springtime Sun' can also be read 'Kasuga.' This must signify that the Kasuga god, the protector of the Hossō doctrines, is watching over Kamatari's descendants," he thought. Just then, he heard the words of a poem, chanted by someone whom he presumed to be the boy:

ika ni sen	Nothing can be done
fuji no sueba no	to save the wisteria tip
kareyuku o	from autumn's decay.
tada haru no hi ni	It must simply place its trust
makasete ya min	in the warm sun of springtime.[22]

He called an attendant close to the carriage, a man named Shindōsaemon-no-jō Takanao. "I've been going over the matter in my mind. The emperor is making this trip, but the retired emperor isn't. It seems to me that the Heike face a dubious future. What do you think?" he said. Takanao signed to the ox-driver with his eyes, and the man, in instant understanding, turned the carriage and sent it flying northward on Ōmiya Avenue.

The regent went into the Chisokuin, in the vicinity of the northern hills.[23]

7.16. Tadanori's Flight from the Capital

Somewhere along the way, Satsuma Governor Tadanori turned back to Shunzei's house on Gojō Avenue, attended by five samurai and a page.[24] The gate was locked.

"It's Tadanori," he announced.

There was agitation inside. "One of the fugitives is back!" voices said.

Tadanori dismounted. "It's nothing special, Shunzei," he shouted. "I've just come back to speak to you. Come out here if you'd rather not open the gate."

"I think I know what he wants," Shunzei said. "He won't make any trouble. Let him in." They opened the gate and Shunzei received him. It was a moving scene.

"I haven't meant to be neglectful since you accepted me as a pupil several years ago," Tadanori said, "but my clan has had to bear the brunt of the unrest in the city and the rebellions in the provinces. During the last two or three years, I haven't been able to pay you regular visits, even though poetry is still very close to my heart. Now the emperor has left the capital, and my clan's good luck has come to an end. I had heard people say there was to be

22. Puns yield another meaning: "Why are you going away, scion of the Fujiwara? Will you not simply trust the Kasuga god?"

23. The Chisokuin was a Buddhist establishment to which Motomichi had family ties. It is conjectured to have been located in the area of Murasakino.

24. Fujiwara no Shunzei (1114–1204) was the most prestigious poet of the day.

a new imperial anthology, and I had thought it would be the greatest honor of my life if you might include even one of my poems. What with all this turmoil, no commission has been handed down, but there's sure to be one after peace is restored. If this scroll contains one suitable poem, and if you should see fit to include it, I'd rejoice in my grave and act as your guardian spirit."

When he was about to leave home, he had snatched up a scroll in which he had recorded more than a hundred poems—to his mind the best of the many he had composed and saved over the years. Now he withdrew it from the armhole in his armor and gave it to Shunzei. Shunzei opened it and looked inside. "I couldn't possibly consider this a keepsake of no importance. Please don't have any fears about that. Your coming here at a time like this shows how much the art of poetry means to you; it moves me to tears," he said.

Tadanori was delighted. "Now I won't mind drowning in the western waves or leaving my bones to bleach in the wilds. Nothing remains to bind me to this transitory existence. Goodbye!" he said. He mounted his horse, tied his helmet cords, and rode off toward the west. Shunzei watched until his figure receded far into the distance. Someone was chanting a *rōei* in a resonant voice that sounded like his:

> Distant lies the way ahead;
> My thoughts run on to the evening clouds at Yanshan.[25]

Moved again by the sorrow of parting, Shunzei had to restrain tears as he went inside. Later, after the restoration of peace, he compiled the *Collection for a Thousand Years*; and then, with a full heart, he remembered how Tadanori had looked and what he had said. There were many eligible poems in the scroll, but he limited his choice to one, taking cognizance of the fact that the author was someone who had suffered imperial censure. Its topic was "Blossoms at the Old Capital." He labeled it "Anonymous."

sazanami ya	It lies in ruins now—
shiga no miyako wa	the old capital at Shiga
arenishi o	of rippling wavelets—
mukashi nagara no	but the cherries at Nagara
yamazakura ka na	bloom as they bloomed long ago.

Tadanori was an enemy of the throne, so there's nothing more to be said. Still, the story is a pathetic one.

7.20. *The Flight from Fukuhara*

Munemori and all the other Heike nobles except Koremori had brought their wives and children, but there was a limit to the number of people who could be taken along, and the men of lower rank had had to leave their

25. Lines from a poem in Chinese by the literatus Ōe no Asatsuna (WKRES 632).

families behind, with no idea of when they might be reunited. A separation seems long enough when the day and hour of the traveler's return are fixed, but these had been final goodbyes—eternal farewells—and those who went and those who stayed had all wept until their sleeves were drenched.

For the hereditary Taira retainers, obligated to the clan for many years of unforgettable favors, there was no question of refusing to follow their lords. But all of them, the old and the young alike, looked back again and again, unable to progress as they should have. Some of them slept on the waves near rocky shores and spent their days on boundless sea paths; others crossed the vast plains and braved the perils of rugged mountains. Each man fled as he thought best, some raising whips to horses and others working poles on boats.

When they reached Fukuhara, Munemori summoned his principal samurai of all ages, a total of several hundred men. "The prosperity of accumulated merit has come to an end; the calamity of accumulated evil has fallen on us," he told them. "We have left the capital to lead wanderers' lives, repudiated by the gods and abandoned by the retired emperor. There seems to be nowhere for us to turn. But a powerful karmic tie from a previous existence binds those who merely take shelter under the same tree; a firm link from another world connects those who merely scoop water from the same stream. What must be the nature of the bond that unites us?

"You didn't declare allegiance to our house yesterday for some temporary gain; you are hereditary retainers, serving as your fathers did before you. Some of you share our blood; others have received our favors for generations. You lived by our bounty while we prospered; can it be that you don't need to honor your obligations now? And can it be that you wouldn't want to travel to the end of any plain, or to the innermost recesses of any mountains, in attendance on His Majesty the Emperor, who bears with him the sacred regalia?"

All the old and young samurai answered in the same way, with tears streaming down their faces. "Even the humble birds and beasts know how to requite favors and repay kindnesses. How could men be ignorant of their duty? It was solely because of your beneficence that we were able to support our families and look after our retainers for more than twenty years. Disloyalty shames a warrior. We'll go with His Majesty to the death, whether the destination is inside or outside of Japan—whether it's Silla, Paekche, Koguryŏ, Bohai, the farthest reaches of the clouds, or the farthest reaches of the sea," they said.[26]

The Taira nobles seemed reassured.

They spent a night in the old capital at Fukuhara. It was late in the first month of autumn, the time of the crescent moon. As the lonely, still night

26. Silla, Paekche, and Koguryŏ were early kingdoms on the Korean peninsula; Bohai was a Tungusic state that occupied parts of eastern Manchuria, the former Soviet Maritime Province, and northern Korea between 700 and 926.

wore on, dew and tears mingled on the travelers' pillows, and everything in their surroundings seemed a source of misery. They looked at the buildings Kiyomori had erected, wondering if they would ever return to see them again. Within the space of three years, all had fallen into decay—the hill palace designed for viewing blossoms in the spring, the beach palace for viewing the moon in the fall, the hall of the bubbling spring, the hall of pine shade, the racetrack hall, the two-storied viewing-stand hall, the palace for viewing snow, the reed-thatched palace, the residences of members of the aristocracy, the temporary imperial palace that Major Counselor Kunitsuna had been commanded to build, the roof tiles shaped like mandarin ducks, and the fine pavements made of stone. Thick moss covered the roads; autumn grasses choked the gates. Ferns sprouted from roof tiles; ivy overran fences. Only the pine wind visited the sagging, mossy halls; only the moonlight entered the exposed bedchambers with their tattered blinds.

The next morning, they set fire to the imperial palace at Fukuhara, and the emperor and all the others boarded boats. This was another painful farewell, even though the grief was less sharp than the anguish they had felt on leaving the capital. The smoke plumes where fisherfolk boiled seaweed at twilight, the cry of a deer on a mountaintop as dawn approached, the waves murmuring toward beaches, the moonbeams reflected in wet sleeves, the cricket choruses in the grass—every sight evoked melancholy, every sound pierced the fugitives' hearts.

Yesterday, they were a hundred thousand horsemen aligning their bridles at the foot of the eastern barrier. Today, they were but seven thousand men untying their mooring lines on the waves of the western sea. The sky was overcast, the water calm, the day nearing its end. Evening mist shrouded lone islands, the moon's reflection floated on the sea.

Cleaving the waves of the distant horizon, drawn ever onward by the tide, the boats seemed to climb higher and higher into the cloudy sky. Already, the passing of time had interposed mountains and rivers between the travelers and the capital, which now lay far behind the clouds. It was as though they had reached the limits of the earth, the point at which all had ended save their endless tears. A flock of white birds resting on the waves gave rise to pathetic speculations. "They're probably capital-birds, the waterfowl with the nostalgic name—the ones Narihira questioned at the Sumida River," they thought.[27]

It was on the twenty-fifth day of the seventh month in the second year of Juei [1183] that the Heike withdrew completely from the capital.

27. Ariwara no Narihira (KKS 411): na ni shi owaba / iza koto towamu / miyakodori / wa ga omou hito wa / ari ya nashi ya to ("If you are in truth what your name seems to make you, I will put to you, capital-bird, this question: do things go well with my love?"). The poem is said to have been composed when the author, traveling in self-imposed exile, reached the Sumida River (now in Tokyo), where a ferryman identified an unfamiliar bird by the name *miyakodori* ("capital-bird").

Chapter 8

Time: late months of 1183
Principal subjects: difficulties of the Taira in western Japan; the contrasting
    characters of Yoritomo and Yoshinaka
Principal characters:
    Go-Shirakawa, Retired Emperor. Head of the imperial clan
    Kanehira (Imai). Yoshinaka's foster-brother and chief lieutenant
    Koreyoshi (Okata). Powerful local warrior in Kyushu
    Munemori (Taira). Son of Kiyomori; now head of clan
    Shigeyoshi (Ki). A powerful local figure
    Sukemori (Taira). Second son of Shigemori (Kiyomori's son and original
        heir, now deceased)
    Tokitada (Taira). Member of a branch family; brother of Kiyomori's
        widow
    Tomomori (Taira). Son of Kiyomori
    Yoritomo (Minamoto). Heir to the chieftainship of the Minamoto clan;
        leader of anti-Taira forces in the east
    Yoshinaka (Minamoto). Cousin of Yoritomo; leader of anti-Taira forces
        in the north
    Yukiie (Minamoto). Uncle of Yoritomo and Yoshinaka; presently allied
        with Yoshinaka

[Retired Emperor Go-Shirakawa has returned to the capital, escorted by
Yoshinaka. Initially welcomed as saviors, Yoshinaka and his uncle, Yukiie,
have begun to behave with the arrogance of conquerors. Yoritomo is still at
his headquarters, the town of Kamakura in eastern Japan. The Heike are in
Kyushu, where a local figure, Okata no Koreyoshi, has just mustered all the
principal warriors of the island against them.]

8.4. The Flight from the Dazaifu

The news of Koreyoshi's revolt was a devastating blow to the Heike, who
had been planning to establish a capital and build the emperor a palace at
the Dazaifu.[1] "Koreyoshi used to be Shigemori's retainer," Major Counselor

1. A special government office in Kyushu. See Glossary.

Tokitada said. "I wonder if it wouldn't be a good idea for one of Shigemori's sons to see him and try to talk him around." The others agreed, and Suke-mori took five hundred horsemen into Bungo Province. But Koreyoshi chased him back the way he had come, unmoved by his arguments. "I ought to take you prisoner here and now, but I'll let you go. I can't be bothered with trifles when I have important matters to take care of. What harm can you do, anyway? Get on back to the Dazaifu and die with your friends," he told him.

After that, Koreyoshi sent a message to the Dazaifu by his second son, Nojiri no Jirō Koremura. "I have enjoyed the bounty of the house of Taira and bear a correspondingly heavy obligation; it would be fitting for me to doff my helmet as your vassal, unstring my bow, and place myself at your disposal. But the fact is that the retired emperor has commanded me to expel you immediately. You'd better leave while you can."

Tokitada went out to receive Koremura, wearing a formal tunic with flame-red wrist cords, a divided skirt made of kudzu cloth, and a high cap. "Our master is the eighty-first human mikado, a direct descendant of the sun goddess in the forty-ninth generation. There can be no doubt that Ama-terasu and Hachiman watch over him. Furthermore, the late Chancellor Kiyomori even brought men from Chinzei into court service after he ended the disturbances of the Hōgen and Heiji eras. You'll be making a mistake if you obey an order from old Big Nose, the governor of Bungo, just because those rebels in the east and north, Yoritomo and Yoshinaka, have sold you the idea that you'll get provinces and estates if we lose," he said. (He used that language because Yorisuke, the governor of Bungo, had an uncom-monly large nose.)

Koremura took the message back to his father. "Forget it!" Koreyoshi said. "The past is the past; the present is the present. If that's their attitude, we'll chase them away right now."

Upon learning that Koreyoshi was recruiting allies, two Heike samurai, Gendayū no Hangan Suesada and Settsu no Hangan Morizumi, took three thousand horsemen to Takano-no-honjō in Chikugo Province. "That fel-low's insolence is setting a bad example. We'll take care of him," they said. They attacked for a day and a night, but Koreyoshi had an immense force at his disposal, and they were forced to retreat.

Then the Heike learned that Koreyoshi was about to attack them with thirty thousand horsemen. There was no alternative; they had to rush away from the Dazaifu. Sick at heart, they bade farewell to the shrine of Tenman Tenjin, the deity on whom they had pinned their hopes. For lack of bearers, the onion-flower and phoenix palanquins were now mere names, and the emperor had to ride in a hand-litter.[2] The imperial mother and the other

2. As the name suggests, the passenger compartment of the onion-flower palanquin (*sō-karen*) was surmounted by a golden onion-flower, considered auspicious because the blossom was long-lived. The phoenix palanquin (*hōren*), surmounted by a gilt phoenix, was used for

noble ladies tucked up their divided skirts, the minister of state and the other senior nobles and courtiers hitched up their baggy trousers, and all of them passed barefoot through the Mizuki portal, fleeing in desperate haste toward the harbor at Hakozaki.[3]

As it happened, the rain was pouring down and a wind was whipping up the sand. Blinded by falling tears and falling rain, they worshipped at Sumiyoshi, Hakozaki, Kashii, and Munakata, each time devoting all their energies to prayers for the emperor's return to the capital. Then they struggled past Mount Tarumi, with its precipitous heights, and past Uzura Beach to a vast expanse of sand. Because they were unused to walking, blood from their feet stained the sand, their red skirts took on a deeper hue, and their white skirts turned red. The famous Xuanzhuang's torments in the deserts and mountains could not have been more agonizing.[4] But Xuanzhuang amassed undoubted merit for himself and others by traveling in search of the sacred doctrines. Most pitifully, the Heike were merely being given an advance taste of the suffering that awaited them in the next world, because enmity was the motivation for their journey.

Much as they would have liked to flee to the farthest reaches of the clouds or the farthest reaches of the sea—if need be, to Paekche, Koguryŏ, or Bohai—they were thwarted by the winds and waves. With Hyōdōji Hidetō as escort, they sought refuge in the Yamaga stronghold.[5] Then they received word of approaching enemies, and traveled nightlong in small boats to Yanagi-ga-ura in Buzen Province, where they had decided to build an imperial palace. But the site proved to be too small. Furthermore, there were new rumors of a Genji attack from Nagato Province, forcing them to hurry out to sea in fishermen's boats.

Shigemori's third son, Middle Captain Kiyotsune, had always had a tendency to brood. "The Genji drove us out of the capital, and Koreyoshi expelled us from Chinzei," he said to himself. "We're like fish in a net; no matter where we go, we can't escape. What chance do I have of living out my life?" He calmed his mind in the moonlight and went to the side of the cabin, where he played a melody on his flute and chanted a *rōei*. Then he intoned a sutra in a low voice, murmured the name of Amida Buddha a few times, and sank beneath the sea. Everyone wept and wailed, men and women together, but it did no good.

---

great occasions of state. The hand-litter (*tagoshi*), which resembled a small raft with a low railing, was used for emergencies, such as evacuation in case of fire. It was carried at arm's length by four men; the palanquins were carried on the shoulders by larger groups.

3. The Mizuki portal was the exit from a moat built in the 7th century to protect the Dazaifu against possible foreign invasion. It was about 15 km from the Dazaifu to Hakozaki (now a part of the city of Fukuoka).

4. Xuanzhuang (602–64) was a Tang monk who traveled through Central Asia to India in search of Buddhist instruction and scriptures.

5. The seat of a local clan, the Yamaga, on a hill near a river mouth, in what is now the town of Ashiya, Fukuoka Prefecture.

Nagato was the province of which Middle Counselor Tomomori was governor. Upon learning that the Heike were afloat in small craft, the deputy governor, a man named Kii no Gyōbu-no-tayū Michisuke, presented them with more than a hundred large vessels. They transferred into the ships and crossed to Shikoku; and at Yashima in Sanuki Province, under Shigeyoshi's direction, the local inhabitants were pressed into service to build a shingle-roofed house for the emperor—a palace in little more than name. In the meantime, they designated a ship to serve as His Majesty's residence, since he could not very well stay in a crude commoner's dwelling.

Munemori and the other senior nobles and courtiers spent their days in fishermen's thatched huts, and their nights in humble laborers' sleeping quarters, while the imperial vessel floated on the sea, an unquiet wave-borne travel palace. Their gloom was as deep as the tides engulfing the moon; their fragile lives were as vulnerable as frost-stricken reeds. The cries of plovers on sandbars at dawn intensified their wretchedness; the sound of nearby oars at midnight shriveled their hearts. When they saw white herons flocking in distant pine trees, they wondered fearfully if the Genji might have raised their banners; when they heard wild geese crying at sea by night, they trembled lest warriors be rowing toward them in the darkness. Blackened eyebrows and pink faces gradually faded as salt winds roughened their skin; tears of longing for the far-off capital rose in eyes transfixed by blue waves. Instead of green curtains in elegant chambers, reed blinds hung in mud-daubed hovels; in place of smoke rising from incense burners, reed fires smoldered in shacks. The miserable ladies could not restrain red tears, which smeared their black eyebrow-paint and rendered them almost unrecognizable.[6]

8.5. *The Retired Emperor Appoints a Barbarian-Subduing Commander*

Meanwhile, Retired Emperor Go-Shirakawa decided to bestow the title of barbarian-subduing commander on Yoritomo, who was still in Kamakura. His messenger, the documents clerk Nakahara no Yasusada, arrived in the east on the fourteenth of the tenth month.

"I've been under imperial censure for years, but now the retired emperor is recognizing my military exploits by naming me barbarian-subduing commander," Yoritomo said. "I can't accept his edict at a private residence; I'll do it at the new shrine." He went to the new Hachiman Shrine, which had been built at Tsurugaoka on a site exactly like the one at Iwashimizu, with galleries and a two-story gate, overlooking a formal approach more than thirty-six hundred feet long.

A conference was held to decide who should receive the edict. "Miura no

6. "Red [i.e., bloody] tears," a conventional term for tears of intense grief or indignation, is used here to balance "black eyebrow-paint."

Suke Yoshizumi would be the right man," they concluded. "He claims descent from Miura no Heitarō Tametsugi, a warrior famous all over the eight provinces. Also, the honor will be a comforting light in the black nether regions for his father, Ōsuke Yoshiaki, who gave his life for Yoritomo."

The imperial envoy, Yasusada, brought with him two kinsmen and ten other retainers. The bag containing the edict hung from a servant's neck. Yoshizumi also had with him two kinsmen and ten other retainers. The two kinsmen were Wada no Saburō Munezane and Hiki no Tōshirō Yoshikazu; the other ten retainers had been requisitioned in haste from ten of the great landholders.

That day, Yoshizumi wore a dark blue tunic and a suit of armor laced with black silk. At his waist, he wore a magnificent sword; on his back, he carried a quiver containing twenty-four arrows fledged with black-banded white feathers. His rattan-wrapped bow was at his side; his helmet was tied to his shoulder-cord. He bowed to receive the edict.

"Who receives His Majesty's edict? Give your name," Yasusada said. Yoshizumi did not identify himself as Miura no Suke. Instead, he gave his true name, Miura no Arajirō Yoshizumi.[7] He presented Yoritomo with the edict, which had been placed in a wickerwork box. When the box was returned after a short time, Yasusada was surprised by its weight. He opened it and discovered a hundred taels of gold dust.

Wine was offered to Yasusada in the oratory, with Saiin no Jikan Chikayoshi as the attendant. A man who held fifth court rank brought the food.

Three horses were led up, one of them saddled. The saddled horse was led by Kudō Ichirō Suketsune, who had once served Empress Tashi as a samurai. An old rush-thatched house had been prepared for Yasusada's reception. A clothing box, filled with two thickly padded sleeping garments and ten short-sleeved robes, had been placed in readiness; and a thousand bolts of cloth had been stacked as a gift, some white and others with rubbed designs in different shades of blue. There was an abundance of food and drink, presented with the utmost elegance and magnificence.

On the following day, Yasusada went to Yoritomo's residence. There were quarters for the samurai both inside and outside the grounds, each sixteen bays long. In the outer quarters, rows of kinsmen and other retainers sat cross-legged, shoulder to shoulder; in the inner ones, the lords of the Minamoto clan occupied the upper seats, and rows of large and small landholders the lower. Yasusada was given the seat of honor in the Minamoto section.

After a short interval, Yasusada proceeded to the main hall. They seated him in the eave-chamber, on matting edged with purple. The blinds were raised to reveal an elevated seat, with matting edged in black and white damask, and Yoritomo entered the room, attired in an unfigured hunting

7. Presumably because Miura no Suke was an informal name. Miura is a surname derived from a locality; Suke, a courtesy title derived from a court office. Arajirō means "Valiant Second Son."

robe and a high cap. His face was large, his figure small, his appearance handsome, and his speech unaccented.

"Yoshinaka and Yukiie have seized the chance to go in and claim whatever ranks and offices they happen to like, and they haven't hesitated to turn down provinces that didn't suit them. The situation is ridiculous. Furthermore, Hidehira in the north disobeys my orders because he's been made governor of Mutsu Province, and Satake no Shirō Takayoshi does the same because he's now vice-governor of Hitachi Province. I'd like to have a command from His Majesty to subjugate both of them immediately," he said.

"I'd give you my name certificate now if I could, but I'm here as an imperial messenger, so I'll present it as soon as I get back to the capital.[8] My brother, Major Recorder Shigeyoshi, tells me he wants to do the same," Yasusada said.

Yoritomo laughed. "As things stand at the moment, I'm not thinking about receiving name certificates. But I don't object if you really want to do it," he said.

Yasusada had announced that he would leave for the capital on that same day, but Yoritomo detained him. "By all means, stay just this one day," he said.

On the following day, Yasusada went to Yoritomo's residence. There he was given a corselet laced with green silk, a sword with silver decorations, a rattan-wrapped bow with hunting arrows, and thirteen horses, three of them saddled. His twelve kinsmen and other retainers received tunics, short-sleeved robes, wide-mouthed divided skirts, and even saddles. So numerous were the gifts that thirty pack horses were needed to carry them. Fifty bushels of rice were provided for the party at every post station, all the way from Kamakura to Kagami—so much too much that they gave away some as alms.

8.6. *Nekoma*

When he returned to the capital, Yasusada went to the retired emperor's palace, presented himself in the inner courtyard, and gave a detailed description of his experiences in the Kantō. The retired emperor was greatly impressed, and the senior nobles and courtiers all smiled in approval.

In contrast to Yoritomo's admirable conduct, the manners and speech of Kiso no Yoshinaka, the present protector of the capital, were indescribably rude and vulgar. Of course, nothing else was to have been expected. What knowledge of civilized deportment could have come the way of someone who had lived at Kiso, in the mountains of Shinano, from the time he was two until he was thirty?

A man known as Nekoma Middle Counselor Mitsutaka visited Yoshinaka to discuss a certain matter.

8. The name certificate (*myōbu*) was a card listing a man's office, rank, name, and age. Its presentation was a symbolic act, pledging unlimited service in return for patronage.

"Lord Nekoma has arrived. He says he wants to see you about something," the retainers said.

Yoshinaka burst out laughing. "A cat wants to talk to a man?"[9]

"This is a senior noble called the Nekoma middle counselor. Nekoma is probably the name of the place where he lives," someone said.

"In that case, I'll see him," Yoshinaka said. But instead of referring to the visitor as Lord Nekoma, he said, "Lord Neko is treating us to a rare visit. Get some food ready."

"Please don't dream of bothering about that now," said the middle counselor.

"You've come at mealtime, so naturally I'll feed you," Yoshinaka said. In the erroneous belief that the word "unsalted" might refer to any fresh food, he said to his people, "We have some 'unsalted' finger mushrooms. Hurry up and fix them."[10]

Nenoi no Koyata acted as waiter. He presented the middle counselor with three vegetable side dishes, some finger-mushroom soup, and a big, deep country-style bowl heaped with rice. Then he placed a similar repast in front of Yoshinaka. Yoshinaka seized his chopsticks and began to eat. Lord Nekoma hesitated, repelled by the squalid appearance of the bowl.

"That's the bowl I use for religious purposes." Yoshinaka told him.

The visitor thought it would be worse to refuse the meal than to eat it, so he picked up his chopsticks and toyed with the food.

"Lord Neko's a small eater," Yoshinaka said. "He's just like the cats we hear about who don't finish their dinners. Eat up!"

Mortally offended, Lord Nekoma hurried away without mentioning his business.

In the thought that a man who held office and rank could not go to court in a tunic, Yoshinaka put on a hunting robe and hunched himself into a carriage, unaware that his costume was devoid of taste from the fit of his cap to the hem of his trousers. His appearance was dreadful—a far cry from the figure he cut on horseback, wearing armor and quiver and holding a bow.

The carriage and the ox-driver had both belonged to Munemori, who was now at Yashima. Bowing to the changing times like everyone else, the ox-driver had let himself be impressed into Yoshinaka's service, but not without resentment. When the carriage left the gate, he whipped up the ox, a fine, spirited beast, which had not been driven recently. As was only to have been expected, it lunged forward, and Yoshinaka fell flat on his back. He struggled to right himself, his sleeves extended like butterfly wings. "Hey, ox-boy!" he yelled, unable to think of the word "ox-driver." "Hey, ox-boy!"

The ox-driver chose to interpret "Hey!" as "Make him run!"[11] He kept

---

9. The place-name Nekoma is partially homophonous with *neko*, "cat."

10. *Buen*, "unsalted," was a term properly used only of seafood.

11. *Yare*, the word translated as "Hey!," is homophonous with the imperative of the verb *yaru*, "cause to run."

the ox galloping for another half mile, until Imai no Shirō Kanehira over-took them with flailing whip and flapping stirrups. "What's the idea of making him run like that?" Kanehira demanded.

"He was too strong for me," the driver said. Then, perhaps in an effort to patch things up with Yoshinaka, he said, "Your Excellency, please use the handhold in there."

Yoshinaka grabbed the handhold. "This is a great contraption! Was it your idea or the minister's?" he asked.

After the carriage was unhitched at the retired emperor's residence, Yoshi-naka started to alight from the rear. "A carriage is supposed to be entered from the rear and left from the front," said a city-dweller he had taken into his service.

"Why should I bypass a place just because it's in a carriage?" Yoshinaka said. He got out through the rear.

Many other ridiculous things like this happened, but people were afraid to talk about them.

Chapter 9

Time: first and second months of 1184
Principal subjects: the battle for control of the capital and the battle of Ichi-
    no-tani
Principal characters:
    Atsumori (Taira). Son of Tsunemori; nephew of Kiyomori
    Go-Shirakawa, Retired Emperor. Head of the imperial clan
    Kanehira (Imai). Foster-brother of Yoshinaka
    Michimori (Taira). Son of Norimori; nephew of Kiyomori
    Munemori (Taira). Son of Kiyomori; head of the Taira clan
    Noritsune (Taira). Son of Norimori; nephew of Kiyomori
    Noriyori (Minamoto). Son of Yoshitomo; half-brother of Yoritomo
    Shigehira (Taira). Son of Kiyomori
    Tomomori (Taira). Son of Kiyomori
    Yoritomo (Minamoto). Heir to the chieftainship of the Minamoto clan;
        leader of anti-Taira forces in the east
    Yoshinaka (Minamoto). Cousin of Yoritomo; controls capital as chapter
        begins
    Yoshitsune (Minamoto). Son of Yoshitomo; half-brother of Yoritomo
Prominent Eastern warriors figuring in battle episodes:
    Kagesue (Kajiwara). Son of Kagetoki
    Kagetoki (Kajiwara). Trusted lieutenant of Yoritomo; presently with
        Yoshitsune's army
    Naozane (Kumagae). Originally with Noriyori's army; later with
        Yoshitsune's
    Sanehira (Toi). A subordinate commander in Yoshitsune's army
    Shigetada (Hatakeyama). With Yoshitsune's army
    Takatsuna (Sasaki). With Yoshitsune's army

[The Heike have twice defeated forces sent against them by Yoshinaka, and
are gaining strength in the west. They are now holed up with the boy-emperor
Antoku in Sanuki Province. Meanwhile, after a falling out and a clash of arms
in the capital between Yoshinaka and Retired Emperor Go-Shirakawa, Yoshinaka has gone his own way and taken control of the city and the court, causing Yoritomo to dispatch two of his brothers, Noriyori and Yoshitsune, to

"put an end to Yoshinaka's excesses." At this point, the Genji are effectively warring on themselves.]

9.1. *The Matter of Ikezuki*

At Naritada's house near the junction of Rokujō and Nishi-no-tōin, where Retired Emperor Go-Shirakawa was staying, the lack of amenities made it impossible to hold ceremonies on the first of the first month in the third year of Juei [1184].[1] Thus there were no felicitations; and because there were no felicitations at the retired emperor's residence, there were no congratulations at the imperial palace.[2]

The Heike, for their part, saw out the old year and welcomed the new on the beach at Yashima in Sanuki Province. The ceremonies prescribed for the first three days could not be performed in satisfactory fashion. Although the emperor was there with them, there were no banquets and no obeisances to the four directions. No trout were offered to the throne, nor did the villagers from Kuzu in Yoshino present their music.[3] "In spite of all the disruptions, things were never this bad in the capital," the Taira nobles said to one another.

Verdant spring had come, with ever softer breezes from the shore and ever milder sunshine, but the Heike felt as though they were *kankuchō* birds trapped in eternal ice.[4] They indulged in long, pathetic reminiscences about life in the capital, and tried to while away the interminable days with memories of how "the willows on the east and west banks did not put forth leaves at the same pace, nor the plum blossoms on the south and north branches open and fall together"[5]—of how they had amused themselves with blossom-viewing in the morning and moon-viewing at night, and with poetry, music, kickball, small-bow competitions, and contests matching fans, pictures, plants, and insects.

On the eleventh of the first month, Kiso no Yoshinaka visited the retired

---

1. Retired Emperor Go-Shirakawa's residence, the Hōjūji Mansion, had burned down during the fighting between Yoshinaka and the retired emperor's supporters. The house mentioned here was one that had been put at Yoshinaka's disposal when he first entered the capital. Naritada was the head of the Palace Table Office.

2. That is, at the residence of the young Emperor Go-Toba (1180–1239; r. 1183–98), Emperor Takakura's fourth son, whom Go-Shirakawa had put on the throne after the abduction of Emperor Antoku by his Taira relatives (Sec. 8.1; not translated). The felicitations at the retired emperor's residence were supposed to precede the congratulations at the reigning emperor's palace.

3. The obeisances to the four directions (*shihōhai*) was a calamity-averting ceremony performed by the emperor on the first day of the year. The trout came from the Dazaifu; the Kuzu villagers played old-fashioned flutes and sang their folksongs. For information about New Year's ceremonies, see McCullough and McCullough, *Tale of Flowering Fortunes*, 1: 380–85.

4. The *kankuchō* was a mythical Himalayan bird. It was reputed to cry, "I'll build a nest today" when suffering from the cold at night, and to say, "I'll do it tomorrow" after sunrise.

5. A slight variation on a couplet by the literatus Yoshishige no Yasutane (WKRES 11).

emperor to announce that he was ready to march westward and subdue the Heike.

On the thirteenth, just as Yoshinaka was reported to be leaving, word arrived that fifty to sixty thousand horsemen had already reached Mino and Owari provinces, sent from the east by Yoritomo to put an end to his cousin's excesses.

In great consternation, Yoshinaka took out the bridges at Uji and Seta and divided his forces for defensive action. His strength was negligible at the time. To the Seta Bridge, where the frontal assault would come, he sent Imai no Kanehira with eight hundred horsemen. To the Uji Bridge, he sent Nishina, Takanashi, and Yamada no Jirō with five hundred horsemen; to Imoarai, he sent his uncle Yoshinori with three hundred horsemen. It was reported that the commanders-in-chief of the frontal and rear assault forces from the east were Gama no Onzōshi Noriyori and Kurō Onzōshi Yoshitsune; also that more than thirty great local landholders were marching with them, and that their combined armies numbered more than sixty thousand horsemen.

In those days, the Lord of Kamakura, Yoritomo, had in his possession two famous horses named Ikezuki [Ill-tempered Biter] and Surusumi [Inkstick]. Kajiwara Kagesue asked for Ikezuki more than once, but Yoritomo gave him Surusumi instead. "I'm saving Ikezuki for the day when I might need to put on armor and ride. Surusumi is an excellent horse too," he told him. Then, for some reason, he gave Ikezuki to Sasaki Takatsuna when Takatsuna came to make his formal request for permission to leave. "Take the horse in the knowledge that other people have wanted him," he said.

Takatsuna bowed. "I'll be the first man across the Uji River on this horse. If people tell you I died at the river, you'll know somebody got ahead of me. If they tell you I'm still alive, you can be sure I was the first," he said. Then he withdrew.

"That was a rash boast," the assembled landholders whispered among themselves.

Leaving Kamakura in independent parties, the easterners traveled toward the capital as they pleased, some by way of Ashigara and others by way of Hakone. When Kajiwara Kagesue reached Ukishima-ga-hara in Suruga Province, he reined in for a while on top of a hill, watching as thousands of horses were led past by their mouth and bridle ropes, each with a colored crupper and a saddle to suit its owner's fancy. He congratulated himself. In all that mighty procession, there was no better mount than Surusumi, the horse Yoritomo had given him. Just then, he spied a horse that looked like Ikezuki. It wore a saddle trimmed with gold and a crupper with a short fringe, and it was champing white foam and prancing as several grooms struggled to control it. He rode down the hill.

"Whose horse is that?" he asked.

"It's Lord Sasaki's," they told him.

He was outraged. "I was going to go to the capital and stake my life in a wrestling match with one of Yoshinaka's famous Four Heavenly Kings, Imai, Higuchi, Tate, and Nenoi. Either that, or I was going to head westward and risk death against one of the Heike samurai—those fellows who are supposed to be as good as a thousand ordinary warriors. But what's the point if this is how His Lordship feels? I'll wrestle with Sasaki and draw on him right here; thanks to me, His Lordship will lose two good men," he said. He waited, muttering.

All unsuspecting, Takatsuna rode into view, taking his time. Kagesue debated with himself. Should he ride alongside and grab him? Would it be better to hit him head-on and knock him to the ground? He decided to speak first.

"Well, Sasaki, I see His Lordship has made you a present of Ikezuki!"

Sasaki remembered immediately that he had heard people talk about Kagesue's desire for the horse. "As a matter of fact," he answered, "that's not quite what happened. When I was getting ready for this campaign, I realized that Yoshinaka would tear up the bridges at Uji and Seta. I didn't have a horse that could get me across the river. I wanted to ask for Ikezuki, but I knew it would be a waste of time, because I'd heard that His Lordship wouldn't even give him to you when you asked about it. I didn't have a prayer. So I decided to act and take the consequences. I was leaving just before dawn. Earlier that night, I came to a meeting of minds with a groom, stole his precious Ikezuki, and brought him with me. What do you think of that?"

Kagesue cooled down. "Damn it! I wish I'd stolen him myself!" He rode off with a laugh.

9.2. *The First Man Across the Uji River*

The horse Sasaki Takatsuna had received was a dark chestnut, very stout and brawny. He was named Ikezuki because he refused to let either horses or men approach him. People said he stood eight inches taller than an ordinary mount. Surusumi, the horse Kajiwara Kagesue had received, was also very stout and brawny. He was named Surusumi because he was pure black. Both were superb animals, inferior to none.

In preparation for the attack on the capital, the easterners broke up into frontal and rear assault forces in Owari Province. The commander-in-chief of the frontal assault force, Noriyori, advanced to Noji and Shinohara in Ōmi Province with a total of more than thirty-five thousand riders, including these men:

> Taketa no Tarō Nobuyoshi
> Kagami no Jirō Tōmitsu
> Ichijō no Jirō Tadayori
> Itagaki no Saburō Kanenobu
> Inage no Saburō Shigenari
> Hangae no Shirō Shigetomo

Kumagae no Jirō Naozane
Inomata no Koheiroku Noritsuna

The commander-in-chief of the rear assault force, Yoshitsune, swooped down on the approach to the Uji Bridge, coming by way of Iga Province with a total of more than twenty-five thousand riders, including these men:

Yasuda no Saburō Yoshisada
Ōuchi no Tarō Koreyoshi
Hatakeyama no Shōji Jirō Shigetada
Kajiwara Genda Kagesue
Sasaki Shirō Takatsuna
Kasuya no Tōda Arisue
Shibuya no Uma-no-jō Shigesuke
Hirayama no Mushadokoro Sueshige

The bridges at Uji and Seta had both been pulled up, and there were barricades made of tree branches floating on the current, tied to ropes between stakes driven at random in the riverbed. As was natural for the time of year, which was past the twentieth of the first month, the last of the snow had melted from the peaks of Hira, the Shiga Mountains, and Nagarayama. The ice had melted in all the valleys, and the river was in full flood. Angry white waves raced downstream; rapids roared like waterfalls; former eddies had become whirlpools. Dawn was just breaking, but a dense fog had risen from the river, dimming the colors of the horses' coats and the lacings on the riders' armor.

The commander-in-chief, Yoshitsune, went to shore and looked out over the water. It may be that he wanted to find out what his men were thinking, for he said, "What shall we do? Would it be best to go around to Yodo and Imoarai? Should we wait for the river to subside?"

At that time, Hatakeyama Shigetada was only twenty-one. He came forward and spoke. "We used to hear lots of stories about this river in Kamakura. It's not some unknown body of water, looming up out of nowhere. It's the outlet of Lake Biwa, and it won't go down, no matter how long you wait. Nobody can bridge it for you, either. Was Ashikaga Tadatsuna superhuman when he rode across it during the battle in the Jishō era?[6] I'll test it for you!" His five hundred horsemen surged forward and lined up bridle to bridle—members of the Tan League and others.

Just then, two warriors galloped into view from the tip of Tachibana-no-kojima, northeast of the Byōdōin. One was Kagesue and the other was Takatsuna. Neither of them had revealed his intentions, but each had secretly made up his mind to be the first across the river.

Takatsuna hailed Kagesue, who was about thirty-five feet ahead of him.

6. See "The Battle at the Bridge" (Sec. 4.11).

"This is the biggest river in the west! Your saddle girth looks loose; tighten it up!"

Kagesue must have feared that the girth really needed tightening. He stiffened his legs in the stirrups to hold them away from Surusumi's belly, tossed the reins over the horse's mane, undid the girth, and tightened it. Meanwhile, Takatsuna galloped past him into the river. Kagesue followed, possibly feeling that he had been tricked.

"Look out, Sasaki!" Kagesue yelled. "Don't mess up trying to be a hero! There must be ropes on the bottom."

Takatsuna drew his sword, cut the ropes as they touched the horse's legs, one after another, and rode straight across the Uji River and up the bank on Ikezuki, the best horse in the world. Kagesue's mount, Surusumi, forced into a diagonal course at the halfway point, landed far downstream.

Takatsuna stood in his stirrups and announced his name in a mighty voice. "The first man across the Uji River is Sasaki Shirō Takatsuna, fourth son of Sasaki Saburō Hideyoshi and ninth-generation descendant of Emperor Uda! If anybody here thinks he's as good as I am, let him wrestle with me!" He charged, yelling.

Shigetada dashed into the river with his five hundred men. From the opposite bank, Yamada no Jirō released an arrow that sank deep into the forehead of his horse, and the animal began to falter. With the aid of his bow, Shigetada dismounted in midstream and made his way along the bottom to the other shore, ignoring the white water leaping toward his helmet flaps from the rocks. As he was about to climb up, he felt a sharp tug from the rear.

"Who's that?" he asked.

"Shigechika," a voice answered.

"It's you, Ōkushi?"

"That's right."

Ōkushi Jirō Shigechika was Shigetada's godson. "The current was too swift for my horse; it got swept away," he said. "I had to catch onto you."

"You boys are always expecting somebody like me to get you out of trouble," Shigetada said. He grabbed Shigechika, dangled him in the air, and tossed him onto the bank.

Shigechika straightened up and identified himself. "The first man to cross the Uji River on foot is Ōkushi no Jirō Shigechika of Musashi Province!" A roar of laughter went up from both sides.

Afterward, Shigetada mounted another horse and left the river. A warrior dressed in an olive-colored tunic and a suit of armor laced with flame-red leather, and riding a white-dappled reddish horse with a saddle trimmed in gold, advanced to the forefront of the enemy ranks.

"Who's this fellow galloping in my direction? Give me your name," Shigetada said.

"I'm Nagase Shigetsuna, a relative of Lord Kiso."

"You'll serve as today's offering to the god of battle!" Shigetada rode alongside, seized the man in a powerful grip, pulled him down, and twisted off his head. Then he gave the head to Honda no Jirō to tie to Honda's saddle rope.[7]

After this prelude, all the other easterners crossed and took up the attack. The men who were defending the bridge for Yoshinaka put up a brief resistance, but were routed and forced to flee toward Kohatayama and Fushimi.

Thanks to a plan devised by Inage Shigenari, the easterners at Seta got across the river at Kugonose, in the area of Tanakami.

9.3. *The Battle at the Riverbed*

After Yoshitsune had defeated Yoshinaka's forces, he sent a courier to Kamakura with a written account of the battle. Yoritomo's first question was about Takatsuna. The courier answered, "He led the way across the Uji River." And when Yoritomo opened the report, he read, "The first man across the Uji River was Sasaki Shirō Takatsuna; the second was Kajiwara Genda Kagesue."

When Yoshinaka learned about the defeats at Uji and Seta, he hurried toward the retired emperor's residence, the Rokujō Mansion, to make formal announcement of his departure. The retired emperor, the senior nobles, and the courtiers at the mansion were wringing their hands and making all kinds of vows. "This is the end of everything!" they said. "What are we going to do?"

Just as Yoshinaka got to the gate, he heard someone say that the easterners had already reached the dry bed of the Kamo River. Without leaving any message worth mentioning, he turned away and paid a long farewell visit at a house near the intersection of Rokujō Avenue and Takakura Street, the home of a woman he had been seeing recently. One of the men with him was a new retainer named Echigo no Chūta Iemitsu. "Why are you wasting so much time, Your Lordship?" this Iemitsu asked. "The invaders are already at the riverbed. You'll die like a dog!" Yoshinaka still lingered inside. "All right," Iemitsu said, "I'll wait for you at the Shide Mountains!" He cut open his belly and died. Then Lord Kiso rushed out of the house. "He killed himself to put some fight in me," he said.

Lord Kiso's force numbered no more than a hundred horsemen, chief among them Nawa Hirozumi from Kōzuke Province. When they rode out onto the riverbed at the end of Rokujō Avenue, they saw thirty riders who looked like easterners. Two of the thirty were riding in front, Shionoya Korehiro and Teshigawara Arinao.

"Do you think we ought to wait for some reinforcements?" Korehiro said to Arinao.

"Now that their vanguard's been beaten, the ones in the rear must be demoralized," Arinao said. "Charge!" He galloped forward with a yell.

---

7. Honda was Shigetada's right-hand man. He also appears in other military tales.

Yoshinaka met him in desperate combat, and all the rest of the easte
pressed forward, each hopeful of being the one to take his head.

Meanwhile, Yoshitsune turned the fighting over to his subordinates and
galloped toward the Rokujō Mansion with five or six fully armed men, planning to mount guard over the retired emperor's residence and ensure its
safety.

Naritada, the master of the Palace Table Office, had climbed onto the
eastern wall at the mansion. As he surveyed the surroundings, shaking with
fear, he saw a white banner shoot up above five or six warriors who were
galloping toward him in a cloud of black dust, their helmets loose from
combat and their bow-arm sleeves fluttering.[8] "Terrible news! Kiso's back!"
he said. The retired emperor and his retinue despaired. This was bound to
be the end! But then Naritada informed them that the warriors were wearing a different kind of helmet badge. "I think they must be some of the
easterners—the ones coming into the city today," he said.

Even as he spoke, Yoshitsune galloped up to the entrance, dismounted,
and pounded on the gate. "Kurō Yoshitsune, the younger brother of Yoritomo, has arrived from the east. Open up!" he shouted.

In a transport of joy, Naritada jumped off the wall and landed on his
buttocks. The fall hurt, but he hobbled inside with the message, too happy
to mind. The delighted retired emperor issued orders for the gate to be
opened immediately.

That day, Yoshitsune wore a red brocade tunic, a suit of armor with
purple-shaded lacing, and a horned helmet. At his waist, he had fastened a
sword with gilt bronze fittings; on his back, he carried a quiver containing
arrows fledged with black-banded eagle feathers. An inch-wide strip of paper was wound leftwise around the left-hand grip of his rattan-wrapped
bow, apparently as a sign that he was the commander-in-chief for the battle
that day. The retired emperor scrutinized him and his companions from
behind a slatted window in the middle gate. "They look like gallant lads.
Have them all give their names," he said. The warriors identified themselves
as first, the commander-in-chief, Yoshitsune, and, next, Yasuda Yoshisada,
Hatakeyama Shigetada, Kajiwara Kagesue, Sasaki Takatsuna, and Shibuya
Shigesuke. There were six of them, counting Yoshitsune, and although the
colors of their armor-braid may have differed, not one was inferior to any
of the others in bearing or character.

At the retired emperor's direction, Naritada summoned Yoshitsune to the
threshold of the eave-chamber. His Majesty asked for a full description of
the battle. Yoshitsune bowed and reported in a matter-of-fact voice. "Yoritomo was amazed when Yoshinaka revolted. He sent out sixty thousand
horsemen against him, commanded by Noriyori and me and including more

---

8. During a battle, the weight of the plates gradually loosened a helmet's cords, forcing it
toward the back of the head. The armor on the bow (left) arm was particularly susceptible to
damage, not only because it was exposed during shooting, but also because it was used as a
shield.

l warriors. Noriyori is coming by way of Seta; he isn't
Yoshinaka's men at Uji and hurried along to defend this
a has fled north along the riverbed, but I've sent men
t have killed him by now."

eror was well pleased. "Excellent! But I'm afraid that
hinaka's army might come here to cause trouble. Guard
aid. Yoshitsune made respectful assent. He secured the
hile, warriors kept galloping up to join him, and his force
soon numbered more than ten thousand horsemen.

Yoshinaka had stationed twenty shaven-headed laborers at the retired emperor's residence,[9] planning, if worst came to worst, to carry him off to the west and make common cause with the Heike. But now he learned that Yoshitsune had already secured the mansion. Resigning himself to the situation, he galloped shouting into the midst of the thousands of enemy warriors. Time after time, he hovered on the brink of death; time after time, he managed to break through.

"I'd never have sent Kanehira to Seta if I'd known things would turn out like this," he said in tears. "Ever since the days when we played together on bamboo horses, we've always promised each other that if we had to die we'd die together. I can't bear to think of the two of us going down in different places. If only I could find out where he is!"

He galloped northward along the riverbed. Again and again, between Rokujō and Sanjō, he turned to meet enemy attacks; five or six times, he drove back the foe's cloudlike host with his meager force. Then he crossed the Kamo River and made his way to Awataguchi and Matsuzaka. Last year, when he departed from Shinano Province, he commanded fifty thousand horsemen; today, as he passed the Shinomiya riverbed, he and his companions numbered but seven riders. And how infinitely more pitiful was the prospect of his solitary journey through the intermediate existence!

9.4. *The Death of Kiso*

Kiso no Yoshinaka had brought two female attendants, Tomoe and Yamabuki, with him from Shinano Province. Yamabuki had fallen ill and stayed in the capital. Tomoe was the more beautiful of the two, with white skin, long hair, and charming features. She was also a remarkably strong archer, and with a sword she was a warrior equal to a thousand, ready to confront demon or god on horseback or on foot. She handled unbroken horses with superb skill; she rode unscathed down perilous descents. When there was a battle to be fought, Yoshinaka sent her out to act as his first captain, equipped with stout armor, an especially long sword, and a strong bow, and she performed more deeds of valor than any of his other warriors. Now she was one of seven who remained after all their comrades had either fled or perished.

9. "Shaven-headed laborers," or *rikishi*, were used as palanquin-bearers and porters.

There were rumors that Yoshinaka was making for the Tanba Road by way of Nagasaka, and also that he was heading north through the Ryūge Pass. As a matter of fact, though, he was retreating toward Seta in the hope of finding Imai Kanehira. Kanehira had lost all but fifty of his eight hundred defenders at Seta, and had started back toward the capital with his banner furled, worried about his master. The two arrived simultaneously at Uchide Beach in Ōtsu, recognized each other from a distance of three hundred and fifty feet, and galloped together.

Lord Kiso took Kanehira's hand. "By rights, I ought to have died on the riverbed beyond Rokujō Avenue, but I broke through an enemy host and retreated because I wanted to find you," he said.

"It's a great honor to hear you talk like that," Kanehira said. "I ought to have died at Seta, but I've come this far because I was worried about you."

"I see that our karmic bond still holds. My warriors scattered into the mountains and woods after the enemy broke our ranks, but some of them must be near here. Tell your man to raise that furled banner!" Yoshinaka said.

When Imai's banner was unfurled, more than three hundred riders responded—men who had fled from the capital or Seta, or who had come from some other place. Yoshinaka's spirits rose. "We have enough for one last battle. Who's the leader of that band I see over there?" he said.

"They say it's Ichijō Tadayori from Kai Province," someone answered.

"What's his strength?"

"He's supposed to have six thousand riders."

"Then it's just the right match! If we have to die, let's do it by attacking good men and going down because we're outnumbered," Yoshinaka said. He rode forward in the lead.

That day, Lord Kiso wore a tunic of red brocade, a suit of armor laced with thick Chinese damask, and a horned helmet. At his side, he had strapped a magnificent long sword; high on his back, there was a quiver holding the few arrows that remained from his earlier battles, all fledged with the tail feathers of eagles. He grasped a bow wrapped with rattan and sat in a gold-edged saddle astride his famous horse Oniashige [Roan Demon], a very stout and brawny animal. Standing in the stirrups, he announced his name in a mighty shout. "You must have heard of Kiso no Kanja; take a look at him now! I am the Morning Sun Commander, Minamoto no Yoshinaka, director of the imperial stables of the left and governor of Iyo Province. They tell me you're Ichijō no Tadayori from Kai. We're a good match! Cut off my head and show it to Yoritomo!" He galloped forward, yelling.

"That fellow who's just named himself is their commander-in-chief," Tadayori said. "Wipe out the whole force, men! Get all of them, boys! Kill them!"

The easterners moved to surround Yoshinaka with their superior numbers, each hoping to be the one to take his head. Yoshinaka's three hundred horsemen galloped lengthwise, sidewise, zigzag, and crosswise in the middle of the six thousand, and finally burst through to the rear. Only fifty were left.

As the fifty went on their way after breaking free, they came to a defensive position manned by two thousand horsemen under the command of Toi Sanehira. Again, they broke through and went on. Again, they galloped through enemy bands—here four or five hundred, there two or three hundred, or a hundred and forty or fifty, or a hundred—until only five of them were left. Even then, Tomoe remained alive.

"Hurry up, now!" Lord Kiso said to Tomoe. "You're a woman, so go on off. Go wherever you please. I've made up my mind to die fighting, or else to kill myself if I get wounded, and it wouldn't be right to let people say I kept a woman with me during my last battle."

At first, Tomoe refused to leave. When she could resist no longer, she pulled up. "If I could find somebody worth bothering with, I'd fight one last battle—give His Lordship something to look at," she thought.

As she sat there, thirty horsemen came into view, led by Onda Moroshige, a man famous in Musashi Province for his prodigious strength. Tomoe galloped in among them. She rode up alongside Moroshige, seized him in a powerful grip, and pulled him down against the pommel of her saddle. Holding him motionless, she twisted off his head and threw it away. Then she abandoned her armor and helmet and fled toward the eastern provinces.

Tezuka Mitsumori died fighting and Tezuka no Bettō fled. Only two riders were left, Kanehira and Lord Kiso.

"I've never noticed it before, but my armor feels heavy today," Lord Kiso said.

"You aren't tired yet, and your horse is still fresh. Why should the weight of a suit of armor bother you? You're discouraged because there's nobody left on our side. But don't forget—I'm worth a thousand ordinary warriors. I'll hold off the enemy awhile with my last seven or eight arrows. That place over there is the Awazu Pinewoods. Kill yourself among the trees," Kanehira said.

As the two rode on, whipping their horses, a new band of fifty warriors appeared. "Get into the pinewoods! I'll hold these fellows off," Kanehira said.

"By rights, I ought to have died in the capital. The only reason I ran off here was because I wanted to die with you. Let's not be killed in different places; let's go down together," Lord Kiso said. He brought his horse alongside Kanehira's, ready to gallop forward.

Kanehira jumped down and took Lord Kiso's horse by the bit. "No matter how glorious a warrior's earlier reputation may have been, a shameful death is an eternal disgrace. You're tired; you haven't got any followers. If you get isolated, and if somebody's no-account retainer drags you down to your death, people will say, 'So-and-so's retainer killed the famous Lord Kiso, the man known throughout Japan.' I'd hate to see that happen. Please, please, go into the pinewoods," he said.

"Well, then . . ." Lord Kiso galloped toward the woods.

Kanehira dashed into the fifty riders alone. He stood in his stirrups and announced his name in a mighty shout. "You must have heard of me long ago; take a look at me now with your own eyes! I am Imai no Shirō Kanehira, aged thirty-three, foster-brother to Lord Kiso. The Kamakura Lord Yoritomo himself must know that I exist. Kill me and show him my head!" He fired off his remaining eight arrows in a fast and furious barrage, felling eight men on the spot. (It's hard to say whether or not they were killed.) Then he galloped around, brandishing his drawn sword, without finding anyone willing to face him. Many were the trophies he amassed! The surrounding easterners released a hail of arrows, hoping to shoot him down, but none of their shafts found a chink in his armor or penetrated the stout plates, and he remained uninjured.

Lord Kiso galloped toward the pinewoods, a lone rider. It was the twenty-first of the first month. The evening shadows were gathering, and a thin film of ice had formed. Unaware that a deep paddy field lay in front of him, he sent his horse plunging into the mire. The horse sank, head and all, and stayed motionless, despite furious flogging with stirrups and whip. Lord Kiso glanced back, worried about Kanehira. As he did so, Ishida Tamehisa, who was hard on his heels, drew his bow to the full and sent an arrow thudding into his face. Mortally wounded, he sagged forward, with the bowl of his helmet against the horse's neck.

Two of Tamehisa's retainers went up and took Lord Kiso's head. Tamehisa impaled it on the tip of his sword, raised it high, and announced in a mighty shout, "Miura no Ishida no Jirō Tamehisa has slain Lord Kiso, the man known throughout Japan!"

Kanehira heard the shout as he fought. "I don't need to protect anybody now. Take a look, easterners! This is how the bravest man in Japan commits suicide!" he said. He put the tip of his sword in his mouth, jumped headlong from his horse, and perished, run through. Thus, it turned out that there was no fighting worth mentioning at Awazu.

9.9. *The Old Horse*

[Earlier, during 1183, the Heike won a battle against forces dispatched by Yoshinaka, another against Yukiie, Yoshinaka's uncle, and others against local opponents, thanks in large part to the prowess of Kiyomori's nephew Noritsune. Then, during the first month of 1184, as the Genji forces fought among themselves, the Heike moved back to the old capital at Fukuhara and established a formidable stronghold nearby at Ichi-no-tani (now in Suma-ku, Kobe). "Flanked by mountains to the north and by the sea to the south, the position at Ichi-no-tani was narrow at the entrance and wide in the interior.

High cliffs rose above it like folding screens. From the base of the mountains on the north to the shallow waters on the south, the defenders had erected a high wall of huge boulders, and had installed branch barricades made by felling great trees. Where the sea deepened, a line of large vessels formed a rampart. At the front of the stronghold, a cloudlike host of armored bowmen from Shikoku and Chinzei stood in rows on archery platforms, each of them reputed to be worth a thousand men. Ten or twenty rows of saddled horses waited below the platforms, and there was a constant din of drums and battle cries. The drawn bows were like half-moons at the warriors' breasts; the glittering swords were like streaks of autumn frost across their hips. The countless red banners on the heights danced in the spring breeze like leaping flames" (Sec. 9.5).

It is now early in the second month of 1184. Noriyori and Yoshitsune, Yoritomo's deputies, have marched westward, Noriyori toward the eastern front of the Taira stronghold, and Yoshitsune toward the rear; and Yoshitsune has just overrun an outlying Heike position at Mikusa, a mountainous area near the junction of Settsu, Tanba, and Harima provinces.]

Munemori sent a message to the Taira lords by Yoshiyuki, the assistant director of the stables of the right. "I have received intelligence that Yoshitsune has already routed the forces at Mikusa and penetrated our lines. The mountain sector is crucial; I want all of you to head for it." But every one of them asked to be excused. Then he dispatched a message to Noritsune, the governor of Noto. "I know we've called on you time and again, but won't you please go?" he asked.

Noritsune's answer was reassuring. "If a man wants to succeed in battle, he can't have anything else on his mind. He'll never win if he's like a hunter or fisherman, always thinking about his own comfort and avoiding inconvenience. I'm perfectly willing to have you send me into danger as often as you like. You can be sure there's one sector, at least, where the enemy will be wiped out." Munemori was delighted. He sent him ten thousand horsemen under the command of Etchū no Zenji Moritoshi.

Noritsune took along his older brother Michimori, the governor of Echizen, and established defensive positions in the hills (that is to say, the terrain below the Hiyodorigoe Road).[10]

Michimori had somebody bring his wife to the camp so that he might bid her a final farewell. Noritsune gave him a tongue-lashing. "They sent me to this front because they thought it was dangerous, and dangerous it certainly is. If the Genji dropped down out of those heights right now, there would be no time to take up arms. Even if a man has a bow in his hand, he won't get anywhere unless he fits an arrow to it; even if he fits the arrow, he won't

10. Hiyodorigoe appears to have been a road from Fukuhara across the Rokkō Mountains to Minō District in Harima, too far north to have served as a point of departure for Yoshitsune's surprise attack (described below). According to some *Heike* texts, the Genji descended from a hill in the vicinity of Tekkaiyama, just above the coast at Ichi-no-tani. See Tomikura, *Heike monogatari zenchūshaku*, 3(1): 145–48.

do any good unless he pulls the bow. If he's as feckless as you, he won't be worth a damn!" Michimori may have felt the justice of the rebuke, for he threw on his armor and sent his wife away.

At dusk on the fifth, Noriyori's Genji army began a slow advance toward Ikuta-no-mori from Koyano.[11] Looking out toward Suzume-no-matsubara, Mikage-no-matsu, and Koyano, the Heike could see places where groups of the enemy had bivouacked and lit beacons. As it grew darker, the fires resembled stars in a clear sky. Not to be outdone, they went through the motions of lighting beacons of their own at Ikuta-no-mori. When dawn approached, the fires in the distance were like the moon rising over the hills. For the first time, they understood the old lines about fireflies in a marsh.[12]

The Genji went about their work in businesslike, deliberate fashion, here pitching camp and resting horses, there pitching camp and feeding horses. The Heike, their nerves on edge, expected an attack at any moment.

At dawn on the sixth, Yoshitsune divided his ten thousand riders into two forces. He sent Toi Sanehira toward the western approach to Ichi-no-tani with seven thousand horsemen, and he himself circled around from the Tanba road at the head of three thousand horsemen, planning to swoop down from the Hiyodorigoe Road onto the rear of the stronghold.

"Everybody knows how dangerous Hiyodorigoe is," the warriors all said. "We're ready to be killed in battle, but we don't want to die in a fall. Isn't there somebody around here who knows these mountains?"

Hirayama Sueshige of Musashi came forward. "I do," he said.

"You were raised in the east," said Yoshitsune. "You can't know anything about mountains in the west that you've never laid eyes on before today."

"I don't think you mean that," Sueshige answered. "Poets know about blossoms at Yoshino and Hatsuse; brave men know what's behind an enemy stronghold." It was an arrogant-sounding speech.

The next person to come forward was Beppu Kiyoshige of Musashi, a youth of eighteen. "My father, Yoshishige, told me, 'When you lose your way in the mountains, whether it's because an enemy has attacked or just during a hunt, simply toss the reins over an old horse's neck and drive him ahead of you. You'll always come out onto a path.' "

"That's excellent advice," Yoshitsune said. "The classic tells us, 'Even when snow covers the plain, an old horse knows the way.' "[13] He put a gold-trimmed saddle and a polished bit on an old whitish roan, tossed the tied

---

11. Ikuta-no-mori (now in Ikuta-ku, Kobe) was the eastern terminus of the Taira stronghold, about 10.5 km from Ichi-no-tani, the western terminus. Koyano, the place where Noriyori had camped, was in the area of the present city of Itami, Hyōgo Prefecture.

12. Anonymous (SKKS 1591): haruru yo no / hoshi ka kawabe no / hotaru ka mo / wa ga sumu kata no / ama no taku hi ka ("Might they be stars in the clear night or fireflies by the riverbank? Or are they fires, kindled by the fisherfolk where I dwell?") The *Heike* author apparently knew the slightly different version recorded in a variant *Shinkokinshū* text, which reads "by the marsh" (*sawabe no*) instead of "by the riverbank" (*kawabe no*).

13. Unidentified.

reins over its neck, and drove it ahead of him into the depths of the unfamiliar mountains.

As was to have been expected so early in the second month, there were places where lingering patches of snow dappled the peaks like blossoms, and others where the warriors heard warblers in the valley and made their way through thick haze. When they climbed, they were among cloud-capped peaks; when they descended, they encountered rugged, forested slopes and towering cliffs. The snow had not melted from the pines; the narrow, mossy track was all but invisible. Snowflakes scattered like plum blossoms in the blustering wind. Darkness settled down over the mountain trail while they whipped their steeds this way and that, and they all dismounted to make camp.

Musashibō Benkei brought an old man to Yoshitsune.

"Who's this?" Yoshitsune asked.

"He goes hunting in these mountains."

"Then you must know the area very well. Tell us the truth."

"Yes, of course I know it."

"I want to get down from here to the Heike stronghold at Ichi-no-tani. Can that be done?"

"Absolutely not! There's no way for a man to get down the gorge; it's three hundred feet long. Or the rock face, either; it's a hundred and fifty feet. It would be out of the question on horseback."

"Do deer go through?" Yoshitsune asked.

"Yes. When the weather turns warm, deer from Harima Province cross into Tanba Province to lie in the deep grass, and when it turns cold, deer go from Tanba Province to Inamino in Harima Province to feed where the snow is shallow."

"Why, it sounds like a regular racetrack! A horse can certainly go where a deer goes. All right, you'll be our guide."

The hunter protested that he was too old.

"You must have a son?" Yoshitsune asked.

"I have." He presented an eighteen-year-old youth called Kumao. They proceeded to put up the boy's hair, named him Washinoo no Saburō Yoshihisa (his father's name being Washinoo no Shōji Takehisa), and sent him to the vanguard to guide them. When Yoshitsune met his end in Ōshū, estranged from Yoritomo after the defeat of the Heike, it was that same Yoshihisa who died at his side.

9.10.   First and Second Attackers

Kumagae Naozane and Hirayama Sueshige stayed with Yoshitsune's rear assault force until around midnight on the sixth. Then Naozane summoned his son, Kojirō Naoie. "Nobody will be able to get out in front when this force rides down the mountain. Let's head for Toi's route, the Harima Road, so we can be the first to attack Ichi-no-tani," he said.

"That's a great idea," Naoie said. "I've been wanting to suggest the same thing. Let's start right away."

"Come to think of it, Hirayama Sueshige is marching with this force. He's a man who doesn't care to fight in a crowd," Naozane said. He told one of his men to check on Sueshige's activities and report back.

Just as he had suspected, Sueshige was already getting ready to leave. "Others can do as they please," he was muttering. "I'm not going to fall one step behind." A subordinate who was feeding his master's horse cuffed the animal. "How much longer are you going to keep eating, you big slob?" he said. "Don't treat him like that," Sueshige said. "You're seeing him for the last time tonight." He rode off.

Naozane's man ran back and blurted out the news. "All right!" Naozane said. He too left at once.

Naozane was wearing a dark blue tunic, a suit of armor with red leather lacing, and a red cape, and he was riding his famous steed Gondakurige [Chestnut Gonda]. Naoie was wearing a tunic decorated with a faint design of water-plantains, and a suit of armor laced with blue-and-white rope-patterned leather, and he was riding a whitish horse named Seirō [White Tower]. Their standard-bearer was wearing an olive-gray tunic and a suit of armor laced with re-dyed cherry-patterned leather, and he was riding a blond chestnut horse. The three proceeded at a walk toward the right, observing on their left the gorge where the others were planning to make their descent, and came out onto the beach at Ichi-no-tani by way of an old path called Tai-no-hata, which had not been used for years.

Because it was still only around midnight, Toi Sanehira had halted with his seven thousand horsemen at Shioya, near Ichi-no-tani. Naozane slipped past him in the dark, following the beach, and rode to the western gate of the Ichi-no-tani stronghold. Not a sound was to be heard in the peaceful enemy camp at that hour, nor was a single Genji warrior following Naozane's party.

Naozane called Naoie over. "There must be plenty of fellows who want the honor of leading the attack," he told him. "We can't leap to the conclusion that we're the only ones. Some others are probably waiting around near here for morning to come. We'd better announce our names." He walked his horse to the barricade of shields and announced their names in a mighty shout. "The first men to attack Ichi-no-tani are Kumagae no Jirō Naozane of Musashi Province and his son Kojirō Naoie!"

The Heike refused to answer. "Just keep quiet," they told one another. "Let them wear out their horses and use up their arrows."

Meanwhile, a warrior came up behind Naozane. "Who's there?" Naozane asked.

"Sueshige. Who wants to know?"

"Naozane."

"Kumagae, is it? How long have you been here?"

"I got here during the night."

"I ought to have been right on your heels, but I was delayed because Narida Gorō tricked me. Narida said he wanted to die wherever I did, so I took him along, but he tried to slow me down after we started. 'Don't be in a hurry to attack first, Hirayama,' he said. 'Nobody will know how well you fought unless you have friends watching behind you. What would be the use of dashing into the middle of a lot of enemies and getting killed?' I thought he had a point, so I went ahead of him to the top of a little rise, turned my horse's head downhill, and waited for some of our men to show up. When Narida came along behind me, I expected him to bring his horse up beside mine and talk about the battle, but he galloped on past with an unfriendly look. 'Damn it!' I thought, 'that fellow's tricked me so he can take the lead.' He was about two hundred feet ahead. I saw that his horse seemed weaker than mine, so I whipped after him. I overtook him and yelled, 'You have a lot of nerve to think you can fool somebody like me!' Then I came on alone to attack the enemy. He must have fallen way back; I'm sure he couldn't keep me in sight."

Naozane, Sueshige, and the others waited, a party of five. When the first light appeared at last, Naozane again walked his horse to the barricade of shields and called out in a mighty shout. (He had already announced his name, but he may have wanted Sueshige to hear.) "Kumagae no Jirō Naozane of Musashi Province and his son Kojirō Naoie, the men who announced their names earlier, are the first to attack Ichi-no-tani! If any Heike samurai thinks he's as good as I am, come on out and face me!"

"Come on! Let's drag those two off their horses! They've been yelling their names all night long." Who were the Heike samurai who came forward with those words? They were Etchū no Jirōbyōe Moritsugi, Kazusa no Gorōbyōe Tadamitsu, Akushichibyōe Kagekiyo, Gotōnai Sadatsune, and other prominent warriors. They opened the gate and galloped out, more than twenty strong.

Sueshige was wearing a tie-dyed tunic with white spots, a suit of armor with flame-red lacing, and a cape with a design of two bars, and he was riding his famous steed Mekasuge [Gray-ringed Eyes]. His standard-bearer was wearing a suit of armor with black leather lacing and a helmet with the neck-guard well down, and he was riding a rust-brown horse.

Sueshige announced his name. "I am Hirayama no Mushadokoro Sueshige, the man from Musashi who led the attacks in the Hōgen and Heiji eras!" He galloped forward, shouting, side by side with the standard-bearer.

Where Naozane galloped, Sueshige followed; where Sueshige galloped, Naozane followed. Neither was willing to be outdone, and they took turns at dashing in, whipping their mounts and attacking until the sparks flew. The hard-pressed Heike samurai must have decided that they were overmatched, for they hurried back inside the stronghold to fight from its shelter.

An arrow hit Naozane's horse in the belly. The horse reared, and Naozane dismounted by swinging his leg over its back. Naoie jumped down and stood beside him, wounded in the bow arm, after he had announced his age as sixteen and had fought until his horse's nose touched the shields of the barricade.

"Are you wounded, Kojirō?" Naozane asked.

"Yes," Naoie said.

"Keep pushing your armor up. Don't let an arrow get through. Keep your neck-guard low. Don't get hit in the face."

Naozane pulled out the arrows stuck in his own armor, tossed them aside, and scowled at the stronghold. "I am Naozane, the man who left Kamakura last winter determined to give his life for Lord Yoritomo and bleach his bones at Ichi-no-tani! Where's Etchū no Jirōbyōe, who brags about what he did at Muroyama and Mizushima? What's happened to Kazusa no Gorō-byōe and Akushichibyōe? Isn't Lord Noritsune there? Fame depends on who you fight; it doesn't come from meeting just anybody who happens along. Come out and face me!" he yelled.

Etchū no Jirōbyōe Moritsugi was wearing his favorite garb, a blue-and-white tunic and a suit of armor laced with red leather. He advanced slowly on a whitish roan horse, staring at Naozane. Naozane and his son did not give an inch. Instead, they raised their swords to their foreheads and advanced at a steady pace, staying side by side to avoid separation. Moritsugi may have thought he was overmatched, for he turned back.

"Isn't that Etchū no Jirōbyōe?" asked Naozane. "What's wrong with me as an adversary? Come on! Let's wrestle!"

"No, thanks," said Moritsugi. He withdrew.

"Coward!" Kagekiyo said. He started to gallop out to grapple with Naozane, but Moritsugi seized his shoulder-guard. "This isn't the only battle Lord Noritsune has to think about. Don't throw away your life here," he said.

Afterward, Naozane got a fresh mount and galloped forward, yelling, followed by Sueshige, who had been letting his horse rest while Naozane and Naoie fought. Not many of the Heike warriors were mounted. The men on the archery platforms aligned their bows and released showers of arrows, but the numbers of the Genji were far fewer, and Naozane and the others escaped harm, lost in the melee. "Ride alongside and grapple with them! Grapple!" came the orders from the platforms. But the horses of the Heike were exhausted from having been overridden, underfed, and made to stand in boats for long periods of time. One collision with Naozane's big, well-nourished beast, or Sueshige's, would have been enough to knock any of them flat, and nobody tried to wrestle with either warrior.

An arrow pierced Sueshige's standard-bearer, a man he valued as he did his life. Sueshige burst through the enemy ranks, took the slayer's head swiftly, and came out again. Naozane also amassed many trophies.

Heike at a disadvantage in battle

Naozane, the first to arrive on the scene, had been kept outside because the gate was closed; Sueshige, the second, had been able to gallop inside because the gate was open. So each claimed to have led the attack.

9.11.   *The Double Charge*

Meanwhile, Narida Gorō arrived.

Toi Sanehira galloped forward at the head of his seven thousand horsemen, and the whole force attacked, yelling, with their colored standards raised.

The fifty thousand Genji horsemen under Noriyori had taken up positions on the main front, at Ikuta-no-mori. Among them, there were two men from Musashi Province named Kawara Tarō Takanao and Kawara Jirō Morinao. Takanao called over his brother, Morinao. "A great landholder wins glory through his vassals' exploits, even though he may not do anything himself, but people like us have to earn their own reputations," he said. "It galls me to wait around like this, without even shooting an arrow, when we have an enemy in front of us. I'm going to sneak inside the stronghold and shoot. I haven't got a chance in a thousand of getting back here, so you'll have to stay; otherwise there won't be anybody to testify later."

Tears ran down Morinao's cheeks. "I can't listen when you talk that way. Do you think a younger brother would prosper if he stayed behind and let an older brother be killed? Let's not die in different places; let's face the end together," he said.

The two told their subordinates to carry word of their last moments to their wives and children. Then they went forward on foot, shod in straw sandals. With their bows as staffs, they clambered over the barricade of branches at Ikuta-no-mori and got inside the stronghold. In the dim starlight, even the color of their armor-lacing was invisible. Takanao announced their names in a mighty shout. "Kawara Tarō Kisaichi no Takanao and Kawara Jirō Morinao of Musashi: the first men from the frontal assault force of the Genji to attack at Ikuta-no-mori!"

None of the Heike warriors felt like fighting. "Nothing is as fearsome as an eastern warrior," they said. "They're just two men in the middle of our huge force. What harm can they do? Let's humor them awhile."

The brothers were first-rate archers, and they let fly a fast and furious barrage of arrows.

"We can't put up with this! Kill them!" somebody shouted.

There were two brothers from the west who were famous archers, Manabe no Shirō and Manabe no Gorō from Bitchū Province. Shirō was at Ichi-no-tani; Gorō was at Ikuta-no-mori. Gorō quickly drew his bow to the full and sent an arrow whizzing off. The shaft drove straight through the breastplate of Takanao's armor to his back. Takanao stood paralyzed, clinging to his bow for support. Morinao rushed up, slung Takanao over his shoulder, and started to climb the barricade. Gorō's second arrow penetrated a gap in the skirt of Morinao's armor, and the brothers fell together. One of Gorō's men went over and decapitated them.

When New Middle Counselor Tomomori saw the heads, he said, "They were brave fellows! Each of them deserved to be called a warrior worth a thousand. I wish they could have been spared."

At that point, the brothers' subordinates shouted, "The Kawara brothers have just become the first men to die in battle against the stronghold!"

"If the Shi League hadn't been negligent, those two wouldn't have been killed," said Kajiwara Kagetoki. "The time has come. Attack!" He and his men shouted a mighty battle cry, which was taken up at once by the rest of the fifty thousand horsemen. Foot soldiers were ordered to clear away the branches, and Kagetoki and his five hundred horsemen charged, shouting.

Kagetoki saw that his second son, Heiji Kagetaka, seemed inclined to get too far ahead. He sent a messenger to say, "The commander-in-chief has announced that there will be no reward for any man who gallops ahead with nobody behind him."

Kagetaka pulled up for a minute. "Tell my father this," he said.

mononofu no	I can no more turn back
toritsutaetaru	than can an arrow in flight,
azusayumi	shot when a warrior
hiite wa hito no	extends the bow of birchwood
kaeru mono ka wa	handed down from his fathers.

Then he galloped on with a shout.

"Don't let Heiji be struck down! Follow, men! Don't let Kagetaka be struck down!" Kagetaka's father, Kagetoki, and his brothers, Genda Kagesue and Saburō Kageie, rode after him.

The five hundred horsemen of the Kajiwara galloped into the great enemy force, pressed it without mercy, and beat a swift retreat, their number reduced to a mere fifty. Kagesue had somehow dropped out of sight.

"What's become of Genda?" Kagetoki asked the retainers.

"He must have penetrated too deep. It looks like he might have been killed," somebody said.

"My sons are the only things I have to live for. Why should I go on if Genda's been killed? I'm going back!" Kagetoki said. He turned around and announced his name in a mighty shout. "I am Kajiwara Heizō Kagetoki, a warrior worth a thousand men! I claim descent from Kamakura no Gongorō Kagemasa, the same who earned everlasting renown by felling an adversary with a return shot, after an arrow had gone through his left eye to the top layer of his neck-guard! If anyone here thinks he's as good as I am, let him kill me and show his commander my head!" He charged, shouting.

"Kajiwara is a warrior famous all over the east," Tomomori said. "Don't let him escape! Don't miss him! Kill him!" The Heike surrounded and attacked Kagetoki with their great numbers.

With no regard for his own fate, Kagetoki galloped through and around the innumerable enemies in search of Kagesue, using sidewise, lengthwise, zigzag, and crosswise maneuvers. Meanwhile, Kagesue had fought until his helmet sagged. Then, having lost his horse to an arrow, he had dismounted and backed against a twenty-foot cliff, where he and two retainers, one on either side, were fighting a desperate defensive battle, with their eyes straight ahead, hemmed in by five adversaries.

Kagetoki caught sight of him. "You haven't been killed!" he shouted. "Here I am! Don't show the enemy your back, Genda—not if it costs you your life!" Together, father and son killed three of the five enemies and wounded two.

"There's a time for a warrior to advance and a time for him to withdraw," Kagetoki said. "Come on, Genda!" He took Kagesue on his horse and retreated.

That's what people mean when they talk about "Kajiwara's double charge."

9.12. *The Assault from the Cliff*

Other eastern warriors advanced after those encounters—the Chichibu, the Ashikaga, the Miura, the Kamakura, and, among the leagues, the Inomata, the Kodama, the Noiyo, the Yokoyama, the Nishitō, the Tsuzukitō, and the Shinotō. The massed armies of the Genji and the Heike mingled in combat, their riders charging in turn and competing to announce their names. Their shouts and yells made the mountains ring; the hoofbeats of their galloping horses reverberated like thunder; the arrows they exchanged fell like rain. Some men retired to the rear, carrying wounded comrades on their shoulders; some sustained light injuries and fought on; some suffered mortal blows and perished. There were those who rode alongside enemies, grappled with them, fell, and died in dagger fights; there were those who seized others, held them down, and cut off their heads; there were those who had their heads cut off. Neither side revealed a weakness for the other to exploit, and the main Genji force seemed unlikely to win without help, valiant though it was.

Now Yoshitsune had circled around to the rear, and had climbed to the Hiyodorigoe Road, behind Ichi-no-tani, toward dawn on the seventh. As he was getting ready for the descent, two stags and a doe ran down to the fortifications of the Heike, probably because they had been frightened by his men. Their appearance caused consternation in the stronghold. "Even the deer that live near here ought to be fleeing way back into the mountains to get away from us," they said. "It's very odd for these three to come down into the middle of a big army like this. The Genji must be going to drop down from those mountains up there."

Takechi no Kiyonori of Iyo Province stepped forward. "Whether they're up there or not, we can't ignore anything that comes from a hostile direction," he said. He shot the two stags and let the doe go.

Etchū no Zenji Moritoshi reprimanded him. "It was foolish to shoot the deer. You could have held off ten enemies with one of those arrows. You wasted precious arrows in order to commit a sin."[14]

Yoshitsune surveyed the distant stronghold. "Let's try sending some horses down," he said. They chased some saddled horses down. Some of the animals broke their legs and fell, but others arrived safely. Three reached the roof of Moritoshi's quarters and stood trembling.

"The horses won't get hurt if the riders pay attention," Yoshitsune said. "All right, take them down! Do as I do!" He galloped forward at the head of thirty horsemen, and all the others followed, down a slope so steep that the edges of the rear riders' stirrups touched the armor and helmets of the men in front. After slipping and sliding at great speed for seven hundred feet through a mixture of sand and pebbles, they pulled up on a ledge above a huge mossy crag, a vertical drop of a hundred and forty or fifty feet. They sat aghast, ready to give up.

Sawara no Jūrō Yoshitsura came forward. "In Miura, we gallop over places like that all day long, even if we're only chasing birds. This is a Miura racetrack!" he said. He dashed ahead, and all the others followed.

"Ei! Ei!" They encouraged the horses in muffled voices, their eyes closed for the terrifying descent. What they were attempting seemed beyond mortal capacity, something demons might do.

Even before the last man reached the bottom, the party shouted a tremendous battle cry. There were only three thousand of them, but the echoes made them sound like a hundred thousand.

Murakami no Yasukuni's men put the torch to all the sleeping quarters and camps of the Heike. As luck would have it, a gale was blowing. Clouds of black smoke billowed up, and great numbers of Heike warriors panicked and galloped into the sea, desperate to save themselves.

There were many vessels ready to receive them at the water's edge, but what good could come of it when four or five hundred men in armor—or even a thousand—tried to crowd into a single ship? Three big ships sank before the onlookers' eyes when they were no more than three hundred and fifty yards from the shore. After that, orders were issued to let men of quality come on board, but to fend off those of lesser worth with swords and spears. Even though they knew what to expect, the ordinary soldiers clung to the vessels from which they were barred. Some lost whole arms and others forearms, and they ended as rows of corpses, reddening the water's edge at Ichi-no-tani.

Noto Governor Noritsune was a man who had fought time and again without suffering a defeat, but now, for some reason, he fled westward on his charger, Usuguro [Dusky Black]. He got on board a ship at Akashi Shore in Harima Province and made the crossing to Yashima in Sanuki Province.

14. Buddhist doctrine proscribes the taking of life.

9.13. *The Death of Etchū no Zenji*

In reckless disregard of their lives, the warriors from Musashi and Sagami took the offensive on both the main front and the seaward side.[15] The Kodama League sent a messenger from the mountainside to Tomomori, who was fighting with his face toward the east. "The men of the Kodama League tell you this because you once governed Musashi Province. Look behind you!" Tomomori looked, and he and the others saw a cloud of black smoke bearing down on them. Without even waiting to exclaim about the defeat on the west, they all took to their heels in desperate haste.

Etchū no Zenji Moritoshi, the samurai commander on the cliffward side, halted his mount and sat motionless, possibly because he thought it was too late to try to escape. Inomata no Koheiroku Noritsuna marked him as a worthy adversary, galloped forward with flailing whip and flapping stirrups, and rode alongside him. Then he gripped him as hard as he could and crashed to the ground with him. Noritsuna was a man famous in the eight eastern provinces for his great strength, a warrior who was reputed to have torn apart a deer's double-branched antlers with ease. Moritoshi let other people think he was merely as strong as twenty or thirty ordinary fellows, but he could actually haul up or send down a ship that needed a crew of sixty or seventy. Thus, Moritoshi succeeded in gripping Noritsuna and holding him fast. Lying underneath, Noritsuna tried to draw his dagger but could not grasp the hilt with his splayed fingers, tried to speak but was pinned too tight to get out a word. But although his head was about to be cut off, and despite his physical inferiority, he kept his valiant spirit. After collecting his breath for a few seconds, he spoke in an offhand manner.

"Did you hear me announce my name? When a man kills an enemy, it doesn't mean much unless he waits until he's identified himself and made the other fellow do the same. What are you going to gain by taking an anonymous head?" he said.

Moritoshi may have thought that he had a point. "I am Etchū no Zenji Moritoshi, born a Taira, but now become a samurai because of my inadequacies. Who are you? Announce your name; I'd like to hear it," he said.

"I am Inomata no Koheiroku Noritsuna of Musashi Province," Noritsuna said. He continued, "If we look at the way things stand now, it seems that the Genji have the upper hand—that you on the Heike side are going to lose out. Unless your masters prosper, you aren't going to get any rewards by taking heads to show to them. How about stretching a point and letting me go? I'll use my exploits to save the lives of any number of Heike men—dozens, if you like."[16]

Moritoshi was outraged. "Unworthy or not, I'm still a Taira. I have no

15. That is, both at Ikuta-no-mori and at Ichi-no-tani.
16. A warrior with documented exploits could expect appropriate rewards. Noritsuna offers to ask for the lives of captured Heike in lieu of material rewards.

intention of looking to the Genji for help, and no intention whatsoever of helping one of them. Your proposal is dishonorable!" He got ready to cut off Noritsuna's head.

"You're disgracing yourself! How can you take the head of a man who's already surrendered?" Noritsuna said.

"All right, then, I'll spare you," Moritoshi said. He pulled Noritsuna upright, and the two sat down to rest on a footpath that ran between a sun-baked field and a deep, muddy rice paddy.

Presently, a warrior in a suit of armor with black leather lacing came galloping toward them on a white horse. Moritoshi eyed him with suspicion. "Don't worry," Noritsuna said. "That's Hitomi no Shirō, a friend of mine. He must have seen me." But he thought to himself, "If I begin wrestling with this fellow after Shirō gets close, Shirō will be bound to attack him, too." He bided his time.

Meanwhile, the rider advanced until he was only thirty-five feet away. At first, Moritoshi tried to keep an eye on both men, but the one on horseback engaged his full attention as he gradually approached, and he lost track of Noritsuna. Noritsuna seized his opportunity. He sprang to his feet with a yell, dealt a powerful blow to Moritoshi's breastplate with both hands, and toppled him backwards into the paddy. As Moritoshi tried to get up, Noritsuna clamped him between his legs, snatched the dagger from Moritoshi's waist, and lifted his skirt. Then he plunged the weapon into his flesh three times, hilt, fist, and all, and took his head.

In the meantime, Hitomi no Shirō had come up. "It's cases like this that bring on disputes," Noritsuna thought. He stuck the head on the tip of his sword, held it high, and announced his name in a mighty shout. "Inomata no Koheiroku Noritsuna has slain Etchū no Zenji Moritoshi, the Heike samurai known in these days as a demon god!" His name led that day's list of exploits.

9.15. *The Capture of Shigehira*

Middle Captain Shigehira, the deputy commander at Ikuta-no-mori, had been deserted by all of his men but one. That day, he was wearing a dark blue tunic, embroidered with bright yellow plovers, and a suit of armor with purple-shaded lacing, and he was riding a famous charger named Dōji Kage [Child Deerskin]. His foster-brother, Morinaga, was wearing a tie-dyed tunic with white spots and a suit of armor with flame-red lacing, and he was riding Shigehira's prized horse Yomenashi Tsukige [Night-eyeless White].[17]

Recognizing Shigehira as a commander-in-chief, Kajiwara Genda Kagesue and Shō no Shirō Takaie pursued him with flailing whips and flapping

17. A horse with a white node (*yome*, "night-eye") behind its front knee was said to be able to run well at night, the reason being (according to one theory) that the node served as an extra eye. Shigehira's horse, which was white all over, could presumably do even better.

stirrups. Too hard-pressed to escape to one of the many rescue vessels at the water's edge, Shigehira crossed the Minato and Karumo rivers, galloped between Hasu Pond on the right and Koma Woods on the left, passed Ita-yado and Suma, and fled westward. His splendid mount forged farther and farther ahead, until there seemed little chance that the battle-weary Genji horses could overtake him. But Kagesue stood in his stirrups, drew his bow to the full, and sent off an arrow, hoping for a lucky hit. The arrow sank shaft-deep into Dōji Kage's rump. When the horse faltered, Morinaga raised his whip and fled, possibly because he feared that Shigehira would take his horse.

"What are you doing, Morinaga? This isn't the way you always swore to act! Where will you go after you desert me?" Shigehira asked. Morinaga pretended not to hear. He got rid of his red armor-badge and rode away as fast as he could.

The enemy was approaching and the horse was weakening. Shigehira rode into the sea, but the water was shoaling, too shallow to drown in. He dismounted, slashed his belt, and unfastened his shoulder-cord. Then he took off his armor and helmet and got ready to cut open his belly.

Takaie came up ahead of Kagesue, galloping with flailing whip and flapping stirrups. He jumped down. "It would be a mistake to kill yourself," he said. "I'll attend you wherever you go." He mounted Shigehira on his own horse, tied him to the pommel, and escorted him back, riding a remount.

Thanks to his splendid, long-winded steed, Morinaga got away without any trouble. Later, he sought refuge with a Kumano monk, the Onaka Dharma Bridge. After the monk's death, he went to the capital with the widow, a nun who was prosecuting a lawsuit, and everybody recognized him as Shigehira's foster-brother. "He's a shameless rascal!" people said. "Shigehira thought the world of him, but he refused to face death at his master's side. Instead, the wretch turns up with a nun, of all things!" We are told that the criticism seems to have embarrassed even so dishonorable a man, and that Morinaga hid his face with a fan.

9.16. *The Death of Atsumori*

After the defeat of the Heike, Kumagae no Naozane walked his horse toward the beach. "The Taira nobles will be fleeing to the shore to get on board the rescue vessels," he thought. "I wish I could wrestle with one of their high-ranking commanders-in-chief!" Just then, he saw a lone rider splash into the sea, bound for a vessel offshore. The enemy was wearing a silk tunic embroidered with cranes, a suit of armor with shaded green lacing, and a horned helmet. At his waist, there was a sword with gilt bronze fittings; on his back, he carried a quiver containing arrows fledged with black-banded white eagle feathers. He held a rattan-wrapped bow and rode a white-dappled reddish horse, with a saddle trimmed in gold. When the horse had swum out a hundred and fifty or two hundred feet, Naozane beckoned with his fan.

"I see that you're a commander-in-chief! It's dishonorable to show your back to an enemy! Come on back!" he shouted.

The warrior came back. As he left the water, Naozane rode up beside him, gripped him as hard as he could, and crashed with him to the ground. Holding him motionless, he pushed aside his helmet, intending to cut off his head, and saw that he was only sixteen or seventeen years old, with a lightly powdered face and blackened teeth [18]—a boy just the age of Naozane's own son Naoie, and so handsome that he could find no place to strike.

"Who are you? Announce your name. I'll spare you," Naozane said.

"Who are you?" the youth asked.

"Nobody of any special importance: Kumagae no Jirō Naozane of Musashi Province."

"Then I don't need to give you my name. I'm the kind of opponent you want. Ask about me after you take my head. Somebody will recognize me, even if I don't tell you."

"He's bound to be a commander-in-chief," Naozane thought. "Killing this one person won't change defeat into victory, and sparing him won't change victory into defeat. When I think of how I grieved when Naoie got just a little wound, it's easy to imagine how this young lord's father would feel if he heard that he'd been killed. I have a notion to let him go." Casting a swift glance to the rear, he discovered Sanehira and Kagetoki coming along with fifty riders.

"I'd like to spare you," he said, restraining tears, "but there are Genji warriors everywhere. You can't possibly escape. It will be better if I'm the one to kill you, because I'll offer prayers for you."

"Just take my head; don't waste time," the boy said.

Overwhelmed by compassion, Naozane could find no place to strike. His senses reeled, his brain seemed paralyzed, and he was scarcely conscious of his surroundings. But matters could not go on like that forever. In tears, he took the head.

"No life is as miserable as a warrior's. It's only because I was born into a military house that I've had this terrible experience. What a cruel thing I've done!" He pressed his sleeve to his face and wept.

But matters could not go on like that forever. He started to remove the youth's tunic, preparatory to wrapping the head in it, and found a flute in a brocade bag tucked in at the waist. "Poor fellow! He must have been one of the people I heard playing inside the stronghold just before dawn. There are tens of thousands of riders in our eastern armies, but I'd be willing to bet not one of them carried a flute to the battlefield. Those court nobles are men of refinement," he thought.

---

18. Court nobles began to blacken their teeth early in the 12th century.

When Naozane's trophies were presented to Yoshitsune for inspection, they brought tears to everyone's eyes. It was learned later that the slain youth was Atsumori, aged seventeen, a son of Tsunemori, the head of the Palace Repairs Office.

After that, Naozane thought increasingly of becoming a monk.

The flute in question is supposed to have been a present from Retired Emperor Toba to Atsumori's grandfather Tadamori, who was an excellent musician. I believe I have heard that Tsunemori inherited it, and that he turned it over to Atsumori because the boy played so well. Saeda [Little Branch] was its name. It is deeply moving that music, a profane entertainment, should have led a warrior to a life of religion.

9.18. The Flight

Shigemori's youngest son, Moromori, the governor of Bitchū, got into a small boat with six companions. As they were starting off, one of Tomomori's samurai came galloping up, a warrior named Seiemon Kinnaga. "Isn't that Lord Moromori's boat?" he asked. "Let me go with you."

They went back to the beach. But what good could come of it when a huge man dressed in full armor tried to jump from a horse into a boat? The tiny vessel veered and capsized, and one of Hatakeyama's retainers, Honda no Jirō, galloped up with thirteen or fourteen men, raked Moromori from the water where he was struggling, and cut off his head. Moromori was fourteen.

Michimori, the governor of Echizen, had been one of the commanders-in-chief in the hills. That day, he was wearing a tunic of red brocade and a suit of armor laced with thick Chinese damask, and he was riding a blond chestnut horse with a saddle trimmed in silver. Wounded in the face and separated from his brother, Noritsune, he was fleeing eastward, looking for a quiet spot where he could commit suicide, when he was surrounded and killed by a party of seven riders led by Sasaki no Naritsuna of Ōmi Province and Tamanoi no Sukekage of Musashi Province. One of his retainers had stayed with him, but even he fled at the last.

The fighting at the eastern and western entrances continued for an hour, claiming the lives of countless Genji and Heike. Piles of dead horses and dead men rose like clustered hills in front of the archery platforms and under the branch barricades; the green bamboo-grass in the meadows at Ichi-no-tani turned pale red. Quite aside from those who were felled by arrows and swords at Ichi-no-tani and Ikuta-no-mori, or in the mountains or on the beaches, more than two thousand heads of the Heike were taken by the Genji to be exposed. Among the Taira dead were Michimori; his younger brother Narimori; Tadanori; Tomoakira; Moromori; Kiyosada; Kiyofusa; Tsunemori's heir, Tsunemasa; and Tsunemasa's younger brothers, Tsunetoshi and Atsumori.

Bowed down by grief, the defeated Heike embarked in boats and set out, taking the emperor with them. Some of their vessels headed toward Kii Province, driven by the tides and winds; some rowed to the offing beyond Ashiya, there to toss on the waves. Others voyaged aimlessly along the coast from Suma toward Akashi, while those on board used oars for pillows, bedewed their lonely beds with tears, and gazed at the misty spring moon with grieving eyes. Others passed through the Awaji Straits and floated off Eshima Shore, their passengers comparing themselves to plovers crying faintly over the waves by night in search of lost comrades. Others hesitated in the offing beyond Ichi-no-tani, as though unable to decide on a destination.

Thus, drawn by the tides and blown by the winds, the fugitives drifted toward many different shores and islands, each group ignorant of the fate of the others. They had held high hopes for the future when they were masters of fourteen provinces and a hundred thousand horsemen, with the capital itself only a day's journey away, but now Ichi-no-tani had fallen, and every heart despaired.

Heike warriors lose
morale after the
fall of Ichi-no-tani

Chapter 10

Time: second and third months of 1184
Principal subjects: aftermath of the battle of Ichi-no-tani; Koremori's fate
Principal characters:

Go-Shirakawa, Retired Emperor. Head of the imperial clan
Kagetoki (Kajiwara). Trusted lieutenant of Yoritomo
Koremori (Taira). Son and heir of Shigemori
Munemori (Taira). Son of Kiyomori; head of the Taira clan
Noriyori (Minamoto). One of the two leaders of the eastern forces dispatched by his half-brother Yoritomo against the Taira
Nun of second rank. Widow of Kiyomori
Sanehira (Toi). A subordinate commander in the eastern forces
Shigehira (Taira). Son of Kiyomori
Shigemori (Taira). Deceased son and heir of Kiyomori; father of Koremori
Yoritomo (Minamoto). Heir to the chieftainship of the Minamoto clan; leader of anti-Taira forces
Yoshitsune (Minamoto). One of the two leaders of the eastern forces dispatched by his half-brother Yoritomo against the Taira

10.1. The Parade of Heads

On the twelfth of the second month in the third year of Juei [1184], the heads of the Taira men who had been slain on the seventh at Ichi-no-tani, in Settsu Province, made their entry into the capital. All the people with personal ties to the clan lamented and grieved, afraid that terrible things were in store for them. In her hideaway at the Daikakuji, Middle Captain Koremori's wife felt especially uneasy. She had heard a rumor that only a few Heike had escaped death at Ichi-no-tani, and that a single senior noble, a middle captain of third rank, would be coming to the capital as a prisoner. Convinced that the prisoner must be Koremori, she lay prostrate with a robe pulled over her head. A certain lady came and said, "The prisoner isn't your husband; it's Shigehira, the senior middle captain," but she was as anxious as ever, for then she felt that Koremori's head must be among the ones the Genji had brought with them.

On the thirteenth, a police lieutenant named Nakayori went to the river-bed at Rokujō to receive the heads. Noriyori and Yoshitsune recommended to Retired Emperor Go-Shirakawa that the heads be taken north along Higashi-no-tōin Avenue and hung in trees outside the prison. The retired emperor was uncertain about how to proceed, so he consulted the chancellor, the ministers of the left and right, the palace minister, and a major counselor. Of those five senior nobles, every one said the same thing: "Never has there been a precedent for parading the heads of senior nobles along the avenues, not since ancient days. We note particularly that the dead are men who served the former emperor for a long time as his maternal relatives. You should absolutely refuse to grant this request from Noriyori and Yoshitsune." It seemed then that there would be no parade. But Noriyori and Yoshitsune made further representations. "When we think of Hōgen in the past, those men were enemies of our grandfather Tameyoshi; when we consider Heiji in bygone days, those men were foes of our father Yoshitomo," they said. "We risked our lives to destroy the court's enemies—to calm His Majesty's wrath and redeem the honor of our forefathers. If we can't parade the heads of the Taira through the avenues now, what incentive will we have to subdue traitors in the future?"

The retired emperor had no choice but to yield to their pressure, and the heads were paraded. Huge throngs viewed the spectacle. In the past, many had experienced fear and awe when the Taira lords presented themselves at court, the sleeves of their formal robes aligned; now, none but felt pity and grief as their heads were exhibited in the public streets.

Saitōgo and Saitōroku, the attendants of Koremori's young son, Rokudai, went to watch the parade in plebeian disguise, worried about their master's fate. They recognized the heads of other men but saw nothing of Koremori's. Still, they could not help shedding copious tears at the sights they witnessed, and they hurried away toward the Daikakuji to avoid drawing attention to themselves.

"Tell me! Tell me!" Koremori's wife said.

"Of all Shigemori's sons, Moromori's was the only head we saw. Among the others, there were So-and-so and Thus-and-so," they answered.

"I can't help mourning every one of them as my own loss," she said, choked with tears.

Presently, Saitōgo restrained his tears and spoke again. "I've been hiding since last year; there aren't many people who recognize me. I probably should have stayed longer, but I met a man who knew the whole story. 'During the recent fighting,' he told me, 'Shigemori's sons were defending Mount Mikusa, which is supposed to mark the boundary between the provinces of Harima and Tanba. Yoshitsune defeated their force, and Sukemori, Arimori, and Tadafusa went by boat from Takasago in Harima to Yashima in Sanuki. I don't know how Moromori got separated from the rest, but he was the only one of the brothers who died at Ichi-no-tani.' 'What about

Koremori?' I asked. 'He apparently went to Yashima before the battle because he was quite ill; he didn't take part in the fighting,' he said. He seemed
to know all about it."

"It must have been worry about us that caused Koremori's illness," the
lady said. "Whenever we have a windy day, I'm frightened to death that he
may be on a boat; whenever they fight a battle, I'm frantic for fear he's just
been killed. But now there's really something to be alarmed about. He's
desperately ill, without anyone to take proper care of him. If only we
knew more!"

"Why didn't you ask the man what disease he has?" the little boy and
little girl asked pitifully.

Knowing what his family must be going through, Koremori decided to
send a samurai to the capital. "They'll be worried about me in the city," he
thought. "My head wasn't there with the others, but they'll still believe I
was drowned or shot; they won't dream I've survived. I have to get word to
them that this dewlike life of mine has been prolonged." He wrote three
letters. In the first, addressed to his wife, he said, "I can imagine how
wretched it must be for you, now that the capital is overrun with our enemies. There must be no place for you to turn, especially with the children
to take care of. I wish I could bring you here to share my fate, but it would
be too cruel to subject you to this life, even though I can bear its hardships
myself." The letter ran on at length in the same vein. At the end, there was
a poem:

izuku to mo	You must look on them
shiranu ōse no	as a memento from me—
moshiogusa	these traces of the brush
kakioku ato o	from one like sea plants drifting
katami to mo mi yo	to meet they know not where or when.

To the children, he sent identical messages: "What are you doing to keep
from being bored? I'll bring you here very soon to be with me."

The messenger took the letters to the capital and delivered them to the
lady, who received them with renewed lamentations and grief. After a stay
of four or five days, he asked permission to leave, and she wrote a tearful
reply. The children, their brushes inked, asked their mother, "What shall we
say in our answers to Father?" "Just say whatever you think of," she answered. Both of them wrote the same thing: "Why haven't you sent for us
yet? We miss you terribly. Send someone right away."

Back at Yashima, the messenger reported to his master with the letters.
Koremori seemed overwhelmed when he saw the children's notes. "I don't
have the heart to take religious vows now," he said, weeping. "The bonds
of affection chaining me to this world are too strong. I don't even feel like
praying for rebirth in the pure land. My only desire is to cross the mountains
to the capital, meet my dear ones one more time, and take my own life."

10.6.   The Journey Down the Eastern Sea Road

Because Yoritomo had made a great point of it, it was decided that Middle Captain Shigehira would have to go to Kamakura. First, they moved him from the custody of Toi Sanehira to Yoshitsune's quarters, and then, on the tenth of the third month, he set out toward Kamakura in Kajiwara Kagetoki's train. He had already tasted the bitterness of returning to the capital from the west as a prisoner, and now, all too soon, he was to suffer the even worse experience of traveling east of Ōsaka Barrier. It is sad to imagine how he must have felt.[1]

At the Shinomiya riverbed, he was moved by memories of the old straw-thatched hut where Emperor Daigo's fourth son, Semimaru, had played the lute, cleansing his mind while the wind howled through [Ōsaka] Barrier, and which Hakuga of third rank had frequented for three years, on windy days and calm, standing and listening, until Semimaru taught him the three compositions. They crossed the barrier, clattered over the long bridge at Seta, and passed Noji village where skylarks soar. Spring had come to the waves on the beach at Shiga; haze veiled Mirror Mountain. The heights of Hira towered to the north; the peak of Ibuki loomed close. Nobody could have intended to detain travelers at the Fuwa Barrier post with its shingled eaves, but there was elegance in the very ruins.[2]

Beset by dismal forebodings, Shigehira passed Narumigata as the tide ebbed; wringing tears from his sleeves, he reached the eight bridges in Mikawa Province, where, so the story goes, a man of the Ariwara clan gazed in pensive thought, reciting, "familiar to me as skirts of a well-worn robe"; and his own sad thoughts seemed as innumerable as the branching streams.[3] When he crossed the bridge at Hamana, a cold wind whistled in the pine trees and sent waves crashing ashore in the inlet. He arrived at the Ikeda post station at twilight, the time of day when the sorrows of travel weigh

1. What follows is a famous example of the narrative pattern called "journey eastward" (*azuma kudari*) or "journey along the Eastern Sea Road" (*tōkai kudari*). Such narratives enumerate the post stations and natural landmarks along the way, touching on scenic, historical, and literary associations, in order to show their moving effect on a traveler who is usually gloomy, apprehensive, and homesick.

2. Fuwa ("Enduring") Barrier, at what is now Sekigahara, Fuwa District, Gifu Prefecture, had been abandoned in 789. Fujiwara no Yoshitsune (SKKS 1601): hito sumanu / fuwa no sekiya no / itabisashi / arenishi nochi wa / tada aki no kaze ("Crude eaves made of wood at Enduring Barrier, where no guard remains: none here but the autumn wind, now that all lies in ruins").

3. Narumigata is an inlet of the sea in the vicinity of the present city of Nagoya. It was famous for its strong tides. The eight bridges (*yatsuhashi*, now in the city of Kariya in Aichi Prefecture), were established as an *utamakura* ("poem pillow," allusive place-name) by a poem attributed to a court noble traveling along the Eastern Sea Road in self-imposed exile. Ariwara no Narihira (KKS 410): karakoromo / kitsutsu narenishi / tsuma shi areba / harubaru kinuru / tabi o shi zo omou ("I have a dear wife, familiar to me as skirts of a well-worn robe, and thus these distant travels darken my heart with sorrow").

heaviest, even on the hearts of people whose circumstances bear no resemblance to his.

He lodged that night with Jijū, the daughter of the brothel-keeper Yuya. When she met him, she said, "How strange that you should have come to a place like this today! I could never have hoped to greet you in the past, not even through an intermediary." She offered a poem:

tabi no sora	How painful must be
hanyū no koya no	your longing for the city,
ibusesa ni	here in the squalor
furusato ika ni	of an earthen-floored hovel,
koishikaruran	lodging under travel skies.

He replied:

furusato mo	I cannot hope
koishiku mo nashi	to make the royal city
tabi no sora	my last peaceful home,
miyako mo tsui no	and thus I feel no longing
sumika naraneba	for the place where once I lived.

"That was a poem of some refinement. Who is this person who's composed it?" Shigehira asked.

"Hasn't Your Lordship heard?" Kagetoki said respectfully. "She was summoned and made a favorite by Lord Munemori, the minister of state who is now at Yashima, when he governed this province. She begged to be granted leave because her aged mother was still here at Ikeda, but Lord Munemori wouldn't let her go. She finally won his permission with this poem, which she composed early in the third month:

ika ni sen	What am I to do?
miyako no haru mo	Springtime in the capital
oshikeredo	is precious to me,
nareshi azuma no	yet I fear the scattering
hana ya chiruran	of cherished eastern blossoms.

"She's the best poet on the Eastern Sea Road."

Many days had slipped by since their departure from the capital. Spring was already drawing to a close, the third month more than half spent. The blossoms on distant hillsides might have been mistaken for lingering snow; the beaches and islands were swathed in haze. Shigehira pondered his past and his future, shedding endless tears as he wondered what karma from a previous existence had brought him to his present pass. His mother, the nun of second rank, had always lamented his lack of offspring, and his unhappy wife, Lady Dainagon, had offered fruitless petitions to all the gods and buddhas. Now he found some small comfort in his childless state. How could he have borne it if it had been otherwise?

When he reached Saya-no-nakayama Pass, it was saddening to realize that there was scant prospect of his going that way again, and he wept until his sleeves were drenched.[4] In dismal spirits, he traversed the ivied path at Mount Utsu and passed Tegoshi.[5] Snowy peaks came into view far to the north; and upon making inquiry, he learned that they were the Shirane Mountains in Kai Province. He expressed his feelings in verse, restraining tears:

oshikaranu	I do not desire
inochi naredomo	to cling to this wretched life,
kyō made zo	yet I have survived,
tsurenaki kai no	survived until today, to see
shirane o mo mitsu	the Shirane Mountains of Kai.

When they emerged from Kiyomi Barrier onto the plain below Mount Fuji, a wind moaned in the pines where green heights rose to the north, and waves sighed on the shore where blue seas stretched vast and wide to the south. They crossed the Ashigara Mountains, where the god had first sung:

koi seba	If you had missed me,
yasenubeshi	you would be thin.
koi sezu mo	It is plain to see
arikeri	you did not miss me.[6]

Past the Koyurugi woods they journeyed, past the Mariko River, the beaches at Koiso and Ōiso, Yatsumato, Togami-ga-hara, and Mikoshi-ga-saki. They had not hurried, but many days had elapsed, and at last they came to Kamakura.

10.7. Senjū-no-mae

Yoritomo received Shigehira promptly. "The destruction of the Heike entered my planning because I wanted to calm His Majesty's wrath and re-

4. Saya[Sayo]-no-nakayama was a steep, dangerous mountain pass in what is now Kakegawa City, Shizuoka Prefecture. It is associated especially with a poem by the monk Saigyō, written when he crossed it for the second time at the age of 68 (SKKS 987): toshi takete / mata koyubeshi to / omoika ya / inochi narikeri / saya no nakayama ("Never had I dreamed of crossing the Pass of Saya a second time in ripe old age—this is the span of life I have been vouchsafed!").

5. Tegoshi was a post station in what is now the city of Shizuoka. Mount Utsu, on the high border between Shida and Abe districts in Shizuoka Prefecture (Suruga Province), is associated in classical literature with a poem ascribed to the author of the "eight bridges" poem above (IM, sec. 9): suruga naru / utsu no yamabe no / utsutsu ni mo / yume ni mo hito ni / awanu narikeri ("Beside Mount Utsu in Suruga Province, I can see you neither when I am awake nor even in my dreams"). The poem, which puns on the name Utsu and a verb meaning "be awake," is prefaced by this explanation: "At Mount Utsu, the road ahead was dark, narrow, and overgrown with ivy and maples. They were eyeing it with foreboding when a wandering ascetic came into view. 'What are you doing on a road like this?' he asked. Recognizing him as someone he had known in the old days, the man gave him a message for a woman in the capital."

6. Back home after a three-year sojourn in China, the god of the local shrine was so annoyed to find his wife looking plump and pretty that he divorced her.

deem my father's honor, but it never occurred to me that the two of us might meet here. Judging from the way things are going, I can probably expect to see Munemori, too," he said. "Now tell me, did you raze Nara because Kiyomori ordered you to, or was it a spur-of-the-moment decision on your own part? It was an incredibly wicked thing to do."

"It was not my father's idea to burn Nara—not mine, either. It happened by accident, when I went to restore order among the monks. There was nothing I could do to prevent it," Shigehira said. He continued, "As I need hardly say, there was a decline in the fortunes of the Genji not so long ago—a change from the old days, when Minamoto and Taira protected the throne as equals. After Hōgen and Heiji, my clan subdued enemies of the court on more than one occasion, and our rewards were beyond our deserts. We became maternal relatives of an emperor; more than sixty of us won preferment. Words can't describe the prosperity that was ours for more than twenty years.

"Now our luck has turned, and I've come down here as a prisoner. They say that when a man crushes a ruler's enemies, he and his posterity enjoy imperial favor until the seventh generation, but it's a monstrous lie. My father risked his life for the emperor time after time. Was it right for our happiness to end with his generation? Was it right for his descendants to come to this? Once our luck ran out and we left the capital, I resigned myself to drowning in the western waves or leaving my bones to bleach in the wilderness, but the thought of coming here never entered my head. What can I do but lament the evil deed in a former life that gave rise to this karma? The classic says, 'Tang of Yin was captured at Xiatai; King Wen was captured at Youli.'[7] If such things happened even in ancient times, what else can we expect in the latter days of the Law? It's common enough for a warrior to fall into enemy hands and die; there's no real disgrace to it. All I ask is that you cut off my head with as little delay as possible." He fell silent.

"There speaks a true captain of men!" said Kajiwara Kagetoki. He wept, and the men seated in rows all drenched their sleeves.

"I don't regard the Heike as my personal enemies, not at all," Yoritomo said. "I'm just obeying the retired emperor's orders."

In the expectation that the monks at Nara would ask for the enemy who had burned their city, Shigehira was turned over to the custody of Kano no Suke Munemochi, a man who lived in Izu Province. It was sad to realize that the middle captain was in much the same situation as the sinners from this world who must pass to a different one of the ten kings every seventh day in the land of the dead.

Munemochi was a kindhearted man. Instead of abusing his prisoner, he paid him numerous attentions. Then he took him to bathe in a specially

7. From *Shi ji* (Records of the Grand Historian). The captors of those sage rulers were later overthrown.

prepared bathroom. His purpose, Shigehira thought, was probably to cleanse his body of the sweat of travel before killing him. But someone pushed open the door and entered—a white-skinned, graceful, pretty lady-in-waiting about twenty years old, dressed in a figured bath apron over a tie-dyed singlet. Soon afterward, a basin containing combs was brought in by an attendant in a blue-and-white singlet—a girl fourteen or fifteen years old, with hair hanging to the hem of her jacket. The lady saw to Shigehira's needs while he took a leisurely bath and washed his hair. After he had finished, she excused herself. "His Lordship was afraid you might consider him a boor if he sent a man," she said in parting. "He sent me because he thought you would find a woman more agreeable. 'If there's anything he wants, find out what it is and tell me,' he said."

"I'm not in a position to ask favors. My only desire is to become a monk," Shigehira said.

When the lady went back to report, Yoritomo said, "That's out of the question. It would be different if he were my enemy, but he's an enemy of the court who's been entrusted to my care. I can't consider anything like that."

"That was an elegant lady who came here just now. What's her name?" Shigehira asked the warriors who were guarding him.

"She's the daughter of the brothel-keeper at Tegoshi. His Lordship took her into his service two or three years ago because he liked the refinement of her appearance and manner. Her name is Senju-no-mae," they told him.

That evening, during a dreary drizzle, the same lady returned, accompanied by servants with a lute and a zither. Munemochi made a presentation of wine, and also came in person to pay his respects, bringing with him a dozen or so of his kinsmen and retainers.

Senju-no-mae served the wine. Shigehira took a little with a listless air. "You may have heard this before," Munemochi said, "but His Lordship told me, 'See that you do everything you can to make things pleasant. Don't blame me for what happens if you're not careful.' I live in Izu Province, so Kamakura isn't my home, but I'll do everything I can think of to be of service to you." To Senju-no-mae, he said, "Sing something before you offer him the wine."

Setting the wine aside, Senju-no-mae chanted a *rōei* twice:

> The delicate gauze of her robe seems heavy;
> She resents the weaver's heartlessness.[8]

"The Kitano god has vowed that if anyone chants that *rōei*, he'll fly to protect him three times in a single day," Shigehira said. "But he's washed his hands of me in this life; there's no point in my joining in. I'd accompany you if the song were one that might lessen my burden of sin."

8. From a poem about a dancing girl, composed in Chinese by Sugawara no Michizane, who was worshipped at the Kitano Shrine as a patron of literature after his death in exile.

At once, Senju-no-mae began to sing the *rōei,* "He leads to the pure land even those guilty of the ten evils."[9] She continued with an *imayō:*

gokuraku negawan	All those who desire rebirth
hito wa mina	in paradise
mida no myōgō	must intone the sacred name
tonaubeshi	of Amida Buddha.

Finally, after she had repeated the words four or five times, Shigehira tipped the wine bowl and drank. Senju took the bowl, offered it to Mune-mochi, and played a pleasant melody on the lute while he drank.

"That tune is usually called 'The Song of the Five Constant Virtues,' but I'll have to think of it as 'Happy Rebirth.' I'd better hurry up and play the 'Ōjō' finale," Shigehira joked. He took the lute, tuned it, and played the last movement of "Ōjō."[10]

As the night wore on, Shigehira found that his mind was perfectly at ease. "It's a pleasant surprise to discover such refinement in the east. Please sing another song—anything's all right," he said. Senju-no-mae chanted a *shirabyōshi* in a truly accomplished manner: "A bond from another world unites all those who merely seek shelter under the same tree, who merely dip water from the same stream."[11] Then Shigehira sang a *rōei,* "The lamplight is dim, tears stream down Lady Yu's face."

Long ago in China, when Gaozu of Han and Xiang Yu of Chu contended for the throne, they fought seventy-two battles, all of them won by Xiang Yu. But at last Xiang Yu suffered a disastrous defeat. Determined to escape with his consort, Lady Yu, he mounted his horse Zhui, a charger that could fly a thousand leagues in a day, but Zhui planted his feet and refused to budge. "My puissance is no more; now I lack even the means to flee. I don't worry about an enemy attack; the only thing that bothers me is this parting with my wife," Xiang Yu said, with tears in his eyes. He lamented all night long. When the lamplight dimmed, Lady Yu shed tears of sorrow; as the night deepened, enemies shouted battle cries on all four sides. There is a Chinese poem on the subject by Tachibana Consultant Hiromi, which Shigehira had apparently called to mind. It was a tasteful allusion.

When the night ended, the warriors excused themselves. Senju-no-mae also withdrew. Senju proceeded to wait upon Yoritomo, who happened to be reading the *Lotus Sutra* in his private chapel that morning. Yoritomo smiled. "My efforts as a go-between bore interesting fruit, don't you think?" he said to her.

"Did something in particular happen?" asked Saiin no Jikan Chikayoshi, who was there to perform scribal duties.

9. From a poem in Chinese by Prince Tomohira (WKRES 591).

10. "Happy Rebirth" is a possible interpretation of "Gojōraku," the name of the tune performed by Senju-no-mae. "Ōjō," another piece of court music, takes its name from a place in China, but could be interpreted to mean "rebirth."

11. From a Buddhist text, *Seppō myōgenron.*

"I'd always thought the Heike were out of their depth in everything except warfare, but I stood and listened all night while Shigehira played the lute and chanted. He's a man of great cultivation," Yoritomo said.

"I ought to have been listening last night, too, but I was feeling ill," Chikayoshi said. "I don't intend to miss the next opportunity. The Heike have produced generations of poets and other talented figures. People used to compare them to flowers—and Shigehira was the peony, they said."

"Yes, he's accomplished," Yoritomo answered. From that time on, he never ceased to praise the manner in which Shigehira had played the lute and chanted *rōei*.

For Senju-no-mae, the encounter seems to have led to sorrow. As soon as she learned that Shigehira had been sent to Nara and executed, she pronounced Buddhist vows, put on robes of deep black, and devoted herself to prayers for him at the Zenkōji Temple in Shinano Province. In the end, she attained rebirth in the pure land.

10.8. Yokobue

Meanwhile, it was in body only that Middle Captain Koremori stayed at Yashima; in spirit, he was a perpetual commuter to the capital. Left behind at home but not forgotten for an instant, his wife and children were never absent from his thoughts. He decided that it was meaningless to go on living that way, and shortly before dawn, on the fifteenth of the third month in the third year of Juei [1184], he stole away from his quarters at Yashima, accompanied by three attendants—Yosōbyōe Shigekage, the page Ishidōmaru, and a groom known as Takesato, whom he chose because people said he was knowledgeable about boats. They set out from Yūki Shore in Awa Province aboard a small craft, rowed across the Naruto Straits toward Kii Province, passed Waka, Fukiage, and the Tamatsushima Shrine, where Sotōrihime had once appeared as a divinity, and arrived at Kii Harbor.

He would have liked to cross the mountains to the city—to meet his beloved family one last time—but it was bad enough for Shigehira to have been captured, paraded through the avenues, and humiliated in the capital and Kamakura. It would be a terrible disgrace for his dead father, Shigemori, if he were captured too. Many times, he felt the urge to set out, but he always fought it down, and in the end he went to Mount Kōya.

On the mountain, there was a holy man named Saitō Takiguchi Tokiyori, a son of Saitō Mochiyori of Sanjō. He had been a samurai in Shigemori's service, and Koremori had known him a long time. He had won a post in the palace guards as a boy of thirteen, and there he had fallen in love with one of Kenreimon'in's lesser attendants, a girl named Yokobue. His father gave him a severe scolding when he heard about it. "I intended to marry you into an influential family so you could rise in the world. Now I find you've got yourself involved with a nobody," he said.

"There was once a Queen Mother of the West, but she isn't around any longer; and though we hear about Dongfang Shuo, we can't see him," the youth thought.[12] "In a world where a young person may die before an old one, a man's life is like a spark from a flint. Even when we say somebody has a long life, it doesn't amount to more than seventy or eighty years, and the prime of life only lasts for twenty years or so. In this dreamlike, fleeting existence, what would I gain by spending even a little time with a wife I didn't care for? Yet I'll seem undutiful if I marry the girl I love. This situation is doing me a favor; it demonstrates that I ought to renounce the harsh world for the path of truth." At the age of nineteen, he had cut off his hair and gone to live a pious life at the Ōjōin Cloister in Saga.

"I could have accepted it if he'd broken with me," Yokobue thought when she heard the news. "But it was cruel to go to such lengths. If he'd made up his mind to be a monk, why couldn't he have told me so? He may not want to see me, but I'm going to find him and tell him how I feel." Late one afternoon, she left the capital and took her uncertain way toward Saga. As was usual for the season, midway through the second month, the spring breeze from Umezu carried the nostalgic fragrance of plum blossoms, and haze veiled the moonlight on the Ōi River. She must have felt that her misery was all Tokiyori's fault.

People had told her that the "Takiguchi novice" was at the Ōjōin, but she had no way of knowing which cloister was his, and she began a pathetic search, hesitating here and stopping there. At last, she heard someone chanting a sacred text inside a ruined cell. The voice sounded familiar. She told the maid who had accompanied her to take in a message. "I've looked everywhere for you. Please let me see you as a monk, just this once."

The Takiguchi novice peeped through a crack in the sliding partition, his heart racing. Even the most resolute seeker after enlightenment would have been moved by her appearance, which bore pitiful witness to her long, fruitless search. But he turned her away without a meeting. "The person you want isn't here," he had someone say. "You must have come to the wrong place." Yokobue resented his coldness, but she had to contain her tears and go home.

"This is a quiet place where a man can recite the sacred name in peace," the Takiguchi novice said to one of his cloister mates. "But I parted from a girl I still loved, and now she's found out that I'm here. I hardened my heart once, but I don't think I can do it if she comes again. I must say goodbye." He left Saga, went to Mount Kōya, and took up residence at the Shōjō-shin'in Cloister.

Presently, he learned that Yokobue had also entered the religious life. He sent her a poem:

12. The Queen Mother of the West (Xiwangmu), a Taoist goddess, gave Wudi a peach from a tree that took 3,000 years to produce fruit; Dongfang Shuo was a paradigm of mortal longevity in the Former Han dynasty (206 B.C.–A.D. 8).

soru made wa	Although you harbored
uramishikadomo	such feelings of resentment
azusayumi	that you shaved your head,
makoto no michi ni	what happiness to know
iru zo ureshiki	you have entered the true Way!

Yokobue answered with this:

soru tote mo	That I shaved my head
nani ka uramin	was not because I harbored
azusayumi	resentment toward you.
hikitodomubeki	Yours is a heart praiseworthy
kokoro naraneba	for steadfast devotion.

Before long, Yokobue died at the Hokkeji nunnery in Nara, where she had gone to live. (Perhaps it was her heavy burden of sorrow that caused her death.) After he heard the news, the Takiguchi novice prayed harder than ever, displaying a zeal so fervent that his father recognized him as his son again. Everyone who knew him revered him; they called him "the holy man at Mount Kōya."

Koremori went to visit this holy man. In the old days in the capital, he had been an elegant gentleman in a hunting robe and high cap, his garments stylishly draped and his hair smooth. Now, when Koremori saw him as a monk for the first time, he must have felt a pang of envy. Here was a true seeker after enlightenment, someone who looked like an emaciated old monk (although he was not yet thirty), dressed in a robe of deep black and a black surplice. Not even one of the seven sages of the bamboo grove, the men of Jin, could have been a more impressive sight—nor could one of the four graybeards of Mount Shang in the Han dynasty.

10.9. The Book of Kōya

When the Takiguchi novice saw Koremori, he said, "I must be dreaming! Why have you fled here from Yashima?"

"I made the trip westward from the capital like all the others, but I was always miserable because of the children I'd left behind," Koremori answered. "I didn't say anything, but my feelings probably showed, because Munemori and the nun of second rank both suspected that I was going to turn traitor like Yorimori.[13] There didn't seem to be any point to my life, and I felt less and less like staying in Yashima. I finally left, not knowing exactly where I was going, and that's how I happen to be here. I'd like to follow the mountains to the capital to see my dear family just one last time, but I don't dare run the risk of suffering Shigehira's fate. It will be better for

---

13. Yorimori was the son of Kiyomori's stepmother, Lady Ike, who had saved Yoritomo's life at the time of the Heiji Disturbance. He had received messages of friendship from Yoritomo, and had stayed behind in the capital when the rest of the clan fled (Sec. 7.19, not translated).

me to take religious vows here and kill myself, either with fire or with water. There's only one problem: for a long time, I've wanted to make a pilgrimage to Kumano."

"It matters very little how a man passes through this dreamlike, fleeting world. What is truly hard is to suffer rebirth in eternal darkness," the novice said.

Guided by the novice, and proceeding by way of the various halls, Koremori at once made a pious visit to the inner cloister.

Mount Kōya stands two hundred leagues from the capital, remote from habitations and undisturbed by mortal voices. The treetops rustle in the mountain winds; peace shines in the rays of the setting sun. True purity of the spirit can be achieved on the eight peaks and in the eight valleys. Flowers bloom where mists touch the groves; handbells resound where clouds hang above the peaks. Ferns on tiles and mosses on fences bear witness to the temple's antiquity.

During the time of the sovereign who reigned in the Engi era [901–22], the emperor gave Great Teacher Kōbō a dark brown robe, in response to a request from the great teacher in a dream. The imperial messenger, Middle Counselor Suketaka, took Archbishop Kangen of the Hannyaji with him to Mount Kōya. When the two opened the door of the tomb to put the robe on the body, a dense mist concealed the great teacher. Kangen shed tears of distress. "Never have I violated one of the commandments—never since I left the womb of my kind mother and entered the chambers of my teacher. Why am I denied the privilege of worship?" he asked. He flung himself to the ground and abandoned himself to tears. Then, very gradually, the mist cleared away, a light shone as of a rising moon, and the great teacher became visible. Kangen robed him, shedding tears of joy. The great teacher's hair had grown very long, and the archbishop also received the honor of shaving his head.

The archbishop's disciple, Ishiyama Palace Chaplain Jun'yū, was much chagrined because he was unable to see the great teacher, even though the imperial messenger and Kangen could do so. The archbishop took his hand and touched it to the great teacher's knee. And we are told that a fragrance emanated from that hand for the rest of Jun'yū's life. People say it still clings to the sacred texts at Ishiyama.

The great teacher replied to the emperor with these words: "In the past, I met the bodhisattva Fugen, and from him I received all the mudras and mantras in direct transmission. An unparalleled vow has brought me to this distant foreign land. I seek to accomplish Fugen's compassionate vows in everlasting pity for mankind. Still retaining corporeal form, I have entered the realm of contemplation to await Maitreya's coming." Even thus, it seemed, must Śākyamuni's disciple Mahā-kāśyapa wait in the Kukkuṭapāda grotto for the spring breeze at Shizu.

The great teacher died during the hour of the tiger [3:00 A.M.–5:00 A.M.]

on the twenty-first day of the third month in the second year of Jōwa [835]. More than three hundred years have passed since then, but he will have to wait another five billion six hundred and seventy million years before Maitreya comes to deliver the three sermons—a long time, indeed.

10.10. *Koremori Becomes a Monk*

Koremori was in a pitiful state. "I don't seem to be able to set a time to end it all. I'm just like the Himalayan bird, always thinking, 'Today! Tomorrow!' "[14] he said. With his skin blackened by salt winds and his body emaciated by incessant worry, he little resembled his old self, but he was still handsomer than other men. That night, he went back to the Takiguchi novice's hermitage and talked about the past and present until dawn. When he watched how the holy man behaved, he saw the pearl of truth being polished with unswerving diligence and faith; when he heard the bell ringing for the morning devotions, he perceived the hope of an awakening from the slumber of birth and death. He must have wanted to escape worldly ties and live in the same way, for the next morning he asked to receive a visit from Chikaku Shōnin, of the Tōzen'in, with the intention of becoming a monk.

He summoned Shigekage and Ishidōmaru. "I've had something in mind that people didn't know about, but I'm in a difficult position now, and I won't be able to survive.[15] There's no reason why my death should keep you from making your way in life; lots of people are prospering nowadays. Once you've seen me to the end, hurry on back to the capital and find some way to support yourselves. Take care of your wives and children, and pray for my wellbeing in the next life," he said.

At first, Shigekage and Ishidōmaru were too overcome to answer. Then Shigekage spoke up, restraining his tears. "During the rebellion in the Heiji era, my father, Kageyasu, your late father's man, died at the hands of Akugenda Yoshihira while he was wrestling with Kamadabyōe Masakiyo near the intersection of Nijō Avenue and Horikawa Street. How can I reveal myself to be a lesser man? I don't remember him, because I was only two at the time. My mother died when I was seven, and there weren't any close relatives to look after me, but Lord Shigemori said, 'This is the son of a man who gave his life for mine.' I was reared near his presence, and at the age of nine, on the same night you assumed the cap of manhood, I had the privilege of having my own hair put up and receiving the name Shigekage. '*Mori* is always a part of a Taira name, so I'll give it to Godai,' His Lordship said. 'The *shige* in my name I'll give to Matsuō.'[16] So my father's brave death turned out to be a blessing for me. Furthermore, the other retainers were all very kind.

14. See Chap. 9, n. 4.

15. This is probably a reference to his desire to return to the capital to see his family. By leaving Yashima, he has cut himself off from the rest of the Taira.

16. Godai and Matsuō were presumably the childhood names of Koremori and Shigekage.

"When His Lordship was dying, he put away thoughts of worldly things and lapsed into silence. But then he called me over. 'Poor lad!' he said. 'I've been a memento of your father for you, and you've been a memento for me. At the next distribution of offices, I was going to make you a guards lieutenant so I could call you by his old title. That won't happen now, and I'm sorry about it. Remember, always do as Lesser Captain Koremori wishes.' Did you just assume that I'd run away and leave you at the hour of your death? It's a terrible humiliation to find out what you've been thinking. You say many people are prospering nowadays, but those are all retainers of the Genji. And could I hope to live a thousand years, even if I did thrive after you became a god or buddha? Even if I prospered for ten thousand years, wouldn't the end come someday? What better chance will I have to enter the true path?" He cut off his hair with his own hand, and tearfully called on the Takiguchi novice to shave his head.

After witnessing these sights, Ishidōmaru cut off his hair at the clasp. He had served Koremori since he was eight years old and had enjoyed favors equal to those bestowed on Shigekage; thus, he asked the Takiguchi novice to shave his head too.

When Koremori saw his two retainers precede him into the religious life, he felt even more miserable than before. But he could not procrastinate forever. Three times, he chanted a Buddhist adage: "He who transmigrates through the three worlds cannot sever the bonds of attachment to family; he who rejects attachment and enters the Way receives the reward of true attachment." Then, at last, he shaved his head. "I wouldn't have minded if only I could have done this after letting my dear wife and children see me one last time as I used to look," he said. It was a sinful thought.

Koremori and Shigekage were the same age, twenty-seven that year. Ishidōmaru was eighteen.

Koremori called in the groom Takesato. "Go straight back to Yashima," he told him. "Don't go to the capital. What I've done will have to come to light sometime, but I'm afraid Her Ladyship might rush into holy orders if she heard the whole story from your lips. This is what I want you to say for me at Yashima: 'As you must have noticed, I've come to hate this life. I've felt that I could only grow more and more wretched, so I've taken religious vows without telling you. My only regret is that you must all be feeling very forlorn, now that this has happened after Kiyotsune died in the west and Moromori at Ichi-no-tani. If, by some miracle, we should regain our old preeminence, please see that Rokudai gets the armor Karakawa [Chinese Leather] and the sword Kogarasu [Little Crow], the heirlooms that came to me from Sadamori as the heir in the ninth generation.' "[17]

"I'll wait to witness your death before I go to Yashima," Takesato said. Koremori acquiesced and kept him with him. He also asked the Takiguchi novice to accompany him, that he might provide religious guidance at the

17. Rokudai was Koremori's son.

end. Then he left Mount Kōya for Sandō in the same province, wearing the garb of a mountain ascetic.[18]

He paused and knelt at all the Kumano branch shrines—Fujishiro and the others. Just in front of the Iwashiro Shrine, north of Senri-no-hama, he met a party of seven or eight horsemen in hunting attire. Fearing capture, he put his hand on his dagger to slash his belly, and his companions did the same. But after the strangers drew closer, they leaped from their horses with no sign of hostility, made respectful bows, and went on their way.

"They must have recognized us. I wonder who they were," Koremori thought. Fearing the worst, he hurried toward Kumano.

The leader of the party on horseback was a man named Yuasa no Munemitsu. When his retainers wanted to know who the pilgrims were, tears ran down his cheeks. "It's nothing for the likes of us to talk about. That was the middle captain of third rank, the son and heir of Minister of State Shigemori. I wonder how he managed to get here from Yashima. He's already taken the tonsure. Shigekage and Ishidōmaru were with him, and they were both monks, too. I wanted to go up and pay my respects, but I went on to save him from embarrassment. He looked so pathetic!" He sobbed with his shoulder-guard pressed to his face, and all his retainers wept.

10.12. *The Suicide of Koremori*

After Koremori had visited the three shrines of Kumano without incident, he got into a small boat in front of the branch shrine at Hama-no-miya and set out on the vast blue sea.[19] Far in the offing, there was an island called Yamanari-no-shima. He went ashore there, peeled some bark from a great pine tree, and inscribed his name. "Grandfather: Chancellor Taira no Ason Kiyomori, religious name Jōkai. Father: Palace Minister–Major Captain of the Left Shigemori, religious name Jōren. Middle Captain Koremori of third rank, religious name Jōen, aged twenty-seven, drowns himself offshore from Nachi on the twenty-eighth day of the third month in the third year of Juei [1184]." Then he rowed toward the open sea again.

Now that the hour had arrived, he could not help feeling miserable and forlorn, determined though he was to die. As was natural for the date, which was the twenty-eighth of the third month, haze veiled the sea far into the distance, a moving sight. Even in an ordinary spring, it is sad to watch a season wane. And we may imagine the feelings of someone who would not see the dawn of another day.

When Koremori saw a fishing boat offshore come back into view after seeming to plunge into the waves, he may have been reminded of what was in store for him. And when he heard the cry of a homing goose, leading a line of its fellows toward the northern regions, he longed to send a mes-

18. Sando is now within the city of Wakayama.

19. The Hama-no-miya Shrine was in the present town of Nachi-katsuura in Higashimuro District, Wakayama Prefecture, near the mouth of the Nachi River.

sage home, no less disconsolate than Su Wu in the land of the Xiongnu barbarians.

He reproved himself for thinking about such things. "What's wrong with me? Am I still fettered by worldly attachments?" He faced the west, joined his hands, and intoned the name of Amida Buddha. But even as he chanted, he thought, "They can't know in the capital that this is my last hour. They must be frantic for any word, even a rumor. What a terrible blow it will be when the news spreads—as it's bound to—and they find out I'm dead!" He fell silent, separated his hands, and spoke to the Takiguchi novice. "It's a mistake to have a wife and children. They're only a cause of anxiety in this world and a hindrance to enlightenment in the next. Mine have come back into my head at this very moment. I've been told that it's a grave sin to let such things linger in one's mind; I confess my guilt."

The holy man pitied him, but he felt that it would never do for him to show weakness too. Wiping away a tear, he spoke with an assumption of calm.

"It's not surprising that you should feel that way. Love is an emotion we can't control, whether we're noble or base. And the karmic bond between husband and wife is especially strong: a single night together is said to signify a bond going back through five hundred lives. It's the way of this fleeting world that those who are born must perish, that those who meet must part. 'Dew on the tip of a branch, a drop of moisture from a stalk.'[20] The parting may be early or late, but one person will go before the other. The vows spoken at the Lishan Palace on autumn nights led to heartbreak at last; the love that inspired the portrait in the Ganquan Hall didn't endure forever. Even Songzi and Mei Fu knew the bitterness of dying; the highest bodhisattvas themselves follow the law of life and death. Even if you were to enjoy the blessing of a long life, you couldn't escape that sorrow; you must remember that you would face the identical grief if you lived for another hundred years.

"Ruling as he pleases over all six heavens in the world of desire, the heretic demon king in the sixth heaven resents the efforts of that world's inhabitants to escape the cycle of life and death, and he hinders them by assuming the form of a wife or a husband. The buddhas of the three worlds, who regard all mankind as their children, and who seek to lead us to the pure land from which there is no return, have issued strict injunctions against loving the wives and children who have chained us to the wheel of transmigration from remote antiquity to the present.

"You mustn't lose heart. In a single twelve-year period, while he was trying to carry out an imperial command to subdue Sadatō and Munetō, the barbarians in Ōshū, Yoriyoshi of the Genji cut off the heads of sixteen thou-

20. Archbishop Henjō (SKKS 757): sue no tsuyu / moto no shizuku ya / yo no naka no / okuresakidatsu / tameshi naruran ("Dew on a branch tip, a drop of moisture on a stalk—even thus, it seems, some in the world go after and some go before").

sand men and killed thousands and thousands of the beasts of the fields and the fish of the rivers. And yet we're told that he was reborn in the pure land because he became a true believer at the end of his life. The merit amassed by the act of renouncing the world is exceedingly great; I'm sure all your sins from previous existences have been washed away. Even if a man builds a jeweled pagoda high enough to reach the heaven of the thirty-three divinities, he won't equal the merit that accrues from a single day in holy orders. And we are also taught this: even if a man makes offerings to a hundred arhats for a hundred or a thousand years, he won't equal the merit that accrues from a single day in holy orders. Yoriyoshi's faith was strong, so he achieved rebirth in paradise despite his heinous sins. And you who have committed no truly evil acts—how could you possibly fail to reach the pure land?

"Furthermore, the god of Kumano is a manifestation of Amida Buddha, whose vows are all dedicated to the salvation of sentient beings, from the first, 'There shall be no more three evil paths,' to the forty-eighth, 'They shall attain the three forms of patience.' The eighteenth vow says, 'Even though I attain the qualifications for buddhahood, I will not become a buddha unless the sentient beings in the ten directions, believing and rejoicing in my vows with fervent hearts, and desirous of rebirth in my pure land, achieve rebirth by reciting my name ten times.' From those words, in particular, we may rest assured that ten buddha-invocations will save us—or even one, for that matter. You must simply have complete faith, and never, never let a doubt enter your mind. If you intone the sacred name ten times with a pure heart, or even once, Amida Buddha will reduce his immeasurable stature to sixteen feet and come forth promptly from the eastern gate of his paradise to meet you, accompanied by Kannon, Seishi, and a countless host of heavenly beings and bodhisattvas in temporary manifestations, who will surround him a hundredfold, a thousandfold, playing musical instruments and singing. Though you may expect to sink to the bottom of the blue sea, you will surely mount a purple cloud.[21] If you become a buddha and attain deliverance, there can be no doubt that you will return to your earthly home as a guide for your wife and children—that you will 'visit the impure world to save men and devas.' "[22] He rang his bell and urged Koremori to chant the sacred name.

To Koremori it seemed a supremely favorable opportunity for rebirth in the pure land. He put away distracting thoughts immediately, intoned Amida's name a hundred times in a loud voice, and entered the sea with "Hail!" on his lips. The Hyōe novice and Ishidōmaru followed him into the waves, chanting, "Hail, Amida Buddha!"

21. Amida and his attendants ride a purple cloud when they come to escort a dying believer to the pure land.
22. From *Hōjisan*, a Buddhist text.

Chapter 11

Time: second to sixth months of 1185
Principal subject: the battles of Yashima and Dan-no-ura and their aftermath
Principal characters:

> Go-Shirakawa, Retired Emperor. Head of the imperial clan
> Emperor. Antoku, son of Emperor Takakura and Kiyomori's daughter Kenreimon'in
> Kagetoki (Kajiwara). Trusted lieutenant of Yoritomo
> Kiyomune (Taira). Son of Munemori
> Munemori (Taira). Son of Kiyomori; head of the Taira clan
> Noritsune (Taira). Son of Norimori; nephew of Kiyomori
> Nun of second rank. Widow of Kiyomori
> Shigehira (Taira). Son of Kiyomori
> Tokitada (Taira). Member of a branch family of the Taira clan; brother of the nun of second rank
> Tomomori (Taira). Son of Kiyomori
> Yoritomo (Minamoto). Principal opponent of the Taira; head of the Minamoto clan
> Yoshitsune (Minamoto). Younger half-brother of Yoritomo; leader of Genji forces at Yashima and Dan-no-ura

11.3. The Death of Tsuginobu

[Yoshitsune has landed with a small force on Shikoku Island, marched to the rear of the enemy stronghold at Yashima, and bluffed the Taira into retreating to their boats.]

That day, Yoshitsune wore a tunic of red brocade and a suit of armor with purple-shaded lacing. At his waist, there hung a sword with gilt bronze fittings; on his back, he carried a quiver containing arrows fledged with banded black-and-white eagle feathers. He grasped a rattan-wrapped bow in the middle, scowled toward the boats, and announced his name in a mighty shout. "I am Minamoto no Yoshitsune, fifth-rank lieutenant in the imperial police and envoy of the retired emperor!" Next, Tashiro no Nobutsuna of Izu, Kaneko no Ietada of Musashi, Kaneko no Chikanori of Musashi, and Ise no Yoshimori identified themselves. Then others gave their names and galloped forward: Gotōbyōe Sanemoto, Sanemoto's son Moto-kiyo, Satō Tsuginobu of Ōshū, Tsuginobu's brother Tadanobu, Eda no Genzō, Kumai Tarō, and Musashibō Benkei.

"Shoot them down!" the Heike shouted.

Some of the Heike in the boats shot powerful arrows from far away; others released streams of lighter arrows. The Genji warriors attacked with shouts and yells, shooting as they galloped through the Heike ranks, and resting their mounts in the shelter of beached vessels.

Instead of joining the fighting, the veteran warrior Sanemoto burst inside the imperial palace, told his men to set fires everywhere, and burned the buildings in no time.

Munemori summoned his samurai. "What's the Genji strength?" he asked.

"Only about seventy or eighty now."

"This is a disaster! Even if we counted every hair on their heads, we'd still outnumber them. Why didn't we surround them and cut them down? We should never have taken to the boats in a panic. We should never have let them burn down the palace. Where's Noritsune? Go ashore and fight!"

Noritsune bowed and obeyed. Accompanied by Etchū no Moritsugi, he transferred his men into small boats and took up positions on the beach, in front of the charred remains of the main gate.

Yoshitsune's eighty-odd horsemen advanced to within arrow range and pulled up.

Moritsugi hailed the enemy from the deck of a boat. "I think I heard you identifying yourselves, but I was too far out at sea to catch your names. Who is the honorable commander-in-chief of the Genji today?"

Ise no Yoshimori rode forward at a walk. "You need somebody to tell you? It's Lord Yoshitsune, a descendant of Emperor Seiwa in the tenth generation and a younger brother of Yoritomo, the Kamakura Lord!"

"Right! You're talking about the stripling who was orphaned when his father died in the Heiji fighting—the one who served as a temple page at Kurama, and then tramped off to Ōshū as a gold merchant's servant, carrying food on his back," Moritsugi said.

"Shut your mouth about my master! You fellows are the ones that took a licking at Tonamiyama and then straggled onto the Northern Land Road, lucky to be alive, and begged and sniveled your way back to the capital," Yoshimori said.

"Why would we have to beg? A generous lord gives us everything we need. They tell me you support yourself and your family by robbing travelers in the Suzuka Mountains of Ise!"

Kaneko no Ietada spoke up. "This bickering is a waste of time! If you're just going to fight with bombast and insults, neither one of you will lose. I think you had a chance to test the mettle of our young warriors from Mu-

sashi and Sagami at Ichi-no-tani last spring." Before he finished, his younger
brother Yoichi, who was beside him, drew his bow to the full and sent off
an arrow twelve handbreadths and two fingers long. It whistled through the
air, pierced the breastplate of Moritsugi's armor, and lodged in his flesh. So
ended the battle of words.

Noritsune had dispensed with his tunic, observing, "Fighting on a boat
has its own methods."[1] Instead, he wore a suit of armor laced with thick
Chinese damask, and a short-sleeved robe with a handsome roll-dyed design. At his waist, he wore a magnificent big sword; on his back, he carried
a quiver containing twenty-four arrows fledged with black-banded eagle
feathers; in his hand, he held a rattan-wrapped bow. He had been the best
archer in the capital; no man escaped who came within the range of his
arrows. Now his purpose was to shoot Yoshitsune down, but the Genji anticipated him. A group of warriors, each worth a thousand, swiftly aligned
their horses' heads to make a shield: Satō Tsuginobu of Ōshū, Tsuginobu's
brother Tadanobu, Ise no Yoshimori, Genpachi Hirotsuna, Eda no Genzō,
Kumai Tarō, Musashibō Benkei, and others.

"Out of the way, scum!" Noritsune shouted. He vented his frustration
with a barrage of arrows, and more than ten armored warriors went down
in an instant. One of them was Tsuginobu, who had advanced to the forefront. He plummeted headlong from his horse, mortally stricken by an arrow that penetrated from his left shoulder to his right side.

In Noritsune's service there was a strong, courageous page named Kikuō,
who this day was attired in a corselet with green lacing and a helmet with
three plates. This Kikuō unsheathed a spear with a plain wooden handle
and went running up to decapitate Tsuginobu. Determined to keep his
brother's head from being taken, Tadanobu drew his bow to the full and
sent off an arrow that struck the back joint of Kikuō's corselet and ran him
through. When Noritsune saw the page fall to his hands and knees, he
leaped from the boat, with his bow still in his left hand, picked up Kikuō
with his right hand, and tossed him into the boat. Kikuō's head was saved
from the enemy, but he died of the wound. Originally the page of Michimori, the boy had been taken into service by Noritsune, Michimori's
younger brother, after his master's death. He was eighteen. Noritsune withdrew from the battle, overwhelmed by grief.

Yoshitsune gave orders for Tsuginobu to be carried to the rear. He dismounted, took his hand, and asked how he felt. Tsuginobu spoke in a faint
voice, hardly breathing. "This will be all for me."

"Is there anything weighing on your mind?"

"Nothing. My only regret is that I have to die before I see my lord rise to
prominence. Otherwise, any man who uses a bow and arrow has to expect

1. As indicated in the Glossary, the "tunic" actually consisted of two pieces. The point here
seems to be that the trousers would have been a hindrance to a man moving in a small boat or
standing on a tidal flat. Noritsune's costume left his legs bare from the knees down.

death from an enemy shot. And to have it told in later generations, 'During the fighting between the Minamoto and the Taira, a man from Ōshū, Satō Saburōbyōe Tsuginobu, exchanged his life for his master's on the beach at Yashima in Sanuki'—for a warrior, that will be an honor in this world and the next." The words faltered on his lips, and he weakened by the moment.

"Is there a holy man anywhere near here?" Yoshitsune asked, with tears streaming down his face. They found one, and he gave him a stout and brawny black horse with a saddle edged in gold. "A wounded man is dying. Make arrangements for a day of sutra-copying," he said. The horse was one that had been given fifth rank on its own, with the name Tayūguro [Fifth-rank Black], when Yoshitsune had become a police lieutenant of fifth rank—the very one on which he had made the descent from Hiedorigoe at Ichi-no-tani.[2]

Yoshitsune's conduct brought tears to the eyes of Tsuginobu's brother, Tadanobu, and all the other warriors who witnessed it. "We wouldn't think dying for this master was any more important than a dewdrop or a speck of dust," they said.

11.4. *Nasu no Yoichi*

Meanwhile, men from Awa and Sanuki provinces, warriors who had turned against the Heike and were awaiting the Genji, came riding up from various peaks and caverns in groups of fourteen or fifteen or twenty, and Yoshitsune's force soon numbered more than three hundred horsemen.

"It's getting late," both sides said. "We can't settle anything today." But just as they were drawing apart, a small, well-appointed boat came toward the shore from out at sea. To the bewilderment of the Genji, it swung around broadside, two hundred and fifty or three hundred feet from the beach, and from inside the cabin there appeared an elegant, beautiful maiden of eighteen or nineteen, wearing a red divided skirt and five white robes lined in green. She produced a pole, topped by a red fan decorated with a golden sun, wedged it between the prow and the planking, and beckoned shoreward.

Yoshitsune summoned Sanemoto. "What's that all about?"

"She seems to be inviting us to shoot at the fan. If you go within arrow range to look at their fair lady, they'll probably have an expert archer shoot you down. Still, you probably ought to order somebody to hit it," Sanemoto said.

"Do we have anybody who's up to it?" Yoshitsune asked.

"We have plenty of good men. Yoichi Munetaka, the son of Nasu no Suketaka of Shimotsuke Province, is a short fellow but a wonderful shot."

"Give me some proof."

"In competitions to shoot birds on the wing, he always brings down two out of three."

2. Called Hiyodorigoe earlier (Sec. 9.9).

"All right, call him," Yoshitsune ordered.

Munetaka was about twenty years old then. He was wearing a suit of green-laced armor over a dark blue tunic, which had lapels and cuffs of red brocade. At his waist, he wore a sword with a silver cord-loop; high on his back, he carried a quiver containing the few arrows left from the day's battle, all fledged with black-banded white eagle feathers, and also a humming-bulb arrow, made of deerhorn and fledged with hawk feathers and gray-banded white eagle feathers. He bowed before Yoshitsune, his rattan-wrapped bow pressed against his side and his helmet tied to his shoulder-cord.

"Now then, Munetaka!" Yoshitsune said. "I want you to shoot that fan right square in the middle. Show the Heike what you can do!"

Munetaka spoke with respect. "I'm not sure I can hit it. If I missed, we'd never outlive the disgrace. You'd better pick somebody who's more likely to succeed."

His reply angered the commander. "Now that you men have left Kamakura for the west, it's up to you to obey my orders. If anyone wants to haggle, he can head for home right now," he said.

Munetaka may have been afraid to refuse again. "I can't say whether I'll miss or not, but I'll try, since that's what you're telling me to do," he said. He withdrew and mounted a stout and brawny black horse, which was fitted out with a short-fringed crupper and carried a saddle with a circular mistletoe design. Then he took a fresh grip on his bow, pulled up the reins, and moved toward the shoreline at a walk.

"That boy can do it!" said the Genji warriors, with their eyes on his receding figure. Yoshitsune also watched with a confident expression.

The target was a little beyond bowshot. Munetaka rode thirty-five feet into the sea, but it still seemed to be about two hundred and fifty feet away. It was around the hour of the cock [5:00 P.M.—7:00 P.M.] on the eighteenth of the second month. There was a strong north wind, and the waves were running high at the shore. The fan on its pole fluttered and wavered as the drifting boat swung up and down. In the offing, the Heike aligned their vessels to view the spectacle; on the land, the Genji watched bridle to bridle. For both sides, it was an occasion of moment.

Munetaka closed his eyes in silent prayer. "Hail, Great Bodhisattva Hachiman and ye gods of my province at Nikkō, Utsunomiya, and Nasu Yuzen! Let me hit the center of that fan! If I miss, I'll smash my bow and kill myself; I'll never show my face again. If it's your will for me to return home, keep my arrow from going astray!" When he opened his eyes, the wind seemed to have died down, and the fan looked easier to hit.

He took out his humming-bulb, fitted it, drew his bow to the full, and sent the arrow whizzing on its way. Short though he was, the arrow measured twelve handbreadths and three fingers, and his bow was powerful. Singing until the bay resounded, the arrow flew straight to the fan, thudded into it an inch from the edge of the rivet, and cut it loose. The humming-bulb went into the sea; the fan flew toward the heavens. For a time, the fan fluttered in the air; then it plummeted toward the sea, tossed and buffeted by the spring wind. The red fan with its golden orb floated on the white waves in the glittering rays of the setting sun; and as it rocked there, dancing up and down, the Heike in the offing beat their gunwales and applauded, and the Genji on the land struck their quivers and shouted.

11.7. *The Cockfights and the Battle at Dan-no-ura*

Yoshitsune crossed over to Suō Province to join forces with his brother Noriyori, and the Heike arrived at Hikushima in Nagato Province.

The Genji had won the battle of Yashima after going ashore at Katsuura [Victory Beach] in Awa Province, and now, oddly enough, no sooner was it rumored that the Heike were at Hikushima [Retreat Island] than the Genji went to Oitsu [Pursuit Harbor] in the same province.

Unsure about which side to support, Kumano Superintendent Tanzō offered prayers and a program of sacred music at the Tanabe Imagumano Shrine. The oracle commanded, "Adhere to the white banner." Still doubtful, he matched seven white cocks against seven red ones in the presence of the gods, and not a single red bird won a victory; all were put to flight. He then decided to cast his lot with the Genji. He mustered his kinsmen, embarked in two hundred boats with two thousand men, took the god of the shrine on board, and proceeded toward Dan-no-ura, with a picture of Kongō Dōji on the wooden strip at the top of his banner. When he came into view, both the Genji and the Heike paid him reverence. To see him join the Genji was a sad blow for the Heike.

Kawano no Michinobu of Iyo Province also joined the Genji, bringing with him a hundred and fifty fighting boats.

The reinforcements gave Yoshitsune renewed hope and energy. The Genji had three thousand vessels and the Heike a thousand, including a few large Chinese-style ships. The strength of the Genji was increasing, even as that of the Heike was declining.

The arrow exchange was to take place at the Moji and Akama barriers during the hour of the hare [5:00 A.M.–7:00 A.M.] on the twenty-fourth day of the third month in the second year of Genryaku. It was on that same day that Yoshitsune and Kajiwara Kagetoki almost came to blows.

"Let me lead the attack today," Kagetoki said.

"I might if I didn't intend to be there myself," Yoshitsune said.

"You're making a mistake. Remember, you're the commander-in-chief."

"That's ridiculous. Yoritomo is the commander-in-chief. I just hold his commission, so my status is the same as yours."

Kagetoki muttered in frustration. "That fellow doesn't have the character to lead samurai."

Yoshitsune overheard him. "You're the biggest fool in Japan!" he shouted, gripping the hilt of his sword.

Kagetoki grasped his own sword. "Yoritomo is the only superior I recognize!"

Kagetoki's heir, Kagesue, his second son, Kagetaka, and his third son, Kageie, went to their father's side. At the sight of Yoshitsune's face, a group of his warriors surrounded Kagetoki and moved forward, ready to kill him—Satō Tadanobu, Ise no Yoshimori, Genpachi Hirotsuna, Eda no Genzō, Kumai Tarō, Musashibō Benki, and other warriors, each of them worth a thousand men. But Miura no Yoshizumi caught hold of Yoshitsune, and Toi no Sanehira held Kagetoki. Both clasped their hands in supplication. "It will encourage the Heike if two Genji get into a fight just before a crucial battle. And what happens if Yoritomo hears about it?" they said. Yoshitsune regained his composure, and Kagetoki had to control himself. But people say that Kagetoki hated Yoshitsune afterward, and that it was his lies that led to Yoshitsune's eventual destruction.

The opposing positions were about two miles apart on the surface of the sea. A turbulent ebb tide was running at Moji, Akama, and Dan-no-ura, and the boats of the Genji, breasting the flow, were carried toward the sea despite the best efforts of the crews. The Heike took advantage of the current to move forward.

Because the water was swiftest in the offing, Kagetoki hugged the shore. He and his sons and other followers snagged an oncoming enemy vessel with rakes and boarded it. Fourteen or fifteen strong, they ranged from bow to stern with drawn weapons, laying about mercilessly and seizing great quantities of booty. Their deeds were the first to be recorded in the written account of that day's exploits.

When the two sides finally confronted each other and shouted their battle cries, the noise must have reached the ears of Bonten above and amazed the king of the sea dragons below.

Tomomori appeared outside the cabin of his boat. "This is our last battle!" he shouted. "Don't even think about retreating, men! Even the best of commanders, the best of warriors, is helpless if his luck runs out! It's the same everywhere—China, India, or Japan. But honor means something! Don't look weak in front of the easterners! What is there to save our lives for? That's all I have to say."

Kazusa no Kagekiyo came forward. "The eastern warriors may boast when they're on horseback, but they don't know anything about sea battles. They'll be like fish trying to climb trees. We'll grab them one at a time and give them a bath in the ocean," he said.

Etchū no Moritsugi said, "When you wrestle somebody, try to pick their commander-in-chief, Yoshitsune. He'll be easy to spot; he's fair-skinned and short, with buck teeth. They do say, though, that it's hard to recognize him at first, because he keeps changing his tunic and armor."

"He may be brave enough," Kagekiyo said, "but a stripling like that is nobody to worry about. I'll clamp him under one arm and throw him into the sea."

After Tomomori had issued his orders, he went to see Minister of State Munemori. "The morale of the samurai seems to be high today, but I'm afraid Awa no Shigeyoshi has had a change of heart. I think we should cut off his head," he said.

"If there's no proof of treachery on his part, I don't see how we can kill him. You know what a faithful servant he's been. Call him in," Munemori said.

Shigeyoshi was wearing a dark yellow tunic and a suit of armor with white leather lacing. He bowed respectfully to Munemori.

"Well, Shigeyoshi, have you had a change of heart? You're strangely dejected today. Tell your men from Shikoku to put up a gallant fight. You seem nervous," Munemori said.

"No, not at all," Shigeyoshi said. He withdrew.

"I only wish I could cut off that fellow's head," Tomomori thought. He grasped the hilt of his sword and looked hard at Munemori, but Munemori withheld his permission, and there was nothing he could do about it.

The Heike divided their thousand vessels into three groups. Yamaga no Hidetō advanced in the vanguard with five hundred boats, the Matsura League followed in second place with three hundred, and the lords of the Taira clan followed in third place with two hundred. Hidetō was the best archer in the Nine Provinces. He selected five hundred men who were excellent shots (although not, of course, his own equals), posted them in lines at both ends of his boats, and ordered them to shoot in unison. The Genji had the numerical advantage with their three thousand boats, but their fire came from many different directions, so that it was impossible to tell where the best archers were. Even with Yoshitsune fighting in the forefront, the Genji faltered under the barrage of enemy arrows, an onslaught too fierce for shield or armor to withstand. The Heike beat a wild tattoo on their attack drums and shouted in victory. "Our side is winning!"

11.8. *Distant Arrows*

One of the Genji warriors, Wada no Yoshimori, decided not to embark in a boat. Instead, he rode to the shoreline, gave someone his helmet to hold, pressed his feet into his stirrups, drew his bow to the full, and dispatched arrows with tremendous force. Nobody within a thousand feet escaped injury. When one of his shots traveled even farther than the others, he beckoned to the Heike, daring them to return the arrow. Tomomori called for it. It was a plain bamboo shaft, thirteen handbreadths and two fingers long, fledged with a mixture of stork feathers and black-tipped white crane feathers. A handbreadth from the head, there was a name inscribed in lacquer: "Wada no Kotarō Taira no Yoshimori."

It would seem that few among the ranks of the Heike were capable of so long a shot, for there was some delay before a man from Iyo Province, Nii no Chikakiyo, was chosen to send the arrow back. It sped more than a thousand feet, from open water to the beach, and lodged in the left arm of Miura no Tarō, who had pulled up his horse more than thirty-five feet behind Yoshimori. The Miura warriors burst out laughing. "Yoshimori thought nobody could outshoot him. He doesn't like being humiliated! Look at him!" they said. Stung, Yoshimori got into a small boat, had himself rowed out, and sent off a fast and furious barrage of arrows toward the middle of the Taira fleet, killing and wounding great numbers of men.

Again, someone out at sea shot a big unlacquered arrow into Yoshitsune's boat and signaled for its return, just as Yoshimori had done. Yoshitsune pulled it out to look at it. It was a plain bamboo shaft, fourteen hand-breadths and three fingers long, fledged with pheasant feathers, and bearing the name "Nii no Kishirō Chikakiyo, a resident of Iyo Province."

Yoshitsune summoned Sanemoto. "Is there somebody on our side who can shoot this arrow back?" he asked.

"Lord Asari no Yoichi of the Kai Genji is a powerful archer."

"All right, call him in."

When Yoichi presented himself, Yoshitsune said, "The Heike shot this arrow from out at sea. They want us to return it. Would you mind?"

"Let's see it." Yoichi tested it with his finger. "It's a little bit weak—also a little short. If nobody objects, I'd like to use one of my own," he said. With a huge fist, he gripped a lacquered shaft, fifteen handbreaths long and fledged with black eagle feathers, fitted it to a lacquered, rattan-wrapped bow, which was a good nine feet long, drew the bow to the full, and sent the arrow whizzing through the air. It flew more than fourteen hundred feet, thudded square into Nii no Chikakiyo's torso as he stood in the bow of the big boat, and sent him head over heels into the bilge. (I can't say whether he was killed.) Asari no Yoichi was a born archer. People said he never missed a running deer at seven hundred feet.

After these events, both the Genji and the Heike attacked and fought with reckless courage, shouting and yelling. Neither side seemed the weaker, but the Heike had the emperor and the imperial regalia with them, and the Genji wondered if they could be defeated.

Just then, something appeared in the sky. For a while, it looked like a white cloud, but that was not what it was. It was a mysterious white banner, and it floated downward until its cord seemed almost to touch one of the Genji bows.

"This is a sign from the Great Bodhisattva Hachiman!" Yoshitsune exclaimed. Overjoyed, he rinsed his mouth and performed an obeisance, and all his warriors did the same.

Furthermore, a school of dolphins surfaced and swam from the Genji position toward the Heike, a thousand or two thousand in all. Munemori summoned the learned doctor Harenobu. "Dolphins always travel in schools, but we've never seen numbers like these," he said. "Use your divining arts to find out what it means."

"If they stay on the surface and turn back, the Genji will be destroyed," Harenobu said. "If they dive and go on past us, we'll be in danger." He had no sooner spoken than the dolphins passed directly under the boats of the Heike. "This is going to be the end for us," he said.

During the last three years, Awa no Shigeyoshi had acted as a loyal vassal of the Heike, fighting battle after battle without regard for his own safety, but now he suddenly went over to the Genji. (It may be that he saw no alternative, considering that his son Noriyoshi had been captured.) The Heike had put their men of noble birth on the fighting boats and their less important warriors on the Chinese-style ships, hoping in that way to surround and crush the Genji when they attacked the ships. But thanks to Shigeyoshi's defection, the Genji ignored the ships and aimed at the boats carrying the disguised commanders-in-chief. Tomomori wished a thousand times that he had cut off Shigeyoshi's head and thrown it away.

Meanwhile, all the warriors from Shikoku and Chinzei deserted the Heike for the Genji. Yesterday's vassals used their bows against their emperor and drew swords against their masters. High seas barred the way to distant shores; lines of enemy archers denied access to nearby beaches. That day, it seemed, was destined to witness the end of the contest between the Genji and the Heike for mastery of the realm.

11.9. *The Drowning of the Former Emperor*

Genji warriors had already begun to board Heike boats that were veering out of control, their sailors and helmsmen lying slain in the bilge. Tomomori crossed in a small craft to the emperor's ship. "This seems to be it! Get rid of everything unsightly," he said. He ran around from stem to stern, sweeping, mopping, dusting, and tidying the ship with his own hands.

"How is the battle going, Lord Middle Counselor? How are things going?" the ladies asked.

He answered with a sarcastic laugh. "You're going to get acquainted with some remarkable eastern warriors."

"How can you joke at a time like this!" They all began to shriek and scream.

The nun of second rank had decided on her course of action long ago. She draped her two gray inner robes over her head, hitched up her divided skirt of glossed silk, tucked the Bead Strand under her arm and the Sword into her belt, and took the emperor in her arms. "I'm only a woman, but I don't intend to fall into enemy hands. I go where His Majesty goes. Follow me, you whose hearts are loyal to him!" She walked to the side of the ship.

Eight that year, the emperor seemed very mature for his age. His face shone with radiant beauty, and his abundant black hair reached below his waist. "Where are you taking me, Grandmother?" he asked, with a puzzled expression.

She turned her face to the young sovereign, holding back her tears. "Don't you understand? You became an emperor because you obeyed the ten good precepts in your last life, but now an evil karma holds you in its toils. Your good fortune has come to an end. Turn to the east and say goodbye to the Grand Shrine of Ise, then turn to the west and repeat the sacred name of Amida Buddha, so that he and his host may come to escort you to the pure land. This country is a land of sorrow; I'm taking you to a happy place called paradise," she said.

His Majesty was wearing a robe of olive-gray, and his hair was done up in a boy's loops at the side. With tears swimming in his eyes, he joined his tiny hands, knelt toward the east, and bade farewell to the Grand Shrine. Then he turned toward the west and repeated the sacred name of Amida. The nun snatched him up, said in a comforting voice, "There's a capital under the waves, too," and entered the boundless depths.

Ah, how sad that the spring breeze of impermanence should have scattered the august blossoms in an instant! Ah, how heartless that the wild waves of transmigration should have engulfed the jewel person! We are told of an imperial hall, Longevity by name, that was designed to be a permanent imperial residence, and of a gate, Eternal Youth, through which old age was powerless to enter—yet now a sovereign less than ten years old had become debris at the bottom of the sea.[3] Words cannot express the wretchedness of such a karma! A dragon above the clouds had descended to become a fish in the ocean depths. In the past, he had held sway over kin by blood and by marriage, with state ministers and senior nobles on every side, dwelling as it were on the heights of Bonten's lofty palace and within Taishaku's Joyful-to-see City; now, alas, he went from shipboard life to instant death beneath the waves.

11.13. *The Parading of the Heike Along the Avenue*

[Most of the prominent Taira men not killed in battle have died by their own hand at Dan-no-ura, but the clan chieftain, Munemori, has been taken alive, as have Tokitada, Munemori's sons, Kenreimon'in, and some lesser figures. It is now a day or two after the battle.]

Meanwhile, it was learned that the Second Prince had returned.[4] Retired Emperor Go-Shirakawa sent a carriage to fetch him. Carried off willy-nilly

3. Longevity and Eternal Youth were the names of a building and a gate at the Chinese imperial palace.

4. Emperor Takakura's son Morisada (1179–1223), the younger half-brother of Emperor Antoku and the older full brother of the new emperor, Go-Toba.

by the Heike, the prince had drifted on the western waves for three years, his plight a source of great distress to his mother and his guardian, the Jimyōin consultant, but now they were reunited, and they all rejoiced tearfully in his safe return.

On the twenty-sixth, the captive Heike entered the city, riding in wickerwork carriages decorated with designs depicting eight-petaled lotus blossoms. The front and rear blinds were raised, and the left and right windows were open.

Minister of State Munemori wore a plain white hunting robe.[5] His son, Kiyomune, rode in the rear of the same carriage, dressed in a white tunic. The carriage containing Taira Major Counselor Tokitada followed. The plan had been for Tokitada's son, Tokizane, to ride with his father, but he was excused on grounds of illness. Director of the Palace Storehouse Bureau Nobumoto, who had been wounded, entered the city by a side street.

The dashing, handsome Munemori was thin and worn, almost another person, but he looked around in seemingly good spirits. His son lay prostrate with lowered eyes, the picture of misery. Wearing light armor over a dark yellow tunic, Toi no Sanehira guarded them with the thirty-odd riders of his personal escort, whom he posted at the front and rear of the carriage.

Spectators of all ages had assembled—not merely from inside the city, but also from provinces near and far, and from mountains and temples. Their countless thousands and myriads formed a solid mass along the entire route, from the south gate of the Toba Mansion to Yotsuzuka. A man could not look behind him; a carriage could not turn its wheels. The famine in the Jishō and Yōwa eras [1177–81] and the battles in the east and west had exacted a dreadful toll in human life, and yet there seemed to be huge numbers of survivors.

The onlookers had not forgotten the former splendor of the Heike lords in the short time since their departure from the capital, a mere year and parts of two others. They scarcely knew whether they were awake or dreaming when they saw the present condition of the men who had once inspired such great fear and trembling. All of them wept until their sleeves were drenched—even coarse, humble men and women who lacked the finer feelings. We may imagine the emotions of people who had been on intimate terms with the clan! Of the prisoners' old associates—men who had enjoyed their favor for years and rendered them service for generations—many had turned to the Genji to save themselves, but they could not forget past kindnesses overnight, and their hearts must have been heavy. There were many in the crowd who pressed their sleeves to their faces and lowered their eyes.

Munemori's ox-driver was Saburōmaru, the younger brother of that Jirōmaru who had had his head cut off for not driving Kiso no Yoshinaka properly when Kiso called on the retired emperor. Saburōmaru had changed

5. Circumspect attire considered suitable for grave circumstances.

to a man's hairdress while he was in the west, but he had set his heart on driving Munemori's carriage that one time. "I realize that grooms and ox-drivers are the lowest of the low and can't have refined feelings, but I'm indebted to my master for being kept in his service all these years. If it's all right, I'd like to guide the ox during his last carriage ride," he pleaded with Yoshitsune at Toba.

"I don't see anything wrong with it. Hurry up!" Yoshitsune said.

Saburōmaru was delighted. He put on a handsome robe, drew a lead rope from his breast, and attached it to the ox. Then, blinded by tears, he set out with his sleeve pressed to his face, depending on the ox to lead the way.

Retired Emperor Go-Shirakawa watched the procession from a carriage near the intersection of Rokujō and Higashi-no-tōin avenues, where the carriages of senior nobles and courtiers were also drawn up in rows. He could not help feeling sorrow and compassion at the sight of the men who had once been among his closest attendants, and the members of his entourage felt as though they were dreaming. High and low shed tears. "Back in the days when everyone was desperate for a glance or a word from one of those men, who could have thought they would come to this?" people said.

In a bygone year, on the occasion of Munemori's formal expression of gratitude for his appointment as palace minister, the carriages of the Ka-zan'in major counselor and eleven other senior nobles had followed in his train, and Head Chamberlain Chikamune and fifteen other courtiers had ridden on horseback in his vanguard. Senior nobles and courtiers alike had decked themselves out in dazzling array because they considered it a great public event. Among them, there were four middle counselors and three middle captains of third rank. The present Taira major counselor, Tokitada, who had been a guards commander at the time, had been called before the emperor, given gifts, and otherwise entertained with splendid ceremony. But not a single senior noble or courtier accompanied the two today. Their only attendants were twenty samurai in white tunics, men who had been captured with them at Dan-no-ura, and who rode tied to their saddles.

After the prisoners had been paraded to the riverbed and back, Munemori and his son were installed in Yoshitsune's quarters at Rokujō Horikawa. Food was offered to them, but they were too upset to use their chopsticks. They merely wept, exchanging silent glances.

At nightfall, Munemori spread out a sleeve and lay down without loosening his robes. His guards, Genpatsuhyōe, Eda no Genzō, and Kumai Tarō, noticed that he had covered Kiyomune with the other sleeve.[6]

"Whether a man's sphere in life is high or low, it's love for a child that causes him the most grief. What can a sleeve do to protect the boy? It's easy to see how much he loves him," one of them said. Fierce warriors though they were, they all wept.

6. Kiyomune (1169–85) was 16 years old.

11.18. The Execution of the Minister of State

[Yoshitsune has delivered Munemori to Yoritomo, but he himself has been forbidden to enter Kamakura because Kajiwara Kagetoki's slanders have made Yoritomo suspect him of treacherous ambitions.]

Yoritomo received Minister of State Munemori. He had him seated in one of the wings, across a courtyard from his own room, and looked at him from behind his blinds. Then he sent over Hiki no Yoshikazu with a message. "I have no personal grudge against the house of Taira. I know very well, too, that I couldn't have survived if your father had not permitted it, no matter what Lady Ike might have said to try to save me. It was entirely due to Kiyomori's kindness that my sentence was reduced to distant-exile, and it was for that reason that I stayed here quietly for over twenty years. But your clan rebelled against the court, and the retired emperor commanded me to strike you down. Nobody born in this country can ignore an imperial edict; I had to obey. I'm glad to be able to meet you."

When Yoshikazu delivered the message, Munemori sat erect and bowed to the floor in a highly inappropriate manner. There were a number of men from the capital among the large and small landholders seated in rows, and also some former vassals of the Heike. "Does he think he can save himself by straightening up and bowing?" they all sneered. "No wonder he's come here as a prisoner instead of dying in the west, the way he should have."[7] But other people wept. "It says in the book, 'When a fierce tiger roams the deep mountains, all the other animals live in fear and trembling; when the tiger is caged, he wags his tail and begs for food.'[8] In the same way, even the bravest commander may change when he gets into a situation like this. That must be what's happened to Munemori," someone said.

Because of Kagetoki's slanders, Yoritomo refused to give a clear answer to any of Yoshitsune's many pleas. Instead, he ordered him to go straight back to the capital.

Yoshitsune left on the ninth of the sixth month, taking Munemori and Kiyomune with him.

Munemori was delighted by the prospect of any reprieve, no matter how short. He lived in constant dread of being put to death somewhere along the way, but they passed one province and post station after another. In Owari Province, there is a place called Utsumi. It was there that Yoritomo's father, Yoshitomo, had been killed, and Munemori felt certain that he would die on the same spot. But Utsumi too was left behind. A faint hope stirred in his mind, pathetically groundless. "Maybe they're going to spare us!"

"We can't possibly live," Kiyomune thought. "They're just waiting until

7. Most of the Taira men had committed suicide at Dan-no-ura.
8. From the literary anthology *Wen xuan*.

we get close to the capital; they don't want our heads to rot in this heat."[9] But he kept his opinion to himself, touched by his father's appearance of abject misery. He merely devoted his time to reciting the sacred name of Amida Buddha. The capital drew near as time passed, and they arrived at the Shinohara post station in Ōmi Province.

Yoshitsune was a kindhearted man. While they were still three days away from the city, he sent ahead for an ascetic from Ōhara, a monk called Hon-shōbō, to serve as the prisoners' religious guide. Munemori and Kiyomune had been kept together until the preceding day, but on that morning they were separated and put in different places. Munemori's spirits sank even lower as he contemplated the likelihood that this would be their last day. With tears streaming down his face, he said, "Where's Kiyomune? I thought I'd be holding his hand when I died. I thought that after our heads were cut off, at least our bodies would lie on the same mat. It's terribly hard to be separated while we're still alive! We've never spent a day apart for seventeen years. It was only for his sake that I disgraced myself by not drowning."

Although the holy man felt sorry for him, he felt that it would be a mistake to show weakness. Wiping away a tear, he spoke in a matter-of-fact voice. "Don't trouble your mind about your son now. It would be agonizing for both of you if you saw each other at the end. Not many men have ever been as happy and prosperous as you were, from the day of your birth on. You became related to an emperor by marriage, you served as a minister of state, there was no worldly glory you didn't enjoy. The thing that's about to happen is your karma from a previous existence; you shouldn't blame society or men. When we stop to consider, even the pleasures of deep contemplation in King Bonten's palace are transitory, so what can we say about human life in this world, a flash of lightning, a dewdrop in the morning? A life span in the heaven of the thirty-three divinities lasts a hundred billion years, and yet it's only a dream; your own thirty-nine years of life have been a mere instant. Who has tasted the elixir of eternal youth and immortality? Who has prolonged his life like Dongfang Shuo or the Queen Mother of the West? Despite his overweening arrogance, the First Emperor of Qin was buried in a tumulus at Lishan; desperately though he clung to life, Emperor Wu of Han rotted into moss at Duling. We're told, 'Whatever lives must perish; Śākyamuni Buddha didn't escape the sandalwood smoke. Happiness ends, sorrow follows: even for heavenly beings, there comes a day when the five signs of decay appear.'[10] Thus the Buddha teaches, 'Our minds are void of themselves; sin and blessedness lack true existence. When we meditate on the mind, there is no mind. The laws do not dwell in the Law.'[11] To regard

9. Time has elapsed since the battle of Dan-no-ura in the third month; it is now midsummer, the sixth month of the lunar year.

10. From a Buddhist petition composed by Ōe no Asatsuna (WKRES 793).

11. *Kanzeongyō Sutra.*

good and bad as unreal is to be in accord with the Buddha's mind. Isn't it a supreme cause for regret, a supremely pitiable folly, that we should transmigrate through life and death for billions of kalpas—that we should find a treasure trove and leave empty-handed—even though Amida Buddha has pronounced his difficult vow after five kalpas of cogitation?[12] Don't think about anything but salvation now." It was in this manner that he administered instruction and urged Munemori to invoke Amida's sacred name.

Munemori recognized the wisdom of the holy man's precepts. He promptly closed his mind to distracting ideas, faced westward, folded his hands, and recited the name of Amida Buddha in a firm voice. Kitsuumano-jō Kinnaga went around behind him from the left, a drawn sword held inconspicuously at his side, and stood poised to strike.

Munemori stopped chanting. "Have you already killed Kiyomune?" he said pathetically. Kinnaga moved in from the rear, and the minister's head fell forward in an instant.

The ascetic broke down in tears. Nor could the other spectators help feeling moved, fierce warriors though they were. Everyone criticized Kinnaga, a hereditary Taira retainer who had served Tomomori morning and night. "We all know that a man has to adapt to the times, but his behavior was shameless," people said.

Afterward, the holy man gave Kiyomune the same kind of instructions and urged him to invoke the sacred name. Most touchingly, the boy asked, "How did my father behave before he died?"

"His conduct was admirable. Please don't be concerned."

Tears of happiness came to Kiyomune's eyes. "There's nothing left for me to worry about now. Just hurry up!" he said.

The swordsman that time was Hori no Chikatsune.

Yoshitsune went on to the capital with the heads. At Kinnaga's direction, the bodies of father and son were buried in a single grave. That was because Munemori had been insistent about wanting to be with Kiyomune, sinful though his desire was.[13]

The two heads were brought into the capital on the twenty-third [of the sixth month]. Members of the imperial police took custody of them at the Sanjō riverbed, paraded them along the avenue, and hung them in the China tree to the left of the prison gate. There may have been some foreign precedent for parading the heads of men of third and higher rank, but I have yet to hear of any such thing in this country. Nobuyori had been decapitated for criminal conduct in the Heiji era, but his head was not hung at the gate. The Heike nobles were the first. When they entered the city alive from the

12. Amida took a vow to save mankind. According to *Maka shikan*, a basic Tendai text, not seizing an opportunity to escape from the cycle of transmigration is like finding a treasure trove and leaving it empty-handed.

13. Desire is an impediment to enlightenment.

western provinces, they were paraded eastward on Rokujō Avenue; when they returned dead from the eastern provinces, they were paraded westward on Sanjō Avenue. In life and death alike, theirs was the greatest imaginable humiliation.

11.19. *The Execution of Shigehira*

The monks of Nara had been insistent in their demands for Middle Captain Shigehira, who had been living in Izu Province since last year as Kano no Munemochi's ward. It was decided that their requests would have to be granted, and orders to escort the prisoner to Nara were issued to Yorikane, a grandson of Minamoto no Yorimasa. Instead of taking him into the capital, Yorikane went from Ōtsu along the Yamashina-Daigo road, which passed close to Hino.

Shigehira's principal wife, Lady Dainagon-no-suke, was the daughter of Torikai Middle Counselor Korezane, the adoptive daughter of Gojō Major Counselor Kunitsuna, and the nurse of Emperor Antoku. After she learned that the dewdrop of his life had yet to vanish—tremble though it did on the tip of the leaf—she longed to meet him one last time in real life, not merely in her dreams; but that was impossible, and she spent the days with tears as her only distraction.

Shigehira asked his warrior-guards for a short leave. "I appreciate all the consideration and kindness you've shown me; it's been quite extraordinary. If you don't mind, I'd like to ask one last favor. Being childless, I don't have anything to chain my thoughts to worldly things, but I've heard that my wife is living at Hino, and I'd like to see her just once, so that I can ask her to pray for me after my death," he said.

The warriors were not rocks or trees incapable of feeling. They wept as they assented. "There can be no objection."

Shigehira was delighted. He sent someone inside with a message. "Is Lady Dainagon-no-suke there? Shigehira is on his way to Nara; he would like to speak to her from the courtyard." His wife came running out before the messenger finished. "Where is he? Where is he?" she asked.

He stood there near the veranda, a thin, sunburned man wearing a folded cap and a tunic with an indigo-leaf design. She moved forward to the edge of the blinds. "Am I awake or dreaming?" she asked. "Come in!"

Tears filled Shigehira's eyes at the sound of her voice, and she was too agitated to say anything more.

Thrusting his head inside the blind, he spoke through his tears. "Perhaps it was because of that frightful sin that I was captured and paraded through the streets this last spring, when I ought to have died at Ichi-no-tani. It was bad enough to be humiliated in the capital, and again in Kamakura, but now I'm on my way to be handed over to the Nara monks for execution. I wanted to take religious vows and give you my hair as a keepsake, but they

ouldn't let me." He separated out a lock of hair from his forehead, bit
f what he could reach, and handed it to her. "Take this as a keepsake,"
e said.

His wife felt even more wretched than in the days when she was living a
of frantic anxiety. "I ought to have drowned myself after we parted, just
Michimori's wife did when he died. My life became a terrible burden, but
e was no certainty about your death, and I kept hoping that somehow,
ugh some quirk of fate, I might see you again as you used to look. I
bear to think this is your last day! I've just stayed alive because I hoped
ight be spared," she said.

They talked of the past and present, and it was only their tears that
seemed to have no end.

"Your clothes look so shabby," she said. "Please change into something
else." She produced a wadded short-sleeved robe and a white hunting robe,
and Shigehira put them on. He left her his old robes, telling her to think of
them as keepsakes.

"I'll do that, of course," she said. "But if I could have just a scrap of your
writing, it would be something to treasure forever." She brought out an
inkstone. Weeping, he set down a poem:

sekikanete	That they may become
namida no kakaru	mementos for the future,
karagoromo	I have taken off
nochi no katami ni	these garments, wet with the tears
nugi zo kaenuru	I have sought in vain to stem.

Her response was prompt:

nugikauru	When I consider
koromo mo ima wa	how they but commemorate
nani ka sen	today's last farewell,
kyō o kagiri no	what solace might they offer now—
katami to omoeba	those garments you have taken off?

"People who exchange vows are bound to meet in the next life." Shigehira
said. "Pray for the two of us to be reborn on the same lotus. The sun's going
down. It's still a long way to Nara; I don't want to keep the warriors waiting." He started to go.

She caught hold of his sleeve to detain him. "Please, please. Stay just a
little while longer."

"Try to imagine how I feel! But there's no way out for me. I'm sure we'll
meet in another life." As he started away, he was tempted to turn back, for
he realized that they would never meet again in this world. But he made
himself leave, determined not to look like a weakling. In an agony of grief,
she flung herself onto the floor near the blinds. Her shrieks and screams
carried all the way to the gate, and he found it impossible to put the spurs

love

to his horse. It seemed to him that it would have been better not to see her at all; the brief visit had merely made him feel worse. She lay prostrate, a robe pulled over her head. If only she might have run after him!

After the monks took custody of Shigehira, they met in general council. "This man is guilty of a crime so heinous that there is no provision for it in the three thousand varieties of the five punishments. It's only right for him to suffer the consequences. He's a traitor to the doctrines and scriptures, so first of all, he ought to be paraded around the outer walls of the Tōdaiji and the Kōfukuji. Then we should either cut off his head with a saw or bury him alive and behead him," some of them argued. But the senior monks demurred. "Those would be questionable acts for monks. You'd better simply turn him over to the warrior-guards and have them execute him near Kotsu," they said. Thus, they returned him to the warriors.

Once the warriors took charge, they got ready to behead Shigehira on the bank of the Kotsu River. Great throngs of spectators assembled, among them several thousand monks.

There was a certain samurai, one Moku Tomotoki, whom Shigehira had employed for a number of years, and who was now in the service of the Hachijō imperial lady.[14] This Tomotoki whipped his horse toward the river, determined to be with his former master at the end. Just as the execution was about to proceed, he dashed up, pushed through the thousands upon thousands of onlookers all around, and made his way to Shigehira's side. "I've come to be with you at the end," he said, weeping.

"I can't tell you how much I appreciate your loyalty," Shigehira said. "I'd like to worship a buddha before I'm put to death. Can anything be done? My sins are so heavy . . ." "Nothing easier!" Tomotoki said. After consulting with the guards, he fetched an image from somewhere nearby. Fortunately, it was a representation of Amida. He set it down on the sandy beach. Then he drew a sleeve-cord from his hunting robe, attached it to the Buddha's hand, and gave Shigehira the other end to hold.

Shigehira faced the Buddha, the cord in his hand. Then he spoke. "We're told that Devadatta was assured by Śākyamuni of eventual rebirth as the buddha Ten'ō, even though he had committed the three deadly sins and destroyed the scriptures preserving the eighty thousand teachings—that despite the enormity of his deeds, his very transgressions had ensured his salvation by bringing him into lasting association with the sacred teachings. I wasn't acting of my own free will when I committed my grave sins; I was merely trying to do my duty. What human being can spurn an imperial command? What person born in this world can ignore a father's order? There's no way to refuse either one. The buddhas must judge between right and wrong.

14. A daughter of Emperor Toba.

"The retribution for my sins has been swift; my luck has run out. No lamentations could express the full measure of my regret. But compassion reigns in the Buddha's world; many paths lead to salvation. I well remember the text that says, 'The perfect teachings tell us that resistance is the same as compliance.'[15] A single invocation of Amida Buddha's name immediately wipes out countless sins. I ask that my resistance may be transformed into compliance, and that these final invocations may bring about my rebirth in the pure land of the nine grades."

He stretched out his neck, meanwhile reciting the sacred name ten times in a loud voice, and the executioner struck off his head. Grave though his transgressions had been, all the monkish thousands and warrior-guards shed tears.

The head was nailed up in front of the great torii at the Hannyaji, because it was there that Shigehira had stood when he destroyed the temples during the fighting in Jishō [1177–80].

Shigehira's wife, Lady Dainagon-no-suke, sent a palanquin to fetch the headless corpse so that she might hold a memorial service. As she had expected, the body had been thrown away. Her men retrieved it, put it into the palanquin, and carried it on their shoulders to Hino. We can imagine her feelings when it arrived. It had retained its old handsome appearance until the day before, but now it was already decomposing in the heat.

Since things could not go on like that forever, the lady prevailed on a group of worthy monks to hold prayer services at the Hōkaiji Temple, which was close by. She also persuaded Shunjōbō, the Daibutsu saint, to get her husband's head from the monks and send it to Hino. She cremated head and body, sent the bones to Mount Kōya, and made a grave at Hino. And then, most touchingly, she took religious vows and prayed for Shigehira's welfare in the life to come.

15. From *Hokke monguki*, a commentary on another important Tendai text, *Hokke mongu*.

Chapter 12

Time: late 1185–early 1200's
Principal subject: fate of Rokudai, the heir of the main Taira lineage
Principal characters:

    Kamakura Lord. Yoritomo

    Koremori (Taira). Eldest son of Kiyomori's late heir, Shigemori; now deceased

    Mongaku[bō]. Monk who had encouraged Yoritomo to rebel against the Taira

    Rokudai (Taira). Heir of Koremori

    Saitōgo, Saitōroku. Retainers of Koremori

    Tokimasa (Hōjō). Yoritomo's deputy in the capital

    Yoritomo (Minamoto). Head of the triumphant Minamoto clan

[On the orders of Yoritomo, now the de facto ruler of Japan, the Taira who managed to remain in the capital have been banished. The Kamakura Lord has also moved against Yoshitsune, dispatching a huge force of riders led by Hōjō Tokimasa to take control of the city. Yoshitsune is now a pariah, with a price on his head.]

12.7. *Rokudai*

Hōjō no Shirō Tokimasa conceived the idea of proclaiming in public that anyone who discovered a Taira child would receive whatever reward he wanted; and large numbers of victims were ferreted out by the greedy local inhabitants, who knew every inch of the city. Even children from the lower classes, if they happened to be well-favored and fair-skinned, were called in and identified as the offspring of this or that middle captain or lesser captain; and when the parents wept and lamented, the informers said, "That child was identified by his guardian," or "He was identified by his nurse." Tokimasa's men drowned or buried the babies, and strangled or stabbed those who were a little older. It would be impossible to describe the grief of the mothers and the misery of the nurses. Tokimasa had many children and grandchildren of his own, and the policy he had adopted was not to his taste, but there seemed to be no help for it. Men must adapt to the times.

Of the Taira children, Tokimasa especially wanted to capture Koremori's son, Rokudai, the heir of the main lineage, who was nearing adulthood. His searches were unsuccessful, but a woman came to Rokuhara just as he was about to leave for Kamakura.

"Koremori's wife, son, and daughter are at Shōbudani, north of a mountain temple called the Daikakuji, which is west of here, behind the Henjōji," she announced.[1]

Tokimasa hastily sent off someone with her to investigate, and his man found a cloister occupied by a group of women and children, who seemed to be trying to keep out of sight. Watching through a chink in the fence, he saw a handsome boy come out in pursuit of a white puppy.

A woman who looked like a nurse yanked the boy back inside. "What if somebody saw you?" she said. "That would be a disaster!"

Convinced that the boy must be Rokudai, the man rushed back to report.

On the following day, Tokimasa surrounded the cloister. He sent in a message: "Hōjō Tokimasa, the Kamakura Lord's deputy, has learned that Lord Koremori's son, Rokudai, is living here. He has come for him; send him out at once."

Rokudai's mother almost fainted. Saitōgo and Saitōroku ran around to look, but the warriors had surrounded the house, leaving no avenue of escape. The boy's nurse fell flat in front of him, uttering piercing shrieks.

Everyone in the cloister had been vigilant about avoiding detection, careful even to refrain from loud speech, but now the whole household broke into tearful lamentations. Tokimasa waited quietly, wiping away tears of pity.

After a while, Tokimasa repeated his demand. "Things are still unsettled. I've come for the boy to be sure he'll be safe from any possible act of violence. It's nothing to get excited about. Send him out now," he told them.

"There's no hope of escape," Rokudai told his mother. "You'd better send me out right away. If the warriors came in and searched, they'd see you and the others looking upset. Even if I have to go now, I can probably get permission to come back if I survive at all. Don't carry on so." It was a pitiful attempt at consolation.

Things could not go on like that forever. In tears, the boy's mother smoothed his hair, dressed him, and prepared to send him out. She gave him a string of dainty little blackwood prayer-beads. "As long as you live, use these to recite Amida's name. Then you can go to paradise," she said.

Rokudai accepted the beads with a pathetic speech. "I'm parting from my mother today. All I want now is to join my father." His ten-year-old sister came running out when she heard him. "I want to go to Daddy, too," she said. The nurse restrained her.

Rokudai had only turned twelve that year, but the elegance of his face and figure made him seem more mature than most youths of fourteen or

1. These were all places in Saga (Ukyō-ku, Kyoto).

fifteen. Determined not to show weakness in front of the enemy, he kept his sleeve pressed to his face, but the tears trickled through.

After he got into the palanquin, the warriors surrounded it, and the party set out. Saitōgo and Saitōroku accompanied him, one on the left side of the palanquin and one on the right. Tokimasa ordered two of his men to dismount so that they could ride, but they ran barefoot all the way from the Daikakuji to Rokuhara, unwilling to accept his offer.

In an agony of grief, the mother and the nurse raised their eyes to heaven and cast themselves to earth. "The authorities are collecting the children of the Heike and killing them in different ways nowadays—drowning, burying, strangling, and stabbing," the mother said. "I wonder how they'll do it to Rokudai. He's rather grown up, so they'll probably cut off his head. All parents love their children, even when they send them to live with nurses and just see them once in a while, as some do. But Rokudai has never been away from me since he was born. His father and I raised him together morning and evening, happy to have such a treasure; and after I suffered the terrible loss of the man I relied on, it was my two children I turned to for comfort. Now there's only one left; the other's gone. What will I do after this? I lived in terror of this very thing for three years, but I never expected it would happen today. All this time, I counted on the Hase Kannon to protect him, but now he's been taken away. He's probably dead already." She ran on in the same vein, shedding endless tears.

The hour grew late, but the grief-stricken mother was beyond settling down to rest. "I dozed off just now," she told the nurse, "and I dreamed Rokudai came riding up on a white horse. 'I missed you so much that I asked for a short leave. Here I am!' he said. He sat down beside me, crying, for some reason, as though his heart would break. In the next instant, I woke up. I looked all around, just in case, but there was nobody there. I wish I hadn't waked up so soon, even though it was only a dream." The nurse wept.

As the long, miserable night wore on, the lady's bed seemed in danger of floating away on a river of tears.

Because all things come to an end, the timekeeper proclaimed the approach of dawn, and a new day began. Saitōroku came back. "What's happened? Tell me what's happened!" the mother said.

"So far, nothing. I've brought a letter." He handed it over.

She opened it to find a very adult-sounding message. "I know you must feel awfully worried. Nothing much has happened so far. I miss everybody already." Without uttering a word, she thrust it into her bosom and fell prostrate. It's sad to think of how she must have felt.

After much time had elapsed in that manner, Saitōroku spoke up. "I feel nervous about being away, even for a little while. I'd better be getting back." With tears in her eyes, the mother wrote out an answer, and he left.

Just to be doing something, the nurse ran outside and began to wander around the neighborhood, weeping. As she walked, she heard someone talking. "Back in the hills from here, there's a temple called Takao, and its monk, Mongaku, is a great favorite with the Kamakura Lord, Yoritomo. I hear he's looking for a son of a noble family to be his disciple." Her spirits rose, and she went off to Takao alone, without saying anything to her mistress.

"Yesterday, a warrior took away a young lord twelve years old, a boy I've cared for ever since he was born," she told Mongaku. "Please, please! Ask for his life and make him your disciple!" She threw herself at his feet, sobbing and uttering piercing shrieks. Moved by her desperation, he asked to be told more. She rose and spoke through her tears. "He's the son of somebody close to the wife of Koremori, the Komatsu middle captain of third rank. An informer must have said he was Koremori's son, because a warrior arrested him yesterday and took him away."

"Who was the warrior?" Mongaku asked.

"He was called Hōjō Tokimasa."

"All right, I'll go and look into the matter." He set out promptly.

The nurse felt a little better, even though Mongaku had said nothing on which she could rely. Back at the Daikakuji, she told Rokudai's mother what had happened.

"I thought you must have gone off to drown yourself," the lady said, "because I was also thinking about jumping into some deep pool or river." She asked to hear the whole story. After the nurse had carefully repeated Mongaku's words, she joined her hands in prayer. "May the request for him be granted!" she said. "May I see him once again!"

Mongaku went to make inquiries at Rokuhara.

Tokimasa told him, "Yoritomo said to me, 'I hear that many Taira children are hidden in the capital, including a son of Koremori by Narichika's daughter. That child is the heir of the main lineage, and he's almost an adult. Be sure to hunt him down and kill him.' I captured a few children of distant relatives, but I couldn't find out where Koremori's son was staying. Then two days ago, an unexpected bit of information came in, just as I was about to go back to Kamakura empty-handed, and yesterday I went to get him. He's an extraordinarily appealing little fellow; I haven't brought myself to do anything about him yet. He's still here."

"I'd like to see him," Mongaku said. He went to Rokudai's quarters. The boy was wearing a double-patterned damask tunic, with the blackwood prayer-beads dangling from his wrist. The curve of his hair, his figure, his bearing—all bespoke a refinement and charm that seemed to come from another world. A drawn face, hinting of broken sleep the night before, made him look even more pathetic and touching. For some reason, tears sprang to his eyes when he saw Mongaku, and the holy man could not help weeping until his black sleeve was drenched.

"No matter how dangerous an enemy this boy might become someday, it would be unthinkable to kill him," Mongaku thought. To Tokimasa he said, "I feel terribly sorry for the child; I wonder if we might have been together in a previous existence. Please let him live twenty days longer; I'm going to visit Yoritomo and ask for him. Even though I was an exile myself, I set out toward the capital to get an edict from the retired emperor and help His Lordship rise in the world. I almost drowned when I tried to cross the unfamiliar lower reaches of the Fuji River in the dark; I begged for my life with joined hands when I met some highwaymen on Takaichi Mountain. I went to Fukuhara, to the Prison Palace, and got the edict through Mitsuyoshi, the former commander of the military guards.[2] And His Lordship made me a promise when I gave it to him. 'You may ask for anything, no matter how important,' he said. 'As long as I live, I'll grant any request you make.' I don't need to mention the things I did for him later; you know all about that. Promises are important; life isn't. His Lordship will never have forgotten unless the appointment as constable-general has gone to his head."[3] He set out before daybreak.

When Saitōgo and Saitōroku heard what had happened, they burst into tears, joined their hands, and worshipped the holy man as though he had been a living Buddha. We can imagine the joy of Rokudai's mother when they rushed back to the Daikakuji with the news. There were still grounds for concern, because the decision would be made in Kamakura, but Mongaku's words had been immensely reassuring. Furthermore, the boy was safe for another twenty days. The mother and the nurse breathed a little easier, trusting that it was all coming about through Kannon's help.

Meanwhile, the sun continued to rise and set, and the twenty days passed like a dream, with no sign of Mongaku. What could have happened? The optimism of the mother and nurse turned to despair. Again, they fretted and agonized.

"Mongakubō's period of grace has expired," Tokimasa said. "I can't go on wasting time in the capital until the year ends; I'll have to leave now." His men busied themselves with preparations for the departure. Saitōgo and Saitōroku clenched their fists, trembling with apprehension, but there was nothing they could do. Mongaku had neither come nor sent a messenger.

The two went to the Daikakuji. "The holy man hasn't arrived in the city yet. Hōjō plans to leave tomorrow morning before daybreak." They wept as they spoke, with both sleeves pressed to their faces.

We can imagine the grief of Rokudai's mother. "Isn't there any wise older man who might advise Hōjō to take Rokudai with him to wherever he meets Mongaku?" she asked. "It would be so sad if they put him to death while Mongaku was on his way with the pardon! Does it look as though they're going to kill him right away?"

2. "Prison Palace" was an epithet for the retired emperor's residence, which the Heike had kept under guard.

3. A little earlier, Yoritomo had been granted this office, which gave him nationwide police and military authority.

"We think they'll do it just before daybreak tomorrow morning. Hōjō's men on night duty seem to be feeling unhappy. Some of them are invoking the name of Amida Buddha; others are shedding tears."

"And Rokudai? What is he doing?"

"When people are watching him, he tells his beads in a matter-of-fact way, but when nobody's around, he presses his sleeve to his face and sobs."

"Yes, that's how he'd act. He's only a boy, but he has a man's spirit. It must be devastating for him to realize that this is his last night of life. He said he'd get leave to come home if he survived even a little while, but we haven't seen anything of him here. And I haven't been able to go there either, even though twenty days have passed. After today, there'll never be a day, never an hour, when we might meet again. What are you two going to do?"

"We'll go where he goes. If he dies, we've made up our minds to gather his bones and deposit them at Mount Kōya. After that, we'll renounce the world, enter the path of enlightenment, and pray for him."

"Hurry back, then. I'm dreadfully worried about him," she said. They went off, weeping.

Hōjō Tokimasa set out from the capital on the sixteenth of the twelfth month, taking Rokudai with him. Saitōgo and Saitōroku also went, scarcely able to see through their tears, but determined to stay with their master to the end. When Tokimasa offered them horses, they turned him down. "We're waiting on our master for the last time; we're not going to notice any discomfort," they said. They walked on, weeping.

It is sad to imagine Master Rokudai's feelings as he faced the eastern road for his farewell journey, mourning the separation from his dear mother and nurse, and looking back toward the familiar capital, which now lay beyond the clouds. Whenever a warrior set spurs to his horse, he trembled in fear of having his head struck off; whenever two men exchanged a few words, he wondered in dismay if this would be his last moment. He had surmised that he might die when they reached the riverbed at Shinomiya, but the party crossed the mountains beyond Ōsaka Barrier and fanned out onto the beach at Ōtsu. Then he guessed that it would be on the plain at Awazu, but the day ended without incident. One after another, they passed many provinces and many post stations, until at last they reached Suruga Province. And that day, people said, was to mark the end of the young master's dewlike life.

The warriors all dismounted among the pine trees at Senbon-no-matsu-bara. They set down the palanquin, spread out a fur rug, and placed Rokudai on it. Tokimasa went up to him.

"I've brought you this far in the hope of meeting Mongaku on the way, but I can't do anything more for you. I don't know what the Kamakura Lord might think if I brought you over the Ashigara Mountains, so I'm going to let people believe I executed you back in Ōmi Province. You share the karma of the Taira; nobody could plead successfully for your life, no matter who." He wept as he spoke.

Rokudai made no reply. He called Saitōgo and Saitōroku to him. "When you go back to the capital afterward, don't let them know I was executed during the journey. I suppose the truth will come out in the end, but Mother would break down if she heard it from your lips. I wouldn't be able to keep from feeling sorry for her under the grass, and that would be a hindrance in the afterlife. Tell her you escorted me all the way to Kamakura," he said. For a time, the two were incapable of speech. Then Saitōgo said, "We're not going calmly back to the capital alive after our master has died before us." He hung his head, trying to hold back the tears.

The last moment had come. Rokudai turned his face to the west, joined his palms, recited the sacred name in a tranquil voice, and waited with extended neck. Kano no Chikatoshi, the designated executioner, went around behind him from the right, with a naked blade held inconspicuously at his side. He prepared to deal the blow, but his mind clouded and he could find no place to strike. He threw down the sword and stepped back, scarcely conscious of his surroundings. "I can't do it. Order somebody else to kill him," he said.

"Well, then, let So-and-so kill him. Let Thus-and-so do it."

As they were debating, a monk in black robes and a divided skirt came galloping up on a white horse, flourishing his whip. He dashed to the execution site, leaped down, and paused an instant to catch his breath. "The Kamakura Lord has pardoned the young master!" he said. "Here's his letter!" He handed it over, and Tokimasa opened and read it:

I am told that you have discovered a son of Lord Koremori, the Komatsu middle captain of third rank. The Takao holy man Mongaku wants him. Have no doubts about handing him over.

> To Hōjō no Shirō
> From Yoritomo

Tokimasa read and reread the letter, which bore Yoritomo's seal. "It's a miracle!" he said as he put it down. I need not describe the feelings of Saitōgo and Saitōroku. And all of Tokimasa's kinsmen and retainers also wept for joy.

12.8. *Hase Rokudai*

Mongaku arrived soon afterward, elated by the success of his pleas. "His Lordship said, 'That boy's father, Koremori, acted as commander in the first battle. I can't spare his life, no matter who asks me.' I tried to frighten him—warned him that he'd lose divine protection if he ignored my wishes—but he told me it was out of the question and left on a hunting trip to Nasuno. I made sure that I went to the hunting grounds, too, and kept after him until he agreed. You must have wondered what was taking me so long," he said.

"The twenty days had gone by, and I'd decided that His Lordship must have turned you down. Fortunately, I didn't kill the boy on the way, even though I almost made a mistake here," Tokimasa said. He mounted Saitōgo and Saitōroku on two saddled horses, which his men had been leading, and started Rokudai off toward the capital. He escorted him for a considerable distance. Then he made his farewell and set out eastward. "I'd like to accompany you awhile longer," he said, "but there are some important matters that I need to lay before His Lordship as soon as I can. I'll say goodbye." He had been most considerate.

After Mongaku received custody of Rokudai, he galloped toward the capital night and day. The year ended while the party was near Atsuta in Owari Province. They reached the capital after nightfall on the fifth of the first month, and Mongaku gave the boy a brief rest in his house, which was near the intersection of Nijō Avenue and Inokuma Street. Then, around midnight, they went to the Daikakuji.

When they rapped on the gate, there was not a sound; the cloister was deserted. Rokudai's white puppy dashed through a break in the wall and came up, wagging its tail. "Where's my mother?" Rokudai asked in a pathetic voice.

Saitōroku climbed the wall to open the gate for his master. It looked as though nobody had been living there for some time. "My life isn't worth anything; I just wanted to preserve it so I could see the people I love. What's happened to them?" Rokudai said. Naturally enough, he spent the rest of the night in wretched spirits, weeping and grieving.

As soon as morning arrived, they made inquiries at a nearby house. "We heard they were going to visit the Great Buddha before the end of the year, and then it seems they were planning to spend the first month in retreat at Hasedera," the neighbors said. "It looks as though nobody's gone near the place since they left."

Saitōgo hurried off to Hase, found the women, and told them the news. The mother and the nurse could scarcely believe their ears. "Is this a dream?" the mother said. "Can it be a dream?"

They rushed back to the Daikakuji, saw Rokudai, and burst into tears of joy. "Hurry up! Take religious vows right away!" the mother said. But Mongaku felt that it would be a pity to make a monk of the boy. Instead, he bundled him off to Takao. And I have heard that he also helped with the practical concerns of the mother's quiet life.

Whether in the past or in the present, many have received succor from Kannon's supreme mercy and supreme benevolence, which extend to sinful and innocent alike, but there can have been few instances to compare with this.

12.9. *The Execution of Rokudai*

So Rokudai grew until he was fourteen or fifteen, a youth whose ever-increasing beauty of face and figure seemed to bathe the surroundings in light. "If only these were the old days, he'd be an officer in the bodyguards by now," his mother said, uttering words that would have been better left unspoken.

Yoritomo was never easy in his mind about the boy. "What of Koremori's son?" he kept asking Mongaku at every opportunity. "You once said, judging from my physiognomy, that I was a man destined to destroy the court's enemies and avenge old dishonors. Is he the same kind of person?"

"That one's spineless; don't worry about him," Mongaku always answered.

But Yoritomo seemed dissatisfied. In an eerie display of prescience, he said, "Mongaku wouldn't think twice about joining a rebellion. Nobody could overthrow us while I'm alive, but who knows what might happen after my sons succeed me?"

Rokudai's mother heard about Yoritomo's remarks. "You've got to take your vows right now. There's no way around it," she said. And thus at the age of sixteen, in the spring of the fifth year of Bunji [1189], Rokudai cut off his beautiful hair at the shoulders, using a pair of scissors. He provided himself with a pilgrim box, donned a robe and a divided skirt treated with persimmon tannin, bade Mongaku farewell, and set out on a pious journey. Saitōgo and Saitōroku went with him, equipped in the same way.

First, he went to Kōya, where he asked his father's religious mentor, the Takiguchi novice, to tell him the whole story of how Koremori had become a monk, and of his end. Then he went to Kumano, a sacred place doubly important to him, he said, because he wanted to retrace his father's footsteps. Standing in front of the Hama-no-miya Shrine, he looked out toward Yamanari-no-shima, the island to which Koremori had crossed. He would have liked to visit it, but an unfavorable wind was blowing, and he could only gaze toward it helplessly, longing to ask the incoming waves where his father had drowned. Even the sand on the beach evoked nostalgia, for it might contain his father's bones. Tears drenched his sleeves. His robes were not those of salt-makers dipping water from the ocean, but there never seemed a time when they were dry. He spent the night on the shore, reciting Amida's name, chanting sutras, and drawing sacred images in the sand with his fingertip. When morning arrived, he summoned a holy man to recite prayers for his father, transferred to Koremori's spirit all the merit amassed by his good deeds, and asked leave of the dead to depart. Then he started back toward the capital in tears.

Now it happened that the reigning emperor [Go-Toba] was a man obsessed with poetry and music. He let Lady Kyō-no-tsubone dominate the government, and there was no end to all the appeals and petitions. Because a king of Wu admired good swordsmen, there were always men in his realm who suffered wounds; because a king of Chu loved slender figures, there were many ladies in his palace who starved themselves to death. Those below follow the taste of those above. People of discernment all worried about what might come of this perilous state of affairs.

Mongaku was a holy man of formidable character, and he took it on himself to meddle where meddling was impermissible. He conceived the idea that the throne should pass to Retired Emperor Takakura's second son, a prince who respected learning and prized principle above all else. No attempt to install the prince could succeed during Yoritomo's lifetime, but Mongaku attempted to stage a revolt soon after his death, which occurred on the thirteenth of the first month in the tenth year of Kenkyū [1199]. The plot was uncovered immediately, and the police were sent to Mongaku's house at the Nijō-Inokuma intersection to arrest him. The holy man, then in his eighties, was banished to Oki Province.

Mongaku uttered a frightful speech as he left the capital. "I won't put up with this! What does that ball-playing kid think he's doing, banishing me to Oki?[4] Some place near the capital would have been right if he had to insist on punishing a man of my age, a person who might die today or tomorrow. I'll greet him in that same province someday!" Oddly enough, it was to Oki, of all places, that Retired Emperor Go-Toba was sent after his rebellion in the Jōkyū era [1219–22].[5] People say Mongaku's dead spirit raged in the province and never stopped badgering the former sovereign.

Master Rokudai devoted himself with great zeal to his religious pursuits at Mount Takao, where he was known as the meditation master of third rank. Nevertheless, Yoritomo kept after the court about him. "He's Koremori's son and Mongaku's disciple," he said. "Shaven head or not, he's no monk inside." So the authorities commanded Anhangan Sukekane to seize him and take him to the east. And at the Tagoshi River, Okabe no Yasutsuna of Suruga received orders to cut off his head. People said it was entirely due to help from the Hase Kannon that he had managed to survive from his twelfth year until he was past thirty.

Thus did the sons of the Heike vanish forever from the face of the earth.

4. "Ball-playing kid" is a reference to the 19-year-old Go-Toba, who had abdicated in 1198 and established an *innochō* (Retired Emperor's Office; see Introduction). He was proficient at the aristocratic sport known as *kemari* (kickball).

5. Go-Toba's "rebellion" in 1221 was an attempt to overthrow the Kamakura shogunate.

The Initiates' Chapter

[Treated as a secret text by the Ichikata-ryū, this chapter is believed to have originated in the late 13th century, after the *Heike* proper, and to have been given its present form by Kakuichi and his Tōdōza senior Joichi. It brings together information about Kiyomori's daughter Kenreimon'in, the mother of Emperor Antoku, which is supplied in Chapters 11 and 12 by other *Heike* texts—namely, her taking of Buddhist vows and retirement to the Jakkōin in 1185, a visit paid her by Retired Emperor Go-Shirakawa in the summer of 1186, and her death in 1191. Although it is divided into five sections, it constitutes a single literary entity—a tale in the old *monogatari* style, rich in poetic imagery, rhythmic passages, *waka*, and melancholy associations.]

Principal characters:

> Dainagon-no-suke. Widow of Kiyomori's son Shigehira; former nurse
> of Emperor Antoku; lady-in-waiting to Kenreimon'in
> Go-Shirakawa, Retired Emperor. Head of the imperial clan
> Kenreimon'in. Daughter of Kiyomori; consort of Emperor Takakura;
> mother of Emperor Antoku. Taken prisoner at Dan-no-ura

I.1. The Imperial Lady Becomes a Nun

The imperial lady Kenreimon'in had gone to stay in the district of Yoshida, at the foot of the eastern hills. The place where she lived was a deserted cloister, the property of a Nara monk called Kyōe. Rank grasses grew in the courtyards, ferns clustered on the eaves, and the tattered blinds left the bedchambers exposed to the wind and rain. Flowers of many different colors blossomed, but there was no master to enjoy them; moonlight streamed in at night, but there was no owner to watch until dawn. It is sad to imagine how she must have felt, that lady who had lived surrounded by brocade curtains in splendid mansions, and who now found herself in so dreadfully dilapidated a habitation, separated from all her relatives. She was like a beached fish, like a bird torn from the nest—nostalgic, in her misery, even for the cheerless shipboard life at sea. Her thoughts dwelt on the distant clouds of the western ocean beyond the boundless blue waves; her tears fell when moonlight illumined the courtyard of the mossy, thatched cloister in the eastern hills. No words could describe her melancholy.

The imperial lady became a nun on the first day of the fifth month in the first year of the Bunji era [1185]. The monk who administered the precepts was Inzei, the holy man from the Ashōbō Cloister at the Chōrakuji Temple. As an offering, she gave him one of Emperor Antoku's informal cloaks. The emperor had worn it until the hour of his death; it still carried the scent of his body. She had brought it all the way from the west to the capital, meaning to keep it always beside her. But now, for lack of anything else that might be suitable, she produced it tearfully, telling herself that the deed might help the emperor attain enlightenment. The monk took it, too moved to speak, and left with tears drenching his black sleeve. People say it was made into a banner to be hung in front of the Chōrakuji Buddha.

The imperial lady had been named a junior consort at the age of fifteen, and an empress at sixteen. Always at the emperor's side, she had urged him to preside over the dawn levees and had shared his love with none at night. At twenty-two, she had given birth to a son who had become the crown prince; and after her son's accession, she had received the palace name Kenreimon'in. She had enjoyed the very greatest respect as both the daughter of Kiyomori and the mother of the emperor.

In this present year [1185], she had turned twenty-nine. The beauty that reminded others of peach blossoms remained unmarred; the freshness that recalled lotus blossoms had not faded. But there was no longer any reason to preserve the tresses reminiscent of black kingfisher feathers, and so, at last, she became a nun. Alas! Her grief knew no end, even after she rejected this transitory world for the true path. Never, not in all the lives to come, could she forget how her despairing kinsmen had cast themselves into the sea; never could she forget the faces of her son and mother. Why had her own dewlike existence dragged on, a mere source of misery? She never ceased to mourn, never ceased to weep.

The nights are short in the fifth month, but the dawns seemed slow to arrive. Not even in dreams could she recapture the past, for she never dozed. "Dim was the waning light of the lamp by the wall, lonely the nightlong beat of the dismal rain against the window."[1] It seemed that not even the lady of Shangyang could have been more wretched when she was imprisoned in the Shangyang Palace.

The wind carried the nostalgic perfume of a flowering orange tree at the eaves—transplanted, perhaps, because the former occupant had sought a reminder of the past[2]—and a cuckoo sang two or three times. Recalling

1. Paraphrased from "The White-haired Lady of Shangyang," a poem by Bo Juyi. The Shangyang Palace, in the southwest corner of Emperor Xuanzong's residential compound at Luoyang, was where the potential rivals of Yang Gueifei were consigned.

2. Anonymous (KKS 139): satsuki matsu / hanatachibana no / ka o kageba / mukashi no hito no / sode no ka zo suru ("Scenting the fragrance of the orange blossoms that await the

the words of an old poem, the lady scribbled them on the lid of her ink-stone case:

> hototogisu   That you raise your voice,
> hanatachibana no   cuckoo, seeking the fragrance
>   ka o tomete   of the flowering orange—
> naku wa mukashi no   is it from nostalgia
> hito ya koishiki   for that "someone long ago"?

Less resolute than the nun of second rank and Michimori's wife, Ko-zaishō, the other Heike women had not drowned themselves in the sea, but had been captured by rough warriors and brought back to the capital. Young and old alike, they had taken Buddhist vows, put on rude attire, and gone to eke out miserable existences in deep valleys and rocky wilds, places of which they had never dreamed. Their old homes had all gone up in smoke, leaving only gutted, deserted sites, fast turning into overgrown fields. The poor ladies must have felt much as did those men who returned from an immortal's dwelling, only to encounter their own descendants in the seventh generation.[3]

Meanwhile, the great earthquake on the ninth of the seventh month had crumbled the tile-capped earthen walls and tilted the rundown buildings at the imperial lady's abode, rendering it even less habitable than before. There was not so much as a green-robed guard at the gate.[4] Already, the depressing voices of insects made officious announcement of autumn's coming, crying from ruined brushwood fences that were even dewier than the lush fields. The nights, as they gradually lengthened, seemed more interminable than ever to the wakeful lady. It was too much that the melancholy of autumn should be superimposed on her never-ending sorrow! In the transitory world where all had changed, not one remained of the old connections who would once have felt bound to take pity on her; not one seemed left who might come to her assistance.

I.2.   *The Imperial Lady Goes to Ōhara*

The imperial lady's younger sisters, the wives of Takafusa and Nobutaka, found discreet ways to express their sympathy. "In the old days, it never

---

fifth month, I recall a perfumed sleeve, worn by someone long ago"). The "old poem" below (SKKS 244) also alludes to this famous composition.

3. According to legend, two Chinese men of the 1st century A.D. met a female immortal on Mount Tiantai, stayed with her for six months, and returned to "encounter their own descendants in the seventh generation." The immediate source of the present allusion is probably WKRES 545.

4. Kenreimon'in was worse off than the lady of Shangyang, whose "palace gates were secured by green-robed guards." The great earthquake of 1185, which had wrought much damage in the capital, is described in a section of that title (Sec. 12.1; not translated).

occurred to me that I might have to depend on those two for a living," she said, weeping. Her attendants all drenched their sleeves.

Her abode was close to the capital, near a road where there were many inquisitive passersby. She longed in vain for an opportunity to move somewhere far back in the mountains—to find a refuge too remote for distressing news to reach her ears, where she might remain while the dew of her life awaited the wind. Then a certain feminine caller told her about the Jakkōin, a very quiet place far back in the mountains at Ōhara, and she resolved to go there. "It's true that a mountain hermitage is lonely, but life is far better there than in a world full of vexations," she said.[5] I believe I have heard that Takafusa's wife made arrangements for the palanquin and other necessities.

It was late in the ninth month of the first year of Bunji [1185] when the imperial lady went to the Jakkōin. Perhaps because the road wound through mountains, the twilight shadows began to gather as she journeyed, her eyes lingering on the colored leaves of the surrounding trees. A lonely sunset bell tolled at a temple in the fields, and the thick dew on the wayside plants added its moisture to her tear-dampened sleeves. Leaves scurried in every direction, blown by a violent wind, and a sudden shower rained down from the cloud-blackened sky, accompanied by the faint belling of a deer and the barely audible plaints of insects. It was all unspeakably depressing. "Nothing was as bad as this before, not even when we were going from bay to bay and island to island," she thought piteously.

The mossy rocks at the Jakkōin evoked an atmosphere of tranquil antiquity. It was a place in which she could willingly settle down. We may wonder if she thought of her own situation when she saw the frost-stricken clumps of dewy bush clover in the courtyard, or gazed at the withering, fading chrysanthemums by the rough fence. She went before the Buddha to pray: "May the Son of Heaven's holy spirit achieve perfect wisdom; may prompt enlightenment be his." Her son's face was before her as she spoke. Would she ever forget him in all the lives to come?

She built a ten-foot-square cell next to the Jakkōin, with one bay as a bedroom and the other as a chapel, and there she spent the days in diligent performance of the six daily devotions and the perpetual buddha-recitations.

Toward evening on the fifteenth of the tenth month, she heard footsteps in the courtyard, which lay buried under fallen oak leaves. "Who can have come to this hermitage? Look and see. If it's someone I need to hide from, I'll hurry and hide," she said.

The intruder proved to be a passing stag. When the lady asked, "Well, what was it?" Dainagon-no-suke replied in verse, suppressing her tears:

5. A slight alteration of an anonymous poem (KKS 944): yamazato wa / mono wabishiki / koto koso are / yo no uki yori wa / sumiyokarikeri ("It is true that a mountain hermitage offers small comfort, yet life is far better there than in a world of vexations").

iwane fumi	Who might be coming,
tare ka wa towamu	treading on rocks, to call here?
nara no ha no	The visitor whose step
soyogu wa shika no	rustles through fallen oak leaves
wataru narikeri	is but a passing stag.

With a full heart, the lady wrote the poem on a small sliding door next to her window.

Despite all its hardships, her tedious existence suggested many interesting comparisons. She likened the rows of native trees at her eaves to the seven circles of trees surrounding the pure land, and she thought of the water collecting between rocks as the waters of the eight virtues.

The ephemerality of worldly things is like springtime blossoms scattering in the breeze; the brevity of human existence is like an autumn moon disappearing behind a cloud. On mornings when the lady had enjoyed blossoms at the Chengyang Hall, the wind had come and scattered their beauty; on evenings when she had composed poems about the moon at the Zhangqiu Palace, clouds had covered the moon's face and hidden its radiance. Once she had lived in a magnificent mansion with jeweled towers, golden halls, and brocade cushions; now her brushwood hermitage drew tears even from the eyes of strangers.

I.3. The Imperial Journey to Ōhara

Meanwhile, around the spring of the second year of Bunji [1186], Retired Emperor Go-Shirakawa decided that he would like to see Kenreimon'in's hermitage at Ōhara. But there were tempests during the second and third months, and the cold weather dragged on, with unmelted snow on the peaks and lingering icicles in the valleys. Spring passed, summer came, and the Kamo Festival took place. Only then did the former sovereign set out under cover of darkness for the recesses of Ōhara. He traveled without ceremony, but his retinue included Tokudaiji no Sanesada, Kazan'in no Kanemasa, Tsuchimikado no Michichika, and three other senior nobles, as well as eight courtiers and a few north guards. They took the Kurama highroad, and he viewed Kiyowara no Fukayabu's Fudarakuji Temple, as well as the former residence of the Ono Grand Empress.[6]

He changed to a palanquin at Ono. The white clouds on the distant hills recalled the cherry blossoms that had now scattered; the green leaves on the trees were poignant reminders of the end of spring. The time was late in the fourth month, a season of lush summer growth. Since he had never traveled there before, all the sights were unfamiliar as his palanquin made its way

---

6. The Fudarakuji (in the mountains of the present Sakyō-ku, Kyoto) had fallen into ruins soon after the death of its builder and principal resident, the poet Fukayabu (fl. ca. 900). The Ono grand empress, a consort of Emperor Go-Reizei (1025–68; r. 1045–68), had lived as a nun at Ono, in what is now Kita-ku, Kyoto.

through the dense foliage. Deeply moved, he realized that the area was completely off the beaten track.

A lone Buddhist structure at the foot of the western hills proved to be the Jakkōin. The venerable garden pond and ancient trees made it seem a place with a noble history. Might it have been of just such a one that the poet wrote these lines?

> The roof tiles are broken, the fog burns perpetual incense;
> The doors have fallen, the moonbeams light eternal lamps.[7]

Young grasses burgeoned in the courtyard, green willow branches tangled in the wind, and the duckweed on the pond, drifting with the waves, might have been mistaken for brocade set out to be washed. The wisteria clinging to the pines on the islet had put forth purple flowers; the late-blooming cherries, interspersed among the green leaves, seemed a novelty more delightful than the season's first blossoms. The kerria on the banks bloomed in profusion, and a mountain cuckoo sang from a rift in the many-layered clouds, as though to welcome the awaited imperial guest. The retired emperor composed a poem:

ikemizu ni	Wave-flowers in full bloom:
migiwa no sakura	on the surface of the pond,
chirishikite	blossoms have scattered
nami no hana koso	from the cherry trees
sakari narikere	along the water's edge.

It was a place where everything seemed endowed with a special charm, even to the sound of water gushing from a cleft in time-worn rocks. The fences were overgrown with green ivy; the mountains appeared etched with an eyebrow pencil. It was a scene to which no painter could have done justice.

When the retired emperor turned his attention to the imperial lady's hermitage, he saw ivy and morning-glory vines climbing the eaves, and "forgetting-grass" day lilies mingling with "remembering-grass" ferns.[8] It was an abode of which someone might have said, "The gourd and rice tub are often empty, the grasses riot as at Yan Yuan's house." The crude cryptomeria thatch on the roof seemed scarcely able to keep out the rains, frosts, and dews, which vied with the infiltrating moonbeams for admittance.

To the rear, there were mountains; in front, barren fields where the wind whistled through low bamboo grass. The bamboo pillars, with their many joints, recalled the manifold sorrows of those who live apart from society;

7. The quotation has not been identified.

8. *Wasuregusa*, a name for the day lily, can be translated as "forgetting grass," *shinobu[gusa]*, a kind of fern, as "remembering grass." The next sentence is paraphrased from a document addressed to a superior by Tachibana no Naomoto (fl. ca. 950), a scholar and minor bureaucrat, in which the author complains about his poverty and failure to win promotion.

the brushwood fence, with its loose weave, brought to mind the long intervals between tidings from the capital. By way of visitors, there were only the
cries of monkeys swinging from tree to tree on the peaks, and the sound of
woodcutters' axes felling timber for firewood. For the rest, those who came
were rare, unless we might count the curling tendrils of wild vines.[9]

"Is anybody home?" the retired emperor asked.

At first, there was no answer. Then, after a long delay, a feeble old nun
appeared.

"Where has the imperial lady gone?" he asked.

"To the mountain up there, to gather flowers," she said.

"Wasn't there anybody she could send on an errand like that? Even
though she's a nun now, it's not right that she should have to do it herself."

"She suffers her present hardships because there has been an end to the
good karma she earned by observing the five commandments and ten good
precepts," said the nun. "Why should she mind performing austerities that
mortify the flesh? The *Cause and Effect Sutra* instructs us, 'If you want to
know past causes, look at present effects; if you want to know future effects,
look at present causes.' If Your Majesty understands past and future causes
and effects, you will feel no grief at all. Prince Siddhārtha left Gayā at the
age of nineteen, covered his nudity with leafy garments at the foot of Mount
Daṇḍaka, climbed to the peaks for firewood, descended to the valleys for
water, and finally achieved perfect enlightenment through the merit of his
hard and painful austerities."

The retired emperor could not tell whether the ancient scraps of cloth in
the nun's patchwork robe were silk or some other material. It was odd, he
thought, that one thus attired should have spoken so. "Tell me, who are
you?" he said.

The nun began to weep, and for a time was too moved to reply. When she
managed to control her tears, she said, "It hurts to have to admit it, but I
am Shinzei's daughter, the one who used to be called Awa-no-naishi. My
mother was the Kii lady of second rank. You used to be so very kind, but
now I'm such an old crone that you don't even recognize me! Oh, I can't
bear it!" She was too pathetic to watch as she held her sleeve to her face, no
longer able to suppress her feelings.

"Awa-no-naishi! I didn't know you. This is so much like a dream!" The
retired emperor could not keep from crying.

"No wonder she didn't seem like an ordinary nun," the senior nobles and
courtiers in the entourage said to one another.

The retired emperor looked around. Heavy with dew, the bushes in the
courtyard leaned against the brushwood fence; on the flooded rice paddy
outside, there was not even enough space for a longbill to alight. He entered
the hermitage and opened the sliding door. The first room contained the

9. There is a pun on *kuru*, a verb that can mean either "come" or "wind" (as on a reel;
translated as "curling").

welcoming triad, with a five-colored cord attached to the hand of the central deity. To the left, there was a painting of Fugen; to the right, there were pictures of the teacher Shandao and the former emperor. There were also the eight scrolls of the *Lotus Sutra* and the nine scrolls of Shandao's writings. Instead of orchid and musk fragrance, smoke ascended from offering-incense. Even thus, it seemed, must have been the ten-foot-square cell where Vimalakīrti aligned thirty-two thousand seats for the buddhas of the ten directions. Noteworthy passages from sutras, inscribed on bits of colored paper, were pasted here and there on sliding doors. There were also two lines of Chinese verse, said to have been composed at Mount Qingliang by the monk whose lay name was Ōe no Sadamoto: [10]

> From a lone cloud, mouth organs and singing resound in the distance;
> In front of the setting sun, the divine host approaches to bid me welcome.

Somewhat apart, there was a poem that seemed to be from the imperial lady's brush:

omoiki ya	Did I ever think
miyama no oku ni	to find myself dwelling
sumai shite	deep in the mountains,
kumoi no tsuki o	gazing at the moon on high,
yoso ni mimu to wa	far from the royal palace?

Off to the side, the retired emperor saw what looked like the imperial lady's bedchamber. A hemp robe, a paper quilt, and similar articles hung from bamboo rods. It seemed only a dream that she had once worn damask, gauze, brocade, and embroidery, the choicest stuffs of Japan and China. The senior nobles and courtiers had all witnessed her former splendor, and they wept until their sleeves were drenched, recalling those earlier scenes as though they had just taken place.

Presently, two nuns, dressed in robes of deep black, came picking their way down the steep, rocky path from the mountain above.

"Who are they?" the retired emperor asked.

The old nun tried not to cry. "The one carrying the basket of rock azaleas on her arm is the imperial lady. The one with the firewood and bracken is the former emperor's nurse, Dainagon-no-suke, the daughter of Torikai Middle Counselor Korezane and the adopted daughter of Gojō Major Counselor Kunitsuna." She burst into tears as she spoke. Profoundly moved, the retired emperor also shed involuntary tears.

The imperial lady would have liked to disappear. Nun or not, it was too embarrassing to have him see her in her present attire. She stood helpless, choked with tears, neither returning to the mountain nor entering the hermitage. Perhaps she despaired of drying her sleeves, which she had soaked

---

10. Sadamoto's name as a monk was Jakushō. He lived in China from 1003 until his death in 1034.

during the nightly drawing of holy water, and which had been drenched again after she had risen before dawn to tread the dewy mountain path. Awa-no-naishi went up to her and took the flower basket.

I.4.   *The Matter of the Six Paths*

"You wear the kind of clothing that's customary for someone who has renounced the world. It's quite all right to appear in it," Awa-no-naishi said. "Hurry up and meet with His Majesty; he needs to get started back to the capital."

The imperial lady entered the hermitage. When she met the retired emperor, tears came to her eyes. "I have expected the radiance of the saving Buddha to shine before the window whenever I have recited a single invocation, and I have waited for the divine host to appear at my brushwood door whenever I have recited ten invocations, but never have I anticipated anything as remarkable as this visit," she said.

"Even those who dwell in the Bhavāgra Heaven, where the life span is eighty thousand kalpas, must face the affliction of inevitable death; not even those who dwell in the six heavens of the world of desire can evade the sorrow of the five signs of decay. The wonderful pleasures of the Joyful-to-see Palace, the delights of Bonten's lofty palace—all are but the good fortune of a dream, the happiness of a phantasm, subject to eternal change. They resemble the turning wheels of a carriage. Sadly enough, the grief of the heavenly beings' five signs of decay has visited the world of men, too," the retired emperor said. "But tell me, who comes to see you? There must be many things to remind you of the old days."

The imperial lady restrained tears. "Of course, this present state causes me temporary distress, but I look on it as a blessing when I think about my future enlightenment. I've hurried to become Śākyamuni's disciple, and have reverently placed my faith in Amida's vow; thus, I escape the sorrows of the five obstacles and the three subordinations, I purify my six senses during each of the six divisions of the day, and I pray with all my heart for rebirth in the pure land of nine grades. There's no time when I don't wait for the welcoming triad, no time when I don't offer fervent prayers for the enlightenment of my kin. But I shall never forget the former emperor's face, not in all the lives to come. I try to forget, but forgetting is impossible; I try to control my anguish, but that is impossible too. Nothing causes as much sorrow as a parent's affection; that's why I pray faithfully, morning and evening, for the former emperor's enlightenment. I believe my love for him will guide me to enlightenment, too."

"These remote islands of ours are as tiny as scattered grains of millet," the retired emperor said. "Still, the merit remaining from obedience to the ten good precepts has conferred on me the awesome title of Lord of a Myriad Chariots; and as befits my status, there's nothing that isn't the way I want it. In particular, there can be no doubt about my entering paradise in the next life, because I've been born in a land where men disseminate the Buddhist teachings, and my desire to follow the Way is fervent. There's no reason why evidence of this world's evanescence should come as a shock to me now. And yet I find it unbearable to see you like this."

The imperial lady spoke again:

As Chancellor Kiyomori's daughter, I became the imperial mother and held the country in the palm of my hand. From the New Year's felicitations through the two changes of dress to the Buddhist names services at year's end, I was attended by the regent, the ministers of state, and the other senior nobles, as though surrounded by the eight myriad celestial beings above the clouds in the six and four heavens; of all His Majesty's many officials, not one but looked up to me in awe. Pampered behind jade curtains in the Seiryōden and the Shishinden, in spring I spent days watching the cherry blossoms on the tree in the Shishinden courtyard, in high summer I found relief from the heat by dipping water from a welling spring, in autumn I wasn't allowed to watch the moon above the clouds by myself, and in black winter, on frigid nights of white snow, I slept warm under layers of bedclothing. My only desire was to live on and on—to petition the gods, if necessary, for the immortals' art of ensuring long life and eternal youth, or to search out the elixir of immortality from Penglai. I believed that the bliss of heaven could be no more sublime than the pleasures I enjoyed day and night. But in the autumn of that year in Juei [1183], I couldn't help feeling miserable when my clansmen, terrified of a man called Kiso no Yoshinaka or some such, left the familiar capital behind the clouds, turned their homes into a blackened wilderness of plains, and traveled along the seashore from Suma to Akashi, places known to me only by name. In the daytime, my sleeves were drenched as we cleaved the boundless waves; at night, I cried until dawn with the plovers on the long sandspits. Seeing famous shores and islands wasn't enough to make me forget the capital. I thought that our forlorn state must surely resemble the sorrow of the five signs of decay.

If we speak of the world of men, I have known the sad suffering caused by separation from those we love; also the hateful suffering caused by association with those we dislike. Not one of the four and eight sufferings has remained outside my experience. At the Dazaifu in Chikuzen Province, we were ousted from the Nine Provinces by a man called Koreyoshi or something like that. The mountains and fields were vast, but there was no place for us to take shelter and rest. As autumn waned that year, we gazed from the eightfold tidal paths on the moon we had watched above the clouds at the ninefold palace. Time passed, and then, around the tenth month, Middle Captain Kiyotsune cast himself into the sea. "Genji attackers drove us out of the capital and Koreyoshi expelled us from Chinzei," he said to himself. "We're like fish in a net; there's no escape, no matter where we go. What chance do I have of living out my life?" That was our first great sorrow.

Our days were spent on the waves, our nights in the boats. We possessed no tribute goods; nobody prepared food for me. If something did come to hand, I couldn't eat it because there was no water. It's true that we were afloat on a mighty sea, but people can't drink salt water. I felt that I was experiencing the sufferings of the world of hungry spirits.

Thanks to the victories at Muroyama and Mizushima, our men seemed to regain their spirit, but many of them died at Ichi-no-tani. Those who remained exchanged informal and formal robes for iron armor and helmets, and there was never a time, early or late, when the shouts of battle stopped. I felt certain that the fighting between the *asura* kings and Taishaku must be just the same.

After the defeat at Ichi-no-tani, parents were left childless and wives husbandless. If we saw a fishing boat in the offing, we trembled lest it be an enemy vessel; the sight of snowy herons flocking in some distant pine grove made our hearts faint with terror lest they be the white banners of the Genji. And I recall how, when we were at Moji and Akama-no-seki, and we all realized that the day of our last battle had come, the nun of second rank said to me, "There isn't a chance in a thousand myriad that any male member of our house will survive. Even if some distant relative did happen to be left, we couldn't expect him to perform memorial services for us. It's always been the custom to spare women. Do your best to come through the battle safely so that you can pray for His Majesty's salvation. I hope you'll also say a prayer for the rest of us." I listened as though in a dream.

A sudden wind sprang up, and a blanket of drifting clouds came down on us, striking terror into the warriors' hearts. Our fate was sealed; no human effort could change it.

When my mother saw the end approaching, she clasped His Majesty the Emperor in her arms and went to the side of the ship. "Where are you taking me, Grandmother?" he asked, with a puzzled look. "Don't you understand?" she said. "You became an emperor because you obeyed the ten good precepts in your last life, but now an evil karma holds you fast. Your good fortune has come to an end. Turn to the east and say goodbye to the Grand Shrine of Ise, then turn to the west and repeat the sacred name of Amida Buddha, so that he and his host may come to escort you to the pure land. This country is a place of sorrow; I'm taking you to a happy realm called paradise."

His Majesty was wearing an olive-gray robe, and his hair was done up in a boy's loops at the sides. With tears in his eyes, he joined his tiny hands, knelt toward the east, and bade farewell to the Grand Shrine. Then he turned toward the west and recited the sacred name of Amida; and my mother snatched him up and jumped into the sea. Darkness shrouded my eyes as I saw my son sink under the waves; my brain seemed paralyzed. I try to forget, but forgetting is impossible; I try to control my grief, but that's impossible too. Those who were left behind uttered so great and terrible a cry that it seemed not even the shrieks of sinners under the flames in the hot hells could sound worse.

When I was returning to the city after the warriors captured me, we stopped at Akashi Shore in Harima Province. I dozed off, and in a dream I saw the former emperor and the Taira senior nobles and courtiers, all in formal array, in a place far grander than the old imperial palace. I asked where we were, because I had seen nothing like it since our departure from the capital. Someone who seemed to be the nun of second rank answered, "This is the palace of a dragon king." "What a splendid place! Is there no suffering here?" I asked. "The suffering is described in the *Ryūchikukyō Sutra*. Pray hard for us," she said. I awakened as she spoke. Since then, I've been more zealous than ever in reciting the sutras and invoking Amida's name so they can be saved. I think it's all been exactly like experiencing life in each of the six paths.

"We're told that Xuanzhuang of China saw the six paths before he achieved enlightenment, and that the holy Nichizō of our land saw them through the power of Zaō Gongen," said the retired emperor. "But it's truly rare to see them before one's very eyes, as you have done." He choked with tears, and all the senior nobles and courtiers in his retinue wrung their sleeves. The imperial lady also wept, and her attendants drenched their sleeves.

1.5. The Death of the Imperial Lady

Meanwhile, the sound of the bell at the Jakkōin announced the end of the day, and the evening sun sank in the west. Hard though it was to say good-bye, the retired emperor restrained his tears and set out for home. The imperial lady could not help weeping until her sleeves were drenched, her memories now more poignant than ever. After she had watched the procession gradually recede into the distance, she turned toward the sacred image. "May the holy spirit of the Son of Heaven and the dead spirits of the Heike achieve perfect wisdom and prompt enlightenment," she prayed in tears.

In the past, she had faced eastward and said, "May the Grand Shrine of Ise and the bodhisattva Hachiman grant the Son of Heaven a thousand autumns and a myriad years of life"; now, pathetically, she faced westward and prayed with folded hands, "May the holy spirit of the dead be reborn in Amida's pure land." She wrote two poems on the sliding door of her bedchamber:

> kono goro wa
> itsu naraite ka
>   wa ga kokoro
> ōmiyabito no
> koishikaruramu

> How has it happened
> that suddenly of late
>   my heart grows heavy
> with nostalgia for those
> who serve the imperial court?

> inishie mo
> yume ni narinishi
>   koto nareba
> shiba no amido mo
> hisashikaraji na

> Since the past has become
> only a fleeting dream,
>   surely this sojourn
> behind a wooden door
> will prove no more permanent.

I believe I have heard that another poem was inscribed on one of the pillars at the hermitage by Tokudaiji Minister of the Left Sanesada, who was with the retired emperor:

> inishie wa
> tsuki ni tatoeshi
>   kimi naredo
> sono hikari naki
> miyamabe no sato

> This is the empress
> whom we compared to the moon
>   in earlier days,
> but no radiance now brightens
> the lonely mountain dwelling.

At a time when the imperial lady was lost in tearful memories of the past and depressing thoughts of the future, a cuckoo from the hills happened to fly by, its voice raised in song. She murmured:

iza saraba   If we are to meet,
namida kurabemu   cuckoo, in this way—come, then,
hototogisu   let us compare tears,
ware mo ukiyo ni   for I, also, like yourself,
ne o nomi zo naku   cry constantly in this cruel world.

The captives from Dan-no-ura had either been paraded through the streets and beheaded, or else sent into distant-exile, far from their wives and children. Of the male members of the clan, Ike Major Counselor Yorimori remained the only one who had neither been deprived of his life nor been denied the privilege of living in the capital. The forty or more women, to whom no punishment had been meted out, had turned to relatives for aid or gone to stay with other connections. But there was no house free of worrisome winds, not even inside jade blinds; there was no dwelling where the dust never rose, not even beyond brushwood doors. Husbands and wives who had slept on adjoining pillows were as remote from one another as the sky; nurturing parents and their children were set apart, neither knowing the whereabouts of the other. Tormented by longing, they barely managed to struggle through the melancholy days.

It was all the fault of Chancellor-Novice Kiyomori, that man who had held the whole country in the palm of his hand, and who had executed and banished people as he pleased, unawed by the emperor above and heedless of His Majesty's subjects below, with no concern for society as a whole or for individuals. It seemed beyond doubt that the evil deeds of a father must be visited on his offspring.

With the passing of time, the imperial lady fell ill. She recited Buddha-invocations, clasping a five-colored cord attached to the hand of the central image. "Hail, Amitābha Tathāgata, teaching lord of the western paradise! Please admit me to the pure land!" she prayed. Overcome with sorrow as the end approached, Dainagon-no-suke and Awa-no-naishi wailed on her left and right.

After her chant had gradually weakened, a purple cloud trailed through the western skies, a marvelous fragrance permeated the chamber, and music sounded on high. Man's time on earth is finite, and thus it was that her life drew to a close at last, midway through the second month in the second year of Kenkyū [1191]. The parting caused agonies of grief to the two attendants who had never left her side, not since the days when she was empress. They had nowhere to turn for help, for the grasses of old ties had withered long ago, but somehow, in a most touching fashion, they managed to perform the periodic memorial services. People said both of them attained the wisdom of the dragon girl, emulated the wife of King Bimbisāra, and achieved their goal of rebirth in the pure land.[11]

11. The dragon girl was a dragon king's daughter who grasped the Buddhist doctrines and attained enlightenment at the age of seven. Her story is told in the *Lotus Sutra*. The wife of King Bimbisāra reached the pure land by listening to one of Śākyamuni's disciples preach.

Reference Material

Offices, Ranks, and the Imperial Palace

The highest court offices for male subjects, in descending order of importance, were imperial regent (*sesshō* or *kanpaku*), chancellor (*daijō daijin*), minister of the left (*sadaijin*), minister of the right (*udaijin*), palace minister (*naidaijin*), major counselor (*dainagon*), middle counselor (*chūnagon*), and consultant (*sangi*). Other prestigious titles included major captain (*taishō*), middle captain (*chūjō*), guards commander (*hyōe no kami, emon no kami*), and head chamberlain (*kurōdo no tō*). There were nine major ranks, each with subdivisions, descending from senior first through junior eighth lower to lesser initial lower. Unofficially, every male aristocrat also belonged to one or more of the following three groups:

1. Senior nobles (*kugyō*). This group, defined partly by rank and partly by office, consisted of the ministers of state (i.e., the chancellor, the ministers of the left and right, and the palace minister); the major and middle counselors; the other holders, if any, of the top three ranks; and the consultants, who sat with the others on the council of state, even though their prescribed rank was only senior fourth lower. Together with members of the imperial clan, this small group constituted the cream of court society.

2. Courtiers (*tenjōbito*). These were men who had been authorized individually by the reigning sovereign to enter the courtiers' hall of the Seiryōden. The group ordinarily included all senior nobles, certain holders of fourth and fifth rank, and one special category of lower-ranking officials, chamberlains of sixth rank, who frequented the courtiers' hall in the performance of their duties.

3. Non-courtiers (*jige*, "gentlemen of low rank"). This large group consisted mainly of holders of sixth and lower rank.

The women at court fell into three main overlapping categories:

1. Imperial consorts and concubines. An official consort bore the title junior consort (*nyōgo*) or empress (*kōgō* or *chūgū*), and might eventually be named grand empress (*kōtaigō*) and senior grand empress (*taikōtaigō*). An unofficial consort was often known as the lady of the bedchamber (*miyasudokoro*).

2. Female officials. The most important of these were the mistress of the wardrobe (*mikushigedono*), who often served as an imperial concubine, and the members of the handmaids' office (*naishi no tsukasa*), who were in constant attendance on the emperor.

3. Ladies-in-waiting of the emperor and his consorts. In the case of the emperor, these included the mistress of the wardrobe and the leading members of the handmaids' office.

Imperial lady (*nyōin*) was a title of respect sometimes conferred by an emperor on his mother, his sister, or a woman of comparable standing.

Women were eligible for appointment to court rank, but few rose above third rank. (A major exception in *The Tale of the Heike* is Kiyomori's wife, who holds second rank.)

The center of court activity, the greater imperial palace (*daidairi*), occupied an area of about 400 acres in the north central section of the capital. Among its principal buildings were the Great Hall of State (Daigokuden) and the structures inside the imperial residential compound—the Shishinden (also called Nanden, or South Hall), a ceremonial building; the Seiryōden, the imperial residence; and various buildings usually occupied by consorts, concubines, and their attendants, such as the Fujitsubo (also called Higyōsha), the Kokiden, the Sen'yōden, and the Kiritsubo (Shigeisha). After 960, repeated conflagrations forced successive sovereigns to live elsewhere, sometimes for years at a time, in private establishments that usually included buildings named after those in the palace. It became increasingly difficult to find the resources to rebuild, and in 1227 the greater imperial palace finally passed into history.

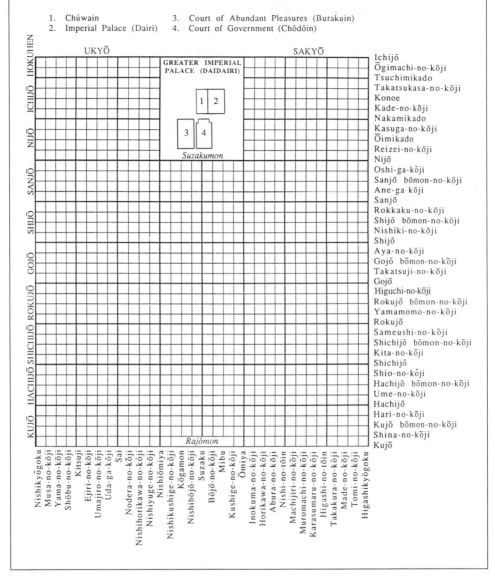

1. Chūwain
2. Imperial Palace (Dairi)
3. Court of Abundant Pleasures (Burakuin)
4. Court of Government (Chōdōin)

UKYŌ

GREATER IMPERIAL PALACE (DAIDAIRI)

SAKYŌ

Suzakumon

Rajōmon

HOKUHEN
ICHIJŌ
NIJŌ
SANJŌ
SHIJŌ
GOJŌ
ROKUJŌ
SHICHIJŌ
HACHIJŌ
KUJŌ

Ichijō
Ōgimachi-no-kōji
Tsuchimikado
Takatsukasa-no-kōji
Konoe
Kade-no-kōji
Nakamikado
Kasuga-no-kōji
Ōimikado
Reizei-no-kōji
Nijō
Oshi-ga-kōji
Sanjō bōmon-no-kōji
Ane-ga-kōji
Sanjō
Rokkaku-no-kōji
Shijō bōmon-no-kōji
Nishiki-no-kōji
Shijō
Aya-no-kōji
Gojō bōmon-no-kōji
Takatsuji-no-kōji
Gojō
Higuchi-no-kōji
Rokujō bōmon-no-kōji
Yamamomo-no-kōji
Rokujō
Sameushi-no-kōji
Shichijō bōmon-no-kōji
Kita-no-kōji
Shichijō
Shio-no-kōji
Hachijō bōmon-no-kōji
Ume-no-kōji
Hachijō
Hari-no-kōji
Kujō bōmon-no-kōji
Shina-no-kōji
Kujō

Nishikyōgoku
Musa-no-kōji
Yama-no-kōji
Shōbu-no-kōji
Kitsuji
Ejiri-no-kōji
Umajiro-no-kōji
Uda-ga-kōji
Sai
Nodera-no-kōji
Nishihorikawa-no-kōji
Nishiyuge-no-kōji
Nishiōmiya
Nishikushige-no-kōji
Kōgamon
Nishibōjō-no-kōji
Suzaku
Bōjō-no-kōji
Mibu
Kushige-no-kōji
Ōmiya
Inokuma-no-kōji
Horikawa-no-kōji
Abura-no-kōji
Nishi-no-tōin
Machijiri-no-kōji
Muromachi-no-kōji
Karasumaru-no-kōji
Higashi-no-tōin
Takakura-no-kōji
Made-no-kōji
Tomi-no-kōji
Higashikyōgoku

The Heian capital (Heian-kyō). Names in capital letters are districts; names in italics are gates.

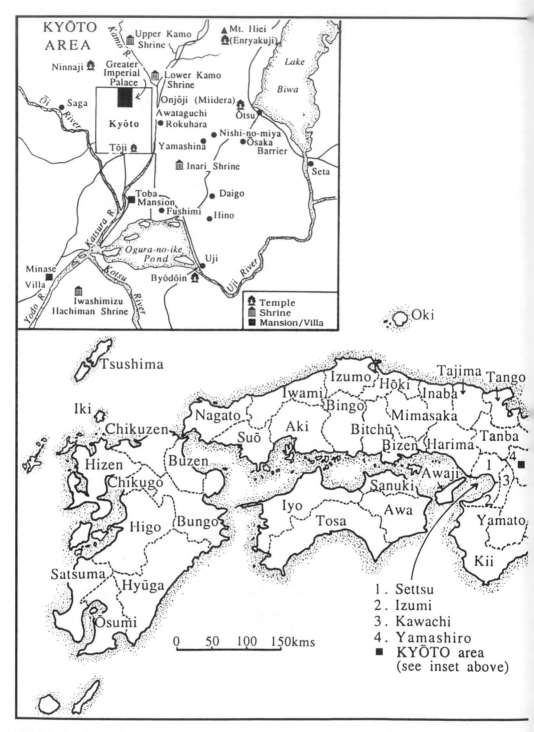

Japan in the classical age

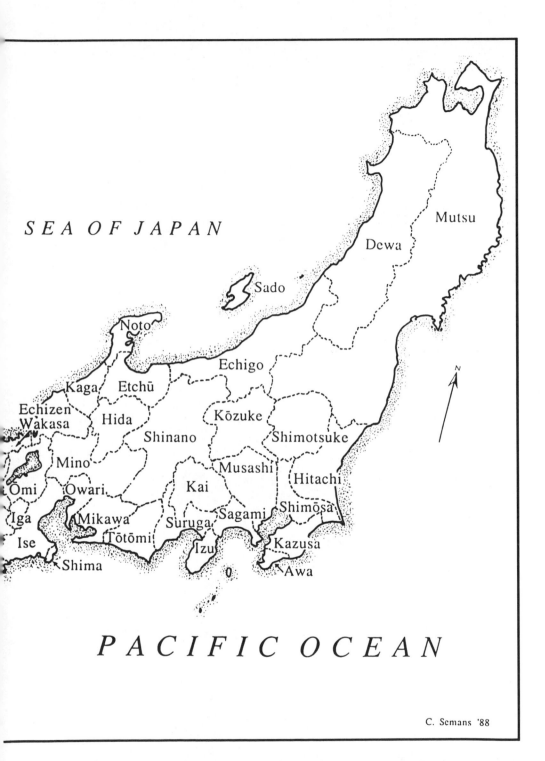

SEA OF JAPAN

PACIFIC OCEAN

Mutsu

Dewa

Sado

Noto

Echigo

Kaga Etchū

Echizen
Wakasa Hida

Kōzuke

Shinano

Shimotsuke

Mino

Musashi

Hitachi

Ōmi Owari

Kai

Iga

Sagami Shimōsa

Mikawa

Suruga

Ise Tōtōmi

Kazusa

Izu

Shima

Awa

C. Semans '88

Glossary

Terms and names listed separately appear in small capitals

Akama Barrier. North of Kanmon Straits; now in Shimonoseki City.

Akashi. A coastal area in Harima Province (now southern Hyōgo Prefecture).

Amaterasu. The sun goddess, claimed by the imperial clan as its ancestor.

Amida (Skt. Amitābha). The Buddha most highly revered at the Heian court. He is the ruler of the Western Paradise (PURE LAND), into which those who believe in him and recite his name are reborn.

Arrow exchange. A declaration by opponents of mutual intent to do battle.

Ashigara Mountains. A low range on the border between Suruga and Sagami provinces.

Assumption of the train (mogi). Like the CAPPING CEREMONY for boys, a rite of passage symbolizing the attainment of adulthood for a girl. The train was a garment worn by noble ladies on formal occasions.

Asuras (ashura). Ugly demons who live by the seashore and dote on fighting. Under the leadership of their kings, they wage constant warfare against the god Indra (TAISHAKUTEN).

Atsuta. Now within Nagoya City. Site of the great Atsuta Shrine.

Awataguchi. The EASTERN SEA ROAD exit from the capital, leading to Ōtsu. The term applied to the area eastward from the Sanjō Shirakawa Bridge to the mountains.

Awazu. A wooded plain in what is now the city of Ōtsu, Shiga Prefecture.

Banshiki, see RITSU

Barrier of Meeting, see ŌSAKA BARRIER

Benevolent King service. A Buddhist rite, usually court-sponsored, in which the Benevolent King Sutra (Ninnōgyō) was expounded. The sutra promised peace and prosperity to countries where it was revered.

Benzaiten (Skt. Lakṣmī or Sarasvatī). Also Myōonten, Daibenkudokuten, Benten. A goddess who guards the lives and fortunes of believers. She has the gift of eloquence and holds a lute on her lap. Sometimes confused with KICHIJŌTEN.

Bhavāgra Heaven (Hiso[ten]). The fourth of the four immaterial heavens; the highest heaven in the THREE EXISTENCES. Existence there lasts 80,000 KALPAS.

Bifukumon'in (1117–60). Empress of Emperor TOBA; mother of the Hachijō imperial lady, Emperor Konoe, and others; extremely influential during Konoe's reign.

Bo Juyi (772–846). Important mid-Tang poet admired in Japan.

Bonten (Skt. Brahman). A Hindu god, ruler of a tripartite heaven in the WORLD OF FORM.

Book of History (Shisho). At *Heike* 3.19, probably *Zhenguan zhengyao*, a moralizing work of the Tang.

Buddha-invocations (*nenbutsu*). Calling on the name of a buddha, usually AMIDA. A believer who chanted "Hail, Amida Buddha!" (*namu amida butsu*) could expect to be reborn in Amida's paradise.

Buddhist names service (*butsumyōe*). Held at the Seiryōden late in the 12th month to expunge sins accumulated during the year. The service consisted primarily of the recitation of the names of 3,000 buddhas, a practice recommended in the *Sanzenbutsumyō Sutra* as a means of expiating sin.

Byōdōin. Originally a villa at UJI. Served as a residence for a succession of prominent court figures, and then became a Buddhist temple in 1052.

Capping ceremony (*genbuku*). A Heian youth's coming-of-age ceremony, held when he was from 10 to 15 years old. Before it, he wore a child's hairstyle and costume and answered to a child's name; afterward, his coiffure, clothing, and name were those of an adult, he was eligible for marriage, and, if his family was sufficiently influential, he obtained court rank and began his official career.

Change of dress (*koromogae*). A ceremony performed twice annually: (1) on the 1st of the 4th month, when tatami mats, lantern screens, and the like were replaced, and the heavy garments, room hangings, and curtains used during winter and spring were exchanged for new, lighter ones; and (2) on the 1st of the 10th month, when corresponding preparations were made for the cold season.

Character parts (*hentsugi*). A game of skill, the exact nature of which is no longer understood. Players were probably required to supply either the left-hand element (*hen*) or the body (*tsukuri*) of a partially concealed character in a Chinese poem or other context.

Chengyang Hall. A building in the women's quarters of the Han imperial palace in China.

Chinzei. A name for Kyushu.

Chōgōdō. A private chapel inside the grounds of Retired Emperor Go-Shirakawa's Rokujō Palace.

Chōrakuji. A temple in present Higashiyama-ku, Kyoto.

Chronicles of Japan (Nihongi, Nihon shoki). 720. First of the official Six National Histories; covers the period from the age of the gods to 697.

Commander-in-chief (*taishōgun*, "great commander of military forces"). In *Heike monogatari*, this title is held simultaneously by numerous members of the Taira clan, and by both Noriyori and Yoshitsune on the Genji side. No

Taira general has a superior title corresponding to "barbarian-subduing commander" (*seii taishōgun*), the title conferred on Yoritomo by Retired Emperor Go-Shirakawa (*Heike*, 8.5).

Congratulations (*kojōhai*). A ceremony honoring the emperor held at the imperial palace on New Year's Day.

Courtiers' hall (*tenjō no ma*). A room in the Seiryōden where senior nobles and courtiers came and went, and which was sometimes graced by the imperial presence.

Curtain-dais (*chōdai*). A curtained platform about a foot high and nine feet square, surmounted by a ceiling supported by pillars about six and a half feet high. The floor was covered by matting, and at night by bedclothing. The structure faced south in the principal room of a residence and served the master or mistress as both private sitting room and bedchamber.

Curtain-stand (*kichō*). Set up inside a room to ensure privacy; usually about three or four feet high and six or eight feet long. It consisted of lacquered supporting members (a foot, two vertical supports, and a top horizontal bar) to which were attached trailing silk curtains decorated with streamers.

Daibenkudokuten, *see* BENZAITEN

Daigo, Emperor (885–930; r. 897–930). Called Engi Emperor, from an era name. Son of Emperor UDA; patron of the arts.

Daikakuji. A temple in SAGA.

Dan-no-ura. A bay in Nagato Province, offshore from the present city of Shimonoseki.

Dazaifu. A special government office in Kyushu charged with military defenses, diplomatic relations with the Asiatic mainland, and local administration.

Dengyō, Great Teacher (Dengyō Daishi). Posthumous name of the monk Saichō (767–822), founder of the Tendai sect.

Devadatta (Chōdatsu). A disciple of ŚĀKYAMUNI who turned against Buddhism, committed heinous sins, and fell into hell while still alive.

Dharma Bridge, Dharma Eye, Dharma Seal (*hokkyō, hōgen, hōin*). The three ranks conferred by the court on outstanding Buddhist monks. Dharma Seal was the highest, Dharma Bridge the lowest.

Double Yang Banquet (*chōyō no en*). Held on the 9th of the 9th month; so called because nine was a yang number. It imitated the chrysanthemum banquets of China, where legend attributed to chrysanthemums, and to their scent, the ability to ward off disease and prolong life. In Murasaki Shikibu's day, the observances consisted primarily of an official repast for senior nobles and courtiers at the Shishinden, with chrysanthemum displays, Chinese poems, music, and dancing.

Dragon kings (*ryūō*). Rulers of the hosts of dragons (Skt. *nāga*) who are among the eight classes of protectors of Buddhism. Dragons inhabit bodies of water and control clouds, rain, wind, and thunder; their kings live in splendid undersea palaces. Some of the kings are benevolent; others are ill-disposed toward mortals.

Earth deity (*kenrō jijin*). In Buddhist cosmology, has charge of the earth; usually prayed to when buildings are constructed.

Eastern Sea Road (Tōkaidō). The provinces of Iga, Ise, Shima, Owari, Mikawa, Tōtōmi, Suruga, Kai, Izu, Sagami, Musashi, Awa, Kazusa, Shimōsa, and

Hitachi; the road from the capital leading eastward, mostly along the Pacific coast.

Eave-chamber (*hisashi no ma*). In an aristocratic residence, an area under the eaves between the main rooms (*moya*) and the veranda.

Eight expositions service (*hakkōe*). A celebration of the LOTUS SUTRA, usually held to help a deceased relative or in fulfillment of some other vow, the text of which was presented as part of the ritual. There were usually eight sessions, held over a four-day period and involving the participation of as many as 60 eminent monks. Music, bells, incense, sacred images, offerings of precious objects, vestments, and texts, and banquets for the attendant monks added to the pomp of these affairs, which were among the most impressive of Heian Buddhist events.

Eight provinces. The provinces east of Hakone Pass in the ASHIGARA MOUNTAINS: Sagami, Musashi, Kōzuke, Shimotsuke, Awa, Kazusa, Shimōsa, and Hitachi.

Eight sufferings (*hakku*). The FOUR SUFFERINGS plus the sufferings caused by separation from loved ones, by association with those we dislike, by failure to obtain desires, and by attachment to the five skandhas.

Eight virtues, waters of (*hakkudokusui*). Waters that well up in a lake in the PURE LAND. Their eight virtues are purity, coolness, sweetness, lightness, softness, nutritiousness, abundance, and the ability to satisfy hunger and thirst.

Enma (Skt. Yama). Lord of hell; judge of the dead.

Enryakuji. Headquarters of the Tendai sect of esoteric Buddhism on Mount Hiei, on the Yamashiro-Ōmi border. Founded in 788 by DENGYŌ DAISHI, with the Healing Buddha YAKUSHI as principal object of worship. It was situated northeast of the capital to serve as guardian against the "demon gate" used by malignant forces, who were believed to live in that quarter. The head monk was known as the Tendai abbot (*zasu*).

Escort (*zuijin*). An armed guard assigned by the court to accompany an important member of the nobility when he traveled in the city or elsewhere. A retired emperor was entitled to 14, a regent to 10, a minister of state or major captain to eight, etc.

Evil paths (*akudō*). Undesirable forms into which an individual may be reborn. Usually said to include dwellers in hell, hungry spirits, and beasts; may include ASURAS. *See also* SIX PATHS.

Felicitations (*hairei*). A New Year ceremony of obeisance to a retired emperor or regent, similar in import to the CONGRATULATIONS of the emperor on the same day.

Fifteen Great Temples. The SEVEN GREAT TEMPLES plus eight others in the Nara area.

Fifth-month festival, *see* SWEET FLAG FESTIVAL

First Fruits Service. A harvest thanksgiving festival; one of the court's annual ceremonial observances. It was less elaborate than the GREAT THANKSGIVING SERVICE.

Five commandments (*gokai*). Prohibitions against killing, stealing, committing adultery, lying, and drinking intoxicants.

Five deadly sins (*gogyakuzai*). Killing a father, killing a mother, killing an arhat, disrupting the community of monks, and injuring the body of a buddha.

Five obstacles (*goshō*), for a woman. Inability to become a brahma-king, an indra, a māra-king, a wheel-rolling-king, or a buddha.

Five punishments (*gokei*). Tattooing, cutting off the nose, cutting off the feet, castration, and execution.

Five signs of decay (*gosui*). Signs of approaching death in a heavenly being (*tenjin*). Differently identified in different sutras. One text lists robes becoming soiled, flowers on head withering, body beginning to smell, armpits sweating, and uneasiness.

Float-patterned fabrics. "Float-patterned" (*ukimon*) seems to have described primarily damasks and bombycines with patterns that appeared to be raised, in contrast to the flatter, less conspicuous figures of bound-patterned (*katamon*) silks. See McCullough and McCullough, *Tale of Flowering Fortunes,* 1: 263 n.

Forty-ninth day services. It was believed in the Heian period that an individual who died entered a brief INTERMEDIATE EXISTENCE (*chūu*) before being reborn. On each seventh day until the 49th, the soul had a chance at rebirth, and its fate could be influenced by the pious acts of the living. Wealthy aristocrats usually arranged for elaborate rituals on each of the seven days, culminating in a grand event on the 49th, and for offerings of many kinds.

Forty-one stages. Stages on the way to becoming a bodhisattva.

Four births (*shishō*). Four kinds of births: viviparous, oviparous, water-born, and metamorphic.

Four Heavenly Kings (*shitennō*). Jikokuten, Zōjōten, Kōmokuten, and Tamon, warlike servants of Indra (TAISHAKUTEN) who protect Buddhists.

Four heavens (*shizenten*). The four heavens in the world of form (one of the THREE EXISTENCES).

Four lands (*shido*). Four realms recognized in Tendai doctrine: land where all classes dwell together (subdivided into the present world and the PURE LAND); temporary land where certain types of advanced beings are reborn; land of Buddha-reward, for bodhisattvas; and land of tranquility and wisdom, where Buddhas live.

Four mandalas (*shiman*). Those depicting deities, those depicting vows of deities in symbolic form, those using numbers to represent deities, and those identifying deities by their postures.

Four sufferings (*shiku*). Birth, old age, sickness, and death.

Fudō (Skt. Acala). An angry Buddhist divinity who smites evildoers.

Fugen (Skt. Samantabhadra). A bodhisattva attendant of ŚĀKYAMUNI, often shown riding a white elephant. Ideal representative of Buddhist teaching, meditation, and practice; patron of believers in the LOTUS SUTRA.

Fuhito, Fujiwara (659–720). Called Tankaikō. Son of KAMATARI; leading political figure of his day.

Fukuhara. Site of Taira no Kiyomori's villa in what is now Kobe. It became the capital briefly in 1180.

Fushimi. South of the capital; now a part of Kyoto.

Fuzoku. Upper-class adaptations of folksongs, especially those from the eastern provinces.

Ganquan Hall. A palace in which Han WUDI installed a portrait of Lady LI after her death.

Gion Shōja (Skt. Jetavana-vihāra). Said to have been the first Buddhist monastery, built for ŚĀKYAMUNI by a rich merchant. At the four corners of its infirmary, there were four glass bells shaped like handdrums, that rang when a sick monk was about to die. Their sound is said to have ended the dying man's suffering and ensured his future happiness by incorporating the words of a Buddhist verse: "All things are impermanent; they appear and disappear. When an end is put to appearance and disappearance, the bliss of nirvana is realized."

Gosechi. Dances performed by young girls as part of the GREAT THANKSGIVING and FIRST FRUITS services in the 11th month. Although merely auxiliary to the main religious proceedings, they were always a focal point of attention.

Go-Toba, Emperor (1180–1239; r. 1183–98). Fourth son of Emperor Takakura; placed on the throne by his grandfather, Retired Emperor Go-Shirakawa, in 1183, after the flight of the Taira with Emperor Antoku.

Great Buddha, *see* TŌDAIJI

Great Thanksgiving Service (*daijōe*). An elaborate harvest thanksgiving ceremony performed at court during the 11th month of the first year of a new reign.

Great Wisdom Sutra (Daihannya[haramitta]kyō; Skt. Mahā-prajñā-pāramitā-sūtra). The fundamental philosophical work of the Mahāyāna school. It was recited as protection against many kinds of evils.

Hachiman. A Shinto deity worshipped as a war god, as a bodhisattva, and as a reincarnation of Emperor Ōjin (ca. late 3rd–early 4th c.?). Considered a guardian of the imperial clan, he was also especially revered by the Minamoto because of YOSHIIE's connection with the IWASHIMIZU HACHIMAN SHRINE (*Heike*, 6.5).

Hakuga. Minamoto no Hiromasa (d. 980). Grandson of Emperor DAIGO; famous as a musician. He is said to have stood outside SEMIMARU's hut at ŌSAKA BARRIER nightly for three years in the hope of learning two secret compositions for the lute (or three, according to *Heike monogatari*). See Ury, *Tales of Times Now Past*, pp. 143–45.

Hase[dera]. A temple at Hatsuse in present Shiki District, Nara Prefecture. Its eleven-headed KANNON was deeply venerated by the Heian aristocracy, especially the women.

Heiji Disturbance. 1159. An unsuccessful attempt to overthrow Taira no Kiyomori and his ally Fujiwara no Michimori (chief adviser to Retired Emperor Go-Shirakawa; better known by his Buddhist name, SHINZEI). Taking advantage of Kiyomori's temporary absence from the capital, the court noble Fujiwara no NOBUYORI and the warrior Minamoto no YOSHITOMO seized Go-Shirakawa and the reigning emperor, Nijō, and made Shinzei commit suicide, but Kiyomori returned and wiped out their forces. Nobuyori was killed, Yoshitomo was murdered later in Owari Province as he fled eastward, and Yoshitomo's eleven-year-old son, Yoritomo, was captured and exiled.

Hie (or Hiyoshi; also Sannō). General term for a group of 21 shrines at the eastern foot of Mount Hiei. Prominent among them were the Seven Shrines, regarded as protectors of the doctrines expounded in the LOTUS SUTRA: Ōmiya, Ni-no-miya, Shōshinji, Hachiōji, Marōto, Jūzenji, and San-no-miya.

Hiei, Mount, *see* ENRYAKUJI

Hikushima. Now a part of the city of Shimonoseki.

Hill of Meeting, *see* ŌSAKA BARRIER

Hino. Now a part of Fushimi-ku, Kyoto.

Hira. A mountainous area west of Lake Biwa.

Hirugashima. In Nirayama, Tagata District, Shizuoka Prefecture.

Hiuchi. On the bank of the Hino River in present Imajō City, Nanjō District, Fukui Prefecture.

Hiyoshi, *see* HIE

Hōgen Disturbance. A brief clash of arms in the capital in 1156, the first year of the Hōgen era, set off when Retired Emperor Sutoku (1119–64; r. 1123–41) and a court noble, Fujiwara no Yorinaga, attempted to depose Emperor Go-Shirakawa and reclaim the throne for Sutoku. Their forces, under Minamoto no TAMEYOSHI and Taira no Tadamasa, were defeated by loyalists led by the Minamoto and Taira clan chieftains, YOSHITOMO and Kiyomori. Sutoku was exiled to Sanuki Province, Yorinaga was killed as he fled toward UJI, and Tameyoshi and Tadamasa were put to death.

Holy teacher (*ajari*; Skt. *ācārya*). A title conferred on Tendai and Shingon monks by the court. These men, skilled in esoteric rites, were familiar figures in the houses of the great.

Home provinces. The five provinces surrounding a former capital at Naniwa: Yamashiro, Yamato, Kawachi, Izumi, and Settsu.

Hōrai, *see* PENGLAI

Hosshōji. Important Tendai temple. Originally a Fujiwara villa in what is now Sakyō-ku, Kyoto; presented to Emperor Shirakawa (1053–1129; r. 1072–86), who converted it into a temple.

Hossō. A Buddhist sect. The KŌFUKUJI was its chief center.

Humming-bulb arrow (*kaburaya*). An arrow equipped with a turnip-shaped hollow bulb, perforated to make a noise in flight. Used, for example, during a ceremonial ARROW EXCHANGE at the commencement of hostilities.

Hungry spirits, path of (*gakidō*), *see* SIX PATHS

Hunting robe (*kariginu*). So called because a somewhat similar garment had once been worn for hunting. A robe with a high, round collar, voluminous sleeves slit at the top, an apronlike front skirt, and a longer rear skirt. Worn by court nobles and warriors.

Hyōjō, see RITSU

Ichikotsu, see RITSU

Ike, Lady. Widow of Taira no Tadamori; stepmother of Kiyomori; mother of YORIMORI. So called because she lived at Ikedono ("Pond Hall") in the ROKUHARA area. She figures in *Heike monogatari* as the person who persuaded Kiyomori to spare Yoritomo after the HEIJI DISTURBANCE.

Ikeda. A post station on the west bank of the Tenryū River. Now Ikeda, Toyoda, Iwata District, Shizuoka Prefecture.

Imayō ("modern song"). A popular late Heian vocal genre. A composition usually consisted of four couplets, made up of alternating seven- and five-syllable lines.

Imoarai. A strategic area southeast of Yodo.

Imperial Regalia, *see* THREE TREASURES

Incense Burner Peak, *see* YIAISI

Indra, *see* TAISHAKUTEN

Intermediate existence (*chūu*). The forty-nine days between a person's death and rebirth. *See also* FORTY-NINTH DAY SERVICES

Ise (fl. late 9th c.). Lady-in-waiting to a consort of Emperor UDA; prominent *Kokinshū* poet.

Ise, Grand Shrines of. In present Ise City, Mie Prefecture (Ise Province). Dedicated to the sun goddess AMATERASU. At the start of each reign, the court named a new Virgin, selected by divination from among unmarried imperial and princely daughters, to serve there as high priestess and imperial surrogate. *See also* SHRINE IN THE FIELDS

Ishibashiyama. Mountainous area southwest of the Hayakawa River in what is now Odawara City, Kanagawa Prefecture.

Itsukushima Shrine. An ancient shrine situated on a small island in Hiroshima Bay, Hiroshima Prefecture (Aki Province); now better known as Miyajima. Its principal objects of worship are three goddesses regarded as protectors of seafarers. Kiyomori became its patron after his appointment as governor of Aki Province.

Iwashimizu Hachiman Shrine. Yawata Hachiman Shrine. A major Shinto shrine situated on Mount Otokoyama near the capital, in what is now Yawata-machi, Tsuzuki District, Kyoto. Dedicated primarily to the god HACHIMAN.

Jingū, Empress (?–?). Semilegendary widow of semilegendary 14th emperor, Chūai. She is supposed to have invaded and conquered the Korean kingdom of Silla while pregnant with the future Emperor Ōjin (ca. late 3rd–early 4th c.?).

Joyful-to-see Palace, *see* TAISHAKUTEN

Kagami. A post station not far from the capital. Now the town of Ryūō, Gamō District, Shiga Prefecture.

Kalaviṇka. Described in the *Amitābha Sutra* as a human-headed bird. It warbles expositions of Buddhist doctrines in the PURE LAND.

Kalpa. In Hindu cosmogony, a period of approximately 4.3 trillion years.

Kamatari, Fujiwara (614–69). Founder of the Fujiwara clan; highly influential 7th-century political figure.

Kamo Festival (Aoi Festival). Held in the 4th month. A major religious and social event, centering on two processions that attracted throngs of spectators. The first was the Virgin's procession from the imperial palace to the KAMO RIVER, where she performed a preliminary purification; the second, the procession of the imperial messenger, the Virgin, and their magnificent retinues to the KAMO SHRINE on the festival day itself. The houses along the way, the parked carriages and viewing-stands, and the spectators were all decked in garlands of real and artificial flowers, leaves of the katsura tree, and especially the heart-shaped leaves of the *aoi* vine, which gave the festival its popular name.

Kamo Return. Imperial messenger's ceremonial return to the palace after KAMO FESTIVAL. See McCullough and McCullough, *Tale of Flowering Fortunes*, 1: s.n. 50, especially p. 410.

Kamo River. A stream that bordered the eastern edge of the capital. It now flows through eastern Kyoto.

Kamo Shrine. General name for an important Shinto institution centered on two main shrines, an upper and a lower, northeast of the capital on the bank of

the KAMO RIVER (now inside Kyoto). Site of two great festivals, the KAMO
FESTIVAL and the Kamo Special Festival. Its high priestess, the Virgin, was
appointed in the same manner as the ISE Virgin.

Kannon, Kanzeon (Skt. Avalokiteśvara). A bodhisattva who lives on the summit of
Mount Potolaka (J. Fudaraku; thought to be on the southern coast of India) and serves as one of AMIDA's two principal attendants; revered especially because of his compassionate vow to save all beings. Frequently depicted with 1,000 arms, or with 11 heads (the uppermost that of a
buddha), he is the central object of worship at such major temples as KI-
YOMIZU and HASE.

Kantō. The eight provinces east of Hakone Pass in the ASHIGARA MOUNTAINS: Sagami, Musashi, Kōzuke, Shimotsuke, Awa, Kazusa, Shimōsa, and Hitachi.
In *Heike monogatari*, often a term for Yoritomo's headquarters and area
of control.

Kasuga Shrine. Great tutelary shrine of the Fujiwara in Nara.

Katsura River, *see* ŌI RIVER

Kawachi Road. A road that led from the capital to Settsu and Kawachi provinces via
a crossing at YODO.

Kawatake bamboo ("streamside bamboo"). A celebrated clump of bamboo in the
principal courtyard of the Seiryōden. It grew near the stream that flowed
through the garden.

Kazan, Emperor (968–1008; r. 984–86). Son of Reizei. Tricked by the Fujiwara into
abdicating and taking the tonsure; as a monk, traveled to KUMANO and
elsewhere.

Kichijōten (Skt. Śrī-mahādevī). In Buddhism, a beautiful goddess, bestower of happiness and prosperity.

Kinshin. Close attendants in the Retired Emperor's Office (*innochō*), typically rich
provincial governors, relatives of the retired emperor's nurses, talented figures with no future in the democracy, and men who simply enjoyed the
royal favor.

Kinugasa. A Miura stronghold. The area is now a part of the city of Yokosuka in
Kanagawa Prefecture.

Kiyomi Barrier. An area now in the town of Okitsu, Ihara District, Shizuoka
Prefecture.

Kiyomizu Temple. A major temple in what is now Higashiyama-ku, Kyoto. Its principal object of worship is KANNON.

Kōbō, Great Teacher (Kōbō Daishi). Posthumous name of Kūkai (774–835),
founder of the Shingon sect.

Kodama League. One of the Seven Leagues of Musashi.

Kōfukuji. The tutelary temple of the Fujiwara clan in Nara; as such, one of the most
powerful religious institutions of the Heian period.

Kohatayama. A mountainous area on the road from the capital to Nara, in what is
now Fushimi-ku, Kyoto.

Kongō Dōji (Skt. Vajra-kumāra). A protector of esoteric Buddhism. He appears as a
youth with a wrathful countenance, brandishing a vajra (*kongō*).

Kōrokan. An official hostelry for foreign envoys in the southern part of the capital.

Kotsu. North of Nara, where the KOTSU RIVER (Kizu River) turns north in eastern
Sōraku District, Kyoto Prefecture.

Kotsu River. Now called Kizu River. A tributary of the YODO.

Kōya. A mountain in Kii Province (Wakayama Prefecture); chosen as headquarters of the Shingon sect in 816 by KŌBŌ Daishi, who died there in 835 and was buried in the inner cloister, where he is said to remain in a state of deep meditation.

Kudara. From the 4th century to the 7th, a state in the southwestern part of the Korean peninsula.

Kumano. A far-flung religious complex in the area of what is now Higashimuro District, Wakayama Prefecture; unified by the Kumano faith, a form of Buddhism devoted especially to the prolongation of life and rebirth in paradise. The central places of worship were three shrines whose deities were regarded as manifestations of Buddhist divinities: the Main Shrine (Hongū, or Kumano-nimasu, deep in the mountains at Hongū Township); the New Shrine (Shingū, or Kumano-hayatama, on the seacoast at Shingū City); and Nachi (Kumano-nachi, at the Nachi Waterfall in Nachi-katsuura Township). There were also many subsidiary shrines.

Kurama. A mountainous area in what is now Sakyō-ku, Kyoto.

Kyō-no-shima Island. A breakwater constructed by Taira no Kiyomori at FUKUHARA to create a harbor for foreign trading vessels.

Land of Buddha-reward in Reality (*jippō*[*do*]), *see* FOUR LANDS

Land of Tranquility and Wisdom (*jakkōdo*), *see* FOUR LANDS

Laozi (6th c. B.C.). Chinese philosopher regarded as the founder of Taoism.

Latter days of the Law (*mappō, matsudai, gyōki, yo no sue, masse*). A 10,000-year period of decline presaging the final disappearance of Buddhism as a living faith. According to one theory, it began around 1050.

Li, Lady. A secondary consort of Han WUDI. The Zhaoyang Hall (*Heike*, 3.1) was a building in the women's quarters of Wudi's palace.

Lishan Palace. According to BO JUYI's "Song of Everlasting Sorrow," Emperor Xuanzong and his favorite, YANG GUEIFEI, exchanged vows at Longevity Hall, a building in the emperor's Lishan Palace, on the night of the Star Festival (TANABATA FESTIVAL).

Lord of a Myriad Chariots. A Chinese epithet for an emperor, adopted in Japan.

Lotus pedestal, *see* PURE LAND

Lotus Sutra (Saddharmapuṇḍarīka-sūtra; J. Hokekyō). A statement of Mahāyāna Buddhist doctrine revered by the Heian aristocracy. It contains dramatic scenes, anecdotes, and parables, and promises many benefits to those who believe in it and extol it.

Mahā-kāśyapa. One of the 10 chief disciples of ŚĀKYAMUNI; said to be waiting in a state of suspended animation for MAITREYA's coming.

Maitreya (J. Miroku). A bodhisattva who has promised to leave the TUṢITA HEAVEN 5,670,000,000 years after ŚĀKYAMUNI's death, come to earth, attain Buddhahood under a dragon-flower tree, and preach the Law at three assemblies as Śākyamuni's successor.

Masakado, Taira (d. 940). Member of a powerful KANTŌ family. After serving the Fujiwara regent Tadahira in his youth, he returned to Shimotsuke Province with frustrated ambitions and began a series of bloody quarrels with relatives and neighbors. By 939, he was in revolt against the court, styling himself New Emperor and claiming to control the eight eastern provinces.

In 940, as he was moving against Izu and Suruga, he was killed by court forces led by his cousin Taira no SADAMORI and a Shimotsuke police official, Fujiwara no Hidesato.

Matsuzaka. A name applied to the hill road leading out from AWATAGUCHI to YAMASHINA.

Mei Fu. A Han immortal (*sennin*).

Menotogo. A *menoto* was a woman who served as wet-nurse for a child of superior social status; her child of approximately the same age was her charge's *menotogo* ("nurse's child," rendered in the translation as foster-brother or foster-sister). The ties that developed from these relationships were usually close and long-lasting.

Michinoku paper. Thick white crepe paper.

Michizane, Sugawara (845–903). A literatus favored by Emperor UDA; promoted to minister of the right in 899. He was exiled to Kyushu in 901, with the nominal title of provisional viceroy of the DAZAIFU, after Fujiwara no Tokihira and others accused him of treasonable intentions. He died in exile.

Miidera, *see* ONJŌJI

Mikasa, Mount. Just east of the KASUGA SHRINE, in what is now the eastern sector of the city of Nara.

Miroku, *see* MAITREYA

Miyagino. Near the present city of Sendai; famous for bush clover (*hagi*).

Moji Barrier. At the western end of Kanmon Straits; now a part of Kitakyūshū City.

Mototsune, Fujiwara (836–91). Powerful early Heian regent and chancellor.

Murasakino. An area immediately north of the capital (now Murasakino, Kita-ku, Kyoto).

Musashino. The part of the KANTŌ plain extending south from present Kawagoe City in Saitama Prefecture to Fuchū in Tokyo. More broadly, Musashi Province.

Musubu. A divinity worshipped at KUMANO Shingū.

Myōonten, *see* BENZAITEN

Nagarayama, *see* SHIGA MOUNTAINS

Nine grades, *see* PURE LAND

Nine Provinces (*kukoku*). A name for Kyushu.

Ninnaji. A center of Shingon esoteric Buddhism, situated in what is now Omuro, Ukyō-ku, Kyoto.

Ninth-day Banquet, *see* DOUBLE YANG BANQUET

Nishihachijō Mansion. A secondary residence used by Taira no Kiyomori. It was a huge establishment in the Hachijō-Ōmiya area of the western half of the capital.

Nobuyori, Fujiwara (1133–59). One of the leading conspirators in the HEIJI DISTURBANCE.

Noji. Northeast of SETA in Ōmi Province.

Northern Land Road (Hokurikudō, Hokurokudō). Seven provinces northeast of the capital, fronting on the Japan Sea: Wakasa, Echizen, Kaga, Noto, Etchū, Echigo, and Sado. Also, the road leading from the capital through those provinces.

North guards (*hokumen*). A guard force at a retired emperor's palace; also, a member of the force.

Novice (*nyūdō*, "one who has entered the Buddhist Way"). Sometimes called "lay monk." A person who takes the tonsure, assumes clerical garb, and leads a religious life in a private residence.

Nyakuōji. One of the subsidiary shrines at KUMANO Hongū.

Nyoiyama. A mountain on the border between present Kyoto and Shiga prefectures. It was on the road from Shishi-no-tani to the ONJŌJI.

Ōeyama. A hill in what is now Ukyō-ku, Kyoto; the road over it led to Tanba Province.

Ōhara. An area near Mount Hiei favored by recluses; now a part of Sakyō-ku, Kyoto.

Ōi River. A name for the upper reaches of the Katsura, a river that runs through the SAGA area and empties into the YODO.

One Vehicle. The perfect and only way to enlightenment; the teachings in the LOTUS SUTRA.

Onjōji. Often called Miidera. A great Tendai temple near Lake Biwa.

Ōsaka Barrier. A government checkpoint on the EASTERN SEA ROAD, in the mountains between the capital and Ōtsu in Ōmi Province; sometimes referred to simply as "the barrier." It appears frequently in literature, often with a pun on *au*, "meet" (formerly homophonous with "ō"), which may give it the meaning "Meeting-hill Barrier" or "Barrier to Meeting." *Saka* means "hill" or "slope."

Oshiki, see RITSU

Ōshū. Another name for Michinoku Province.

Otagi. A cremation site in the eastern hills outside the capital.

Otokoyama, *see* IWASHIMIZU HACHIMAN SHRINE

Ox-Driver, *see* TANABATA FESTIVAL

Penglai, Mount (J. Hōrai). In Chinese legend, an isle of the immortals in the eastern sea.

Pure Land (*jōdo*). AMIDA's Western Paradise, to which he, his two chief attendants, KANNON and Seishi, and a heavenly host escort dying believers. According to one school of thought, there are three major categories of rebirth into this paradise, each with three subdivisions. They are distinguished from one another by the kinds and locations of the lotus blossoms provided for reborn souls, by the speed with which the blossoms open, and by the length of time required for the individual to attain perfect enlightenment.

Rendaino. Near the western base of Mount Funaoka in present Kita-ku, Kyoto.

Rengedani. A residential area for monks on Mount KŌYA.

Ritsu. One of two basic seven-tone scale structures in Japanese music, the other being *ryō*. Its three modes were called *ichikotsu, sōjō,* and *taishiki*; the three *ryō* modes were called *hyōjō, oshiki,* and *banshiki*. The *ritsu* modes were considered light and modern.

River of Three Crossings (*sanzu no kawa, watarigawa*). A river in hell forded by human spirits on the seventh day after death. The worst sinners were required to use the most difficult crossing.

Rōei. A type of vocal music. The lyrics, sung to the accompaniment of Chinese instruments, consisted of short excerpts from Chinese poems (usually a 14-word couplet) or, less often, of WAKA.

Rokuhara. A region in the vicinity of the Rokuhara Mitsuji Temple, east of the KAMO RIVER; site of the residences and administrative offices of the Taira clan.

Ryō, see RITSU

"Ryōō." Also "Ranryōō." A dance performed on festive occasions. It featured an elaborately costumed dancer who held a golden baton and wore a fierce gold mask surmounted by a dragon. According to one tradition, the dance celebrated the bravery of a 6th-century Chinese king, Gao Changgong, who hid his mild features behind an imposing mask and led 500 men to victory against a hostile army.

Ryōzen. An area in the present Higashiyama-ku, Kyoto.

Sadamori, Taira (?–?). With Fujiwara no Hidesato, defeated Taira no MASAKADO; later became commander of the defense garrison in the east and held provincial governorships. He created a strong Taira military presence in eastern Japan.

Saga. An area west of the capital (in present Ukyō-ku, Kyoto).

Saibara. A major Heian vocal genre. The lyrics were mostly folksongs that had been set to Chinese music early in the Heian period. Four chapters in *The Tale of Genji* are named after *saibara*, attesting to the popularity of the genre during its heyday (late 10th–early 11th c.).

Śākyamuni (said to have died 554 B.C.). The historical Buddha; Prince Siddārtha, son of King Śuddhodana (sovereign of Kapila at the southern base of the Himalaya Mountains) and Queen Māyā. At around the age of 29 (or 19?), he stole away from his father's palace on a white horse, sent the horse home with the groom Chandaka, and embarked on a life of religious austerities. At around 35 years, he attained enlightenment under a sacred pipal tree at Gayā, in what is now Bihar. He preached for 45 years at the Deer Park, the Jetavana-vihāra Monastery (GION), the Bamboo Grove, VULTURE PEAK, and elsewhere, and died at around 80 years in a grove of *ŚĀLA* trees, near Kuśinagara in central India. (In *Heike*, I.3, Gayā is a mistake for Kapila.)

Śāla. A tall evergreen tree, native to India, which bears small, pale yellow flowers. According to legend, as the Buddha lay dying in a grove of these trees, their flowers turned white and fell.

Sannō, *see* HIE

Sanron. A Buddhist sect.

Sarusawa Pond. A body of water in front of the Sanmon Gate at the KŌFUKUJI.

Seinan Palace, *see* TOBA MANSION

Semimaru (fl. 10th c.?). A semilegendary blind musician who was said to have lived near ŌSAKA BARRIER and, in one version of the legend, to have been a son of Emperor DAIGO.

Senbon-no-matsubara. A pine-covered coastal plain in the area of present Numazu City, Shizuoka Prefecture. From there, the EASTERN SEA ROAD crossed the ASHIGARA MOUNTAINS into Kamakura.

Seta. One of the two main approaches to the capital across the river that flows out of Lake Biwa; a settlement on the east bank of the river, which is there called the Seta, just south of where it emerges from the lake. *Compare* UJI, YODO RIVER.

Seven circuits. Aggregations of provinces. (1) EASTERN SEA ROAD (Tōkaidō): Iga, Ise, Shima, Owari, Mikawa, Tōtōmi, Suruga, Izu, Kai, Musashi, Sagami, Awa, Shimōsa, Kazusa, and Hitachi. (2) Eastern Mountain Road (Tōsandō): Ōmi, Mino, Hida, Shinano, Kōzuke, Shimotsuke, Michinoku, and Dewa.

(3) NORTHERN LAND ROAD (Hokurikudō, Hokurokudō): Wakasa, Echizen, Kaga, Noto, Etchū, Echigo, and Sado. (4) Mountain Shade Road (San'indō): Tanba, Tango, Tajima, Inaba, Hōki, Izumo, Iwami, and Oki. (5) Mountain Sun Road (San'yōdō): Harima, Mimasaka, Bizen, Bitchū, Bingo, Aki, Suō, and Nagato. (6) Southern Sea Road (Nankaidō): Kii, Awaji, Awa, Sanuki, Iyo, and Tosa. (7) Western Sea Road (Saikaidō): Chikuzen, Chikugo, Buzen, Bungo, Hizen, Higo, Hyūga, Ōsumi, Satsuma, Iki, and Tsushima.

Seven Great Temples. TŌDAIJI, KŌFUKUJI, Gangyōji, Daianji, Yakushiji, Saidaiji, and Hōryūji, all in or near Nara.

Seven monks (*shichisō*). Performers of leading roles at major Buddhist services: the lecturer, or expounder of texts (*kōji*); the reader, or reciter of texts (*tokushi*); the invoker, or reader of the sponsor's petition (*juganshi*); the performer of the triple bow (*sanraishi*); the hymn-chanter (*baishi*); the flower-scatterer (*sangeshi*); and the transmitter (*dōtatsu*), who handed the petition to the invoker.

Seven sages of the bamboo grove (*shichiken*). A group of wealthy recluses who lived together, free of worldly concerns, during the Western Jin dynasty (A.D. 265–316) in China.

Seven Shrines, *see* HIE

Seventh-day services, *see* FORTY-NINTH DAY SERVICES

Seven treasures. Lists vary. Usually identified as gold, silver, beryl, agate, crystal, pearls, and carnelian.

Shandao (613–81; J. Zendō). One of the Chinese patriarchs of the Pure Land sect; regarded in Japan as an incarnation of AMIDA.

Shang Mountain. In Shanxi Province, China. Remembered as the place to which four men retreated to escape the excesses of the Qin regime (221 B.C.–206 B.C.).

Shide Mountains. Crossed by the spirits of the dead as they make their way through the nether regions to the court of judgment.

Shiga Mountains. General name for the mountains from Hiei on the north to Nagarayama on the south. Sometimes refers specifically to Nagarayama.

Shihuangdi (259 B.C.–210 B.C.; r. 246 B.C.–210 B.C.). First Emperor. Founder of the tyrannical Qin dynasty; first unifier of China.

Shi League (Shinotō). One of the Seven Leagues of Musashi.

Shinohara. 1. A post station, now a part of Katayamazu, Enuma District, Ishikawa Prefecture. 2. A post station northeast of SETA.

Shinomiya riverbed. At YAMASHINA on the road to Ōtsu (now within Higashiyama-ku, Kyoto).

Shinzei (d. 1159). Buddhist name of Fujiwara no Michinori, a court literatus and statesman who was one of Retired Emperor Go-Shirakawa's KINSHIN. He was forced to commit suicide by the perpetrators of the HEIJI DISTURBANCE.

Shirabyōshi ("white rhythm"). A type of dance with accompanying song; also a performer of such a dance.

Shōmeimon. A gate opening into the great south court of the Shishinden at the imperial palace.

Shōtoku, Empress (718–70; r. 749–58 as Kōken and 764–70 as Shōtoku). The last sovereign empress. Remembered especially for having wanted to cede the throne to the monk Dōkyō.

Shōtoku, Prince (Shōtoku Taishi; 574–622). Regent during the reign of his aunt, Empress Suiko; famous as an upright figure and an important early patron of Buddhism.

Shrine in the Fields. After their selection, both the ISE Virgin and the KAMO Virgin moved into the imperial palace compound for a stay that usually lasted until the 7th month of the following year (Ise) or the 4th month (Kamo). Ordinarily, the Ise Virgin then proceeded to a simple Shinto-style residence at SAGA, the Shrine in the Fields, in the 8th month, stayed a year, and went to Ise early in the 9th month. The Kamo Virgin stayed at a similar Shrine in the Fields in MURASAKINO for three years. River purifications preceded the moves to the palace and to the Shrine in the Fields.

Shun. A legendary model Chinese emperor, chosen by YAO as his successor. According to Chinese sources, it was a wicked father, rather than an obstinate mother, as *Heike* has it (3.19), whom he treated with exemplary filial piety.

Siddhārtha, Prince, *see* ŚĀKYAMUNI

Six daily devotions (*rokuji no tsutome*). Buddhist invocations and sutra readings performed in the morning, at noon, at sunset, early in the night, at midnight, and at the end of night.

Six heavens (*rokuyokuten*). The six heavens of the WORLD OF DESIRE.

Six paths (*rokudō*). The six forms in which a being may be reborn: dweller in hell (*jigoku*), hungry spirit (*gaki*), beast (*chikushō*), ASURA (*ashura*), human (*ningen*), and deva (*ten*). *See also* EVIL PATHS

Six supernatural powers (*rokutsū*). The powers to be anywhere and do anything, see everything, hear everything, remember past existences, see into the minds of others, and understand extinction (powers attained by buddhas and arhats).

Sōjō, *see* RITSU

"Song of Everlasting Sorrow," *see* YANG GUEIFEI

Songzi. A Han immortal (*sennin*).

Son of Heaven. An epithet used of the emperor.

Sotōrihime. Favorite mistress of Emperor Ingyō (5th c.); said to have been an expert poet. She is worshipped as a patron of literature at Tamatsushima Shrine, WAKA-NO-URA.

Southern capital. Nara.

Sue-no-matsuyama. Appears in poetry as a mountain near the coast in Michinoku Province. No longer identifiable.

Suma. A coastal area in what is now the southwestern part of Kobe. Site of an old barrier. Famous for its beauty, and as the place where the court noble Ariwara no Yukihira (818–93) lived in exile.

Sumeru, Mount. In Buddhist doctrine, a lofty peak towering at the center of every world.

Sumitomo, Fujiwara (d. 941). An ex-official who stayed in Iyo Province as a local chieftain after his term of office expired in 936. As the leader of the powerful local families ("pirates") in the area, he virtually controlled the Inland Sea for about five years. He became an open rebel in 939 and was suppressed by a punitive force in 941.

Sumiyoshi Shrine. Also Suminoe. On the shore of Naniwa Bay (now Ōsaka Bay). An
    important shrine whose deities were special patrons of seafarers and poets.
Su Wu (d. 60 B.C.). A general sent by Han WUDI to fight the nomadic XIONGNU
    people. When conquered, he refused to submit to the Xiongnu chieftain,
    who thereupon exiled him to uninhabited territory. According to legend,
    he was repatriated 19 years later, during a period of peace, when a message
    carried by a wild goose informed Wudi's successor that he was still alive.
Suzakuin. A residence used by retired emperors. It occupied an area in the capital
    bounded by Sanjō and Suzaku avenues.
Sweet Flag Festival (*tango no sechi*). Celebrated on the 5th of the 5th month to ward
    off diseases that tended to strike with the onset of hot weather. It embraced
    a variety of ceremonies and customs, most of them involving the aromatic
    leaves and roots of the sweet flag, or calamus, to which the Chinese and
    Japanese, like the medieval Europeans, ascribed medicinal properties.
    Sweet flag leaves and/or roots were stuffed under eaves, hung inside rooms,
    used in the preparation of "medicinal balls," worn as hair ornaments, sent
    with poems, and formally presented to the emperor by court physicians at
    a sweet flag banquet.
Tagoshi River. A stream near Kamakura in present Zushi City, Kanagawa Pre-
    fecture.
Taishaku[ten] (Skt. Śakra). A deity who lives in the TUṢITA HEAVEN at the top of
    Mount SUMERU; identified with the god Indra, who fights the ASURAS. His
    palace, called Joyful-to-see (Kiken), is a vast establishment that is some-
    times called a city.
Taishiki, see RITSU
Takao. In present Ukyō-ku, Kyoto. Site of a famous old Shingon Temple, the Jingoji;
    known for its autumn leaves.
Takasago. A shrine in what is now southern Hyōgo Prefecture; known for its pine
    trees.
Tamatsushima. A small island in WAKA-NO-URA Bay.
Tametomo, Minamoto (1139–70). Chinzei no Hachirō. Eighth son of TAMEYOSHI;
    renowned archer; fought many private battles in Kyushu. He joined his
    father's side in the HŌGEN DISTURBANCE, was captured and exiled to
    Ōshima Island in Izu Province, subjugated the neighboring islands, and
    committed suicide when attacked by a punitive force.
Tameyoshi, Minamoto (1096–1156). Son of YOSHICHIKA; adoptive son of YOSHIIE.
    One of the leaders of the military forces on the losing side in the HŌGEN
    DISTURBANCE. He was put to death after the failure of the attempted coup.
Tanabata Festival. A ceremony observed on the 7th of the 7th month. It celebrated
    the brief annual reunion of the Ox-Driver (the star Altair) and his wife, the
    Weaver Maid (the star Vega), who ordinarily had to stay on opposite sides
    of the River of Heaven (Milky Way). In one version of the legend, the Ox-
    Driver rowed across the river; in another, he crossed on a bridge of magpie
    wings. Offerings of calligraphy, poetry, and fruit were presented, together
    with prayers for skill in sewing and other feminine accomplishments rep-
    resented by the Weaver Maid, and for proficiency in the use of the brush.
Tang Yao, *see* YAO
Tankaikō, *see* FUHITO

Tashi, Empress (1140–1201). Adoptive daughter of Fujiwara no Yorinaga. Consort of Emperor Konoe (1139–55; r. 1141–55); later became consort of Emperor Nijō (1143–65; r. 1158–65).

Tathāgata ("Thus-come"). An epithet for a buddha.

Tatsutahime. Goddess of autumn. Associated with Tatsutayama, a place famous for autumn color, and thus also associated with skillful dyeing.

Tenchi, Emperor (626–71; r. 668–71). Important early figure who played a leading role in the institution of the Taika Reforms. See Introduction to the *Heike*, p. 245.

Tendai, *see* ENRYAKUJI

Ten directions (*jippō*). North, east, south, west, northeast, southeast, northwest, southwest, up, and down.

Ten evils (*jūaku*). Killing, stealing, adultery, lying, clever talk, duplicity, slander, ill-will, covetousness, and perverted views.

Ten good precepts (*jūzenkai*). Strictures against the TEN EVILS.

Ten kings (*jūō*). According to the *Ten Kings Sutra*, a dead person goes from the INTERMEDIATE EXISTENCE to hell, where 10 kings judge him in turn over a three-year period. Their conclusions determine the nature of his rebirth. (Other texts name one of the 10, ENMA, as the sole judge.)

Tenman Tenjin. The deified Sugawara no MICHIZANE, who was worshipped as a god after his death in exile.

Tenmu, Emperor (d. 686; r. 673–86). Succeeded Emperor TENCHI after a brief succession war; reigned at Kiyomibara in Yamato Province.

Tennōji. Shitennōji. A major Buddhist temple in what is now Osaka. Said to have been founded by Prince SHŌTOKU.

Ten precepts (*jikkai*). Prohibitions against taking life; stealing; committing adultery; lying; drinking intoxicants; wearing adornments and using scent; singing, dancing, or watching or listening to performances; using a high, wide bed; eating at improper times; and acquiring gold, silver, and gems. Prescribed for new monks and nuns. As in Murasaki's case (*Genji*, "New Herbs: Part Two"), the first five could be administered while the recipient was still a lay person.

Thirty-three divinities, heaven of. Tōriten (Skt. Trāyastriṃśa). Situated on top of Mount SUMERU, where the god Indra lives in a great palace surrounded by the mansions of 32 lesser divinities. One of the six heavens of the WORLD OF DESIRE.

Three bodies (*sanjin, sanshin*). The threefold nature of a buddha: the essential nature, the form assumed in paradise, and the form assumed to assist sentient beings.

Three deadly sins (*sangyaku*). Killing an arhat, shedding a buddha's blood, and disrupting the community of monks.

Three evil paths, *see* EVIL PATHS

Three existences (*san'u, sannu*). Also three worlds (*sangai*). The existences, or worlds, into which sentient beings are ceaselessly reborn; identified as desire, form, and spirit.

Three insights (*sanmyō*). Insights into past, present, and future.

Three subordinations (*sanjū*), for a woman. Subordination to father, to husband, and to son.

Three Treasures (*sanshu no jingi*). Hereditary symbols of imperial authority, believed to go back to the age of the gods: the Bead Strand (*shinshi, yasakani no magatama*), the Sword (*hōken, ama no murakumo no tsurugi*), and the Mirror (*naishidokoro, yata no kagami*).

Three virtues (*santoku*). The virtues of the eternal aspect of the Buddha's body, of his wisdom, and of his freedom from bonds.

Three worlds, *see* THREE EXISTENCES

Toba, Emperor (1103–56; r. 1107–23). Controlled the court from the death of his grandfather, Retired Emperor Shirakawa (1053–1129; r. 1072–86), until his own death. Father of three emperors (Sutoku, Konoe, and Go-Shirakawa), two high Buddhist prelates (Kakushō and Kakukai), and two imperial ladies (Jōsaimon'in and the Hachijō imperial lady).

Toba Mansion. Built as a retirement residence at Toba, south of the capital (now in Kyoto), by Emperor Shirakawa, great-grandfather of Go-Shirakawa. Also called Seinan [Detached] Palace. It was a luxurious establishment, with many buildings and extensive grounds.

Tōdaiji. A major temple in Nara, founded by Emperor Shōmu in the mid-8th century; site of a huge statue of VAIROCANA known as the Great Buddha (*daibutsu*).

Toi. The mountainous area between ISHIBASHIYAMA and Hakone.

Toribeno. A cremation site in the general area of the present Kiyomizu Temple, Kyoto.

Totsukawa. The wild, mountainous region along the upper reaches of the Kumano River (Totsukawa River) in southern Yoshino District, Nara Prefecture.

Tsurayuki, Ki (ca. 872–945). Poet; principal compiler of *Kokinshū*; author of *Tosa nikki*.

Tsurugaoka. In Kamakura.

Tunic. Term used in this book for *hitatare*, the name of an amply cut two-piece costume often worn by warriors. In *Heike monogatari*, *hitatare* is usually short for *yoroi hitatare* ("armor *hitatare*"). *Yoroi hitatare*, designed for wear under armor, consisted of a relatively tight-fitting narrow-sleeved shirt and matching pants, both made of brocade, glossed silk, raw silk, or the like, with drawstrings at the wrists and ankles.

Tuṣita Heaven (Tosotsuten). The fourth of six heavens in the WORLD OF DESIRE. Said to be the abode of MAITREYA.

Twelve-linked chain of causation (*jūni in'en*). Links in the chain of existence: ignorance, action, consciousness, name and form, six sense organs (eye, ear, nose, tongue, body, and mind), contact, feelings, craving, grasping, becoming, birth, and death.

Twelve Places (*jūnisho*). A general name for 12 shrines in the KUMANO complex, including the three main ones.

Uda, Emperor (867–931; r. 887–97). Teijiin Emperor, Kanpyō Retired Emperor. Son of Emperor Kōkō. Took the tonsure in 899. Patron of Sugawara no MICHIZANE; sponsored literary activity.

Uji. One of two main approaches to the capital across the river that flows from the south end of Lake Biwa; the area on both sides of the river (there called the Uji) where it emerges from the Ōmi mountains. The Uji Bridge crossed the river in what is now the city of Uji. The area was the site of many aristocratic villas, including the one that became the BYŌDŌIN.

Ukishima-ga-hara. A stretch of sand dunes on the coast between the Fuji and Kisegawa rivers in Suruga Province (now inside the cities of Numazu and Yoshiwara in Shizuoka Prefecture).

Umezu. On the west bank of the Katsura (Ōi) River.

Unmeiden. A building in the imperial palace compound, situated just west of the
Sen'yōmon Gate. It was important as the repository of the emperor's rep-
lica of the Mirror, one of the THREE TREASURES, which was in the care of
the handmaids' office.

Urin'in. A well-known Tendai temple at MURASAKINO.

Vairocana (J. Dainichi Nyorai). The Buddha who is the main object of worship in
the Shingon sect; regarded as the embodiment of the truth.

Vimalakīrti (J. Yuima). A rich disciple of ŚĀKYAMUNI. Through the exercise of supernatural powers, he made room in his tiny hut for 32,000 buddhas.

Vulture Peak (Skt. Gṛdhrakūṭa; J. Gishakutsusen, Ryōjusen, Ryōzen, Juhō, Washi-
no-miyama). An Indian mountain where the Buddha is said to have
preached many sermons; site of the convocation described in the LOTUS
SUTRA.

Waka ("Japanese poem"). A poem in Japanese, as opposed to one in Chinese. Often
a synonym for *tanka* ("short poem"), a poem in 31 syllables.

Waka-no-ura. A scenic coastal area bordering Waka-no-ura Bay in Kii Province
(now a part of Wakayama City). Sometimes used as a metaphor for the art
of poetry because the name is translatable as Poetry Beach or Bay of Poetry.

Watanabe. A warrior band known as the Watanabe League lived in Settsu Province
at a place of this name (now a part of Osaka).

"Waves of the Blue Sea." A court dance. Two helmeted performers imitated the
undulations of the sea, wearing splendid wave-patterned robes decorated
with embroidered plovers.

Weaver Maid, *see* TANABATA FESTIVAL

Welcoming triad (*raigo no sanzon*). AMIDA, KANNON, and Seishi. *See* PURE LAND

Western Paradise, *see* PURE LAND

Whizzing arrow (*hikime*). A hollow wooden arrowhead that made a loud noise in
flight; used to frighten malignant spirits. It was a larger version of the
HUMMING-BULB ARROW.

World of desire (*yokkai*). One of the THREE WORLDS. Among its subdivisions is a
celestial realm inhabited by devils who disturb mortals' peace of mind to
hinder them from attaining enlightenment.

World of form, *see* THREE EXISTENCES

World of hungry spirits, *see* SIX PATHS

Wudi, Han (156 B.C.–87 B.C., r. 141 B.C.–87 B.C.). Best-known emperor of the
Former Han dynasty in China.

Xiongnu. A warlike nomadic people who lived north of China for about 500 years,
beginning around the 3rd century B.C.

Xuanzong, Emperor, *see* YANG GUEIFEI

Yakushi (Skt. Bhaiṣajya-guru). Healing Buddha. An early object of worship in Japan
because of his vow to cure illness. He rules a paradise in the east, the Jōruri
Pure Land. His image is the principal icon at the ENRYAKUJI.

Yamashina. Now a part of Higashiyama-ku, Kyoto.

Yamato. A name for Japan.

Yanagi-ga-ura. Now a part of the city of Kitakyūshū.

Yang Gueifei (719–56). Beautiful favorite of the Tang emperor Xuanzong (685–762; r. 712–56), whose infatuation with her led to extravagance, corruption, and diminished imperial authority. A revolt cost the emperor his throne and Yang Gueifei her life. Their love and its tragic conclusion is the subject of BO JUYI's "Song of Everlasting Sorrow," a poem to which both *Genji* and *Heike* make repeated allusion.

Yao. A legendary Chinese ruler of exemplary probity. He selected SHUN as his heir because his own son was unworthy. There is no known source for the statement that he especially "revered an aged, infirm father" (*Heike*, 3.19).

Yashima. In the northern part of the present city of Takamatsu on Shikoku Island.

Yawata, *see* IWASHIMIZU HACHIMAN SHRINE

Yellow Springs (*kōsen*). Destination of the dead; hades. Originally a non-Buddhist concept, it came to be equated with the Buddhist hells.

Yiaisi. A temple north of Xianglu (Incense Burner) Peak in what is now Jiangxi Province, China. Classical Japanese literature contains numerous allusions to a couplet by BO JUYI in which the two are mentioned: "Propping up my pillow, I listen to the [evening] bell of the Yiaisi Temple; rolling up the blind, I gaze at the [morning] snow on Incense Burner Peak."

Yodo. A strategic area at the confluence of the UJI, Kizu (KOTSU), and Katsura (ŌI) rivers.

Yodo River (75 km). A stream known as the SETA between its source (Lake Biwa) and UJI, as the Uji between Uji and YODO, and as the Yodo between its confluence with the Katsura (ŌI) and Kizu (KOTSU) rivers and its mouth (Ōsaka Bay).

Yoriyoshi, Minamoto (988-1075). Clan chieftain; powerful eastern warrior. In 1062, after an arduous series of battles that had begun in 1051, he put down the rebel Abe brothers, Sadatō and Munetō, in Michinoku.

Yoshichika, Minamoto (d. 1108). Son of YOSHIIE; a provincial official in western Japan who rebelled against the court. He was attacked and killed by the governor of Inaba, Taira no Masamori, whose exploit helped pave the way for the Taira ascendancy.

Yoshifusa, Fujiwara (804–72). Called Chūjinkō. Powerful 9th-century political figure. First subject to serve as chancellor and imperial regent; father-in-law of Emperor Seiwa.

Yoshihira, Minamoto (1141–60). Called Kamakura no Akugenda. Oldest son of YOSHITOMO; captured and killed after the HEIJI DISTURBANCE.

Yoshiie, Minamoto (1039–1106). Called Hachiman Tarō. Oldest son of YORIYOSHI; clan chieftain. He earned military prominence by campaigning successfully for the court against powerful local figures in eastern Japan.

Yoshino. A mountainous region in Yamato Province, known for cherry blossoms and deep snows, and as a traditional destination of ascetics and recluses.

Yoshino Palace. An imperial villa near a waterfall on the Yoshino River in Yamato Province.

Yoshitomo, Minamoto (1123–60). Son of TAMEYOSHI; father of Yoritomo. He was on the winning side in the HŌGEN DISTURBANCE but was killed when he espoused the losing cause in the HEIJI DISTURBANCE.

Yotsuzuka. Old site of the Rajōmon Gate at the south end of Suzaku Avenue in the capital.

Yu Shun, *see* SHUN

Zenkōji. A temple in Shinano Province (now in Nagano City, Nagano Prefecture). After obscure beginnings, it became esteemed in the late Heian period as a source of miracles.

Zhangqiu Palace. A building in the women's quarters at the Han imperial palace.

Bibliography

Abe Akio, Akiyama Ken, and Imai Gen'e, eds., *Genji monogatari*. Vols. 12–17 of *Nihon koten bungaku zenshū*, ed. Akiyama Ken et al. 51 vols. Tokyo, 1971–76.

Aston, W. G. *Nihongi: Chronicles of Japan from the Earliest Times to A.D. 697*. London, 1956.

Birch, Cyril, ed. *Anthology of Chinese Literature from Early Times to the Fourteenth Century*. New York, 1965.

Bowring, Richard. *Murasaki Shikibu: Her Diary and Poetic Memoirs*. Princeton, N.J., 1982.

———. *Murasaki Shikibu: 'The Tale of Genji.'* Cambridge, Eng., 1988.

Bynner, Witter, and Kiang Kang-ku. *The Jade Mountain*. New York, 1929.

Field, Norma. *The Splendor of Longing in 'The Tale of Genji.'* Princeton, N.J., 1987.

Hurvitz, Leon. *Scripture of the Lotus Blossom of the Fine Dharma*. New York, 1976.

Jigu, Monk. *Saikai yotekishū*. Ed. Tomikura Tokujirō. Tokyo, 1956.

Kitagawa, Hiroshi, and Bruce T. Tsuchida. *The Tale of the Heike*. Tokyo, 1975.

Konishi, Jin'ichi. *A History of Japanese Literature*. 3 vols. to date. Princeton, N.J., 1984–.

Liu, Wu-chi, and Irving Lo, eds. *Sunflower Splendor: Three Thousand Years of Chinese Poetry*. Bloomington, Ind., 1975.

McCullough, Helen Craig. *Classical Japanese Prose: An Anthology*. Stanford, Calif., 1990.

———. *Ōkagami, the Great Mirror*. Princeton, N.J., 1980.

———. *The Tale of the Heike*. Stanford, Calif., 1988.

McCullough, William H., and Helen Craig McCullough. *A Tale of Flowering Fortunes*. 2 vols. Stanford, Calif., 1980.

Nagano Jōichi. *Heike monogatari no kanshō to hikyō*. Tokyo, 1975.

Okada, H. Richard. *Figures of Resistance: Language, Poetry, and Narrating in 'The Tale of Genji' and other Mid-Heian Texts*. Durham, N.C., 1991.

Ōta Seiroku. *Shindenzukuri no kenkyū.* Tokyo, 1987.

Ramirez-Christensen, Esperanza. "The Operation of the Lyrical Mode in the *Genji monogatari.*" In Andrew Pekarik, ed., *Ukifune: Love in 'The Tale of Genji,'* pp. 21–61. New York, 1982.

Sadler, Arthur L. "The Heike Monogatari," *Transactions of the Asiatic Society of Japan,* Tokyo, ser. 1, 46.2 (1918), pp. 1–278; 49.1 (1921), pp. 1–354.

Schafer, Edward H. *The Divine Woman.* Berkeley, Calif., 1973.

Seidensticker, Edward G. *The Tale of Genji.* 2 vols. New York, 1976.

Shirane, Haruo. *The Bridge of Dreams: A Poetics of 'The Tale of Genji.'* Stanford, Calif., 1987.

Takagi Ichinosuke et al., eds. *Nihon koten bungaku taikei.* 102 vols. Tokyo, 1957–68.

Tamagami Takuya. *Genji monogatari hyōshaku.* 12 vols. Tokyo, 1964–68.

Taniyama Shigeru et al., eds. *[Shinpen] kokka taikan.* 5 vols. Tokyo, 1983–87.

Tomikura Tokujirō. *Heike monogatari zenchūshaku.* 4 vols. Tokyo, 1966–68.

Tsuchihashi Yutaka and Konishi Jin'ichi, eds. *Kodai kayōshū.* Vol. 3 of Takagi et al., *Nihon koten bungaku taikei.*

Ueda, Makoto. *Literary and Art Theories in Japan.* Cleveland, Ohio, 1967.

Ury, Marian. *Tales of Times Now Past: Sixty-two Stories from a Medieval Japanese Collection.* Berkeley, Calif., 1979.

Waley, Arthur. *The Tale of Genji: A Novel in Six Parts.* 2 vols. New York, 1976. First published 1925–33.

Watson, Burton. *The Complete Works of Chuang Tzu.* New York, 1968.

Yamashina, Yoshimaro. *Birds in Japan.* Tokyo, 1961.

Genji and Heike: selections from The tale of Genji and The
   tale of the Heike / translated, with introductions, by Helen
   Craig McCullough.
   p.   cm.
   Includes bibliographical references.
   ISBN 0-8047-2257-9 (cl.): ISBN 0-8047-2258-7 (pbk.)
   1. Murasaki Shikibu, b. 978?   Genji monogatari.
2. Murasaki Shikibu, b. 978?—Translations into English.
3. Heike monogatari—Translations into English.
4. Japanese fiction—To 1600—Translations into English.
I. McCullough, Helen Craig.   II. Murasaki Shikibu,
b. 978? Genji monogatari. English. Selections. 1994.
III. Heiki monogatari.   English.   Selections.   1994.
PL788.4.G43G27 1994
985.6'314—dc20   93-20623
                                              CIP

∞ This book is printed on acid-free paper

Original printing 1994
Last figure below indicates year of this printing:
07   06   05   04   03   02